Theater in Lebanon

Tarek Salloukh studied drama and theater arts at the Lebanese University in Beirut. As actor and director, he performed in the theaters of the Lebanese capital for many years. He concluded his studies with a Ph.D. at the University of Konstanz in South Germany, where he now lives.

TAREK SALLOUKH
**Theater in Lebanon.
Production, Reception, and Confessionalism**

[transcript]

Bibliographic information published by Die Deutsche Bibliothek
Die Deutsche Bibliothek lists this publication in the
Deutsche Nationalbibliografie; detailed bibliographic data
are available on the Internet at http://dnb.ddb.de

© 2005 transcript Verlag, Bielefeld
and Diss., Univ. Konstanz, 2004
Tag der mündlichen Prüfung: 2. Juni 2004
Erster Referent: Prof. Dr. Hans-Georg Soeffner
Zweiter Referent: Prof. Dr. Kay Kirchmann

All rights reserved. No part of this book may be reprinted or
reproduced or utilized in any form or by any electronic, mechanical,
or other means, now known or hereafter invented, inlcuding photocopying
and recording, or in any information storage or retrieval system,
without permission in writing from the publisher.

Cover Layout by: Kordula Röckenhaus, Bielefeld
Typeset by: Tarek Salloukh
Printed and bound in Great Britain by
Marston Book Services Limited, Oxfordshire

ISBN 3-89942-387-9

TABLE OF CONTENTS

INTRODUCTION 11
  APPROACH, METHOD, AND FIELD RESEARCH 13
    Theoretical framework 13
    A qualitative approach: The »Grounded Theory« 23
    The practical framework 26
    Organization of the research paper 28
    The field research and the database 30
      Observation and protocoling 32
      Interviews 33
      Limitations 35
  A HISTORICAL OVERVIEW 36
    The confessional context 36
    Historical overview of theater 39
    Overview of literature 42

THE ENVIRONMENT OF THEATER (LEVEL I) 45
  CONFESSIONALISM: A MAJOR »SPHERE OF DISCORD« 46
    Terminology and characteristics 46
      Confessional neutrality 48
      Two confessional views of confessionalism 50
    The confessional world: the »Self« 51
      The confessional community ('aṭ-ṭā'ifa) 51
      Family and clan 52
      The individual and the collective:
        a second sphere of discord 53
      Politics of the social world: wāsiṭa and zaʿīm 56
      »Rulers« versus »ruled«: a third sphere of discord 58
      Institutions 58
      Education 59
    Regionalism: the geographical extension of confessionalism 61
    War 62
      Catalyst effect: two areas and two audiences 63
      Generation gap: a fourth sphere of discord 65
      Theater and war 66
    The attitude towards the »Other« 68
      Isolation 68
      Knowledge of the other 69
      Competition and duplication 70
      Tension and relaxation 70

Emotionality	71
The Christian construction of the Moslem	72
The Moslem construction of the Christian	73
Differentiation and identification: two esthetic realms	74
Apportionment	77
Polarization	78
Labeling	78
Globalization	79
Media	81
Newspapers and other media	83
CONCLUSION AND CONSEQUENCES: THE ENVIRONMENT OF THEATER	84
The spheres of discord as on-going »social dramas«	85
Friction	86
Esthetic realms	87
Graphical representation of the environment	88

OUTER-PERFORMANCE PRODUCTION (LEVEL II)   91

THE PARAMETERS OF THE PRODUCTION	91
Freedom, censorship, and restrictions	91
Governmental institutions	93
Confessional Institutions	93
Overriding restrictions	94
Attitudes of the production towards theater	95
The production agents' view of theater	95
Theater as space of the individual	98
The audience and the economic balance between production and reception	100
STRATEGIES OF THE PRODUCTION	103
Selection and composition	103
Approaching the spheres of discord	105
Approaching the esthetic realms	107
Approaching the audiences	108
Marketing	108
Appeal	109
THE ELEMENTS OF PLAY	112
Actors	112
Place: host-guest attitudes	115
Form	116
Text	116
Music	117

Sex and other elements of attraction	118
Heterogeneous and homogeneous plays	120
Topic	121
THE CROSSING PLAY	122
A TYPOLOGY OF THEATER	125
Entertainment Theater—»'al-masraḥ t-tarfīhī«	126
Chansonnier Theater	126
Boulevard Theater	129
Serious Theater—»'al-masraḥ l-ǧādd«	129
Intellectual and Academic theater	130
Political Theater: 'al-masraḥ s-syāsiyy	131
Religious Theater: 'al-masraḥ d-dīniyy	133
Popular Theater: 'al-masraḥ š-šaʿbiyy	134
CONCLUSION: PRODUCTION	136

OUTER-PERFORMANCE
RECEPTION (LEVEL II) — 137

THE PARAMETERS OF RECEPTION:	
THE ATTITUDE OF THE AUDIENCE TOWARDS THEATER	137
Theatrical culture	137
Meaning and role of theater	139
Theater in the relation between the self and the other	141
Differences between the two social worlds	145
The Christian milieu: estheticism,	
exclusivism, and development of the individual	146
The Moslem milieu: functionalism,	
popularism, and conservation of the collective	148
Attitude of the audience towards theater people	150
GOING TO THEATER	151
Acquiring the ticket	151
The circumstantial audience	151
The intentional audience	153
Selecting a performance	153
The place	155
Transportation	155
Beirut as common space	156
The Crossing Audience	156
The financial element	158
CONCLUSION: A TYPOLOGY OF THE AUDIENCE	158

PERFORMANCE (LEVEL III) AND
POST-PERFORMANCE (LEVEL IV) 161
REALITY ONE »R1« AND REALITY TWO »R2«:
THE BASIS FOR INTERPRETATION 161
Identification 164
Interpretation: spheres of discord and esthetic realms 166
Emotional and rational motions 168
THE PERFORMANCE AS FRAME OF INTERACTION
BETWEEN THE SELF AND THE OTHER 169
Actor-audience interaction 170
Audience-audience interaction:
polarization and harmonization 172
POST-PERFORMANCE (LEVEL IV):
EVALUATION AND FEEDBACK 175
CONCLUSION 177

SUMMARY AND CONCLUSION 179

APPENDIX A: EXCERPTS AND EXAMPLES
FROM THE FIELDWORK 199
OBSERVATIONAL PHASE 199
»On Top of it,« fawq d-dakki (Example A) 199
In the South 200
In the Beqā' valley 202
»Alleys,« zawārīb (Example B) 202
»Civil Disorder,« šawāz madani (Example C) 205
»Come boy, eat mğaddara,«
ta'ā kōl mğaddara yā ṣabi (Example D) 205
'Arabsat (Example E) 206
»In front of the door,« 'amāma l-bāb (Example F) 207
»Jazz, crime and punishment,«
Jazz, 'al-ğarīma wa-l-'iqāb (Example G) 208
EXAMPLES OF FIELD NOTES 208
Memo 1: »zawārīb« 208
Memo 2: šawāz madani 209
Memo 3: »The Martyr son of the country.«
'aš-šahīd 'ibn l-balad 211
Memo 4: ğnaynit ṣ-ṣanāyi' 212
Memo 5: »Dream maker,« ṣāni' l-'aḥlām 212
INTERVIEWS 212
Interview guidelines 212

Audience reception interviews	213
Production interviews	213
Partial list of interviewees	214
Translated interviews citations	215

APPENDIX B: DIAGRAMS 235

APPENDIX C: ARABIC TRANSCRIPTIONS 253

APPENDIX D: GERMAN SUMMARY 347

BIBLIOGRAPHY 355

Introduction

»The evil that men do lives after them;
the good is oft interred with their bones...«
(Julius Caesar, III, ii)

Through these lines from *Julius Caesar*, Shakespeare alludes to the conscious selectiveness of remembering. After a series of selection processes, people are able to make choices, take decisions, and eventually construct their own view of the world. These choices are conditioned by several parameters encompassed in time and space. They in turn form limitations through which a fast changing world is conceived. New elements come to life; others die. Our senses are not keen enough to register all these actions. At the same time, we do not usually acknowledge the existence of something, unless there are some sensible indicators to it. At any rate, our disability to detect or observe those indicators by our senses can neither deny nor confirm their existence. We are unable to realize at all time and space that certain things have grown old while others have already turned into artifacts. Left of them are relics, which, though still present in form, are only shadows of ideas living in the mind of their interpreter. Still, departing from these relics, artifacts, words, essays, oeuvres, paintings, or theater dramas, researchers and other people as well try to discern meanings of things. They construct concepts in their minds and attribute to them their own interpretations. In turn, these constitute their conception of reality and set at the same time the borders of what they consider as fiction. For this purpose, objects of the environment change in meaning with different interpreters giving them new dimensions and making more than trivial changes to their esthetics. As is the case in real life, theater presents a field of different types of interpretations especially in Lebanon.

A multifaceted social structure and the civil war are two factors of influence on theater. During the Lebanese civil war (1975-1990), Beirut was divided into two areas separated by a demolished downtown with internal frontiers sustained by snipers' bullets and militias' bombs. The outcome of this situation was a demographic division of the Christian and Moslem populations respectively into East and West Beirut. Within this gloomy description of the environment, a few facts drag the attention of the observer. First, certain types of theater were blossoming like the one known as Chansonnier Theater,[1] which consists of a series of sketches and songs containing political and social satire. Second, we notice that the performances of a Chansonnier play undergo several changes when moving among different areas of the Lebanese territory resided by other religious communities. Adjustments in text, omission of certain scenes, additional sketches, and an eventual replacement of the actors themselves are examples of corrections at this level. Third, these arrangements of the esthetic elements coupled with maneuvers to overcome the delicacy of certain topics are aiming at adapting the theater play to different types of audiences. Fourth, we observe duplication in the production of theater between East and West Beirut. In addition to that, certain forms of theater attract a rising number of audiences in both areas like Popular Theater,[2] while others are struggling for survival like Intellectual Theater.[3] Other aspiring types disappeared completely from the scene like the one known in the 1970's as the Daily Theater.[4] All these are unmistakable changes pertinent to the process of production, which is tightly linked to the way theater is received by the different audiences. They are hence indicators of a change in the reception of theater. Knowing that these changes came together with the creation of two milieus resulting from the war, it is essential to seek links between them and the new environment with its factors of influence.

Other questions rise here about the *raison d'être* of theater, the differences in form and topic pertinent to each milieu, and the relation between the theaters of each milieu. What are the criteria for interpretation of the elements of theater? What are the roles and functions of theater in each milieu? What are the reasons necessitating the above mentioned modifications when changing areas? What are the conditions for a theater play to have success among audiences belonging to various religious communities? On the whole, what are the parameters controlling production and reception of theater?

---

1   The French translation: »Artiste qui compose ou interprète des textes ou des chansons, surtout satiriques ou humoristiques.« (Larousse) . In theater, it refers to a type of play, in which these songs are presented within a frame of dramatic sketches. See section: Chansonnier Theater.
2   See section: Popular Theater.
3   See section: Intellectual and Academic Theater
4   The term »daily theater« was used in the 1970's by the actor Hasan Alaa' ad-Dīn alias »Shoushou.« The idea behind it was to have a theater group making presentations around the year. With the war and the death of the actor, this type of theater vanished.

In this research, I will try to shed a light on theater in Lebanon: its production and reception types, audiences, and interpretations in each of the two social worlds constituting the Lebanese environment: Christian and Moslem.[5]

Approach, method, and field research

Theater presents many unknowns. Some researchers limit theater to a mere artistic context; others approach it from a social perspective. A classical view of theater consists of a continual comparison between art and life. Plato writes in his *Republic*, »Art is imitating life, and life is only a shadow of the ideal forms« (qtd. in Schechner 1988: 37). As art, theater consists of several art forms like architecture, music, dance, acting, directing, writing, lighting, and sound. On the other hand, seeking a role for theater in real life links it to tradition and ritual, through which human groups express their belonging to each other. Theater can also be used as a medium or a mediation tool to contribute to some ideology or system, and this could be for political, humanitarian, economic, or cultural purposes as some Lebanese theater directors would like to define it (329, 619).[6] Theater can be any combination of these interpretations depending on the interpreter. Since choosing a correct approach determines also the method to be used in finding adequate interpretations, it is useful at this stage to have an overview of the relevant theories of drama.

Theoretical framework

In *Theater Audiences*, Susan Bennet (1990) states two paradigms of dramatic emphasis concerning theater. The first is »the performance theorists« represented by a mainstream in North America. To this category belongs the experimental and theoretical work of Richard Schechner and his »Performance Group.« We will return to this view later.

The second area of dramatic theory as stated by Bennet, is semiology, which started in the 1930's and 1940's with Mukărovský and the Prague School, working both from Russian Formalist and Saussurian lin-

---

5 The concept of the social world is used according to the meaning elaborated by Strauss 1987 (230- 40). In our context, the social world reduces to the denomination of the social environment of the religious communities, defined by the interviewees (»in-vivo«) as (ṭāwā'if). Compare to the concept of »social system« (Luhmann 1984).
6 These numbers refer to excerpts from interviews gathered in an electronic database. Those in italics are translated in a separate section. The others are only found as arabic transcriptions. See sections: The Field Research, Translated Interview Citations, and Appendix C.

guistic theory. Semiology extended over the 1960's to the 1980's where it was »launched« again with Pavis, Elam, de Marinis, and others, as Bennet states it. About this approach, Bennet concludes that, »despite the breadth of semiotic interest, the audience has neglected the audience almost as much as elsewhere.« Keir, for example devotes 9 of 210 pages in his work to the audience (Bennet 1990: 9-15). In fact, although most of the semioticians emphasized the importance of the social context and the spectator in theater, they did not offer a practical method to take that into consideration. The manageability of this approach is not evident. Making a code for the signs of theater for each theatrical subject seems as improbable as the universal cultural code that is supposed to be at its foundation. Pavis states the necessity for a ready-made code; however, he swiftly strays away from it (Bennet 1990: 14). In *Semiotik des Theaters: Das System der theatralischen Zeichen, Band 1*, Fischer-Lichte writes:

Bedeutung entsteht dann, wenn ein Zeichen von einem Zeichenbenutzer innerhalb eines Zeichenzusammenhangs auf etwas bezogen wird, sie kann sich ändern, wenn das Zeichen a) in einen anderen Zeichenzusammenhang eingefügt oder b) auf etwas anderes bezogen oder c) von einem anderen Zeichenbenutzer verwandt wird [...] Mit diesem Charakteristikum erklärt sich auch die allgemein bekannte Tatsache, daß verschiedene Menschen demselben Zeichen – sei dies nun ein Wort oder eine Zeichnung, ein Werkzeug oder ein Gebäude – unterschiedliche Bedeutungen beizulegen vermögen. (Fischer-Lichte 1983: 8-9)

Within this frame of the individual interpretations, finding a corresponding schema of meaning to every sign becomes even more difficult and presents practical problems. First, how to detect all the signs composing a performance, and second how to find a common basis among individuals, within which one meaning is assigned to each sign? It is true that the signs can have several meanings acquired with respect to various interpreters, but how to determine a common interpretation relevant to each performance? On the other hand, by attributing constant preset meanings to signs, we are dropping the importance of the differential in meaning due to the specific performance as a unique event on the time axis. These factors consitute shaky foundations for the semiotic approach. Schechner writes:

performances not only play out modes, they play with modes, leaving actions hanging and unfinished, so theatrical events are fundamentally experimental: provisional. Any semiotics of performance must start from, and always stand steadily on, these unstable slippery bases, made even more uncertain by the continually shifting receptions of various audiences. (Schechner 1988: xiv).

Schechner gives at this point the clue to the solution by mentioning different receptions corresponding to different audiences. He thus moves from the individual spectator to the collective audience. In this context, since the relation between the sign (signifiant) and the thing it refers to (signifié) depends on the interpreter, looking for an absolute meaning of the »signifié«—one »right« and »true« meaning—has itself lost its meaning:

> Die im hermeneutischen Erkenntnisstil angelegte Selbstreflexion führte [...] zur Entdeckung und Problematisierung des Lesers und des Interpreten als des ‚Koautors' von Texten. [...] Dabei vollzieht sich sowohl auf der Seite der Interpreten als auch auf der des jeweiligen Dokumentes der Wandel von einer absoluten zu einer historischen Semantik. [...] Folgerichtig verlor die Suche nach der ‚einen' Bedeutung an Bedeutung. (Soeffner 1992a: 14-15)

We recurr thus to a semantic in which the interpretation is based on the historical meaning of the event of the performance in opposition to an absolute interpretation valid for all performances. Departing from the historical perspective, the adopted strategy consists of looking for common patterns of interpretations through the classification of numerous interpretations into types resulting from the social background of the interpreter. Hence, the receptions of the audiences is expressed through patterns of their »understanding process« itself, »how« they formed those interpretations, and the socialization producing it:

> Ging es früher ausschließlich um das »Was« des Verstehens, so ging es nun mehr und mehr um das »Wie«: um das Verstehen des Verstehens selbst, um Verfahren, »Regeln«, »Muster«, implizite Prämissen, sozialisatorisch vermittelte Aneignungs-, »Schulungs«- und Überlieferungsweisen des Deutens und des Verstehens. (Soeffner 1992: 15-6)

Practically, this can be achieved through the construction of the »Idealtypus« as pattern for reception of the different audiences in the case of the performance: »Eine [...] strukturanalytische Rekonstruktion und Darstellung von Einzelfällen erzielt ihren soziologischen Erklärungswert dann, wenn sie einmündet in die Konstruktion eines historisch-genetischen »Idealtypus.« [...] Das Verfahren einer solchen konstruktiven Rekonstruktion ist das der historisch-rekonstruktiven Hermeneutik« (Soeffner 1992: 13-4). This »type« is constructed from the output of the »actors« of a certain phenomenon going through their explanations of their actions and the reasons leading to them. From this »type,« the interpreters' subjective meaning is deduced, which, in Weber's conception, is the meaning sought by sociology as a science:

»Sinn« ist hier entweder a) der tatsächliche α. in einem historisch gegebenen Fall von einem Handelnden oder β. durchschnittlich und annähernd in einer gegebenen Masse von Fällen von den Handelnden oder b) in einem begrifflich konstruierten reinen Typus gedachten Handelnden subjektiv gemeinten Sinn. Nicht etwa irgendein objektiv »richtiger« oder ein metaphysisch ergründeter »wahrer« Sinn. Darin liegt der Unterschied der empirischen Wissenschaften vom Handeln: der Soziologie und der Geschichte, gegenüber allen dogmatischen [...] welche an ihren Objekten den »richtigen«, »gültigen« Sinn erforschen wollen. (Weber 1972: 1-2)

Therefore, we do not seek »the right or metaphysically true meaning,« but in a historical case, the meaning attributed to something by a social actor, a »Handelnder.« In other terms, this is the reconstruction of the *attitude* of the individual leading to his or her line of action, which constitutes a construction of the first order (Konstruktion erster Ordnung) in Schütz' terminology in his *Der sinnhafte Aufbau der Sozialen Welt* (1974). From the potential answers to this raw data, the researcher will try to build a structured view of interrelated factors yielding an adequate meaning of the investigated phenomenon. This, in turn, constitutes a construction of the second order (Konstruktion zweiter Ordnung) as defined by Schütz.

Another question consists in determining the pattern or »type.« The generalization from the individual case to the general pattern is confirmed by G. H. Mead through his view of the socialization process in relation to a »generalized other.« Departing from the concept of *meaning*, Mead makes the link between the individual attitude to the meaning as follows: »The mental processes have to do with the meanings of things, and that these meanings can be stated in terms of highly organized attitudes of the individual. [...] Such an organization of attitudes in reference to what we term objects is what constitutes for us the meanings of things« (Mead 1934: 125). Trying to determine all the backgrounds, single calculations, and future expectations of every individual in order to present the horizon of expectations is extremely complicated and quite impossible. And even then, we are limited to the case of the individual in question. A reduction of those factors in order to attain a certain typology, as we mentioned, is manageable. Adopting this approach implies a transfer from the particular individual and his »organized attitudes« constructing the individual meaning to a more »generalized« idea of this individual himself implying a set of generalized »organized attitudes« of a »generalized« individual. The interaction between individuals is, in this case, reduced to an interaction with a »generalized other,« taking place in the social environment:

> It is in the form of the generalized other that the social process influences the behavior of the individuals involved in it and carrying it on, i.e., that the community exercises control over the conduct of its individual members; for it is in this form that the social process or community enters as a determining factor into the individual's thinking. (Mead 1934: 155)

Since the »organized attitudes« of the individual are stemming from the socialization of the community, thus it should be possible to determine the collective attitude expected from the individual as a pattern relevant to the community and not to a particular individual.

Having set the course of action regarding the construction of meaning starting from attitudes, we come now to the question of the relevant »building blocks of the play«. The building of meaning reduces to a historical reconstruction inducing »types« of interpretations. These, like it is the case with the elements of the environment, can be divided into *esthetic* (form) and *topical* elements (content). At this stage, we need a definition of the esthetic unit, to which qualitative attributes can be assigned. The easiest term coming to mind at this stage is »element,« and it is used interchangeably with the term »signs and symbols.« The elements of the environment and the interrelation between theater and its environment reflect the result of the strategies of the productions in choosing and processing those elements in a theater play, thus converting them from raw elements of the environment into processed *elements of play*. By considering those elements as signs, we come to Schütz definitions of *sign* and *sign system*:

> Zeichen sind Handlungsgegenständlichkeiten oder Artefakte, welche nicht nach jenen Deutungsschemata ausgelegt werden, die sich aus Erlebnissen von ihnen als selbständigen Gegenständlichkeiten der Außenwelt konstituieren oder für derlei Erlebnisse von Gegenständlichkeiten der physischen Welt im jeweiligen Erfahrungszusammenhang vorrätig sind (adäquate Deutungsschemata), sondern welche Kraft besonderer vorangegangener erfahrender Erlebnisse in andere (inadäquate) Deutungsschemata eingeordnet werden, deren Konstitution sich aus polythetischen Setzungen erfahrender Akte von anderen physischen oder idealen Gegenständlichkeiten vollzog. [...] Unter Zeichensystem verstehen wir einen Sinnzusammenhang zwischen Deutungsschemata, in

den das betreffende Zeichen für denjenigen, der es deutend oder setzend gebraucht, eingestellt ist. (Schütz 1981: 168)

In this definition, signs are seen as the elements used to perform a »Handlung.« Their meaning is not determined according to an innate structure derived from a fixed adequate repertoire of experience, but they are defined according to dynamic multivariate experiences. Furthermore, in a Schütz-Luckman context, Soeffner derives three representational means from the sign: the symbol, the emblem, and the ritual (Soeffner 1989: 160). As representatives of social experience, they rank higher as the individual concept, historically based and accordingly varied. They influence their influencer (1989: 161). The symbol as such will not only be a sign for the »seen,« but it will turn to reality: »the wine *is* the blood, and the bread *is* the flesh of Christ. The symbolized *shines* through the symbol (1989: 162). »It is what it is. [...] Not only in the everyday life meaning, but also in the extraordinary one. Symbols are their own concept« (1989: 163). Mead makes the connection between *meaning* and *symbol* according also to past experience.

The meanings of things or objects are actual inherent properties or qualities of them; the locus of any given meaning is in the thing which, as we say, »has it.« We refer to the meaning of a thing when we make use of the symbol. Symbols stand for the meanings of those things or objects which have meaning; they are given portion of experience which point to, indicate, or represent other portions of experience not directly present or given at the time when, and in the situation in which any one of them is thus present (or is immediately experienced). (Mead 1934: 122)

If meaning is inherent in the elements, symbols are defined by the way we refer to them, when they are not immediately in the situation of a conversation. In comparison, both Schütz and Mead present *meaning* as relative to a past experience registered in the subconscious of the interpreter regardless of the immediate situation in which the symbol is used. This immediate experience, however, becomes a future basis for interpretation inducing a differential in meaning increasing through time. Because the meanings of these units are established by the experience of the interpreters, different interpreters can give different meanings to the same sign depending on the »experiencing consciousness« of the interpreter: »[...] der Zusammenhang zwischen Anzeichen und Angezeigtem ausschließlich im erfahrenden Bewußtsein desjenigen konstituiert [ist], welcher das Anzeichen als Hinweis auf das angezeigte interpretiert« (Schütz

1932: 165). It is this meaning that we are seeking in our »type construction.«

As a conclusion, in the adopted approach, meanings of signs and symbols are determined with respect to a historical experience: it could be a theatrical experience, the case of the performance, or a real life one. Again here, we will try to build types of the criteria of use and interpretation of signs and symbols in relation to theater.

Within the frame of the performance, we consider the »performance theory« of Schechner (1988) and the »social drama« of Victor Turner (1982), as stated by Bennet above. The differential in meaning of the signs and symbols pertinent to a particular performance is the outcome of a repetition of a certain *Erlebnis*, which in turn becomes the basis for future interpretations. Victor Turner considers the performance as an *Erlebnis* in five moments. By relating the past experience to the present feelings, the spectator establishes meaning within the *Erlebnis*:

A performance, then, is the proper finale of an experience. Dilthey's presentation of the five »moments« of Erlebnis has a processual structure, being genetically connected. Each Erlebnis or distinctive experience has (1) a perceptual core—pleasure or pain may be felt more intensely than in routinized, repetitive behaviors; (2) images of past experience are »evoked with unusual clarity of outline, strength of sense, and energy of projection« (qtd. in R.A. Makreel 1975: 141). (3) But past events remain inert unless the feelings originally bound up with them can be fully revived; (4) »meaning« is generated by »feelingly« thinking about the interconnections between past and present events. [...] But it is in bringing past and present into »musical relation« that the process of discovering and establishing »meaning« consists. [...] (5) an experience is never truly completed until it is »expressed,« that is, until it is communicated in terms intelligible to others, linguistic or otherwise. Culture itself is the ensemble of such expressions—the experience of individuals made available to society and accessible to the sympathetic penetration of other »minds.« (Turner 1982: 13-4)

Also, in *The Performance Theory*, Schechner states seven magnitudes of the performance, ranging from the smallest to the macro unit of the performance; these are: 1. The brain event, 2. The microbit, 3. the bit, 4. The sign, 5. The scene, 6. The drama, 7. The macrodrama (Schechner 1988: 282). For our purposes, this categorization presents a spectrum of the levels, upon which, the *elements of play* can be examined. Moreover, it suggests a relation between theater and everyday life. This relation, a core concern of this research, is well elaborated by Schechner, who presents also many links to the social sciences. Among those, we find the notion of theater as ritual from Victor Turner, and its role in the daily life—what Turner calls »social drama« (Turner 1982). This approach is also useful in setting the frame of work: first, by approaching the performance itself as a phenomenon, which focuses the area of work, and second by connecting it to the environment, which gives a credibility to any interpretation of the *elements of play* based on their connection with their context. Thus, it is no coincidence that Schechner sees in Lebanon a typical example of a Turnerian drama, confirming therefore the above mentioned arguments with a hint to the role of the media:

Surely the events in Lebanon over however many decades make a well-knit Turnerian social drama, one that can never get beyond crisis and failed redressive action. Media encourages these large scale dramas to be viewed with varying degrees of anxiety and amusement by hundreds of millions of people. A »Rashomon effect«[7] occurs where the same data are woven into many different narratives according to cultural bias, editing, and individual interpretation -- and these become parts of a Geertzian interpretation of cultures by different cultures. (Schechner 1988: 281)

At this stage, a practical approach from the upper discussion starts to materialize. For our purposes, the phenomenon of theater could be linked to its environment through the attitude of its actors. Going through those attitudes, the research, as we mentioned, is oriented towards hermeneutics and the »Verstehende Soziologie.« Here, we find the works of Weber (1972), Berger and Luckmann (1969), and Schütz (1974). To the relation between interpretation in theater and in real life, we consider Goffman (1959) and Soeffner (1992b). For the method, the qualitative analysis based on Strauss/Corbin (1998) and Soeffner (1979, 1999) is of interest. To the work of the actors during the performance, we consider Stanislavsky (1994). For the reception side, the works of Wolfgang Iser (1974) and Hans-Robert Jauss (1982) developed for the interaction between text and reader seems interesting. However, the analogy between text and theatrical performance remains inaccurate. The major difference is that the text itself is static; the reader decides when to move on with reading. The performance on the other hand is dynamic; it goes on with or without the attention of the spectator. Another point is that the performance includes an interaction between actors and audiences; whereas reading a text presents interaction between the reader and the text, in which the interpersonal mode of interaction between the reader and the

---

7 »Rashomon« refers here to a short story by Aktagawa Ryunosuke (1892-1927), which together with other short stories "Yabu no naka," became the highly applauded film Rashomon (1950). Rashomon, directed by Kurosawa Akira, was the first Japanese film to win international acclaim.

writer is indirect, seen through the choice of words and diction.[8] Maintaining the analogy between text and performance under these conditions reveals unrewarding.

Going back to our first argument of the selectiveness of reception, the interpretations related to theater can be retrieved from the actors of theater themselves. Since meanings vary depending on the interpreter, it was left to the participants in theater to determine their views in this regard. Their respective attitudes determine the position of theater in its social milieu and the possible interpretations attributed to its single elements. For practical purposes, those participants can be divided into two categories: the production agents including actors, producers, and playwrights, and the reception agents including the audiences. Those are the *actors*[9] of the phenomenon. The performance represents the field of interaction of all agents and elements of play existing in relation to their environment. This necessitates an inspection of the relation of those elements to their environmental origins, their usage in theater, as well as the structure of the environment producing them. In brief, in order to understand the phenomenon of theater in Lebanon, it is essential to consider production and reception in the different environmental conditions. Moreover, knowing that the meaning of theater and performance is liable to change with respect to each area, it is necessary in the field work to reconstruct this meaning with respect to the different milieus, as a prerequisite for understanding the event of a single performance. Within the performance, an interaction between spectators and actors, which may differ according to their confessional belonging, takes place. Because it is not manageable to list and explain all signs of the performance, we will try to find the criteria upon which esthetic signs change in meaning. In this manner, types of interpretations by the direct actors are constructed. Furthermore, the theater process extends beyond the boundaries of the performance to pre and post-performance phases presented in the »practical framework« section below.

Through this approach, we are not limited to using theater literature to construct a »general,« »true« meaning of theater although similarities between the eventual findings of this research and other drama theories are to be expected. Since other theater theories were developed in different environments, their adaptability to the Lebanese case is also questionable. Hence, starting from a given general theory of theater and applying

---

8 Compare to this effect the »communication triangle« and the »telic modes of meaning« as presented in Kane 2000 (p. 253-261).
9 The word actors here is a designation of the persons or people playing a role in a phenomenon and not necessarily for the »actors« on stage in theater. Used as equivalent to the German »Akteure,« it consists of the production agents (P.A.) and the reception agents (R.A.) of the process of theater.

that on Lebanon is inadequate for our method, in contrast to starting from case studies in Lebanon and moving to the generalization of results.

Using the »grounded theory« as explained in the next section, categories are taken from the field research and rooted in its data as we see from the indicated interview citations in Appendix C; they are derived from and applicable to the Lebanese case. This does not exclude their matching of some other results in another field, but at the same time, it does not mean that they are any direct application of any. The value of the resemblance to a given theoretical model is in and by itself a confirmation of that model, and is accordingly treated as a potential confirmation but not a result.

Through qualitative interviews, the horizons of expectations of the actors and the different attitudes towards theater and its environment are constructed. Those interpreters, actors and spectators, are also considered among the elements constituting the single performance. A direct interviewing was conducted about how they perceive their role in the performance and their understanding of theater and their attitudes towards other actors. To this purpose, particular performances are used as examples, taking into account the interaction impact of other participants in these performances. In addition to that, there are very few statistics about Lebanese theater that are worth mentioning. Since we are involved in the interpretation of meaning, the emerging concepts themselves as determinants of meaning are as important as the quantity of people who acknowledge them.

On the practical level, R. Schechner divides the theatrical process into seven parts: training, workshops, regular rehearsals, warm-up, the performance, the close, and the assessment or evaluation (Schechner 1984: 26). Since »it is impossible to know prior to the investigation what the salient problems will be or what theoretical problems will emerge« (Strauss and Corbin 1998: 49), setting solid thresholds between the processes of theater is also not adequate. The explanation of the processes of theater will eventually consist of interrelated concepts elaborated, explained, and interpreted with respect to the context of their relation to the environment and to each other. For manageability purposes, however, we can manage a working basic division of theater into three main processes: production, reception, and performance.

Two important findings of the first round of interviews—the »open coding« phase according to the method explained hereafter—confirmed these assumptions. The first was that theatrical elements, as defined by the actors, are interpreted in comparison to their environmental equivalents. From this perspective, a satisfactory categorization of the active forces in the environment is deemed necessary. The second was the appearance of an influential factor in the environment: confessionalism. It developed into the main category as the research progressed. These two factors in need of inspection were included in the field research as initial categories to be inspected.[10] Later development of the research revealed their subcategories and characteristics.

A qualitative approach: The »Grounded Theory«

In the »grounded theory,« A. Strauss and later J. Corbin present a methodology for leading qualitative analysis. The »grounded theory« means »a theory that was derived from data, systematically gathered and analyzed through the research process.« The researcher does not begin a project with a preconceived theory in mind, but rather begins with an area of study and »allows the theory to emerge from the data.« The background of this idea is that »Theory derived from data is more likely to resemble the 'reality' than is theory derived by putting together a series of concepts based on experience or solely through speculation« (Strauss and Corbin 1998: 12). Hence, sticking to rigid guidelines whether in qualitative or in quantitative research methods hinders the discovery of new categories outside the frame of a preset structure:

[...] to adhere rigidly to initial guidelines throughout a study, as is done in some forms of both qualitative and quantitative research, hinders discovery because it limits the amount and type of data that can be gathered.[...] Because these early concepts (gathered through quantitative or some methods of qualitative research) have not evolved from »real« data, if the researcher carries them with him or her into the field, then they must be considered provisional and discarded as data begin to come in. (Strauss and Corbin 1998: 205)

In other terms, a quantitative procedure is liable to limit the research to the preset categories acquired from experience, secondary literature, personal inclinations, or, in the best of cases, of the first round of inquiry, the pilot study. Moreover, it is more adequate in the case of preset variables. However, the aim here is to determine properties and dimensions for expectations, nuances, and characteristics. Strauss explains: »by the term ›qualitative research,‹ we mean any type of research that produces findings not arrived at by statistical procedures or other means of quantification.« (Strauss and Corbin 1998: 10-11). Therefore, the use of standardized quantitative means of data collection proves to be inadequate in

---

10 See the explanation about the organization of the research in the introduction.

our case because it will involve having preset values for our unknowns. This is the case in the quantitative approach liable to omitting from its perspective the emergence of new categories initially unanticipated by the researcher. Because the unknowns are by definition interpretations from which we try to construct types, it is not possible to start with the types themselves. This implies that the direction of the construction should be from the data to the categories. With the absence of quantitative data and the scarcity of theory and »technical literature« specific to theater in Lebanon like reports or papers of professional and disciplinary writing serving as background materials against which findings from actual data can be compared (Strauss and Corbin 1998: 35), it is useless to speculate or count on personal experience alone in the purpose of building a preset concept to be tested or elaborated. However, quantification is used in the assessment of the importance of certain categories and their relevance to a potential emerging theory. The relevance of a category and its ranking in the conceptual ordering has been determined by the *frequency* of its occurrence in the different coding procedures resulting from the interviews, especially the phase known as »open coding.« Later, in the »axial coding,« frequency was also an indicator of the relevance and the dimension of a certain property with respect to a category. This is how the »interplay between qualitative and quantitative methods« mentioned by Strauss and Corbin (1998: 31) is applied in the »conceptual ordering« and »theorizing« procedures (1998: 15).

Furthermore, due to the delicacy of the issue of confessionalism, the chances of getting reliable information through questionnaires are tiny. People do not talk freely about this topic, as it was experienced in the field work. Also, we do not have the possibility of following an incoming idea by asking on-the-spot questions in such an approach. The lack of trust in discussing the theme of confessionalism in public would eventually lead to intentional inaccuracies in potential questionnaires. On the contrary, in a direct interview, there are more chances of deducing the effects of confessionalism depending on the interviewer and the analytical method thereafter. Now how does the »grounded theory« become visible in the practice?

The »grounded theory« is a method of leading qualitative analysis, which starts with a case study and then moves to a more general level following a series of abstractions and coding procedures: open, axial, and selective coding. This theory is rooted (grounded) in data acquired in a field research. Silverman (1993) defines »data« in the following manner: »When we say ›data,‹ we mean interviews, observational field notes, videos, journals, memos, manuals, catalogs, and other forms of written or pictorial materials (qtd. in Strauss and Corbin 1998: 58). Practically, data are analyzed and classified in concepts. These concepts are either codified by the researcher or they are assigned codes found in the raw data as pronounced by the actors (in-vivo). By processing the codes, which are attributed to parts of data, we come to categories. The relations of the categories to the phenomenon in question and their interrelations to each other form the theory or the types we are seeking. The first stage, the open coding, aims at the discovery of new codes and categories: »Open coding: the analytic process through which concepts are identified and their properties and dimensions are discovered in data« (Strauss and Corbin 1998: 101). The second phase, the axial coding, aims at finding the relation between those categories: »Axial coding: the process of relating categories to their subcategories, termed »axial« because coding occurs around the axis of a category, linking categories at the level of properties and dimensions« (Strauss and Corbin 1998: 123). The final stage, the selective coding, aims at filling the theoretical blanks in the links and in the main categories: »Selective coding: the process of integrating and refining the theory« (Strauss and Corbin 1998: 143). The ultimate aim of the coding procedure is to reach »theoretical saturation: the point in category development at which no new properties, dimensions, or relationships emerge during analysis« (Strauss and Corbin 1998: 143). After determining the codes and classifying the categories into theoretical frames, we come to building the model. This stage is not compulsory for the explanation of the phenomenon, however, it adds to the theoretical saturation of the desired theory. Throughout those phases, a selective process, the »theoretical sampling,« which determines the direction and sequence of each following stage, is taking place. »Theoretical sampling is sampling on the basis of emerging concepts, with the aim being to explore the dimensional range or varied conditions along which the properties of concepts vary« (Strauss and Corbin 1998: 73). The movement from the specific to the general leads to a more general »theory« with varying explanation power of the phenomenon in question. To the question of generalizing from one case study, Strauss and Corbin stress that a qualitative research consists of studying the concepts and their relationships and not the numbers. Manifestations of these concepts might emerge more than a 100 times in the one case, which might be in different forms according to the writers. If the concepts are abstract enough, then they gain a general aspect (Strauss and Corbin 1998: 284).

The analytic tools of the »grounded theory« turn out to be the most adequate for our research especially if we consider the taboo-nature of the emerging main category »confessionalism,« the delicacy of working on meaning and interpretation, and the need to construct confessional types.

The practical framework

Reaching results through the grounded theory is partly done through analysis based on comparisons, either with personal experience or with literature, and on asking questions like who, where, what, how,... (Strauss and Corbin 1998: 73, 92-3). Here, Strauss and Corbin emphasize: »*It is not that we use experience or literature as data but rather that we use the properties and dimensions derived from the comparative incidents to examine the data in front of us*« (1998: 80). To this purpose, several analytic tools are used to in the coding process.

The first steps of analysis using the »grounded theory« is the »microanalysis.« It consists of a »detailed line-by-line analysis necessary at the beginning of a study to generate initial categories (with their properties and dimensions).« »It is a combination of open and axial coding.« »Although microanalysis sometimes is referred to as 'line-by-line' analysis, the same process also can be applied to a word, a sentence, or a paragraph« (Strauss and Corbin 1998: 57). However, »*not every single bit of data has to be analyzed 'microscopically.'*[...] Usually, microscopic coding of 10 good interviews or observations can provide the skeleton of a theorethical structure« (Strauss and Corbin 1998: 281). The code resulting from this analyzed section form the basic unit of conceptualization and theorizing. After establishing the relation between the different categories and their properties and dimensions, a conclusion about the research problem is liable to emerge. It is usually in the form of an explanation with a generalization potential: a »theory.«

Strauss and Corbin define categories, properties, dimensions, and subcategories as the following:

- *Categories:* Concepts that stand for phenomena
- *Properties:* Characteristics of a category, the delineation of which defines and gives it meaning
- *Dimensions:* The range along which general properties of a category varies, giving specification to a category and variation to the theory
- *Subcategories:* Concepts that pertain to a category, giving it further clarification and specification (Strauss and Corbin 1998: 101)

Starting from the phenomenon »theater in Lebanon,« the aim is to detect and reconstruct categories and subcategories of factors influencing the production and reception of theater, their properties, dimensions, horizontal and axial interrelations. These form the end theory or »type.« With the use of a self-developed computer database application (explained in the following section), excerpts from interviews consisting of single words, sentences, or paragraphs, were assigned adequate codes. Within this coding system, the frequency of occurrence was easy to establish. It is the first indicator of the relevance of a certain concept. The categories, together with their properties and dimensions, emerged therefore from qualitatively assessed data. Their relevance to the phenomenon in question was measured quantitatively through the frequency of occurrence of categories (See Appendix B: Diagram 7). The conceptual ordering of the categories, which was more transparent at the end of the research, suggested the following practical frame: the environment of theater, the pre-performance phase, the performance, and the post-performance. The organization of the research is designed after the entity of the findings in the following way.

The actors of the phenomenon theater, were referred to as the *production agents* for the production part in contrast to *reception agents* for the spectators and audiences. For the period extending *outside (pre/post)* performance, these include: the producer, the playwright, the director, and the actors. During the performance, from the production agents, only the *actual* actors are on stage, interacting with the audiences and the technical elements. The reception is also divided into two phases: *pre/post* performance and *during* performance. The human elements taking part in this process are the audiences, referred to later as *reception agents*.

In the process, four levels corresponding to the phases of the process from the environment to the performance were distinguished.[11] The aim of those levels is to make the organization and the conclusions more manageable.

- *Level I*: designates the general environment where theater is taking place. This includes Lebanon—with its two internal milieus—and the externalities coming from the global environment. The actors at this level are: Christians and Moslems. The relevant institutions at this level are the religious and educational.
- *Level II*: designates the process of production and reception, as a sub-process of theater outside the frame of the performance. The actors at this level are the producers, the playwrights, the directors, and the actors. These can be designated as *production*, or, using to this end the in-vivo terminology from the interviews, *the theater people*. Parallel to those are the potential audiences, to which we assigned the term *reception*. The word *actors*, unless it is explicitly defined in the context as *stage actors,* designates the human factors in the phe-

---

11 See appendix B, diagram 2.

nomenon. Among the institutions involved at this level are the universities, censorship bureau, and the religious organizations.
- *Level III*: designates the performance itself as a sub-process of theater. The actors at this level are the stage actors and their audiences.
- *Level IV*: designates conclusions and consequences. Theoretically speaking, this level is the end product of the other levels. It also situates the effect of the performances and of theater within the general environment. It induces a change caused by cycles, plays, and performances. In the frame of the research, it represents the conclusions derived from data.

Those levels form the framework of the field research; however, they are extendable enough to avoid hindering the discovery of new data. Through the interaction of those levels with each other, a better formulation of the theory is reached.

Organization of the research paper

A question can be asked here: if the core method of the research relies on the »grounded theory,« how come we find a historical elaboration of »confessionalism,«as main category, right at the beginning? With a typical qualitative research, there are points of interest that turn around a certain phenomenon, which can be expressed through a question, which the research is supposed to answer through an explanatory theory rooted in the empirical results. Even if confessionalism would have been considered as a »mini-theory«—which is not the case, since it emerged from data—confessionalism would have had a practical side.

»From a practical standpoint, the mini-theories have merit, especially for practitioners who need knowledge to handle problematic situations on the spot« (Strauss and Corbin 1998: 282). In our case, keeping confessionalism as a background for the interviews avoided endangering both the field research and the interviewer.[12] Besides, confessionalism imposed itself as *the* main category in the open coding, the phase of detection of the relevant categories in the grounded theory, as mentioned above. Since the historical overview is displayed at the beginning of the paper, it was logical to present the historical background of confessionalim also at the beginning. This is not a denial of the emergence of confessionalism as a main category in the empirical data; it simply denotes a more logical way of organizing the data. On the other hand, a sequential presentation of the empirical findings in order of appearance complicates the display of the results as well as the organization of the research.

---

12 See section: Limitations of the research.

Hence, instead of following sequential order, the categories were displayed according to their hierarchy. The properties of each category, including confessionalism, even if they emerged at later stages of coding, were all presented as one section with the category. The relation to other categories were mentioned also within this section. A synthesis of the categories and their interrelations is found in the brief conclusions at the end of each level.

In other words, from the categories that appeared in the open coding, the main parts of the research could be classified within the above mentioned levels, whose purpose is to distinguish between the different processes related to theater. This also helped in defining the frame of the fieldwork. Later, the interrelation between the different fields served to explain the theoretical relations. For practical purposes, results that emerged from the axial or selective coding were also displayed at the beginning. Again, the reason was to overcome the non-practicality of the sequential display of data complicating the deduction analyis. It is therefore likely to find categories that appeared factually in the end of the fieldwork presented before their chronologically precedent emergences. Also, the relations between categories were presented in all cases departing from the category regardless of the chronological sequence. All in all, the paper follows an argumentative organization. Starting from Level I, the environment of theater, we acquire global results of the field research. Based on those, analysis was performed through each section. Historical and background data are limited to the introduction. All categories emerged from the data.

Regarding the Arabic concepts and names of persons and organizations, the transliteration used is according to the »Deutsche Morgenländische Gesellschaft« in its publications and by Hans Wehr (1952/1977). However, the names of persons and organizations that already have a French or English spelling are kept in this spelling. The transliteration is detailed in the following table:

Arabic alphabet	Transliteration
ا	ā
ب	b
ت	t
ث	ṯ
ج	ğ
ح	ḥ
خ	ḫ
د	d
ذ	ḏ
ر	r
ز	z
س	s
ش	š
ص	ṣ
ض	ḍ
ط	ṭ
ظ	ẓ
ع	ʿ
غ	ġ
ف	f
ق	q
ك	k
ل	l
م	m
ن	n
ه	h
و	w, ū
ي	y, ī
ء	ʾ

Table 1: The Arabic transliteration according to the Deutsche Morgenländische Gesellschaft (DMG) and to Wehr (1952/1977)

The field research and the database

The research, as has been said, follows a schema of open, axial, and selective coding of the qualitative analysis. It consists of interviews with the actors outside the frame of the performance, together with the observation of a multitude of performances.

In the fieldwork, interviews with the actors resulted in a mass of field notes, transcription texts, and protocols. The attitudes of actors were found to be varying according to the confessional belonging of the interviewer and the interviewee, the region where the interview is taking place, the structure of the audience and its expectations, and other situational and structural factors. Two social worlds crystallized. They include persons, organizations, and institutions, all having confessional labels. Confessionalism, the first category to appear in the open coding, was gradually categorized. It characterizes the relation between actors and audiences, and in all what is of relation to the concept of the *other*, but most importantly on the level of interaction especially in the performance. The construction of the *other* on the confessional basis is, therefore, part of the relevant attitudes. Those differences were obvious in interviews of multi-confessional mixture of audiences and actors. In addition to that, the categories *other* and *self* were also elaborated as subcategories of confessionalism. In the axial coding phase, the interviews were guided towards the completion of the interrelations between the main categories, which was followed in parallel with theoretical sampling. Reaching the selective coding, the same data was used to detect selective categories, which were in this case, related to the symbolic *elements of play* used in the interaction.

The interviews are classified in a large self-designed database of transcriptions,[13] offering several analytical tools like coding and classifying. Identification numbers are associated with each excerpt. The recovery of any or all of the desired data records can be achieved by a simple entry of the identification number. For data protection purposes, only partial information was included in the text. Translations of selected citations without the complete interview information are found in Appendix A. The Arabic citations are found in Appendix C. They can be used for reference purposes about the way the results were deduced. Throughout the text, references to the direct data are kept through identification numbers. Underlined numbers mean that the excerpt is found in the translated section at the end. Here, a remark about the translation should be mentioned. This translation was made with reservation from the Lebanese spoken Arabic. The intended meaning of the interviewee, along with the interpretation of the interpreter, departed originally from the Lebanese text. The coding procedure was also made based on the Lebanese text as transcribed directly from the taped interviews. The English translation, which came at the end, was used only for illustration purposes. Strauss

---

13 Many programs aim at facilitating the qualitative research like ATLAS, ETHNOGRAPH, and NUDIST. My application, based on Microsoft Access, offers a self-tailored solution to coding and the quantification of results.

and Corbin encourage only a minimal translation in order for the English reader to get a feeling about what the interviewees are saying. This is because »the difficulties of accurate, let alone nuanced, translation are legion.« For this purpose, key passages and their codes can be translated only to a high degree of approximation. One should say that »many of the original subtleties of meaning are lost in translation« (1998: 285-6). For the sake of integrity, however, the Arabic reference numbers are also mentioned in parentheses. These are the non-underlined numbers. The complete Arabic text is found in the database explained hereafter and a hard copy is found in Appendix C. The use of the citations in the text came from the coding procedure. This implies that some citations, which are loaded with more than one code, are cited at different places. Their illustrative power, however, is not equal at all times, and if we take one point, some reference numbers are more illustrative than others. This discrepancy is molded when looking at the sequential context in which the coding was elaborated.

The database program contains all the interviews and makes them easily accessible throughout the research. This helps a lot in the classification of the large amount of interview excerpts, but more important in the coding processes. The retrieval of the results of the coding phases is made faster and easier and the frequency of appearance of a certain category in the open coding was automatically registered. In the following phases, the axial and selective coding, easy access to the root data helped verifying the source at any point, which allowed the double-checking of the data. Moreover, the semantic frequency of relevant words or in-vivo concepts could also be detected. With this, there was quantification of the qualitative results.

Observation and protocoling

In opposition to film or text, we cannot »catch« the performance. Creating a video film of the performance restricts the analysis to the perspective of this film limiting hence the freedom of the potential reception to that particular frame. This aggravates the importance of the observation data, in which a researcher has the chance of living this unique and unrepeatable event, and therefore the freedom of analysis. In any case, there is very little filmed material of theater plays, because of copyright considerations.

Limiting the observation phase to the actual field research period is not quite accurate. The researcher started following the subject already in the early stages of his work in theater. This has two sides: first, he was able to gather a good deal of inside information, which is a positive result; second, during the present evaluation of the interviews, he had to filter out the opinions, which were built during this extended observation. On the whole, the long observation period opened the door towards an in-depth analysis, and helped especially in refraining from hasty, inaccurate judgments. The observation of the latest field research, however, which was accompanied with field notes and protocols, constituted in the bottom line, next to the interviews, the main material on which the results were based.

Interviews

The aim of the interviews was to gather audio material and, when possible, other data to analyze following the methods described above. They consisted of a series of conversations with actors, directors, producers, playwrights, critics, and spectators, with different lengths. At the beginning, there was a sketch of a guide for the interviews, [14] but later it was more beneficial to lead the interview towards an open-end type, where the possibility of getting new categories, especially about critical or taboo subjects, is more likely. As a start, two guidelines explained below, were designed: one for the audience on the reception side and one on the production side.

An interview would start by stating the name and the place where the person comes from. This way one has a fair chance of knowing to which confession the person belongs. The reason is the demographic division issuing from war.

Apart from that there were always other guidelines to knowing the origin of the person, regarding accent, clothes, education, and so on... Of course this means a considerable amount of time to be allocated to each interview according to the guidelines, especially when the interviewee goes astray and wants to talk about other things of interest to him. In the evaluation phase, this time revealed to have been well invested.

On the production side, interviews were conducted with: directors, actors, producers, writers, critics, and other people who work in theater. On the reception side, the different audiences were equally interviewed. This was done either directly before or after the performance, or independently from a specific performance. The length of the interviews varied according to the time allocated to by the interviewees and the saturation level regarding certain points. The range shifted between less than five minutes, in the case of on-the-spot interviews with audiences just before, or right after the performance, to a long argumentation of more than three hours, usually with theater experts. The number of those interviews is about a hundred. This was conceived as a security margin. Two important goals were achieved through this large number. First, no incoming

---

14 A copy of the »interview guidelines« is presented in Appendix A.

data seemed to bring any novelty to the coding procedure. Second, through theoretical sampling and selective coding in the last interviews, a confirmation of the first results took place. No more data about the points that were not satisfied in the beginning came from the last interviews. By moving closer to »theoretical saturation« (Strauss and Corbin 1998: 292) is where the field research came to an end.

During the open-ended interviews, some questions where intentionally used as stimulators for talking in order not to lose the spontaneity of the interviewee. This resulted in long interviews. Confessionalism, which is a taboo-topic, has dictated the use of this method. The conversation aims at determining how theater is received by both audiences and theater people. The points brought up by the interviewees were elaborated. Among other things, they were relevant to the level of their education, theatrical education. The interview starts with a general overview of the meaning of theater and the spontaneous comments on defined points in a particular play. Then it moves to tackle more critical things regarding confessionalism, identity, the war, the political situation, and other themes the interviewees associated with the play. The next step is to get an opinion about other plays they saw, and what they found interesting in those plays. With different degrees of success relative to each interview, the data collected was satisfactory in getting substantial results.

In the transcription, only illustrative sections of the interviews, which do not represent the whole text, were considered in the in-depth analysis. These sections, ranging from one word to a whole paragraph or a series of paragraphs, amounted to 1666 sections of which 1269 sections were coded (76%). A number of 181 sections (10.8%) were translated as illustrations. Strauss and Corbin stress that the amount of descriptive quoting from interviews to be included in the text as a whole and the translated parts are left to the researcher to determine according to his purpose (1998: 283). »In general, however, we think twice about loading a theoretically oriented monograph with too many chunks of descriptive material« (Strauss and Corbin1998: 284). For practical reasons, it is not possible to include all those citations in the text. This would put down the logical sequence and make the text incomprehensible. Once again, we stress here that the value of the data comes from the frequency of the concepts determined hereby through the coding procedure (1998: 284) and not through the microscopic analysis of every detailed piece of data. This coding was best made through the database. A statistical diagram of the frequency of the main categories is found in Appendix B, diagram 7. The written material is usually presented after the analysis is through, it »usually begins with an introductory chapter, followed by a review of the literature, then a presentation of the findings (in two or three chapters), and then the summary/conclusions/implications section. For all that, the thesis writer might be able to think architecturally about the middle chapters« (Strauss and Corbin 1998: 251).

Limitations

There are many limitations to the field research. First, apart from the unwillingness to discuss confessionalism, asking about that subject was also dangerous regarding the precarious status of freedom in the country. It was therefore not advisable to ask certain questions because of the police and a multitude of security systems.[15] This made the interviewees reluctant to talk about things associated with the war like confessionalism or the view of the *other*. The classical answer to such questions would be: »we are all brothers,« and this would practically mean the end of the conversation. One has to be satisfied with what the interviewee narrates about the others and his or her analysis of their line of action. In addition to that, it was not obvious that the interviewer, coming from the domain of theater and personally knowing most of the people working in that field, could tackle certain topics which could be considered as personal. Moreover, to many interviewees, it was not clear why the interviewer would ask questions to which the answers are quite evident for somebody who lived the war and worked in theater. The aim of being objective and wanting to extract all the data from the interviews was not evident. Second, video cameras were not allowed inside theater houses, because the producers usually have an agreement with a certain TV station, to exchange the copyrights of filming the play against advertisement. Third, the production actors are unwilling to reveal certain aspects of their professional methods by openly discussing the own work. It was another challenge to extract that information. Fourth, the translation and transcription of interviews presented another type of problem concerning the accuracy of the translation, as we mentioned earlier. Making the analysis and coding departing from the original language of the interviews solved this problem. The intensity, tone, and delicacies are not always shown in comparison to the original text. Fifth, using the performances as examples present another problematic issue. Due to security and also professional considerations, it is not appropriate to include any names in the confessional or professional context. This created a substantial prohibition to the freedom of using the essential information gotten either from interviews or from observations. Complete anonymity is rather impossible, since any little reference to the story, the place, or the context of a

---

15 Having the private security personnel is a matter of status and power. In many performances, it is not unusual to find many groups of private bodyguards.

theater play immediately reveals the persons involved in it. This had a serious influence on curbing the use of examples and citations, especially in relation to critical topics. On the one hand, creating friction is a confirmation of the analysis presented in the research; on the other hand, it limits the tools used to reach this analysis. This implies some scarcity in the use of examples, citations, and descriptive detail. Sixth, another type of scarcity is also found in the written literature about theater. Only a few books and newspaper articles are available. The rest of the information—also the historical part—was extracted from the interviews with many inaccuracies in the documentation of the interviewees and knowing the problem of the absence of official statistics about theater productions or the audiences.

A historical overview

In this section an overview of the historical context of Lebanon is presented. It also offers an overview of the history of Lebanese theater.

The confessional context

Tracing the roots of confessionalism is a long odyssey in the history of Lebanon. This is due to changing regional, military, and political actions determining its fate. Some stations in this history left undeniable impressions. The confessional context serves as a support to understand the dimensions of some of the terminology used in this research namely the rupture between Christians, Moslems, and Druzes. The narration of history is, however, influenced by the confessional identity of the narrator.[16] This is noted in many instances. At schools, history books avoid mentioning any event from a confessional perspective. They go as far as denying such interpretations. Many are the books, however, that elaborated on the role of confessionalism in shaping the modern history of Lebanon. Most of those were written either by Westerners or from a Western perspective. Taking advantage of the climate of freedom in Europe and America and of the distance from the Lebanese environment, which usually acclimatizes the writers in this context, the narrators of history from this perspective consisted of Lebanese doing their research abroad, together with Westerners associated with Lebanon either through their fields of research or through their fascination in the Orient as a whole,

---

16 In the overview here, I relied on Salibi's (1991), which is considered as the standard work to the history of Lebanon.

with Lebanon being the key to understanding this Orient.[17] We move now to basic background information of the territory.

Lebanon is a small country (10452 km²) on the eastern coast of the Mediterranean. Its population consists of three million Lebanese belonging, with different proportions, to 19 religious affiliations called confessions *(ṭawā'if)*. Derived from Christianity, Islam, and different ethnic groups, these sects can be reduced to two groups: Moslems and Christians. This reduction is dictated by a de facto partition established during the Lebanese civil war (1975-1990) into two major camps, with the higher religious belonging binding the ethnic subdivisions of the camps together.

One common experience among these confessional groups that fled to Mount Lebanon seeking refuge is persecution. They were mostly »Syrians who could not tolerate tyranny« that fled to ›L'Asile du Liban‹ as Henri Lammens, a Jesuit priest of Flemish origin, called it. Those persecuted in Syria were not only the Christians, but also the Shias and the Druzes« (Salibi 1988: 134). Later, under the Shihab regime, »Lebanon became the refuge of the Greek Catholics persecuted by the Greek Orthodox, Armenian Catholics persecuted by Armenian Orthodox, or Druze and Greek Othodox persecuted by the Wahhabis in Syria« (Salibi 1988: 147).

Inside the confessional blanket, we find tribal sections. »the Maronites of one mountain district – that of Aqura – were divided into Qaysi (north Arab) and Yemenite (south Arab) factions, much as other tribal Arabs in Syria were« (Salibi 1988: 85). The Druzes were divided into three parties: the Jumblatis on one side, the Yazbakis on the other side headed by the house of Imad, and the Nakadis in between headed by the house of Abu Nakad« (Salibi 1988: 111).

Over the years, there were trials of peaceful coexistence between the different groups, but it was not much of a success. Tension, conflicts, and massacres occurred between the coexisting communities, especially between the Maronites, a Christian sect, and the Druzes, originally a sect of Islam. Starting as early as the mid 19th century, »the clashes between Druzes and Christians continued for two decades since 1840-1, and ended by the large-scale massacre of the Christians of southern Lebanon and Wadi al-Taym in 1860« (Salibi 1988: 68-9). In this massacre, »the Druzes massacred about 11,000 Maronites in the Shuf and Wadi al-Taym. In other parts of Syria, about 12,000 Maronites were massacred in one day. This led to the French entering the Shuf area, while France con-

---

17 For an elaboration on the Lebanese war, see Hamdan (1997), Hanf (1990), Riek (1989), Petran (1987), Deeb (1980), and Hudson (1968). For a general overview of the Lebanese history, see Salibi (1991, 1988, 1976), and Hitti (1965).

sidered itself the protector of the Maronites for they were considered Roman Catholics. Afterwards came the »Règlement Organique« of 1861 to organize Mount Lebanon, which was convened in Beirut and called for by the French« (Salibi 1988: 16). On the other hand, »The Muslims, quick to take advantage of any weakness among the Maronites, attacked Mount Lebanon every time they heard that its people were divided by heresy« (Salibi 1988: 79). At the heart of this conflict is the historical identity of the common state:

Since the emergence of Lebanon as a state in 1920, the Christian and Muslim Lebanese have been in fundamental disagreement over the historicity of their country: the Christians by and large affirming it, and the Muslims denying it...From the Muslim side, there has been an insistence that whatever history Lebanon can claim for itself is in reality part of a broader Arab history. Yet the notion of what really constitutes Arab history remains confused by the fundamental historical association between Arabism and Islam. (Salibi 1988: 3-4)

The last clash was the latest Lebanese civil war (1975-1990) during which almost every confession had is own militia and fought, in turn, against the others. Also in 1990 there was no solution to the coexistence problem, and what is more important is that the identity problem, the main conflict point, did not find any solution either. However, other factors played a role in ending the war in a sudden way in 1990. The $ṭā'if$ agreement concluded by stopping all military actions, and reduced some of the Christian privileges to the advantages of the other communities.[18]

Hence, the formation of the Lebanese state carried already the seeds of its fall, which are found in the structure of its population. »...most of the Arabs who adopted it (Arabism) were tribal or quasi-tribal communities of different kinds, and also of different religions and sects, who had not undergone a uniform social and civic development, and who were therefore still far from having achieved the attributes of a real nation« (Salibi 1988: 52). However, this structure did have prosperity during a certain period of time before the last civil war. It was a precarious prosperity threatened by political instability and shaky short-term agreements between the leaders of the confessions.

---

18 There are many interesting events that took place, which were not covered by the scope of the research like the withdrawal of the Israeli forces from South Lebanon in May 2000 and the departure of the Syrian army from the rest of Lebanon in April 2005. These had substantial influence on the political and social environment of theater in Lebanon and are for sure worth studying.

Those two lines of identity were reflected socially and geographically in two social worlds resulting in war, regionalism, and isolation. This is the reason why our consideration was limited to two fields of study of theater instead of 19. Also, it is important to mention that, during the war, theater did not cease to exist. Following the example of all the institutions, educational, political, social, etc., theater was geographically located in two zones: West and East Beirut. The Druze areas did not witness any important theatrical activities like those in the other parts of Beirut. Also, the Southern Suburb of Beirut, whose population consist of a majority of Shias did not witness any noticeable theatrical activities.

Historical overview of theater

Classified under »Arabic theater,« on the one hand, and trying to find the links to the Western theater on the other hand, we observe in theater an extension of the historicity and identity conflicts. The literature about theater in Lebanon differs according to the confessional identity of the writer, similar to the entire phenomenon of theater. This divergence is manifest in two directions: an »Arab« line of thought and interpretation presenting an Arab version of the identity of theater and the Lebanese society, paralleled by a »Lebanese« line still looking for a self definition and trying to find it sometimes in the West and at other times in a retrospective reading of the Lebanese history. Literature between those two lines did not cross the border of plain documentation based on interviews and newspaper articles aiming to produce a historical reconstruction of the history of Lebanese theater. They are limited in the realm of highlighting the role of a certain person active in theater. This explains, to a certain extent, the reason why the institutionalization of theater did not succeed till the present. Nevertheless, the history of theater in Lebanon is not detached of that of the Arab countries as we see later.

Depending on our definition of the scope of theater, four forms of theater can be considered:the first is called »'al-ḥakawātiyy« (the narrator), which consists of a one-man-show sitting in the cafés and telling heroic war stories to the visitors of the café. Second, we have »ḥayāl z-ẓill«[19] known in the Western definition as »shadow pantomime.« Third, we have »ṣandūq l-furǧah,« a puppet show coming out of the box (ṣandūq), and fourth »'az-zaǧal,« which is a form of improvised poetry between two groups of poets challenging each other in front of a live audience. These could be seen as the earliest forms of theater in Lebanon. Due to the lack of accuracy in documentation, a great deal of information and illustrative examples are, as mentioned earlier, based on the memory

---

19 For more about » ḥayāl z-ẓill,« see Sa'ad (1993).

of the interviewees. These four forms have sequentially died. The last one is also on its way to extinction. The modern history of theater after these forms is divided in the following phases: the beginning with Mārūn n-Naqqāš in 1847, the phase after Naqqāš extending till 1960, the »theatrical movement of the 60's« which extended from 1960 till 1975, the war phase from 1975 till 1990, and the post war theater from 1991 till the present.

The modern form of theater in Lebanon started with Mārūn n-Naqqāš (1817-1855), who is acknowledged by most of the references (Kurayyim 2000; Yaghī 1999; Rahī 1999; Sa'id 1998; Shaoul 1989) as the pioneer in bringing theater to the Arab world and by all as the first to present what we now call theater in Lebanon. The first play he presented was »'al-baḫīl« an adaptation of Molière's »L'Avare,« in 1847. It was presented in front of an audience consisting of a gathering of his friends and the intellectual elite and a group of politicians in his house in Beirut. In 1849, he presented also in his house in Beirut, the second play, »'abu l-ḥasan l-muġaffal 'aw Hārūn r-rašīd« (The Dumb Abu l-Hasan or Haruun Ar-Rashid). A description of this performance is found in David Urquhart's »Lebanon—the Mount of Syria... History and Memories,« according to Yaghī (1999). The third play came in 1853 »al-ḥasūd s-salīt« (The Naughty Jealous). It was presented in the first theater house which was built next to the house of Naqqāš in Beirut and was later turned to a church after his death (Yaghī 1999: 21-30).

The phase after Mārūn n-Naqqāš was characterized by a heavy emigration of the Lebanese theater people to Egypt. There, the freedom climate under Al-Khedyawī Ismaīl has allowed theater and arts to flourish; whereas Lebanon and the other »Pays du Levant«—according to the French naming—were drowning in a dark era of repression of freedom by the Ottoman regime, anxious to save its empire from the increasing influence of the European missionary schools in the area. Near the end of the 19th century, many Lebanese intellectuals emigrated chiefly in two directions: Egypt and America. The theater people went more to Egypt starting from 1876, because of the language advantage (Kurayyim 2000: 54-56).

During the period, extending approximately from the beginning of the 20th century till the 1960's, theater continued in a less powerful manner than in the Naqqāš period. Kurayyim (2000) cites that since the beginnings of the Western model with Naqqāš, theater did not cease to exist except for the period of World War I (Kurayyim 2000: 60). Apart from that, theater performances were held in schools like the »Ottoman College,« »the Maqāsid schools,« »La Sagesse,« »Les Écoles des Frères,« »zahrat l-'iḥsān,« »the Patriarchal school,« and »the ṯalāṯat aqmār school.« There are no documents indicating the confessional distribution in relation to the reception of theater between Christian and Moslem schools or universities. These schools are Christian in their majority, however, except for the Maqāsid, which is Sunni. They usually presented one performance at the end of the school year. At that time also, theater started in the universities like the »Université St. Joseph« ('al-yasū'iyya), the »Junior College,« and »the American University of Beirut« (Kurayyim 2000: 80-84). Later on, theater was sponsored by religious and beneficiary organizations, but it did not have a long life because it was accused of promoting for »corruption and immorality«—mainly from the religious authorities at that time that felt that theater was getting out of their control. At that stage also, Lebanon witnessed the birth of several theater troupes, the first one to appear was »munazẓamat 'ihyā' t-tamṯīl l-'adabiyy« (the organization of the revival of literary acting), (Kurayyim 2000: 89-90) followed by a series of troupes, which were known according to the founder/leader more than by the types of performances they produced.

Afterwards the most important phase in the history of the Lebanese theater came at the beginning of the 60's with »'al-ḥaraka l-masraḥiyya« (The Theatrical Movement). This was associated with two names: Mounir Abou Debs and Antoine Moultaka.[20] The first was director in the »Troupe of Modern Theater« (firqat l-masraḥ l-hadīṯ), in which we also find Moultaka. Later, Moultaka founded the »Circle of Lebanese theater« (ḥalaqat l-masraḥ l-lubnānī). This period also witnessed the birth of the Baalbak Festivals,[21] »masraḥ mahrağānāt Ba'albak d-dawliyya,« which started its activities formally in 1969.

The productions in the 60's were generally translations from the western theater prospected for an intellectual audience. Since theater then was a novelty, the audience was unknown and the production focused on staging imported europeon classical plays, which reflected a line of translation and adaptation typical to the Lebanese theater. »firqat l-masraḥ l-

---

[20] The Christians were pioneers in starting theater in Lebanon. With this movement of the 60's, the name analysis (see section: A Historical Overview) shows that this did not change. Nevertheless, it is hard to get any clear statement, even from the founders of the movement of the 60's, about the confessional belonging of the entire group of participants in that movement.

[21] The question of the confessional identity of these festivals with their international dominant participation is difficult to answer. On the one hand, their organizational committee follows the internal proportional confessional distribution on the institutional level, and on the other hand, it tries to maintain, to a certain extent, a neutral »national« timbre. Another issue is whether, according to this line of thought, »neutrally« percepted Lebanese artists exist in the first place. Whether, for example, the singer Fairuz, a symbol also of those festivals, is considered in reality as a symbol of a Christian view of Lebanon or of a »national« one.

ḥadīt« presented the following plays: »Oedipus the King« (Sophocles) in 1966, »Macbeth,« (Shakespeare) in 1962, »Les Mouches« (Jean-Paul Sartre) in 1963, »Hamlet« (Shakespeare) in 1964, »Le Roi se Meurt« (Ionesco) in 1965, »Die Physiker« (Dürrenmat), »The Kings of Thebes« (Sophokles) in 1966, »Les Justes« (Camus) in 1967, »The Exception and the Rule« (Brecht) in 1968, »The Celebration of a Killed Nigger« (Arabal), »Faust« (Goethe) in 1968, among others. Facing those classics, there was only one originally by a Lebanese author »'al-'izmīl« in 1964 by Antoine al-Maalouf (Sa'iid 1998: 150-3). Parallel to those, the »ḥalaqat l-masraḥ l-lubnānī« presented in the same line plays like »'anā nāḫib« *(I am a voter)* in 1970 (Caragiale) and »Caligula« (Camus) in 1970 (Sa'iid 1998: 171-7).

This »golden« era of the Lebanese theater was interrupted by the civil war of 1975, whose roots are spread along the Lebanese confessional history from the Ottoman era to the 1860 eruption and the »qā'immaqāmiyyatayn« period. The theater of the war was distinguished by a break in the old »intellectual« orientation, introducing new types like the »Chansonnier Theater« and »Boulevard Theater.« It also strived to have a closer relation with the audience. This implied a more relaxed attitude towards what was previously considered as sacred. The after war period witnessed a general decay in theater, and unsuccessful trials to repeat old »successes.«

Overview of literature

Few are the books dealing with the Lebanese theater. Also, fewer are those that take an analytical approach to add to this literature. Most if not all are limited to portraying a sketch of the history of theater, starting from the persons and names that made this history. Following a chronological order of the phases of history, we start with the most recent publication by Muhammad Kurayyim's, *al-masraḥ l-lubnānī fī niṣf qarn: 1900-1950* (The Lebanese Theater in half a century: 1900-1950). In this book we find a narration of the history of Lebanese theater in this period, along with its historical context of development. The book sheds a light on two areas: the first is »theater in the schools« in Lebanon in the era after Mārūn n-Naqqāš, and the second is the theater troupes that existed in the period from 1900 till 1950. In addition to a survey of the performances of those troupes, the book contains parts of the texts of plays, a description of the theater houses, and other places of the performances. In the second part, there are short biographies of some theatrical figures. In the third part, two full texts of plays are found.

The second book of interest is Khalida Saʿīd's *al-ḥaraka l-masraḥiyya fī Lubnān: 1960-1970* (The theatrical Movement in Lebanon: 1960-1970). Saʿīd's book, in cooperation with the »Commission of the International Festivals of Baalbeck,« is a detailed documentation of the history of Lebanese theater taken mainly from live interviews and newspaper articles. Starting from the names of groups and individuals, the book delineates biographies of actors, directors, playwrights, and the history of theater within the educational institutions like the American University of Beirut, the Université St. Joseph, and others.

Paul Shaoul's *'al-masraḥ l-ʿarabiyy l-ḥadīt: 1976-1989*, (The Modern Arab Theater: 1976-1989) published in 1989, takes the Lebanese theater from an Arab perspective giving a documentation about theater in the Arab world, along with a multitude of biographies of theater people, mostly Lebanese.

Abd ar-Rahman Yaghi's book *fī l-ǧuhūd l-masraḥiyya l-ʿarabiyya: min Mārūn n-Naqqāš 'ilā Tūfīq l-ḥakīm (In the Arabic Theatrical Efforts: From Maruun an-Naqqash to Tuufiq al-Hakiim)* gives another Arabic perspective of theater in which the Lebanese played the major role in creating the Arab theater. It moves from the Lebanese space, with Mārūn n-Naqqāš, to Egypt and Syria as a continuation of this movement.

In the Kuwaiti periodical *'ālam l-ma'rifah* (World of Knowledge), Ali ar-Rahii writes an overview about theater in Lebanon. He based his information mainly on one article in the »*Lebanese Literature Magazine*« of January 1957 written by Abed el-Latīf Sharāra, in addition to a research about »political theater in Lebanon« by Ghassan Salamé and a newspaper interview with Marwan Najjar, a Lebanese contemporary producer and playwright.

Among the books headed at criticizing theater, Abido Basha presents some analytical view of theater. In his *kitāb ar-rāwī* (1995) (The Book of the Narrator) Basha presents biographies of several theater figures. In *bayt n-nār, 'az-zaman ḍ-ḍā'i' fī l-masraḥ l-Lubnānī (Fire House, the Lost Time in Lebanese Theater)* (1995), we find a controversial view of the question if Mārūn n-Naqqāš could be considered as the first pioneer or not. In *mamālik min ḥašab, 'al-masraḥ l-ʿarabiyy 'inda mašārif l-'alf t-tālit* (1999) *(Kingdoms of Wood, the Arab Theater at the Brink of the third Millennium)*, Basha presents a more critical view of Lebanese theater within the context of an Arab experience. He continues to present an overview of theater in Egypt, Tunisia, Syria, Morocco, Algeria, the Arab Golf, Iraq, Palestine, Jordan, and Libya.

The rest of the documented sources consists of newspaper articles and interviews with the actors and directors who lived the beginnings of the theater in the 1960's, their memories, their documents, and photos.

Some of those documents were put together at a later stage in books, like *masraḥī wa l-masraḥ* by Isaam Mahfuuz. The lack of literary works, which was a common problem among those who worked on theater, can be reported to a general underestimation of the importance of theater, as well as the concentration of theater people on theater work more than on documentation. Next to that, we can trace this to a general weakness of the written culture in the Lebanese society compared to the oral one.

THE ENVIRONMENT OF THEATER (LEVEL I)

From this point on, the results of the field research are detailed and classified in four levels.[1] The empirical data gathered through observation, interviews, and unregistered conversations,[2] led to the formation of categories at Level I, whose interplay with the subprocesses of theater at Level II affects the selection and composition of what is denoted as *the elements of play* and their reception parameters. These, in turn, are at the basis of the interaction and interpretation within the frame of the performance at Level III, and the post-performance evaluation at Level IV. Departing from the interviews, we have a reconstruction of the attitudes of the actors, Christians and Moslems, including their determinants of action. Moreover, the categories of the environment of theater (Level I) are summed to be the »first reality« (Reality One or »R1«) in contrast to a »second reality« (Reality Two or »R2«),[3] considered during the performance (Level III). This terminology will help to understand the link between environment and performance as it crystallized from the fieldwork (2273, 2668).[4] The concept behind these levels and divisions will be elaborated gradually in the following sections. We start with the major category at Level I, confessionalism.

---

1 For a quick overview of the resulting categories see Appendix B, Diagram 3. For a graphical presentation and statistical overview of the coding results and frequency of the categories, see Appendix B, Diagram 7.
2 Certain theater producers preferred not to tape parts of their interviews, especially when it came to discuss mentioning the works of other theater people or their opinions about the other confessions. For this purpose, the interviewer recurred to field notes, samples of which are found in Appendix A: Examples of Field Notes
3 See section: »R1« and »R2,« The Basis for Interpretation
4 These numbers correspond to the large database of citations taken from the interviews of the field research explained in section: The Field Research and the Database. Only a representative part (180 citations) is translated in Appendix A, Translated Interveiw Citations. These are the ones in italics in the parenthesis. The rest remained in the original Arabic language in Appendix C. The abstraction and categorizing were effected from the Arabic language; therefore, the abstraction when compared to the translation can contain some impurities.

Confessionalism: a major »sphere of discord«

Confessionalism, a characteristic impressing the modern image of Lebanon, has its roots in the remote past of the country. A refuge for persecuted communities, Lebanon, as shown in the section »Historical Overview«, is composed of a mixture of communities refusing to give up their confessional identities in order to merge in a common national existence. The will to keep the confessional identity created a status of competition among those communities, as well as solidarity and loyalty to the own community on the expense of a common national Lebanese identity. In order to understand the roots of confessionalism, we find that the concept of »'aṣabiyya« as elaborated by Ibn Khaldun[5] and the traditions and culture issuing from it can present fair explanations to this social configuration. However, the properties and dimensions of confessionalism denoted thereafter are the result of interview categories. Their roots may be found in Ibn Khaldun's »'aṣabiyya .« In short, »'aṣabiyya « implies a loyalty based on blood relations in a hierarchical structure whose core unit is the family. In its extension, it means the clan. With 'aṣabiyya, we can also anticipate feelings of rejection or hostility towards other groups, which were later conceived as confessionalism.

Terminology and characteristics

There are several etymological definitions of confessionalism. *Webster's Third New International Dictionary* defines the word as follows: *»Confessionalism*: n. the principle that a church should have a confession of faith: devotion or adherence to a confession of faith.« Next to confessionalism, there is another word close in meaning. *»Sectarianism*: n. sectarian spirit or beliefs: exclusive or narrow -minded attachment to a sect, dedesignation, party, or school <religious ~> <socialist ~>.« *The Concise Oxford Dictionary* defines *»Sectarian*: adj. & n. adj. 1. of or concerning a sect. 2 bigoted or narrow-minded in following the doctrines of one's sect. n. a member of a sect. 2. a bigot.« The definition of confessionalism in the *Wahrig Deutsches Wörterbuch* is oriented towards the object of faith: *»Konfessionalismus*: <m.;-; unz.> Festhalten an einem bestimmten Bekenntnis: theolog. Richtung, die dies als unerläßlich betrachtet.«

In this research, the term confessionalism is used as a translation of the Arabic word *(ṭā'ifiyya)*, which is frequently encountered in discus-

---

5   Abd ar-Rahman Ibn Mohammed Ibn Khaldun (1332-1406), an Arab sociologist and philosopher, elaborated on the concept of 'aṣabiyya in his »muqaddimat Ibn Khaldun,« which he started to write in 1374 and finished later in Cairo (Ibn Khaldun: 1990).

sions at all levels. It came in-vivo in the interviews as a standard concept. *(ṭā'ifiyya)* has many religious, communal, social, and political connotations. It entails the foundations for the definition of the *self* and its separation from the *other* within the Lebanese context. These dimensions were developed extensively over a long period of time, especially during the war period, which covered the period from 1975 till 1991. *(ṭā'ifiyya)* has as consequences the solidarity with the own group, discrimination, aggressiveness, hostility towards the other groups complying thus to a great extent with the concept of »*'aṣabiyya.*« Furthermore, the word commonly used to describe extreme feelings of confessionalism in the Lebanese context is »*ṭa'aṣub,*« which is syntactically related to »*'aṣabiyya.*« »*ṭa'aṣṣub*« is literally translated as *fanaticism,* which can be oriented towards different objects: ideological or religious. The common meaning of »*ṭa'aṣub,*« developed especially during the war, when no other modifier follows the word is confessional fanaticism.

Moreover, the adjective *confessional* is used by both Christians and Moslems, as a quality attributed to persons, like »he is confessional,« for example. Its intensity varies, along a spectrum, a person can be *non*-confessional or *very* confessional or *extremist* in confessionalism. Confessionalism, also, can be denoted as extremism, or fanaticism. The difference between those two words is very thin. Extremism, for the person using it, defines confessionalism as being an attribute of the *other* (not I), and is therefore negatively used. The user is at a distance from that extremity. Fanaticism *(ṭa'aṣṣub)* has the meaning of belonging and high solidarity, it defines confessionalism as being an own attribute, which can be regarded as a positive quality, with which one can even boast about.

Confessionalism represents the first major sphere of discord in the environment of theater. Before going through the effects of confessionalism on theater, we go through the nature of confessionalism as seen in the eyes of the actors. This situates its role in the structure, and discerns its influence on this structure and consequently on theater. The conclusion is that not only did confessionalism present a modifier to the structure, but also it polarized the attitudes of the people towards themselves. Before proceeding to delineate its properties and dimensions, we mention here that in the coming text, several designations are used for the religious communities. Some are deduced from the interviews; others are chosen because they are more adequate for theorizing. The Christian community is denoted as: »the Christians,« »the Christian social milieu,« or »the Christian social world«; in parallel, the Moslem community is denoted as: »the Moslems,« »the Moslem social milieu,« or »the Moslem social world.« In order to avoid misunderstanding, especially for the

Lebanese reader, it is noted that the aim of these designations is solely the designation of the cultural space. They do not have any allusion neither to religion nor to politics, nor do they pretend to encapsulate the structure or concept of any of the communities to any frame. Their origin is the scientific categorizing based on the field research and partly taken from the common language of the people themselves.

Confessional neutrality

The first characteristic we encounter during the interviews is that both production and reception agents are conscious of the existence of confessionalism. Attitudes and reactions, however, show differences depending on confessions. Nevertheless, they vary in their willingness to talk about confessionalism depending on their trust in the objectiveness of the interviewer or if the conversation could lead to problematic consequences. Their attitude towards discussing the subject moves gradually from »total unwillingness,« sometimes directly and bluntly stated at the beginning of the interview, to a degree of tolerance mixed with caution. Caution is reflected in refusing to get into detail or to be involved into a discussion of the sort in front of other people.

When tolerating to talk about confessionalism, the individual usually sets himself at a distance from the topic ensuring personal noninvolvement *(641)*. The attribute of being confessional is rejected from oneself and passed on to the other confession. It is like a contagious decease, a taboo that has to be tossed away. One explanation to this is that confessionalism is associated with the war and its atrocities, which are still fresh in the minds of the Lebanese. Crimes committed during the war were to a large extent linked to confessionalism. Being confessional entails an implicit image of association with those crimes. Moreover, regardless of the role of confessionalism in the war, it grew strong during that period, especially under the geographical and demographic divisions in Beirut and the rest of Lebanon. This created a convenient atmosphere for barriers to freedom and consequently the tabooing of confessionalism both on the social and political levels. To this end, there arises a constant need of justification from the accusation of being confessional or not.

Lifting this accusation is thus a need both in the public and the private spheres, and also in theater in order to gain credit among the audience. In an interview with a Christian play producer and actor, who was presenting his plays solely in Moslem Shia areas (Example A, Appendix A), he emphasized the fact of having a mixture of all audiences and that the actors of his group are also a mixture of all confessions. However, in the areas where the performances are taking place there is a little chance of having Christian spectators. First, this contradiction suggests the necessity to be confessionally neutral in the aim of having more audience (*2547*), and second, it shows another face of confessionalism. A Christian representing the Moslem view of politics on stage or vice versa has more weight than a Moslem pleading for the same matter, because he comes from the *other* camp. Since this would serve the own community, the parties of influence in a certain area have an interest in displaying such a case supporting their point of view about the occupation of the South, where the Shia form a majority. In this case we have a presentation of the *self* by the *other* in the favor of the *self*. The actors gain popularity, since they are an exception to the rule playing outside their natural environment. There are however conditions to be accepted to present the *other* in his area apart from standing for his cause. For this purpose, a theater agent should build good connections with the influential persons in that area in order to get the approval of going there in the first place.[6] Similar to this case, many directors strive for confessional neutrality, but this can have negative effects on the reception of the play. It also reflects fear of the *other* and lack of security regarding critical topics like confessionalism. Assigning neutral non-confessional names to theater characters, which is the case in all plays, is an illustration of neutrality (*820*). It is rare in a theater play to find names like Muhammad (likely to be Sunni), Toni (Christian), or Ali (Shia). Rather we find Fadi, Sami,... and other passe-par-tout names not standing for any religion. As a result, the play becomes void of credibility and misrepresentative of reality for the critical spectator. On the other hand, using confessional names elevates the degree of symbolical confessional friction among the audience. Production agents, as we see later, seek the middle path between neutrality leading to dullness and friction, which is attractive but dangerous. Usually, they stand at the edge of friction.

On the reception side, neutrality has another face. In an interview with a Christian spectator coming to see a Moslem actor performing in a Christian area (example B, Appendix A), he said that he is there for the sake of seeing the actor[7] and not the play, because this actor proves to be »not confessional« due to the fact of presenting his play in a Christian area. By watching a performance of this play, this spectator wants also to declare that he is not confessional (*2810*). The other extreme is not to go to a play because it is done by a Christian or a Moslem. This view was uttered in many off-the-record conversations by spectators of other theater plays.

---

6   See section: Politics of the Social World.
7   The play is a one-man-show, which usually leaves the whole space for the actor to show his talent.

Two confessional views of confessionalism

»The identity of the individual is defined according to his confessional belonging in Lebanon« (Section: Translated Interview Citations, citation *337*)

»We should be in Europe... No, no, in America [...] No, not Arabs... We are not Arabs [...] We have a problem of identity and belonging« (Section: Translated Interview Citations, citation *409*)

»I am looking at this experience [a Moslem play] as one step on the right track in the search for an Arab art which has its identity and specifications, and that, through the serious cooperation between the Arab intellectuals and creators« (Section: Translated Interview Citations, citation *3079*).

These contradictions, which speak for themselves, show only one face of the differences between the two social worlds. Christian statements characterize a major side of the conflict, confirming the historical problem about the identity of Lebanon.[8] Apart from the historical conflict, acknowledging confessionalism as a problem is not seen in the same way in the Christian and Moslem social worlds. In the Christian domain, confessionalism is not highlighted. It is a repressed topic, not so pleasant to mention. It was mainly characterized by denial, rejection and unwillingness to discuss, and this had many forms and excuses. The few individuals who engaged in open conversations about the topic constitute the exception to the rule. In the Moslem milieu, the existence of confessionalism as a problem is acknowledged more openly than in the Christian milieu. Confessionalism and its related issues are considered as a problem in need of discussion in order figure out solutions for it (*961*). Nevertheless, this readiness is mixed with caution and fear, which materialized in avoiding specific details like names, places, political parties, and the like.[9] The same thing is observed in theater where there is avoidance of symbols of confessional nature (*186*).

In the Moslem milieu, confessionalism is blamed on the Christians, who keep holding to their privileges at the disadvantage of the Moslems. During the war, confessionalism played the role of igniter of clashes between the two camps keeping differences active. On the other hand, confessionalism is seen as a barrier to the individual ambitions, especially of the Moslem community. Since most of the public posts in Lebanon are distributed on a confessional basis, the access to these posts can only

---

8 See section: The Confessional Context
9 In one of the interviews with an actor who, after the war was over, was kidnapped, threatened and shot at, in the other area, the person in question refused to give any direct detail about that incident even though it was not much of a secret by the time he was interviewed, and that it was already an old story.

succeed for candidates of the corresponding confession. This is seen as an injustice and disadvantage in the Moslem milieu. In the Christian milieu, these »privileges« are considered as a political guarantee of a »persecuted minority« within a Moslem environment (*2287, 226*).

The confessional world: the »Self«

The social world is held together by feelings of belonging to the *ṭā'ifa*, which in turn conceals a family structure in its background. Within this world, we have internal rules of hierarchy and distribution of power. These are present in two main concepts: *za'īm* and *wāsiṭa*, explained below. Many conflicts are witnessed at the *individual-collective* and the *ruling-ruled* levels. As a result, we notice a weakness of the institutions of the state in comparison to the confessional ones. This section presents the confessional world starting from the confessional community.

The confessional community ('aṭ-ṭā'ifa)

The confessional community in Lebanon represents the frame of identification and belonging to its members. It is the focal point, towards which loyalty is directed. As mentioned earlier, the *'aṣabiyya* enhances these feelings of solidarity and loyalty to the community. Supporting the brother in the *ṭā'ifa* (confession) is a duty of the *ṭā'ifa* member. This support becomes very uncompromising when confronted with a member of another *ṭā'ifa*. About solidarity and hostility, R. Schechner writes:

In humans, substitute in-group and out-group for »my species« and »other species.« Many languages reflect this division by naming the home culture »human,« relegating all others as non-human or barbarian [...] (which) gives rise to two complementary conflict systems: 1) aggressive conflict against outsiders (»not my people«); 2) aggressive solidarity for insiders (»my people«). (Schechner 1984: 246-7)

In the Lebanese case, this has become the nucleus of a » confessional identity« to the members of the *ṭā'ifa* differentiating them from the non-members and hindering them from merging together in a »common identity.« Salibi writes:

In the Lebanese Republic, civil, commercial and criminal law was the same for all, and its administration remained in the hands of the state courts. On the other hand, matters of personal status involving marriage, divorce and inheritance were left to the religious courts of the different sects which were officially recognized as part of the Lebanese judiciary... every Lebanese citizen, regardless of personal wishes, was officially recognized as having two identities, one national, the other confessional. (Salibi 1988: 194-5)

With the weakness of the state, especially during the war, the confessional identity gained ground over the national one. The individual is more likely to identify with the *ṭā'ifa*, his natural environment, than with the artificial structure of a state build on shaky foundations and oral conventions. Within the *ṭā'ifa*, we find a solid family structure, in which inter-confessional marriages are neither encouraged nor desired. The result was that the family structure is in its majority within the *ṭā'ifa*.

Family and clan

The family[10] (*'al-'ā'ila*) and its larger form, the clan (*'al-ašīra*), are the basic units of the confessional community. The family is acknowledged as a natural standard unit of the community in both milieus. The reasons for that can be associated with religion. Both Christianity and Islam call for the unity of the family and the respect of the parents. As a result, the family is the first loyalty factor forming the identity of the individual. Also the confessional belonging dictates and teaches the importance of the family. The family ties rank, however, higher than the confession. Moreover, the type of bond between members of the same confession is different from the type of bonds within the family, especially in the definition of the relation to the confessional *other*. Whereas the implications of confessional loyalty are liable to induce hostility; having a similar family structure implies respect for that structure and acknowledgement of the family as a sacred unit in both milieus. Loyalty and belonging are, thus, not exclusive to confessionalism; they extend to the family structure.

The virtues of the family are an emotional subject and an important source of emotionality, since the family ties are surrounded by a tone of holiness. They are incontestable and do not come easily to public discussion. In public discussions, we find highlighting the merits of the family and religion, leaving no space for critique. The family ligature is obvious and direct, it is taken for granted, and argumentation about those facts are insignificant (*769, 770*). It is in this sense self-justifying. Being taken for granted, nonetheless, does not mean acknowledging the family ties as a positive factor, it is seen as a fact (*2347*).

In theater performances, the family as a unit also affects the constellation of the audience. The collective sense of the family prevails over the individual one. It also affects the motivation for going to theater in

---

10 For more details about the family in the Lebanese system see Farsoun (1970) and Khalaf (1987).

the case of the »circumstantial or casual audiences« as we will see later. With the family structure favoring the collective, the space of the individual gets narrower leading to the second sphere of discord in the environment of theater.

The individual and the collective: a second sphere of discord

The confession and the family are the socializing factors configuring the personality of the Lebanese individual. Here, it is useful to differentiate between two types of the individual: the *person (šaḫṣ)* as opposed to the *individual (fard)*. This designation occuring in the interviews refers to the *person (šaḫṣ)* as integrated in the collective and draws benefit from his situation; whereas the *individual (fard)* is used as opposing this collective represented by the *person*. With the English translation (*fard* = individual), it is phonetically difficult to draw the line between the two.

Hence, the *person(šaḫṣ)* acts in the frame of »the personality resulting from the influencial transmission of psychological capacities of the human being with the values, norms, role expectations, and control of behavior acquired through socialization and the social environment« (Hillman 1994: 661). The situation of this *person (šaḫṣ)* in society is defined by the social role assigned by the family and the religious community. The *person (šaḫṣ)* is at the same time product and representative of the community. If we consider him to be an incarnation of the »traditional,« the *individual (fard)* would be the progressive, rational, scientific, emancipated, and self-aware »change-inducing« factor. In this regard, it is customary to have a conflict between the two developing to be our second *sphere of discord*, whose importance lies not only in the classical opposition between change and conservatism, but chiefly in the overlapping between the traditional and the confessional collective. The conflict between *the individual (fard)* and *the collective* as represented by the *person (šaḫṣ)* is redirected by the confessional authorities towards the inter-confessional sphere of discord, thus obscuring the internal conflict through diverting it to the exterior.

At this level, there is a parallel structure in both communities. The confessional rank defines the role and also the extent of power and authority. Exercising power is done in many cases according to the sole judgment of the *person (šaḫṣ)* in charge of a certain position, giving him more independent authority on the expense of the hierarchical system as required in institutions. The person, in return, pays more consideration to the confessional structure than to the governmental one, since his authority is deduced from the prevailingness of the confessional structure over the national one. This also increases the importance of the *person (šaḫṣ)* with respect to the governmental institutions, which leads to the conflict between the institutions on the one side and the persons on the other side. A common political discussion on the national level sets those two concepts in opposition to each other: »the state of institutions and the state of persons« *(dawlat l-mu'assasāt wa dawlat l-'ašḫāṣ)*.

In contrast, the *fard*, whose nearest conversion is »individual,« is the »opposite value to the collective and society, independent from the social and environmental factors, a 'spiritual' entity with free will, self-judging, and self-referential capacity« (Hillmann 1994: 360). Going against the tide the individual becomes a symbol of non-integration and an anti-confessional element. The will of self-realization of the individual makes way to many strategies aiming to overcome melting in the collective. His characteristics are a reaction to the compelling structure, and they are derived from strategies and tactics aiming at overcoming it. Because of the non-compatibility of a fulfilled individual to the structure, characteristics of this type of individual are found across both social milieus, but also the infiltration of the social role is present within both types. In our context, the »individual« is not merely a mark out of independency from the *collective*. It also represents a will to oppose and differentiate particularly from the confessional *collective*. The *person (šaḫṣ)*, on the other hand, is the one »freely choosing« to be integrated in the *collective*. In a further extrapolation, »individuals« could be hypothesized as a category apart.

Nevertheless, regarding communication, both types have common characteristics. First, we have a tendency towards easy judgment and classification of the confessional *other*. In a society based on differentiation, categorizing, and labeling, the individual tends to be accordingly judgmental. This affects the evaluation process in reception. It enhances »mass judgment« and »collective opinion« at the expense of the sticking to objective criteria and »sound« judgment (2986). The individual, although apparently refusing the imposed »collective opinion,« is nevertheless adopting the method and criteria under which this opinion is generated. Judgment is hence used in a comparable manner in the relations on the individual level. Second, we have the indirect way of communication. In an analogous scenario to the communities adopting indirect communication in order to avoid friction, the inter-individual communication is a reproduction of this scheme, and this not only in order to avoid friction on the collective level, between inter-confessional individuals, but also in the interaction between individual and the community. This is a characteristic of the theatrical communication on all levels, especially in addressing the *other*. It shifts the text from the direct to the abstract or indirect, like using remote analogies or jokes to be able to express simple ideas. As a consequence, the impact on reception is dimmed, because theater offers less of the classical sharp dramatic climaxes (34, 267, 2715); these are, however, replaced by a more elaborated allusive style *(laṭṣāt,* 2811).

In real life, the aim of both »persons« *('ašḫāṣ: sing. šaḫṣ)* and »individuals« *('afrād: sing. fard)* is success and achievement. Here, we witness the striving to transform the effects of power into wealth and money. In other terms, money by itself is an indicator of power and success (*86*), and hence improves the status of the individual in society. It is at the same time the means and the goal. The social ranking is considerably influenced by wealth, the criteria for success. Mercantilism and sense of profit are the consequences of this ideology. Success is usually achieved using the paths set through the structure, and its fruits are therefore hard to reap if one is an *individual (fard)*, in our concept of the »individual.« Success is both an achievement and an implication of achievement. Coping with the structure can be an achievement by itself, and it is distinctively on the individual level. As side effects, it affects the attitude of the individual towards the environment by stimulating arrogance, and show-off with symbols of success and status, which can be material or moral assets like education and culture (2183, *2184*). Theater, classified by society under the elastic term »culture« and part of the »cultural capital«[11] increases in »artistic value« the more the symbols used are »difficult to understand« and »abstract in form.« This opened the door for production to hide some of its incompetence behind the terms »difficult,« »cultural,« »theater is for the educated,« and the like. The reception, by accepting this classification, acknowledges its ignorance of theater (*2994*).

Thus, although the Lebanese have different characteristics leading to Christian and Moslem types on the collective level, we also find common characteristics on the individual level, something that is » typically Lebanese.« A typical example of the sort here would be the Lebanese food, which, apart from slight variations, looks similar in all Lebanese areas. At this level, the differences between the two *collectives* are set aside, and we get farther from the *confessional sphere of discord*. This level also constitutes the nucleus for identification on the reception level in theatrical productions of non-confessional nature. The reproduction of these characteristics on stage is part of the strategy of the production to attain a play that is equally accepted among multi-confessional audiences. This is the basic strategy of what I named the *Crossing Play*.[12]

---

11 Bourdieu 1982: 32 ff.
12 See section: The Crossing Play

Politics of the social world: wāsiṭa and zaʿīm

The misbalance in the power distribution between *persons ('ašḫāṣ)* and *individuals ('afrād)* paves the way for privileges and abuse of authority, the *persons ('ašḫāṣ)* being those complying with the confessional structure to reach personal goals and escalate on the social scale. The power of *persons ('ašḫāṣ)* comes, as has been noted, from going along with a system, which does not support the *individual (fard)* as such.

Within this composition, two concepts have developed: *connections connections (wāsiṭa)* and *patron (zaʿīm)*.[13] *Zaʿīm* means literary *patron* or *chief*, and it is the general designation for the powerful and privileged person, able to exercise authority in a certain domain, where others are not. Around this privileged individual, we find subordinate ones, whom he supports through his power, and in return they help him through loyalty to maintain power and privilege. Those people tend, consequently, to be loyal to persons more than to principles. The individual in this structure is related to the other through a relation of leader and dependents—*patronage*.[14] In this type of relation, there is no respect for the space of the dependents nor for their basic rights in a system of values, the relation is founded on the supremacy of power of the *patron (zaʿīm)* in relation to the dependents. The *patron (zaʿīm)* gains respect from the dependents according to the level of his strength, who, in turn gain a position among each other proportional to their loyalty and servitude to the *patron (zaʿīm)*. The *patron (zaʿīm)*, himself part of the confessional structure, follows its rules unquestionably as means to reach his ends. Striving to reach a better status, the individual aims to be a *patron (zaʿīm)* as ultimate status. To this end, the confessional system of values is more often used as a means and not as an end in itself.

Apart from that, the *patron (zaʿīm)* can acquire the image of a savior or a hero worth fighting for, or even sometimes dying for *(2350)*. This is the case of the political *patron (zaʿīm)*. The *patron (zaʿīm)* takes care of the worries of the people, and tries to keep their loyalty, the source of his strength through finding jobs for the needy, supporting with educational costs, and similar matters *(2724)*. Referring to a strong person in certain matters is very helpful to make even part of the inequality of the system. This means trying to get some of the privileges that are outside the reach of this individual. This can be done through confessional and family connections where the *patron (zaʿīm)* is also a subordinate in the hierarchy. The act of referring to those connections to reach a certain goal is called *wāsiṭa*, which means *medium* or *mediation*. Since in every institu-

---

13 For an elaboration on the concept of (zaʿīm), see A. Hottinger (1966). For a analysis of the Sunni community, see the sociological study of Johnson (1977), and that of Gilsenan (1996).
14 For an elaboration of patronage in Lebanon, see S. Khalaf (1977).

tion there is a *patron (za'īm)*, hence the *patron (za'īm)* concept is an integrated part of the communication between the *individual (fard)* and the institutions, which are dominated by the *collective*. The *za'īm*-subordinate combination and the *connections connections (wāsiṭa)* networking are part of the structure and can be extrapolated within the confessional as well as the political systems. The *patron (za'īm)* can be the confessional leader, the parliamentary deputy, the minister, or the patriarch of the clan. In *Rentiers, Patrone und Gemeinschaft: soziale Sicherunng im Libanon*, Rieger (2003) pleads that the confessional community *(ṭā'ifa)* is a modern form of the *patron (za'īm)*, corroborating thus the compulsory dependency of the *ruled* on the *ruling* in our third sphere of discord presented in the section below.

On the other hand, in order to keep the dependency of the subordinates, an atmosphere of outer threat is propagated among those subordinates, the source of which is typically the other confession. The *patron (za'īm)*, belonging to the same group, presents himself as the one who can protect his dependents. This has created inside both milieus a class of *(zu'amā': sing za'īm)* present at different levels (*229*).

Through socialization, the individual learns to »consider the other,« who becomes a »significant other« whenever the expectations of the other are known to oneself (Mead 1934). Confessionalism, the family and clan structure, which are the basis for this socialization, imply many duties on the individual: accountability towards the peers, a determined attitude towards the individuals of the other confessions, the consideration of the internal and external power balances, and the consequent social control and pressure arising from these implications. All these constitute an »unwritten law« through which the power distribution and accordingly the communication methods function. The pressure is increased or relieved respectively according to the individual acting against or within the confessional concept. This pressure creates direct limitations on the personal freedom of the individual and is reflected in restraints on the freedom of theatrical productions made at the level of this individual.

Theater acts on the thin line between the borders of a reality, as set by society, and fiction, another reality whose borders are solely set by theater actors and their respective audience. Used as a way of self-expression of the weaker individuals, it represents this second sphere of discord on the individual level. The value of this characterization of the common features of the weaker *individual (fard)* versus the *person (šaḫṣ)* is that it appears in theater as the neutral median characteristics creating a large spectrum of agreement and understanding between the different communities and audiences on a non-confessional basis.

»Rulers« versus »ruled«: a third sphere of discord

The structure elaborated above with the *patron (za'īm)* and the individuals in constant need for a *connections connections (wāsiṭa)* paves the way towards the formation of two groups: a class of *rulers* and one of *ruled*. The class of *rulers*, which are also *patrons (zu'amā')*, is resting on the incompetence of the national structure in facing the confessional one. It is also traditionally transmitted through the family, which, internally accepts the authority of the elderly as the *patron (za'īm)* regardless of his competence. The same is observed on the confessional level, the competence of the *patron (za'īm)* is not questionable. The weak institutional structure strengthens the unquestionable authority of this *patron (za'īm)*. Besides, the *patrons (zu'amā')* have got the key positions in the illusory state structure. Since the *patron (za'īm)* does not need legitimization for his authority, but he instead »rules,« the formation of the class of *rulers* is a logical consequence. It is manifested in the political ruling class, formed of traditional, old feudal, and clan *patrons (zu'amā')* together with the new *patrons (zu'amā')* produced during the war.

In the interviews, we notice that the interviewees make the division between *ruler* and *ruled*. This gap creates not only alienation between the two classes, but it also keeps the *ruled* class away from having any influence on the *ruling* system as a whole. This gap could be used to keep the structure safe from changes. One of the would-be roles of theater, as seen by the audiences, is to expose that to the public. In this hypothetical frame of lack of freedom, that same *ruling* class disables this role. Tensed feelings between the confessional communities act negatively in sustaining this status quo.

Institutions

On the institutional level, family ties together with confessional balances play an important role in hiring and recruitment at the expense of productivity, motivation, and expansion of the individual (*216*). Secularism is far from finding its way to the structure of the government; even though it is showing a growing acceptance among the less advantaged groups. In the communication between the institutions and the individual, confessionalism is reflected in a discriminative attitude extending over the Christian-Moslem domain, to Christian-Christian like Maronite-Orthodox or the Moslem-Moslem like Sunni-Moslem (200). Until now, the distribution of the jobs in the public sector follows a strict confessional proportion dictated by the »National Pact« (*'al-miṯāq 'al-waṭaniyy*) of 1943, which is an oral agreement between the leaders of the confessions about the proportional distribution of the confessions in the political participation. This has rapidly extended to the entire public sector. Furthermore, the confessional division is producing more private institutions, winning ground over the national state institutions. Here we find schools and universities, which are the starting point for confessional and religious socialization. In the private sector, the confessional identity of the owners or founders of the institutions determine the confessional proportion of the workers (*995*).

Similar to the case on the levels of actors, the emergence of confessionalism on the surface is repressed also on the institutional level, and this under several alibis. The most common alibi is that confessionalism being a direct cause of war, therefore any »excitement of the confessional feelings and instincts,« is a contribution to war. Therefore, it has become a taboo subject to tackle in public. Consistent with the above terminology, the »rulers,« whose roles may be endangered by a change in the structure, are the ones setting the margin for freedom of expression according to their interests.

Education

Contrary to what one might think, education is not the antidote to confessionalism. In Lebanon, education is an extension of the confessional configuration. Education has a traditional role in socialization and religious, confessional schooling. This can be observed among all communities. »In the Druze schools in Shuf, the history came to be taught according to some new Druze version. The symptoms were that the students didn't honor the Lebanese flag or national anthem, nor they referred to the state as a matter of principle.« (Salibi 1988: 202) On the Shia side, »the works of the Jabal Amil scholars, and the Shia religious teaching in general was meaningful to the Shia themselves and to Iran. They could not be traced as a part of general Lebanese heritage (Salibi 1988: 206). »The Christians adopted the Phoenician origin for Lebanon and elaborated on it as »Phoenicianism,« while in fact the Phoenicians themselves were Arabs. The Moslems, on the other hand, accepted that the Phoenician history would be taught as an integral part of the history of Lebanon, however, noting that the Phoenicians would not be presented as non-Arabs« (Salibi 1988: 175). Between the Arabism of the Phoenicians and the Phoenicianism of the Arabs, the historical conflict was gaining ground in the educational sector. The modern educational scheme is a reflection of this conflict.

On the other hand, education is a continuation of the *differentiation* process arising from confessionalism. One of the main effects on the confessional view of the *other* is that many Moslems consider the Christians more educated than they are. This puts a barrier between the two based on the educational level. Second, within the educational institutions, we find a reproduction of the confessional structure (475, 476). Schools as well as universities make no exception (724). Every *ṭā'ifa* has its own confessionally based schools and universities. Third, due partly to the high costs of private schools, education is regarded as part of the social status. It is important to show—even if only through simulation and pretense—that one is educated (*2994*). The social ranking can be made better through higher educational degrees. Education is, hence, among the show-off characteristics (2183, *2184*).

In theater, education divides the audience into two segments »educated« and »non-educated«, whereas the distinction emerging from the data can be better interpreted in the terms *cultivated (muṯaqqaf)* and *non-cultivated (ġayr- muṯaqqaf)*. Being *educated (mu'allam)* means having gone to school and university and eventually attained a degree. Being *cultivated (muṯaqqaf)*, as distinguished from simply *educated*, means having acquired more than scholarly education through reading and self improvment. Part of being *cultivated* is to go to theater; thus, seeking the acknowledgement of education. Culture creates a motivation of going to theater—and a specific type of theater: the »Intellectual Theater« in differentiation to the »Popular Theater« visited by the »rest.« Going to theater, thus, becomes here part of the differentiation between two types of audiences: *intellectual and popular.*

This distinction resembles Bourdieu's (1982) classification of »going to theater« as one of three ways of differentiation between what he calls the »working« and the »ruling« classes. These differentiation methods are manifest in spending on nourishment, culture (which includes theater), and self-presentation (representation) (Bourdieu 1982: 298-9). These activities form part of the »intellectual capital« (143-150) necessary for social »legitimation« (115). The »ruling-ruled« sphere of discord falls into this category, regardless of whether the »ruled« are at the same time the »working« class in Bourdieu's concept. We should note here that the analogy with Bourdieu, in spite of the apparent resemblance, is not typical of the Lebanese case, where we have a dominance of the confessional structure between communities and the hierarchical systems derived from it regarding family and clan. The structure of the *patron (za'īm)*, which might resemble the class distinction of Bourdieu is but a derivative of this clan configuration, which in turn is part of confessionalism. Hence, reducing the conflict to a sole class conflict is deemed inappropriate.

Regionalism: the geographical extension of confessionalism

Regionalismus bezeichnet Tendenzen zu einer verstärkten oder vorrangigen Orientierung der jeweiligen Bewohner an der eigenen Region, mit entsprechend verringertem Interesse für den umfassenderen Lebenszusammenhang (Staat, Kulturkreis, Kontinent, u.ä.m.) Regionalismus ist um so mehr ausgeprägt, je mehr die jeweilige Kultur mit einer spezifischen Kultur verbunden ist oder hauptsächlich bzw. gänzlich von einer ethnischen oder nationalen Minderheit bewohnt wird (Hillmann 1994: 729).

Webster's Third New International Dictionary defines the word as follows: »*Regionalism*: consciousness of and loyalty to a distinct subnational or supranational area usually characterized by a common culture, background, or interests.«

For our purposes, the word is used as a translation to the Lebanese *(manāṭiqiyya)*. Hence, the meaning of regionalism, as is the case with other categories, is derived progressively from our data, from which *regionalism* emerged in-vivo. The concept, however, is not new to the Lebanese history, where its roots are found. Regionalism is a normal consequence of confessionalism. It was strengthened during the war period, where it reached its peak. Moreover, as a product of confessionalism, regionalism was a factor keeping the divisions among the different Lebanese segments active during the war. It is affecting the Lebanese social environment, and consequently the social worlds of theater. In the following, we find a delineation of the nature, properties, and dimensions of regionalism and its role in theater. Some of the characteristics mentioned in the definitions above will come out to be close to reality.

Two factors contributed to the formation of feelings leading to regionalism: confessionalism and the *'aṣabiyya*.[15] With the war and its physical and demographic consequences, the regional ties grew stronger. Area loyalties grew stronger (*681*), and the environment, social world, extended to add a regionalist complexion to the already existing geographical and demographic distributions. With the weakness of the national identity, social and cultural loyalties are oriented towards the region. Regionalism also contributes to the definition of the identity, in spite of confessionalism being the main element prevailing in this matter. With the expansion of the playground of confessionalism itself, new areas of differentiation within the regional boundaries were formed. Regionalism also set new alliances within those boundaries. Roman Orthodox Christians living in West Beirut, for example, are closer to the Mos-

---

15 As defined by Ibn Khaldun: 1990

lem perspective regarding Arabism and its relation to the West than their counterparts living in East Beirut (*2937, 2951*). This effect is strengthened by the isolation between the areas, and could be explained as a reaction to being marginalized by the other Christian groups.

Nevertheless, the main contribution of regionalism to the Lebanese structure is that it allowed the transition from a cultural space to a physical one. In other terms, a physical area was created to be a home for the cultural space, and the two social worlds acquired physical dimensions and boundaries known as the Eastern and Western areas. This labeling comes originally because the first area to incur such a separation was the capital Beirut, which was divided into East Beirut with a dominant Christian distribution, and West Beirut with a dominant Moslem distribution. This does not mean that all of East Beirut consisted only of Christians and of the same sect, but that the majority was Christian. The same applies for West Beirut. Moreover, we find smaller divisions inside these areas and this into quarters and streets of a high concentration of either confession (*774*). Regionalism, thus, did not stop at the confessional level. It developed to cover other types of divisions. A geographical division, with its regionalist dimensions exists, for example, between »the mountain people« and the »coast people« (*2927*). Other divisions are between the North, the South, Beqā', Beirut, etc. extending the regionalist thinking beyond other feelings of devotion and loyalty. Beirut, however, is acknowledged as the center for all. In any event, regionalism, especially through isolation and separation, contributed to the creation of the two separate social worlds. It also influenced the sets of esthetic elements of the environment as shown later.

War

»You can't understand war until you live one [...] The war released the beasts, the dogs, and the lords in us,« says an interviewee. War extends throughout the Lebanese history and the formation of the Lebanese state. »From the 1930s, the streets of Beirut, every now and then, became the scene of violent clashes between Christian and Muslim gangs, one side brandishing the banner of Lebanism, the other of Arabism« (Salibi 1988: 180). If this were to be the sole problem or not, is a matter of interpretation. However, the description is valid from 1930 through the last events of 1975-1990. Under different banners, the different groups fiercely fought each other.

Whether behind the scenes or on stage, war is the catalyst that brought about all the differences and enhanced them. Without entering into all the psychological and social effects of the war, this section is reduced to the direct effects of war on theater and its relation to the other categories. War constitutes the biggest »social drama« extending to theater. War has clearly defined the groups on the Lebanese political and social scenes.

Catalyst effect: two areas and two audiences

During the war, the population, including the potential audiences, did not have the freedom of motion in all areas. Crossing from East to West Beirut or vice versa, presented particular difficulties. Check points, military of different factions, long waiting time on the *(ma'bar)*, the check point where it was allowed to cross from one area to the other, bad treatment, and the constant danger, made the crossing undesirable and reduced it to pure necessity. Those who did not have to go to the other area stayed gladly in one area in order to avoid the humiliation. Under these conditions, it was unthinkable to cross because of a theater performance here or there. This enhanced the *isolation* and the *divergence* in the development of theater according to the area and its audience, and helped developing a special cultural climate with the geographic separation (*2292*). The respective audiences got used to different living styles. The war played an important role in enhancing this division, which means years of deteriorating communication and agonizing social exchange. The social multiconfessional coexistence turned into pure confessionalism. As a result of the war, confessionalism (*671*), regionalism, isolation, demographic division, and separation (*2408*, *729*, *854*), ignorance and boycotting of the other (*861*) took over communication with the *other*. Many agree that the war ended without solution leaving the people unsatisfied and divided (*862*).

Nevertheless, the division due to war was reduced to two worlds despite the existence of a variety of confessions. The audience, following the example of the tangible regional division, was also divided in two parts: East Beirut and West Beirut audiences (1080). This physical division constitutes a major cleft in the Lebanese environment by building, in a painful and irreversible way, two cultural zones, two social worlds. The multitude of views corresponding to the different confessional communities fused hence together in two opposing camps defined by their geographical areas. This »de facto fusion,« which erased some of the specificity of each of the areas on the one hand, had the positive effect of forced unification of the different confessions in each area. This made it possible to limit the cultural environment of theater to these two cultural milieus in Beirut (East and West) and its surroundings extending on the coast stripe to Jounieh. Outside this area, there are few theater productions worth mentioning. Most of these productions are »moving plays,«

which started in Beirut or the surrounding areas, and moved on to visit those areas, especially in summer, where people leave the coast heading to the mountains.

From another perspective, however, the war can be considered as a unifying factor between the Lebanese. It is believed by many to be a war against Lebanon and not a civil war. Within this view, there is the belief of an intention to destroy Lebanon and its cultures (246, 261, 262). This makes the war a common experience and hence a unifying factor towards the making of the common national identity. This claim among some of the Lebanese intellectuals had little impact in the aftermath of the war. It did not reach any practical materialization. It was superseded by confessionalism.

On the family level, the war enhanced the long existing housing problem, which helped forcibly in keeping the family together because the children had to live with their parents due to the unavailability of houses. This strengthened the solidarity of the family together and helped increasing the family ties.

The separation due to war did not only happen on the geographic level, but also on the vertical structural level. The war helped creating a cleft in socialization between the old and the new generations. This led on the long run to a generation gap, since a big section of the war generation has the tendency to refuse the traditions of the old generation, whom they blame for the war and destruction (*967, 973*). To these particular *segments* of the war generation, and to the forced alliance under the two camps resulting from war, we can observe that the war did decrease the intensity of confessionalism turning it into feelings of sympathy to the »area inhabitants,« of the same camp, thus strengthening *regionalism*. In opposition, the war increased confessionally backed hostility towards the inhabitants of the *other* camp.

In summary, war played the role of a catalyst strengthening the divisions between the different groups on the confessional and regional levels. It also created a forced unification in two camps, thus decreasing *confessionalism* and channeling it into *regionalism* leading to two audiences. Moreover, as a reaction to war, there emerged an opposite attitude within segments of the war generation, which consists of rejecting confessionalism and its corollaries seeking a radical change.

Generation gap: a fourth sphere of discord

With the war building a gap between the two generations, a new sphere of discord is found in the environment. In connection with this sphere, new dimensions of age are developed. *Young,* for example, is used as a synonym for *»young in spirit,«* open, able to accept, and eventually carry out change (101, 102, 103). The *young* is a synonym of a new, non-conservative, structure; whereas *old* is the conservative, the representative of the confessional system with its values like: the enforcement of *respect of the elderly,* the determination of the social role according to age, keeping the authority to the elderly... Accordingly, it is not unlikely to have an elderly leader constellation, forwarding the leadership to their children. Nevertheless, the conservative attitude of the old generations is weakened by the war. The parents' authority has declined (2335). Facing this fact, the new generation finds itself in front of a crossroad centered on the dilemma of accepting or refusing the old structure.

Rejecting the old structure, which means an enforcement of the »I« with respect to the »me,« in Mead's terminology (Mead 1934), could induce social change. This could mean a rejection of the family structure implying a strengthening of the individual on the expense of the family, the main unit of the confessional system. There are vague traces of this kind of *revolution* within the new generation (181). In this case, the young individual finds him or herself fighting against the confessional tide, which supports the family, going back to the initial sphere of discord. As an active component of the structure, life is much easier on both carrier and social levels (2225). Hence, the pragmatic acceptance of the structure is the easier way to reach these goals. Acceptance starts by being a pioneer in serving the community *(ṭā'ifa)* and so accepting the assigned social role within the confessional structure. The potential rebels belong to a segment refused by the two societies, and they are generally individuals living outside the norms and the family system, or to *avant-garde* elements striving for social change. Among those individuals, we find a small part of theater actors and other artists making only an exception to the flux of artists integrated in and consequently benefiting from the structure. With this categorization of the war generation, we find ourselves with a special case of the *individual-person (fard-šaḫṣ)* or individual-collective sphere of discord. The difference here is the age factor, which is not always the case in the individual-collective sphere of discord.

Another category of non-integrated individuals, which increased as a result of the war, is represented through segments of the new generation overwhelmed by *globalization*, and stuck between the refusal of the confessional structure, incited to that by the effects of war on the one hand

and the dead end of non-integration on the other hand. Many of those end up adopting a day-to-day rhythm of life as it was forcibly dictated by the war. They lack the capacity to plan for the future, and the responsibility that goes parallel with such a planning. Many are »lost, have a fear from the future, and an absence of horizon regarding it.« They have symptoms of hesitation, lack of self-confidence, and are caught in a conflict between traditional identity and a vague fiction of a new identity mainly derived from and oriented towards globalization. On the active level, they seem to be pragmatic, non-accepting but at the same time non-revolting, and in a state of chronic waiting for some solution to come from the outside. Regarding theater, there are unjustified hopes that the new generation will be able to have better chances in advancing theater both as potential actors and audiences (624, 101).

Theater and war

Using symbols of emotional impact is at the heart of the communication between actors and audiences. A symbol loaded with emotions taken from the »emotional memory« of the actors (Stanislavski (1994, 167-171) with the appropriate adaptation to the audience can achieve a similar impact on the audience. This applies typically to those elements of play taken from war.

The direct effect of war on theater can be seen on two levels: the formation of a polarizing topic, and signs and symbols with a strong emotional impact, reminiscent and reviving of emotional experiences to all Lebanese. These could be names of persons, areas, and most prominently, topics and scenarios mirroring several façades of this war.

Among those signs, we mention: Kalashnikovs, military uniforms with different patterns indicating several groups, canons, tanks, different shades of the green color as worn by the different militias, smoke coming out of burned houses, broken windows substituted by plastic folders, walls filled with cicatrices of bullets and bomb pieces, half standing buildings... Added to those are the particular esthetic emblem created by the militias themselves: the cross of the »Lebanese Forces,« the main Christian militia, the different flags and colors specific to every group (deep green: Amal; yellow: Hizballah; white: Katā'ib; red: Socialist Progressive Party (the Druze militia); black: the Syrian National Party...), the variety of drawings of the cedar... Next to these signs, there are also situations evoking scenes from war. Examples are: waiting in line to get the bread (the militia people who cross the line without waiting are part of this situation), waiting on a gas station, waiting to get water from a broken pipe in the ground (for whatever reason that water is only available from this pipe), fighting for a place in the above mentioned queues, power cuts, shelter situations, crossing from East Beirut to West Beirut and vice versa, check point inspections... In addition to that, we find war-associated processes: rationing of food and fuel, rationing of electrical power, the substitution of the governmental institutions through confessional ones. These processes manifested in waiting queues, black outs, and chaos [...] Those symbols opened new dimensions of interpretations. Bombarding that starts at 10:00 in the morning, for instance, is considered »mean«; whereas, shelling later in the afternoon became part of »normality,« complying with the »rules.« These descriptions were used in the formal communication channels like newspapers, radio, and TV.

In theater, not only the new symbols were used, but also complete scenarios from the war formed the background for many theater plays. In *(ǧawz l-ǧawz)* »A husband for two,« a taxi driver is married to two women, one in East Beirut and one in West Beirut, was a successful attraction to the audience (2331). This fantasy reversed an ugly side of the war to the benefit of an ordinary person: the taxi driver. The fantasy of the taxi driver of marrying two wives—although, through his confession, he is not allowed to—making use of the separation and isolation between East and West Beirut during the war, made a special background for this Boulevard comedy. Another example we find in a play called *('aš-šahīd 'ibn l-balad)* »The Martyr Son of the Country.« In a scene where the protagonist, a normal citizen who chose not to fight during the war, is waiting in front of the bakery to buy bread, the militiamen from different »national« parties,[16] who are fighting in principle on the same side against other »less national« parties, start a gun fight among each other about who gets the bread first (2344, 2345, 907). Another example is in »'al-ḥalaba« (The Ring), which is a series of conversations between two militiamen on the opposite sides, and their way of seeing the world *(2711)*.

War affected reception on two levels. First, the war symbols, mentioned above, appeal directly to strong emotional experiences, and therefore provide vivid images. Second, the experience of war redefined the relation to the *other* and consequently the meanings of existing signs and symbols. Some acquired more intensity; some lost their meaning (2335). It has created a new perspective based on the reality and culture of war. During the war, for example, some theater houses were used as shelters, where people took refuge against bombing. This gave additional meaning and particular connotation to those places. A spectator, going after the

---

16 The meaning of the word »party,« as developed in the war, is understood in the context of armed militia with »party« as the administrative structure. The interviewees use the words party and militia interchangeably; party denotes here also the »armed people.« In many cases, the militias ended in being self-justifiable entities.

war to such a theater, where he or she was hiding from bombs cannot but make an association between the place and the war (604).

The war had a damaging effect on the emotional structure of the audience (*2278*). As a consequence, it induced a shift in the interests of the audience to the basic elements of survival, among which the role, function, and meaning of theater have to be redefined (1079). There was a strong need for entertainment and forgetting the bad times (*923, 988, 398*). Thus, it has defined the function of theater, as supplying the space for such an entertainment.

The attitude towards the »Other«

The two social worlds, although different in views of the world, are not independent from each other. In fact, they are much influenced by each other. Despite isolation and regionalism, the different communities kept the image of the *other* as a scale of reference for shaping the image of the *self*. This type of relation to the other helped in developing different channels of communication, through which the image of the self is made clear to the other and vice versa. Theater, through its role as presentation of the self, is a dominant figure among those channels. Through theater we have contact with the *other*. In relation to this contact, however, the society is in a constant motion of getting closer and gaining distance. The presence of the other among the audience affects both actors and audiences. The choice of having a certain topic under a certain esthetic form in theater is also affected by the type of company the spectator already has or expects to have within the audience: the peer or the non-peer *other*.

Isolation

Isolation from the *other* is a property of confessionalism strengthened through regionalism. It consists of being reduced to living in the own cultural, here also, geographic milieu. We notice that isolation is stronger with the younger generations, especially the war generation (*928*), rather than with the older ones, which had more chances of mixing culturally with the other side. Due to war, the new generation was forced to remain in the own milieu (*227, 781*). The two areas are physically as well as culturally *eclipsed* from each other. Regionalism, by providing two physical spaces to the confessions of Lebanon, helped in deepening the isolation and separation between them. As a result, people were able to develop different types of living in their respective areas, and hence two different sets of cultural signs and symbols (*523, 2271*). As a consequence of isolation, the *other* is not accounted for in the social cycle of the one milieu.

The social and artistic events remain most of the time exclusive to the peer like in the following example.

A ceremony dedicated to honor to a well-known theater person took place in a hall annexed to a church in an area not far from Beirut, the hometown of that person. The aim of the ceremony was to mark the long years of contribution to the promotion of Lebanese theater as one of the earliest founders. There was an official representation from the ministry of culture, but almost none of the fellow actors or directors of West Beirut was present. They were apparently not invited and the organizers explained that the ceremony is on the village level in spite of the official representation. On the other hand, the character of the place (the church) added to this result (243).

This is one of the reasons why there is little exchange between the two milieus on the cultural as well as on the social levels. This lack of exchange extended to theater as social act requiring tangible contact with the *other*. Moreover, isolation opened the door for the media being the sole interface with the *other*. Here, the confessional media was set free to shape the image of the *other*.

Knowledge of the *other*

The isolation also paved the way for fantasy and imagination about the *other* going beyond the media-constructed image. Consequently, the image of the »non-own« is not based on accurate information or facts (*594*). In opposition to that, the image of the *own* is embellished in differentiation to the *other*. Separation limited the information about the *other* and of involvement in his problems. The degree to which the actors know or are involved with the problems of the *other* became superficial reaching sometimes a high level of ignorance (461, *853*, *1069*, *501*, 502). Moreover, a growing attitude of »not mingling« in the affairs that are considered or labeled as »not belonging« to the own social environment. This tradition was passed on from the old generation to the new one, which had anyhow less chance of interregional mixing. Consequently, this tradition, mixed with an attitude of carelessness, has become more characteristic of the new generation (*2256*). After the war, a curiosity to know the other is slowly developing (*853*).

Limited knowledge of the other augment the sufficiency of relying on minimal degrees of contact, typically expressed through outer appearance and esthetics, through which a discriminative attitude from the *other* is developed. Knowledge remains thus limited to the identification of the confessional belonging of the person; afterwards, the preset opinions prevail. This affects also the patterns of communication. In a normal conversation between two persons who just met, for example, we can easily detect the change occurring once the confessional identities of the participants become clear. These changes can affect, the topic, the choice of words, or could even lead to a sometimes sudden end of the conversation, if the detected identity does not match presumed looks, linguistic fashion, or names of the participants.

Competition and duplication

Competition between Christian and Moslem confessions is present on both the individual and the collective levels, even with limited direct contact *(911, 585, 1065)*. The confessional *other* is always present in the mind as a competitor even when not physically or directly involved *(598)*. This leads to jealousy and encourages the formation of parallel structures within the social worlds. In theater, this competition has two forms: first, it is race on gaining the audience, the essential element for survival in the absence of subventions from the state; second, it is a medium of transmitting the peer values to the other. This is especially critical in friction topics approaching the national identity and the Arab-West views relative respectively to Moslems and Christians. Opposition to the mentality or the allegations of the *other* takes the form of an indirect dialogue in theater. Competition, fundamentally centered on differentiation, is oriented towards the *other*. It stops at that level without wanting further productivity. Personal initiative, freedom, and motivation are consequently limited. Competition and rivalry dominate the process of production, although not always on the surface. On the long run, they led to duplication between the social worlds, on the institutional level, including the existence of theater in both milieus.

Tension and relaxation

Confessionalism induces a feeling of relaxation and security about being among the peers, in the own area. Accordingly, there are also feelings of tension and not being at ease in the presence of the non-peers of the other area. This fact, amplified by the weakness of information about the *other*, increases the demographic isolation and its consequences *(557)*. Apart from being among the peers, being in the own region itself provides feelings of relaxation to the inhabitants. It is the physical boundary of the social world, where the work and the circle of friends exist *(556)*. The regular service-taxi[17] lines, for example, are still set between points of the one area. The old stop at the crossing point *(ma'bar)*, even though it should not be relevant now, years after the end of the war, is factually still exis-

---

17 Public transport cars (service-taxis) take several passengers at a time from A to B regardless of the road taken. It a sort of a shared taxi according to destination. In fact, it opens many possibilities for casual conversations.

tent. It is rare to find a taxi driver who would not consider the old *(ma'bar)* as a turning point. Even if one is near this point, he or she will still have to take a taxi to the »border,« and from there find taxis on the other side covering the other area. Crossing is always accompanied with tension. It is rare, even today, to find a taxi driver whose A and B are not in the one area. Answering my question if he would take me directly from West to East Beirut, a taxi driver said: »Everybody has his area, why should I go there and take the food away from the others? Neither would I want them to come here. I feel better working in my area.«

These feelings are considerably stronger, when progressing from the idea of the temporary visit to the idea of living inside an area dominated by the *other*. The barrier at this point is bigger and the effect is more tangible. The experience of the war, still fresh in memory, show how living outside the own community can be unpredictable, precarious, and insecure. The number of dislocated who lost their houses just because they happened to be a minority in a certain enclave is a witness to this fact. Hence, supplying also a feeling of security for the insiders (*227*), the region is acknowledged as an own domain of social existence (*332*, 781). Consequently, a Christian has little of an opinion about matters related to West Beirut in as much as a Moslem would not have an opinion about matters relevant to East Beirut. Neither wants a social role in the domain of the other.

Emotionality

On the whole, confessionalism is a product of emotions. It also produces emotions. The consequences of those emotions have accumulated with time to form the conditions of new confessional waves. The emotional nature of individuals of both communities and the noticeable extensive irrational behavior fortified during the war have contributed in aggravating confessionalism. The question why people in Lebanon are emotional is difficult to answer. The reasons could be traced to the natural climate of the Orient, to religious traditions, which are more oriented towards spiritual matters than rational ones. However, rationality is progressively gaining ground with increasing levels of education and exposure to globalization (2992). Emotionality is the fuel with which theater finds its way to existence. The Lebanese audience goes to theater to *feel*. The brain games are mostly not popular.

With emotionality comes also nostalgia of the past found not only with the elderly, but also with the war generation. However, this generation is nostalgic of a non-definite past, a past that it neither saw nor lived. In theater, the image of Lebanon is created based on *a* past that in reality may never have existed for the war generation. This leaves the door open for images of the past based on fantasy like in example D: *(ta'ā kūl mǧaddara yā ṣabī)*[18] »Come boy, eat *mǧaddara* « where we find a vision never seen by the author nor the working troupe. Nostalgia of the past for the war generation does not stop at the pre-war period, but it extends also to the war period regardless of the moral and ethical problems caused by and magnified by war (897). The war generation still longs for the war times. One explanation could be the excessive freedom from all commitments related to that period where the only worry is survival. Another is that the war itself covered parts of the best times of life, childhood and youth. The effects of this nostalgia centered on the war period reach the older generation of the theater production, which showed little adaptation enabling it to keep up with the new audiences (2919). There is a degree of nostalgia of the past in theater also. The audiences who were initiated to theater in the 60's kept a loyalty to the old forms of theater; it was then new and they were young. They are yearning for times before the war, where everything was young and beautiful (2813).

Next to those properties of confessionalism common to both milieus, and as their consequence, the construction of the other developed in the following way.[19]

The Christian construction of the Moslem

In the Christian eyes, art, acting, and theater are not accepted in Islam *(752, 1061, 584, 1089)*. They are not compatible. Due to »their« religion, Moslems are seen as »not free to produce theater because of the act of creation involved in theater and the religious hindrance to this act.« Whether this is true or not, the mere existence of theater in the Moslem milieu can be considered as a refutation to it. This idea that appeared frequently in the interviews represents a clear attitude of Christian audiences towards the Moslem theatrical milieu regarding arts and acting. Furthermore, Moslems are seen as unable of producing theater because they lack the philosophical »conflict« necessary to produce theater: religion takes care of all the details of life *(741)*; they simply do not need theater *(755)*. These views present one explanation why Christian audiences do not go often to West Beirut to see a Moslem production. Another view is that the Moslems are trying to »imitate« the Christians, acknowledged to be the pioneers in theater. This makes it less interesting to go to watch an »imitation« *(636)*. Here, we notice also the competition

---

18 See Appendix A, Example D
19 According to the method used in the research, the veracity of all claims used to present the constructions of the other in the following two sections, is not put to question. In the evaluation, some information in the interviews was taken »as it is« without making judgment about its validity in describing the other. It aims at constructing a picture as seen by the interviewee.

factor on the surface. All in all, theater in the Moslem milieu is seen as a dying trade, with no great hopes for the future (*328*).

Next to that, the Moslems are seen as representatives of the Arab identity and belonging to the Moslem world. Whereas the Christians compare themselves and tend to identify more with the Europeans and the Western free thought. They consider themselves as having more freedom and being more open-minded than the Moslems (*134, 731*). The Moslems are seen as closed and radical. This view extends to relate the Christian area to freedom of thought and the other area to a lower margin of freedom (*600*). This includes freedom of expression and action. »The Moslems are limited within the boundaries of their own religion,« concluded one actress (*138*). »They are tied up in many aspects like sex and the view of the woman, which are the most prominent taboos in the Moslem world« (150). The Christian actress is considered by the Moslems as »not decent in clothing and behavior,« says another during an interview (*140*).

The Moslem construction of the Christian

In the Moslem construction of the Christian, we see some parallel points to the preceding section in addition to more contradictions and indicators of ignorance of the other.

The Christians are thought to have educational advantages over the Moslems (*2237*). This has developed into different feelings of tensions and resentment like the inferiority-superiority dilemma in which Moslems think that »Christians think us inferior and look down at us because they, the Christians, are more educated.« (*2286*) These tensions augment especially when the contact increases between the two, like in the case of a Moslem living in the Christian area or vice versa (*225*). The Shias, in particular, consider themselves to be the most disadvantaged among the Lebanese confessions. They argue that the Christians have political privileges due to the » '*al-mītāq 'al-wataniyy,*« »The National Pact,« based on which the political equilibrium of the country was thought to be maintained. Especially the Maronites are seen as most privileged (*226*).

In theater, Christians are acknowledged as having a greater margin of freedom of expression. In example D, a criticism of the social life in old Beirut in a comic frame was presented through mentioning the name of a Christian saint in a comic way, a case not possible in Moslem theater about a holy symbol. »You're so innocent I can see already St. Rita hovering in the room over you,« says the dialogue in the performance. With the implicit confessional restrictions on freedom, putting a saint in such a context could be subject to severe censorship extending to banning the whole play. Later in an interview with a Moslem director who watched the same performance, she explained that the Christians are more privileged than the Moslems since they have a larger margin of freedom, and that, in a Moslem production, such an allusion to a sanctity would not be possible (*888*). »They always make it to have advantage. You can have more freedom in Ashrafieh. It is always the case,« she adds.

Differentiation and identification: two esthetic realms

As a result of confessionalism, regionalism, the attitude towards the *other,* and the definition of the identity of the *self,* two differentiated esthetic realms emerged, in which the own identity is defined through *differentiation* from the *other.* This differentiation, however, implies a certain image of the *other,* of what *is not,* as much as of the *self.* In this perspective, the communities show a parallel structure. The characteristics of this *other* have proved to be of minimal importance compared to the act of differentiation itself, whose roots could be traced back to *'aṣabiyya* and solidarity with the own community and stem, paralleled with negative feelings towards the *other* ranging from differentiation, distinction, and distancing, to hostility and hatred. These extremes were reached mostly during the war.

Differentiation has several forms, in the life style of the communities, their esthetic norms, as well as their moral values. In many cases, some common elements, esthetic, linguistic, and even moral values, evolved with time to meet the requirements of differentiation. These changes can be of different degrees. Some are slight, other more radical. The effects on the moral values were most of the times compensated for in an esthetic manner.

In this regard, Bourdieu defines the represented »social world« as »space for life styles«:

Die wissenschaftliche Einteilung in Klassen führt zur gemeinsamen Wurzel der von den Akteuren geschaffenen klassifizierbaren Praxisformen und ihren klassifizierenden Urteilen über die eigene Praxis so gut wie die der anderen: der Habitus ist *Erzeugungsprinzip objektiv klassifizierbarer* Formen von Praxis *und Klassifikationssystem* (principium divisionis) dieser Formen. In der Beziehung dieser beiden den Habitus definierenden Leistungen: der Hervorbringung klassifizierbarer Praxisformen und Werke zum einen, der Unterscheidung und Bewertung der Formen und Produkte (Geschmack) zum anderen, konstituiert sich die *repräsentierte Soziale Welt,* mit anderen Worten *der Raum der Lebensstile.* (Bourdieu 1982: 277-8)

In their understanding and assessment of style and esthetic taste, the two communities rely on practices within the own social world. The elements produced and the systems of classification and assessment of those elements are both products of this space. In his work based on class differences, Bourdieu describes three ways of differentiation between groups: »nourishment,« »representation,« and »culture.« Nourishment includes eating in restaurants; representation includes clothes, shoes, money spent on cleaning, perfume and the like; culture includes books, newspapers, music material, sport, toys, and cultural events (Bourdieu 1982: 300).

In Lebanon, we notice considerable differences in the same three categories. Some are the result of the existing class differences between a rich Maronite class and a typically poor Shia one. However, by taking a rich class of Maronites in comparison to a Shia rich class, the differences take another turn. *Taste* and *luxury* tend towards Arab esthetical values in the case of the Moslems, the kind we see in Arab countries like Egypt, whose esthetics are transmitted through the film industry and television, or Saudi Arabia. This shows in the architecture, the status symbols, the type of cars, and the like. On the other hand, the majority of the Maronites follow the French and American model regarding taste and choice of style elements. This sets two levels of differences: a classical class level especially between the Maronites and the Shias, and a confessional one prevailing over the esthetic elements like language, clothing, and the »life style.«

Furthermore, differentiation does not stop at the boundaries of the one social world. There are also inner divisions. The Armenians in Lebanon, for example, consider themselves as being »trashed« by the Lebanese including the Christian community. Moreover, they differentiate radically between their culture and the Lebanese one, which they consider as alien to them. Having to live in the alien culture imposes barriers on the development of the own culture, and constitutes a hindrance to their creativity, especially in arts and literature. This is more a characteristic of Armenian-Lebanese nature, regardless of whether Christian or Moslem Lebanese. Nevertheless, inner boundaries drop down in the case of an exterior threat like the case of the war.

Thus, the confessional identity induces the formation of emotional attitudes towards esthetic elements. These stem from the self-other views, but are based to a large extent on the already existing and formally religious systems of values in each milieu. This is because religion, with its esthetic form, is part of the identity and belonging independent of the faith as such.

The different communities have different atmospheres characterized by different sets of signs and symbols. This is manifest in differences on the visual and the audio levels. Churches, crosses, small statuettes of Christian saints in small sanctuaries *(mazārat: sing. mazār)* spread around every street corner, house balconies, road curves, and the like decorate the Christian area. Church bells are heard at all times. In parallel, mosques, flags, paintings of leaders, and the heavy use of green color in the architectural panorama contribute to the image of the Moslem milieu. Quran is heard from the many mosques in the area.

Signs belong to the milieu as part of a set and not on a singular basis. The existence of a sign from the other milieu seems odd and is quite noticeable. A Christian woman coming to visit old relatives in West Beirut, for example, and who sees a priest walking in a main street there will be surprised just by the mere sight of the priest in the »wrong« environment (928). The same sight would not have raised any attention had he been in the Christian area. Especially during the war, this and other combinations related to belonging or being in the wrong place were developed. In a similar manner, after the barriers separating the Eastern area from West Beirut were removed, the sight of veiled women inside Jounieh, on the Christian side, was odd and strange to the Christians living there. The majority of the war generation were never in the Western area to see »veiled women.« Such examples denote a clear division on the visual level.

On the audio level, the language used in daily life differs from one area to the other. Whereas the language in East Beirut is mixed with a good deal of French and a bit less of English *(528)*, the language in West Beirut contains more Lebanese Arabic rarely using any French word *(2262)*. Instead of French, the Moslem community, apart from some odd intellectuals, would prefer using English when they feel the need for a foreign expression. These differences, both on the audio and visual levels, refer to a larger category of esthetic differentiation, which has become part of the identity of each community.

With the structural influence of regionalism on the environment, there is also an influence on the esthetic elements as well as a contribution in introducing new connotations to the names of places. The regional denotation of »down and up,« for example, is used respectively for West and East Beirut. Both communities use and agree to this designation. One explanation is that West Beirut being the old center is denoted as »down town.« There is, thus, a linguistic *separation,* regarding the two areas, reflected in a »*we-them, here-there, up-down*« vocabulary (908). Furthermore, using the area to design the confession, which is frequent, is a strategy to avoid conflict and attenuate the intensity of confessionalism in verbal communication *(2810,* 2814, 2815).

This sort of agreement about terminology came as the result of three subprocesses of differentiation: apportionment, polarization, and labeling.

Apportionment

Apportionment refers here to the process of selecting signs and symbols from the environment and adopting them (Aneignen) as part of the »own« culture, and at the same time acknowledging other signs and symbols as belonging to or the characteristic of the other, »not the own.« The result of this process is the division of the symbols of the environment into two »portions.«

Regardless of the question and degree of faith, religion is in the background of apportionment. The dominant system of values characterizing all communities and functioning as identity is religion. The background of adopting esthetic elements is partly consisting of the esthetic religious ritualistic domains and tradition. Not all the signs and symbols of the environment, however, have religious backgrounds. The choice, adoption, and rejection of a certain symbol, as part of the repertoire of the *own* or *self* symbols is dictated by the need for esthetic differentiation rather than by religious conviction. By the time a group starts adopting new signs, the other group start the differentiation process by rejecting them. In football, for example, if a group of Christians supports Germany, then a group of Moslems existing at the same place would probably support Brazil. In this example, differentiation is brought about on an esthetic basis. The Brazilian flag becomes a *polarized* visual symbol. Mixing the language with French or English, or insisting on Arabic is an example of this divergence. A remarkable example is in the designation of a common religious exercise, »fasting.« Whereas the Moslems denote it as »*ṣiyām*,« the Christians insist that their fasting is »*ṣawm*.« The two words in Arabic have the same meaning. Likewise, the expression »thanks God« is similarly diverted into »*neškur 'Allah*« in the Christian version and »*'al-ḥamdu lillāh*« in the Moslem version.

The divergence in the view of the national identity can be an example of apportionment. The Moslem community supports adopting the Arab culture (*889, 900*), therefore East oriented, whereas the Christian community is West oriented in trying to reach the European model, with more or less accentuation on the French culture. History, religion, and other fields were used to justify a determined view, still emphasizing the Arab culture for the Moslem community, and adopting the Phoenician culture as root for the Lebanese culture in the eyes of the Christian community (375). This is enhanced by the education, from schools to universities, which are private institutions founded by Europeans and Americans i.e. western influenced *(2268)*. With the rise of globalization, English became more and more global, i.e. neutral, losing relatively the American and British »colonial« coloration, and making it more and more accepted by the Moslems *(583)*.

The adoption of new signs and symbols, as fast as it was on the esthetic level, remained very slow on the level of moral values. A Lebanese non-married woman, for example, whether she is Christian or Moslem, is still to stay at the home of her parents, even though she might have a boyfriend, with the unofficial knowledge of the parents. Cohabitation as practiced in the West is not an option in Lebanon *(2284)*. This would belong to the common area between the two communities as derived from tradition and norm.

Polarization

Polarization is the process of adding an emotional component—a charge—to the elements of the environment. This charge overrides, in many cases, the initial meaning of the sign and attributes a confessional taint to the meaning. In Lebanon, the signs and symbols of the environment are polarized between the two social milieus. This implies a *deviation*[20] from the »apparent« insinuation of the sign. The *domain of the sign,* connected to its polarity, becomes thus more important than the sign itself. This applies to individuals whose belonging to a certain group becomes more important than their person. With the globalization and the speeding media, new signs and symbols are entering the environment everyday. These are polarized through the environment on level I (The environment of theater), before they get to theater on levels II (Outer-performance production) and III (Outer-performance reception). In theater, *polarization* starts from the topic, polarized according to the spheres of discord. Following the topic, the esthetic signs and symbols follow a similar procedure like we saw in the football example above *(686)*.

Labeling

Labeling is a continuation of the chain of processes discussed earlier. It denotes the sealing of the sign by giving it a brand name, a *label,* either Christian or Moslem. This applies also to people *(2350)*. Confessionalism enhances labeling and classification of the individual, both *other* and *self.* The tendency to classification and division is a common characteristic in both milieus *(337, 2186)*.

In his explanation of »Stigma,« Goffman considers society as ruler and judge:

---

20 Compare to the concept of »semantic differential« by C.E. Osgood, 1967.

Die Gesellschaft schafft die Mittel zur Kategorisierung von Personen und den kompletten Satz von Attributen, die man für die Mitglieder jeder dieser Kategorien als gewöhnlich und natürlich empfindet. Die sozialen Einrichtungen etablieren die Personenkategorien, die man dort vermutlich antreffen wird. Die Routine sozialen Verkehrs in bestehenden Einrichtungen erlaubt es uns, mit antizipierenden Anderen ohne besondere Aufmerksamkeit oder Gedanken umzugehen. [...]
Der Terminus Stigma wird also in Bezug auf eine Eigenschaft gebraucht werden, die zutiefst diskreditierend ist, aber es sollte gesehen werden, daß es einer Begriffssprache von Relationen, nicht von Eigenschaften bedarf. (Goffman 1967: 9-11)

This complies with the understanding of the concept of *labeling* as used later. In addition to the local factors, globalization has an impact on the environment.

Globalization

Globalization affects both environment and theater. The effects of globalization on theater will be limited here to two areas: the influence of globalization on the relation between the two communities, and its consequences on signs and symbols.

With globalization, new signs are entering the environment through the media. The new communication means have speeded this process. Incoming signs are subject to polar distribution, however, at a lower speed than globalization. The effect was to create a non-processed domain of elements made of global signs, which escaped these processes because their speed was not enough to match the raging globalization, a neutral domain. From this domain, both social milieus use signs according to their degree of exposure to them. The most exposed to this domain is the young generation, for which the global culture has exceeded and overridden, in many instances, the traditional one. Although the Lebanese confessions might be circumscribed in the own social milieu both milieus are characterized by openness to the outer world, which increases the exposure to globalization. Moreover, the progress of the media, satellite technology, the internet, along with the growing tendency to indiscretion, increases this exposure. Private schools and universities, products of the Western missionaries and the weakness of the national—local—sense of belonging of the individual are all factors favoring globalization. In theater, exposure with visiting immigrants presents another type of exposure. The audience has a seasonal aspect of emigrants returning home for the summer when theater festivals take place (2593, 2634). These emigrants are marked in their identities by the different countries to which they emigrated and are messengers of their cultures. The reaction to this exposure, however, is not equal in both social worlds albeit there are some common points.

In both milieus, globalization is seen as a threat to the Lebanese structure, identity, and tradition (2410, 2336, 2267, 2272). It is seen as an outsider culture setting its feet more and more in the life style with new signs and symbols and invading areas not reached so far in the past. Another common point concerns one side of the Western civilization. The West is seen as more developed, especially in placing theater as a tradition and part of daily life (2235). The evaluation of development, however, differs between the two groups, as is also the image of globalization itself.

Specific to the Moslem milieu, religion is put to confrontation with globalization (807). Moreover, the image of globalization is marked exclusively by the USA, Hollywood productions, and the Western civilization (817). As a consequence, globalization is dressed with the image of the West, which is characterized by »loose moral values.« To this effect: »sex, drugs, the dollar, Michael Jackson, Madonna, Bill Clinton's sexual perversity, Monica Lewinsky,« are typical symbols of globalization in the Moslem eyes, which should be rejected (890). By enhancing globalization, the Western influence over the communities will increase at the expense of the actual religious values.

In the Christian milieu, the image of globalization, also related to the West, is not so radically negated. The West is seen as an example for the young generation. It is seen as a paragon of civilization (108). In contrast, the older generation, less influenced by globalization, has a more realistic image of the West. It is true that the West has more freedom but the Western societies are »lost and have no identity« (643, 646). This, of course, depends on the definition of identity, which, in this case, means going back to past roots and traditions in contrast to a new stream in the young generation seeking identity in the present. These conflicting perspectives are the result of a part of the young generation partly refusing the traditions of the past, which led several times to war, and hence finding itself in front of a forced choice of adopting the alternative offered by the global culture. »We should take the best of the West, without losing our identity,« said one interviewee. But, is it possible to discern between the »example of civilization« and the »lost Western identities«? Here, we notice a contradiction between an oriental Christian community, and the rationality of the West. The West is seen as having less emotionality, whereas, the Lebanese are emotional (687). The West is individualistic, whereas the East has collective belonging as a characteristic (737).

The Lebanese Christian individual tries to imitate the Western, particularly the French type (205). This shows in several issues, like »civil marriage« for example. The old generation, under the influence of the confessional leaders, refuses fundamentally the idea of civil marriage, considered as a product of globalization and the West, and aiming at and capable of destroying the family (2260). The new generation is welcoming the civil marriage. This is partly due to conflict between generations, and also to civil marriage seen as a step away from the confessional structure. Moreover, this new generation sees Lebanon as multicultural »like the USA,« and, therefore, it should move further in this direction (207). The image of the West is generally embellished by this generation. Even the controversial issues find positive explanations. »In Europe, for example, sex, when used in the media, is seen by the European audience only »from an artistic point of view,« says one Christian director. »In Lebanon, it is seen as mere sex limiting thus the ›artistic reception‹ of the Lebanese audience« (588).

Apart from the generation conflict more existent in East Beirut as in West Beirut, the globalization and its associations present new horizons of conflict for the Christian and Moslem communities. These conflicts are portrayed in theater through adoption, integration, or rejection of new moral issues, along with their signs and symbols finding their way through globalization. Adoption or rejection of those signs vary from the total rejection of all global signs, to the acceptance of partial signs—filtered from Arab to Western in a classical Moslem-Christian conflict situation—to the indifferent acceptance by the new generation deduced from war and the complete rejection of the old traditional confessional structure.

Media

The media are the windows through which the global culture enters the social worlds. They also serve as interface of communication between the Christians and Moslems in times of isolation. The image of the *other* is to a large extent the product of the media. Theater, a medium itself, is also channelled through other media, especially television.

Television

From newspapers to television and lately the internet, the attitude towards the media is strongly impressed by the war period. Television, the most effective medium in Lebanon, is looked at as a confessional product (602). During the war, television stations were considered to have highly provoked confessional feelings that helped creating conflicts among the confessions (935). The objectivity of the media is, thus, put to question, and seen as being manipulated and manipulatable depending on the circumstances *(2380)*. On the pure information level during the war, the media included a considerable part of political propaganda with little information, especially about the *other* (2748) reflecting negatively on his image in theater (2217, 2218).

Also, television supplied the staff for theater from actors to directors, since television was present before what is seen as modern theater in Lebanon in the 60's (918, 2948). Due to this, television also monopolized the launching of theater actors through intensive publicity (978), which would normally cost a small fortune if endeavored on a private scale, and therefore would render producers outside the television sphere non-competitive. As a consequence, many theater actors are loyal to and therefore labeled under the wing of their supporting television station *(maḥsūbīn)* (979, 980). The effect, in this case, is not limited to the level of individuals; it affects also signs and symbols by adding to their potential meaning a new component corresponding to the confessional identity of the television station. This becomes clear knowing that advertising for a certain theater play is usually exclusive on *one* television station. The reason for that is the customary barter between television stations and theater producers, in which advertisement is exchanged against the play copyrights. As a consequence, the television station helps in shaping the image of the play by supplying it with a confessional label (577).[21] In addition to that, in the case of advertising of a small production on a strong station, there is a disproportion in the »dimension« of the plays, since the publicity label overrides the technical or artistic quality. Personal connections contribute to this effect. This is seen by production as misleading to reception (2297), despite the fact that some producers claim that publicity does not affect the number of spectators coming to theater (494, 333).

Since television was introduced in Lebanon before theater, the audience is initiated to television as the starting point for theater (2984). Theater, cinema, and television are typically classified together in the eyes of the audience (2748, 2351). Nevertheless, where theater is a collective social act (403, 405, 2403, 2212), cinema is seen as entertainment for the individual. The culture of theater is deduced and continued from television and cinema (827). Cinema is considered as a competitor to theater (2984). The common element between those three domains is the actor. The first classification of theater with respect to the audience is, thus, related to this actor element. The people are more attracted by the big name and the personality of the actor than by the drama itself.

---

21 LBC: Maronite, MTV: orthodox; Mustaqbal: Sunni; Manār: Hizballah (Shia); NBN: Amal (Shia); Télé Liban Canal 1: Christian; Télé Liban Canal 7: Moslem...

Due to the regional technical problems of going to theater in addition to the already existing television initiation and familiarity, television is a competitor. It sometimes even substitutes theater. Chansonnier Theater is a typical example to this end. Chansonnier Theater, concentrating on playback of songs (Lipsing), is similar to television shows and therefore does not lose much of its effect when broadcasted on television as a result of copyright barter. Moreover, the same troupes involved in Chansonnier, are presenting parallel to that, a similar television show, with the same sketches and songs. For the spectator, this means an additional hindrance on motivation for going to a theater, in which the entrance prices are usually high. This means a decrease in the number of theater audiences (574, 2412, 239, 240).

All in all, the audience is more in touch with television than with theater. Television is able to enter all houses and impose itself (826, 882). Since the main interest of television stations lies in commercial profit, the door to initiation to theater has also acquired a commercial image in the eyes of the non-experienced potential spectator (881).

Newspapers and other media

Newspapers do not deal with theater any different than television. The production considers newspaper critiques as publicity and not as actual evaluation of their play (2332). This means that personal connections, belonging, and confessionalism define the way the critique goes rather than technical and artistic talent (814, 2339). In their form, some critiques seem to be flexible *passe-partout* valid in all cases like the »horoscope prediction« as one producer expressed it. One strategy to achieve this is by making the critique »difficult« and non understandable, which partly contributes in pushing new potential audience away from theater (2301). To this purpose, we find an extensive use of alien irrelevant terminology, contributing little on nothing to the explanation or approaching a show-off language taken usually from the western critique and hardly applicable to the Lebanese theater. The effect of newspapers remains, however, minor compared to that of television. This goes back to the reading habits of the Lebanese audience in general, since they prefer usually television to newspapers (981). All in all, we find the audiences vulnerable to the media, which is principally dominated by television.

Conclusion and consequences: the environment of theater

To sum up, the environment of theater constituted of several communities is controlled by many forces based in their majority on confessionalism. After the war, geographical areas were divided according to predominant confessional majorities. This has resulted in increasing feelings of regionalism and the creation of confessional social milieus characterized by many »spheres of discord.« The internal configuration of the community is regulated through the concepts: family, *('ašḫāṣ), ('afrād), connections (wāsiṭa),* and *patron (zaʿīm),* as explained above. The *patron (zaʿīm)* of each community regulates the relations between confessions. This leads to exceptions and overriding restrictions in theater productions. In order to be able to present a play in a certain area, a theater agent has to make a *connections (wāsiṭa)* with the local *patron (zaʿīm).* This configuration is infiltrated in the institutional and governmental levels, though it does not always emerge on the surface. Theater production agents have to account for it in order to be able to exist. They can turn it into their favor as is the case in examples A, in which a Christian is able to present his play in a Shia area or example B, a Moslem actor in a Christian area. On the other hand, it can turn against them and lead to stopping the play (Appendix A, Example F). The margin is set by the *patron (zaʿīm),* who is himself under the confessional »unwritten law« together with his subordinates, *('ašḫāṣ).*

On the other hand, the more theater is linked to its environment in topic and form, the more confessionalism grows in importance. The more theater is detached from the environment the less influence confessionalism has on it. Nevertheless, it is tolerated to address the *other* in theater using an allusive style of communication. Also, the construction of the *other* in theater is made easy through using esthetical elements, thus avoiding directness. The position of the esthetical elements in the two social worlds generates a classification in what we called »esthetic realms.«

In conclusion, confessionalism has two major effects on the environment of theater: first, the creation of on-going social dramas around the spheres of discord generated in two social worlds and causing friction, and second, defining meaning for esthetic realms with respect to the social worlds due to apportionment, polarization, and labeling of the esthetic elements of the environment.

The spheres of discord as on-going »social dramas«

The environment of theater presents many *spheres of discord*. The main discord sphere comes as a result of confessionalism. It divides the environment into two social milieus characterized by conflict and friction: these are the Christian and Moslem. Due to regionalism those two social milieus acquired a physical spaces denoted as East and West Beirut. With war, the division between the two social worlds became clearer. As a result of this sphere of discord, an attitude from the confessional *other* was developed in both milieus. This attitude resulted in the need for differentiation, which in its turn ignited three subprocesses: apportionment, polarization, and labeling of the esthetic elements of the environment. Signs and symbols were divided into two esthetic realms: Christian and Moslem.

The second sphere of discord is the ruled versus the ruling classes. The ruling class in Lebanon has a confessional structure. Trying to dispute the authority of the ruling class is usually channeled into a confrontation with the religious authorities, and the ruled class finds itself again in a confessional confrontation with each other.

The third sphere of discord is the individual versus collective. The development of the individual is held within the frame of the family with its extended meaning: the clan. Trying to unfold the individual is faced with the religious authorities favoring the family structure. This reduces these trials to a dispute of the individual with these authorities, and brings back the confrontation to the confessional level, which weakens individuals from all confessions, and restitutes the confessional authority.

The fourth sphere of discord is the war generation versus the old generation, with the first calling for the strengthening of the individual and the refusal of confessionalism. Also, at this level, the confrontation between the two is easily channeled into the third sphere of discord putting the individual against the confession *(ṭā'ifa)*, and hence, bringing this sphere back to the confessional sphere of discord.

As a result, the confessional sphere of discord is the dominant one among the other three. Accordingly, the spheres of discord lead to the formation of different groups of actors in the environment, with a dominance of the Christian-Moslem distribution. By going back to the historical facts leading to the last war, the spheres of discord could be classified as generators of permanent »social dramas« in the Turnerian sense. Theater is in this case the incarnation of the social drama on stage. The extent of this will be discussed in the coming sections.

Friction

Stemming from the discord spheres, a vital factor for theater arises: *friction*. In all the models of drama used by Schechner, we find *conflict* to be a central factor. The »drama« consists of two opposing powers (represented by X and Y) in friction on stage (Schechner 1982: 16-27). In the environment, friction is developed through the increasing *experience* with this other. The most prominent historical manifestation of *friction* on the level of the environment is the »social drama« (Turner 1982) resulting from *war*.

From the impact of the use of the environmental elements in theater, and the perceived changes in meaning with respect to the place of use in the respective social worlds, we can deduce that the following »control formula« determines the meaning of interaction: »Who says what to whom, where and with what consequences?«[22] The answer to those questions sheds a light on the communication. This general formula is confirmed through confessionalism regarding *who* can say *what* to *whom* and *where*. It is also confirmed through regionalism, which gives the value of *where*. Thus, discussing a topic from the focus of this formula means coming across confessionalism, the *self* and *other* in the confessional sense. Using to this purpose Weber's definition of «social action«:

Soziales Handeln (einschließlich des Unterlassens oder Duldens) kann orientiert werden am vergangenen, gegenwärtigen oder für künftig erwarteten Verhalten anderer. [...] Die »anderen« können Einzelne und Bekannte oder unbestimmt viele und ganz Unbekannte sein. [...] Nicht jede Art von Berührung von Menschen ist sozialen Charakters, sondern nur ein sinnhaftes am Verhalten des anderen orientiertes Verhalten.« (Weber 1921: 11)

Not every contact with the *other* is of social character, but a meaningful behavior oriented at the *other*. This is the role of the spheres of discord. They give meaning to the interaction because they are by definition constituted as a function of the *other*. Accordingly, friction areas are formed around the topics related to the spheres of discord. A discussion of those topics is deemed as taboo, especially in the inter-confessional communication. Contact, communication, or interaction between the *self* and the *other*, whose theme reflects divergence in the views of the world with respect to the two groups leads to this friction. Friction can be manipulated with the selection and composition of the type of signs and symbols used in the interaction, the actors of the communication, and the place of the communication.

---

22 See Lasswell (1948).

Friction is also the result of different emotional and cognitive *attitudes* of different groups of actors about themes derived from the spheres of discord. We can comprehend a division of the environment into areas characterized by emotionality resulting exclusively from these attitudes.[23] The differences in attitude between the different actors lead to friction and consequently to »friction areas.« In these areas, we find the topics, symbols, and signs, which, due to their relation to the spheres of discord, present interests, problems, and needs of this society.

Esthetic realms

In view of this discussion, the esthetic elements of the environment acquire an emotional component according to their belonging to either of the environmental friction areas or social milieu depending on *where* and *by whom* they are used. Reciprocally, the belonging to a friction area, which is based on emotionality, is a determinant of these components with respect to reception. The *position* of an element in relation to the discord spheres determines its potential impact when exercised on the audience. This potential impact becomes kinetic whenever it is used and interpreted by the receiver. The term *environment* denotes therefore the circumstances under which the experience leading to collection and classification of signs and symbols occurs. *Selecting* a certain sign or symbol, either for use in production, or as a subprocess of reception, is a decision and an insinuation by itself. The *composition* of signs gives several possibilities of meanings and interpretations.

At this level, we can also distinguish two types of divisions: first, the esthetic signs and symbols affecting the *form*; second, the *topic* itself, which can be directly associated with the spheres of discord. Esthetic signs and symbols can thus be reduced to audio-visual elements. These elements can be of stable nature like moral values, for example, or they can be topical apt to vanish easily with time and are only characteristics of a certain phase. Hence, they can be qualified according to their emotional, symbolic, rational, and structural significance.

By classifying these elements according to their belonging and potential associations, we are faced with esthetic groups or *realms*, which contain certain characteristics of the signs and symbols belonging to them. In relevance to theater, these can be classified as follows: *Christian*, *Moslem*, and *global* esthetic signs and symbols. Topics are constructed using those symbols. For the topic, however, the relevance would be between *polarized* and *non-polarized/neutral* signs and symbols. Due to differentiation, apportionment, polarization, and labeling,

---

[23] Compare Peter Vorderer and Sabine Trepte, Medienpsychologie in »Psychologie in der Praxis« p. 709 for a psychological overview of the media.

processed signs and symbols are apt to be polarized by the environment, which reduces the non-polarized to the non-processed signs and symbols. These include the daily life *(Alltag)* events and the signs and symbols of the *global realm*, both transmitted through the media.

Graphical representation of the environment

Spheres of discord, friction areas, esthetic realms, and signs and symbols of the environment, along with their positions with respect to each other and their magnitude can be presented as a graphical map of the environment. This map represents hence the system of influential forces dominating the social configuration. It is in a constant motion, and hence changing on the line of time. Reconstructing the map and determining its pattern of action give us a clearer idea about the internal processes concerning reception. In the case of Lebanon, we are concerned with the motion of the relevant actors: the confessional *self* and *other*. Accordingly, the strongest poles in this structure map are resulting from confessionalism. The friction areas can also be divided into zones reflecting the value of the applied sign or symbol in terms of friction, tolerance, taboo, and neutrality. These are symmetrical or parallel, common, and polar zones. This division refers to the topics presented in theater and their reception.[24]

On the other hand, three positional coordinates, a magnitude, and a direction, can be used to designate the characteristics of signs and symbols. These add up to form a vector put directly on the environmental chart.[25] Esthetical elements of the environment are then represented by a sign vector (SV), which varies in values depending on the systems of reference—Moslem and Christian coordinates. The value of SV inside the Moslem or the Christian systems alone does not determine all its coordinates; part of them depends on the value of SV in the whole environment, in which the both systems are interacting. By adding the two vectors in each social world, one can reach a resultant value for the whole environment. Reciprocally, this gives SV an added value that could be positive or negative when compared to the own esthetic realm. The mosque, for example, has no meaning alone; it acquires meaning through the existence of an audience. This meaning is enhanced, when the spectator of the one social world knows that the other is watching. In this sense, SV acquires an additional meaning because is has a direction towards the other. Showing a »cross« in a Moslem play has no meaning for the Moslem insider if it is not associated with the Christian *other*. The polarity of

---

24 See Appendix B, diagram 6.
25 See Appendix B, diagram 4.

each vector determines its value in theater and its acceptance in different areas. From the esthetic elements we find symbols used in theater having the representative value of the whole environment, these are names of regions and of people and signs related to the identity of the system or social world. Again, using the vectorial representation has the advantage of being able to add several vectors mathematically in order to reach a resulting vector representative of the summation. This would represent the impact of different signs simultaneously. By adding the prominent vectors used in a performance, one could anticipate a visual indicator of the impact of the performance. Determining the prominent vectors is once again done through the spheres of discord and the esthetic realms.

Outer-performance production (Level II)

From the image of the environment presented above, we move now from Level I, which represents the conditions-consequences level of the »grounded theory,« to Level II, which resumes the processes of theater outside the performance. Hereby, we start with the activities of the production agents in preparation of the performance and their corresponding parameters. Next, we come to their strategies in the compositions of the elements of play. Accordingly we derive our typology of theater.

The parameters of the production

Before launching a theater play, the production agents have to account for certain parameters, derived in their entirety from the environmental structure. These put the agents in conflict between the personal wishes represented in their attitude towards theater and audiences, the financial pressure, and the way censorship is applied.

Freedom, censorship, and restrictions

A theater play has to cross many borders before meeting the stage. A topic or an esthetic form cannot see the light without being compatible with the cultural background of the social world in which it is presented. On the whole, the theater process reflects equilibrium between the producers and the audiences, achieved through harmony between its conditions, process, and consequences. Taking that into account, the producers work on the thin line between three factors: first the possibility of staging in relation to the margin of freedom and its rules of equilibrium allowing a play to staged; second, the interests of the audiences which depend on the reception process as a whole in setting the criteria for the performance, and third, the personal vision, wishes, goals, financial capacities, and technical background of the production agents.

The topic and the form of a theater play are restricted by environmental factors condensing their effects on the production process in two ways. First, they build direct restraints on freedom through governmental institutions having the confessional institutions in the background, and second, they exercise indirect pressure on the producers via financial and technical means. This pressure is due to the dependency of production on the audience—which is under the influence of the confessional leaderships—for their bread and butter. Not having the freedom of expression has become the norm. Freedom is always seen as existing elsewhere, preferably in the West: Europe and America. On the other hand, in comparison to neighboring countries, producers still believe that there is a good margin of freedom in Lebanon (217, 580, 936).

What is at the basis of lack of freedom? The restraints on freedom are manifest in fear and frustration. In the interviews, fear materialized through the refusal to talk especially at the sight of the tape recorder (2804, 2917). As consequences of fear, indirect communication is intensified, and frustration is growing. In reflection on theater, actors are afraid to express themselves both on the private and professional levels (532). The source of this fear is not difficult to detect. The power balance between confessional communities is expressed through an »unwritten law.« Their implementation goes seldom through judicial processes before violence takes over. Violence occurs usually as a result of breaking any of those rules. With the configuration based on *('ašḫāṣ)*, *('afrād)*, and *(zaʿīm,)* rules can be even haphazardly set and reset according to cases and circumstances, especially in the lack of *connections (wāsiṭa)*. Breaking the unwritten law, and the chaos extending from the days of the war, are the grounds for many instances of violence, which, not to the least extent, are monopolized by the government or its institutions. Artists, actors, journalists are not exempted from the consequences of violence; on the contrary, they present a common target on the practical level due to their obvious exposure to public. Instances of physical violence, which were registered in the interviews, include threatening (Appendix A, Example F, *2943*), kidnapping, shooting at, and physically attacking the subject (913). Other kinds of violence include damaging of properties like the car or the house (830, 839), along with reputation and image damage, which can be fatal in many cases for the carrier of actors.

All this encourages a self-imposed censorship especially regarding the *other*. This reflects knowing the own limits and not mingling with the matters and social issues of this *other,* a common knowledge. In one example,[1] discussing the matter of the *(ḥiǧāb)* in a Christian play being not a Christian concern, the working group got criticism from both Christian and Moslem sides. The play, depending on intellectual audience, had to stop after a short while.

---

1 See Appendix A, Memo 4

Governmental institutions

On the technical level, before going on stage, a theater script has to get the approval of the office of control at the »Sûreté Générale.« In most of the cases, this means that the script will be subject to censorship. Connections and the *connections (wāsiṭa)* factor are decisive elements in the extent of the censorship, more than logic and fairness. Most of the time, the censorship is arbitrary and autocratic according to the mood of the officer (592). Moreover, passing the censorship on the text is not enough. There are always controllers from the Sûreté Générale, »inviting themselves«—every other night and mostly with family and friends—and imposing themselves on the production. This abuse of position, initially under the pretext of controlling whether the actors are abiding by the already approved written text, is associated by the implicit threat of »complicating matters,« which can be as bad as stopping the play, if the producers were to object. In other terms, even if the Sûreté Générale has already approved of the text, and that at a later stage, it was found to be altered, or to have a different impact than speculated by the censorship office, the Sûreté Générale is allowed to cancel the actual performance or even stop the whole play (2199, 2424). Again, personal considerations and the subjective judgment of the controlling officer play a major role. Formal censorship, thus, is not a guarantee. If a text passes the censorship of the government, and the background influence of the confessional institutions, this is not a security that it will come through. The street law and fanaticism, applied through other organized or non-organized groups, institutions, persons, or political and religious parties, have the final word on that (937, 938, *2943*).

Confessional Institutions

The criteria setters for theater »censorship« on signs and symbols are in accordance with the religious values on the one hand and the political power balance on the other hand. The confessional institutions normally try to go through the governmental channels, which are anyhow formed on confessional basis, in order to achieve this goal. During war, as the power of the government faded away, their faith diminished in these institutions, and therefore they took matters through the governing powers on the ground, namely the confessionally based militias (2409). In example F, the actors were threatened and a religious militia stopped the play. The intervention of the army and other governmental institutions was useless. The play, in which there is a monologue with God, was interpreted as a blasphemy raising the actor to the rank of the prophets, and hence insulting religion. It was tabooed and eventually stopped. The religious institutions and their corollaries have influence and power to forbid or accept a certain play. The play »waṣiyyat kalb« (A Dog's Testament), an adaptation of the Brazilian playwright Ariano Souasona presented in 1966 (long before the war), was forbidden by order of the Maronite patriarchate (1066). The story is about a millionaire whose dog died. He wanted the dog to have a funeral in the church, so he settles the finances with the bishop and the patriarch to have the funeral done the way he wanted. The play was presented for two or three times, and then it was forbidden to continue.

Parallel to this channel of the pressure on theater productions, there is the financial factor, which plays the opposite role in encouraging the rule-conforming plays. Before the war, there were considerable subventions of theater productions, which helped propagating the religious values (989, 991). Recently, Religious Theater is also the result of subsidy. One example is »wa qāma fi-l-yawm ṯ-ṯālit« (And he rose on the third day), an important religious production of 2001, which fits into this category.

Overriding restrictions

As we mentioned above, the criteria for censorship are not the same for everybody. It follows the rules of »persons« (*'ašḫāṣ*) and institutions (272). Moreover, when it comes to mentioning political or religious personalities in theater, the degree of censorship, depends on the amount of influence the person has in the corresponding institution. By going back to the differentiation between the *person* (going along with the structure) and *individual* (as going against the collective), the *patron (za'īm)*, deriving his power from his position in the structure, is not likely to contradict the elements of this structure. Therefore, the role of the personal connections as a strategy to overcome restrictions is limited by a general acceptance in the own social milieu, which the *patron (za'īm)* is not usually willing to jeopardize. The use of personal restrictions will thus be limited to the bridging of certain incoherent deficiencies of censorship, which can only extend the margin of freedom with respect to the non-networked individuals. This, in turn, opens the possibility of the *connections (wāsiṭa)* system for the subordinates of this *patron (za'īm)*.

Also within the theater process, we have a similar configuration of *(theater-za'īm)* and subordinate *('ašḫāṣ)*. The structure of the theater troupe is based on loyalty to the *patron (za'īm)*, who is usually also the big name in the production. This could be the actor, the playwright, the director, but usually a combination of those with the function of the producer. The personal through the structural and confessional connections overrides certain restrictions (2733). This can also be represented as a ramification between those »who can,« in our context the *('ašḫāṣ)*, and those »who cannot,« the ignored individuals, *('afrād)*. The latter are reduced to passivity and abuse whereas the others are encouraged to have more activity and power, extending sometimes to the abusive limits. A higher rank is here the *(theater-za'īm)*. We should mention here that in most cases, the acknowledgment comes from being powerful in the environmental channels. The Lebanese system, which favors persons to institutions, is also reflected in theater. Those »who can,« have all the capital, the media, and the power, to launch and promote for their product, what is always essential for business. Those »who cannot« are only auxiliaries abiding by the preset rules. This sets the limits for the institutionalization of theater and leaves a greater margin of freedom to the persons to determine the line of theater adequate for their purposes. Consequently, the types of theater are to a great extent a function of personal wishes. On the other hand, acknowledgement in theater can be the result of technical capacities of theater agents. This was the case at the earlier stages of theater, when it was still a new form in the environment. Now theater capacities find themselves forced to subordinate to the *('ašḫāṣ)*.

Attitudes of the production towards theater

The attitude of production towards theater determines its motivation for working in theater. It is hence part of the parameters leading to the actual theater typology.

The production agents' view of theater

The production agents differ in perspective according to their function in the production process and their placement with respect to the spheres of discord. They might have some goals in common like financial and social success and they work together mainly to promote themselves individually (2189). In the following an overview of the functions as seen by theater agents is presented.

The *producer*, the money payer, aims at having a high return on his investment, even if this would sometimes mean abusing financially the other actors in the production (2298).[2] This is normal where the work atmosphere is dominated by limited financial resources and revenues. The strategies used to attain this goal are centered around the direct marketing through channels used to bring audience to theater, like the family,

---

[2] There are many forms of abuse: not paying wages on time or not paying them at all, not giving a copy of the contract to the actors, not keeping the oral agreements regarding publicity and marketing, setting a lower budget to the play then promised at the beginning, expecting the actors to be involved in activities far from their discipline involving physical work on stage in the décor ...

organizations, and clubs more than on improving the quality of the product (2315). By influencing the taste of the vulnerable, non-experienced audience through advertisement, and the faulty assessment of certain plays, ambitious producers aim at gaining their audience (2279). Moreover, producers enjoy the status of being the essential element in the production *('ašḫāṣ)*, whereas all the others are dispensable (1135).

The *playwright* is a real rarity (62, 60, 1140, 2195, 2371). Usually, there are very few, who are only concentrated on theatrical production; they have other more lucrative jobs like writing for television or newspapers (844). Playwrights differ in their personal attitude, from the artistic to the commercial writing (855). Since, they are the last on the line, in making money, they can allow themselves the fantasy of writing according to mere feelings approaching thus poetry (361, 1107, 2932). The word *poet* in Arabic *(šāʿir)* is literally translated as *feeler*. It is rare to find producers for plays that are written without accounting for the audience. They end up usually producing them themselves with low budgets. On the other side, we find more practical playwrights taking their material from everyday life hence appealing more to the brighter segment of the audience *(863)*.

The *director* has a critical function. He is responsible for the entire work (610). The relationship between the directors, and actors, and the producer tends to follow the *zaʿīm*-dependents model found in the environment (2311). In compliance with the one-man-show: the same person is involved in acting, directing producing and writing are often. This person becomes *the big name* in the play (934, 2307).

The *actors* seek money, fame, and status (2708) through focusing on being close to the audience (880). This comes sometimes at the expense of their theatrical performance. In many cases, this ends up in shifting from playing a character in a performance to focusing on being themselves the center of the performance, as a director complains (2189). This is seen in many performances where the character of the actor takes over replacing the original character. This exposure to the public implies also a direct exposure of the confessional identity of the actor to the mood of the audience, which conditions the acceptance of actors to the nature of this identity. In many plays, we notice changes in the actors when the play intends to »cross« from one area to the other.[3]

All in all, there are common characteristics among these actors, which constitute the motivation for producing theater. Some find their joy more with the contact to the spectators, in the moment of identification, which yields emotional satisfaction (696, 697, 698, 699, 700, 701, 705). Some find more satisfaction and express positive feelings towards

---

3 See section: The Crossing Play

the academic theater in opposition to commercial theater (702). These attitudes lead to different types of motivations, classified here from the weakest to the strongest: tradition, religious and political propaganda, *l'art pour l'art*, financial profit, and approaching the spheres of discord from the perspective of the individual *(fard)*, where the theater supplies the »space« for this approach.

Even though theater does not belong to the Lebanese traditions (631), it has, nevertheless, preceding forms, which are still in the collective memory of the audience. These are the *ḥakawātī, ḥayāl z̧-z̧ell,* and *zaġal* (870, 871), as we saw in the section: A historical overview of theater. The present forms of theater, however, are not a continuation of these, and hence not the result of tradition. In spite of that, there is the brink of a theatrical tradition following the example of father-son chain. By extrapolation on the effect of theater on the environment, we see here conservatism in the reproduction of the social image without seeking to induce change or progress.

As a second motivation for theater production, there is the classical *L'art pour l'art*. Turner describes this puritanical view of the artists:

> Artists have no motive for deceit or concealment, but strive to find the perfect expressive form for their experience. [...] as Dilthey writes, 'life discloses itself at a depth inaccessible to observation, reflection, and theory' (Vol. VII, 1927: 207). Once »expressed,« however, as works of art, readers, viewers, and hearers can reflect upon them since they are trustworthy messages from our species' depths, humanized life disclosing itself, so to speak. (Turner 1982: 15)

The production agents consider theater as »art« not for all audiences, and therefore they find it unavoidable to detach theater from the dependency on the taste of the audience (238, 2329). These are usually the academics and part of the younger generation of actors. When faced with the financial consequences, they tend to turn easily to the practical side. In this case we distinguish two types of plays. One tailored according to the taste and liking of the audience, aiming at financial profit, and one tailored according to what the production considers as »art.« As a consequence, the job assignment in the theater group due to having a smaller number of spectators for this type of theater is affected. We find actors working with other activities than their original one: they build the décor, prepare the own costumes, look after the music, and sell tickets (2988). This tendency, depending solely on the willingness of the young actors, is what keeps academic and intellectual theater alive.

Nevertheless, the main motivation for theater production remains *financial profit*. Theater is seen as a profession or a job aiming at making money (241, 1100, 2362, 451, 519). Apart from being a must for the existence of the production, aiming at financial profit has negative effects on the quality of theater productions. It pushes towards commercial productions, in which the quality of the product comes in the second rank compared to the marketable highlights. On the second hand, it spoils the teamwork, because usually only the producer achieves the profit; whereas the actors and other theater people, usually victims of their own good will, end up being *abused* (2300). This explains the tendency towards the one-man-show in aiming at financial freedom for actors.

Theater as space of the individual

Next to the financial profit, theater is an island of the individual *(fard)*. Theater presents, whenever it is not in the hand of the rulers, a space in which ideas not totally compatible with the present structure are expressed. In this case, theater becomes an own world with the own rules and characteristics. It is detached from the two social worlds forming hence an island for the *('afrād)*. This is a result of the general attitude towards »theater people,« being not taken seriously and consequently isolated, as explained in the reception section, and that theater is new to the Lebanese environment (247, 874, 260, 1078, 2393). This off-center space becomes the playroom for a new hierarchical structure, in which we find similarities with the outer structure, especially having a central person, the *theater-zaʿīm,* as has been mentioned. The existence of this latter and the resulting constellation of *zaʿīm*-dependents, the second sphere of discord, are themselves indicators of non-institutionalization of theater.

The world of theater is, thus, still under construction with enough space for newcomers to prove themselves in this new constellation. With time, the structure of Level I tends to infiltrate theater completely, like is the case with other institutions. Level II has still time in its way towards replicating the structure of Level I. Meanwhile, theater can function as a space for achieving what one cannot achieve in real life: being a *patron (zaʿīm)*.[4] One aim of the production would be the self-realization through theater. The difference is that, at this level, the production agents of this category would have the advantages of the *patron (zaʿīm)* within the theatrical structure, without having the serious requirements of power in real life, nor would they enjoy this rank as a consequence of the theater ranking. We notice, to this effect, a repeatable pattern in all productions: a central person trying to be the only *big name* in the play, which comes

---

4   See section: »R1« and »R2,« The Basis for Interpretation

frequently at the expense of the team work. Theater, depending on individuals (803, 819, 2310), is, however, not consistent in its development. In many aspects, it is limited to those persons, and others have to restart the same way once their antecedents have disappeared from the scene.

On the other hand, the confessional sphere of discord is already existent in theater. Since the relation with the *other* is dominated by competition (2657, 2311), we notice here a boycott at the individual level—between the aspiring *(zu'amā')*, similar to the one we saw on the collective level in the environment. As a consequence, the fact of visiting a play produced by the *other* becomes a strategic decision depending on the stage of competition. This boycott between individuals leads also to less continuation in the work on the institutional level. Many of the reasons of the boycott lay also in the discriminative attitude issuing from confessionalism, where the infiltrations of confessional relations from Level I to Level II takes place.

The third sphere of discord, the individual-collective sphere, has a different aspect in theater than in the environment. In theater, the freedom of the individual is one of the main reasons for a person to decide to join the field of theater. As we mentioned earlier, the concept of the *individual (fard)*—not the *persons* complying with the structure and using its channels to his or her own advantages *('ašḫāṣ)*—has no space to develop in the structure. The individual choosing theater is going against the tide. This, in itself, reveals, a certain characteristic of revolt, even in the case where the person in charge is complying tactically with the structure. In this case, we talk about a means-end relation on the individual scale incited both by the personal desire of the human element and the fulfillment of the individualistic tendencies (2415, 2420). By accepting the social role attributed to them, their production would lead to the normalization and fortification of the structural relations. The output here is a pro-collective theater. By refusing this role, they would be swimming against the tide, with all the problems coming out of that. (2652, 2709) The output would be a »pro-individual« theater. Added to that are the financial factors and the mercantilist culture, which are a source of pressure.

Since theater is still in the formation phase, it is to a large part dovetailed by the personal wills and wishes of the production agents, whose personal views do not necessarily represent the collective experience of society. As a result, individual production agents are under the belief, that the audience should be »elevated« to the level of »good, serious, or meaningful« theater. Many productions have a great discrepancy to the audience, especially in »Serious Theater« productions (361). Usually, they discover rather soon, that when it comes to acquiring more audience, the social representation cannot be limited to the individual level of appeal. In addition to that, this leads to a magnification of the individual views and problems, the personal experience, as if they were problems of the collective.

The audience and the economic balance between production and reception

The knowledge of the audience is part of the parameters of the production agents. There are, nevertheless, several criteria, through which the production presents its own typology of the audience: education, age, war, sex, social rank ... the relevance of any classification is measured with respect to the relation to the theatrical process and its actors. Consequently, there are many classifications of the audience. The relevant classification is here the one helping to explain the line of action from the actors' point of view. The image of the audience produced by the production can still be insufficient or failing, but it still explains *their* view and hence determines *their* line of action. In relevance to theater, the ideal classification reflects as many as possible of the factors influencing the attitudes of the audience towards theater, which is shown later in the reception section under the term: experienced versus inexperienced audiences. Since, the main concern of the production is the attraction of the audience, their work is focused on the direct incitement for coming to theater in relation to the two Christian and Moslem audiences. In the following we see the audience from the production point of view covering these two groups.

Although we detect several differences regarding theater and its audiences pertinent to the two milieus, the strategies used by the production are implicitly working from the following perspective: »the Lebanese audiences do not react to the mental processes during the performance as much as it reacts to the emotional appeal, which secures identification and gives meaning to the play« (52, 1131). Whether this claim is true or not, it is the codex based on which the production is acting. Moreover, both sides of production make a distinction between the *own* and the *other* audience. There is also a distinction between the intellectual and the non-intellectual audiences in the two milieus. In the following we find the production view of the audience in each social world.

In the attitude of the Christian production towards its own audiences, we notice two types of classification: first, the *intellectual* versus the *non-intellectual* audiences, whereby *intellectual* has become synonym to »urban and educated,« and the non-intellectual tends towards being first rural and then less educated. Urban extends from Beirut to cover the northern coast, and it stops at the limits of what is known as the Eastern

Area. This is where most of the theatrical activity is taking place. In other cities like Tripoli, Saida, Sour, and Zahlé, theater is limited to children theater in schools and some plays who make to round from the process of production taking place in Beirut to these areas.[5] Naturally, university students count among the intellectuals. »Before the war, it the audience consisted more of university students and a few ideologists. After the war, they became all *confessional* audiences,« states one director (1104). This is an indicator of a transfer in the grouping of the audience according to the main sphere of discord: Christians and Moslems. This intellectual audience is that of the »Serious Theater.« The rest is bound to go to »Entertainment Theater« like the Chansonnier and Boulevard Theaters[6] (1117). Moreover, a common knowledge is that reading is not habitual among the bigger part of the audiences. »Nobody reads,« protests a director (812).

Complying with the general case, the production considers the largest part of the audience to be emotional, thereby seeking laughter and entertainment in theater instead of moral preaching or rational activation (1052, 1054). Addressing the emotions can be thus efficient from the point of view of the production (2306). Sexual attraction, alcohol, a big spectacle, or music shows fall all under this entertainment category (621, 1053). In the difference in response between the audio and visual appeals, the production agents approve of the dominance of the text over the visual (2316).

In evaluating the Moslem audience, Christian theater agents find that they are more innocent and spontaneous than the Christian audience (595, 596). In that case, they »cope better with *easy* things offering them easy identification« (2649). The topic has to reflect the problems and pains of the people (2614, 2624). Therefore, we find a focus on the topic, which represents usually one side of a social problem. The problems on the *national* level are typical theater topics (2655, 2656).

In the Moslem production view of the audience, we notice similarities with those of the Christian agents. First, the Moslem audience is not interested in theater as such, but more in the *topics* discussed in theater (962). Therefore the production is based on topics and not on the esthetic display of artistic composition. The audience is also interested in laughter (220) and entertainment (2697). In the Moslem view of the Christian audience, the actor is a representative of the community (962). This means that the actor is also personally responsible for the content and form of the play as a whole. Moreover, the audience likes »easy« theater, and not

---

5 See section: The Crossing Play
6 See section: A Typology of Theater

the theater requiring hard discipline and continuous concentration (968, 969).

The view of the audience decides about the strategies of the production. However, financial matters are the real engines behind the existing types of theater. These are based on a simple equation: in lack of subsidies, the production depends on the audience in order to survive (*419, 635, 641*). Since theater, as noted, is not being established in the Lebanese society—having only recently been introduced as a required material in schools (402), we have a small number of audiences. Getting more audience is the primary worry of the production (875).

Besides, the type of theater encouraged or subsidized by the confessional institutions is mainly *religious* theater (310, 991). Subventions in general, whether from confessional or governmental confessionally influenced institutions, follow the *wāsiṭa* system, which increases discrimination and orientates the productions in definite directions complying with the subsidizing party (2991). One should mention, however, that the subventions of theater are, in any case, not enough to support its subsistence. Moreover, there is limited commercial investment in theater (63, 64). This is due to the competition of other activities like sport or television. »One single advertisement in a successful sport event, like Basketball, or in a TV series, would make publicity for the sponsor worth months of theater play sponsorship,« says one director about the private sponsoring of theater plays in return for common advertisement (1134). »A sponsoring company would not waste its money in theater, they prefer easy popular events.« In any case, there are few private interested investors (804). Also, there are no subsidies worth mentioning from the state. Only lately, nevertheless, the ministry of culture started offering little financial support to selected people.

With the lack of subsidies, the majority of actors turned their backs to theater seeking financial security in the more lucrative dubbing »doublage« of Mexican soap operas (810, 956).[7] The others, left with a limited choice, are forced to produce commercial theater (802). In this type of theater, we notice an increase in the use of »elements of attraction« and marketing strategies to increase the number of the audience, affecting, at the same time, the nature of the product.

All in all, the production is dependent on the audience for survival (306, 307, 308, 984). Due to the economic balance, the theater process as a whole is based on the reception of the audience. Understanding the reception helps understand the rest of this process. The measure for the

---

7   The Dubbing, which started as a strong wave on all TV stations, is practically inexistent now. All TV stations have stopped it, because it was not cost-effective any more.

success of the production is proportional to its understanding of the reception and the way to use this understanding. These factors in turn decide about the course of action centered basically on marketing.

Strategies of the production

Taking these parameters into account along with the level I, the question now is to determine how the production deals with them and the strategies that they use to achieve their goals.

Selection and composition

The production of theater involves two major processes: *selection* and *composition*. The selection processes in theater production are the result of the attitudes of the production towards theater and its audiences. Consequently, the production acts as a result of its own interpretation of the environment, and theater presents an interpretation of this environment from the perspective of this production. There are limits, however, to the know-how and rationality of this selection process. They act, feel, think in terms of what they know without having the need to realize this knowledge at all times. The production is conditioned by its know-how.

The source of material for theater consists of problems at level I, resulting from conflicts; interests, which are goal-oriented solutions to problems, and different issues, which could be topical and daily events that are not yet processed, interpreted, or classified within the spheres of discord. These are the concerns of society, which, expressed through a variety of symbols *selected* from different *esthetic realms*, defined above as groupings of symbols and elements around an idea or a concept of higher order of the environment, compose the elements of the theater play. Among these, we find the *topic*, characterized by its position with respect to the spheres of discord. The style of composition of the elements chosen from the *esthetic realms* generates the *form* of a theater play. Both form and topic in theater are reflections and results of the production's interpretation of the expectations of the audience.

Selection—and ruling out—of elements is function of the belonging of the element to a certain *esthetic realm*. These include behavioral patterns, manners, style, appearance, clothing, language, names, and other esthetic forms of life, which, in our spheres of discord, can be indicators of recognition, differentiation, and identification of both *other* and *self*. In Lebanese theater, selection is more important than composition. The production prefers to minimize its efforts by choosing »ready-made«

elements rather than composing them.[8] This, we see in all the processes, starting from copying the western world to adapt to the confessional worlds. This is due to the tendency towards easier production, the lack of experience, and the false estimation of the reception of the audience. With the limited choice of ready-made elements, the efficiency of the production is questionable. The direct factors affecting selection—freedom and economic balance—determine the strategies used in composition.

Composition, thus, is reduced to establish meaningful relations between the selected elements. These relations also follow the model of spheres of discord and belonging to the esthetic realms. However, they have to account for the initial relations as they are in real life. In most cases, the production, with its ready-made policy, keeps the relations as established in the environment, forming thus what we defined as Reality One or »R1,« thus limiting the play to changes in events rather than suggesting a structural change. Reality Two or »R2,« which denotes the reality constructed in the performance at Level III, will be thus a mere replica of »R1« leading to the »mirroring effect« or the reproduction of the »social dramas« with their esthetic forms on stage. The closer the elements are to reality, the stronger the identification of the audience.[9]

Hence, confessionalism and other spheres of discord influence the selection of the form and the content of a theater play. Depending on the target audience, the adequate choice of signs and symbols used in the production is determined. The strategy for this selection aims at gaining audience through tangency to the freedom and taboo margins. The attitude towards confessionalism, starting with the awareness of confessionalism is part of the *know-how* of the production. It affects all the selection processes included in the production, as well as the interpretation of elements of the reception. It is an integrative part of understanding the audiences and hence a crucial key to the successful theater production. Selection is found in the production as well as in the reception of theater. The chosen elements, when promoted in the television advertisement, function as pre-performance contact between production and audience.

Next to signs and symbols, the stage characters themselves are a composition from real life, the personal experience of the actors, and their emotional memories (Stanislavsky 1994). The relation between the actor as an individual and the stage character that he tries to incarnate is of phenomenological nature, since it is based on the experience of the actor. Moreover, the common repertoire between the actors and the audi-

---

8 See section: The Text
9 See section: Reality One »R1« and Reality Two »R2«, The Basis for Interpretation

ence is built with the experience of both. The composition is prepared by the actor alone. Real life and experience include also other actors, theater shows, and hence we see theater regenerating itself in theater. Having an original product is a function of novelty. Correspondingly, in phenomenology, an element can be understood only if it is connected to a seen-before element or if it is itself a seen-before element. Creativity, in this context, depends also on the real life elements, and this at two levels: 1. Adding new elements, 2. Composing new relationships between elements. Those real life elements are the signs and symbols received by the human senses, codes, symbols, or even a direct copy of real life persons, which are in the end a composition of both. This complies with Fischer-Lichte's findings:

Wo immer eine Kultur sich konstituiert, schafft sie allein mit diesem Akt bereits die Voraussetzung für die Konstituierung von Theater: die Zeichen, die es braucht, sind mit der Kultur immer schon gegeben. Werden sie in jener neuen spezifischen Funktion verwendet, hat Theater sich konstituiert. (Fischer-Lichte 1983: 20)

Lebanese theater relies more on form than on content to attract the audience. Consequently, it is more selective than relational concerning the elements of the environment, because establishing relational constructs between notions (elements of form), is not what the audience enjoys. Here, a »notion« is the conception of a received element as interpreted by the audience; whereas, the produced element, before becoming a »notion,« is a »construct« that is not yet used, containing a »potential« meaning to be revealed in the interpretation in front of a live audience. Moreover, theater, in the eyes of the audience, is assessed according to its reflection of the environment Reality One »R1.« An abstract theater, in which Reality Two »R2« is structurally distant from Reality One »R1,« is considered as unreal and thus not good processed, as shown later. This encourages the production to stick to the environment as inspiration and source of material.

Approaching the spheres of discord

By getting near the spheres of discord, the production is able to determine three essential factors: the protagonist, the antagonist, and the topic. The first two determine the »identification angle« of the audience; the last determines the burning issue. By selecting signs and symbols from the esthetic realms, the identification of the audience can be anticipated. These two processes are related with a set of strategies.

The first strategy is the *avoidance* of the spheres of discord hence opting for neutrality. The context for this avoidance is dictated by the restraints on freedom. Confessional extremism affects the freedom of production of theater in a threatening manner. It is ideology put to action, and hence plays a restrictive role in theater implementing a strong censorship. Questioning certain moral values, for example, can be labeled as a sort of blasphemy against God and hence forbidden. Under this title, many plays did not see the light, being aborted during the rehearsal period or stopped shortly after the premiere.

This is noticed in both Christian and Moslem milieus with different intensities. Tolerance in the Christian areas is asserted as relatively higher in comparison to the Moslem ones especially in tackling religious issues. Direct confessional statements and elements are repressed in both areas. This makes theater non-representative of the society, and less meaningful. On the other hand, it forces confessional feelings to submerge in an indirect not always refined communication form.

Consequently, the production agents, in their quest for a higher multiconfessional amount of audience, seek a compromise leading to equilibrium. The negative effects of this orientation towards compromise are manifested in an underdevelopment, since they have to stick to and sometimes invent a neutral system of signs trying to reach the compromise. Averaging and approximation of the elements of the environment would weaken the whole effect and dissolute the meaning into naiveté and ridicule, presenting in »R2« a faulty idealistic image of »R1.« Here, neutral expressions denoting the relation to the other appear in communication: »our brothers the Moslems,« and in parallel, »our brothers the Christians,« are typical examples. These are indicators of denial of confessionalism in theater. However, with time, this itself has become an indicator of confessionalism, since these expressions can also be ironically used (*2373*). Furthermore, the names used in theater are confessionally neutral. Sami, Wafiq, Samer, Fadi… are not indicators of any confession (*186*). In real life, these names constitute a small minority of the actual names in the society. More common names are Toni, Maroun, Muhammad, Ali, etc. Each can be easily classified in terms of confession. In theater and television productions, they are presented as the general case. The neutral names have become an established rule of theater production. Breaking that »unwritten« rule can be the subject to confessional interpretations.

At the extreme end of the freedom spectrum comes the forbidden, the *taboo*. Taboo is an indication for what is not allowed by the social structure. It is the result of high friction and high emotional charges. Since, the structure contains a multitude of systems of values, the amount of taboos is accordingly large. This makes the *taboo* a flexible concept, the definition and margin of which are quite dynamic. It depends on circumstances, place, persons, topics, words, and moodiness. For theater, taboos are at the ends of the spheres of discord. Overriding taboos follow the same rules of persons and institutions. Taboos are however more difficult to override. On the other hand, a taboo can be used as a point of attraction in a theater production (549, 554, 563, 547). In this case, the more indirect and abstract the text is, the more it has chances to pass censorship. Taboos also filter the types of audiences of theater between those who accept to break social taboos and those who are limited to their traditional and social roles.

In contrast to the *avoidance* strategy, the production can *utilize* the spheres of discord to achieve their goals. We can differentiate between two streams of theater: one stream is seeking its way towards being a meeting forum for the Lebanese audiences, Christian and Moslem, outside the confessional context; another stream is using confessionalism to generate a snowball effect gaining popularity among audiences belonging to the one »social world,« serving in this manner their financial profit, an end justifying the means of the whole process of theater.

Approaching the esthetic realms

Regarding the esthetic realms, one straightforward strategy of the production consists in sticking to the »local« signs and symbols depending on the place of the production. Moslem production agents would stick to the Moslem signs and symbols and vice versa. This strategy is, however, not unconditional. Exceptions and deviances are elaborated in the regional play versus the »Crossing Play,«[10] where we find an interplay of the signs and symbols according to the type of the audience whether it is homogeneous or heterogeneous.

Another strategy of avoiding the spheres of discord is through *copying*. Copying, duplicating classical plays »as they are« reflects a certain distance from both social worlds, since it is the construction of some non-Lebanese reality. The non-involvement in the spheres of discord is, however, not guaranteed. There are two possible directions here: the Arab and the Western, which are respectively the two views of national identity disputed by Christians and Moslems. As a result, the origin of the copied play can raise this conflict leading to confessionalism, and brings theater back to the heart of the on-going social dramas.

A form of copying is taking complete characters and elements from the environment and bringing them to the stage. Here, we make the dif-

---

10 See section: Strategies of the Production

ference between *using* those elements in theater for the purpose of further composition, and the mere *reproduction* of characters, signs, symbols, and situations, without putting any creative effort worth mentioning regarding the composition of a drama or the study of the interaction of the used elements with one another and with the audience. This presents in most of the time a mediocre »copy« of parts of the environment without the necessary dramatic coherence, associations, and even unity.

As a third major effect of copying, we find the current typology of theater as set by the production agents. This typology is a *copy* of the original French designation. The effect is having similar names to the origin. Thus, theater is classified into Chansonnier, Boulevard, popular, and political theater. The validity of this classification is only through the field to be determined. It can be misleading. Even though the production agents try to introduce new »types« of theater to Lebanon, its background may not be matching any of the Lebanese audiences, the final determinant of the product.

Approaching the audiences

In their approach to the audience, the production agents follow standard procedures in marketing and appeal. In the latter, the fruits of confessionalism yield positively.

Marketing

One marketing strategy of the production addresses a *target* audience according to which the product will be tailored (235, 236, 1048, 2294, 2313). Due to regionalism, and its consequences, the choice of the audience, between Christian and Moslem succeeds according to the area. The young till middle-aged generations are the main targets, since the amount of theatergoers among this generation is larger than that of the old generation (624, 2228). Among the target groups, the production strives to *create* new audiences, not only through modification of the product, but also through direct marketing methods (*1045*). This can be achieved by public relations starting with the small discussion with the audience after the performance, which is a direct link between the audience and the actors, to inviting influential personalities to theater on the hope that they bring other people with them (1048, 2413). Parallel to this strategy, we find the direct marketing prior to the performance, which starts by professional promotion in the frame of schools and religious organizations. In this case, a sales representative, usually on behalf of the producer, makes a tour on schools and organizations presenting the play and looking for the possibility of either presenting the play at the school, or that the members of the organization book up a performance at the theater house *(ḍamān)*.[11] Another strategy is of course the television advertisement. Apart from normal advertisement, which is the fruit of the exchange with the copyright of the play, the production tries to establish a permanent link between television and theater. To this purpose, a theatrical troupe would perform altogether in a television series, creating thus a continuous promotion for their theatrical product (2306, 2329).[12]

After having chosen the target audience, comes the maintenance phase. This is done through »bringing up the newly acquired audience and building a relation with it. The audience becomes thus what you make of it,« say many theater producers (384, 485, 623). One objective regarding the raising up of the audience is to »elevate it to the high standard of the art.« The follow up requires continuity. Building the habit of going to theater (1047, 1049), as a cumulative process, is another phase of the »raising up.« The relation with the audience lives so in the memory of both the active audience and the non-active one. This kind of relation has a cumulative side, which was broken during the war, but it is resurrecting slowly in the years that followed (2214, 2215, 2227). As a result of »bringing up,« theater tends to be disconnected from the real needs of the audience laboring under permanent coaching. The followers of this belief are the academics and the intellectuals. The other trend is »getting down to the standard of the audience,« which is the normal result of the economic balance. The followers of this strategy, would stay close to the environment, and mostly use the spheres of discord, that proved to be popular, even when void of any »artistic« value, in the eyes of the intellectual critics.

Appeal

Targeting the audience through marketing does not determine all the set of strategies of the production towards this audience. Another related strategy referring to the audience, also a condition of success of the performance, is the grouping of the audience around a central idea, appealing thus to the audience as a whole, or as subgroups.

Webster's Third New International defines *appeal* as follows: »the power or property of arousing a sympathetic response.« In the context of theater, we are departing from the assumption that the production cannot in fact produce emotions within the spectators; it can only assume and expect a certain reaction, and then produce the appeal liable to provoke it. Appeal, thus, as defined and used here, is the construct, esthetic or ab-

---

11 See section: Booking up
12 The series »muni'a fī Lubnān« is an extension and a continuous promotion for the Chansonnier group that presented »šawāz madanī,« for example.

stract (concept), oriented at the activation or incitement of a targeted realm of the spectator, through signs, symbols, form, topic, or a composition of those. By defining the target realm of activity of the audience, the appeal opens the door to affecting this audience. It can also be achieved through the definition of the situation of the performance. The appeal adds a constant emotional stimulation that enhances the meaning by »framing« it within an emotional context. In other terms, the appeal helps setting the »emotional context.«

By making a judgment about the spheres of discord, or indirectly about a symbolic topic in favor of one view or the other, the appeal is constructed. It can either bring sympathy or antipathy to the audience. In the case of a homogeneous audience, the case of the regional play, an infavor appeal implies popularity bringing the audience together;[13] in the case of a heterogeneous audience in a Crossing Play,[14] it implies polarity bringing two poles of the audience on opposing views.

This pattern is found in all types of theater and it contributes to the ritualistic aspect of the performance. The theme of the appeal is a common interest related to the social structure presenting, thus, a problem to be solved in the course of the performance. Having lived the duration of the performance with this common theme is a rapprochement of the types of audiences together. This rapprochement is easier to get by the groupings found as a result of the spheres of discord, which represent by themselves, an in-vivo typology of audiences: Christian-Moslem, individual-collective, ruling-ruled, and war-prewar generations.

The more the texture of the audience is evident, the easier it is for the production to manipulate the elements of the play in order to please this specific audience. The more the audience is diversified, the more the production is obliged to turn to a more neutral and standard level, seeking compromise and getting away from the spheres of discord related that could irritate a group of the heterogenous audience. Designing and estimating audience texture is the main factor in this strategy, knowing that the aim is to please the whole of the audience and not only a part of it. The difference between the topic of the play and the theme of the appeal lies in striving to have the agreement of the audience about this theme; whereas, the topic is an idea, about which, parts of the audience can still disagree and eventually polarize. Therefore, the theme, lying in the background and managing a common ground to the audience, is of higher rank than the topic, found at the front of the discussion.

---

13 There are many clichés that appeal to the audience like »we thank you all, you are a great audience«; naming the place of the performance during the play, which touches the nerve related to regionalism, etc.
14 See section: The Crossing Play

The construction of the appeal is thus based on the position of the elements used on the environmental chart,[15] which determines their relevance with respect to the audience. It is oriented towards the needs and the interests of the social groups, and it is emotional in nature. It also contains a promise of activation of a certain realm of the spectator, when introduced in the outer-performance communication, the advertisement in the media.

Since the environmental spheres of discord and esthetic realms are based on emotional reception, the *appeal* to emotions is the most frequent in Lebanese theater. The *interests* of the people also differ in the two milieus. The production is adapting to those interests in choosing the topics, towards which the emotions of people are well studied and known. One realm of emotional appeal is laughter and amusement. Here, the production is using this as a basis for its strategy (924, 2190). There are many ways to make people laugh, one is playing on presenting a comic image of the *confessional other* (825), but this type, even though very implicitly and swiftly constructed found its peak at the time of war. Now, with the strong censorship, it is slowly vanishing to be replaced by indirect allusions.

During the war the friction topics accepted in one area and rejected in the other, were frequently staged. The absence of the government censure enabled the producers to use the negative feelings of a specific confession towards the other, and put those types of plays on stage because they would drag a kind of easy audience wanting only to express certain negative feelings and instincts towards the other milieu. Those negative and positive feelings about certain issues are part of the attitudes of the audience, which are determinants of both production and reception. Usually, the aim of this type of production is commercial benefit.

Second, we find the appeal to social or human sense, what is usually the case in Serious Theater. The ignition, however, is usually not relevant to the confessional feelings, or even keep appealing to the individual *(fard)*. This factor depends on the type of *appeal* in the intention of the production and implemented by the actors. Without the confessional feelings, the appeal to the collective level would not be possible, which represents a different image than that of the environment. The most efficient appeal resides in the ignition or triggering of confessional feelings and lies therefore within the friction zone, which encircles the political domain. This *awakening* of confessionalism is ignited either by certain signs in the performance, or by the place itself; however, it is usually incited by the presence of the *other*, be it the confessional other, or the peer

---

15 See diagram 4, Appendix B

other, and it is enhanced when the person is outside the own social world, represented explicitly by the geographical area.

Finally, the appeal to *nationalism* plays the role of neutralization of confessionalism; it can escape the friction zone under the cover of alleged non-confessionalism. The national emotions, in this sense, are considered as positive and neutral, and are therefore liable to be staged.

The elements of play

The selection of the audience being achieved through choosing to present the play either in West or East Beirut using for this purpose the strategies elaborated above, we discuss in the following the *elements of play*, their criteria of selection, especially their distance to the spheres of discord and their *belonging* to the or the other of the social milieus, what we can name as the »diction« of theater. As has been mentioned, through the remodeling, processing, stylizing, and composing of the *elements of play* and using ready-made material from the environment, the production forms a construct (play), which, when interpreted by the audience in the performance, is denoted as the »second reality,« »R2«, in contrast to the environment, »R1.«

Actors

The main factor in selecting the actors is the *acceptance* of the audience, especially regarding the »star« in the production. Although, it is common to have the »star« and the main actor to be the same, by the term »big name,« any of the working group, producer, playwright, director, or the main actor, can be denoted. In the actual cases, those functions are interchangeably fulfilled by the same person, which becomes the attraction for a certain group of the audience. The more the actor approaches the esthetic *form* required by a certain social milieu, the more his or her acceptance will grow. This gives more relevance to the form on the expense of the content.

In the same line, the confessional identity of the actor affects the identification of the audience. There is a triangle between the actor as a person, the character he is playing, and the symbolism of his confessional identity both in theater and in real life. During the performance, the actors are liable to cross from the symbolism of the theatrical character to the symbolism of real life. The identification is thus limited to one environment, where the actors can also enjoy the privileges of that symbolical value. One strategy used to overcome the confessional identity of the actor is to improvise by using neutral language to cross over critical topics in the case of the Crossing Play; in contrast the use of local, regional language arises the sympathy of the audience (*2660, 926*). In our example A, the barrier of conflicting confessional identity of the main actor and the audience, was overcome through the extensive use of the regional southern accent and local traditional clothes, and through a topic covering the main interest of the area, which was the military occupation of the South. In addition to that, the main actor disposed of good personal connections with the local *patron (za'īm)* compensating for his confessional identity and enabling him to proceed. He highlighted his personal regional background, since he is also from the South, benefiting, thus, from the strong *regionalism*. In this case, it was no more important who takes the main role as long as the *composition* complied with the context of the region.

As a measure to confront the confessional constellation, a director[16] deliberately formed a theatrical group constituted of a confessional mixture of actors. His vision was that this would help eliminate the effects of confessionalism on the reception of the audience, and therefore increase the chances of acceptance of his group of actors among different types of audiences, Christians as well as Moslems. Moreover, pushed by his awareness of the negative effects of confessionalism, he thought this would set a new standard and a message of rejection to it. In an interview, he explained the amount of trouble on the technical level he had while rehearsing for his first play with the group. »The work has almost doubled. Every thing is taking double the time and effort; most of it is spent on coordination and ›translation,‹ between the actors,« as he put it. In this process, the technical terms of theater, which are taken from real life, can have a different meaning. Pouring a glass of whiskey, talking to a prostitute into a nightclub, clothes, etc… have different codes. There was a considerable decline in efficiency resulting from the structure of this troupe. Nevertheless, the mere existence of this group, is both a proof of the awareness of the problem, and a way of the dealing with it, since, a mixed group has more chances of being accepted among the different communities, hence, more spectators. As a result, the gained acceptance from new groups of audiences on the one hand was met by a new rejection from other traditional groups, who are not in favor of hybrid theater troupes.

Besides, confessionally mixed theater troupes strive to show that theater, as an institution, is not confessional and hence to remove the ac-

---

16 A Christian director and actor who converted to Islam. Such a conversion can have many negative consequences in a country where the social and professional life is based on confessional belonging.

cusation of confessionalism hoping to get more audience i.e. betting on a higher acceptance. Sometimes, the practical reason for having mixed troupes is the lack of technical capacities on the practical level forcing the choice of actors from outside the »normal selection.« Such discrimination is also existent in the academic field related to theater. It affects the results of the academic performance and the distribution of scholarships. »In the Lebanese University, a student cannot have the highest grades and respectively have the opportunity of a scholarship abroad unless the religion of the student is compatible with the place of the university,«[17] as I was told by one professor. One should mention here, that due to the demographic division, the number of Moslem students in East and Christian students in West Beirut is in both cases not significant. At the time of the fieldwork, in the Christian section of the Lebanese University in East Beirut there was only one Moslem out of thirteen drama students; in the Moslem section located in West Beirut, there were no Christians at all.

Hence, in choosing the working group the production strives for *internal compatibility*. It is not enough to have the acceptance of the audience; it is also required to be able to function correctly on the internal level among the working group, which is influenced by the confessional constellation. There is also discrimination in selection due to practical as well as confessional considerations. These are found, with varying degrees, on the levels of working, hiring, and salaries. On a practical level, a mixture of confessions inside the one group means having to deal with complications. There is a feeling of comfort in working with the same color faced with discomfort in the opposite case (230). As a result, the working groups are usually constituted of actors of the same confession.

---

17 This is quoted from a non-taped conversation and cited under condition of anonymity. The following explanation helps understanding the institutional division reflected on the actors. The Lebanese University has duplicate sections in both parts of Beirut. In West Beirut, it is section I, in East Beirut, section II. This division was established as a result of the war, like most of the governmental institutions. Another example of institutional division among actors in theater is the splitting of »the syndicate of Lebanese actors and artists.« At the beginning, there was one syndicate whose offices were located in a »border« area in East Beirut next to the old green lines that divided the city into two sections. The president of this syndicate was a Christian Maronite. The actors are required to pay a certain annual fee of membership. Other artists, like dancers and singers were excluded from the syndicate. Later, it came out that those are making good money in respect to the actors. There emerged a new syndicate called »the syndicate of professional artists,« which includes all the actors together with the dancers and singers. A Moslem headed this new syndicate. The entrance was conditioned by quitting the old syndicate. Once more, the confessional structure of the environment repeated itself.

Furthermore, certain actors aim at arousing the confessional feelings towards the *other* in order to achieve popularity within the own community. This can be done by selecting the type of play and the way the character is composed. As a consequence, those plays are limited to one area. Having taken sides for once, it is difficult to shift sides again. They become non-accepted in the other milieu, and are bound to develop in their chosen line. This can happen either because of apparent denial of the values of the own milieu in the case of the Crossing Play, or simply by being non-diplomatic regarding the *other* milieu in the regional play (*1062*).

Family ties are also influencing the selection of the working group. Loyalty and solidarity with family and clan also exist in theater. Certain families are known to have made a traditional business in theater or arts in general (878). These are found in television and music. »Like father like son,« there are in fact many cases, in which the kinship continues the tradition of the father (340).[18] Tradition in theater is not only on the production level, but also affects how the audience will receive the inheritor. This involves, apart from the inheritance of the job of the father also the inheritance of the theatrical image of the father (2427). This has two direct effects: first, it conserves some loyalty to the old generation; second, it preconditions the image of the coming one.

Place: host-guest attitudes

As a decisive element of play, the place of the performance induces host-guest attitudes of the audience and actors, putting thus the conditions for what is denoted below as the Crossing Play.[19]

Selecting the place entails reconsideration to all other elements of the production because it induces a change in the most crucial element: the audience. Religion, belonging, education, and confessional structure of the audience are all elements that change with the place. Apart from the audience, the area itself, urban or rural, imposes its character on the play. As an effect of regionalism, what is accepted in a certain area with a certain audience would not be accepted in another area, even if we, theoretically, take an audience of the same confession. Not only, the audience changes with the area, but also, and most important, the attitude of the audience changes with the place, regarding what they consider as »home« or »host« area, and respectively whether they are the »hosts« or »guests.« The relevant division here is naturally East and West Beirut.

---

18 Three flagrant examples here: Khodr Alā' d-dīn, Milad Rizk, and Ziad Elias.
19 See section: The Crossing Play

Coping with this factor, the role assignment of host-guest reflects in the production itself. A Christian play in a Moslem area should behave as a *guest* play, which implies showing respect to the characteristics of the area and avoiding to mingle or question those characteristics—particularly the system of values related to religion—which is usually left outside the theme of the play. Playing in a Christian or a Moslem area sets therefore the rules for the choice of text, language, visual elements and others. The shift from likeness to acceptance, rejection, or prohibition goes along a continuum. The production agents acknowledge that the content and form of a certain performance should adapt regionally according to the changing emotional interests of the people (*2204*).

Form

Signs and symbols constitute the form of a theater play. They are classified according to their belonging to the esthetic realm. The form is an important factor in the Lebanese theater, because of the symbolic value of the esthetic realms in relation to the self-*other* interaction and the spheres of discord.

Text

Getting a text is a major task in Lebanese theater. There is a scarcity of writers and playwrights. One reason could be that Lebanon has a limited tradition in theater compared to written texts in other fields like journalism, for example. In any case, there is a shortage of texts. As a response to that, ambitious producers compensate for the lack in importing ready-made texts or copying *('an-naql)* (646, 850).

The first problem arising from copying is the discontinuity in the cultural context, which forces the spectator to refer to the remote context in order to understand a theater play. In addition to that, the receptor is alienated from the product, and the attitude of the spectator towards that remote sign is more likely to be of rational nature, provided that this attitude is already formed in the first place. On the long term, this lack of self-creativity changes the attitude towards theater in general also. Copying is not limited to borrowing signs from the global culture. There are plays that are copied in full, i.e. text, scenography, décor, and indications for the directing (77, 381, 951, 1139). One version of copying is the adaptation *('al-'iqtibās)*, which transforms a part of a play of a certain cultural context to a new one. Such an adaptation involves lots of neutralization and »mise en accord« with the corresponding social world. The first grade of adaptation is the translation and in its extension, the lebanization *('al-labnana)*. Lebanization is the translation of a foreign text, including

Arabic, into Lebanese Arabic. This procedure, however, is not a mere textual translation; it goes over to the context translation. As a result of lebanization, many elements of the performance are exchanged for more compatible ones. This includes those that are foreign and hence not liable to be understood by the Lebanese audience, as well as those that cause friction in the respective social worlds.

In choosing the language, the producers make the difference between Moslem and Christian vocabularies (2715).[20] The moral values of the social milieu and its margin of tolerance affect the selection of language. Swearing on stage, for example, is a classical taboo in both milieus; nevertheless, in the Moslem milieu it is less accepted than in the Christian one (141). Names, as already mentioned, are direct indicators of the *self-other* relation.[21] They are the most obviously traceable signs and symbols in the zones of friction, and hence have a direct emotional impact on the audience. Other elements take more processing time on the reception side, and are therefore not immediately inducing friction. Among the names are persons and area names. The names of the characters in the play, especially the hero, have the greatest symbolic value. The same strategy is used in the names attributed to regions occurring in the play. Considering the regional symbolic value, we find dedesignations like »the village,« »the town« filling up for the pseudo-names.

Adopting neutrality, nevertheless, does not mean that the construction of the *other* or of the *self* is not existent. On the contrary, indirect material of signs and symbols acts like metaphors in rhetoric reflecting the confessional reality. The *other* is mostly represented by esthetics rather than by text in order to avoid friction.

Music

Music is among the elements appealing to the audience (2798). It is a source of pleasure for the spectator (2949). Music, dancing, and songs are also the best tools to fill up for the emptiness of the story, the lack of credibility of the topic, and the lack of experience of both production and audiences (1141, 2281, 2283). In our context, they also have symbolic values. They act both within the avoidance-utilization strategies related to confessionalism, and have the possibility to group or to polarize the audience. Music can achieve the required level of neutrality sufficient to evade censorship. To this purpose, classical music or world music can be used. Among the local symbols, we find the Dabké, a sort of folk music accompanied with a folk dance, accepted among all confessions. The songs of Fairuz, the famous Lebanese singer, are also inter-

---

20 See section:Differentiation and Identification, Two Esthetic Realms
21 See sections: Confessional Neutrality and Approching the Spheres of Discord

confessionally accepted regardless of the image of Lebanon that they bring. Such music affects the audience as a unifying factor.

These same elements can achieve a strengthening of the emotional impact through the application of songs with biased connotation to the social worlds, especially the military songs developed through the war and associated with it. Some singers have become themselves symbols of specific milieus. Other insist of singing only in Lebanese dialect, refusing on purpose as a sign of patriotism, the use of standard Arabic *(fuṣḥā)* or Egyptian Arabic. These singers become »stigmatized« with political and confessional labels. They have a polarizing effect among the spectators.

Sex and other elements of attraction

As noted earlier, the most efficient medium for advertising for a play is television. Through barter between the transmission rights of the play on television and the advertisement, many plays with small financial budgets are able to advertise. Since the media is also classified as Christian or Moslem,[22] placing an advertisement in a certain television station is a determinant of the segment of audience addressed by this advertisement. The pre-performance contact with the audience through the media shapes the image of the play and affects reception. But the television advertisement is not the only way to attract the audience. In the composition of the play itself, we find elements made exclusively for the attraction. They are like »added« to the play in order to serve this particular purpose, and are therefore not necessarily connected to the subject of the play, nor do they serve any particular dramatic purpose (2703). Those are denoted here as *elements of attraction*, which are usually highlighted in the television advertisement and function as a trap to the inexperienced audience.

In the commercial theater, we find several points of attraction that act independently of the dramatic sequence of the performance. They represent the *new*, the *unusual*, or the *shocking* that the performance promises to reveal. And so we notice a disparity between the image of the play in the pre-performance communication and the performance itself, which can cause surprise or deception among the audience. Signs related to sex, optical tricks, machinery, and technology are typical examples of common attractions.

Sex is one of the most symbolic forms exploited in theater to attract the audience. Through sex, which is a controversial concept regarding the two worlds, the symbols of the *self* and *other* are sharper and more obvious. It is enough to look at the costumes to know whether an actress is Christian or Moslem. The differences between the two social milieus are

---

22 See section: Television

the source of the symbolism, detected on both the value and the visual levels of the symbols related to sex. On the moral and value levels, the Christian woman likes to enjoy a larger margin of freedom than the Moslem woman. On the visual level, it is enough to have a veiled woman to make a clear connotation to Islam. There are, however, many aspects of sex. One is the relation between sexes, where we find a male dominance in the man-woman role relation. In both milieus, we find that the role of the woman is marginalized with respect to the man's role (2683), and the idea of sexual taboo is more applied to what the woman does and not to the man (258). This role distribution has at its origin the family background typical of the confessional structure along with the age hierarchy. The image of the man and woman in theater is defined accordingly. In the Moslem milieu, the woman, as actress, is not well seen (257). She has considerable social and familial pressure. Also, Christian actresses are seen as »indecent« by the Moslem society, as we mentioned earlier.

The reception of sexual signs and symbols change drastically with the area. Remarkable is that the Moslem audience would accept sexual allusions coming from male actors but not from female actresses (*534*). This could be reported to the value system allowing more liberty to men than to women. Accordingly, it is more shocking to hear a woman talk about sex than a man. Moreover, the production agents in the Christian milieu would consider the Moslem audience as totally non-accepting for sex (253). Common to both milieus, nonetheless, is that the strong socialization regarding sex has also made a psychological barrier that the actors cannot easily cross. For the actresses, they are afraid of not being able to get married later, if they reveal that they are open to discuss sex in public (252, 255, 256). On the other hand, sexual frustration (818) increases the value of sexual elements proportionally to the strong pressure emerging from the social control, which is stronger on the Moslem side than in the Christian one.

Sex is, therefore, acknowledged as an element of attraction (813, 853, 2239). Since it belongs to the taboo subjects, it is the implicit motivation to go to theater for certain segments of the audiences. As a topic, sex is not accepted. It is tolerated to sneak through the back door finding its indirect way to the stage. In one academic play, incest was presented on stage. We noticed that the people only clapped on the daring scenes, and that most of the photos were made there (2245). Of course, the play did not go out of this academic frame, but this experience shows the importance sex enjoys with respect to other elements.

Not only in theater, but also in the general public discussion, the degree to which sex is accepted differs largely between the Moslem and the Christian milieus (149, 586, 2610, 2612). Allusions to sex cause friction, especially when coming from the *other*. The value of sexual symbols is left to the audience and the place to define: in some situations it could be as trivial as showing a thigh to irritate part or the whole audience (251, 587, 904). Nudity, kissing on stage, and physical contact are strictly not allowed. The only acceptable sexual symbols are indirect and allusive. These refer to a general static appearance like wearing a miniskirt (254), or to an action considered as containing a sexual connotation like eating, showing the tongue, or licking ice cream, etc... Even some objects are loaded with sexual connotation like milk (587). The resulting sexual frustration is in turn channeled in theater by the production as main elements of attraction.

Next to sex, technology is also used as a mere element of attraction. In certain plays, lighting, sound, machinery, and décor seldom serve any dramatic purpose. Due to initiation from cinema and television, these factors have become the criteria of a *good* play (2196, 2197, 2766, 2865). People await special effects (2985), and they usually consider it as a good sign to have more machinery and a prestigious décor. These are indicators of success, and are hence important elements of attraction regardless of their dramatic functionality (2896).

Heterogeneous and homogeneous plays

As a consequence of the selection of the esthetic signs and symbols, we can discern two variations of plays: the »heterogeneous« and the »homogeneous« play.

A *heterogeneous* play is one in which elements of both social worlds are compounded. It contains signs and symbols from both Christian and Moslem social worlds. In most cases, the purpose of such a mixture—which could extend also to actors and other elements of the production—is to gain the acceptance of several types of audiences and hence achieve the »crossing effect.« This suggests thus that a certain form of mixed play is attracting more than one type of audience. Another type of mixed play is that of achieving a representation of the *other* on stage, designed for the *own* audience. This type of indirect contact through the construction of the *other* gained popularity especially during the war. The indirect dialogue with the *other*, and the ability to present the own view of this *other* are a source of pleasure and attraction to audiences on both sides—taking into account of course the limitations on freedom.

The *homogeneous* play, in opposition to the mixed play, and as its name suggests, is made of one set of elements and is rarely designed to be seen by the *other* audience but rather made for local consumption, therefore, intersecting with the insider play explained below (see section: The Crossing Play).

Topic

In Lebanon, the topic of a theater play is usually coupled with a social problem. Reciprocally, problems, which also invoke a need for solutions, are typical potential topics of theater. Most of the problems lead to a confrontation with the spheres of discord. They are magnified in the production through the choice of the esthetic elements having symbolic values in relation to the *self-other* interaction. These are the expectations from Serious Theater, in contrast to those from Entertainment Theater, where the main aim consists in making the spectators forget their problems. Both present mechanisms of coping with social problems. As a result, the topic in theater is chosen according to its distance to the spheres of discord. Hereby, we find two types of topics: those derived from daily life, described here as *topical,* and those concerned with the spheres of discord, denoted as *structural.*

Topicality is better expressed in French by *actualité.* It is the event-tied construct denoting a category of *topics* related directly to *current* events and is therefore understandable only in the context of these events. They are used to produce a momentary effect, usually easily gained emotional reactions having no continuity or duration. The intention of topicality, which is the link between the daily life and theater, is to produce an easy-to-follow plot; however, it wipes off the development of the characters of the play and the innovation of ideas that go beyond the daily and the common (2984, 189). Topicality also indicates neutrality, because it is still in the phase precedent to the apportionment and labeling, and the door is still open for different interpretations. Depending on the approach, topicality is found in Entertainment Theater.

Next to the topicality, we have the *structural topic.* The main concern of this type is not the daily event, but it tries to deal with subjects beyond the ephemeral ones. This sort is in constant friction with religion, philosophy, and moral values. As a result of restrictions on theater, it is bound with excessive neutrality leading to emptying it completely from sense. Nevertheless, we still find neutral, middle space topics concerning the human or global domains and corresponding mostly to Serious Theater, specifically to the academic type. In any case we find in these topics, and as an illustration of neutrality, an avoidance of the opposition of Christian and Moslem. Typically, these include the abuse of the ruled class by the political elite, i.e. the second sphere of discord, bureaucracy, criticism of the *patron (za'īm)* structure, approaching the individual-collective sphere of discord. Due to the parameters of production cited above, this approach usually ends up by flattering the *patron (za'īm)* and discovering new criteria for the perfection of his image, apart from making him gain acknowledgment for his position as *patron (za'īm)*. Among those topics, related also to the spheres of discord, we find themes related to external factors, like the military situation in the country, for instance. In principle, the topics are general, even if they have the shine of being critical. They are treated in a most general manner in order to avoid censorship.

From the perspective of the confessional sphere of discord, we can discern three types of topics: relational, internal, and external. Relational topics contain elements relevant to the relation between the two social worlds. These include the structural and esthetic features of this relation: confessionalism, regionalism, and war. The relational topics are the ones creating most friction. They function against the principle of gathering the audience around one common factor. Therefore, they are either tabooed, or they get little approval by one of the audiences. The internal topics contain elements referring to the structural relation inside the one social world like the image of the *self*, the system of values, and internal politics, both issuing from the religion controlling the social world. Typical examples of this domain are the individual-collective and the ruling-ruled spheres of discord, which are internal with respect to the confessional one. The external domain represents structures and elements that are not directly related to the social worlds. These include the global issues, which, due to their neutrality inspire material for theater (845, 849, 920, 945).

The Crossing Play

The awareness of the necessity of inducing fundamental changes on the play in order to be able to cross to the other social milieu paved the way for a new concept: the *Crossing Play*. Apart from the regional connotation, the Crossing Play summarizes the strategies of the production agents and their choice of the elements of play. A Crossing Play is a play that has successfully crossed the cultural borders and found an audience in the other milieu. One can divide it into two categories: plays presenting *regional editions*, i.e. modifying its elements according to regional needs (*2346*), and *passe-partout* versions of the same play designed neutrally to fit all regions. The general strategy of the Crossing Play is the avoidance of the confessional sphere of discord. A premeditated agreement with the local authorities represented by the *(zu'amā')* of the different areas, in which the performance will eventually take place, is essential. This agreement sets, however, additional restrictions on the elements of play regarding the person of the *(zu'amā')* in question. Usually, the aim of these plays is to produce laugher and entertainment.

The *regional edition* is a play that undergoes reforms when shifting areas in compliance with the social world. There can be several symmetrical editions of that play, whose compatibility is limited to a specific milieu *(538, 542, 1062)*. The corrections are effected mainly at level II— outside the performance. The actors do the rest adaptation on the spot at level III during the performance. The corrections include the *elements of play* and therefore induce a change in the consequent interaction. On the audiovisual level, the regional edition implies using signs and symbols exclusive to each social milieu, whenever the play moves from the one milieu to the other. This can impose considerable changes in text, actors, and visual elements. The more the signs used in the play are relevant to one milieu, the more the required change is flagrant. The change in the language happens often whenever it concerns the names of political leaders in the areas. The incentive behind the change remains the power-fear equilibrium implemented to avoid upsetting the audience (575). This is where the agreement with the *patron (za'īm)* is necessary. Irritating or friction words that could upset the region or the *patron (za'īm)* are taken off or changed. This is done in order not to have unpleasant consequences that could sometimes endanger the entire troupe. As a rule, when the play is changing areas and therefore audiences, it is advantageous and necessary to reconsider the names of the *patrons (zu'amā')* appearing in the dialogue.

On the other hand, the change could aim at pleasing the regional audience. Sometimes this could mean mentioning names of families or even persons taken directly from that area along with an extensive use of regional language *(2654)*. This can be seen as a sign of respect of the values of the other system, but sometimes it represents an abuse of those values. Changes occurring with the only purpose of pleasing, regardless of esthetic rules, could induce a repulsion among the aware audience, who feel itself »tricked« (2346). When the change is technically difficult, the production agents count on the stage actors to adjust the intensity of their performance in order not to have a provocative effect. In the worst of cases, a complete section has to be removed.

Hence, in a Chansonnier type of theater running in East Beirut and wanting to move to West Beirut, for example, it is necessary to take the political figures being criticized into consideration. The type of criticism involved originally in such a situation is worth considering. The apparent criticism, usually used to ease off a political frustration of an audience on the second sphere of discord, turns out in the final analysis to be a kind of an implicit flattering complot between these political figures and the production. Taking all three parties involved, the political figures, the audience, and the production agents, they all have an interest in Chansonnier Theater. The political figures are satisfied because they get to be represented on stage. Since the kind of direct criticism is anyhow forbidden due to the lack of freedom we mentioned earlier, the mere fact of being represented on stage means an acknowledgment of the political authority of those persons and their implicit acceptance as existing on the political stage. This is an advantage worth the sacrifice of being the object of a passing joke. The second party involved, the part of the audience that is fooled by the fake criticism is also happy because it eases off the frustration induced from the lack of freedom of expression and the political performance of those politicians. This part of the audience is the real target of the Chansonnier production agents. The intellectual audience is targeted in other types of »intellectual« plays designed for another level of »criticism,« in which the same political figures would be abstracted to match the Western example. In our example of Chansonnier (Appendix A, Example C), political figures of both milieus were represented. The actors worked on the intensity of their performance in order to adjust to any of the two milieus.

The *passe-partout* play is initially designed to be able to move between borders without incurring any change. This, of course, implies, a degree of neutrality, enabling it to maintain such a status. Moreover, even if using the same signs and symbols, the reception is regionally different. In one play discussing indirectly the disadvantages of the military dominance over the civil population, for instance, the interpretation concretely corresponded to the local military in each area (1058). Due to the abstraction of the name of the military presence, every audience filled in the blanks with the regional militia.

In any event, the composition of the Crossing Play depends also on the structure of the audience. The adopted strategy reflects the basic attitude of the production towards the *other* and the spheres of discord. It has to account for the balance of power inside every region represented by the *('ašḫāṣ), ('afrād), connections (wāsiṭa),* and *patron (za'īm)* configuration.

In contrast to the Crossing Play, we have the insider plays. Avoiding the spheres of discord can here be achieved through the complete avoidance of the interaction with the *other*. We notice a rising stream towards one color productions moving in a divergent manner towards the adoption of the *non-other* as identity leaving behind the construction of the *self*. This is a direct effect of the yearning towards differentiation forgetting the need for compromise with the *other*. This type of plays is usually made for only one social milieu and it remains in its realm. It could even attract more audience from this same milieu by presenting the exclusive view of the world corresponding to the social milieu, and hence consolidating the own ideas. In this case, we have an indirect utilization of the confessional sphere of discord, aiming at gaining popularity. This is usually the case with Popular Theater. During the war, for example, there was an abuse of the confessional emotions of people in theater, by portraying the *other,* directly or indirectly, in a nasty way (*1082*), aiming at financial profit (801, 873). The selection of signs and symbols is usually done from the one social milieu. However, we find a presentation of the other, using the esthetic realms of this *other*.

A typology of theater

It is difficult to set a sole criterion for the typology of theater. In fact, the Crossing Play, the Insider Play, the Heterogeneous and Homogeneous Plays are the typology resulting from the field work. However, they did not appear as such in the in-vivo naming of the interviewees. Also, it is logical to have »Christian Theater« and »Moslem Theater« as potential names of the Insider Play. This naming, apart from the repulsing confessional character,[23] is also avoided in the in-vivo terminology of the interviewees. The common alternative was to say: »Theater in the Western Area« or in the »Eastern Area,« which leaves little characteristics about the nature of this theater, apart from the Christian-Moslem differentiation. Aiming at being consistent with the current in-vivo designation, the types were therefore explained according to the existing naming. Nevertheless, the constructed types above are used as characteristics to explain current designations, which are neutrally adopting the French or American origin. Due to copying and duplication, they were attributed in both milieus to the existing types of theater. On the other hand, in the literature about Lebanese theater, a common scheme for typology is reduced to telling the biography of the production agents and naming the type after the director or writer. Since we relied on the interviews, it was logical to consider the designation of theater as presented in-vivo by the reception agents. This, however, is not the only *raison d'être* of the existing types of theater, which depend also on the will of the production agents. The motivation of the production in theater, as we saw above, is torn between two main tendencies: first *l'art pour l'art,* which produces Intellectual Theater not yielding enough money for self-financing, and second the commercial profit, which leads to »commercial« theater dependent entirely on the taste of the audience.

---

23 See section: Confessional Neutrality

The following main groups of theater, »'*al-masraḥ t-tarfīhī,*« Entertainment Theater, and »'*al-masraḥ l-ǧādd,*« Serious Theater, crystallized in the interviews. Theater is here classified according to its *purpose*, which corresponds to two needs of the audience: social, political critique and entertainment as we see below in the reception section. Their subcategories, however, classify theater through its *theme* like the religious, political, and intellectual theater. Joining common characteristics of the two, »'*al-masraḥ š-ša'biyy,*« Popular Theater, came into existence. It is classified according to its *audience*. In the field research, a play of every group was the object of repetitive observations: different performances with different audiences and abundant interviewing. Other theater types like »spectacle theater« '*al-masraḥ l-'isti'rāḍiyy,*« which is a mixture of dance and music, and »children's theater,« which is introduced in the schools on a commercial basis, were omitted from the scope of the research. »Spectacle theater« focuses on the audio-visual effects with little importance given to the topic. It imitates Western shows. Outside all domains, it has little connection to the social worlds and has therefore a special type of audience not relevant to our focus. Children's theater has also a special type of audience, which is not covered by the scope of the research.

In the following, we find explained the strategies of the production as well as illustrations about the elements of play used in the current types.

Entertainment Theater—»'al-masraḥ t-tarfīhī«

Amusement or Entertainment Theater corresponds to the *avoidance strategy* in the selection of topic and form keeping a distance from the spheres of discord. It joins two types of theater, Chansonnier and Boulevard. It is considered by some production agents as less valuable from the artistic point of view than Serious Theater (1045). In this research, Chansonnier Theater was chosen to represent this category. Floating on the surface, this category of theater does not induce friction and complies with neutrality. Moreover, the aim of this type of theater being entertainment, the central idea around which the production gathers its audience is *laughter*. The neutrality and distance from the spheres of discord help setting the mood of relaxation needed for this purpose.

Chansonnier Theater
Several factors contributed to the rise of Chansonnier Theater. It started with the need for entertainment as a result of the war, the economic situation, and the lack of theatrical culture, which led many people to satisfy themselves with the topicality staying at a distance from the ideological

and philosophical debates. The Chansonnier play consists usually of a series of independent sketches (2427), whose aim is to make people laugh and forget the outer reality. The link between the sketches is most of the time nonexistent, however, a repeating pattern, *topicality*, constitutes the main material for Chansonnier. This theater takes the themes from the news, and, with each performance, improvisation actualizes the text to the current novelties. It constructs sketches that are easily understood, because they require only a minimal mental effort complying thus with the wishes of a certain segment of the audience and with the frame of the performance usually presented in a restaurant. It exposes the obvious social and political needs of society that people do not dare discuss at the political level (189, 2942). Nevertheless, Chansonnier Theater remains at the level of displaying the problems without presenting a judgment about them, except the statement that this is negative, not good, or not beautiful. Substantial analysis is absent. Usually, it is performed by a group of five actors: two to three of which are females wearing as a rule short skirts. This is used as the main attraction to the audience. To illustrate topicality, we consider the play »Civil disorder«.

In »Civil disorder,« *šawāz madanī*,[24] there was a sketch entitled by the actors as »Labné,« a sort of Lebanese food. The actor starts by singing a patriotic song of the well-known Lebanese singer, Wadī' ṣ-ṣafi, »ya bnī« (my son), changing the word to Labné. For the non-informed spectator, the sketch can be interpreted as mocking the idea of identity and patriotism. In fact, the sketch is an allusion to a speech of some minister on television, calling for the people to enhance their savings by eating Labné because it is cheaper. Typical of Chansonnier Theater, this example illustrates the use of topicality to have a quick link to the audience (2942). On the other hand, it is an illustration of the connection between theater and the other media, especially the link between television and the stage, since the topicality *(actualité)* is transmitted to the audience through the media.

Among the topics constituting this *actualité*, the most flagrant are parody representations of politicians (195). Since politics is a hot topic on the Lebanese agenda and in the daily life discussions, to which the audience is already initiated through television, it is easier to relate theater whose topic is around politics to the daily life of the audience. This achieves easy connectivity between what the audience knows from everyday life and what is presented on stage (3, 171). In this way, theater production is meeting the audience at their playground of choice: their daily life interest. The lack of the bridging and interaction between the political, social, and individual levels, however, reduce the politics in

---

24 See Appendix A, Example C

theater to a repetition of the daily events found in the media, and to an emotional, shallow explanation attributed to them, in order to find the most attractive way to present them to an audience not so much counting on a real discussion but rather on being amused by the form.

Nevertheless, this easy connectivity has other requirements. In Chansonnier Theater, the production expects from the audience a certain degree of education (4, 114, 117), a follow up of topicality, and a minimum level of intelligence to be able to make those associations between the stage and daily life. These are mainly requirements met typically by Beirut audiences—whether East or West Beirut depending on the place of the production. Typical targets of Chansonnier Theater are university students, who fulfill easily those requirements. This type is typical to the Eastern area of Beirut and is characterized by a dominance of young audiences.

Songs and music (from which the name is derived: chanson) are the main characteristics of Chansonnier Theater. They are mainly well known melodies remade with new words according to the political or social context. The bone of the theme is the critic of political leaders, however, in reality it is only tangent to those persons as to the political topics themselves. In this regard, Chansonnier approaches the ruling-ruled sphere of discord, in which the problems of interest to both Christian and Moslem potential audiences are present. By its reluctance to suggest any solution to those problems, and satisfying itself with the portrayal stage, Chansonnier is able to come across the confessional sphere of discord, keeping its acceptance from both sides. Chansonnier, thus, is a potential *passe-partout Crossing Play* for all audiences.

When moving from one area to the other, the production agents, and here usually the actors, adapt both text and acting in relevance to the place. This adaptation consists mainly of changing persons names, when necessary, to avoid friction with the local *patron (za'īm)*. These adjustments depend on the mood of the *(za'īm)* and his tolerance to jokes about his personality. Playing on topicality, it tries, when changing locations, to adapt to the place of the performance by adding »local« expressions to the text. It is tolerable for the dialogue to contain some dirty words. They are attenuated or removed on the spot by the actors according to the type of audience and its reaction to the first occurrence of such words. The signs and symbols used in Chansonnier are a »mishmash« of the Christian, Moslem, and global esthetic realms, producing a fast changing rhythm similar to television series.

Regardless of these qualities, Chansonnier has a negative connotation among the intellectual circles (960, 894, 647). It is sometimes looked at as »a combination of thighs and alcohol and not theater. It is corrupting the moral values of the audience and destroying the taste of people« (894, 960, 2341). The criterion for a successful Chansonnier is *laughter*, which can be seen as a war-associated effect, a reaction to frustration. This disparity between the critique and the facts on the ground is found in the other types too.

Boulevard Theater

The theater of the Boulevard, also a French naming, can be classified in the same category of Entertainment Theater »*'al-masraḥ t-tarfīhī*.« The structure of Boulevard Theater is, however, different. This type is completely imported from the French scene and adapted *('iqtibās)* to the relevant Lebanese social contexts. The play is usually a comedy based on misunderstandings and deriving its comical factor from the situation, what the French call »comique de situation.« It usually involves marital betrayal, infidelity, and a multitude of extramarital affairs. It is generally more tolerated in the Eastern Christian area than in West Beirut. The plot turns around the marital betrayal and consists of one complete story. The sole aim of Boulevard is amusement and laughter; the audience forgets »R1« for the time of the performance to be plunged in »R2.« Boulevard Theater creates a »non serious« frame through which the degree of tolerance of the audience is expanded. A typical example is the play »A husband for two,« *(ğawz l-ğawz)*,[25] in which, even a situation resulting from war, itself a social drama and an incarnation of many spheres of discord, was used as a setting to present a harmless comedy based on a comical situation. It ignores totally the spheres of discord and groups the audience around one idea they cannot disagree about: laughter. To this purpose, the production uses neutral elements all through in order to get the required distance from the spheres of discord, and hence it is able to focus on entertainment. Entertainment, laughter, and the distance from the spheres of discord are, thus, the joining elements of the audience.

Serious Theater—»*'al-masraḥ l-ğādd*«

The *utilization* of the spheres of discord as a strategy of the production leads to a second typology of theater. Those strategies leaed to the following categorization. Serious/Striving theater, »*'al masraḥ l-ğādd*,« is a category including several subtypes: intellectual, political, and religious. These designate theater that does not aim at laughter but conveys a certain »message« to the audience. It plays on the borders of freedom, since

---

25 »A Husband for Two« or (ğawz l-ğawz) is the story of a taxi driver, who is moving between the two areas and has a wife in each one, who finds himself stuck with the unification of the two Beiruts at the end of the war. See section: Theater and War

it is trying to convey the taboo, to express what generally causes friction. This makes the topic attractive to the different audiences, but at the same time liable to harsh censorship, which can lead in the end to the deception and frustration of the spectator, who does not find the wanted satisfaction in reflecting his opinion.

The topics of this theater vary between the social and the political. It starts classically at the level of the ruling-ruled sphere of discord and slides down to the confessional sphere, ending up by not being able to propose solutions to the discussed topics. Since the basic problems of discussion proposed by this type are subject to create friction between Christian and Moslem audiences, it is not convenient for a heterogeneous audience. Furthermore, being tangent to the moral values principally regulated through religion, it comes to many direct collisions with the confessional institutions. In opposition to the » 'al-masraḥ t-tarfīfī,« the themes of this theater are *structural,* and the *topical* elements used there, are a mere vehicle to reach this structural dimension. It follows the scheme of a story containing a plot, a climax, and a dénouement. Themes of war are also frequent.

The theme, around which the formation of the audience occurs, depends on the type of theater. In the case of Intellectual Theater, it is the fact of discussing a certain topic, that is of interest to the intellectual audience. In Political Theater, the topic is the common enemy, which is usually centered around the political ruling elite and the bad economic situation resulting from the performance of this elite. In Religious Theater, we are left with the religious ideology as a joining factor for the audience.

The drive behind these productions is usually the individual and personal attitudes on the production side. Its strategies vary between the individual and the emotional appeals. The presentation of the self is also eminent in this category, and the friction between the *self* and the *other* is always present as a result to the closeness to the spheres of discord.

Intellectual and Academic theater

The large audience sees this type of theater as concerning a group of self-appointed intellectuals (383, 881, 1139, 2367). Its target audience consists of university students (879) already initiated to theater, and the production expects an educated, almost academic sphere audience, mostly from people related to the field of arts or theater. The performance is usually followed by a discussion (2954). The production strives the freedom of expression at the expense of ignoring the taste of the large audience. This complies in their eyes to the example of the Western theater, including the avant-garde, happening, and experimental theater (1107,

2933). The focus in this theater is not on the emotions and the story, but on the happening itself, complying thus with Schechner:

> While in the orthodox theater the focus was on the emotions, the focus in the new theater is on the »happenings.« This means that the emotions and the characters are only by-products, the existence of which may not even be necessary. This has decreased the effect of the narrative, and increased the importance of a variation of programmed events. (Schechner 1988: 23)

This type of development as presented by Schechner has reached the Lebanese theater due to copying. It did not develop in this environment, and hence, its audience is limited to the same circle of intellectuals. Moreover, it is dominated to a large extent by the personal factor on the production side, and therefore does not always comply with the interests of the audiences, be it on the Christian or the Moslem collective levels. Most of times, it takes the individual-collective sphere of discord, where the collective represents an abstract concept of society not necessarily linked to the Lebanese environment. Its audience are bound to a certain educational standard. This is the case of example D, which reflects a nostalgic but degenerated vision of Beirut before the war. The interest of the audience during the play was focused on the degree of daring in breaking the sexual taboos in theater. Apart from its being not approved by the religions, as a result of its philosophical thoughts (example F), Intellectual Theater depends on the tolerance of the academic field. To this effect, we take into account the short duration of the theater festivals, in which it is usually performed and their corresponding academic frame. In example G, the play had no success because of its total disconnection from the ongoing social dramas and the lack of substitute rising the interest of the audience. The same we find in example K.

On the other hand, it suffices to have theater in French or in English to be ruled out by the large audience and therefore having to stay within the »intellectual circle.« This can be the case regardless of other elements of play that might be set otherwise. This is the case in example I. The setting of the play would have pleased an average French audience, but the fact of presenting it in French excludes this segment labeling the play under »intellectual.«

Political Theater: 'al-masraḥ s-syāsiyy

Politics is a hot topic on the Lebanese menu due to the geographical, economic, and cultural situation of the country. Lebanon has earned several political nicknames like the »thermometer of the Middle East,« the Swiss of the Middle East, the »laboratory of the West in the East,« etc.

These varied according to the political situation and its attempted interpretations. Politics thus play a main role in the Lebanese social life. Political discussions are part of daily life. The war, with its different ups and downs, has made out of politics a main interest of the people. Under Political Theater, the audience understands every type of theater whose topic deals with political concerns. With a few exceptions, it can also intersect with Chansonnier and Popular theater.

Political topics are an important attraction to the audience (2239, 853). Nevertheless, the lack of the bridging between the political discussion and its echo on the social scene has reduced the politics in theater to a repetition of the daily events found in the newspapers and to emotional, shallow explanations attributed to them, in order to find the most attractive way presented to a public more focused on the form. This draws the boundaries for the political taboo. On the esthetic level, Political Theater remains in the *ruler-ruled* sphere of discord away from the direct *Christian-Moslem* sphere of discord. Remaining at the level of the esthetics, political taboos can be overcome. The imitation of personalities of politicians is widely accepted and rather popular. On the one hand, the politicians would still consider imitating them on stage as a kind of publicity; on the other hand, it lessens the general popular anger about the important point, the labor of those politicians in real-life. To this end, newspaper politics remains more tolerant in expressing opinions and adopting them (2620). Thus, Lebanese Political Theater is reduced from the ideological interaction of political concepts to the shy allusive characterization of political figures on stage. In most cases, this increases the chances for a clientelistic flattering attitude towards those figures: either through embellishing their image or carefully teasing that of their opponents. In this regard, it gets nearer to Chansonnier Theater with the exception of setting and form, since it is presented in a normal theater house and has one coherent topic instead of sketches.

Nevertheless, there are also »politically committed« theater houses representing the political views of certain parties (*2942*).[26] These, however, are bound to a strong censorship. A play propagating communist ideas, for example, is not compatible with religion and is at constant confrontation with the confessional authorities. It creates alienation between this theater and the audience because, to a large majority, the Lebanese are religiously oriented. On the other hand, a political critique does not find its way to stage. The political situation in Lebanon is conditioned by the regional politics, which eventually produce taboos (859). This leaves Political Theater with a lesser margin of expression and a minor connec-

---

26 The play »Jeḥa fi-l-qurā l-'amāmiyya« is a remake of Brecht's »Der aufhaltsame Aufstieg des Arturo Ui.«

tion to the environment. Its shallow existence can be explained as representative of the image of »political freedom,« which the confessional structure likes to highlight but refrain from implementing. At its best, Political Theater is able to make shabby allusions about certain points. *Avoidance and neutrality* constitute the main strategies of the production here. They play on the ruling-ruled sphere of discord grouping the audience under its label. The little margin of freedom has the effect of increasing the frustration of the audience, in contrast to Chansonnier Theater, which uses the same sphere of discord more subtly to ease off this frustration. In example E (Appendix A), the two obvious strategies of the play were to gather the audience as the »ruled« party, presenting to that purpose a common enemy: poverty and the bad economic situation resulting from the »ruling« party. The direct approach to this sphere of discord, however, made it questionable if the play will continue to be working or not.

In conclusion, the political aspect of this theater is upstaged by censorship. It has become void of any analytical perspective desired by the audience. This is the main reason behind its gradual »extinction« form the scene. Politics, however, is used as a »spice« in Chansonnier and Popular Theater because of its attractiveness and variety in relation to the spheres of discord.

Religious Theater: 'al-masraḥ d-dīniyy

Religious Theater or »'*al-masraḥ d-dīniyy*« has the function of keeping the solidarity with the confessional identity, and hence has an »internal« perspective within the community. It belongs to the sacred domain of religion in which every community accepts the holiness of both the *self* and *other*. Knowing its capacity to produce friction, this theater remains clear in its religious message without confusing it with political connotation.

Faith usually characterizes the audience of this type of theater, which focuses on revealing the benefits of each religion having a universal human message. In this sense, it succeeded in reaching universal neutrality enabling it to survive. Here, it is important to make the difference between religion and confessionalism. Religion is different from confession. Many people who claim to be non-believers show strong feelings of confessional solidarity. Others who have faith, stress that they are not confessionally oriented. Those, however, are a small minority and not the typical case. The general conclusion is that religion as such does not necessarily encourage confessionalism.

Nevertheless, the importance of confessionalism as a sphere of discord and the taboos and restraints of freedom resulting from it are at their peak whenever it comes to religion. In one play, there was even a division of the audience between women and men in order to maintain a religious aspect (952). The delicacy of religion leads to the exclusion of vital issues from public discussion because they are regulated by religion. In addition to that, since religion is freely exercised in the environment, there is little need of expression for it on stage, in contrast to other repressed social dramas using theater as their medium of expression.

Religious Theater falls under the category of »avoidance strategy« of the production. It is produced for the inner social milieu, and is not oriented at self-other communication. It preaches the audience the beliefs of the confession. The result is an obvious division between the two lines of theater with respect to each social milieu. Moreover, confessional institutions subsidize Religious Theater. This enables it to survive the economic balance between audiences and production. During the war, the confessional militias used theater for confessional promotion. The plays »ṭa'r l-llāh,« (God's Revenge), »Charbel,« (the name of a Lebanese saint), »yasū' bn-l-'insān,« (Jesus, the son of man), and »wa qāma fī l-yawm ṯ-ṯālīṯ« (And he rose on the third day), are examples of religious plays. Those plays are directed towards the peer group to enhance solidarity with the own community, and are hence typical Insider Plays.

Popular Theater: 'al-masraḥ š-ša'biyy

The Popular Theater, *('al-masraḥ š-ša'biyy)*, represents a successful strategy of the production aiming at increasing the number of the audience. This is reached through the utilization of the spheres of discord, without inflicting strong friction, and aiming at entertainment. The emotional energy is directed towards a constructed image of the antagonist. This is usually an abstract theme like poverty, ignorance, corruption, or occupation like in example A. In the case of a mixed audience, diverting the emotions of the two groups of audiences towards the common enemy leads to a harmonization effect between the two. Nevertheless, a reduction of the conflicts of the spheres of discord to the single image of the enemy decides for the success of harmonization. This effect resembles political populism, in which big promises and simple solutions are presented. Nevertheless, the target audience of Popular Theater belongs usually to a certain social world. It reproduces the second reality »R2« according to their vision of »R1« (2951, 2668, 2670), using to this purpose indirect methods of mentioning the *others* and the symbols of their social milieu. In example A,[27] the signs of the *other* were used allusively in association with the common enemy. They appeared under the esthetic characterization of the people who were claiming the house, working un-

---

27 See Appendix A, Example A

der the orders and with the complicity of the enemy. The mentioning of the *other* was used in a pure esthetic presentation of a television group shooting a video clip. In the play, they start using the house of the Shia main character as if it was theirs. After a while, the owner of the house notices that he has become a stranger in his own house. He is represented as a Southern Shia person through the accent, language, and clothes; whereas, the adversary and his local accomplices were represented as Christians only through the same stylistic and esthetic tools. Playing on the edge of this sphere of discord, the play becomes more attractive to the specific audience since it falls within their vision of the *other* and the world. Moreover, the easy-to-track symbolism used in the play is analogous to the theatrical experience of the mentioned audience. With little experience in theater, this audience is in fact satisfied with easy symbolism, and the play fits their vision of theater.

On the other hand, Popular Theater is a hybrid combination of the previous categories. It gathers both the amusement and comedy, and is at the same time touching the needs and problems of the audiences. Sometimes, Popular Theater is even striving to present a solution to these needs and problems, within a comic and irrational frame. It usually fulfills the function of saying and doing on stage, in »R2,« what is not possible in »R1.« This gives satisfaction to the audience, by relieving, for the time of the performance, the frustration accumulated in »R1.« Working for large audiences, which is also the criterion for its naming (2657), this theater is characterized by a shallowness of the political and social discussions, and is hence seen as »cheap and idiotic« by some academics (2977, 2981). Among the strategies to oversimplify the *identification* process, there is always the presence of a hero, »from the people and to the people,« with whom the audience can directly identify (1137). This implies that: first, by the choice of actors, Popular Theater has to consider the confessional acceptance of the hero and his strong representation function, and second, that the stage character of this hero should be clearly and directly identifiable, even at the expense of uncovering a confessional identity. This implies a step away from the dull abstract neutrality of Intellectual Theater generally unpleasant to the large audience. The themes of this theater are taken from the *political domain,* since politics is the most urgent need at the collective level. It is, hence, directed towards the confessional sphere of discord, using to this purpose the ruling-ruled one. It, nevertheless, avoids direct discussion, and gives simplified solutions to the proposed problems in order to refrain from frustrating the audience.

Conclusion: production

While theater in Lebanon plays on the environmental conflicts to gain popularity, in theater itself, we find the same basic conflicts as in the environment, creating a mirror effect between theater and everyday life (2639). This is expressed in our terminology as Reality Two mirroring Realtiy One. Although these are affecting theater negatively, they can, however, have a positive effect by creating a contra-reaction, which is all the same more attractive to the audience.

The production is using the charged significant symbols from the environment »R1« and staging them in the performance »R2«. Systems and structures of the environment are hence reproduced in theater. The processes reconstructed as types of production present direct similarities with their analogues in the environment. This procedure depends on the degree of know-how of the production regarding the environment and the audience. Neutrality and keeping an »official cover« are the two main means of the production in dealing with freedom. To this purpose, the production adopts strategies of *avoidance* or *utilization* of the spheres of discord, taking into account not to present a dull product unable to attract the audience or to overcome the economic barrier. Another strategy is to gather the audience, with its different segments, around one central agreed upon idea. The selection of signs and symbols from the esthetic realms of the environment follows the strategies related to the spheres of discord and belonging to a specific social milieu. This is achieved according to their emotional significance characterized by friction issuing from the *self-other* interaction and other conflict areas. Appealing to the confessional belonging of the audience is used indirectly by the production to achieve representation and identification, especially in Popular Theater. The production uses themes related to the problems, the values, norms denoted here as *spheres of discord*, together with *actualité* characterized by a short life and flexibility regarding change.

The Crossing play between the two social worlds recurs to effecting changes in the elements of play if it wants to avoid dull neutrality. This requires subtlety on behalf of the actors who are asked to execute many on-the-spot changes according to the situation at level III. Other elements of play are also altered at level II in anticipation of the audience. Changes vary from lines in text, to complete scenes, and sometimes to a change in actors. Gaining acceptance in the area of the *other* requires getting the agreement of the local *patron (za'īm)* and abiding by the role of the guest. The difference between the intention of production agents regarding the structure of the performance and the expectation of the reception is the cause of satisfaction, dissatisfaction, or frustration.

Outer-performance reception (Level II)

Since the process of production is oriented towards the reception in the Lebanese case, it is expected to find out that this latter is also dependent on the spheres of discord in the environment. Those social dramas affect the reception in the first place before going further to the production.

The outer-performance reception at Level II, can be divided into two processes: selecting a performance and going to theater. The attitude of the audiences towards theater determines the selection of a specific performance. Going to theater is also influenced by this attitude, the place of the performance, the financial element, and the direct incentive or motivation of going to theater, denoted here under »acquiring a ticket.« These end up in forming the typology of the audience.

The parameters of reception: The attitude of the audience towards theater

The attitude of the audience towards theater determines the parameters of reception. It is hereby divided into the following categories: theatrical culture, the perception of theater, the relation to the other in theater, the differences between the two social worlds, and the attitude towards the »theater people.«

Theatrical culture

Situating theater in society involves determining its function along with shedding a light on its *raison d'être*, the conditions of its existence. *Theatrical culture,* the term used by the production to describe the degree of know-how of the audience in theater (343), is still on is its way to development. Theater is not rooted in the traditions, neither it is part of the daily life (2440). It is still a new not finally defined element of the environment (448).

The lack of theatrical education is, as with other teaching subjects, inflicted by general delays in reforming the educational school programs:

a result of confessional balance considerations (837). Although theater has recently entered schools (221, 2378), the results are questionable: first, some schools are simply using theater as a means of commercial benefit; second, foreign schools are expected to teach an alien view of theater, increasing the gap between theater and its direct environment, the source of its repertoire of signs and symbols (626, 2928). On the other hand, commercial universities allocate usually a low budget to theater in comparison to other majors (2275). Since working in theater is not beneficial on the economic level, parents paying for the university education of their children do not see in theater a serious academic major. We also notice that more females than males want to major in theater, due to the fact that the education of females is still considered as less important than that of males in the first place (2255). All this portrays a skeptical aspect of the rank of theater in society and the theater people.

Although the production sees education as a requirement to understand and produce theater (168, 170, 171, 264, 1039), it is questionable whether this latter is equivalent to theatrical culture. The conditions of constitution of theater are not necessarily coupled with education, but more with a social need for the existence of theater. It is noticed, however, that educated spectators are more initiated to theater than their less educated counterparts. This creates a partition between an inexperienced audience and an experienced audience. This partition is not necessarily dependent on the level of education, since, many educated people are not initiated to theater, and others who are not so educated, but are already acquainted with it. The effect of education is more in the type of theater each type visits. Intellectuals, who are both educated and initiated to theater, constitute the normal audience for Intellectual Theater. The educated but inexperienced constitute the typical Entertainment Theater audience. The least educated are the typical Popular Theater audience. This classification emerged from observation, interviews, photo and video analysis. The audience of intellectual theater would like to be differentiated from that of entertainment and popular plays.

Inexperienced or »virgin« audiences have less trained seeing and hearing habits regarding the elements of theater. In their interpretation of signs and symbols, they are most liable to make a direct comparison between those elements and their real life equivalents, without accounting for their artificial components. The border between theater and real life itself is not obvious in their regard. Reshaped, remodeled, stylized, signs and symbols are interpreted at three stages: first, during the performance as part of the interpretation process; second, in the evaluation of the performance by the audience in the post-performance phase, and third, in the placement of the role of theater as a phenomenon in the environment.

Knowing that, in those three phases, this audience is vulnerable to all the »marketing offensives« of the production, including faulty assessment in the newspapers critique and especially the elements of attraction. Nevertheless, inexperienced audience is partly initiated to certain elements existing in theater, like music, songs, and dance. Also, »beautiful words« and poetry are positively received and appreciated by the audience (2316, 2835, 2843).

As for the language, the spoken Lebanese, used exclusively in Popular and Entertainment Theaters, is easier to understand than the standard Arabic, used in most of the intellectual plays. The discrepancy between standard Arabic and the spoken Lebanese used in the first two types of theater frames this latter within the context of daily language and daily life situations, which the average spectator prefers in order to easily understand the play. By remaining distant from Entertainment and Popular Theater, standard Arabic, with its potential scientific capacity, truncates part of the topics, in which this tool is needed, from theater. On the other hand, using standard Arabic in Entertainment or Popular types of theater does not solve the problem, since the discrepancy between the two languages keeps the biggest part of the potential audiences away from theater in that case. They can understand standard Arabic, but they cannot »feel or have fun« in this language as said in one interview. The development of the spoken language is handicapped through being not written. Some even count on theater to offer a frame for this development.

All in all, the lack of theatrical education, together with the language problem, encouraged a type of *easy* theater for the less educated limiting their tastes and interpretations to easy symbolism, refraining theater from entering the sphere of the abstract level of symbols and theatrical conventions needed for more developed phases. Furthermore, this paved the way towards *realism* in theater as a means of reaching the largest part of the audience, and defines it as a criterion of the quality of theater productions.

Meaning and role of theater

Theater appreciation depends on the types of audience. By excluding the intellectuals, who constitute a minority, the following was observed. The typology of theater as seen by the audience is based on an *emotional* understanding of theater oriented towards a *functional* role in society. It varies according to the *effect* of the performance, which is the determinant of the role and meaning of theater in society. This reflects also the pragmatic and goal-oriented mentality of the Lebanese in general. The first partition made by the audience regarding theater is: »comedy« versus »drama.«

Under the term *comedy*, all types of theater related to laughter, entertainment and amusement are categorized. The main aim of these types is to make people laugh like in Chansonnier and Boulevard (2889) and to stimulate certain emotions like in Serious and Popular Theaters (1082, 2977). The word *drama,* as used by the audience, corresponds to Serious Theater, which is expected to deal with serious topics of life. It is also seen as a difficult type of theater (1105), because »it demands brain work, is heavy, tiring,« and for a certain laughter-seeking audience »boring.« This connotation corresponds to Serious Theater in general, and the intellectual in particular.

However, Popular Theater can express serious topics without »being boring.« Through realism, this theater presents the easy identification for the broad audience. Due to its *realism*, it becomes a representation of the social reality—i.e. becoming the »mirror of society.« It interacts with social reality, and is thus an active factor in society. Departing from this viewpoint, theater is a tool in need of a cause in order to function as part of a social movement. It is part of the environment, and it acquires a meaning only in this tight connection to it. The audience would recognize in the theater play parts of their own reality (390, 391, 2886, 2878, 2915, 2683). This aspect of theater is »serious« because it affects society. Form this perspective, separating between fiction and reality (2675, 2676) would be theoretically sufficient to induce a larger margin of freedom of expression. This separation is not obvious in Lebanon, where theater is not traditionally established and the thin difference between the signs of the environment used in theater and their actual values in the environment is not respected. Certain signs and symbols used in theater are taken seriously depending on their direct closeness to the spheres of discord. The same elements used in abstract manner are rather noticed. This makes their use delicate implying a tighter margin of freedom and a widening of the taboo domain. Despite the seriousness of the use of some theatrical elements related to the spheres of discord, theater itself remains not serious (2601). Depending on its type, we can discern two major roles for theater: a medium of expression of the needs of society and also a space for entertainment (211, 386, 505, 678, *893,* 373, 2210, 2934).

Expressing the social and political needs of the society is the first function attributed to theater. Being a medium of expression, the theatrical action is oriented towards a central object, the topic. This assigns another function to theater: displaying social problems for the public, which could potentially lead to a public discussion between the *self* and the *other* (959, 218). The closer the topic to reality, the more meaningful it becomes (1128).

Entertainment, the other function attributed to theater, suggests that the aim of theater is making people laugh (400). This can also be seen as part of the social needs (481), defining the goal of the theatrical action as that of giving pleasure to the biggest amount and variety of people (*848*). Thus, theater fulfills an entertaining function bringing pleasure to the audience (893, 2304, 2388). Defining entertainment can differ from the mere effect of laughter to the complete transportation from »R1« to another reality »R2,« the type of entertainment achieved through making the spectator forget »R1.« To this purpose, the production has to present a more appealing alternative reality »R2.« This is usually achieved through shaping »R2« after the will of the spectator (2815), which includes the construction of the self and the other, enabling him or her to reach a »state« of satisfaction not achieved in »R1.« This is done by taking antagonists from real life like politicians in Chansonnier Theater, for example, and ridiculing them. The stage, through identification, becomes a way for the audience to express how they see, feel about, and want to have reality. The protagonist is usually the »normal average citizen,« who becomes a hero for the time of the sketch giving the audience the opportunity, though unreal, to thrust feelings out. The success of this transportation depends on the »credibility« of the scenario and the strength of identification of the spectator, which, in its turn, is a function of the connectivity between »R2« and »R1.« During the war, for instance, this entertainment function relieved the audiences, by diverting them from the reality of war (*1046*). Through entertainment also, the audience goes to theater in the aim of forgetting the worries of daily life (2600).

In both functions *entertainment* and *expression*, theater has a cumulative effect (387) both on the environment »R1« and on the theatrical experience, which helps developing »R2« in the long run. Nonetheless, this effect is slow and remains in the subconscious of the spectator. It does not materialize in immediate action or change.

Theater in the relation between the *self* and the *other*

Theater is an important axis between the two social worlds. Regarding the meeting with the *other*, due to psychological separation, the direct interaction remains at a low level. Complying to the host-guest attitudes, parts of the audience are like »tourists« in the area of the *other*, neither having an influence nor wanting to have one (2221). This role will be more elaborated in the Crossing Audience below. More important here is the symbolical interaction found in theater.

Whether it is a representation of the *self* or a construction of the *other*, theater is a field of friction between the two. Depending on the actors, the audience, and the place of the performance, this *self-other* construction acquires different dimensions. The actors no longer represent themselves, but the community they belong to. Due to this representation also, the relation between the actors and what they symbolize determines the course of the interaction in the performance. The way this is done contributes to form an image of this community. Theater can be a medium of *self*-presentation (*853, 1069*). It introduces the community to the *other*, and serves in shaping the image of the community to its members (2731, *757*).

This, however, does not always function as a representation on the collective level; in many cases, the representation could be independent of the community and work thus on the individual level (2973). This can be the case in Serious Theater that appeals to the individual rather than the collective or in Entertainment Theater in which the representation is avoided in order to preserve neutrality. In Popular Theater, it is rarely the case that a hero represents the individual.

In order for the performance to succeed in this representation, feelings of solidarity with the community have to be aroused first. Here enters confessionalism the frame. In both milieus, the audiences have the potential to exert strong confessional feelings (*1059, 841*). The way those audiences see the production of each other sums up to the credit of confessionalism. Theater is thus feeding on emotions in a society less liable to consider mental effort as »amusing« (2798). Confessionalism is so used behind the scenes. Pleasing the confessional side of the audience is done using confessional symbols under a certain camouflage in the form. The examples are many in this regard: »Tanious Chahine,« which was presented in the theater »George V« in Jouniéh in the Eastern area in 1997, was the story of a Maronite historical political figure of Mount Lebanon, »ğabal lubnān.« The audience were brought from the mountains in busses to see this play. The play contains many allusions to general Michel Aoun,[1] who was a popular Chrisitan leader in the last phase of the war. His popularity was basically among a segment of Christians and as a result the audience was also Christian. There is also symbolism in this example. The person of Michel Aoun is used as a symbol to achieve the effect of popularity based on patriotic feelings.

---

1   The example of General Michel Aoun is used here in the frame of discussing the type of audience interested in such a play. This is analyzed apart from of his political background refusing to be a mere Christian figure but rather national patriotic one.

In example B (Appendix A) from Serious Theater, there is an illustration of this representation function. In the play we find a Moslem actor presenting—as seen by the Christian audience—an image of the Moslems, containing many elements that comply with the image of the Shia constructed by the Christian milieu like the lack of education, ignorance, view of the woman,... These elements lay behind the acceptance of the play in the Christian area (*488*). When presented in Moslem areas, this play did not please the audience. This could be interpreted in two ways: it is either that the Eastern area sets the criteria for what a good play is through its more powerful media means, or that the Christian construction of the Moslem, as presented in the play, is not what a Moslem audience wants to see. The fact that, after its presentation in the Eastern area, the Moslem audiences came to see it, speaks in favor of the first interpretation. Taking into account the solidarity with a Moslem raising actor—*representing the community* in the *other* area—is in the favor of the second. Nevertheless, many phases were indicating a non-confessional character.

Throughout the play, the actor, in his role as a retired trash collector, comes back to the quarter of his old activity. He starts looking in the trash bins and making up imaginative stories about the neighborhood relying on his findings. In one scene, he accidentally drops a plate breaking it into three pieces. He tries to fix the pieces together but it does not work. Turning to the audience and addressing it directly, he says that if a plate of three pieces cannot be fixed together, how can one fix a whole country in three pieces. This direct reference is a symbolic statement about the complications issuing from confessionalism. Such allusions group the audience from both sides around the common idea that confessionalism and its implications are not a good structure to build unity in the country. On the one hand, this is an accepted statement in both milieus; on the other hand, it opens a dialog about the meaningfulness of such a structure. It does not give an answer nor suggests a solution; that is how it passes censorship. This type of dialogue would not be understood in this manner had it not been to the *representation* effect of this actor. Within one social world, this statement would have been a normality and not a dialogue. A probable interpretation would be that »the *other* is confessional that is why we cannot build a state.« The meaning it got here is derived from representation.

Apart from this message, when indicating the snobbish people of the street, and whenever it came to imitate his daughter-in-law, the characters presented were typical of the Eastern area. He tries to transmit the carelessness of the Christian society towards important issues considered as affecting more the *other* society. One of those is the occupation in the

South, which is ignored by the Christian community as »non of their business.« In a »discotheque scene«—a cliché of the Eastern area as perceived by the Moslems—he presents the dancers as rubbish bags. Playing the role of the moderator, he cuts in one song reminding the dancers of the suffering of the people of the South under the occupation. They all clap, and the dance goes on, with most of the dancers not even noticing why they clapped. This critical and sharp message would only have been accepted when declaring a clear non-confessional level. Nevertheless, it is known that personal connections in the field are the ones who paved the way towards bringing the play to East Beirut in the first place. Through opening the space for the mutual expression of ideas, this kind of theater acts like an inter-confessional »forum.« No doubt, the play itself is a monodrama of a good artistic level less known to the non-experienced audience of the South, which increases the curiosity factor. The type of audience, however, was restricted to the intellectual audience showing their non-confessionalism and booked up performances by certain organizations *(ḍamān),*[2] reached through public relations.

In a parallel example from Popular Theater (Appendix A, Example A), Christian actors are able to create an identification space in the Moslem Shia milieu in the South (757). Due to the regional belonging of the main actor to the South, to personal connections on the individual level, and working on a straight »representation« technique using original signs and symbols from inside the social world, the Moslem esthetic realm, the play did succeed, to a large extent, in presenting an image of the Shia hero as a *self* definition in the own community. The actor dropped the own Christian image of the Moslem and adopted a Moslem view of the *self*. Nevertheless, the play did still contain certain allusive remarks well covered behind layers of adopting the Moslem »cause« in the South. These were seen as »mocking the image of the Shia,« as a Moslem actor of Popular Theater says, who found in the Christian actor, apart from being a competitor, »an abuser of the feelings and the cause of the people.« This reality was not obvious to the inexperienced audience. Consequently, the play was still a success, achieved through a good know-how of the image the *other* wants to show.

The success of this play caused amazement among the Christian production agents. Normally, Christians are supposedly identifying with Christians and vice versa. It is either that the actor should have concentrated on his normal audience, the Christians, or that the Shia audience should not have identified with him. According to this frame also, Christian actors are expected to be working in the same sphere, and Christian audience is supposed to identify with Christian producers, and vice versa.

---

2 See section Two Confessional Views of Confessionalism

In this case, however, we find a precedent in this type of theater to achieve this representation effect, where the belonging of the actor himself normally plays a decisive role. The actor, as we mentioned, compensated for that through his »regional belonging,« and playing on an evident theme of the Shia: the occupied South[3] and the resistance against the occupation. In the last scene, the farmer, the original owner of what was later a »disputed« property, takes a plough, the only weapon at his reach and a symbol of honesty and work, and raises it in the face of the occupiers of his house, symbolizing thus the continuation of the resistance with present means. Moreover, the Shias, usually neglected on the political scene, gained a new role due to the resistance in the South. This was reflected also in theater. This also proves the relation between the real events on the social and political scenes and their reflection on stage. Before this phase there was little interest in theater from the Shia audience.

In summary, presenting the *self* or constructing the *other* on stage can only function whenever it *complies* with the pre-constructed image of the respective audience. Its acceptance by the audience is also a function of the place, which determines the host-guest identity.

Differences between the two social worlds

As a matter of fact, theater exists in both social worlds. Due to religious considerations, theater has, however, less or different reasons to exist in the Moslem milieu than the Christian milieu. The existence of theater in the Moslem milieu under its present forms can be explained through the duplication existing between the social worlds emerging from rivalry and competition. This duplication was able to maintain the parallelism between the structures, even regarding issues of discord. The existence of theater in the Christian milieu is, in itself, a necessity of its existence in the Moslem milieu, and vice versa. If theater exists in the Christian milieu as a result of the tendency towards copying the western model, it exists in the Moslem milieu as a result of the duplication effect, similar to the case with other institutions. This complies with the difference in the Arab theater where we had the »shadow play« and the »puppet show« avoiding human personification on stage.

Furthermore, in evaluating this theater in the Moslem environment, the Christian view pleads that the Moslems should be closer to the people in their production (2366, 2950). Of course, being close to the people is the ultimate aim. Which people and why is there a discrepancy? Here, these questions are legitimate to be asked. On the other hand, the same complaint is heard on the Moslem side, that Christian theater should be

---

3 The play was presented in 1999 before the Israeli withdrawal in May 2000.

closer to the people (909). Seeing the theater of the *other* as lacking closeness to the audience reflects two factors: first, a duality in the view of the theater itself, and second, a duality in the view of the other audience. Moreover, it reflects a misunderstanding of the *other*—a false image—and also of the *self*, suggesting a misconception of theatrical action on the production-reception communication level.

Between the two lines of the function of theater being a medium of expression and a way of entertainment common to both communities, the thin differences can be traced on two levels: the dimensions of the functionality of theater and the role of the individual in theatrical representation. Regarding functionality, the difference is between the could-have-a-function in the Christian milieu and the should-have-a-function in the Moslem milieu. The individual is more present in the Christian theater than in the Moslem milieu. By extrapolation, those differences, increasing in divergence with time, will reach two concretely different concepts of theater in the long run.

The Christian milieu: estheticism, exclusivism, and development of the individual

The Christian environment accepts theater as a phenomenon that *could* have a social function, but this function is neither necessary to justify its existence nor does it exclude or replace *l'art pour l'art* as justification and raison d'être of theater. In »*Die feinen Unterschiede*« (La Distinction), P. Bourdieu reaches a similar result when inspecting the response of the lower classes in France to art in general. The lower classes aim at finding a reason or a function to justify the existence of art and theater; whereas, the upper classes strive to show their differentiation through accepting *l'art pour l'art* as self-justifying (Bourdieu 1987: 63, 591, 594 ff). Nevertheless, reducing the difference between the Christian and the Moslem social milieus to a class difference is not applicable in the case of Lebanon. The tendency of functionality is found, with a few exceptions, at the upper class levels in the Moslem milieu, whereas the *l'art pour l'art* is found within the lower class levels in the Christian milieu. This adds a clear exclusiveness to theater as a whole associated with exquisiteness and refinement in taste. Despite the fact that theater could have a social function (*2348*), and that its existence is not a mere coincidence; nonetheless, this function approaches estheticism. Estethicism is defined as »the acceptance of beauty and taste as a fundamental standard, ethical and other standards being secondary. 2. an exaggeratd or excessive devotion to art, music or poetry, with indifference to practical matters« (Webster's Encyclopedic Unabriged Dictionnary of the English Language). At its best, estheticism can only reflect reality, but it does not implicate change or revolution in its environment (194, 335). Theater can be the mirror of reality without necessarily being active in it itself. The mirror reflects thus only an esthetic perspective of reality.

By associating art with the creativity of the individual, the tendency of *l'art pour l'art* leads to an increasing role of the individual artist, whose gains on importance. This explains the different definitions of the function of theater in society according to individual visions. In parallel, for the individual spectator, theater is an island outside the collective, an escape from a pressing collective. Christian theater tends more towards individualism found in Intellectual Theater, away from the collective, the case of Popular Theater. The existence of Popular Theater in the Christian areas is hardly remarkable in comparison to the Moslem milieu. Being a medium of expression at the individual level, we approach more the idea of the artist as sole creator, whose world constitutes both means and goal. The theater play becomes, thus, a window on the unique world of this particular individual, and the meaning of the performance resides in the communication and interaction. This suggests also that the Christian social needs expressed through theater can be metaphysical or philosophical (504). Entertainment should also involve creativity communicated through esthetically expressed feelings, hence, polishing the feelings of the spectator (499). Under the form of a pure incitement to laughter, entertainment is at the lower scale of the functions of theater.

In this context, we can deduce more appreciation of acting as an independent art regardless of its realism in the Christian milieu (2733, 2841, 2860). There is, thus, a focus on the performance of the actor itself more than on the conveyed meaning (872). Some views reduce theater as a whole to the »art of the actor.« This makes the actor the focus of attention of the audience. Consequently, it shifts the identification from the focus on the drama of the performance as a whole to the emotional following of this particular hero adopted as sole emotional object for identification. We also notice an increasing importance of directing (2898), which can also be the attraction in theater. All this suggests a drift in theater getting farther away from *realism*.

In conclusion, theater is classified as an art, and it is a standalone entity (2833). It is the aim of being in the performance and thus, spectators go to see acting and directing for the sake of their esthetical values (2784). Through the concept of theater as *art*, the Christian theater encourages the development of the individual, because its creativity is based on breaking everyday life conventions. This coincides in our context to the concept of the *individual (fard)* rather than the *person (šaḫṣ)* as explained above.[4]

---

4 See section: Politics of the Social World

The Moslem milieu: functionalism, popularism, and conservation of the collective

In opposition to the Christian environment, the Moslem environment necessitates that theater *should* have a social function; otherwise it becomes meaningless and superfluous. This function, similarly to the Christian milieu, can vary between the expression of the needs of society as a primary function and entertainment as a secondary function.

In expressing the needs of society we detect another difference between the two milieus. Whereas the needs of the Christian society can be maintained at the individual level, in the Moslem milieu, the needs are away from the existential or metaphysical questions. They come from a pragmatic perspective related to less structural topics like the political injustice, social criticism, identity problems and conflicts. The topic in the case of what is denoted in this milieu as »drama« should be handling a problem of the community. This line tends to assign a functional role to theater in society. The nature of the social topics to be dealt with is determined by the acceptance, tolerance, and position of the topic in the environment.

As we said above, the necessity for existential questions is lower in the Moslem milieu than in the Christian one. Whether it is a matter of freedom, need, or both, we notice that those topics, typical of the individual level and more elaborated in the Christian milieu, appear only seldom and in a very minimal form on a Moslem stage. This can be interpreted as a dominance of religion in the Moslem milieu in being exclusively responsible for regulating those issues, having therefore a greater influence compared to the Christian milieu. This creates a general difference both in the nature of the topics and in the perspective from which those topics are dealt with. This pragmatic approach, when applied to the issue of functionality of theater, can also explain the futility of *l'art pour l'art* as *raison d'être* of theater.

Departing from this perspective, theater can have a social as well as a political function depending on the changing pragmatic needs of society. It can even work as part of a political movement aiming at and able to induce change (866). It could be used as a weapon, like other media, against »the corruption and things harming society moving from the political need to the political cause« (222). Theater represents therefore the social worries of society (342, 903), and it becomes itself a worry, whenever it is not able to fulfill those functions. It drifts away from the futility of »living some event« and puts more focus on the topic, which should also be connected to daily life (2609). This is also a push to Popular Theater in the Moslem milieu (2693), which feeds on expressing the needs of the masses of people. More precisely, it is a push of the *popu-*

larization of theater to reach more audience. Reciprocally, theater tends more towards reflecting a »popular culture.«

Entertainment as a function of theater in the Moslem milieu is achieved in a pragmatic way. It aims at making the spectator laugh, which is acknowledged as a social need even though less important than expressing serious problems. The form of laughter is nonetheless simple in its structure. Since laughter in theater is usually induced by the breaking of a habit or norm, many of which fall in the Moslem milieu under the strong dominance of religion, the limit at this level refrains from using the moral values or traditions presenting the object of the ridicule, like in Boulevard Theater presents the marital betrayal as frame for creating comic situations. This mode is substituted in the Moslem milieu by the clowning and farce, as it was the case with the theater of Shoushou,[5] or is the case in current Moslem comedies.

Hence, laughter, should be explicitly stated and defined as an end in itself. This is due to the slight contradiction it represents to the ought-to-be function of theater. Inducing laughter is far from the »social cause« and »expression of needs,« that are used to justify the existence of other forms of theater in a Moslem milieu, where—strictly considered—the idea of creation, the representation of characters on stage, »being left to God alone,« is not accepted. This weakens the justification of the social need of laughter for breaking this »rule,« since laughter could be achieved through other means.

In contrast to the Christian milieu, the focus on the »person«—the hero—in the Moslem milieu is deduced from the representative capacity of the character in the community. In our context, we have the representation of *persons ('ašḫāṣ)* and not *individuals ('afrād)*, especially when it comes to the role of the woman. It is seldom to find an independent woman character at this stage. The identification of the audience is achieved through the matching of the character with the social problems. The individual itself is of less importance.

In conclusion, this »functionalism of theater,« its rooting in the real life, and its conservation of its structure, leads the Moslem theater towards increasing realism, which, in its turn, is becoming the scale of evaluation of theater plays by the audiences.

---

5 Shoushou is the nickname of a theater actor, Hassan Ala'a ad-Dīn, who started, what was later known as the »daily theater.« This theater died with the death of its founder, although the son of Shoushou, Khodr Ala'a ad-Dīn, hardly tries to revive the style of the father. The topics dealt with in this theater are light social critiques in a comic form. According to Berge Fazlian, one of the directors who worked with Shoushou, Shoushou's audience was mostly predisposed to laughter regardless of the topic. »The audience used to laugh as soon as he, going down the stairs in one performance, would stretch his hat from the scenes.«

Attitude of the audience towards theater people

Apart from the general attitudes controlling the social worlds regarding the *self* and the *other* based on the confessional distribution, the attitude of the audience towards the production can be narrowed to the view of the actors and of acting as a job. Of course, all the factors cited concerning theater have their impact at this level; the attitude towards theater itself is reflected more or less also on the actors.

»Theater does not feed bread« is a frequent saying spread among both theater people and audiences. Acting is not accepted as a serious job. The idea of a serious job is a synonym here for yielding money and conveying stability (2986). Theater people are not accepted in society, because they are considered as not having a »serious« job. This pushes them to try harder to compensate for having a non-lucrative job (2958, 2986), either by leaving theater, or by trying to prove that it *is* a serious job, through a rising tendency to focus on the financial profit. Moreover, the image of theater itself as »not serious« is also carried on to the actors. The actors are seen as »capable of lying correctly,« »we don't know when they are lying or when they are telling the truth,« etc... These prejudices, aggravated by the distance between the society and theater, the lack of »experience in theater,« and the non-clear definition of art in general, especially in the Moslem milieu, contribute to creating a rift between production and reception.

In addition to that, the image of the woman actress, which is also the most prominent friction between the two social worlds, is at its worse in theater. As an example, the French word »artiste« is used in the colloquial language as an equivalent for »prostitute.« As a result, it is substituted by »comédien« or »comédienne« to avoid falling into this category. Since the word is a derivation from »art,« we can deduce, in which context the idea of art was initially associated. In other terms, even if some types of »art« are »tolerated« and »respected,« this remains on a theoretical abstract level, because »the artists« themselves as persons are not taken seriously. Moreover, the image of theater as act of creation reflects negatively on the theater people themselves.

On the other hand, the increasing initiation to theater is working slowly towards correcting and improving this image, especially now that the acting field—especially the »doublage« (dubbing of Mexican soap operas)—proves to be lucrative on the financial level, which works positively in restituting the faith in acting as a serious job.

Going to theater

Whereas most of the work of the production is concentrated in the outer-performance preparations, the outer-performance work of the audience is reduced to two subsequent processes, *selecting* a play according to certain criteria and *going to theater*. The selection of the play is a general result of the cumulative of attitudes emerging from Level I and continuing to form primary expectations, which lead eventually to the motivation of »going to theater.«

Going to theater is a designation of the processes incurred by the spectator leading him or her to the performance. It is parallel to the physical trajectory of the spectator from home to the theater house, and it includes a number of factors affecting reception—especially in the case of a change in the area. This trajectory and its connotation contribute to form an attitude at the beginning of the performance denoted as the initial state of the spectator; it depends on the trajectory known as »going to theater.« This trajectory starts with »acquiring a ticket,« it is affected by the place of the performance and the financial element, and it determines the selection of the performance. After the performance, the impact is done through evaluating the final state of the spectator.

Acquiring the ticket

The context of »acquiring the ticket« is a designation of the processes leading the audiences to the theater houses. This creates a division of the audience between circumstantial and intentional audiences.

The circumstantial audience
As funny as it might look, going to theater has more in it than a personal choice (2407). Being in a theater performance in Lebanon does not necessarily mean you have paid for your ticket or that you have chosen to be there. Social pressure and solidarity with the collective play a decisive role here.

Organizations
This category represents the audience going in groups to theater. They either belong to certain religious, social, or political organizations or parties, or they simply sympathize with those. The effect on the structure of the audience is that we have blocks with similar social, political, or religious orientations. In this case, the spectator is under a certain peer pressure that creates the motivation to go to theater as a part of the activities of the organization. Mostly, these organizations get special group discounts.

Booking up: ḍamān

Booking up means here buying all seats in a performance in the intention to resell them at a profit. In Lebanon, it is known under the word *(ḍamān)*. This category represents one or more persons, or a group, club or organization buying all the tickets of a specific performance and selling them again with a margin of profit. The aim of such a transaction ranges from making personal benefit, to collecting funds for the so-called organization. It can be part of the above mentioned category, but the usual case is that the actors and other people working in the play would get a discount on tickets for a certain performance and try to sell them using their personal and public relations as part of the marketing strategy of the play. The people who buy the tickets do it for the sake of the actors in this case, and, in many cases, they do not even go to see the play. In this instance, we can talk about and act of social solidarity highly related to the family and the social structure.

This audience consists of groups of interrelated people, among which we find also family members going together, or seizing the opportunity to meet with their relatives at the place of the performance. Here, the performance is not the purpose in itself, but the social meeting in the background. In addition to those categories, spectators come to the theater box office either because of price incentives of direct sales or by coincidence. Usually, the box office remains open for the advantage of the person who booked up the performance. Another negative effect of this method is that it decreases the number of people who go willingly to theater, since they wait to buy the ticket, unavoidably, from some acquaintance or relative who got involved in *(ḍamān)*. This way, many spectators find themselves in theater, waiting for the curtain to lift and also impatiently for it to fall again, praying meanwhile for a shorter agony. The same can be true for the next category: invitations (982, 983).

Invitations, public relations for the theatrical sphere

This represents the category of invited audience. Of course, there are many reasons why one would be invited to see a play, depending on the relation to the working group. As a marketing concept, one should avoid having an empty theater house, because this would eventually harm the image of the play. Therefore, the production tries to keep each performance at a certain tolerable level of audience through the distribution of invitations. Some producers went to the extent of paying a pseudo-audience to keep this image. This is particularly the case, when scenes of the performance are recorded for advertisement purposes. A full house is always an indication of the success of the play and therefore gives a good marketable image. The producer can control the timing and amount of invitation tickets to be given away.

Another classical type of invited audience is the theatrical sphere and their connections and relatives, who usually wait to be invited in order to go to theater. In comparison, they would always expect to pay for eating in a restaurant, where there is a singer or dancer. This is also an indication of the rank of theater in society in general.

The audience issuing from invitations has a different motivation of coming. The theatrical sphere comes for two reasons: first, to be informed about what is going on in the milieu, and second, for the sake of public relations, since it is an opportunity to meet other people from the sphere. Invitations to people outside this sphere are used to enhance business relations with organizations that would potentially book up the play. In any case, the interest of the audience is far from the value of the performance itself, and its reactions during the performance are conditioned by this factor. The number of invitations can be known, by observing the people staying after the performance for a small talk with the persons who invited them. In many cases, I witnessed the majority of the audience waiting (including me).

The intentional audience

This category represents the theatergoers who willingly pay for their ticket in the sole aim of seeing the performance. These are, in a way, the »real audience.« Their direct motivation is related to two factors: interest in theater and in the particular performance depending on their initiation to theater. In their majority, they are families or couples. In the latter case, going to theater is part of a cultural »going out« among the educated audience. This audience goes into the processes of selecting a performance.

Selecting a performance

In choosing a performance, the spectator is affected by the long-term incentives resulting from the attitude towards theater and short-term ones. Parallel to the selection process, the spectator starts forming expectations about the performance in question (2427). The expectations pertinent to the particular performance can be divided as follows: expectations focused on during-performance effect, expectations focused on post-performance effect, and expectations based on outer elements, the social effect. The reasons for selecting a play and the formation of expectations about it constitute the motivation to see this play.

Who selects a performance? The reason of being in a certain performance, as classified through the interviews, came to two types of circumstances: curiosity and social circumstances. The latter being included in the circumstantial audience, the first type constitutes the intentional audience.

From the interviews, one can deduce that the process of selection itself comes first as a manifestation of the response to the elements of attraction set by the production. These start in the advertisement, which is the outer-performance standard communication between the two sectors production and audiences. Among those we can also include: the appeal, especially the part shown in the advertisement acting as a promise to the audience, the big name in the performance, and the topic.

From the social contact point of view, the curiosity about the *other* can sometimes play the role of an attraction. This is what makes *Crossing Plays* interesting, because it is a contact with the *other* and a window on the social world on the other side. Of course, this can have also a reverse function when the curiosity fades to be replaced by a refutation of the close encounter with the *other*.

Also affecting the expectations is the frame in which a performance is presented. The festivals of theater, for example, usually taking place in summer, constitute a special frame. It is not the normal daily theater, but plays that are made specifically for festivals. This frame limits the type of audience going to theater as well as their expectations, which drift towards the uncommon and the unfamiliar. It also extends the span of tolerance of the audience (434, 435, 438, 429, 430). However, this frame induces a limitation on the type of audience since it is then exclusively the academic and university circle.

Related to the »theatrical culture,« *curiosity* represents a motivation for going to theater in Lebanon (2764), since theater has still the glance of something new to many people. There are even people who have never been to theater in their lives (2829). This is also related to the question of availability of theater, especially in the villages outside the cities, where a theater performance as such is a special attraction (2672). Curiosity increases also in the case when the spectator is not able to expect something determined, but is rather left with expecting the unknown, which is a different type of motivation based on little information.

Among the social factors working as a motivation, theater functions as an intellectual »going out« for couples, and a social meeting with friends and relatives (449, 442, *2211*). The personal relations to the actors are also a motivation of coming to theater (2640), and the meeting with the *other* in the case of Crossing Audiences. Choosing to go to theater in this case means choosing social contact with other people. It is a choice related to the *other*, peer or non-peer.

The place

By changing areas we have two processes that start in this shift and affect, at a later stage, the frame of the performance. The attitude of the audience is not always constant. It changes with the social world on two levels. First, the type of audience changes with the changing area between Moslem and Christian. Second, the same spectator incurs a shift in the attitude once moving between West and East Beirut. This is due to the awareness of the spectator of the shift in the social environment when knowing that he or she will face another environment. Therefore, for every spectator, and according to the region where the performance is taking place, there are Eastern and Western modes. What a Moslem accepts to see in East Beirut, where he is a tourist, he would probably refuse at »home,« as a host. We find here two borders, one between the own system of values and that of the *other*, and the second border is between the own system of values and the practical requirements of daily life. As a result of this shift in mode, the spectators go through a correction of the image of the *other*. Due to the separation in the war, most of the attitudes about the *other* are based on prejudice. Being in the other area means having an updated input about the other, which, compared with the preformed image is liable to changes.

In addition to that, the area as such has connotations differing with respect to the respective audiences. The names of areas are symbols having historical connotations by themselves related to the experience of the people living in those areas and to the outsiders. This connotation becomes part of the performance. West Beirut, for a Christian, has a connotation of *war* and Moslems. These become part of his reception of the signs and symbols of the performance. A regional component of the meaning is, thus, relevant to the area itself. Moreover, regionalism implies changes in meaning incurring when changing cultural constellations represented here by the physical boundaries.

The change in the area works, thus, as a catalyst regarding the effects on theater performances. The longer the spectator has to drive to get to the theater house, the greater the alienation.

Transportation

Related to the place we have also technical problems. The transportation difficulty increases when having to change the area. The audience would have to travel a longer way with increasing costs and a longer time spent on the road (877). Another technical problem related to transportation is availability of theater. In this case, we can talk about an urban-rural division. Most of the theater plays are based in the cities and on the coast. In the mountains we find only seasonal visiting plays (2672, 2583), which have the aura of the unique opportunity. All this necessitates a stronger »incentive« on behalf of the audience since the way to get to the performance gets physically longer and harder, mixed with the feeling of meeting the *other* (2922).

Beirut as common space

Before the war, Beirut used to provide a common space for the *self-other* interaction. This common space, made it possible for art and production to flourish (781). With the impoverishment of this space in the time of the war, the question arises whether theater can assume the role of a virtual space to replace the physical space? This, nevertheless, would mean having a theater that is detached of the geography and demography of society, and thus conflicts with theater dependency on the environment as source of material. The result was limited to some shy and unsuccessful attempts by some optimistic theater producers to try to assign this role to theater. A neutral area where no color is dominating remains, therefore, unrealistic.

The Crossing Audience

Parallel to the Crossing Play elaborated earlier, there are Crossing Audiences moving across areas in the purpose of seeing theater performances. Being in contact with the *other* initiates many processes among which we find differentiation, identification, and confessionalism. This opportunity is intensively present in theater, because, by bringing to the public discussion the views of different orientations, we have a more intense meeting and interaction between the *self* and the *other*. There are two reasons for this crossing. First, certain plays never *cross* to the other side and hence are only available in the one area. This forces this audience to cross to see the play at the expense of being in the other area. Second, some audience would like to see the play in the other area regardless if the play would come to the own area or not. These two audiences are here denoted as Crossing Audiences. The first type is crossing because of the performance itself, not necessarily with the intention of meeting the *other*, and risking for this purpose—in his view of course—a potentially unpleasant meeting. The second type is crossing with the intention of a meeting, motivated by the will to see the performance from his perspective. The performance would then be seen as a joining factor between the two, since this audience is usually tolerant, being aware of the situation.

In this frame, it accepts deliberately what is presented on stage without constant juxtaposition between the systems of values of the self to that of the other. Another aspect of this phenomenon is the refusal of the »regional edition« of the play, where the signs and symbols would be adapted according to the production's view of the *other* not necessarily approved by the target milieu. This resembles seeing the original play in its natural environment, with its *normal* audience. Experiencing the *other* in his milieu becomes, hence, part of the performance.

Within this context, it is noted that the number of Christians that go to West Beirut to see a play is less than that of the Moslems going the reverse way (1071). Moslems have a better rate in participating in the cultural life of East Beirut. After the end of the war, there was a Moslem interest in discovering the other area. Pushed by curiosity and by the fact that the number of theater productions in East Beirut was larger than that of West Beirut, the cultural exchange was more in the direction West-East than East-West. This phenomenon was explained in the interviews as follows: one explanation to the direction of motion of the audience is that the Christians have less interest in sharing in the cultural life of the other side. The reasons for that are certain beliefs mixed with, if not based on, the view of *other* and isolation (*861*). Here, it is noted that during the war, part of the Christians were also called the »self-isolated,« (*'al-'in'izāliyyīn)* Another explanation is the lack of freedom reproached to be in the Moslem area. Consequently, it is »useless and futile« to go to see theater there. With the lack of freedom, the theatrical experience is neutralized and hence distanced from reality. A third explanation is related the religious factor, which denies the discussion of certain topics in West Beirut. This factor, imposed on the production side, has affected greatly the taste of the audience, which was forced to suffice itself with what is available, at the expense of the own interests. On the other hand, the topics discussed by the Moslems do not interest the Christians and are sometimes of no relevance at all to them. A fourth explanation to this fact is that the Christians have little motivation to go to theater in West Beirut, since they perceive it to be in the best of cases an imitation of that of East Beirut. This goes along a *superior-inferior* view of the *other*. A fifth explanation of this boycott would be a general depression on the Christian side after the end of the war, with the feeling that the Christians lost the privileges they believed to be entitled to discouraging contact with the *other*. The boycott came also as a consequence of separation between the areas. This term, reminiscent of war and political tensions, reflects to a certain extent this atmosphere. It came in vivo in the interviews: »the Christians are boycotting the Moslem theater,« as one playwright stated it (*2379*).

The financial element

With the shrinking middle class due to the war among other factors, it has become more difficult for the audience to spend money on luxuries like theater. The audience now, due to the poor economic performance of the country and the uneven distribution of money, is more or less divided between those »who have and those who don't« (157, 158, 955) This means that only a minority of the potential audience can allow itself to pay $21 for a performance (355, *2375*, 2935), which is normally the entrance fee for Chansonnier Theater, or $7 to $10, the average for other types, reaching up to $30 per ticket. Added to that are the transportation costs. The typical spectator would go with the own car and then try to find a parking place, knowing that parking costs are higher at night in the vicinity of theater houses (around $2 to $3). The theater houses offer no reduction for students or pupils; they have to pay the full tariff. In comparison, a cinema ticket costs about $6.5 normal tariff and can go down to $3 on Mondays or special cinema days.

Conclusion: A typology of the audience

There are many criteria according to which we can make a classification of the audience, most of which emerged in previous sections. The chief division is derived from the environment according to the main sphere of discord resulting in Moslem and Christian audiences. With the »crossing factor« we are liable to have heterogeneous versus homogeneous audiences in the case of the regional play. The differences between those two were elaborated in the course of the research. Second, the audience can be seen according to the categories listed under *going to theater* resulting in *intentional* and *circumstantial* audiences. The intentional audience is going to theater for the sake of theater itself and not because of its social aspect. On the other hand, the circumstantial audience are those who do not have theater as a goal; they *happen* to be there due to family, social pressure, or other reasons. Between those two we find the *casual audience,* visiting theater on an irregular basis. Going to theater also implies another category of non-theatergoers. This category represents, thus, non-active audiences due to the lack of initiation to theater and the technical problems related to the region, financial status, transportation, information, and the like. Third, another approach to the typology of the audience is through education and theatrical culture, the result of which is the intellectual, the educated, and the non educated audience, characterized by conflicting views about theatre itself. Next to those, the emigrants represent another category. They are in general a very tolerant audience, since they come full of positive attitudes towards Lebanon (2593, 2603, 2634, 2635). Their presence among the audience has a seasonal aspect because they are usually there in summer to visit their families, and are typical audiences of summer theater festivals. Those spectators have a different theatrical culture and expect to see the long missed Lebanon through theater. In different forms, the confessional shadow prevails over these categories. It is the main worry of the production and the main determinant of the reception.

Performance (Level III) and Post-performance (Level IV)

With the performance, we move from Level II, defined as the pre- and post-performance activities and originally linked to Level I through the attitudes towards theater and its meaning in society, to Level III, which describes the activities happening during the performance: *interpretation* and *interaction*.

These two processes help giving an insight of the performance. They in turn depend on the type of the given audience, the topic and form of the play, and the place. As mentioned earlier, the constellation resulting from those parameters as conceived by the spectators forms a »second reality« »R2«, in which the spectator is eventually immersed for the time of the performance. The field research showed that the activities of the audience are centered on the comparison of »R2« to that of the environment, denoted as »reality one« »R1.«

Reality One »R1« and Reality Two »R2«: the basis for interpretation

»All the world's a stage,
And all the men and women merely players;
They have their exits and their entrances...« (As You Like It, II/vii)

In the eyes of the Lebanese audiences, the theater performance is or is supposed to be a reflection of real life (2273, 2668). The most prominent aspect of that resemblance is the reproduction of style elements of the environment in the performance. With those elements, the audience is able to construct a new »space« with its own rules, through which a new reality comes into view. The transition from »reality one« to »reality two« resembles the following description by Luckmann/Berger:

Das Theater ist ein besonders gutes Beispiel des Spiels der Erwachsenen. Der Übergang von einer Wirklichkeit in die Andere wird durch das Auf- und Niedergehen des Vorhangs markiert. Wenn der Vorhang aufgeht, wird der Zuschauer »in eine andere Welt versetzt«, eine Welt eigener Sinneinheit und eigener Gesetze, die noch etwas oder gar nichts mit den Ordnungen in der Alltagswelt zu tun haben können. Wenn der Vorhang fällt, kehrt der Zuschauer »in die Wirklichkeit« zurück, das heißt in die oberste Wirklichkeit, in die Alltagswelt, mit deren Wirklichkeit verglichen die auf der Bühne jetzt dürftig und ephemer erscheint, wie lebensvoll sie auch wenige Augenblicke früher gewirkt haben mag. (Luckmann/Berger 1969: 28)

The interesting point in this description, apart from confirming the daily world as »upper reality« and the performance as »other world,« is that the transition of the spectator from one reality to the other is marked by a theatrical element: the movement of the curtain as indicator of transition. The transition reduces the role of the spectator to a participant in a game, a fictitious reality well separated from the »upper reality.«

The passive voice used above, »the spectator is transported,« indicates a passivity of the role of the spectator in this transition. A more active role of the spectator is found with Schechner, who approaches the performance as a phenomenon close to the ritual. In describing the state of the spectator, he compares the ritual, which includes a »transformation,« to the theatrical performance, which induces »transportation« from one state to the other (1990: 236). He defines the change resulting from the performance, and interprets it as a transformation similar to that of the ritual. This change consists of three elements: 1. in the drama (story); 2. in the spectators (transportation which is the rearrangement of body and mind for a period of time), and 3. in the audience where the change may be either temporary (entertainment) or permanent (ritual) (1988: 170-1).

Whereas in the first approach, what we designated as »R2« implies the participation of the spectator within a non-serious gamely frame, the second approach does not leave much space for the will of participation of the spectator, but considers the transportation as a *factual* effect of the performance. The question in both views remains the following: to which extent is the performance another reality »R2« to the audience in comparison to the first reality »R1«? And how does the spectator make the connection between the two? More explicitly: To which extent are the elements of theater different in their reception to those in »R1,« and to which degree do we have differentiation, on the side of the Lebanese audience, with its poor theatrical culture and extra sensitivity towards signs and symbols related to the spheres of discord, between fiction and reality in the space of the performance and that of the outer environment? To this Schechner writes, »It is hard to define »performance« because the boundaries separating it on the one side from theater and on the other side from everyday life are arbitrary« (1988: 85). In the Lebanese case, these factors, including the willingness to join the »transportation,« are related through the same factor: the »theatrical culture.« Furthermore, the »actual time« of the performance, during which »R2« takes place, is, in the end, »real time« taken from »R1.« Hence, »R2« will be considered according to the *interpretation* of the different audiences, which issue exclusively from »R1,« in a typical functional Moslem case, and can extend to a *gamely frame* within a fictitious reality with the own rules and regulations in a typical Christian case. In other terms, Level III is rooted in Level I through mechanisms developed in Level II, the most relevant of those mechanisms being the theatrical culture and the relation between the two realities. Since theater presents differences from one milieu to the other, it is normal that »R1« of the Christian turns out different than that of the Moslems. Here we can distinguish two sorts of interpretations: one with respect to the reality of the own milieu and another with respect to the relation to the *other* milieu. The relation between the two is channeled through the spheres of discord and the esthetic realms from which signs and symbols are used in theater.

The lack of theatrical culture indicates a transparence between the context of the performance »R2« and the context of everyday life »R1.« The performance is not acknowledged as a frame by itself having criteria that can be different from the evaluation criteria of everyday life. On the contrary, we find that some of its elements are subject to the same judgment criteria as the environmental elements. Their processing by the audience is done according to similar rules and laws. In contrast to audience not taking theater as a serious business, they are apt to apply a pretty serious criteria to the message transmitted through the performance. What an actor would say on stage can sometimes be interpreted, as if it were the personal opinion, the own responsibility. The difference between fiction and reality is not clearly cut. This enhances the acuteness of the performance regarding different structures of audiences and actors, especially in the case of heterogeneous audiences and Crossing Plays. An overdeveloped sensitivity towards the on-going social dramas can be noted depending on the realism of the play itself and the proximity of its topic to the spheres of discord.

To sum up, we can say that the audience builds a relation between »R1« and »R2.« The nature of this relation depends on the type of audience, on the realism of the play, and on the theatrical culture. These create the context in which the audience *experiences* another reality in theater. Reciprocally, the performance is conceived as the »experience« of a new reality. About this experience in theater, Turner writes:

»Experimental« theatre is nothing less than »performed,« in other words, »restored« experience, that moment in the experimental process -- that often prolonged and internally segmented »moment« -- in which meaning emerges through »reliving« the original experience (often a social drama subjectively perceived), and is given an appropriate aesthetic form. This form then becomes a piece of communicable wisdom, assisting others (through Verstehen, understanding) to understand better not only themselves but also the times and cultural conditions which compose their general »experience« of reality. (Turner 1982: 18)

Thus, every performance adds to the theatrical culture of the audience. This, in turn, increases the space for more distinction between »R1« and »R2« enhancing the frame of »R2.« Reciprocally, in the performance, we find a different experience of everyday life reality, »R1.« Different descriptions of this experience crystallized from the empirical research. The common factor among those descriptions was the juxtaposition of »R2« and »R1.« The performance was seen as a space for experiencing the fantasies of the spectator that are not realized in »R1.« It is a *risk free* experience in a non-serious world (799). »R2,« thus, is a subjective construction of a reality according to the will of the spectator, unlike the structure of the »R1,« over which the spectator has no influence, especially the social and individual problems. Moreover, if theater is an escape to the production agents, the performance is an *escapade* for the spectators. Also, since »R2« offers what is not possible in »R1,« achieving the *patron (za'īm)* image is possible through theater. In addition to that, »R2« varies according to the actors issuing from the spheres of discord: a Christian-Moslem, an individual-collective, a ruling-ruled, and generations experiences. These determine clear positions about the interpretation focus of the different audiences, and constitute at the same time the perspectives of identification. On the other hand, in the case of the Crossing Audience, on can enjoy an intersubjective experience, seeing the performance from the perspective of the *other*.

Identification

Identification is essential for the success of a theater performance. Without identification, the audience does not share the experience of reality, since they do not make part of it. This is done through choosing a certain perspective, from which the spectator sees the performance. The choice of the perspective complies with the general attitudes in »R1,« especially the belonging of the spectator to the social world. The position from the spheres of discord determines the group to which the spectator chooses to belong to at least for the time of the performance. Identification depends, in the first place, on the actual classification of the spectator within the groups resulting from the dominant *Christian-Moslem* confessional sphere of discord. The attitude of the spectator towards those conflicts determines his or her rank in the categories. This would be enhanced by the *representation* factor conditioned by the theater troupe and the rest of the audience, which are able to ascribe a role to the spectator putting pressure on his initial choice regarding identification. The identification helps to keep contact between the performance and the spectators thus maintaining the communication process running by offering several grips for the understanding of the *other* before moving to interpretation. Hence, the identification process is not only dependent on the initial attitude of the spectator, but also on the role ascribed to this spectator within the performance itself. The acceptance or denial of this role shapes the rest of the reception during the performance. This role ascription hangs, as has been said above, between pole pairs issuing from the spheres of discord. In this regard, R. Dahrendorf writes:

Am Schnittpunkt des Einzelnen und der Gesellschaft steht *homo sociologicus*, der Mensch als Träger sozial vorgeformter Rollen. Der Einzelne *ist* seine sozialen Rollen, aber diese Rollen *sind* ihrerseits die ärgerliche Tatsache der Gesellschaft. Die Soziologie bedarf bei der Lösung ihrer Probleme stets des Bezuges auf soziale Rollen als Elemente der Analyse; ihr Gegenstand liegt in der Entdeckung der Strukturen sozialer Rollen. (Dahrendorf 1958: 20)

Apart from the social role influencing identification and issuing in the case of Lebanon from the spheres of discord regarding the topic, identification is influenced by the use of signs and symbols from an adequate repertoire. The relevant repertoires in Lebanon are the esthetic realms. »The essential thing to achieve identification is to talk the language of the audience and to be close to them,« as one production agent expressed it. This was achieved in example A, by the use of a regional accent, the representation of the concerns of the specific audience, the topic, and the form of the play. The main actor succeeded in appearing as »one of them.« He talks like they do. He talks about their concerns. The use of Lebanese folk music added to his identity, knowing that his audience is initiated to the *mawwā,l*[1] the *nāy*, and the *zağal*,[2] three elements used by

---

1 The mawwāl is a sort of improvised piece of poetry. Inspired by a certain occasion, the poet improvises and sings a few verses, usually in the aim of expressing sudden grief or joy. Nowadays, the mawwāl is found as an introductory part of some Lebanese songs. The »nay« is a musical instrument resembling the flute often used as accompaniement to the mawwāl.
2 See section: Historical Overview of Theater

the actor. In this manner, the actor was able to create a part of Lebanese tradition and heritage with a contemporary concern. This made it easy for them to identify with him, apart from the fact that he played a simple style, and used regionalism obviously by changing the name of the area in the play as he moves from one place to the other. The name of the region, its inhabitants, and *patrons (zu'amā')*, became by itself a symbol with a wide range of meanings. The effect of regionalism in the performance went as far as the mentioning of names of local families and of specific persons. This constitutes only a small part of the extensive use of the regional language. As a result of transparency between the performance and its direct environment, the language used in the performance acquires a symbolic significance related to the actual place where the performance is taking place more than the mere context of the dramatic text alone. By presenting the same play, in a different area, there is a change in the meaning of those names pertinent to the change in the geographical context with different definitions of those symbols in addition to new ones comprised within the new space (536).

In conclusion, the *identification* succeeds when we have a *match* between the *belonging* of the spectator to a certain social world and the reality presented on stage. This is best achieved through the use of regional and local esthetics and the representation of the spectator's point of view regarding the spheres of discord. Identification leads to the interaction of the spectator with the on-going action on stage. It constitutes the spectator's perspective of interpretation.

Interpretation: spheres of discord and esthetic realms

Next to the identification process, *interpretation*, the meaning as constructed by the spectator, is a result of the attitudes at the Levels I and II and the phase denoted above as »going to theater.« These constitute the »interpretative frame« of the spectator. From this perspective, the performance, rooted in the environment, is able to produce meaning. In spite of this connection between the performance and real life, trying to make a one-to-one coordination between the elements of real life and those of the performance fails to give a significant explanation to their reception without making the link between those elements and the »frame« of this latter.

With identification as the perspective of interpretation, this latter follows the general classification of signs and symbols in the »structural map,«[3] which gives them potential values; their actual values being determined during an actual performance as a unique event. The potential

---

3   See Appendix B, Diag. 4.

value of signs and symbols are derived from their reception in the environment, which constitutes the justification of the existence of the circles of emotionality: the spheres of discord causing both emotional friction and esthetic differentiation, and the esthetic judgment typified in the esthetic realms.

A sign or a symbol does not acquire its actual dimension until it is actually *used* within the frame of a performance. Changing the frame would eventually change the meaning. A cross put on by a Christian actor as a necklace on stage is normality; a Christian audience in East Beirut would not even notice it. The same cross has to disappear in West Beirut, if the play is to cross to that side. A crossing Moslem audience from West to East Beirut notices this cross very well. Their interpretation is part of the image of the Christian, therefore of the *other*. Its significance gets more importance, if it is combined with a construction of the Moslem on stage. In this case, even the tolerant Crossing Audience feels itself directly addressed, all this happens before the actor utters a word. In a Chansonnier performance with a heterogeneous audience in Antelias, an area in East Beirut, this symbolism was made through a less direct symbol than the cross. The Christian troupe, in one sketch, presented a »rebellious« Southern woman in her typical clothes wanting to fight with the military resistance. She was wearing a colorful dress, under which she wore her home pajamas. This construction, typical of the decent country Shia women, is an indicator of bad taste for Christian eyes. Upon the appearance of the actress on the small stage of the restaurant where the Chansonnier was taking place, half the audience blew in laughter (the Christian part). The others (obviously the Moslem part), not knowing at the beginning what happened, took a grim face for the rest of the sketch. The message behind the sketch is still in favor of this Shia woman, since it compares her to the nonchalant Christian woman, who does not care for nor wants to know about what happens in the South. In a comparison with the same figure, constructed in example A, the same style in clothes didn't seem to erect any reaction among the Shia audience of the South, who took it as part of normality, appreciating the realism in the play. The audience also accepted the fact, that the hero is married to four women, what he declares as a joke in the play. Also in example A, in two separate interviews with Shia theater people about this play, one director, using bad language (after the tape recorder was turned off), considered the construction of the woman and her accent as a way too exaggerated mocking construction of the actor. The other director said that *nobody* in the South would marry four women due to the economic crisis, and that the actor in question is simply making fun of the Shias in a cheap manner, which the inexperienced audience couldn't detect. Of course, due to the place of the performance, the few Christian spectators who happened to be there could not blow in laughter about those issues.

All in all, the interpretation, effected from the perspective of identification, depends, as a consequence, on the spheres of discord and the esthetic realms. The work done to achieve identification and interpretation is activating for the spectator. It is on two levels: emotional and rational.

Emotional and rational motions

If the performance has anything to offer as a direct motivation for the spectator, it is to make this latter *actively* participate in it. This participation depends on the attitude of the spectator, the »going to theater« phase, but also on the performance itself, i.e. the work of the production represented here by the actors. The effects on the spectator vary between several standings as appeared in the direct results of the field research, which vary between boredom, tiredness, entertainment, and brain work.

Boredom is a manifestation of the loss of interest in the action on stage. This happens when the topic is of no concern and accordingly of no meaning to the spectator. Boredom results in cutting the participation of the spectator. The second observed symptom is tiredness. This is related to the fact of excessive demand of the performance from the spectator either in relation to the brain activity or to the emotions (2893). And the ultimate result of the two is sleep, which is a denial of any activity at all. Of course this kind of passivity can hardly be called participant audience. Nonetheless, the activity of the spectator depends on his or her own attitude. In one interview, a spectator made a simple statement about the audience: »It is divided into two categories: those who like to think (444), and those who like to be entertained.« As simple as it might seem, we can here discern two types of activities: activation of emotions and brainwork (2681).

Emotions play a crucial role in theater. First, the process of identification is based on feelings and emotions (568). Second, confessionalism, as we saw earlier, is emotional in nature. Third, the main motivation for the Lebanese spectator to be in theater reduces in many cases to emotions (2898), and the main tool in the hand of the production is also the emotionality of the audience (2902). The source of emotions arises out of the relation between »R1« and »R2.« This is manifested in satisfaction resulting from conditioning »R1« according to the will of the audience within the framework of »R2.« Being engulfed in the performance provides nervous relaxation leading to laughter and amusement. This gives a relief from the daily life worries (2600), and highlights the importance of having a choice that one can implement. Theater provides the opportunity for the spectator to choose his own reality, which gives a feeling of freedom. In addition to that, we find the arousing of strong emotions related to the topic (2821, 2835), and sometimes even sensual emotions like sex (587).

Next to the emotional activation, we have the brainwork. In all the interpretation processes, the brain is activated, and the »seeing and hearing habits« are in constant training. The result influences the interpretation process, since it gives new dimensions to the esthetics besides those already existent in »R1.« Moreover, the spectator is learning during the performance. Some theater plays are designed to teach (many end up in plain preaching) the spectator (2817). Through identification, the spectator learns about the own *self* and the problems that concern him (2808). The performance thus functions as a mirror of the *self* within the first reality (2668).

Apart from the changing interpretations, which show the differences between Christians and Moslems, the performance acts as a frame of interaction between the two.

The performance as frame of interaction between the Self and the Other

The performance offers the time-space frame for two things: creation of *meaning* and *interaction*. The course of interaction, however, depends on the types of actors and audiences engaged in an act of co-creation of meaning. The shift from the »absolute« to the »historical« meaning, in our cases, restitutes the performance as a unique »historical« event, in which, the »scenic space« embedding the *meaning* is constructed simultaneously by both participants. Schechner writes, »More than in 'product arts' (painting, sculpting, writing, film) 'process arts' (live performing) are co-created by performers and spectators. A reader may complete a written text in each reading, but only during live performances do artists and audiences co-create together in exactly the same time-space« (1988: 202-3). The range of this joint work extends from the actor-audience to the audience-audience. In our case, both types of interactions lead to a friction between the *self* and the *other*.

Actor-audience interaction

The interaction between actors and audiences is centered on two concepts: the transmission of meaning and the representation of the *other* on stage.

Describing the reaction of the audience to a joke played by the actors, Schechner writes, »It (the joke) stunningly erases the gap between audience and performer: the audience hears the performers, laughs as a response; the performers hear the audience laughing, perform as a response, and so the farce progresses.« (Schechner 1988: 244). The interaction between actors and audience resembles a chain reaction. It is a session of interaction, a mental and emotional exercise, an exchange of feelings and ideas between the actors and the audience—which is orchestrated by the actors under the direct influence of the audience.

The audience conceives the symbols transmitted by the actors. Through the image of the reaction of the audience captured by the actor, this latter redesigns the course of the coming step. In his work, *La Formation de L'Acteur*, Stanislavsky describes the transition between the image as conceived by the actor, and the conveyed symbolical form. »Cette neige blanche, comme le jour tragique, c'était la vie; et cette forme noire que je revoyais, étendue devant moi, c'était la mort. Ce soleil, ce ciel bleu, l'éternité... Le souvenir avait grandi. L'image avait pris figure de symbole« (Stanislavski 1994: 175). This type of transitions is at the basis of the emotional exchange between the actors and the audience. The actor draws emotions from his own emotional experience and presents them as symbols to the audience. The audience, in turn, uses those symbols as a door to get to the experience of the actor based on their own emotional memory. Thus, we have a retransformation from symbol to meaning through the common work of actors and spectators. With a Lebanese peer audience comes also the family effect present in booked up performances. With the performance turning into a family meeting, the interaction between the actors and the audience is broken. The performance becomes a background for the family meeting. The actors, in this case, have little chance in capturing the audience and therefore resign to continuing their texts amidst the chaos emerging from a well-acquainted audience with little active interest for the performance. In this case, the work of the actors turns to the technical side reproducing mechanically their lines and gestures. The performance continues without the interaction hence losing a component of its meaning. The transition between meaning and sign is linked by G. H. Mead as follows: »Meaning arises and lies within the field of the relation between the gesture of a human organism and the subsequent behavior of this organism as indicated to another human organism by that gesture« (Mead 1934: 75-6). Through this »symbolic interaction,« the meaning is *symbolically* transmitted to the individual.

Since the signs are captured by the senses, they have, therefore, an emotional value depending on the way and ease they can be captured with. The way the actor produces those signs, regardless of the technical parts of rehearsing and personal capacities, depends on his *attitude* towards the audience and the amount of his information about it, but most important, according to the progress of the symbolical exchange taking place between the two parties during the performance. The *reception* and understanding of the audience determines the way the actor plays, and consequently the course of the interaction. This applies also to the audience. The *reception* of the audience, based on its attitude, determines its part of the interaction as well.

The actors focus on *how* to perform signs and symbols more than on *what* they are saying or the gestures they are doing (28, 416, 417). Stanislavsky explains this through the process of »adaptation.«

A partir de maintenant, nous adopterons le terme d'adaptation, pour designer les moyens tant physiques que spirituels mis en œuvre pour s'adapter les uns aux autres dans un jeu très varié de circonstances, et dans le but d'accomplir un objectif précis. (Stanislavsky 1994: 224)

The emotional content expressed by the actor necessitates a certain adaptation, whose basis is sometimes not obvious. This differs if the contact is with a group, a person, an imaginary or a real object. The communication uses to this end the senses along with all the physical and mental elements. In this emission and caption of »waves,« the eyes, the voice, the facial expression, the hands, and all the body, contribute to the modifications appropriate to adaptation (Stanislavsky 1994: 226).

This confirms the earlier argumentation about the insignificance of the sign outside the frame of the performance. Taking this latter into account (2612), the actors mention a sort of emotional ability, through which they are able to scan the emotions of the audience (2203). This develops their adaptation strategy, which may differ even with the same text. The intensity and focus of the text are liable to change and can be regulated—through the tone of voice and body gestures—to match the frame of the performance (2835), which has a general form related to place and expected audience and a specific form related to the particular situation of the event. This style of acting reveals an application of the Stanislavsky system, in which the relation between the actor and real life is channeled through emotions—what Stanislavsky calls the »emotional memory.« The emotional content that actors attribute to their performance is hence derived from their experiences in real life. With adequate training, the actor is able to recall emotional moments from his repertoire of emotional memories. The application of the Stanislavsky system in Lebanon is typical regarding its influence on the acting schools. The mechanism of interaction between actors and audiences is a confirmation of the validity of that system.

Audience-audience interaction: polarization and harmonization

The most important effect of the performance on the audience emerges out of the audience-audience interaction on the collective level, which can have the form of a *direct* communication in the case of a *heterogeneous* audience or an *indirect* one in the case of a *homogeneous* audience.

Situating the processes of the performance chronologically, we notice the following: Already at the beginning of the performance, just as the audience starts to meet in the outer hall waiting to be seated, the face-to-face interaction among the audience starts. It is subject to evolution during the time of the performance to become a common experience of the particular audience either bringing it together around a certain view or idea—harmonization effect, or, the frequent case in a multiconfessional Lebanese audience, polarizing it around the topic. These two phenomena depend on the position of the topic to the spheres of discord in »R1« on the one side, and on the balance in the form affecting the identification procedure. The polarization reverts the effect of the fictitious »R2,« and replunges the audience in »R1.« In this sense, we can comprehend the meaning of the transparency between »R1« and »R2« as stated earlier. On the other hand, the harmonization of the audience around a central idea is what Victor Turner calls »spontaneous communitas.« It is manifested, in its ultimate form, in the »dissolution of boundaries shutting people off.« It is a movement toward the ritual (Schechner 1988: 141), and it forms the trajectory »from theater to ritual,« drawn by Turner.

Enhanced through the representation effect in front of the *other*, polarization, as mentioned, is the central phenomenon happening during a performance with a heterogeneous audience. Through representation, »...the individual maintains a show before others that he himself does not believe, he can come to experience a special kind of alienation from self and a special kind of wariness of others« (Goffman 1959: 236). The individual is »dragged« into a certain attitude and a certain behavior, dictated, not by the own beliefs, but by what the individual, at the time of the performance, believes to be his or her own role in the presence of the peer and non-peer *others*, matching thus the following characterization: »Soziale Rollen sind Bündel von Erwartungen, die sich in einer gegebenen Gesellschaft an das Verhalten der Träger von Positionen knüpfen. Wie Positionen sind auch Rollen prinzipiell unabhängig vom Einzelnen denkbar« (Dahrendorf 1958: 33).

In our inspection of the environment at level I, considered as »R1« in the context of the performance, level III, *polarization* is characteristic of the process of adoption and rejection of signs and symbols of the environment. It is at the basis of the said two esthetic realms. The topics around which the polarization takes place are the same ones denoted as in the vicinity to the spheres of discord. At level III, the polarization is related to the division of the audience starting from the first encounter with each other, as well as during the lapse of time of the performance, »the neighboring chairs.« It is enhanced through increasing interaction between Christian and Moslem audiences. It affects the audience of the one color, regardless of their beliefs, to retreat to their self-definition in front of the *other*, especially at the occurrence of friction signs and symbols on stage. This supposes a mixed audience, among which the theatrical reception is conditioned through the presence of the *other*. It also enhances the *pre-selection* of the *other* audience achieved by the choice of the place. And the peer group accompanying the prospected spectator intensifies it. A Moslem father, for example, would not likely go to see a Chansonnier in the Eastern area with his daughter. His tolerance to the same Chansonnier is greater, however, had he been with other fellows. This is rendered obvious in the choice of place of the performance, which is also related to the choice of the persons accompanying him to theater. This also applies to different signs and topics especially related to sex, the presence of people drinking alcohol, and the role of the woman in society (2664), which constitute the most evident separation signs between Christians and Moslems. In any case, getting near any of the friction areas around the spheres of discord would cause a polarization of the audience during the performance (199). Some of them would refuse a part while others would adopt it. This product of confessionalism makes every performance unique depending on the place and the constellation of the audience.

As a result of polarization, we notice a shift in the perspective of the spectator between the individual and the collective. The actor or actress, due to the representation effect, has a double function: the person and the character he or she imitates. Both, with different degrees can contribute to being a *symbol* of the collective, the own confession. In this instance, the Arabic word for *actor, (mumaṯṯil = representative)*, is adequately indicating this representation role of the actor (715, 716). The shift from the individual to the collective perspective reaches all the mechanics of the performance, which include the identification, the representation effect of the actor, and the interpretation of signs and symbols. Being an individual *self* or representing the collective *self* at the time of the performance changes the degree of emotionality during the performance among both actors and audience.

Together with the presence of the other comes the social control influencing the behavior, reaction, and eventually the interpretation process (2798). It is imposed from both the peer and the non-peer other. This includes differentiating matters between Christians and Moslems like Alcohol. Alcohol is not accepted in theater in the Moslem milieu. This factor, characteristic of Chansonnier Theater, is one of the flagrant indicators of the separation of the audience between the two social worlds. The Chansonnier when moving to West Beirut is presented in a normal theater without the possibility of drinking alcohol or eating, the case in East Beirut where it is presented in restaurants with food and alcohol. This change in the setting induces a change in the frame of the performance, since the disposition of the Christian audience to alcohol is different from that of the Moslem one. The role of alcohol also differs from a pure physical one in the case of a Christian audience to a combination of a break in morality, an opposition to the religious values, and a physical effect with a Moslem audience. Even in the case of a Moslem non-drinking audience, they still come to see how the other audience would drink and be affected by alcohol. Parallel to that, we have a Moslem drinking audience that enjoys coming to East Beirut to drink and watch Chansonnier Theater. Alcohol, next to its direct effect on the performance through the enhancement of emotionality, has still a strong symbolic value. Together with the difference in role distribution between man and woman, it is the second strong symbol of non-seriousness and loose moral values characteristic of the Christian milieu as seen by the Moslem social world.

In addition to that, the *individual-collective* sphere of discord appears during the processes of the performance. By extrapolating the idea of weakness of the individual, the actors carrying a revolting tendency against the extinguishing of the individual find on stage a chance to revolt. This implies an inflation of the representation of the individual in theater plays more than its level in real life. The fulfillment of the idea of the individual on stage is shared with the spectators through identification. This is characterized by the freedom of choice in the identification process with an inflated representation of the individual. Identification differs among spectators, depending on if they come alone and isolated, which is rarely the case in theater, or if they come accompanied by family and friends, which is the normal case. The average spectator is bound to the social act of communication, which can be conditioned by the mere presence of the *other,* the »non-centered communication« using Goffman's terminology.[4]

To sum up, being in the presence of the *other* means: 1. The revival of the relation with this *other* whether it is the peer or the confessional other 2. A change in behavior and reactions conditioned by the other and the topics produced on stage 3. A crossing of the threshold from the individual self to the collective self which leads to an effect of representation of the community and its related emotional constellation like solidarity and rejection; this crossing depends on the way the appeal of the actors to the audience is constructed 4. A reproduction of the image of »R1« with respect to »R2« 5. A revival of the criteria used for differentiation from the *other,* friction, tolerance margin, etc. All these factors contribute in making the performance a *confessional Erlebnis* adding to the general credit of *confessionalism* in the environment. Hence, the performance, with the heterogeneous audience, will be producing another cycle of differentiation due to the direct meeting with the confessional *other;* also, the homogeneous audience, through its regional character, will be enhancing the gap between the Christian and the Moslem communities especially on the esthetical level.

Post-performance (Level IV): evaluation and feedback

After the performance, actors and spectators enter the phase of cooling off, prior to the evaluation and the integration of the performance into real life. »Cooling off is getting both performers and spectators out of the performance. The aftermath includes spreading news, evaluating, writing, and in many ways showing how performances can feed into systems of social and aesthetic life« (Schechner 1988: xiv). The criteria for evaluating a performance by the audience differs in as much as the general attitudes towards theater and the »going to theater« phase are different. The play is subject to juxtaposition with the expectation of the spectator, and it varies with the degree of theatrical culture. It is noted here, that even the non-experienced audience is active in criticizing the work of the production, its analysis relying, to a large extent, on their general experience in »R1,« as is the case with interpretation during the performance (2639). The comparison between »R1« and »R2« sets the scale for the quality of the play (2860, 2874, 2878, 2886). Experienced audiences evaluate, ac-

---

4   Goffman 1959.

cording to »expectations« also, the quality of the time spent in the performance, comparing thus the »actual time« of »R2« as part of »R1,« measuring the degree of »having a good time.« Parallel to those are Christian and Moslem criteria for evaluation. The functional Moslem approach imposes a direct useful connection between »R1« and »R2«; whereas, the Christian objective approach to art implies a greater distance between the two.

It is worth mentioning here that a discrepancy exists between the real opinion of the spectators and what they say in public (2742). The reason for this discrepancy is that the expression of opinion is conditioned by the rules of indirect communication. Saying something positive or negative about a play does not always reflect reality, more than it does reflect the nature of relations between the persons involved and in which frame it is said. This gains more importance, for example, in the case where the person involved in expressing the opinion belongs to the theatrical sphere. In this case, we notice a standard tendency to say a positive opinion about the play in public, whereas, the real opinion is difficult to get. This made it difficult to get any objective or honest opinion, when conducting the interviews, for example. The audience were not feeling free because many of them thought that the interviewer is working with the theater troupe, which led them to say something »nice« about it (2619), falling into indirect communication pattern. Certain attributes given in this context have become standards in evasiveness of giving a straight opinion. The words »*mumayyaz,*« (special), or »*mahḍūm*« (nice) for example, initially a product of the journalist language, are repeated expressions in the theatrical evaluation, which hardly express a meaning at all. They reflect ready answers covering for the refusal to make any public statement (2910).

Moreover, we notice a tendency on the part of the spectators to attribute *one* categorical judgment to the whole performance (2845, 2862, 2919, 2773): »good« or »bad,« »negative« or »positive,« »our side« or »theirs.« Consequently, the performance, which is a collection of signs and symbols, becomes itself another sign or symbol in its larger environment. Its evaluation follows the same criteria of other environmental elements resulting in its *labeling* and classification in the one or other repertoires. Thus, apart from being a confessional experience for the audience, the performance acts as a confessionalized sign with respect to its environment.

Consequently, a change in the cycle of performances induces a change in the environment. Both production and audiences are learning for the next cycle of processes. Theater is a repeatable and cumulative experience. With every new cycle, the production acquires new feedback from the audience. The sensibility of the production to the reception mainly depends, in the evaluation phase after the performance, on the number of audience and the preset standard of success of the performance. The audience, knowing more about theater, is changing in attitudes and behavior. The production is adapting with them. The production, attempting with more or less success to base itself on the wavelength of the audience and its classifications, is working on renovation in theater according to the summation of the elements discussed above.

Conclusion

In this section we have seen that the controlling elements affecting the interpretation of topic and form in the performance can be reduced to the following: the place, the presence of the other, and the confessional identity of actors and audiences. The theatrical elements of the performance acquire different symbolical values according to the change in these factors. These are denoted as the »frame of the performance,« which can be thus seen as a »symbolic interaction« within this particular frame.

Based on this frame of the performance and with the presence of the *other,* a polarization of the audience takes place. Moreover, we notice a shift in the perspective from the »individual« spectator to the collective. The performance, however, can also constitute an »individualistic experience,« since, apart from the confessional conflict on the collective level, there exists an individual versus collective conflict that shows also in theater. The activated realms of the spectators change between the cerebral to the emotional activities. This results in tiredness, boredom, sleep, entertainment, amusement, relaxation, laughter, etc. Another transition takes place from the reality of the environment to the reality of the performance through identification. In this substitution, the spectator has the chance of escaping the own reality, and thus has a diverting effect in a reality mostly designed to fit his or her wishes. With the presence of the *other,* two phenomena can take place: *polarization,* a division of the audience around certain elements of performance, or *harmonization,* the »spontaneous communitas« achieved in the case of agreement about elements of the performance. These depend on the type of audience, whether it is homogeneous or heterogeneous.

In the post performance phase, both production and reception incur an evaluation phase increasing their respective experience in theater. The effect of the performance on the social world is, as a result of this experience, cumulative. Due to the tendency to be categorical in judgment, the performance, apart from being a confessional experience in the case of a heterogeneous audience, is also part of the confessional signs and symbols constituting the elements of the environment.

Summary and Conclusion[1]

According to the method used in the research, its theoretical background, and manageability considerations, the theatrical process can be divided into four levels. The environment is considered as Level I, the processes of theater excluding the performance are denoted as Level II, Level III corresponds to the performance itself, and the post-performance Level IV coincides with Level I considering the performance as one cycle in a theatrical process taking place in the environment.

This concluding chapter will start sequentially from Level I to Level IV with a summary of the resulting categories and their interrelations at each level. Conclusions are presented throughout the mentioned levels as well as at the end.

Level I: The environment of theater

At Level I, the empirical work showed that the key to understanding theater in Lebanon is the multi-confessional environment in which it is rooted and whose social dramas it reflects. A short description of the environment and the forces acting in it is therefore essential in the building of implications. Here, we encounter the classical conflict between Christians and Moslems on the view of a national identity of Lebanon respectively between plain Lebanese and Lebanese Arabic.

The Lebanese environment is the result of a history of *confessionalism, regionalism,* and war between multitudes of religious groups *(ṭawā'if)* forming the Lebanese society. During the last war (1975-1990), these groups crystallized into two major categories: Christians and Moslems. The main conflict field between the two has been the vision of the national identity and its political implications in a politically and militarily active area like the Middle East. Whereas the Moslems would like to take for granted the Arab origins as a determinant of their belonging and commitment to the large Arab world, the Christians are heading towards building a pure Lebanese identity based, though, on a Western example. Resulting from the catalyst effect of the war, the geographic division,

---

1 For a visual summary of the results, see appendix B, diagrams 5 and 7.

which started from East Beirut with a Christian demographic dominance and West Beirut with a Moslem dominance, became a generic naming of the other parts of the country. The Lebanese coast was de facto divided into Eastern and Western areas becoming a synonym for respective Christian or Moslem demographic majorities. As an immediate result of this division, regionalism added to confessionalism through enforcing the isolation between the war-created regions. This paved the way towards the conception and later the growth of two social worlds, which, though apparently separated from each other, kept several channels of communication witnessing to their inextricable structure. Institutions, including the educational ones, were also divided into two sections: Christian and Moslem, creating duplicate institutions in both areas.

The spheres of discord: social dramas related to confessionalism

Due to this divergence in views, to the different religions and beliefs, and to the traditional codes within each social world, many friction issues came into being. They are denoted in the course of the research as the *spheres of discord*. Confessionalism, diverting Christians and Moslems apart, became more profound in the last war and is at the basis of the creation of the two social worlds. It is hereby denoted as a sphere of discord characterizing many of the relations between the two milieus. In addition to that, as the results showed, every sphere of discord, whether it focuses on an issue situated between the two worlds or is related to an internal conflict within the boundaries of the one world, can be converted into a confessional issue extending outside these boundaries, ensuring thus an eventual necessary divergence from intra-milieu politics to extra-milieu conflicts. The spheres of discord are hence social dramas related directly or indirectly to the Moslem-Christian conflict manifested by confessionalism. Specific to the intra-milieu relations of both social worlds are three other major spheres of discord.

The first among those is the *individual-collective* sphere of discord, which is not surprising in a structure supporting the collective confessional at the expense of the expansion of the individual. A conflict in this circle can be easily diverted towards the confessional sphere of discord. Since religion preserves the holiness of the family, any contradiction with the family structure—even if it were in reality against the feudalism represented also by the family—would be considered as attacking religion, classifying its author among the enemies of the confession, the *(ṭā'ifa)*. Another direct implication on theater is the creation of taboo themes regarding the family and of course the *(ṭā'ifa)* issues. The individual-collective sphere of discord is seen as a conflict between the *(fard)*, the individual revolting against the collective confessional structure, and the *(šaḫṣ)*, the person going along the confessional collective tide. In its developed form, the *(šaḫṣ)* becomes the *patron (za'īm)*, the ultimate rank in the confessional collective configuration. This leads the way towards the second major sphere of discord issuing from confessionalism: the *ruling-ruled* sphere of discord.

Thus, the internal political configuration of the community is characterized by the concepts: family, *('ašḫāṣ)*, *('afrād)*, *connections (wāsiṭa)*, and *patron (za'īm)* leading to the *ruling-ruled* sphere of discord.[2] These divide each social world into *ruling* and *ruled* classes of society. As the empirical results show, this exists in a parallel structure in both social worlds. It is manifested in the *za'īm*-dependents structure, in which the *ruled* have no choice but to recur to the *connections (wāsiṭa)* in order to be functional in managing their everyday life matters. This traditional structure, extending from the time of the feudalism in the Ottoman era, found its continuation through the religious *(ṭā'ifa)*. This latter dictates the coordinates of the *patron (za'īm)*, and is at the same time his main source of authority. The *patron (za'īm)*, hence, represents the success within the confessional structure. He is bound to support the foundations of the *(ṭā'ifa)* including confessionalism in order to maintain his privileges.

Consequently, due to the undeniable dominance of the religious authority in the political field according to the power they possess over their communities, the ruling-ruled sphere of discord amounts to being an arrangement resulting from the confessional sphere of discord. The *ruler*, whose political power is derived from his religious belonging and authority, tries to maintain his position by diverting any internal critique towards the external enemy, aiming hence at keeping the obedience through portraying the other confession as the »danger.« In opposition, the *ruled* demonstrate a certain awareness of that manipulation, which is, however, not mature enough to overcome the confessional trap. Any conflict on the ruling-ruled level can thereby be diverted to one against the religious authorities and hence religion, whereas the *other* is the »real problem.« It becomes easy to revive the confessional animosities kept fresh through many political and historical open wounds tarnishing any political or social conflict with a confessional turn and diverting it to the main sphere of discord.

The last main sphere of discord, emerging in the field research as a direct consequence of war, is the cold conflict between the *war* and the *pre-war* generations, based on the former blaming the latter for the war

---

2 See section: Politics of the Social World, for the definitions of the Arabic terms.

and its consequences. Due to the confessional turn taken by the war,[3] any appearance of the theme »war« in theater is enough to refresh confessional disputes, diverting so the generations conflict also into the confessional cycle.

We can conclude here that the spheres of discord created hot issues of conflict in the environment based on confessionalism. These issues, when they arise as topics in the public discussion like is the case in theater, turn into confessional conflicts between Christians and Moslems drawing away from the original aim of the discussion. But this is not the sole effect of the spheres of discord. They also divide the production and reception agents in theater, the actors of the phenomenon, according to their model: Christians and Moslems, rulers *(zu'amā')* and ruled (subordinates), pro-individualist *('afrād)* and pro-collective *('ašḫāṣ)*, war generation and pre-war generation. At each extremity of a given sphere of discord, we find potential production or reception agents, whose strategies and view of theater differ considerably from the other extremity. Level II can only be understood in the light of this configuration.

The division on the esthetic level: the esthetic realms

Furthermore, the environment of theater witnessed a division of a different order. With competition, tension, isolation, increasing ideological conflicts, and a lack of knowledge of the *other* characterizing the relation between the two social milieus especially in the aftermath of the war, Christians and Moslems have strived towards differentiation from each other on the esthetical level. The *esthetic* elements present in the environment witnessed a series of processes which could be summarized under the term *confessionalization*, which resulted at first into two main esthetic realms, Christian and Moslem. As soon as the one side would »adopt« a certain sign or symbol as belonging to the own realm and as a reference for self-identification, the other side would seek a parallel but possibly different equivalent. As expected, the Christians headed towards a westernized esthetic, whereas the Moslems opted for an *arabized* form. The race towards *differentiation* can be divided into three processes concerning the elements of the environment: *polarization, apportionment,* and *labeling*. Esthetical elements were polarized towards either side. Through apportionment, the elements were acknowledged as »Moslem« or »Christian« and were labeled accordingly. Hence, each party was able to set the elements with which it identifies, and which guarantee at the

---

3   This is not meant here to be a judgment on the war reducing it to a mere conflict between Christians and Moslems. It is a statement of the fact that confessionalism did have a role in the war.

same time the differentiation from the *other*. Differentiation also reached the esthetical elements coming from outside the two social worlds. Elements issuing from globalization, which invaded both worlds are also subject to the preceding processes. The criteria for their polarization are the same axial division between the Arab-oriental world and the Western world. Nevertheless, part of the incoming global signs and symbols remained neutral. These are included in both milieus and form the *global* esthetic realm, which is used in theater for its neutral value.

Despite this differentiation, theater does exist in both milieus. Its existence is due to the parallelism and duplication on the institutional level in the two social worlds. After inducing the necessary changes, both worlds form, according to self-approved criteria, an own version—a pseudo duplicate—of the other. The existence of a certain form of theater in a certain area is to a great extent the justification for its reproduction in the other area. All types of theater were duplicated taking little account of the different types of audiences, which created a gap between the production agents and the audience. This widened the alienation between theater and the audience.

Theater and environment

To sum up, the environment affects theater in several ways. First, the spheres of discord and their related social dramas constitute the material from which theater chooses *topics* attractive to the audience. At the same time, these constitute the taboos imposed by the *rulers* as restrictions on the freedom of production. As a result, theater is forced either to use indirect methods of communication, in which an indirect *form* can have significant advantages over a direct *content,* or to try to escape restrictions through building connections in the political configuration of the place of the performance. In many case, this leads to flattering of the image of the regional *patron (za'īm)*.

Second, the spheres of discord created frustration and friction seeking an outlet at the one extremity, and a need for the restitution of power and authority through brightening of the image and deliberate »coaching« of the audience at the other extremity. In both cases, theater was used as a medium to fulfill those needs even if not on equal terms. There are more productions resulting from frustration as from image embellishment.

Third, the actors in the environment, which are the potential production and reception agents, are divided in a similar configuration according to the extremities of the spheres of discord: Christian/ Moslem, ruling/ ruled, pro-individual/ pro-collective, and war/pre-war generations.

This affects their strategies, their reception of the role of theater, their focus of identification, and their interpretation.

Fourth, *signs and symbols* used in certain types of theater like the Popular and parts of the Serious and Entertainment Theaters are usually chosen from the confessional *esthetic realms*. Here, we can talk about the confessionalization of theater through estheticism. The creation of meaning in an indirect communication model takes place through the selection of signs and symbols belonging to the adequate esthetic realm.

Fifth, the mechanism of production and reception in theater is a reflection of the structures existing in the environment. This is best illustrated in the *za'īm-subordinates* structure. The team is usually reduced to *one* person in charge, upstaging the rest of the group to the benefit of being the pseudo-*za'īm* on the theatrical scene: the *theater-za'īm*. One impact on theater production is the elimination of the concept of the troupe, replacing it by a compulsory association with the *theater-za'īm*. Consequently, the confessional identity of the troupe is structured according to that of the *theater-za'īm*, leading to an alteration in the course of the interaction between the audiences and the actors and the labeling of the image of the play with a confessional identity. On the other hand, the *theater-za'īm* is the one who negotiates an agreement with the local *patron (za'īm)* in the case of the Crossing Play. The potential agreement reflects additional restrictions on the play, but at the same time it enables the production to conquer new audiences in the other areas.

Denoting the environment as the first reality »R1« in contrast to the second reality »R2« presented in the theater performance, we come to the following results. In the evaluation of theater with regard to its relation to the environment, theater can act as an escape from »R1,« representing entertainment and diversion away from the worries of real life. Otherwise, it can be a reflection or a reproduction of »R1.« It is a stage for the realization of things not possible in »R1« like the expansion of the individual inhibited in »R1,« and the shaping of »R1« according to the wish of a specific audience. Theater could also extend to be a revolution against »R1« or a solver to problems in »R1.« Those attitudes exist in the environment, but are not equally present in both social worlds. All this depends on the theatrical culture developed by the audience, which affects their comparison between »R1« and »R2« and their criteria for understanding theater.

The other main function of theater is within the relation between the two social worlds as traced with respect to the spheres of discord. The replication of »R1« in »R2« leads also to the continuation of the conflicts between the two social worlds in theater, hence the enhancement of the confessional sphere of discord. Next to television and written media theater could play an important form of contact between Christians and Moslems however indirect and informal it tends to be. It offers the stage for the customized presentation of the self as well as the construction of the other. This construction, as it showed, is characterized by a falsification of both *self* and *other* not quite achieving what we can call a forum of communication.

Used as a medium, theater has a double function depending on which party of the *ruling-ruled* sphere of discord is handling the production. In the hand of the ruling authority, it can be used to ensure the convergence of an intra-milieu issue to an extra-milieu one. It suffices to present the *other* as approving of something in order to incite its refusal by the own milieu regardless of its value. In the hand of the ruled, theater is an outlet of frustration, or even a revolution against reality. The spheres of discord, as has been noted, constitute burning areas of conflict and cause constant sources of frustration necessitating a social outlet. Theater, despite tremendous restrictions on freedom and the lack of subventions on the financial level, functions as this outlet. It supplies the necessary space for the expansion of the individual and acts as a contra factor to a system expanding the collective, family and clan, at the expense of the individual. It can also be the outlet for the generation conflict.

Thus, theater plays the role of an outlet to the frustration issuing from the spheres of discord. It is a way of expression of the social needs, interests, and problems turning around the conflict topics present in the environment. At the same time, these make up the necessary conditions for the existence of this theater, and shape its topics, types, and esthetical form.

In the light of this configuration of the environment, it becomes difficult to join theatrical forms and activities in Lebanon under the banner of »Lebanese Theater« but rather under »Theater in Lebanon.« More specifically the different types of theater existing due to copying and duplication in both milieus can be labeled as: »Theater in the Eastern Area« or »Christian Theater« and »Theater in the Western Area« or »Moslem Theater.« Those yield the typology of theater presented hereafter.

Level II: Outer-performance theatrical activities

At level II, the attitude of the audience towards theater is the main determinant of the processes of production and reception outside the frame of the performance. In order to survive financially, the production depends totally on the audience, because theater does not benefit from any subventions worth mentioning from the government. At the same time, the attitudes of the reception regarding theater assign to it a role and a function as shown above in the situation of the role of theater between the environment and the two social worlds. These functions cited above do not apply in the same degree to both social worlds.

Differences between the two social worlds regarding the view of theater

Here, we discern considerable differences between the two social milieus regarding the vision of theater and its social function. The Christians, tending towards the Western ideal in which *l'art pour l'art* is a sufficient justification for the existence of theater, put more stress on the *form*. Also, the concept of the individual in the Christian theater is growing. In the Moslem milieu, for reasons linked to religion, theater ought to possess a social function in order to justify its existence. Functionalism therefore conditions theater through associating its topic and form directly to real life elements. The more theater is connected to real life, the more important, justifiable, and compatible is its role. This implies an increasing *realism* in the Moslem theater, whereas in the Christian milieu, theater advances more *estheticism*, which can be sought separately from the worries of real life and even from the existence of the topic in and by itself.

By looking at this *estheticism* and *realism* from the perspective of the modern history of theater in Lebanon, we find that this result is not a coincidence. The seeds of theater were brought from the Western theater through the Christians, who kept this copying tradition until recently. Classical as well as modern theater were thus imported to the Lebanese society from, for instance, Molière, Chekhov, Shakespeare regardless of the interests of the audiences, theater was at the time totally new and unknown. It was at a later stage that the adaptation came, exceeding a little more the mere translation to some changes in the names of places and characters. It is important here to mention that with the import of theater, the *western* attitude regarding the meaning of theater was also imported to the Christian milieu. Theater, thus, did not have the time and space to mature and develop according to the will of the audience of its environment. The audience as well did not have the free environment to develop its own attitude towards theater. They were coached to learn about the attitude towards theater in the same way they learned about theater itself. Under theater, the Christian milieu, till now, refers to this learned attitude imported with the adapted plays.

The Moslems, for their part, did not continue the Arabic beginnings of theater in ḥayāl ẓ-ẓill and 'al-ḥakawātiyy,[4] instead they followed the

---

4 See section: Historical Overview of Theater

same steps of theater in the Christian milieu. They tried to develop theater following two contradictory lines: esthetic art reshaped to meet the Arabic esthetics, and functional realism more compatible with the Islamic thought. In a way, they tried to reproduce the phenomenon of inventing theater in an Arab Islamic form. For their part, the attitude towards theater was settled through functionalism. Later, the developed types of theater in both social worlds showed resemblance due to the duplication effect. The interests of the audiences regarding the »form« remain, however, divergent between Christian estheticism and Moslem realism.

Going back to the lack of freedom resulting from the *ruling-ruled* sphere of discord, we find that the taboos as defined by the rulers pushed towards more estheticism of theater complying with the indirect communication strategy. This is incompatible with the Moslem orientation towards *realism,* but it matches Christian *estheticism*. Here we can say, that due to reasons related more to a coincidence, the Christian choice proved to be more successful than the Moslem one at least in the present period.

The types of theater

By looking at the relation between the two social worlds, taking into account the duplication effect, we come to the actual repertoire of types of theater: Serious Theater, Entertainment Theater, and Popular Theater. In fact, these types match the in-vivo termini used by reception and production agents and defined through fieldwork. At the same time, they are the answer to two detected social needs of the audience: »serious« social and political critique and »entertainment.« A dominant realism resides in Popular Theater and Serious Theater; a tendency towards taking a distance from real life—forgetting the outer reality—dominates Entertainment Theater.

To maintain the interest of their audiences, those types act in different ways as a function of the spheres of discord. The audiences are divided into two categories: estheticism-oriented Christians and realism-oriented Moslems. The configurations of estheticism and realism in a given type of theater determine its »natural« audience and thereby the appropriate social world, in which it is better presented.

The topics chosen in Serious Theater, whether presented in a realist or abstract form are taken from real life close to the spheres of discord. Apart from Intellectual Theater, which has little audience compared to the other types but considerable number of productions within the academic circle, other forms of Serious Theater like Political Theater are on their way to extinction due to the lack of freedom and the socio-political taboos. Intellectual Theater guarantees its existence through the university students who are tolerant and ready for experimentation. Financially, though, it would have had very little chance of survival. Regarding the larger audience, it is based on »coaching« by the production pretending to teach the audience more about the meaning of theater.

Entertainment Theater aims at the deliberate diversion from those spheres of discord using two strategies. The first strategy is achieved through fully ignoring the real life »R1« and submerging the spectator in an alternative reality »R2« totally detached from »R1.« This is the case of Boulevard Theater, whose topics are in their majority still imported from the French »Théâtre de Boulevard.« The second strategy, found in Chansonnier Theater, portrays sketches and scenes from daily life in which certain political figures are caricaturized. The effect is the transformation of »R2« into a surmounted form of »R1,« where the *ruled* become *ruler* and make fun of this latter. With the choice of the adequate esthetic form, a successful form of theater keeping a distance from directly tackling the spheres of discord has evolved. It is accepted by the political figures in question since the represented political caricatures are not critical but esthetical. They function as political publicity keeping them alive in the minds of people. Relying on a strong estheticism, it is no wonder that this type of theater started in the Christian milieu. Later, with its duplication in the Moslem milieu, realism slowly replaced estheticism, which negatively affected the detachment from reality necessary in entertainment, something that resulted in more restrictions and less success. One result is that the »Chansonnier Theater« is still evaluated as an exclusive Christian development to which a potentially equivalent duplicate still lacks in the Moslem milieu.

In Popular Theater, entertainment and realism are mixed. Its codex seems to be »un peu de tout, passe-partout.« Being »serious,« its topics are close to »R1,« and are therefore engaged in the social and political critique. Its »entertainment« potential comes from making fun of the political situation, which is achieved without any direct portrayal of a definite political figure like in Chansonnier Theater. However, since it cannot satisfy the political interests of the two social milieus, Popular Theater ends up representing the point of view of its own milieu. It can therefore only be located at one side of the confessional sphere of discord in order to maintain its popularity within one world. Its audience is from one social milieu, and it contains vague allusions to types of politicians belonging to the other milieu without designating them openly, the case of the obvious symbolism of Chansonnier Theater. Being more serious and functional, it is more compatible with the Moslem milieu and its functionalistic theatrical culture.

Now, how do the *production agents* deal with the selection and composition of a theater play? Upon which criteria do they act in choosing adequate *elements of play?* First of all, the strategies of the production agents differ depending on their position with respect to the extremities of the spheres of discord. Accordingly, we discern two goals of the production: *coaching* the audience towards a certain end and supplying an *outlet* for social needs. Apart from Religious Theater and a few unsuccessful »ideological« plays aiming at coaching, the dominant type of theater consists of profit-seeking productions based on satisfying the social needs of the audience. Here the production faces other difficulties.

As has been noted, the freedom of the production in considering the topic is limited due to the multitude of critical subjects, the diverging political and social points of view, and the political and social taboos. In theater, like in real life, much depends on »who says what to whom and where.« The topics related to the spheres of discord, when presented in public, cause friction and conflict. In as much as these two qualities are attractive to the audience, there is a limit to the capacity of the production in displaying them in a performance. The governmental institutions apply hard censorship set by the ruling authorities with great discriminative measures. There are two major determinants of taboos to which all the spheres of discord lead: the ruling authority and the religious one. Both can implement censorship on theater, as it was shown in the recent history of theater,[5] and they have many a common point and political interest.

Hence, Christian and Moslem religious authorities are both competent in commanding censorship. Apart from that, discrimination is also found in the way the few financial subventions of the government are distributed, next to the clear subventions of Religious Theater through religious authorities. To override the restrictions, the production agents are faced with two alternatives. The first alternative is to join the *connections (wāsiṭa)* system according to the relation of the big name of the production—the *theater-za'īm*—with the local *patron (za'īm)*. As a result of which the margin of freedom can be extended, however, only to a limited span and at the price of flattering the *patron (za'īm)*. This extension turns in a vicious circle, since, if the freedom would be extended, it would make sense to criticize the corruption of this same *patron (za'īm)*, for example. This would not be possible if the extension results from a *connections (wāsiṭa)* coming from the same *patron (za'īm)*. The second alternative is to forfeit this freedom and to apply neutrality in form and topic.

---

5 See Appendix A, Example F, and section: Freedom, Censorship, and Restrictions

Here, the production is either limited to Boulevard Theater or the play is doomed to be dull and empty of meaning.

The Parameters of production

On the whole, the parameters of production consist of reaching the economic equilibrium between finding enough audience to cover the costs of production and the margin of freedom defined through the religious and governmental authorities. Other factors like the personal wishes of the theatrical production agents, *l'art pour l'art*, in which we also find the tendency towards the expansion of the individual artist, and the relatively influential tradition, issuing from a father-son or family tradition in the theatrical field, have all a much smaller influence as an incentive for production agents.

The strategies of production

The above-mentioned parameters of the production are the determinants of the strategies used in order to surmount the various restraints. These strategies are concerned with the selection and composition of what is denoted as the *elements of play* consisting of the addressed segment of the *audience*, the *place* of the performance, the *actors*, the *topic*, and the *form*. For each of these elements, the production has developed a set of strategies to overcome incoming challenges.

The producers are concerned first of all with the type of audience, mainly Christian or Moslem. Accordingly, the place of the production should be decided first. A theater house should be chosen either in East or West Beirut. There, host-guest attitudes come out according to the types of audiences with regard to the confessional identity of the group of actors. The guest attitude expands the capacity to tolerate the other audience and the acceptance of the local system of values hosting the performance. This is the case of the Crossing Audience, whose aim is to see the performance in its »original version,« i.e. in the eyes of the *other* and from his perspective. It is noted here that the Crossing Audience consists more often of Moslem audiences visiting East Beirut, whereas the reverse case is restricted to some presentations of »intellectual theater« taking place mostly in a border area in West Beirut still functioning as a middle space for this intellectual circle. One reason for the direction of the Crossing Audiences refers to the aftermath of the war and the boycotting and differentiation attitudes of the Christians towards the Moslems; another refers to an implicit difference in what is denoted by both milieus as the »artistic standard« of the *other* theater. However, the main reason behind that is the original difference of interests between the ordinary, and realistic popular tendency in the Moslem milieu and the exclusivism and estheticism of the Christian audience.

Moreover, the host has a stricter judgment towards values strange to his social world. The Crossing Play has then to abide by the rules implied by the choice of place and the requirements of the local *patron (za'īm)*. This includes considerable esthetical and topical changes carried out while seeking compatibility. Esthetically, this includes changes of straight references like names and obvious symbols, and the neutralization of social and most important religious values. The actors exercise, on the spot, changes in the intensity of certain lines in order to fade *out* or *in* a certain effect. Apart from that, the costumes, especially those of women, are grandly revised. A Chansonnier taking place in Jounieh and intending to move to rural Moslem areas in summer has at least to account for providing longer skirts for its actresses. Critical words, swearing, and daring scenes have to disappear. Some actors, whose past could be associated with a certain militia, cannot be part of the crossing team. All this goes under the name of *neutrality*, the main strategy of the Crossing Play. Moreover, topics should be appropriately designed from the beginning in order to suit these purposes.

The second concern of the production is the choice of the adequate *actors* who are suitable for the audience and the place, and at the same time possessing the artistic qualifications to fit their role in the intended play. The choice of the actors is also affected by the internal compatibility of the group of actors together. Mixed groups of actors are seldom formed alone; they belong usually all to the same confession as the *theater-za'īm*. Having mixed actors entails more work and complexity of coordination to attain the desired results.

Third, the most important work of the production remains in topic and form. In this regard, their strategies are related respectively to the spheres of discord on one side and the esthetic realms on the other side. The subtlety of the production resides in achieving the closest distance to the spheres of discord without reaching the explosive climax. They recur to allusive tactics in tackling certain topics; examples here are found especially in Popular Theater having a historical or analogous theme derived from the political situation in Lebanon. The allusion is made from those events having a plot that can be easily connected to the present. The most attractive sphere of discord in this regard is the ruling-ruled, since it provides, as is the case in Chansonnier Theater, a political publicity for the current political figures making it even more attractive to them. The closer a topic is to the spheres of discord, the more friction it assembles, and the more audience it gathers. If the play has a certain judgment over the topic corresponding to the viewpoint of either social world, then it is impregnated with a confessional label and its audience belongs exclusively to that milieu. If the judgment is left to the audience, we have a *polarization* of this latter in the course of the performance, but the play keeps its attractiveness. This is how the spheres of discord are utilized by the production. The play can, nevertheless, be conceived as a diversion from reality. In this case, the topic in question has no connection to the spheres of discord. This is the case of avoidance of approaching the spheres of discord illustrated in Boulevard Theater, for example.

The esthetic realms are the guiding grips for the *identification* process of the spectator. Depending on the milieu from which signs and symbols are used, the spectator recognizes and identifies the *self* and the *other*. Having a topic with a one-sided judgment and whose signs and symbols belong to one esthetic realm implies a regional, insider play unable to cross to the other region. By mixing those combinations, we can produce the passe-partout play able to cross. The differences in esthetic realms are on the audio and visual levels. In the spoken Lebanese, different accents, usage, and vocabulary characterize each social world. The use of standard Arabic, French, or English has also acquired different meanings with respect to each milieu. Distinction is as well present in music, the choice of musical instruments, costumes, haircuts, moustaches, and women's make up. Those are enhanced by the race towards differentiation and vary between Arabic and Western orientations. Due to the lack of knowledge of the other, his construction is based more on prejudice than on knowledge or historical research. The type of Arabic music present in the Moslem milieu, for example, diverges notably from that used in a Christian play intending to describe a Moslem milieu. The same goes for Western music between the Moslem use in theater as an allusion to the Christian milieu, and its use in the Christian milieu itself.

Adding that to the indirect communication imposed on theater production due to the lack of freedom, the construction of the *other* in theater is deviating significantly from the image of this *other* in reality. A sort of unstudied mutilated caricature is substituting it. On the other hand, the construction of the *self*, away from being faithful to reality, contains a hidden *coaching*, similar to the one found in the media regarding globalization, towards a projected ideal self-image notably diverging from the actual image. With the imposed indirect communication, the lack of freedom, the mutilated construction of the other, and an idealized self-image, theater can hardly achieve the acceptable contact between the two social worlds necessary to establish communication. On the contrary, due to those factors, theater achieved a state of miscommunication based on these artificial images of the *self* and a prejudiced image of the *other*.

It is hence bound to incur more isolation within the boundaries of the own milieu.

Fourth, the strategies of the production regarding the audience are based on marketing techniques. Due to the degrading economic situation and the difference in theatrical culture, these strategies aim at attracting new segments of the public to theater rather than having more audience from the same segments. To this purpose, many elements of attraction are introduced in the composition of a theater play without any dramatic necessity, in the intention of making the link between the production's view of the taste of the audience in »R1« and the new things they intend to »teach« them about theater. Cheap sexual allusions, indirect stepping over the religious tabooing, common jokes, vulgar dresses for women, and performing theater in restaurants are all elements aiming at attracting new audiences meanwhile attributing a commercial tan to theater. Another strategy consists of direct marketing. Groups, clubs, religious organizations, and scouts are the typically targeted audiences. Producers, directors, actors, and outsiders, all engaged in the marketing process, strive to get the acceptance of those organizations to attend a performance. Performances are sold to groups or individuals who will try to resell the tickets with a profit margin *(ḍamān)*.[6] Due to the family structure, this circumstantial audience is forced to come to theater to encourage their family member. They end up not buying any tickets at the box office, waiting to eventually encourage a given relative by buying it from him. In this way, they become conditioned both by the time of the performance and the accompanying audience. Apart from that, to cover for the nights with »thin« audience, the production uses invitations serving also as part of their public relations policy resulting in more circumstantial audience. The family-meeting atmosphere and the feeling of duty towards a given member of that family dominate the performance and influences the freedom of the reception because of the social role imposed by the presence of the peer group. This makes the difference to the intentional audience, buying its ticket at the box office, showing interest in the play itself, and feeling free to choose the time, and place, regardless of the rest of the audience.

The types of audiences

The audiences are divided into several categories. First, we have the Christian-Moslem division. Second, theatrical culture and education determine, with changing degrees, the typology of the audience. Here, we

---

6   See section: Booking up

can distinguish a theater-initiated audience to a »virgin« audience. Third, comes the crossing versus the local audiences.

To the first division, we can attribute the estheticism versus realism and the consequences derived from it. By theatrical culture, we mean the orientation of the development of the concept of theater within a certain milieu, in addition to the frequency of exposure to theater. In the Christian milieu, we notice a learned attitude towards theater, whereas in the Moslem milieu we notice a trial towards the formation of an own attitude based on the own experience. Intellectualism, however independent from the religious milieu, depends on this initial classification. The theater-initiated audience, which can entail intellectuals as well as merely educated spectators, requires novelties in productions. The non-initiated (virgin) audiences are themselves the new conquests of the strategies of the production. The two categories differ hence in taste, the type of visited theater plays, and the transparency they exercise in linking real life »R1« to the reality of the performance »R2«. The less they are initiated, the more »R1« and »R2« are transparent, and the more we approach the spheres of discord in general and confessionalism in particular. The third categorization refers to a special type of audiences seeking the contact with the *other*. This contact is usually reduced to attending the performance »in the perspective of the other.«

The criteria of the audience in »going to theater« are affected by the *elements of play,* the attitude of the audience towards theater, and the given confessional label of the play. Transportation, crossing from one area to the other, and financial difficulties are also decisive technical as well as psychological factors. Downtown Beirut, which used to play the common space between the »two« Beiruts, still carries traces of this old neutrality making it a candidate for hosting *mixed* audiences, Christian and Moslem.

By juxtaposition to the theater types, we can roughly say that the audiences for »Popular Theater« consist mainly of the Moslems seeking a popularized political theater, which has little chance of crossing and is therefore regional. The audiences of »Serious Theater« can be of both types, but the audiences, apart from the »intellectual theater« do not usually mix. The audiences of the »Entertainment Theater« can be of both milieus; it has the most chances of mixing.

However, the theatrical culture remains divergent between Christians and Moslems. The Christian initiation to theater is based on a learned western estheticism, whereas the Moslem initiation is based on a mixture of a functionalism duplicating the esthetical values of the West in an adapted Arabic-oriented form. Mixing those audiences becomes progressively difficult for the production agents, showing themselves different points of view according to the countries, in which they learned about theater. This gap between production agents and audiences leads to a gap between audiences and theater itself and affects their view of this latter. It also does not give theater the chance to develop according to the environmental factors affecting production and reception presented at Level II.

Level III: The performance

At Level III, the performance, we observe two main processes: *interaction* and *identification*. The actual composition of the audience at the time of the performance next to the *elements of play* forms the *frame* of the performance. Accordingly, heterogeneous or homogeneous audiences, the place, and the situation of the play (crossing, insider) are all determinants of the interaction in the performance.

In the case of a heterogeneous (mixed) audience, the interaction leads usually to *polarization* of the audience depending on the topic and form. To this effect, we notice: a shift within the individual spectator from the individual to the collective attitude, representation, and role-playing, all ignited by the presence of the *other*. The more friction the topic causes, the more the identification process approaches the perspective of the spheres of discord, and the more »R2« approaches a segment of »R1.« In this case, the transportation effect from »R1« to »R2,« which is ideally the aim of the performance for the individual spectator, is replaced by more »serious« friction setting the audience back into »R1.« In the case of the Crossing Play and the types of Entertainment Theater detached from »R1« like Boulevard Theater, the *harmonization* effect among heterogeneous audiences is achieved by gathering the audience around one central agreed-upon idea. This also enhances the chances of transportation from »R1« to »R2.« In an ideal situation, we can even reach a »spontaneous communitas« for the lapse of time of the performance. In the case of a homogeneous audience we have a shift from the collective to the individual. The performance plays consequently the role of an oasis of the individual within the collective. This, however, is the case of the intentional audience. In the case of the *ḍamān* and other circumstantial audiences, the performance takes the form of a family meeting, in which it only plays in the background of this meeting.

Level IV: Post-performance

The aftermath of the performance can be estimated at Level IV in our conceptualization. In many cases, the evaluation of the performance by the audience is subject to categorical judgment depending on the own personal experience. However, judging a theater play is also part of the indirect communication cycle existing between the two social worlds. In the case of mixed audiences, the real opinion can only be known after the audience had returned to its own social milieu. In the case of a performance with a topic close to any of the spheres of discord, we notice a labeling of the performance as a whole as Christian or Moslem constituting thus the *confessionalization* of the process of theater.

The more theater is related to the environment, the more the effect of confessionalism grows in the theater process. The more theater can be detached from the environment (»R1« and »R2«), the less it is confessionalized.

Conclusion

In general, the process of theater starts at Level I with confessionalism of the environment under the form of spheres of discord and esthetic realms. Level II relates to Level I through the confessionalism of topics and esthetics as defined by the spheres of discord and the esthetic realms. The closer theater production approaches the spheres of discord, the more attractive the theater performance is to the audience, and the higher is its capability of reviving confessionalism. Confessionalism here is noticed in the signs, symbols, and topic of the theater play, especially in the construction of the image of the *self* and the *other* and the presentation of their interaction in real life. Level III is the product of a confessional balance between production and reception at Level II. The performance as an experience with the *other* and its echo in the environment usually contribute to the renewal of confessionalism in the wider environment of theater. Confessionalism is here present in the interaction with the *other* implied by the performance. Level IV, the aftermath of Level III, constitutes another confessional cycle in Level I, in which the performance and the play themselves become polarized symbols. All this results in confessionalism being omnipresent throughout the whole process of theater, making it, therefore, the guiding factor in the production and reception of theater. Without confessionalism, the elements of the play, which are expressed through signs and symbols used in the performance, would lose a substantial component of their meaning. The image of theater in Lebanon as we know it would be different.

Due to the lack of freedom, theater productions are forced to recur to indirect allusive methods of communication based mainly on esthetical constructions replacing direct quotations. On the other hand, theater plays a major role in the construction of the image of the *self* and that of the *other*. However, these images present strong divergences from reality: the *self* is idealized according to confessionalization processes (differentiation, apportionment, polarization, and labeling) in the two social worlds producing theater, whereas the image of the *other* is mutilated based on little knowledge and lots of prejudices issuing from confessionalism. Depending on the place of the performance and the potential audience, there is a variation in the degree of the tolerance of the milieu to theater.

Adding to that, Christian and Moslem theatrical cultures present differences regardless of the degree of initiation to theater; they are heading in diverging directions. The Christian milieu is heading towards learned estheticism, imported from the Western culture, together with other elements of theater. The Moslem milieu is hindered by a tendency towards functionalism, which results in realism. Both theaters are inhibited through the lack of freedom. Due to duplication effects, we find similar types of theater in both milieus with different degrees of success due to diverging tastes of the audiences. Since estheticism is more compatible with the method of indirect communication imposed by the lack of freedom, the Christian theater encouraging estheticism has more chances of development than the Moslem theater based on realism and repressed by the lack of freedom and by the religious environment.

Outlook

Only with the erasure of the view of the *other* as presented by the *(ṭā'ifa)* we can decrease the importance of confessionalism *(ṭā'ifiyya)* in the environment eliminating it from the perspectives of theater. With the institutionalization of the theater and its environment, the Crossing Play will no longer be dependent on the agreement of the *theater-za'īm* with the area *za'īm* for its existence, but will have the chance of reaching areas that were restricted so far by this configuration. On the other hand, theater would have to show ability in finding new spheres of interest and hence a new meaning to its existence. These will open other horizons repressed at the present by confessionalism. So, theater could make a decisive step having more weight in the daily life of the Lebanese. Aiming at shedding a light on a dark area regarding the reality of theater, the future will reveal the extent to which this research has achieved a step towards improving »theater in reality.« More effort is required if theater in Lebanon is to have a prospering future in its line, its way, and its meaning.

Appendix A: Excerpts and Examples from the Fieldwork

In this appendix, the raw data of different phases of the fieldwork are presented. They are an application of the »grounded theory« as elaborated by Strauss and Corbin (1998). The data consists of observations, field notes, interview transcriptions, and audio-visual material.

Observational phase

In this section we find a description of attended performances along with the remarks jotted in the field notes. The descriptions are concentrated on the three performances that formed part of the field research.

»On Top of it,« fawq d-dakki (Example A)

The first thing we notice about the play is its popularity. The number of spectators reached sometimes 3000 spectators for the one show, which is quite high with respect to other plays. It belongs, hence, to the »Popular Theater,«[1] whose success criteria are the high number of audience.

The play is not presented in a permanent theater house. It is turning from one place to the other, mainly in South Lebanon, where it finds the most audience. The shows did not take place every night, but they were organized and advertised for every performance separately. Despite of the group of actors being mainly Christian, it played in Moslem areas away from its »normal« environment. The majority of the performances took place in villages of the South. It had little or no success in West Beirut where it was launched at the beginning, and was never presented in East Beirut, even though the group of actors is Christian. The text was written by the Russian playwright »Stanislav Strateyev« and adapted to the Lebanese situation in the South. The facts of reception observed during the attended performances were confirmed with the interviews later.

---

1   See section: Popular Theater

The first scene starts with Ismāʻīn and Um Taʻān, his wife, at the taxi station in Beirut waiting to return to their village »ṣafad l-me'ti« (a fictitious village) in South Lebanon. The taxi driver who finally takes them happens to be Syrian. On the road, the driver plays Syrian popular songs on the radio. ʼUm Taʻān wants eagerly to change the music, so she asks her husband to talk to the driver to that purpose. He asks the driver to play some *baladī* »national« songs, the driver nods in agreement, but then he puts the same song again. Ismāʻīn asks him for a second time, and the same thing happens again. On the third time, the driver turns angry with them, and says: »This is national. Did you understand now, or didn't you?« The intended meaning of this scene is the Syrian »occupation« of Lebanon.

Once the two arrive at the village, they find lots of foreigners inside their own house. They try to chase them out, but they refuse to go. The house, as it seems, has a historical value, and that is why they do not want to leave. There are some archeological findings inside of it, in which those »occupiers«—direct allusion to the Israeli occupation of South Lebanon—are interested. Since they are simply of a higher number, the two cannot not force them to go. Taking this occupation as a matter of fact, they try helplessly to get used to the idea of living with the occupiers. It turns out that the people who invaded the house come from all kinds of official and non-official authorities and they all have papers »legitimizing their existence« and delegating them to do research and to live in the house. The play continues with comic scenes and more political allusions. Finally, Ismāʻīn asks them which right legitimizes their occuppation of his house and ruins his peaceful life. They show their papers to Ismāʻīn. This latter, frustrated and helpless, is left at the end with one choice: fight and resist. In the last scene of the performance Ismāʻīn lifts his plough as a symbol of resistance.

With a good degree of entertainment and a strong message easily transmitted to the audience, the play achieved hogh popularity.

In the South

I had the opportunity to see performances of this play in two different areas. The first was in South Lebanon in dayr qānūn n-nahr, a village lying in an area bordering the part of Lebanon controlled at that time by Israel. It was summer, which made it possible to organize such an open-air event. The place of the performance was a big garden on a hill belonging to a restaurant. The organization of that event was a joint effort between the producer of the play and the owner of the restaurant. At the other side of the hill, one could see Israeli tanks. People say that the military atmosphere is always tense in that area and that nobody knows when the Israeli bombs start falling, something that can happen at any time.

The majority, if not all, of the spectators were of the Shia confession. The greater part of the villages in the South are under control of either Hizballah or Amal or both together. To that effect, we could notice a good number of bearded men dressed with simple costumes like it is usual in summer obviously sympathizing or belonging to Hizballah. In opposition, not all Amal partisans have beards. The audience consisted basically of the population of the village of all ages and of the neighboring villages, mainly families and relatives. There were women with their children, teenagers, young girls and boys. Among the people I interviewed were also a few Lebanese American emigrants who usually return home for the summer vacation, together with a family living in Düsseldorf in Germany. The two main actors in the play are Christians. Ismāʻīn himself is a Maronite, and Um Taʻān is an Armenian. The rest is a mixture involving also Moslems.

Before the performance started, a series of patriotic songs praising the deeds of the resistance against the Israeli army were played. A good number of the spectators were already an hour or so before the start on the scene. There were more than 2000 chairs placed in the open air. Later they were all full and additional chairs were brought in to the site. When the play actually began, there were more than 2500 spectators. The performance started.

The people were reluctant to show any reaction to the first scene, the one alluding at the Syrians in Lebanon. Later in the interviews, nobody wanted to comment about it. As I dropped the term »Syrian occupation of Lebanon,« I got no answer. The Syrians in Lebanon are denoted differently according to the area. Among the Christians they are »occupation.« Officially, they are denoted as the Syrian »presence« in Lebanon, The Moslems would simply say »the Syrians.«

The audience, to whom the Israeli occupation is a daily reality, reacted most at this type of occupation. With the hero returning home to find it occupied by people he did not know with certificates from around the world telling him that he has to accept that, the identification of the audience was at its peak.

In one daring scene, Ismāʻīn makes it clear to his wife that he wanted to sleep with her. There was of course no question of nudity or anything of the sort, except some vague hints. The two lie at different sides of the bed and the lights turn off. The language was totally adapted to the class of the audience, and contained no words that could be denoted as »dirty« or »immoral« even to such a sensitive audience. The intention of the scene is to produce laughter. In the interviews later, some interviewees did not refrain from trying to allocate a sense of low morality to this scene, which came implicitly from the confessional identity of the main actors. »A Moslem would not do that« was in the background of the argument. It was not said clearly because the confession of the interviewer was not known. We could conclude that the scene as a whole was not accepted in the current frame of the performance.

In the Beqā' valley

The performance attended took place in the Beqā' valley in a village called in Bar Elias, a village not far away from the »Damascus Road.« The Beqā' valley is the stronghold of the Syrian army. The village itself has a Christian majority. As in the other case, the audience also consisted of all age segments, families, children and relatives. They came from the village and the neighboring areas. In difference to the performance in the South, the music played before the start of the performance was joyful, consisting of popular songs.

The actors played the taxi scene hastily, and when the allusion to the Syrian occupation was to be clear, the main actor interrupted the actress through improvising: »did you forget that we are in the vicinity of Anjar?« (Where the »Damascus road» is) this was enough to end the first scene without continuing the rest of the dialogue. The scene did, however, have a different echo, because the Christian audience started cheering and clapping right after it. In opposition to that, they showed little interest in the last scene with the resistance and occupation of the South. It is worth mentioning here that Israel also occupied West Beqā' during the big invasion in 1982, so the people suffered also under this occupation. Nevertheless, throughout the whole performance, they concentrated on jokes and scenes invoking laughter. Adapting to that fact, the actors increased the accentuation on those jokes and cut short the serious and in the given context »heavy« message of resistance. In opposition to the performance in the South, laughter dominated the place during the »daring scene.«

»Alleys,« zawārīb (Example B)

The play has several points of attraction for the research. It is performed by a Moslem Shia from the South in Jounieh, a town in the Eastern Area. The play is a monodrama, a type not well known in Lebanese theater. At the time the play was first presented in the South for the Shia audience, it did not have the expected success. Later, it moved to Jounieh, and it had surprizing success among the audience there. Some of the Moslem audience who did not attend performances presented in the South, came the longer way to Jounieh to see it in the Christian area. It is produced by the Lebanese Broadcasting Corporation (LBC), the Christian TV station and the first in the country. It belongs to the *serious* experimental theater, which, due to the lack of subventions from the government, is usually concentrated within the academic circle, where students and professors have the chance of experimenting.

The story of the play is that of a lonely man, whose name is not mentioned at the beginning, has worked in his past life in gathering garbage from the streets of a given neighborhood in Beirut. Now that he is retired, he returns to his old locality. His old habits of searching in the garbage still at hand, he is able, through analyzing the garbage, to imagine stories taking place in the locality. The play is a long monologue, in which, the man, dressed differently from things gathered from the garbage, tells these stories. From his narration, we know that he has a son, Adnān, who is married and has recently had a child. The nameless man, Abu Adnān, finds himself babysitting the child when the parents are not there. As the couple was in a night club one evening, the child got very sick, and the man, who does not know much about medicaments, got into a big panic and did not know what to do. He goes looking in vain for the parents. Running from one corner to the other, he remembers he had the address written on a piece of paper. He starts looking for the parents. After a long search, he finds them in the night club, surrounded by people dancing and laughing. Abu Adnān ends by finding his daughter-in-law dancing with a strange man, so he quarrels with him. His son appears at the end. He realizes with bitterness that the child, whom his father carried under his arm all the time, has already expired. It was too late.

Even though the topic of the play seems like a family drama, it contains a direct critique of a society careless of the happenings on the political and social levels. The occupation of the South came through a scene in the night club, where the moderator, between two songs, announces that the people should not forget the South, the dancers clap, and the music goes on. There is then the portrayal of a society careless and self-centered to the point of neglecting the own child. The interests of this society are centered along having »sinful« fun in a nightclub: a society more like the one in East Beirut. At one place came the question of honor, where he quarrels with a man he saw dancing with his daughter-in-law. In a way, the play seems like a conflict between generations, but it is also the confessional conflict, since the contradicting values that are presented could be identified to either social worlds. Behind the human facet of the child dying because of the carelessness of the parents, lies the greater problem of opposing points of view regarding the »dying« country.

The performance I attended took place in a theater house in Jounieh 15 km north of Beirut. It belongs geographically to Kesrouan in the »Eastern Area.« During the war, Jounieh and Kesrouan were not much affected by bombs. It was relatively more secure than Beirut. The majority of the military actions and bombing was centered in Beirut, and that is why Jounieh enjoyed a certain prosperity at the expense of old Beirut. In the times of war, the people of Jounieh had houses to rent for the Beirut inhabitants who were tired of war. The rent was set at a high price for even the lowest quality apartments or rooms, under the slogan »we are selling you security.« The name of Kesrouan and Jounieh was later related to this saying. The »stranger of Jounieh« is also a common expression designing all those who are not originally from Jounieh; they will never be integrated there. Even if one lives there for years, one will always be a stranger to the original inhabitants because they do not accept anybody as part of them.

The audience who attended this performance was mainly of East Beirut originally. One of the actors had booked the performance *(ḍamān)*[2]. Among the audience was a group of Christian scouts. The audience, as observed, was disposed for tolerance and patience. They know what they are going to see and they do not expect it to be compatible with their ideas. The critique of the way of life was not accepted, because it was clearly directed at the Christian community. At the climax of this critique, the audience was silent. Certain values came out to have different meanings between the actor and the audience. Those were symbols or concepts like: *night club, bar, pub, honor, sex, going out at night, and dancing*, which were all presented in a negative image in accordance to the Moslem view of those concepts. In Jounieh, people live from those businesses, and they are not negatively seen by the Christian community in East Beirut. The general human allusions were more accepted, like the sick child, the panic, and the situation of medical care in Lebanon. His interfering in the life and the privacy of his daughter-in-law was also not well digested by the audience. All in all, we can say that the audience accepted the common human values, in their simple form, and rejected the symbolical critique to their society, coming from an outer source.

---

2   The ḍamān has an effect on the type of audience, and on the reception in general, since the free choice of going to theater to see a play is put to question in this case. See section: Booking up

»Civil Disorder,« šawāz madani (Example C)

»Civil Disorder« is a typical regional Chansonnier Theater. The use of language, songs, political allusions *(laṭšāt)*, is obviously made for the Eastern Area. The Eastern Area is divided into several sub-atmospheres. The area where these types of performances take place is Jounieh. I attended about eight performances of this play, all in one place. The type of audience barely showed any indicator of change in type. It was a mixture between yuppies and older people with a certain financial standard extending from the nouveau riches to the richer categories. The majority, however, consisted of young people. Since the performances took place in Jounieh, the audience was in its majority Christian.

The action on stage itself was not the central interest of the audience. Apart from drinking and eating, the spectators were more conversing with each other and sometimes with the actors. This was made possible due to the small size of the stage, the immediacy of space between audience and actors, and the effect of alcohol. As I noticed, the object was not the theme of the play but rather to enjoy the time of the performance, using it as a bridge to this goal. The initial attitude is the readiness to have a good time. The presentation of heavy topics, or the heavy handling of serious things would create an immediate turn off, since it contradicts with this spirit. This was noticed in one sketch. It started with a Phoenician ship crossing in the Mediterranean; unfortunately it reached nowhere. The sketch, ended rather abruptly. The idea of identity was shyly present. Nevertheless, it was enough to detect the Moslem audience, since they were the only ones who suppressed any reaction, since they negate the Phoenician idea and consider it as opposing the Arabic identity of Lebanon.

»Come boy, eat mğaddara,« ta'ā kōl mğaddara yā ṣabi (Example D)

The play *ta'ā kōl mğaddara yā ṣabi* was presented within »The September Festival 1999« at the »Théâtre Monnot,« of the Université St. Joseph in Ashrafieh, a district of East Beirut. The play is a recreation of the social scene of old Beirut before the war. It evokes nostalgia of the past, even if this past is unknown for the majority of the audience consisting of the university students and the academic circle. The fact of having the play within a *festival frame* shifted the spectrum of expectations of the audience to the unusual and extends their span of tolerance. The story contains an incest case, which is usually tabooed. The many reporters, always present in such festivals, were particularly interested in daring scenes, presenting sexual connotations and presenting some »thighs« as directors would express it. The cameras did not stop flashing at those scenes. Silence reigned over the place. The audience, intellectuals and academics, accepted those scenes as experimental.

'Arabsat (Example E)

This example illustrates more the freedom restraints through the governmental institutions. Regarding the atmosphere: as I entered the theater to make interviews with the star and producer of the play, I couldn't help noticing three to four people with guns under their jackets, the type easily recognized as »security.« They were in fact from the Sûreté Générale, as I knew later, and they came to control that the actor does not make any changes to the play. The performance was tense, I couldn't make any photos except for one hasty group photo at the end, and as for interviews I restricted myself to two people from the audience, whom I happen to know from before. After a hasty interview, no one of the other spectators gave it a second thought about staying after the play for a chat.

I interviewed the actor at the beginning, as I said, and he was also tense and not really willing to divulge the reasons why the Sûreté Générale was there. His father, Shoushou, was very known in Lebanon before the war; he died at an early age. The son studied acting and directing in the United States and got back to Lebanon to work there. With the reputation of his father, and the incredible resemblance between the two in shape and voice and acting style, he started working in Beirut loyally continuing the line of the father.

The play was quite different from a typical East Beirut Chansonnier although the content and form showed similarities. Here, we find a political topic in a comic form, which proved to be popular at the end of the war, but whose popularity decreased as soon as it was spread in both areas. The subjects delineated did not make any exception from the topics that are usually presented in Chansonnier Theater: occupation, without naming directly which type of occupation, freedom of expression, social topics like the medical care, the confessionalism in opposition to the national identity. What was different from an East Beirut Chansonnier is the place of presentation, which is not a restaurant where they would clear up a small corner and call it a stage and where the actors would play while the people are eating and drinking. It took place in a normal theater house selling tickets ranging from 15 000 L.L to 25 000 L.L. ($10 to $17). The sex factor was downlighted. The actresses were not presented as the center of attraction; they wore more decent clothes and their bodies did not reflect the shape of aspiring modeling or publicity stars.

Alcohol also was not the attraction either, since it was not available in the theater. The central point of attraction for the audience was the star himself and, in this case, his incredible physical resemblance to his father. This was enough of a motivation to go to theater, even if the majority of the audience did not actually see the father on stage but rather on TV. However, the aspired impact of Chansonnier Theater, entertainment, was dimmed by the contradiction between the form and the heavy political message.

»In front of the door,« 'amāma l-bāb (Example F)

In »'amāma l-bāb,« a play presented right after the war ended at the beginning of the 90's in Beirut, we find a critical example about freedom as a result of a power balance between confessional and governmental institutions and the strength of confessionalism and regionalism. It also shows the weakness of governmental and national laws in opposition to the unwritten law issuing from the confessional power balance. The street law is the one that applies in the end. Moreover, it shows the strength of religion in defining the frontiers of freedom. In this case, the law could neither protect the theater house nor the rest of the working troupe.

The text is an adaptation of a German play. A Nazi soldier who was captured as a prisoner in Siberia during the war had the luck of escaping execution. When returning to Berlin, he sees the destroyed city and starts blaming God for it. This critical monologue triggered the religious powers against the play. »Only prophets can talk to God. This is not acceptable.« It was considered as blasphemy. The director was »ordered,« as he expressed it, by a local militia to stop showing the play, which was taking place at a university campus in West Beirut. The actors received threats of killing if »ever they set foot again in that theater.« By recurring to the governmental channels, the army, holding security in Beirut, proposed that he should continue with the already approved play, but after the threats he was obliged to stop. We see here that even when the army wanted the play to continue, they couldn't hinder the militias from threatening the actors. The play was stopped.

»Jazz, crime and punishment,« Jazz, 'al-ğarīma wa-l-'iqāb (Example G)

This is another example of »festival« plays. It shows more the irrelevance of Intellectual Theater to the large audience. Even though the audience was tolerant, within the framework of the festival, the reactions that came were artificially provoked, like clapping, which came exclusively from friends of the actors present in the theater, and the production highlights were limited to a few daring acrobatics on stage, to which the audience clapped.

Examples of field notes

Following are examples of field notes used to illustrate the analysis based on the »grounded theory« method. These represent the first impressions and the corresponding analysis right after the performances. They are reported authentically here as they were taken the first time in the purpose of illustrating the method.

Memo 1: »zawārīb«

The audience: Coming to see this monodrama is »à la mode.« They didn't come out of knowledge or passion for theater but for the mere fact that he is an actor acting alone, and that ›it is good to see him‹ to show off with being up to date.

Intellectuals would come to confirm that they are educated and they know. Intellectual show off.

Dominance of the person, star, »vedette«

The people respond more to music than to the social critique of the play. Dancing in the Night Club is negatively presented in the play. Whereas it is normal in East Beirut.

His language is from South Lebanon. His social critique applies to the society in East Beirut. He played »down« when the audience did not react to his critique.

The audience showed tolerance invoked by the frame of the performance.

His values are old and do not correspond to the new post-war generation.

When I asked if she liked the play, she answered that *he* was great. She did not mention any other elements in the play.

»It is funny how he talks in the trash.« »It is good to know about the South.« The South was mentioned only one time. It is not the topic at all. Only, the actor is from the South. Ignorance, immaturity, show off, snobbism.

Memo 2: šawāz madani

The main actor: He came to theater after having studied engineering. Then he went to France and did not continue his studies there but stayed in Lebanon to do theater.

He classifies older theater people as a monopoly.

Through our socialization, confessionalism has extended to be an attitude of:

discrimination based on belonging to a certain sect, community, or confession. This type of religious discrimination is no more based on belief but on belonging.

discrimination based on belonging to a certain region (regional discrimination)

Social discrimination, ranking, social status (prejudice.)

(Forced?) separation between the people done by: peer pressure, lack of information, false information, ignorance of the other.

Hostility is one characteristic of this division

From the belonging idea we come back to the identity problem. The historical identity of the Lebanese, the false history, that one learns in schools, knowing that it is false, would lead to not taking the state and its rules seriously. Later in life one sees that this is anyhow the case on the practical level, discrimination in theater related to persons and not to laws or regulations.

This discriminative attitude, is derived initially from confessionalism, and fostered through the upbringing in the family, school, and later in life on the practical level in the relation with the representatives of the government (discrimination according to persons and *wāsiṭa*, and to the confessional, regional, family, clan, and related to a central figure, the *za'īm*, and also hierarchy and social status. The action of automatic classification of people according to the above mentioned data, although a clear derivation of confessionalism and the initial differences specific to the different communities, has nevertheless become part of the »Lebanese» character and this showed in the »judgemental attitude» of another actress, for example. It is not based on deductive judgements, but on a need of being judgemental about the *other*.

Being open minded, accepting the other, not judging, remain words with no meaning on the practical level. The *other*, in confessional terms, is seen uniquely from this perspective, this synthetic interface. Ignorance of the *other* has created hostility. With education this hostility has been more and more buried under layers of »civilized appearances,« but it did not really change.

The idea of the state is considered as unreal, a lie that should not be taken seriously.

The heads of the confessions with their related hierarchical dependents adopted the policy of remaining in the shadow. Their strength in theater appear through the institutions of the government, here through the Sûreté Générale who can approve or disapprove of the subject and the text chosen for this topic.

There are explicit red lines in Chansonnier. It is forbidden to:

Criticize, oppose, mention, any information about the confession. This taboo runs under the banner of morality or security.

Criticize a *patron (za'īm)* directly or make any kind of statement specific to specific events, involving person, even if this is already in the newspapers. The more integrated a person is in the system, the less reachable he is.

Mention directly: Syria, South Lebanon, the Palestinians, the Iranians, God, ...

Need for protection *(za'īm, wāsiṭa)*: working in theater means that you are exposed to any *patron (za'īm)* who would want to prove his power on the political scene or his place in the system through hassling you. This can go as far as to prohibit you, with the tools of the system or with direct threat, from presenting your play.

Self-censorship: the theater people have learned these rules by heart, and they are forced to abide by them. The only political criticism we see in theater reduces to flattering the politicians. This is a promotion for them, since it keeps them alive in the minds of people.

Implications on *production*:

Tying down the subjects within the limits set above.

Not being able to express a free opinion about vital topics, which leads to loss of interest of the audience, and therefore less audience

The relation between the actors, producers, casting (choice of people), is subject to the above mentioned rules: personal relations *connections (wāsiṭa)* override the technical capacities, discriminative attitude,...

The relation between the actors and their audience is based on the judgemental part derived from above i.e. on prejudice with respect to the *patron (za'īm)*.

Trying to attract people to survive, the production (actors, directors,...) appeal to the audience (give the people what they want), this leads into falling automatically into the trap of confessionalism.

In relation to confessional media, especially TV, (owned by confessional institutions, also through the new regulations of the law of information). The image of the play is shaped according to where its advertisement appears.

The existence of plays that break those rules, is possible, however, their survival is not likely. They depend either on audience or on sponsorship from charity or religious organizations.

Implications on *reception*:

Classification of plays according to the belonging of the actors.

By seeing the confessinal trend, the performance plays the role of confirming the prejudice in one direction or the other. This is specifically done when there is an obvious representation of Christian or Moslem characters on stage.

This leads to:

The theater tends towards having a role in socialization, i.e. a role in the system.

The performance is a place where one would compare what he »learned« or »experienced« in real life i.e. his repertoire of knowledge to the »reality« as seen on stage. The fact of having those specific confessional in nature prejudices would limit the performance to those comparison and lessen the degree of other dimensions in the mind of the receiver

The emotional reactions of the receiver are delimited within the spectrum of his socialization. The reactions of the audience are also liable to be learned.

Memo 3: »The Martyr son of the country.« 'aš-šahīd 'ibn l-balad

In one scene of this play, the main character is waiting in front of the bakery to get bread, when the militiamen of the same region started fighting among each other, who will take his bread without having to wait. This scene is typically taken from the war culture.

Confessionalism is brought symbolically on stage through the main character. Her name was *ṭawā'if,* »Confessions.« It is a symbolic characterization of a woman having intimate relations with six men at the same time, each from a different confession. They spend their life fighting all the time with each other, and still going back to her as a refuge. The ultimate message of the play finished at saying *no* to her, but did not reveal how to stop her. We see here more an attempt of political critique of confessionalism that did not develop to go beyond the complaint. It is acceptable that confessionalim as a vague concept is a problem, but any further elaboration of it is not welcome.

Memo 4: ğnaynit ṣ-ṣanāyi'[3]

The separation between the two milieus is present also through an implicit respect of the domain of the *other*. Not mingling, not interfering, with the »affairs of the other,« found its way to theater. In »*ğnaynit ṣ-ṣanāyi'*« the topic of *ḥiğāb* veiled women was mentioned. The actors are Christian and they tried as much as possible to keep the discussion within an objective, scientific frame. The echo was, however, contrary to their will. The Christian critique was that the topic is not of »our concern«; whereas, the Moslem critique was that the Christians are interfering in affairs not belonging to their prerogatives. The confessional character of the relation with the *other* was able to override this level.

Memo 5: »Dream maker,« ṣāni' l-'aḥlām

This play, presented in 1987, has had a certain festival prize, and was presented in two festivals in Baghdad and Carthage. When it came Beirut, it closed after a week because of lack of audience. In 1987, there was war. Regardless of the accuracy of the narration of the interviewees, this could be seen as a typical case of incompatibility between the taste of the audience and the assumptions of the production.

Interviews

Following are the interview guidelines, a list of the interviewees on the production side, and cited sections from the interviews from both production and reception after transcription and translation.

Interview guidelines

There were two guidelines for the interviews, one for the audience and one for the production agents. Both tried to cover similar points like identity, construction of the other, freedom, confessionalism, war, regionalism, in theater and the performance in question. Since free interviewing is liable to reveal new categories, the guideline was not strictly followed. It was enhanced with time to meet the upcoming categories.

In the period from July to September, about 50 long interviews (from 30-150 minutes) on the production side were effected, and 50 short interviews (less than 10 minutes) with the audience. The reason for the gap is that the audience was best available either short before the performance,

---

3 The name of the central park area in West Beirut.

or late in the night afterwards. This timing was important, because it keeps the direct impressions related to the performance in question.

Audience reception interviews

The initial guideline for the audience interviews looks like the following:

- Name?
- Are you coming from a far place to see this play?
- Did you like the play?
- What exactly did you or didn't you like?
- What do you think of the audience?
- What does theater mean to you?
- Do you go often to theater?
- What do you think of Lebanese theater?
- What, in your opinion, are the problems of Lebanese theater?
- The conversation changes according to his cited points. Usually, war comes as a problem.
- How do you think the war affected the theater in Lebanon?
- Do you think there is freedom to say whatever you want on stage?
- If the answer to the previous question is »yes,« then I go to: what about political things, or sexual things, or religious things.
- How do you classify the audience of this play?
- How do you see the audience in Lebanon?

The rest of the interview is devoted to specific spots in the performance related to the main categories, which are either established in previous interviews like confessionalism, or politics, or freedom, or which came up on the spot through the same interviewee. These were different with respect to each play.

Production interviews

The guideline for the interview on the *production* side goes slightly in a different way, even though some questions are similar.

- What is your opinion of the play? Are you satisfied with your work?
- What are your personal problems in this play?
- What does theater mean to you?
- Since when are you actor, (producer, director, ...)?
- What do you think of Lebanese theater?
- In your opinion, what are the problems of Lebanese theater?

- Usually the talk would always lead to a discussion of the war, and there I would start tackling the idea of confessionalism related to the war.
- How do you think the war affected theater in Lebanon?
- Do you think there is freedom to say whatever you want on stage?
- If the answer is »no,« then I ask what are exactly the topics that one is not free to talk about?
- If the answer to the previous question is »yes,« then I go to: what about political things, or sexual things, or religious things?
- Do you think that over the years we have built a certain identity to theater?
- If yes, what kind of identity? (Usually, it is always a debate about Arabism, and Lebanism, related to an old debate between Christians and Moslems☐
- What do you think of the audience?
- How do you classify the audience? According to what criteria?

Then the conversation continues along different lines, which I didn't stop. In the case where I knew the people personally, I would go to more direct questions, but only at the end. Specific questions turn around what the person would do exactly in theater i.e. how he or she would prepare for his or her role, in the case of actor or actress, or what are the criteria, he takes into consideration when doing his job, and if the audience is part of them.

Partial list of interviewees

The following is a partial list of names in alphabetical order on the production side, whose interviews were evaluated as expert interviews. Many other interviews were conducted with experts whose names are not mentioned due to data protection. These include all the audience interviews and part of the production experts. I cordially thank each and everyone of the intervieewees and all those who helped make this research possible.

- Abou Jaoudé, Toni
- Alā' d-Dīn, Khodor
- Ali Ahmad, Rafiq
- Assaf, Roger
- Basha, Abido
- Bassil, Mario
- Bou Nassar, Joseph
- Chedrawi, Yaacoub

- Dagher, Patricia
- Dick, Renée
- Ez-Zein, Ahmad
- Fazlian, Berge
- Gébara, Raymond
- Haddad, Carla
- Hadichian, Varoujan
- Hamdan, Jamal
- Jabre, Michel
- Kassis, Jean
- Kesrouani, Mounir
- Khayat, Sami
- Khoury, Chakib
- Khoury, Jalal
- Kourayem, Mouhamad
- Maalouf, Maurice
- Moultaka, Antoine
- Moultaka, Latifé
- Najjar, Marwan
- Plisson, Alain
- Saad, Farouk
- Saaid, Ziad
- Salameh, Kamil

In addition to those, there were quick non-anticipated interviews made shortly before or after the performance with the actors and the spectators. From these interviews, information was deduced according to the methods listed above.

Translated interviews citations

The numbered sections here are part of a larger collection of transcriptions taken from the interviews. These were then coded and formed the categories following the »grounded theory.« The number at the beginning is the identification number in the »database.« Through this number, all the information relevant to the section can be found as one record in the database. This information was omitted for anonymity purposes.

86 money... which is the thing... the serious right thing in Lebanon...
134 it is another way of thinking ... mm... they are ashamed of expressing their ideas like we express them...

138 religions matters... they are limited by religion... not all of them... the majority... for sure...

140 they consider us girls ... that we are indecent because we work in theater...

186 there are lots of forbidden things... you have **17** confessions... if you want to talk in this line notice... all the names are neutral neither Moslem nor Christian... the identity is gone...

200 they are the heads who divided us... I don't make the difference between Moslem and Christian...

216 everything is by inheritance... *patron (za'īm)* son of a *patron (za'īm)*... maybe it works... but artist son of an artist is not always successful...

225 confessionalism is a decease we are suffering from... All of us... Here we are here... You and me ... I am from one confession and you are from the other... And unfortunately we know that everybody belongs to the other confession although we shouldn't have known... So are the relations in this country...

226 Confessionalism is a form of injustice in Lebanon... the proof... last time when the issue of civil marriage was under discussion in Lebanon... the first thing they agreed on was to hinder the project ... the heads of the confessions... if one speaks a word about the other [...] they swear at each other in public... but with civil marriage they were together...

227 during the war ... there was a demographic isolation of each confession... you come to ask me would you live there... I would not state names of the areas... I tell you ...no my brother... there they are all from this or that confession... no they are all from this sect... even sects... why? they made the citizen feel... it has come to a state where the citizen would subconsciously tell you no... If you insist more he tells you I feel more secure among the sons of my confession...

229 the people are divided... the confessions in particular... the people can be divided either confessional or into classes... we here... the weapon that is used in the Middle East and the retarded countries is the confessions...

230 they tell me to propose names for a play or a TV series... I say »George« they ask for one from the confession... why is it that George would have $4000 in LBC and Mohammed only $1000 and this without that Mohammed could even notice...

328 the Moslem society does not need theater... everything is solved through religion...

330 all is solved with religion...

332 ...in an area that is not my area...

337 the identity of the individual is defined according to his confessional belonging in Lebanon...

409 we should be in Europe...No, no, in America [...] Not Arabs... we are not Arabs [...] we have a problem of identity and belonging...

419 (Regarding the subject of women wearing veil in Islam.) The Christians: the subject is of no concern to us. The Moslems: you are mocking the veil and Islam.

488 Rafic Ali Ahmad succeeded because they like to see somebody who is less than them...

501 ...they don't see the work of the other... and they want to subdue the other...

506 our life... our inheritance... our causes... geography... thought... tradition...

523 we have a different type of life here in East Beirut than the one in West Beirut...

528 I am Lebanese... but not Lebanese at the same time...westerner... America. The language... how they speak... their accent...

534 About the sex question: if the sex talk comes from men you hear lots of laughter, they stand, enthusiasm and everything... but if the actor is a female... they neither like it nor accept it.

538 I hope we don't have any prejudice... and that we can make theater for all Lebanon... and not only regional theater... where we have to change in every area because our theater is connected to a certain category...

556 I feel good here... why I feel better here? I don't know... because I got used to it... my work is here... my friends are here... I don't go often down... I have nothing to do in that area... but I feel relaxed here... may be now if we do down and work down I would feel more relaxed but I feel better relaxed here... now...

557 I feel more relaxed here... why do I feel more relaxed here... I don't know... Because I got used to it... My work is here my friends are here... I don't go often down... I have nothing to do... In that region... But I am relaxed here... Maybe now if we go down and work down I would feel relaxed down... but I here feel more relaxed now...

570 Lebanese theater... at least it should have an identity...

583 the Christians have the »affectionate mother« France heading towards the Francophonie... Western loyalty... The Moslems have an Arabic opening... but they are heading towards the Anglophonie.

584 in Islam as a religion... theater is forbidden ... even painting is forbidden... incorporating the human is forbidden as an Art...

585 those who founded theater in the Arab countries... I am sorry to say it like that... because I am not confessional... and my way of belief is very special... are the Christians... they are the pioneers in the Arabic culture... nobody comes to tell me you should consider yourself as non Arabs... may be I am not Arab... but I am better than you are in Arabic...

594 Hermel... where the roots of Hizbullah are... you should know that it is more related to Syria than to Lebanon...

598 there is the factor that I am Moslem for example... screw the Christians... and I am Christian screw the Moslems... this is a Christian who has a play... his play is no good... and this is a Moslem... apparently he wouldn't say that... he would be ashamed... (of being confessional)... but inside he would be biased...

600 the Moslem... I think he knows himself... he knows very well that the Christian area is the area of freedom of thought... I mean... for that reason... the majority of them... I mean... the Christians and the Moslems come to spend the evening here... (in the Eastern area)... nobody goes there...

635 you can't say because of the existence of the religious fanatism... Especially the existence of the Moslem element... It has evolved a lot no doubt ...but the Moslem element which is against the representation... Acting...

636 the Islamic element is against representation...

641 this I can't say in any place... I say it in front of people that understand it... because if I say in the street... they would say, he is against the Moslems and Islam...

671 the normal people are very confessional... the war awoke confessionalism in the minds of people...

681 My education is foreign... but I feel myself Lebanese... the structure has to do with the land... the climate... the language does not change the identity...

683 the Lebanese are oriental... and they see with all their body the relation with the place of the performance...

685 the way of expression is the identity...

686 the topic is the responsible for polarization...

706 I am still discovering if my identity...I see it as a Lebanese...I don't know?

713 at the beginning I felt myself the odd man out... later, day after day, I felt more and more... I'm sharing with them

719 the K family... when we had K among the audience, it used to show... or for example somebody from Reyfoun... you feel a different response...

728 may be the Christian has more belonging to the European environment than to the Arab problems happening here...

731 the Christian is more liberated than the Moslem in making theater...

732 The communism is a cover... with Ziad Rahbani... he cannot get out of himself...

736 the Palestinians would catch you and tell you... Screw you... you are a Christian... I tell them hey people listen... I am on your side... I am with you I am one of you... doesn't help...

741 in the Islamic world... there is no conflict... that is why there is no theater...

747 the belonging defines identity... the belonging to the Nation... to the clan... the family... if you have a high rank officer of the Druzes and a Joumblat... he would dictate on the commandant what to do...

752 they (the Moslems) say they prohibited personification... it is not true... they didn't need it (theater)... what would they do with it?

755 Fadel al-Jaayiby was saying we are telling stories to people who do not need our stories...

757 now there are only the Shias that go to theater ... Because they are in a state of social promotion... They see themselves in theater... they are put again on the scene... they come from the Southern Suburb and see KK... a Maronite that does... does... Ismail... and the girl who is doing Oum Tahan is an Armenian... but they are seeing themselves... that is new for them but it will not last… that is our chap AA... they turned their back to him and swore at him... and when he came here…I brought him here and ... make him work and run in E. Beirut... he became better in their eyes... I was with somebody who is a relative of Kamel El-Assaad... she was telling me... what a dog this AA... we are the best people ... we are educated ... he made goatkeepers out of us...when the play functioned after six months… I saw her coming to see the play... they are applauding him… that's one of us... in fact take my word... whatever happens for the Christians... it is a pioneer... it will happen for the Moslems... after so many years... it means that Aoun and Geagea will still happen there…

768 Saida for example is considered as Arab, Beirut not.

769 here I am, living here... I will have children... I will habitate them here... we are a clan... we don't get far from each other...

770 we start riding on each other... you find quarters...there are Assabi-yaat inside the city... this is the Arab town...

771 It does not mean that it is a city with Moslems and not Christians... the European city... that is the abstract individual...

772 »my son is gone«... it means... he cut all the ties to the community...

774 Ashrafieh is Orthodox... Caracon Ed-Druze... Jemmayzeh is Maronite... Nahr is Armenian... the confessions are still there…

781 the absence of the common space... there is still East and West... I, the son of E. Beirut... when I go to W. Beirut... I have no opinion... and the son of West whenever he goes to Jounieh he has no words there...

like my students whenever they go to the Shouf they start telling me about the Shouf as if they're talking about Cyprus... the crisis is a crisis of the society... the absence of the space for variety and interaction...

815 A confessional... sectarian... and regional divisions... every quarter has something different... we are now at the beginning of the 21st century but we are still Uurbaan, clans, Bedouins...

820 especially the Christians couldn't name George in a play... they kept on naming neutral names... Raymond Gebara staged »Kandalaft goes to heaven«... but not for here (West Beirut)... for there... (East Beirut)... he put it in the Picadelly... they (the Moslems) don't come to see it ... all who go are you and I and a few others...

821 such a society will produce such an audience...

822 Rahbani have a formula... they make their calculations for example that they would want their play to be presented in the Druze area... just like that... we are people who like to hear... we want to hear... we like to hear the beautiful word... if you make theater with casual words... nobody will accept it...

825 why... do they put Abou El-Aabd? TS: here? No... there in your area (East Beirut)... why do they put inside the chansonnier Abou El-Aabd... to make fun of the Moslems... and there they laugh on him and pay him money...

829 there are common things... tireness, hunger, sickness, food, sex,...

836 theater without freedom... how can it be ... theater without freedom...?

839 if you want to go for confrontation... you hit your head with the wall... they put in jail... they boycott you... they kick you out of you job...

840 I had a Magister in theater... he wouldn't let to the university... here I am considered as a Christian Nasaretarian... and there a communist... I got my doctorate degree... I needed connections... this world is quota... Kamil Chamoun... Franjieh... the Patriarch... Hoss... Joumblat... last I brought him a recommendation from the door keeper... they wanted them all to be Moslems in the area... the parties... Mourabitoun... Amal... confessionalism exists... it can always be moved... any time... you talk with the people here (West Beirut)... they tell you »our brothers the Christians« excuse me for the expression... and in our village, if they see a fly... they tell you »look... look this is Oum Mouhamad«... it is a sponge... and they are able to move at any hour... historically... confessionalism has a history...

841 if you would talk about the snow of Alaska... They would find something for it...

848 at the beginning I had a political goal... with time we got modest and I saw the importance of theater as art aiming at pleasure and a medium to regain thought... and moving the emotions and thoughts of the spectator... who will not be paying money to go and hear some political or ethical preaching but looks for entertainment... this entertainment is different between the educated and the average employee... the playwright should give a common pleasure to the biggest amount of different spectators...and not to be limited to intellectuals or only popular categories...

853 AA... Al-Jaras... he made it about the South... in fact, this piece did not have success in the first stages in front of this audience... which is its normal audience... he had the idea to present in Jounieh... he did so... there was... I mean with the beginning of the peace phase... and the beginning of the opening of the Lebanese on each other after separation... the people were interested in ... those who did not know the people of the South... they don't know their suffering... they were interested in seeing it... and get to know those people... it came... the fact that you are presenting something to an audience... that doesn't know you... that came to get to know you... to what you represent on stage... the people liked this piece... and they came in numbers... till it reached... I've seen the play several times... that people came from Tyr... when the play was there... they didn't see it... when it came to Jounieh and found this success... they came from Tyr to Jounieh to see it... imagine to which extent... they recognized its value late...

854 I can say that the civil war... has produced some kind of psychological division in the mind of people...

861 a few of the intellectuals in West Beirut... if we can reduce Lebanon to Beirut... are sharing in the cultural life in East Beirut... to the contrary of what is happening in the Eastern areas... to a large extent... they are still boycotting the plays showing in West Beirut...

862 after Taa'if... the Christians thought their rights were gone... by the Moslems... they don't come to them... we could work with them but there is a barrier...

863 the playwright takes his material from the people and returns it to them...

869 here with us... with the Arabs...

878 there is the family Itani... they used to present theater in the Piccadelly and the Orly houses... you have Fairuz and her sister...

885 a clash of identities...

888 I am a citizen of the Lebanese South... I was born in a country where there is a farm of confessions and arrivists and... the... wrong system... full with injustice and oppression... where there is no justice...

889 Ibn al-Balad is the Lebanese or the Southern... Ibn al-Balad is the popular conscience... is the Arab conscience...
893 theater is the stand from which I express my political and human position...
900 this country... we... we... are Arab... we have convictions...
908 the region has nothing to do with the success of the play... and the most prominent evidence is that »Al-Jaras« found success dort... before it succeeded here... the audience... the more you respect it... the more it respects you...
911 I don't want to talk about him...not one word... not one word... when we are alone we talk.... (after turning off the tape recorder)... what a shitty... what a shitty person... this would represent the South... in this manner... this... this... there is nobody in the whole South that talks like this woman with him...
923 the audience was living in fear... of the death in the war... they wanted and easy theater... they are not ready to work out their minds... because they are tired... that is why we have theater during the war... a theater aiming at making people laugh and entertaining them...
925 I think that the Lebanese is Lebanese... they all eat Tabbouleh and drink Arak...
926 In »Hizb Saadallah« with Antoine Ghandour in »Chateautrianon«... we had regional expressions... Kesrouani expressions... »sim smaimek«... »skot wala kelmeh«... a Kesrouani would understand them... for me, they don't have any meaning...
928 the woman was astonished that there is a priest walking on Korniche El-Mazraa... and my neighbour under is Christian... and we are living together like brothers... but this new generation... the woman of this young guy belongs to the new generation... maybe she never saw a Moslem... she was isolated in Jounieh... and all the environment are Christians... she was very much surprised to see a priest in an Islamic area...
929 the people stayed mixed here... the Western area was not emptied from the Christians... in opposition to the Eastern areas... the Moslems got scared they came here to the West... the line of the American University... it was always like that... an Arab line... the students of course... not the university... the Jesuit University has Lebanese and only Lebanese... no Arabs... all from one confession.
941 the conflict is national... the Moslems say we are Arabs and they preach the one national Arabism and the Arab unity... and the Christians say... we have nothing to do with the Arabs... those Arabs are a bunch of underdeveloped people... we are closer to Europe... we are Western in our way of thinking...

952 »... for the first time in the history of theater in Lebanon... and may be also in the world... the audience was divided into two parts... one for the women and one for the men... the name of the play was »Tha'ar Allah« -- The Revenge of God« -- so theater is part of a general movement...«

959 the Christian would see how the Moslem would think about the subject and vice versa...

961 No No No No the audience in a way till now... even in the private circles... we are discovering confessional people I mean... They don't know who we are ... they start talking about the confessions as if we belong to their confession I mean... one should admit the existence of confessionalism so that one can come over it... we keep on saying there is no confessionalism... We are Lebanese we have no confessions... no there is confessionalism.... And confessionalism that exists in places were one would not think it should exist I mean... and there are hatreds and there are tensed feelings and there is tension... and there is whatever you want in the end.

962 people are not interested in theater as such... they are interested in the topics presented in theater... no more nor less... to a certain extent they are interested in stars... they go to see Antoine Kerbage and they want him to say things complying with them...

963 I mean...where is Lebanon...? shall I move Lebanon to put it in Europa?... idiots... those are idiots... and those who insist that the identity of Lebanon is Arabic are also idiots at the same time... because Lebanon... in general... Lebanon is retarded...

967 the intellectual audience left me... even though I didn't change... because the intellectual audience is old now... then came the war... this audience knew Beirut before the war... and is still seeking Beirut before the war...

973 the war is related to age... there is no culture... they want just to make up for the lost time in the war... we have a lost generation now... may be in **5** years we have something better with more education...

983 invitations... some salesman comes and tells you: did you bring some invitations to your play this year?... xyz brought us **20** invitations yesterday...

995 I am an Orthodox... I taught two years at Kaslik (a university in the Eastern area)... the Maronites discovered that I am Orthodox... I am telling you this story for fun... they told me... for fun... what a loss... what a loss... it means that it is not only confessionalism... it is also sectarian... with sects...

1000 I personnally would not do a play against Christians or Moslems... because I don't deal with religion... because religion as such is untouchable...
1045 we used to call the schools and the clubs and that is how we made our audience...
1046 during the war we had nothing to do but war... either theater or being lost... it was a defoulement that prevented us to think of what is happening outside...
1059 the audience will never get out of confessionalism... never... as long as the situation is like that... it will never get out...
1061 Islam as a religion prohibited theater... because of its pagan origin... the theatrical form... that is why the first form of Arab theater is the shadow play »Khayaal az-Zill«... it is forbidden to make theater... because he who is involved in theater in Islam is considered as outside the religion...
1062 Wassim Tabbarah and Mohammed Shbaro... two Sunni Muslims that worked in E. Beirut... and alike... One Druze... God bless his soul... Nabih Abou El-Hosn whose theater was at most in E. Beirut... and those did not dare going to the Moslem area... to the contrary of Ziad Rahbani whose theater was the most prominent in W. Beirut ... and who did not dare coming to ... to...E. Beirut thus the concept of confessionalism did not infiltrate the theater game.
1065 the Moslems recognize that the Christians... and the Maronites in particular have a big credit in conserving the Arabic language in the days of the Turks... there was a fear of »turkization«...
1068 I don't like the clergy but I like religion...
1069 all the people who came to see the play of AA came unwillingly... »alone and something about the South... and I don't know what«... but after they saw the play... everybody... I am 100% sure and certain because I got this feedback from many people who bought all the seats for a certain night... and many told me straight... all the people who left after the performance regretted not having come earlier... totally... totally... they had a total change in the image... the people in the area... when they are ignorant of people in the other area...
1082 during the war there was a cheap theater... they make a play in East Beirut swearing at the West and vice versa...
1084 I... by Got... I worked theater here during the war... I criticized the authoritarianism here in the area... in »Zaradushta became a dog«... they asked to have the play in West Beirut... ehm... I told them there is a religious character in the play... Christian... If I would want to move the play to West Beirut... I want to put a Moslem religious character... they didn't accept... they said they can't... see...

1089 there are religions... there are religions whose structure is against art... theater for example... it means the Islamic religion... the Christian religion allows... that you make a play about Christ or something... the Islamic religion doesn't allow you to mention the prophets or Mohammad... even the common prophets... Ibrahim for example... I produced the play »Tahta Rihayat Zakkur«... Ibrahim goes down from heaven... The Moslems do not accept it...

1100 a Shia wave... he rode that wave... you know... these are merchants... I don't like to talk about merchants...

2184 the parents would teach their children to show off with them... they give them education in America in order to come back and build a villa better than that of the neighbors...

2186 I produced a series about Ramadan... In LBC, as soon as they knew it was Islamic... they classified it as a midnight show...

2204 In every area, the people laugh according to their social reality... in Nabatieh for example, people laugh for small things... because they lost a bigger thing... it means... it means they don't have a permanent theater there... they consider it a big thing if somebody comes to them and presents anything... the audience was very good... and there was a lot of direct communication between us to the extent that there are several dialogues that took place between me and the audience... I mean you have to break the fourth wall... in Nabatieh the audience was different ...and here (West Beirut) is another type of audience...

2211 theater has a special place in the urban society... the rural society doesn't need theater... the city needs theater because it needs social meetings...

2221 there is no real meeting... those who go to that area are visitors... there is no real meeting... they visit Jounieh... they visit Hamra... tourists...

2237 if the Maronite would come to tell me that he considers himself a God... I wouldn't communicate with him... it is not hatred... it is not that I don't like the Christians... I was raised in a nun school... and I learned their principles... we pray each time we go to class... but there is a barrier of communication. With all the... the play would have a barrier in communicating... with everybody... the director doesn't know to whom he is producing...

2238 ...RR used to do plays in the Centre Culturel Francais in French... etc... he shifted to Hakawati theater... then he shifted back to something like Hizballah... then he shifted back again to a certain formula between human level in general and... because he is lost between he is still a Shia and his wife is still veiled... but he returned to speaking French although he quit talking French for a while... now he has become French... and be-

cause he is French... his wife Hanan is French... they have the French nationality all of those stories... these people they are also victims and executioners of theater... you understand me when I say executioners... it means they decided they decided how to imprint it how to emboss it...
2240 the Orthodox are like Moslem and Christians... the Sunnis of Beirut are really special... I thought at a school full of Sunnis from Beirut... urban people and open to the West... they make you feel they are not confessional even though they stick to their religion... in contrary to the Sunnis in Tripoli...
2246 the Maronite is a boaster...
2248 the Shias are always weeping...
2249 the Orthodoxes have the complexes of inferiority typical of the minorities...
2250 the Armenians I can't describe them... they are very ugly...
2256 people who are living only 20 km away from Moslem areas... they don't know what Ramadan means... how do you see it? This comes from schools... from culture, from the educational policy of the government... I am against something... eh... remove the confessions... because... Lebanon... don't forget is made out of confessions... you should protect the dignity and respect for all confessions...
2257 there should exist some supra nationality... it should not be that the confession gives you your identity...
2258 My children would say: »We are American citizens and we are Lebanese too, my father and my mother are from Lebanon« ...
2259 we at théâtre Monnot, we always have a mixture of religions...
2262 the cultural and linguistic pluralism... there are people who speak one word of English one Arabic... and others speak one French word and one Arabic word... I am against that...
2268 Lebanon... America and France... France because... we are culturally imperialized... because the state doesn't help to wipe off this thing... it doesn't support the Lebanization... it doesn't support the Lebanese University... or our Arabism... French... it's too much...it's too much... we are forced to learn... it is not wrong to learn... English... everything is in English... in my university... we don't learn Arabic... everything is going too far... too far...
2271 yeah sure... regions... complexes... from Ashrafieh and up they speak French... down they speak English...
2277 we are so to say European... we are... we should not be in the Middle East... I don't know we should be in other... I don't know they should move Lebanon and put it next to something else... we are not like the Arabs... we are not Arabs... I what we are not but I don't know what we

are... I am still searching for what we are... I still didn't reach a solution... but I know what we are not...

2278 we are French and American and Italian and Phoenicians (she laughs)...

2284 we eat like Europe we dress like Europe... we buy the TVs of Europe... but let a girl live alone like the European girl... by Got they make hell on earth the Lebanese... cohabitation... no... we take the skin like always... Lebanon is very complex.

2286 because the Arabs are like that... we... Lebanon is Arab in principle... now the culture... the imperialism came later... but we are in Beirut , a conservative city...Beirut and the Beirutis... conservative families... even Ashrafieh... Ashrafieh are Beirutis... Beirutis not in the sense of Sunnis... Beirutis from Beirut... I mean the Moslems are more conservative... I am Moslem... no I am not Moslem... my father is Moslem... I am nothing... no religion... they are more strict because their religion imposes that on them... the Chritians are different... they are different ... also fundamentalists... but they went to Europe earlier... they learned more than the Moslems... The Moslems are newly there... that is why the Christians underestimate the Moslems because they think they are ignorants...

2287 ... this play... do you know if any Moslem would have done it?... the sky would have fallen on earth ...it would have been doom's day... but because it is a Christian who has done it...I mean... apart that the TV and other things are... but the Chritians have the priority...I don't know why... but this is the truth... I don't know why... may be because they are political and diplomatic more than the others... and the war... the war did not end yet...

2292 there was a separation between the areas... we didn't know what was being produced in the other area...

2346 not only you can say there is a play here and an equivalent play there... they resemble each other but they change names... the same play... the audience would see the perfomance of the play »Kazzab« (liar) done at the beginning of the 80s... they see it... in the Eastern area critisizing the Syrian role... later the same play with the same actors moved to Ras Beirut... it became against the Israelis... there is an abuse... there is arrivism... exercised on the feelings of the people according to the area in which they are...

2347 we have a project of a play that establishes the individual... on the expense of the clan... because ... in my opinion... the only solution is to establish the individual... our problem in the Orient is that we don't have individuals... our problem in the Orient is that Oedipus is not from our country... here our God says to Ibrahim: you shall kill your son and offer him for sacrifice... Ibrahim does not try to ask his son what he thinks of the subject... The individual doesn't exist... while, if Oedipus comes from here... and that the Oracle tells him you shall kill your father and marry your mother... he would have told her: mama wait for me in bed... I am going to kill papa and then come... he wouldn't have resisted...

2348 I in my opinion... the role of theater is to establish the individual...

2350 the individual has a brand... we want to label the Lebanese citizen... he's branded ... labeled as individual... nobody goes on the street because of one of his civil rights... he goes on the road because of the *patron (zaʿīm)*... not because of the bread or some unjust legislation... I know from the media that is mutilating my life... in another country they would have destroyed many TV stations... the individual is not fulfilled... the major concern in theater or in TV productions should be the fulfillment of the individual...

2366 Qualité du texte. Une pièce qu'il faut écouter autant de voir. J'estime qu'au Liban nous avons passé de l'ignorance totale du théâtre à un théâtre avant gardiste en oubliant toute la trajectoire que le théâtre a suivi, ce qui fait que nous avons une forme de théâtre batarde que je deteste pronfondément parce que ça ne correspond à rien finalement. Ca ne trouve ses racines dans rien... ni dans les traditions populaires... ni dans les traditions sociales... ça ne trouve ses racines que dans les traditions commerciales et c'est très triste...

2367 Ensuite faire du théâtre pour une chapelle de pseudo... de pseudo-intellectuels qui viennent et qui croient déchiffrer dans des rebus intellectuelles dans pensées on ne peut plus ténébreuses [...] je n'aime pas cette forme de spectacle non plus...

2368 C'est pour cela que je vais essayer de faire dans ma seconde tentative une forme de théâtre très simple pour habituer les jeunes à venir voir au théâtre ... des choses simples dites facilement mais toujours en prenant en considération que l'enfant est le public le plus difficile qui existe... et qu'on ne peut pas le tromper et qu'on n'a pas le droit de le tromper... et qu'on a une très grande responsabilité en tant que metteur en scène vers le public d'enfants ... il ne faut pas déformer son goût... il ne faut pas chercher à l'influencer... il faut lui présenter des choses simples dans lesquelles il se trouvera et il comprendra de lui-même... on n'a pas besoin de lui ascéner des messages...

2369 Le Petit Prince... ils ont tout compris... Molière... j'ai monté »Le Bourgeois Gentilhomme«...»Le Malade Imaginaire«... je vais monter »Les précieuses ridicules«...La princesse Thurandaud...

2370 Le Bourgeois Gentilhomme»... tout le monde a retrouvé les côtés negatives d'une société libanaise qui est tournée vers l'Occident... qui qui se pique de vouloir jouer au bourgeois avant-gardiste... et qui n'a aucune

culture et tout est superficiel ... c'est un vernis de la société artificielle... c'est la seule pièce où j'ai ... parce que le texte le permettais joué sur un côté oriental parce que il y a une turquerie dans le bourgeois gentilhomme... dans la scène la plus spectaculaire... j'ai fait une Haflé à l'orientale avec ... du du ... Derbakké du Tablé avec danse orientale... ça a été un côté très libanisé dans la pièce et d'ailleurs la pièce a commencé en arabe et s'est terminée en arabe également... ce n'ai pas un mélange... j'essaie au contraire à travers de prototype de personnages humains de faire passer cela auprès des jeunes et ils le comprennent parfaitement... scolaires à partir de 7 ans...
2371 Ce qui nous manque c'est des auteurs dramatiques... ce sont toujours des adaptations...
2372 Qu'est ce que c'est que libanais? Traditions qui remontent si loin... ouvert à la mer ce qui fait que le libanais ne ressemblent à aucun autre pays de la région ni du monde... c'est un mélange de culture... sens de l'argent... sens du gain... c'est resté dans l'âme du libanais...
2373 Ce sont des nuances d'après moi... le chrétien a pris du Musulman ... tout le monde a pris de tout le monde...
2374 Rarement le public se mélange parce que les productions qui sont faites qui sont faites au Liban sont faites en fonction d'un public... ils ne sont jamais faites dans l'absolu ... on ne monte pas une pièce de théâtre parce qu'on aime cette pièce de théâtre... il y a ceux qui font le théâtre de facilité ... dans lequel le spectateur entre et sait d'avance qui'il ne va pas se casser la tête... qu'il entre ayant pay 15000 LL. Veut s'amuser pour ces 15000 L.L [...] il y par contre un autre genre... le théâtre politique... et se veut posant des questions mettant en cause le système dans lequel on vit et prenant partie pour une cause determinée... il y a un public... pour ce genre... il ne pense pas avoir des réponses à ses questions mais se retrouvera dans sa façon de penser et de revoir la société libanaise sous cet oeil critique... ces deux sont des productions ciblées vers le public... et automatiquement qui reçoivent en échange ce public pour lequel ils sont destinées... il y finalement très peux de pièces qui ne correspondent ni à ça ni à ça [...] ce genre de productions visent à attirer vers elle le spectateur qui veut s'amuser en essayant de lui donner quelque chose de plus serieux sans tomber dans l'excès contraire de lui donner des recettes politiques... de prises de positions... tranchées nettes et catégoriques... ce genre de spectacle est malheureusement le grand sacrifié au Liban... parce que jusqu'à présent il ne trouve pas un public... il cherche... mais ne trouve pas encore...
2375 Quand vous faites payer 20$ pour voir une pièce... je trouve cela une barrière qui empêchent beaucoup de monde qui aimeraient venir [...] et le théâtre est un plaisir que l'on partage... il y a très peu de gens qui

viennent seules au théâtre ... et cela revient trop chèr... le théâtre n'est populaire que dans une forme que je deteste c'est le théâtre de chansonnier... la les gens paient 21$ parce que on leur donne à boire on leur donnent à manger... on leur donne un spectacle qui ne coutent rien parce que ça se déroule sur un scène de 2 x 3 m. où l'on ne peut faire rien du tout... il n'y a pas de costumes, d'éclairage, de mise en scène, rien du tout...(the extended version of restaurant)... c'est de l'anti-théâtre... mis chemin entre le populaire et le politique... c'est une forme batarde... un mélange...

2376 Censure dans le domaine de la liberté sexuelle... on est plus libre politiquement... cela relève du fait que il ne faut au Liban ne heurter aucune susceptibilité [...] qui est une forme de qualité... on réagit souvent par susceptibilité et pas par sensibilité [...] et c'est dans les moeurs orientales...

2377 Le merchantilisme n'a pas réussi à imposer une liberté sexuelle dans le théâtre et dans la vie de tous les jours au Liban... c'est une forme hypocrite de présenter le sexe...

2378 Le théâtre est entré dans les écoles... dans quelques années nous allons avoir un public averti... chacun pourra retrouver dans ce monde du théâtre quelque chose qui le touche... option dans le baccalauréat... on les envoie voir des pièces de théâtre ... il n'y a qu'au Liban que ça se passe dans le monde arabe...

2379 Il y a eu des choses intéressantes qui n'ont pas été vues par tout le monde... elles ont été vu par des spectateurs qui savaient qu'est ce qu'ils allaient voir et donc c'est dommage parce que Il y a eu des pièces qui reflétaient une réalité que l'on ignorait dès qu'on était de l'autre côté de Beyrouth... Beyrouth Est ignorait ce que vivait Beyrouth Ouest et Beyrouth Ouest ignorait ce que vivait Beyrouth Est... Il aurait fallu au contraire que les gens de Beyrouth Est sachent ce qui se passait et comment vivaient les gens à Beyrouth Ouest et les gens de Beyrouth Ouest méritaient de voir ce que pensaient et peut-être de cette rencontre de deux choses complètement différentes il y auraient pu avoir des solutions à beaucoup de problèmes...

2380 Les médias ont été manipulées... il faut donner aux gens tout le temps de choses sensationelles... la presse est devenue merchantile... il faut lui donner du sang et du sexe... le public ne réagit plus qu'à ça [...] les médias désinforment... pour un but lucratif... politiquement ... socialement ... moralement... religieusement... il n'y a plus de conscience journalistique...

2400 Shoushou est un clown mais un clown inimaginablement fort [...] . le caractère qu'il a fait est pris ni de l'Egypte ni des Arabes ni de rien... c'est un caractère typiquement qui se trouve à Beyrouth... une sorte de charlatan... on voit le public au théâtre de Shehrazade... en descendant les

retardataires entendent la voix de Shoushou et commencent à rire... Shoushou est un génie... grand... comme Fairouz... on entend la voix et on est pris...
2403 D'abord... le théâtre c'est quoi... ? C'est un endroit où la société se ramasse [...] c'est un spectacle... seul art qui peut être vivant devant une société pas devant un individu... même le cinéma est individuel... quand on est seul dans une salle de cinéma on rit seul... si c'est une comédie... mais quand c'est la même situation dans le théâtre on ne réagit pas... mais quand tout le monde rit... on rit [...] donc le théâtre c'est un acte collectif... pas individuel... comme dans une église ou bien un mosquée... il y a une communication... aujourd'hui... l'homme est devenu individuel trop individuel s'assit devant la télévision... et mange... voit dans l'Internet... la nécessité du théâtre... il faut à tout moyen chercher a soutenir le théâtre parce que c'est un rassemblement collectif... l'église a aujourd'hui perdu de valeur... qui a remplacé... côté sentiment... le football... oui c'est la même chose... sentiment de collectivité... manifestation... collectivité... c'est cela qui est important dans le théâtre [...] Rock ... Beatles... ils sont géniaux... les idéologies ont toutes fait faillite...
2408 during the war... there was a threat to the people ... self conservation... existence... all religions... there was a segregation on all levels... confessional... ideological... familial... everything...
2419 we are a small country based on families... there is the relatives factor... we should not be afraid of it... when the family breaks down, lots of other things break down with it... freedom is existing in a very strong way...
2547 audience of all confessions... Our theater. Has audience from all confessions... Even the actors are from all confessions... And one family... Even lately we were performing in Syria... Even though the accent is strange for them but we had lots of Success...
2654 no doubt in Jounieh... they wouldn't be appealed like here... they would't be like here... I don't know... I didn't try in Jounieh yet...
2660 If I blow my belly (the guy is fact with a big belly) in Palestina, I will destroy Israel... Bar Elias... Bekaa... South... I will send you a patrol of the family »Hamiyeh« to ruin it for you...
2711 Al-Halaba was about two militia people meeting in the street... in the war talking about each other... about their relation to the street to the people to killing... it was a cry against the militias in the war...
2724 you cannot find a job with a doctorate unless you go to the confessional *patron (za'īm)*...he should give you a reference of acceptance... an OK... who is your *patron (za'īm)*?
2738 Field Note based on personal observation.

2810 regarding me personally... No... I mean I don't know him personally but from what I follow of his news... Of his theater... I feel he is a little bit away of what you mean with regionalism... Or confess... I don't want to say confessionalism... Related to him... Yeah... I feel him away like that... That is why I am coming to see him...

2855 the topic is very beautiful... the topic of our lives ... a live topic... not a fictitious one... we are all living this topic... we felt it because we live it...

2927 there is a difference between the mountain people and the coast people who are open to all streams...

2930 the meaning of tradition... the theatre... we are interpreting our life and our inheritance... on stage... we are incorporating these local issues... they are local but at the same time universal... but in geography,... thought, tradition..., logic, in a philosophy of life... Lebanese...

2937 the Arabs are nothing... they are pupils compared to the western cleverness... and the western crualty ... and the western egoism... and the western double-cross... and the western fraud... and the western treason... the westerner would sell God... but you will not write these things yourself... the westerner would sell God... to win... he slaughters his mother to gain 5 dollars... the Lebanese society...if we go back to theater... is an elitarian society ... if we consider theater in the absolute... i.e. when we take out the folklore and the Chansonnier... theater in Lebanon never had this interest... a large audience like football I mean... it was never so...

2942 there are theater houses that are also committed... those who took Brecht and worked on it... And...and imitated him and imitated others and they took Lupe de Vega... the stories of popular heroism... All had the same aim... and others... those who take the newspapers headlines and blow it in the play... as if you are reading daily things. Daily events... You laugh over a big event... a big scandal ... Politicians... This ends... as soon as the play is over it dies... even the audience... by going out start thinking about what to do next.

2943 »Amama al-Baab« all the parties are in this matter... the left-wing parties... in Lebanon and the confessional parties...[]... imagine people coming out of war... coming from Jounieh to present a play here... young women... going back home after the performance... are followed by cars...and threatened... by people coming out in the middle of the night...

2945 I am Christian Orthodox...because I am an Oriental... I live and hear the sound of the Mou'azzin and I feel it entered my heart... and my chest while asleep... I feel secure...in my plays you always find the Moslems and the Christians... I can say that I am Lebanese...

2947 ...there is a variaty of things...theater should be seen socially outside the hierarchy of the political leaders... those are forced to work on a confessional basis in order to keep their servants...if the Orthodox did not take care of the Orthodox community he will never become a minister for the Orthodox... and the Armenian... and the Shia... and Chakib as Orthodox the same... now I revealed myself... you will swear at me...

2951 with the globalization they throw at us and idea... a color... a movement... the specific will suffer but will revolt... because globalization is not able to wipe off the specificity of individuals and civilizations... and that's why... there is an Islamic resistance to globalization... the Moslem today in America... there are campaigns against him...

2994 they are not honest... there is something artificial... disgusting... they claim ... they claim they have something... and then they say that the people did not understand it...

3079 I am looking at this experience as a step on the right track in the search for an Arab art which has its identity and specifications, and that through the serious cooperation between the Arab intellectuals and creators.

Appendix B: Diagrams

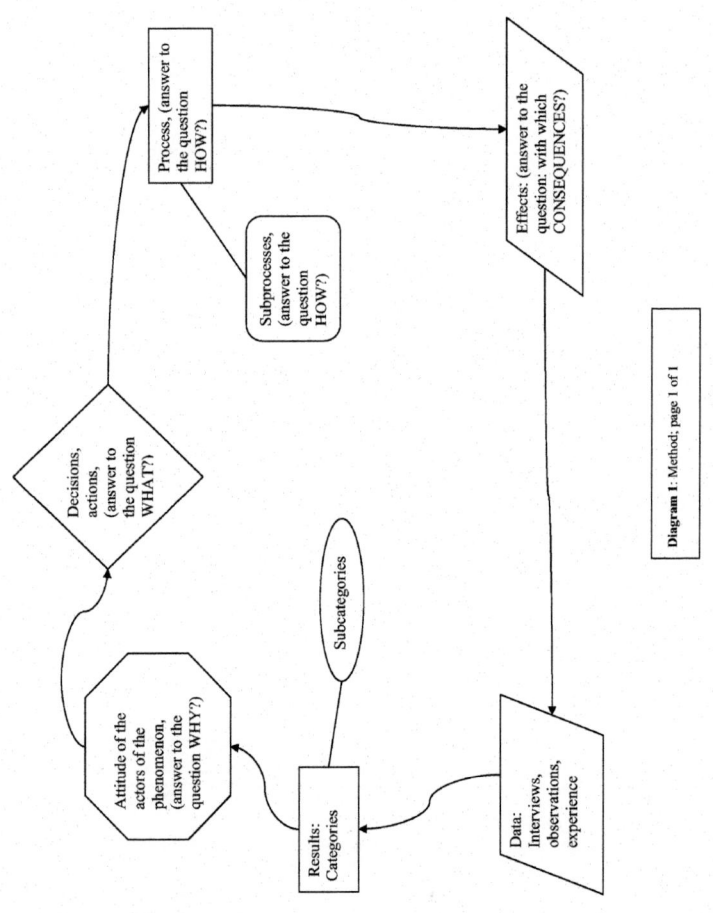

Diagram 1: Method; page 1 of 1

DIAGRAMS

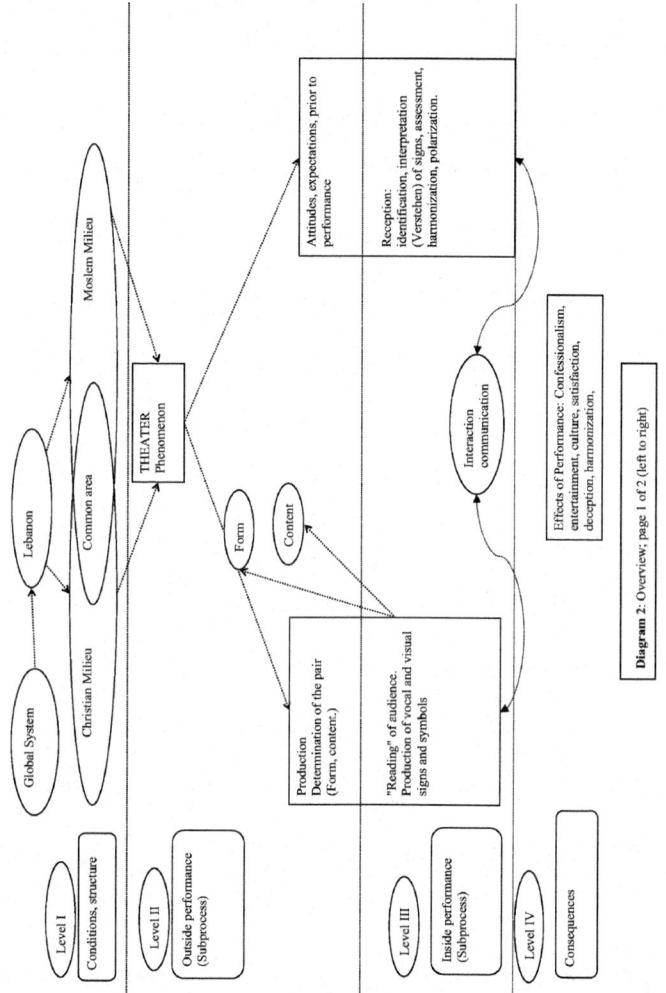

Diagram 2: Overview; page 1 of 2 (left to right)

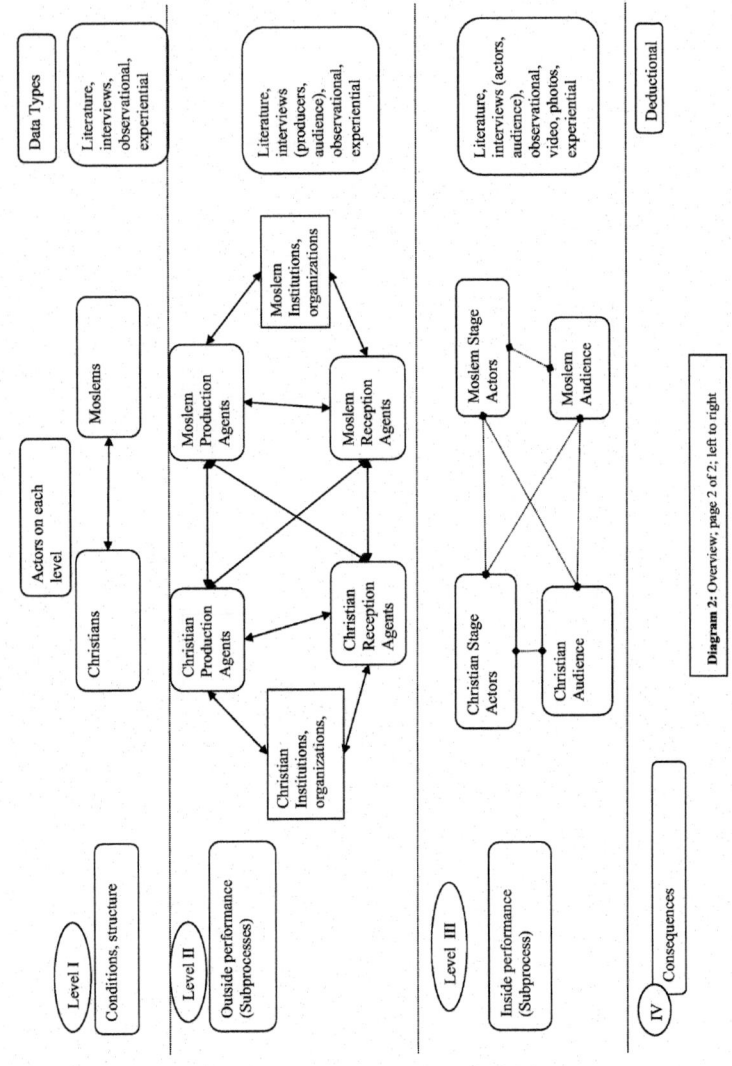

Diagram 2: Overview; page 2 of 2; left to right

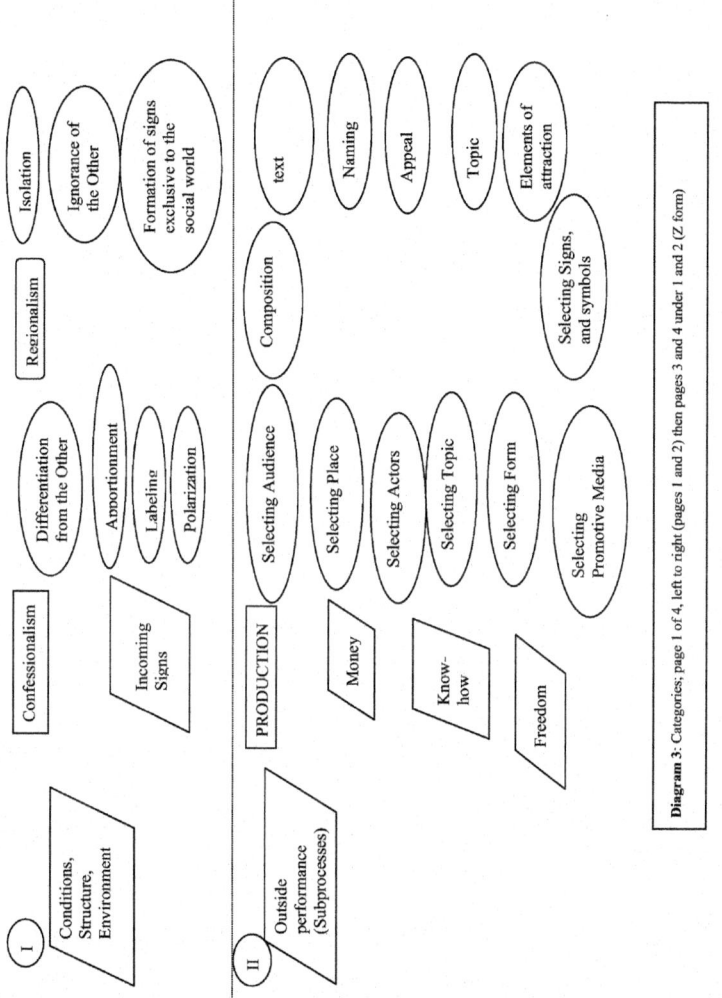

Diagram 3: Categories; page 1 of 4, left to right (pages 1 and 2) then pages 3 and 4 under 1 and 2 (Z form)

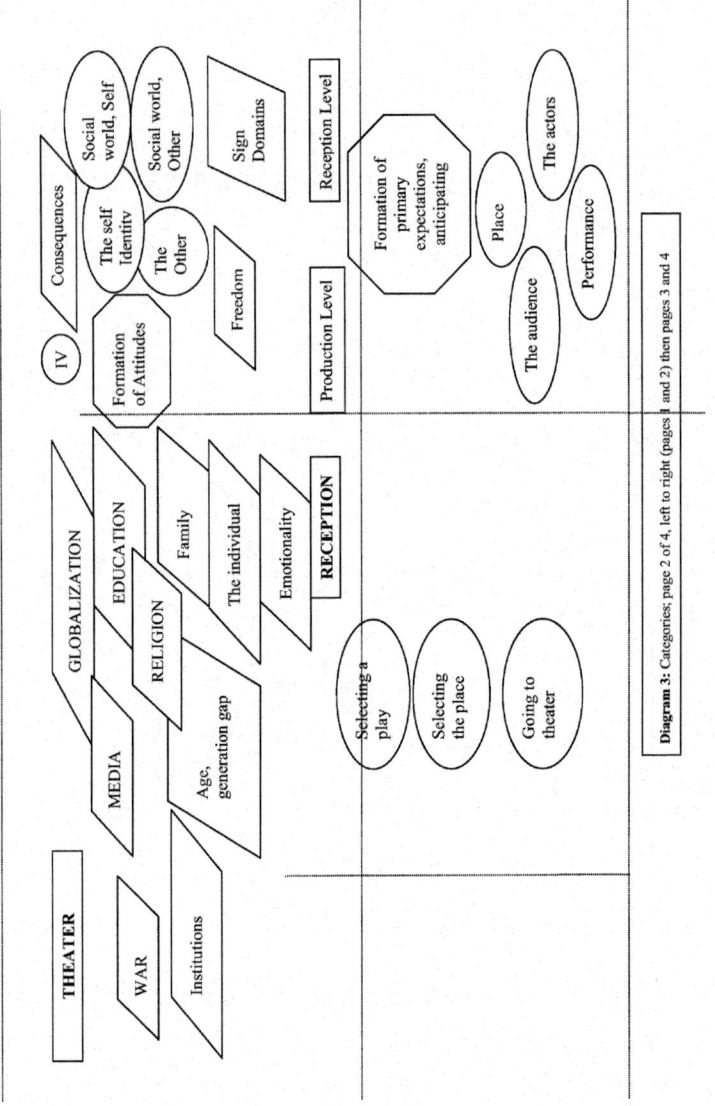

Diagram 3: Categories; page 2 of 4, left to right (pages 1 and 2) then pages 3 and 4

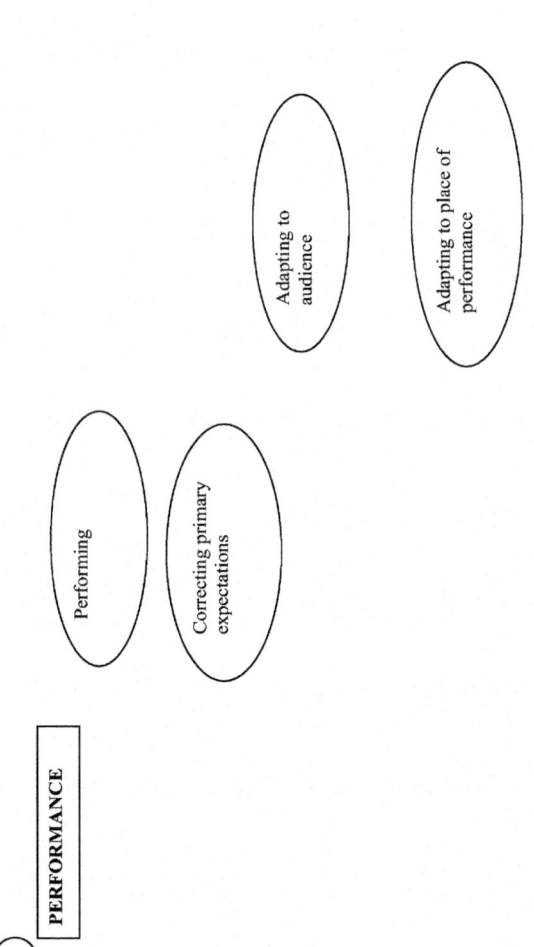

Diagram 3: Categories; page 3 of 4, left to right (pages 1 and 2) then pages 3 and 4 under 1 and 2 (Z form)

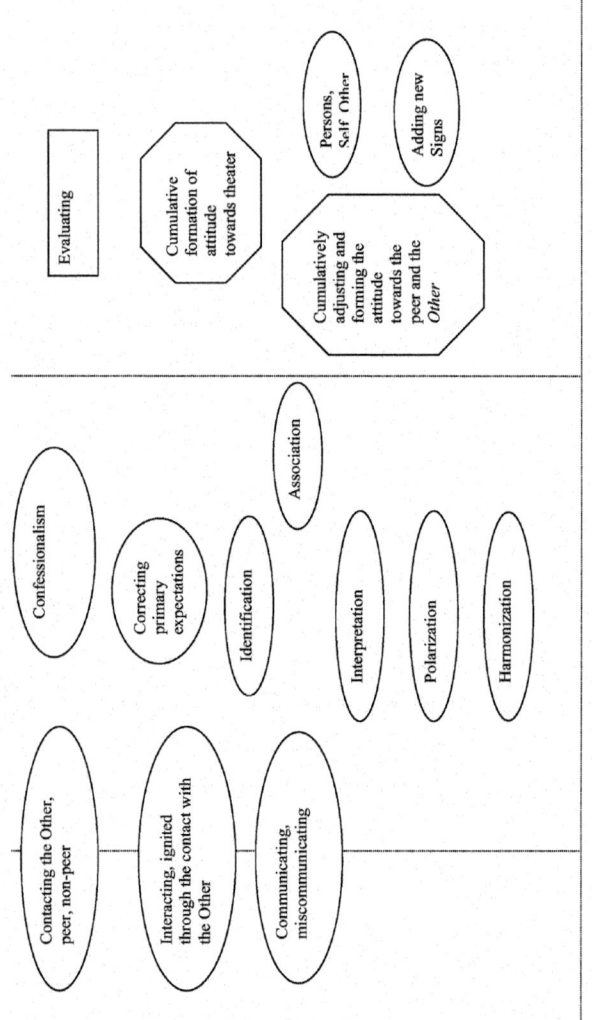

Diagram 3: Categories; page 4 of 4, left to right (pages 1 and 2) then pages 3 and 4 under 1 and 2 (Z form)

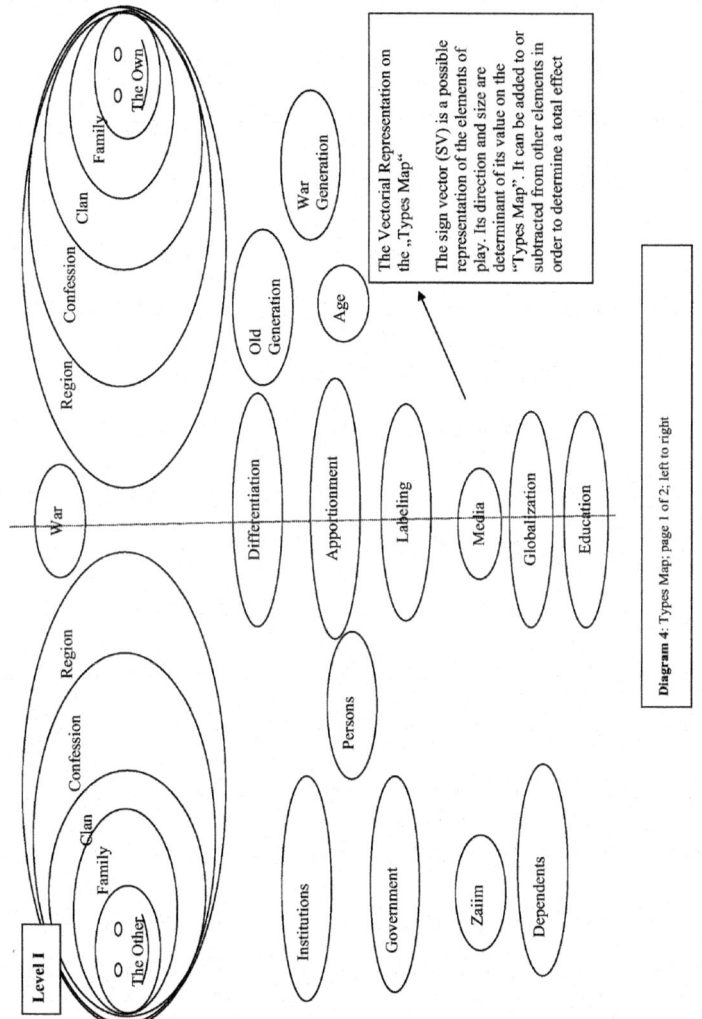

Diagram 4: Types Map; page 1 of 2; left to right

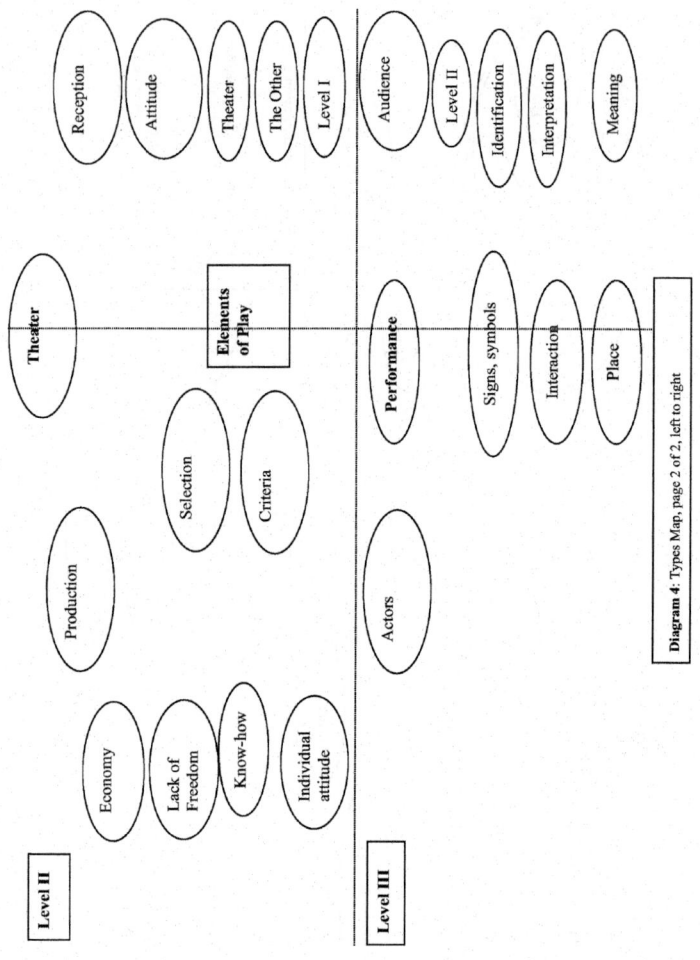

Diagram 4: Types Map, page 2 of 2, left to right

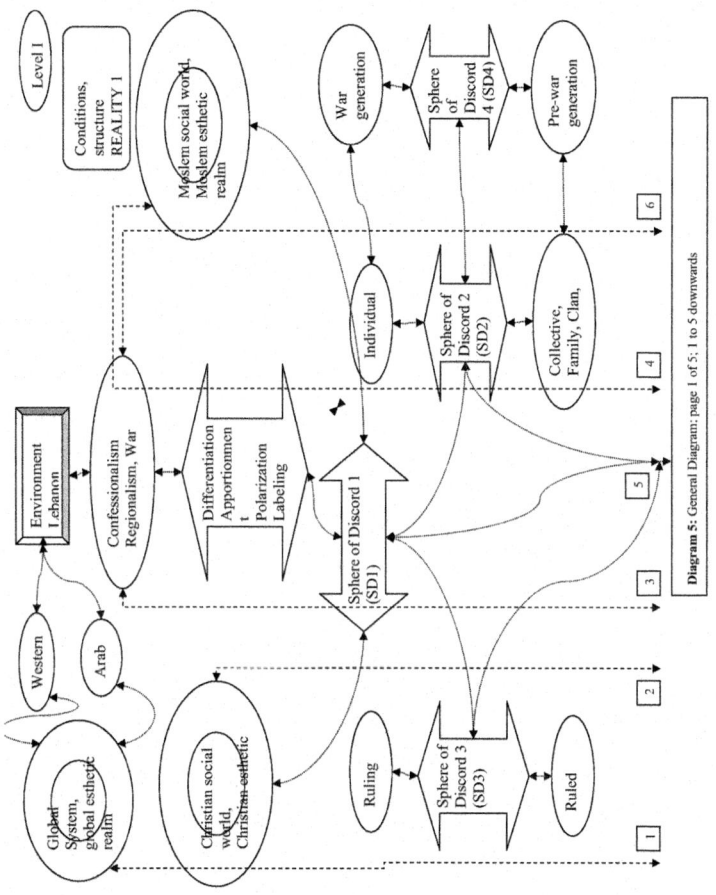

Diagram 5: General Diagram; page 1 of 5: 1 to 5 downwards

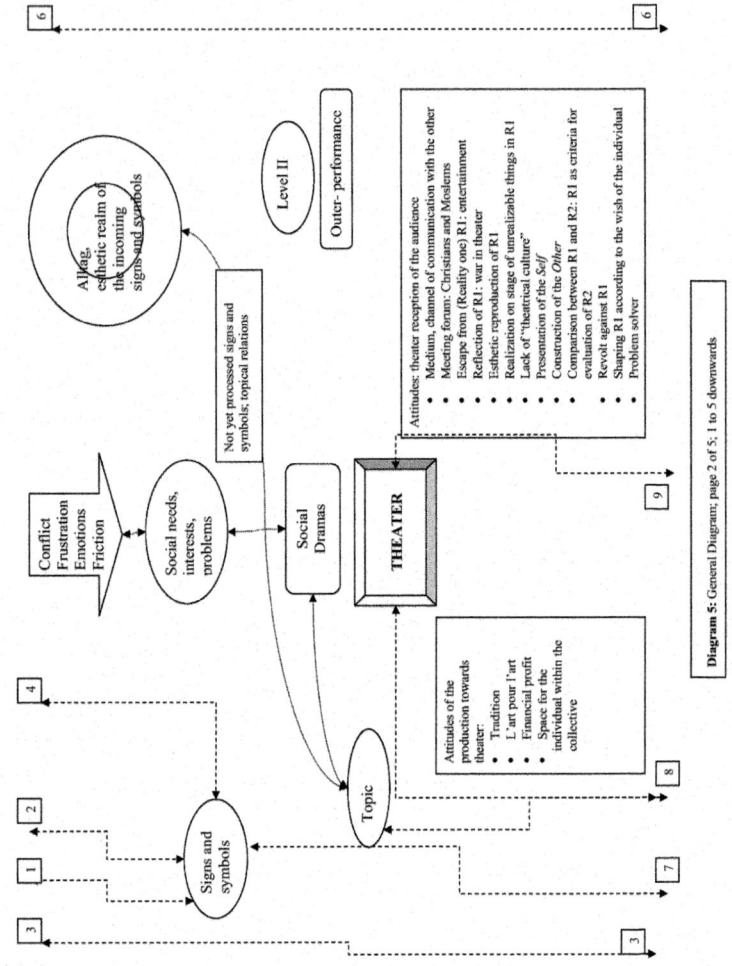

Diagram 5: General Diagram; page 2 of 5; 1 to 5 downwards

DIAGRAMS

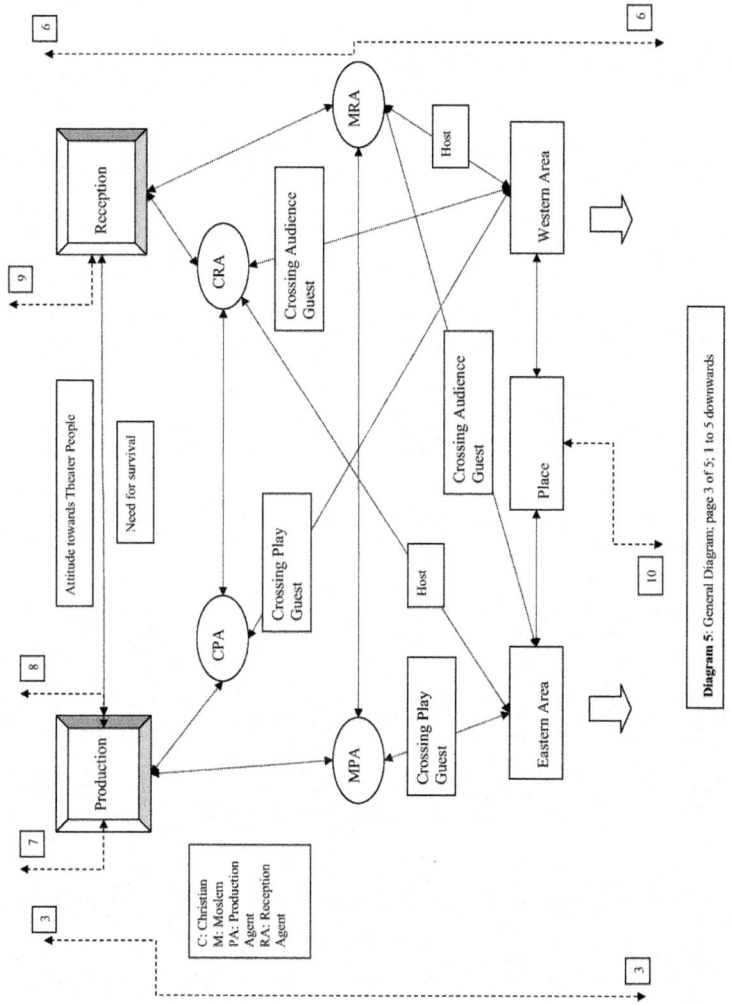

Diagram 5: General Diagram; page 3 of 5; 1 to 5 downwards

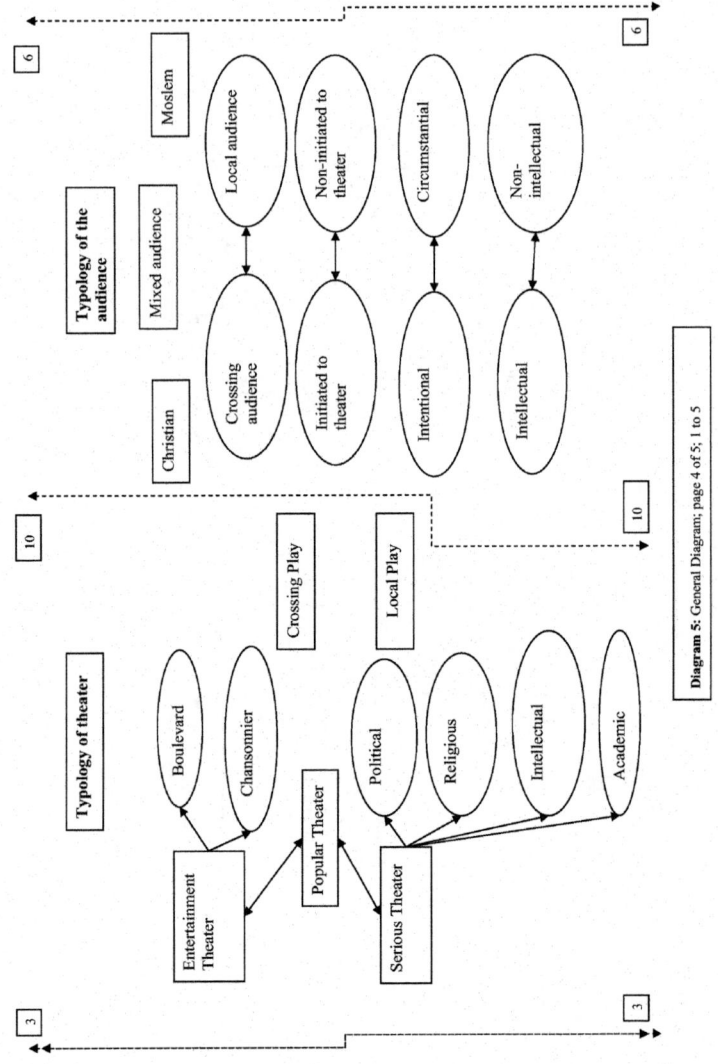

Diagram 5: General Diagram; page 4 of 5; 1 to 5

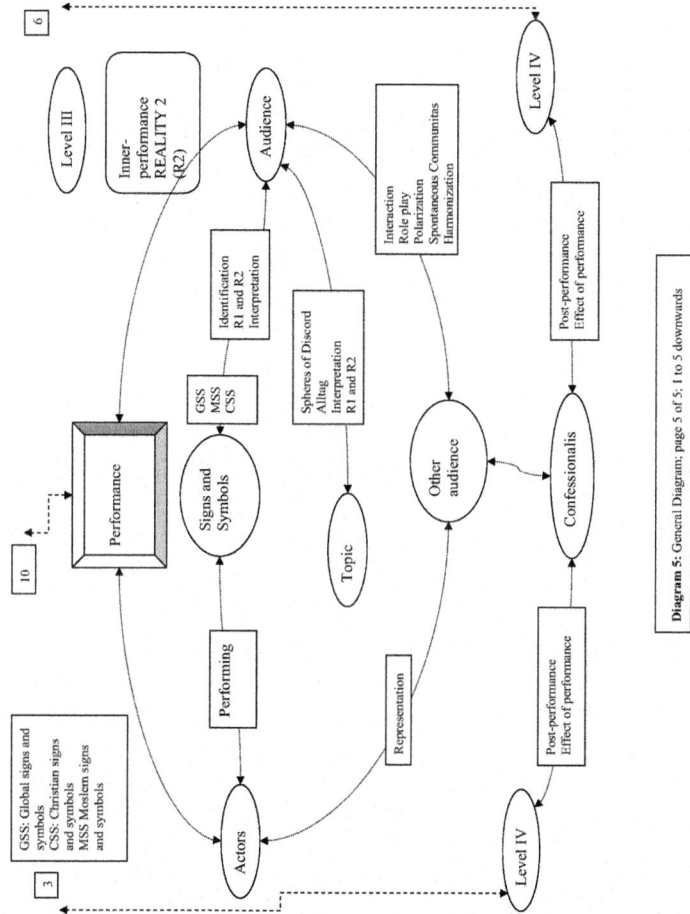

Diagram 5: General Diagram; page 5 of 5; 1 to 5 downwards

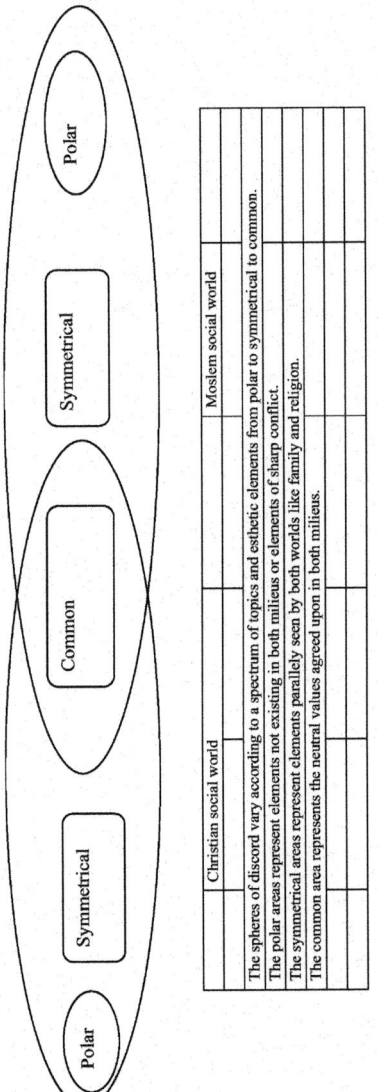

Diagram 6: Zones; page1 of 1

DIAGRAMS

Diagram 7: Statististical Figures		Frequency of occurence in coding	
Total citations from interviews	1787	**Category**	**Freq.**
Total non coded sections	518		
		1 Confessionalism	193
		2 War	107
		3 Role of theater in daily life	59
		4 Regionalism	59
		5 Identity	56
		6 Freedom	50
		7 Education	48
		8 Meaning of theater	36
		9 Age	35
		10 Globalization	34
		11 Money	33
		12 Sex	29
		13 The other	24
		14 Media	21
		15 Language	18
		16 Waasita and Zaiim	17
		17 Christian Vs Moslem	16
		18 Theatrical culture	14
		19 Family, clan	13
		20 Politics	8
		21 Individual	7
		22 Emotions	6
		23 Religion	2
		24 Moslem Vs Christian	2
		25 Alcohol	2

APPENDIX C: ARABIC TRANSCRIPTIONS

In the following, we find the transcribed sections of the interviews used in the analysis. All these sections were coded in order to reach the results presented in the research. The identification number, once entered in the electronic database, gives the name of the interviewee, the place, date, and other information. Numbers void of text are the result of automated numbering of the software used. They should be ignored, because they contain no data originally. Some were removed in order to keep anonymity. Through this numbering, we notice the evolvment from the line by line analysis in the first phases to section analysis at later stages of axial and selective coding.

Identification number

Text

1 The integral transcription of interviews
2
3
4
5
6
7
8
9
10
11
12
13
14 رقم Interview1
15 Cassette # 1 – Face A
16 س. ... 26 سنة ... اييم ... .س
17 ط. س.: شو دارسة وأديه عمرك؟
18 س.: دارسة حقوق... سمرا...... شوف كيف بعرّف عن حالي
19 كيف...
20 ط. س: OK مثلا؟ حقوق دارسة اذا مسرح تعملي عم ليش
21 س. : كرمال... اييم... لإنو اساسا ما بحب الحقوق... أمم درستا لانو لازم ادرس شي... اييم وعم
22 ...بعمل مسرح لانو سنحتلي الفرصة وبحب التمثيل
23 ط. س.: بتحبي التمثيل
24 س. : بحب أكيد ايه... وما كان فيه عندي... ما...ما كنت عارفة أساسا انو فيي ادرس تمثيل ويكون فيه
25 ...عندي شهادة تمثيلية... هلق يمكن ارجع ادرسا بعد وقت معين
26 ط. س. : مم... طيب ما زالنا حكينا عن المسرح بشكل عام... شو بيعنيلك المسرح؟
27 direct س. : المسرح هو تعبير عن ... فكرة ...()... جامدة... بتعبرها بطريقة حركة معينة بتعطيها

253

28 لشعب... بط... مسرحنا بطريقة ضحكة يعني... بتع... بتمثلهن أفكار عن حياتنا وبطريقة
29 مضحكة مسرحنا يعني.
30 ط. س. : أفكار عن حياتنا، طيب شو هي الافكار اللي برزت شوي بالمسرحية معنا؟
31 س... : اوه.. أكتر شي فيه كتير منها سياسي
32 ط. س. : سياسي
33 س. : ايم لانو هوي عايشين نحنا بمصخرة سياسية معينة ... ايبم ... كل العالم شايفتها بس ما حدا
34 بيسترجي يحكيها... بتفوتها عن طريقة نكتة بتسير تمرق سلسة أكتر
35 ط. س. : كبت حريات يعني؟
36 س. : أمم... مش كبت حريات يعني... استغلال بس... استغلال حلو... بطريقة حلوة... عرفت كيف؟
37 ...أنو
38 ط. س. : طيب شو بيعنيلك المسرح اللبناني بالذات؟ كيف بتشوفي انت المسرح اللبناني؟ فيه مسرح...
39 س. : المسرح اللبناني... فاشل
40 ط. س. : لبناني... ما فيه مسرح... فاشل؟
41 مسرح اساسا... ما فيه حدا يقدر الفن... اساسا public ما فيه... لانو ما فيه
42 ط. س. : يقدر الفن؟ بس انو بالمسرح العالم مش كلهن بيجوا منشان الفن؟
43 س. : ايه مش كلهن بيجوا منشان الفن... بس... انو... اللي اللي بيجوا ...عم بيجوا ليتسلوا وهني
44 أقليات... اللي بيجوا... اللي عم يدفعوا ويجوا ليتسلوا... هني أقليات... اللي بيقدروا يسمحوا
45 لنفسهن يدفعوا ليتسلوا... ايم
46 ط. س. : أهه... أقليات لانو العالم...؟
47 س. : عادة الواحد لازم يكون المسرح ببلد م... متمدن وبيقدر الفن... لازم يكون المسرح هوي
48 الأكل... هوي غدا هوي عشا... عرفت كيف بس عنا بلبنان ما ... مش المسرح منو منيح... انو
49 عادة الواحد بيفضل ما يتعشى يروح يحضر مسرحية لانو كمان بتغذيلو عقلنا d'un cer-tain
50 بس بلبنان ما فيه منها فيه واحد بيروح بيدفع عالمسرح تيتسلى point de vue
51 يعني Entertainment ط. س. : تيتسلى
52 س. : وأكترية المسرحيات اللي بتشغل المخ ما حدا بيحضرا وبتعتبر فاشلة بلبنان
53 ط. س. : فاشلة بلبنان... أي... اذا بدنا نعمل بس تحديد لمسرح لبناني... فينا نحددو اذا كان الموضوع
54 لبناني او اذا كانوا الممثلين لبنانيين او اذا كان معمول بلبنان او باللغة اللبنانية او كيف منحدد
55 مسرح لبناني؟ يعني اذا جبنا مسرحية لتشيكوف...
56 س. : ايه؟
57 ط. س. : وعملناها باللغة اللبنانية... صار مسرح لبناني؟
58 س. : لا أكيد أنا بعتبر أنا ما بعتبر انو
59 ط. س. : ايه حسب رأيك
60 س. : مسرح لبناني لا ليش ما فيه حدا بيجي بيكتب مسرحية مظبوط هوي بيكون لبناني وبيكتبها
61 مظبوط بجذور لبنانية بآثار لبنانية بتاريخ لبناني بكل شي لبناني سبق علينا أو هلق عم نعيشه...
62 ليه... ليه أصلا ما حدا بيكتب أولا لانو ما حدا بيقدّرو اذا كتب تانيا لانو اذا كتب وحدا قدّرو
63 بتجي بتدفع عالمسرحية وما فيه منتجين يعني بتتعذب لحتى يجي حدا ينتجلك المسرحية و...و
64 ...والجمهور ما بيرد هالانتاج يعني
65 ط. س. : الجمهور ما بيرد الانتاج ...يعني فيه مشكلة انتاج؟

ARABIC TRANSCRIPTIONS

66 س. : ايه فيه مشكلة انتاج لانو الواحد بينتج وبيشتغل شي ف...فن حلو بيلاقي انو ما فيه مردود يحوي

67 بالسينما صار نفس الشي ما فيه سينما لبنانية لانو بيشتغلوا وبيحطوا انتاج معين ما بيردوه... ما

68 حدا بيشتريه...

69 ط. س. : اذا كان فيه فيلم لبناني أنت بتحضريه؟

70 س. : .... اذا كان فيه فيلم لبناني... حسب فكرتو... انو اذا كانت فكرة كل العالم عم تحكي عنها... اذا

71 كان نص مم... مهم اذا كان... وخاصة اذا كان بيحكي عن عن لبنان يعني اكيد بحضرو

72 عن... مش ضروري لبنان كتاريخ... عن مجتمع لبناني ايه

73 ط. س. : يعني عن موضوع لبناني؟

74 س. : عن موضوع معين انو عايشينو نحنا

75 تبعك هوي اشيا يمكن عايشينا نحنا؟ intérêt ط. س. : الـ

76 أكيد غير هيك لا يعتبر لبناني... ليش لبدي جيب مسرحية من برا وأعملها ولبننها قول هاي

77 ...لبنانية... هاي منا لبنانية هاي لاني أنا منى قادر أعطي بقوم بجيب من برا

78 ط. س. : طيب برأيك ليش ما فيه حدا عم يكتب؟

79 س.. : لانو اللي بدو يكتب فيه كتير كاتبين...

80 ط. س. : امم

81 س. : وكاتبين اشيا حلوة... ومسكرينها... فيه كتير بعرف كتير عالم كاتبين بيقولو ليكو هالمسرحية

82 ليكو لوين بتودي ليكو شو أبعادها ليك... بالحكي. بس بالفعل تعا بيع هالنص ما حدا ما حدا

83 بيكب مبلغ تيشتري نص... عرفت كيف؟... وما فيه مش كل مؤلف هوي مخرج ومنتج... فيه

84 عندك مؤلف فيه مخرج بيتقبل انو انا ... ب بخرجها لهاي المسرحية لانو عجبتني فكرتها

85 فيه مخرج ومؤلف بس هني عطوا بس انا ok فيه منتج بيجي بيقلك انو bonsoir (للجرسون)

86 بدي اعطي المصاري اللي هيي... الشغلة... المظبوطة بلبنان اللي بدو يعطي المصاري

87 ...مصرياتو ما رح يرجعولو اذا رجعولو ما بيرجعولو مع ربح

88 ط. س. : امم

89 س. : يعني تشغيل المصاري بالمسرح ... ما الو ...مردود ... يعني حرام الواحد يعني... عم يقتل

90 ...مصرياتو بيكون

91 public اللبناني... كيف انتي بتقسمي الـ public ط. س. : طيب حكيلي شوي عن الـ اللبناني؟

92 اللبناني public س.. : ...الـ

93 ط. س. : الجمهور اللي انتي بتحسي انو هيدا جمهور بيفهم مسرح هيدا ما بيفهم مسرح او بتقسمي مثلا

94 مثلا من منطقة لمنطقة؟ public حسب المناطق ... بيفرق الـ

95 هوي اللي منبسطلو منبسبط فيه هوي اللي public نحنا public س. : امم... بيفرق الـ

96 بيفهم النكتة السريعة... هيدا ... صار غير نوع مسرح... ما فينا نحكي عن المسرح

97 لانو انا مش ممثلة مسرح général

98 ط. س. : لا ايه هيدي المسرحية بالذات

99 اللي بيهمنا نحنا هوي اللي بيتقبل النكتة السريعة وبيفهما public س. : ع مسرحنا... الـ بسرعة

100 ط. س. : مين بيكون اجمالا؟ ممكن من كل طبقات الاعمار؟

101 ...وال... العالم الكبار بالعمر... المتمدنين اكتر من غيرن الـjeunesse jeunesse س. : الـ

102 ط. س. : المتمدنين

103 يعني ... مش اللي ... مرق عليهن jeune س. : ايه... انو يعني... اللي... اللي عايشين حياة الوقت

104 ...وبعدهن لبنانيي وماع... ومن ايام زمان وهيك

105 ط. س. : هااللي بدي اسأل عنو بالذات... هل العالم اللي اعتبرناهن متمدنين هني العالم يللي... انو كيف فينا نقسم؟ 106
107 س. : هني مش العالم اللي معن مصاري... لا... هني العالم ... اللي عايشين بالحاضر يعني ... اللي عم بيشوفو برا شو فيه ... اللي عم بيشوفو كل المجتمعات كيف عايشة... يعني ... هوي المجتمع 108 معين ثقافي niveau اللي بيفهم ... اللي عندو 109...
110 ط. س. : ثقافة
111 س. : ايه اكيد ... انو غير هيك ما فيه... واحد مش مثقف ما فيه يستوعب كل الافكار ... بدو يحسنا كمان enchaînement d'idées ناس فاشلين عم نحكي عم نحكي تنحكي... بدو يكون اول شي عندو 112 بدو منطقي يتابع الش... لان نحنا كمان مسرحنا منو ... انو منو نكت بايخة عم logique يكون 113 نضحك العالم من خلالها لا هني نكت ازكيا ... فيه كتير فيه كتير ايام بتقطع نكتية زكية ما حدا 114 بيضحك عليها 115
116 ط. س. : هيدا كنت بدي اسألك لانو لاحظت مرتين مرق
117 س. : ايه ما حدا بيضحك عليها لانو ما فهموها امم بس نحنا مش شغلتنا نعلم نحنا شغلتنا عم نعطي ...اللي عنا واللي فهم فهم واللي ما فهم ما فهم 118
119 ط. س. : اجمالا أي public مثلا؟ اكتر شي بيتجاوب بأي منطقة
120 س. : بعد ما عملنا tournée؟
121 ط. س. : بعد ما برمتو
122 من 4 5 سنين ما فيني ما بتذكر كتير منيح... ايم... بس tourney?t س. : عاملي
123 ط. س. : كيف تقدريك؟ الجبل ... المدينة...؟
124 س. : لا المدينة اكيد اهم...
125 ط. س. : المدينة يعني بيروت؟
126 س. : ايه بيروت اكيد
127 ط. س. : وبيروت بكل...
128 س. : ضواحيها؟
129 ط. س. : ضواحيها؟ نفس الشي والا
130 س. : لا مش نفس الشي (واثقة من نفسها) يعني أنا بحس ... الضاحية الشرقية...
131 ط. س. : ها ها
132 س. : غير يعني بعتبر الضاحية الغربية هيي من الجبل كمان... ايه
133 ط. س. : من الجبل كمان لانها غير طريقة تفكير والا لانو...
134 س. : لانو... ايه... غير طريقة تفكير... أمم...بيستحوا يعبروا عن افكارن متل ما نحنا منعبرها...
135 ط. س. : من ناحية؟
136 س. : من ناحية الدين
137 ط. س. : الـ sex مثلا؟
138 س. : ايه قصص دينية يعني...انو... الدين حاددن لدرجة انو... مش كلن اكيد بس تلات ترباعن... اكيد تلات ترباعن... يمكن اقل شوي ما بعرف... تلات ارباعن بعدن عايشين بمجتمع كتير 139 متحفظ...
140 يعني بيعتبرونا نحنا البنات ما منسوا يمكن (تعبير اسلامي – افلام مصرية)... بيعتبرو انو الشاب يللي بيقول كلمة بذيئة كمان عيب (تأثير دراسة الحقوق) و... وقلال اللي بيجوا 141 يحضرونا
142 منن ... لانو معتبرينا هيك... عرفت كيف... بس ... فيه مجتمع معين منن بيجي بيحضر وبينبسط...143
144 ط. س. : بينبسطوا؟

145 س. : ايه

146 على الـ référence ط. س. : امم ايه بس بشو بينبسطوا انا لاحظت مثلا بالمسرحية فيه كتير sex مثلا

147 انكليزي) وكذا وتقريبا مرقت بكل السكتشات تخصصت للـ) indirect او direct (french)
148 sex؟

149 انو ... بيخافوا يحكوا ... sex س. : لقلك شغلة لبنان اساسا... اللبنانيي كلن ... بيخافوا من الـ عن السيكس

150 كلن بينفذوه بطرق كتير بشعة... وبيخافوا يحكوا عنو لانو بيعتبروا انو اللي بيحكي عنو
151 عيب... بس ما هوي اللي بينفذوا كمان كتير عيب اذا (بسرعة مستدركة) اذا بيعتبروا اللي
152 اهين الواحد يحكي عنو ولا ينفذوا عنا لا بيفذوا donc... بيحكي عنو عيب اللي بينفذوا عيب
153 بس صعب يحكي عنو يا ريت منوصل لمرحلة نحكي عنو متل موضوع متل حياتة مواضيع
...

154 ...انو ... شغلة... أنو sex متل موضوع اه... المدرسة... متل موضوع... كلو هيدا... كمان الـ
155 ...بدا تفكير بدا ذكا بدا تحليل بدا... منو شغلة عيب لا... مش عيب

156 ط. س. : فيه موضوع تاني مرق بالمسرحية... فيه 3 4 مواضيع مرقوا بالمسرحية فيه الكذب والفقر

157 س. : ايه الفقر لانو كلنا عايشينو... فيه كتار اللي عم يشتغلوا وما عم بيكفوا حالن... فيه كتار عم
158 يحترق دينن ليل نهار شغل وما عم يقدروا يكفوا ... اول ما يجي المعاش بيطير... هيدي كمان
159 حالة فقر... بس انو اكيد كلنا عايشين بس عالقد... عالقد عالقد عالقد... ايه وطبيعي نحكي عنو...

160 الكذب لانو كمان عايشين ببلد كلو لوفكة وكذب كلو تمثيل... ايه... السياسة تمثيل المجتمعات
161 تمثيل كلو تمثيل كلو كذب...

كل الليالي؟ بيختلف حسب public ط. س. : بدي اسأل كمان شغلة هلق هوني الـ
162 س. : ايم
163 public اكتر عم بيستوعب اكتر او اذا jeune ط. س. : حسب انت بتلاحظي انو اذا كان
164 universitaire اكتر اذا ناس

كتير مهضوم ... كتير بيتقبل كل شي و publique l universitaire س. : الـ165
166 او système américain مثلا AUB ط. س. : طيب الناس اللي بيتعلموا اذا كانوا تلاميذ système
نفس الشي والا بتحسي فرق اوقات؟ 167 USJ

168 س. : لا نفس الشي لا كل اللي بيتعلموا عندن نفس الـ... هلق نحنا عنا المجتمع مقسوم لناس معلمة
169 وناس مش معلمة وناس عايشة بالمجتمع بلا ما تكون معلمة بس بتفهم... واذا فهمت من الحياة
170 وهيك... انو تلات ترباعن العالم اللي هني مركزين حالن يعني... هني علموا حالن او معلمين
171 ...ايمم public نحنا اللي منعتبرن احسن public بالجامعات ... هني هو العالم الـ
172 وصار فيه كتير منن يعني اكتيرة اللبناني صاروا معلمين واكتيرة اللبنانيي صاروا اذا مش
173 معلمين ... يعني بيستحي بحالو بيعلم حالو يعني ... عرفت كيف يعني و... هيدا احسن
174 public...مهم يعني public عنا ايمم... وتلات ترباع المجتمع اللبناني صار

175 اساسي يعني thème اساسي أو problème ط. س. : طيب اذا بدنا ناخد بها المسرحية صارت مقسمة ع
176 طغا عالكل thème هودي بالتساوي او فيه
177 الطاغي عالكل ... أنو... البلد مجنون thème س. : الـ
178 ط. س. : هاها

179 س. : اييه... عايشين ... منعتبر حالنا عايشين... كلنا منعتبر أنو... من برا بتتطلع بالكل بتلاقيهن ع
180 يضحكوا من جوا بتلاقيهم كلن عم يبكوا... ايه... هلق هيدا هوي المجتمع اللبناني طول عمرو

257

181 مقتنع بالحالة اللي هوي فيها ولا مرة طلع منها ولا مرة قال انا بالقوة بدي اطلع اذا مش بالمنيح

182 بدن يطلعوني من هالحالة بدي اطلع بالقوة هيي حالة سياسية اكيد اساسا يعني... بلشنا فيها ...وبعدنا مكملين 183

184 وبالخبريات بتعرفي كيف... trio ط. س. : طيب هلق السياسة دايما كانت مرتبطة بلبنان بالـ تقسيمة

185 البلد والوفاق الوطني direct ... و...هالخبريات ... هلق هودي ما ذكروا بالمسرحية بشكل بس

186 فيه ممنوعات كتير... عندك 17 طايفة.. اذا بدك تحكي هيك لاحظ.. كل الاسامي بتكون نص ع نص لا اسلام ولا مسيحي... راحت الهوية...

187 فيه ممنوعات كتير... عندك 17 طايفة.. اذا بدك تحكي هيك لاحظ.. كل الاسامي بتكون نص ع نص لا اسلام ولا مسيحي... راحت الهوية...

188 ليه ما عملوا شي كوميك... يا خيي اللبناني طالع من حرب بدو يضحك... لا ما بدن يضحكوا بدن يبكوا

189 يزيدو قط يعني four cats المسرحية انتقادية بتعالج اشيا عايشينا العالم (...) مثلا هون الـ 190 لانو فيه كتير تلطيش anglais أو بالـ francais كل جمهور لازم يكون عندو فكرة شوي بالـ عهالناحية

191

192

193

194 المسرح منو شي اساسي... يعني الواحد اذا كان مرتاح بيحضر... اذا كان تعبان ما بيحضر... المسرح بيتأثر بكل شي...

195

196

197 هيدا بيحجب طبقة شوي منا فلتانة تجي عالمسرح

198 هيدا بيحجب طبقة شوي منها فلتانة تجي عالمسرح

199 الكلام زفر

200 هني اللي فرقونا الرؤساء... ما عندي مسلم ومسيحي

201 نحنا وقفولنا مسرحية... من سنة سنتين... اذا حكيت كلمة بيوقفولك مسرحك...

202 مصاري مصاري business كلو بالنهاية

203 مسرح ثقافي بس كمان بيدق بالشعب... مش محصور بـ 30 40 شخص بكل لبنان... مسرح ثقافي فيه يكون شعبي كمان...

204 العالم بتقول انو الشانسونييه منو مسرح لانو فيه أكل وشرب... لا الشونسونييه مسرح...بس مختلف عن المسرح

"المتعودين عليه... "مطار شارل ديغول

205 الغرد اللبناني بشكل عام اللي عطول بيفتش يشبه حالو للفرنسي أو للأجنبي وهالعوايد المترسخة عنا اللي منا عوايد من تراثنا...

206 التطرق للشي اليومي... والحديث عن سياسيين حاليين...

207 بلد متشعب الثقافات... خود أميركا...

208

209 Interview مع ج. ح

210

211 المسرح بيعنيلي حياة كاملة... أنا بقدر عبر من خلال المسرح...

212 اللبنانيي كانوا سباقين بالمحيط العربي بالمسرح

213 يمكن الحرب ... مع الاسف... أغنت المواضيع الكتيرة...

214 المسرح تتحكم فيه التجارة لانو ما فيه دعم من الدولة... واذا حصل الدعم بدو معارف وما فيه مسرح وطني
وما فيه مسرح وطني

215 ريمون جبارة بيشتغل مسرح... أحمد الزين بيشتغل مسرح... منير كسرواني... بيشتغل مسرح بس هودي خلي رأي
بس هودي خلي رأي

[...] الناس فيهم... نشوف كيف الناس بتشوفن

216 نحنا عنا كل شي بالوراثة... زعيم ابن زعيم يمكن بتظبط... بس فنان ابن فنان يمكن ما دايما بتظبط...
بتظبط...

217 نحنا عنا هامش واسع من الحرية...

218 نحنا اللبنانيي عنا هم بدنا نقولو فينا نقولو بالمسرح...

219 كان عنا جمهور ناضج... الظروف الاقتصادية انعكست عليه... هلق جمهور المسرح قليل...

220 العالم بيهمها تروح تضحك...

221 هلق بالمناهج الجديدة ... في شغلة مهمة... انو حطو المسرح مادة الزامية بالمدارس والثانويات...
والثانويات...

222 بدو يمرق جيل وجيلين... ليعرف الولد المسرح شو أهميتو... شو منافعو للشعوب... وين فيك تستعملو سلاح بوج
تستعملو سلاح بوج

223 ...الفساد... بوج الطغيان... بوج الانحطاط... بوج الجهل... بعدين بيصير في عنا جمهور لوحدو زياد بس غرب بطل حدا يفهم عليه... العالم عنا كمان مش مطلوب منها تفهم كل شي... بدك تفهمها...
تفهمها...

224 الواقع عنا كتير صعب... وبدك تفوت فيه بدك تكون مسؤول عن كل كلمة تقولها... زياد ما كان يهمو شي... كان يقول كل شي...
يقول كل شي...

225 الطائفية مرض عم نعاني منو كلنا... وهياني قاعد انا واياك... أنا من طائفة وانت من طائفة... مع الاسف منعرف انو
مع الاسف منعرف انو

كل واحد من طائفة مع انو ما لازم نعرف... وهيك العلاقات بالبلد...

226 ما الطائفية شكل من أشكال الظلم بلبنان... والدليل على ذلك... وقت اللي انطرح هيديك المرة... الزواج المدني بلبنان...
المرة... الزواج المدني بلبنان...

أول شي توحد... أول شي اتفقوا عليه رؤساء الطوايف... واذا واحد حكي كلمة عن التاني... بينشروا حريم بعضهم ليشبعوا...
ليشبعوا...

227 فيه شكل المفروض اذا واحد صار فنان... يطلع من هالقصة... ما بعتقد طلعوا منها عالآخر... لانو نحنا فيه بعض
لانو نحنا فيه بعض

الناس حملوا موروثات من الاهل... من البيئة... من المحيط... انت بتعرف لبنان... يعني بالحرب... تأثروا صار فيه
تأثروا صار فيه

ديموغرافيا لكل طائفة... يعني صار فيه تجمعات سكنية من طائفية ... بتجي بتقول طائفة بتعمر مجمعات سكنية
مجمعات سكنية

لطائفة معينة...بتجي انت بتسألني...بتقللي ولا بتسكن هونيك... ما رح سمي... بقلك لا يا خيي هونيك كلن من هول
هونيك كلن من هول

الطائفة... لا كلن من هيدا المذهب... لا حتى مذاهب يعني... ليه.؟. صاروا وصلوا لمرحلة للمواطن يعني بدون لا
يعني بدون لا

شعوريا بيقلك لا... اذا جيت زركتو بيقلك انو انا بحس بالامان بين ولاد طايفتي... مع انو أكتر شي بيبعصوا للواحد
بيبعصوا للواحد

ولاد طايفتو... لانو اذا انت الك حق بشي... ورايح تعملو بشهاداتك ما بتاخدوا لانو بيجي واحد من ابن طايفتك...
ابن طايفتك...

بياخدو على اسمك... ع اساس انو لازم يكون بالطايفة بس هوي عندو علاقات... انتي ما عندك علاقات... فمين عم
علاقات... فمين عم

يبعصك؟ ... ابن طايفتك [...] التقسيم الطائفي موجود... بنفسيات كتير من الناس... الفنانين... موجود... والدليل على
موجود... والدليل على

ذلك انو فيه بوط وفيه فرق... وفيه محسوبيات... هلق عملوا مسلسل عن عاشورا وهيدا بيخص الطائفة الشيعية
جابو... وهيدي شغلة كتير منيحة... جابوا موارنة... وجابوا روم ... وجابوا سنية... وجابوا دروز... وجابوا شيعة
وعملوا مسلسل...وهيك لازم تكون القصص... أنا ضد اللون الواحد... مش بالمسرح ... بالمؤسسات الاعلامية... بتفتح
عالاسامي بتلاقيهم كلهن من لون واحد... لتقلي انو ما في ... فيه... الطائفية معششة بالبلد... ...معششة... بكل البلد
التركيكة ركبها الانتداب وبعدا راكبة لهلق وفيه ناس عم بيغذوها... اذا ما كان فيه طائفية... في ناس ما الهن مطرح
بالبلد... ما انا واياك بدنا نجي ناخدلن مطرحن... واللي متلنا... فيه كل شي... حتى التجنيس عم بيتم عأساس انو
...رصيد هالطائفة... وغيرو... منشان الانتخابات
منير كسرواني جمهوره من لون واحد... بيعمل حفلة بالجنوب بيجي 2500 شخص... بيعمل **228** حفلة بمطرح تاني...
بيجي 300 شخص... لانو كمان الجمهور عندو اهتمامات تانية... ريمون جبارة يعرض شربل بصيدا يمكن ما حدا
بيجي يحضرا... يعرضها بجونية بيجي يمكن 2000 واحد... خلينا بكسرواني... ليه ما عرض بجونية...؟ لانو
جمهور جونية ما بتهمو هالقصة... آخر هم... ما فيه وعي وطني... صرلو فترة كبيرة مغيبين عنو هالمعلومات... ما
...ذنبو الجمهور... ذنب نحنا المثقفين اللي مندعي الثقافة... ومنتسلح ورا الطوايف
الناس مفرقين... الطوايف بشكل اساسي... الناس بيتقسموا يا طائفي... يا طبقي... نحنا عنا **229** السلاح اللي بيستعملوه
...بالشرق الاوسط والدول المتخلفة هوي الطوايف
بيقولولي أطرح أسماء... بطرح جورج... بيقولولي ما فيه حدا بالطائفة بينفع لها الدور... **230** وهيك صارت التركيبة... ليه
بيكون معاشي 4000 واذا اسمي محمد بيكون LBC يا جماعة ... ليه أنا اذا اسمي جورج بالـ معاشي 1000 بدون
...ما حس
231 Interview.
232 First let me talk about Armenian audience, and then I come to the Lebanese audience
233 Taste, some want to laugh, others want to have psychological plays
234 We don't have musicians here, [...]
235 I have had 10000 audience and now 2000
بيار شمسيان... مسرح لبناني أوطى منا... مع منير كسرواني بوزارة للهوارة... 700000 **236** ...حضروها
الرحابنة عم بيحطوا 250000 دولار ويبطلعوا 1000000 دولار **237**
238 الـ to please the audience لمستوى الفن... مش نحنا ننزل audience نحنا بدنا نشيل منير هيك it's easy
...عم يعمل هلق
...جمهورنا تعود ع المكسيكي... ما بيروح عالمسرح... بدو يشوف شو صار **239**
كمان... dish صار كل واحد يقعد بالبيت... يحط الكاس... يحضر تلفزيون... هلق صار فيه **240** يلي بدك... كبوس هاي
...هاي [...] شو بدو يروح عالمسرح هيدا
241 the theater is serving the public, giving what the audience needs, they are surviving

but not the art ... حيث بدن يعيشوا ... they must grow as an actor, producer, director [...]

242 we taught Lebanese theater, folk dance, to have an orchestra...

243 now we've gone down, we are not creating anymore, because one should be in his own
land to create... the Armenians in Armenia are very poor, but they very creative
because they are in their own land [...] not like us... we are forced to speak Arabic
French ... English... Turkish... and study in the schools 3 4 languages... they don't have
time to study those people [...] what to study [...] if we want to study the arabic culture...
that's not our culture [...] yes if you want to create you have to create through your own
culture [...] this is our problem... and they blame us [...] my students... they say they don't
like Armenians [...] this Tommy the one I liked very much... told me he liked two only
Aznavour and me... the Armenians he doesn't like [...] your don't know the problems of
Armenians here so that you don't like them [...] we came like [...] زبالة لهالبلد 1920 the
Turks slaughtered 1.5 Millions of us... the Lebanese don't know about the Genocide...
they know about 6 Millions of the Jews that were killed... this they know...

244 we have no tradition [...] we are a mixture with English and French traditions [...] if we
have christians and moslems... it makes no difference [...] there must be tradition [...]

245 there should be a continuation [...]
اسرائيل بتضرب ساعتين... بتروح الكهربا... أنا ليه بدي اعرق هون؟... بس حسوا انو بلشت 246
الثقافة ترجع... مع
مهرجانات بعلبك... دغري اجو ضربوا... حتى يروح كل... شي

247 my best audience were the rich people [...] why... because they have the means to go to
all sorts of theater [...] (relate to continuation)...

248 [...] إيكو بيروت ... كانوا يحطوا اشيا حلوة... راحوا وقطعوا

249 the christians are more advanced...

250 religion effect...taboo... سكرت [...] عيب the horizon of the people...
بيبلشوا يقولولها للوحدي عيب... عيب... غطي فخادك... بيكون عمرها سنتين... خلص سكر 251
... كل شي

252 you give them their freedom [...] they become like white paper... you can register what
you want on it... but if it is registered don't do this ... that... that... you close them

253 they used to look like dunkeys whenever they saw a skirt...

254 we also used to be dazzled when we see a minijupe... but you should give a chance to

get immune to it [...]
255 I told her please [...] leave just **5** cm up and we are OK... how would you work... she has

talent... and everything... but this is closed...

256 بيخافوا انو يمكن بكرة ما بقدر اتجوز [...]
257 بيقول AUB بعد ما حضرها دكتور من الـ ...Who's afraid of Virginia Woolf تعرفنا هلق عشرموطة

جديدة.. مش المدرسة بس العقلية وكيف واحد تربى [...]
258 if the girl kisses a boy... she is a whore now... he can fuck whoever he wants ... and it is

no problem... since I was **20** years old... it is like that [...]

259 كل واحد وحدو ما بيقدر يغير...
260 Chute libre [...] back to zero every time...

261 بدن نحنا حمار... جحش يركبوا عليه... مين عم يخرب ليش عم يخرب ما بعرف... مشروع الاوبرا... قال مليون دولار ما فيه...

262 theater and music should be part of education...
263 (proudly made in Lebanon; Israel destroying the culture of Lebanon)...

264 كان فيه عندي واحد بيصبغ صباطي... كان عندو 7 8 أولاد... قلتلوا كيف بدك تطعميهن... قلي... الله

بيبعت...شو اذا ما بـ [...] بيبطل الله يبعت... علمتو انو يوم الـ 14 ما بتـ [...] ... هلق كل ما يشوفني بيقللي 14... هيدا بدو يحضر مسرحية؟...

265 my mother...we were not allowed to kiss our children... that means not allowed to kiss

your sin [...] but I am ... her son... see the difference...

266 ما عم يتركونا نكبر... منشان هيك ضربت اسرائيل [...]
267 لانو : س. déjà يعني المسرحيات بكل يذنكروا عم كانوا...direct قصص نذكر فينا ما direct لانو
268 واللي تعجبت انو كان فيه ناس مثلا ذكرت indirect ط. س. : ايه اكيد بس انو انذكروا بشكل اسامي انو
269 اشخاص...

س. : ايه هلق نحنا فينا نذكر اسامي اشخاص... اييمم...اسم رئيس جمهورية قديم منعونا **270** نذكرو لانو

رئيس جمهورية فينا نسمي بنص اسمو مش بكل اسمو... بيعلقو على ابيخ القصص... في **271** قصص بالامن العام كان لازم ما تقطع قطعوها... وفيه القصص اللي بتضايقن من ناحية **272** انو...

الشخص ... بيأثر عليهم اذا عرف عم ينحكى عنو... عرفت كيف؟... هيدولي الاشخاص **273** القانون والاشخاص ودولة المؤسسات) اللي منعونا نحكي عنن ... بس اكثرية السياسيي مش) **274** ممنوع نحكي عنن الا الناس اللي... نوعا ما مهمة **275**...

...ط. س. : بس اسألك شغلة هلق اذا نقلتو من منطقة لمنطقة ... بتلعبوا نفس الشي والا **276** س. : ايه لا ما منغير اسم فلان لانو هوي حاكم هون ولا نايب هون **277**

تنقول sex ط. س. : لا مش هيك لانو فيه نكت مثلا فيه نكت كانت بموضوع معين مثل **278** حساس بمنطقة
س. : لا لا لا لا لا أكيد **279**
ط. س. : ما **280**
مرقت عالامن العام déjà س. : أكيد **281**
الجرسون : عملنا قهوة **282**
س. : merci... thanks **283**

284 ط. س : merci كتير
285 س. : وسط ولا مرة
286 الجرسون : لا مرة
287 س. : انا بدي سكر اذا ما فيه ازعاج بدي عذبك
288 ط. س. : انا لا مظبوطة
289 س. : انت بدك مرة... اييه بقى... لا مبدئيا بكل المناطق نفس الشي... نفس الشي لانو déjà مرقت
290 ...عالامن العام ووافق فيها بحياالله منطقة معينة عرفت كيف ع كل... المناطق اللبنانية donc
291 ما ح télévision ما منخاف من حدا هودولي افكارنا ومنقولون [...] عم منقولن على الـ نسترجي
292 ...نقولن عالمسرح
293 ط. س. : ok احسن نقطة عجبتك او بتحسي انو الجمهور دايما بيتجاوب عليها؟ أي احسن شي عجبك بالمسرحية...
294 س. : امم... الانتقاد السياسي... ممم ... كلن بيحبوا... كلن بينبسطوا... كلن بيقولوا برافو... بس ...
295 المشكلة انو ما عم نقدر نوصل انو نخلي اللي عم نفكر فيه يسير واقع مظبوط او اللي عم نقولو
296 يسير جدي... حتى نحنا... حتى نحنا... حتى نحنا انو منمثّل بس بتجي لقناعتنا انو... ما فينا
297 نعبرن بطريقة حقيقية اكثر... عرفت كيف (قطشة قهوة)
298 ط. س. thème؟ يعني : كيف قلت بتحددي المسرح اللبناني قلنا حسب الـ
299 س. : بحدد المسرح اللبناني كيف يعني حسب الـ thème؟
300 ط. س. : يعني أي منعتبرو مسرح لبناني قصدي بس؟
301 س. : المسرح اللبناني هوي المسرح المسرح... يعني ما بدنا نعتبرو... ما فيه مسرح لبناني ... بس انو
302 اذا بدو يكون فيه مسرح لبناني لازم يكون المسرح اللي كل العالم بتحكي عنو هوي ... المسرح
303 الفكري المسرح اللي بيعبر عن افكار ... المسرح اللي فيه يقوّم شعب معين هيدا المسرح بس ما
304 فيه منو ما حدا بيسترجي يعملو واذا ما حدا بيفهمو واذا فهموا ما حدا بينفذو...
305 ط. س. : مع انو هلق الشانسونييه هلق بكل لبنان
306 س. : الشانسونييه اللبناني اكتريتو مادي... اكتريتو تيطلع مصاري... ايه ما ما فيه لانو... ما فيه ع
307 لانو لو ما فيه مشكلة مادية بالبلد... حتى لو واحد بيحب الفن للفن ما ح déjà عالم بتسترجي
308 يجي يعطي مصرياتو كرمال الفن للفن لان بيموت من الجوع... عرفت كيف انو... يا ريت
309 منوصل لمرحلة حدا يجي يقلنا فيه تمويل مسرحي بلبنان وعوا هالشعب بس حتى اللي بيقدر
310 يمول ما بدو يوعي الشعب لأن اذا وعاه بيبطل هوي ممول... (تضحك). عرفت كيف...؟
311 ط. س. : ok طيب thank you very much
312
313
314
315
316
317
318
319
320
321

322
323
324
325
326
327
328 المجتمع الاسلامي لا يحتاج للمسرح... كل شيء محلول بالدين...
329 المسرح بحاجة لقضية
330 كل شيء محلول بالدين
331 عنصر الطرب يغني عن المسرح
332 منطقة غير منطقتي
333 الاعلان ما بيجيب حدا ع المسرح
334 طروحات غير طروحاتي
335 المسرح يعكس الواقع، هو ليس عنصر تغيير ولا يعمل ثورة
336 العلاقة بين العمل المسرحي والجمهور ليست بحاجة للـ LBC
337 هوية الفرد تحدد بانتمائه في لبنان
338 لا يوجد تفاعل بين المنطقتين
340 المسرح محسوبيات، وراثة
341 لا مسرح وطني
342 المسرح هم اجتماعي
343 نقص في الثقافة مسرحية
345 المسرح اداة توصيل نظريات يسارية، فشل
346 العقلية
347 الذوق
348 المسيحيون لا يحضرون المسرح هنا
350 المسرح مرتبط دائما بحركة فكرية
351 علاقة الفلسطينيين بتدمير الدولة اللبنانية
354 يعاني من حالة قرف
355 الناس في حالة جوع
357 تقسيم الجمهور حسب العمر
358 لا يذهبون الى المسرح 18-22
359 جمهور استهلاكي 23-40
361 بكتب متل ما بحس
363 أزمة مواضيع في المسرح
364 Joindre l'utile à l'agréable
366 رموز طائفية، ربطها بجمهور طائفي، أسباب تجارية
367 ثقافة
368 حرية
370 اللبناني يسعى الى تقليد الفرنسي (الاجنبي)
371 الحياة اليومية خليط
372 حرية
373 تعبير عن الرأي
374 عصر انحطاط
375 طائر الفينيق
376 تشاؤم
377 نعم يوجد اختلاف
380 الذوق العام وذوق العامة
381 استحضار المسرح من الخارج
382 المسرح الدائم

383 مسرح ثقافي يعني المعنيين ولا علاقة له بالجمهور
384 أنا اربي علاقة مع الجمهور
385 المسرح ظاهرة
386 Theater is a collective need
387 Theater is cumulative
388 Educational
389 Strategic
390 Quality of life
391 Celebration of life
392 الجمهور له أعضاء تناسلية، له عقل، مشاعر، وغيره...
393 الجمهور بحاجة للترفيه بعد الحرب...
395 يعاني من مشكلة حرية
397 الحرب: توقف المسرح، ظهور الشانسونييه
398 جمهور الحرب: خوف من الموت، مسرح سهل
399 تجارة
400 أضحاك الناس
402 دور الدولة: ادخال المسرح في المدرسة ما قد حصل مؤخرا
403 Le théâtre est un acte social
404 au cinema le spectateur est un individu
405 au theatre il est en collectivité avec les autres
406 Besoin
407 Nécessité
409 نحنا لازم نكون بأوروبا بأميركا مش عرب. مشكلة هوية وانتماء
410 we are culturally imperialized
411 The medium is the message
412 theater is an instinctive need
413 نقص بالثقافة المسرحية
415 ما فيه مسرح، كلها محاولات افرادية
416 لو بتحكيها بصدق وعاطفة
417 نفس الكلمة بتقولها بطريقتين مختلفتين بتعطي مفعول مختلف
418 مسرحية "جنينة الصنائع": موضوع الحجاب
419 (بالنسبة للمسرحية المتعلقة بالحجاب)
المسيحيون: الموضوع ما بيعنينا
المسلمون: عم بتنمر ع الحجاب والاسلام
420 المسلمون: عم بتنمر ع الحجاب والاسلام
422 المسرح مهتم بالتجارة
424 يختبئ وراء اصبعه
425 جاهل
426 كذاب كما قال عنه ريمون جبارة
428
429 الجمهور لم يصفق الا عند انطفاء الانوار وبدافع من أحد المشاهدين دائما
430 لم يهتم الجمهور بشيء سوى ببعض الحركات الجريئة على المسرح
431 مسرحية تثقيفية
433
434 أجواء بيروت قبل الحرب
435 incestالجمهور صفق للحظات الجريئة: قبلة،
436 faire l'amour avec une mineure
437 culotte on stage
438 المصورون اخذوا صورا عند هذه المشاهد

265

440
441 "منطقة مقطوعة على الحدود مع "الحزام الامني
442 الناس بتحب تجتمع
443 هيدي المواضيع بتهم كل الناس
444 فيه ناس بتفكر وبتفهم
445 فيه ناس بتحب البسط والضحك
446 فيه ناس كانت لاول مرة عم تحضر مسرحية
447 فيه ناس ما فهموا شي
448 مفهوم المسرح جديد
449 الناس تذهب الى المسرح بهدف لقاء اجتماعي وليس بهدف المسرح أو المسرحية
451 المسرح مهنة
452 ترفيه وضرورة في الحياة
453 لا يلغي الفرد
454 passif
455 tradition
456 لا يوجد مشاهد فرد
457 هوية المسرح تتأثر بهوية الجمهور
458 مشكلة تواصل
459 مشكلة تراكم
460 نعم يوجد طائفية
461 جهل بالشخص الأخر
462 عقليات مختلفة والعمل معها يتطلب جهدا مضاعفا
463 يقولون انهم غير طائفيين ولكن تركيبتهم كذلك
464 المسرح افراز هذا المجتمع لذلك: فهو طائفي بقدر ما المجتمع طائفي
465 في الفرع الاول، لا يمكن أن يطلع مسيحي أولا
466 في الفرع الثاني، لا يمكن أن يطلع مسلم أولا
468 مسلمة في منطقة مسيحية
469 الحرب
470 ثقافة مسرحية
471 تعويد الجمهور على الالعاب المسرحية
472 النظام الاقطاعي
474 globalisation
475 تعددية ثقافية
476 تعددية لغوية
477 الحرب
478 الحرية
479 الطائفية
481 المسرح حاجة تثقيفية، ترفيهية
482 معلومات
483 حياة اشخاص
484 الحرب
485 the audience is what you make of it
487 christian communist in Moslem area
488 نجاح لرفيق علي احمد: لانهن بيحبوا يشوفوا واحد اقل منهم
489 مشكلة اندماج
490 غير مقبول في المنطقتين
491 twilight zone
493 انقطاع بين المناطق
494 مع أو بدون اعلان نفس الجمهور عدديا

ARABIC TRANSCRIPTIONS

495 أنواع المشاهدين
496 guichet minority
497 ضمان: بيحس حالو مبلوص
498 نخبة مثقفة
499 المسرح تهذيب للغرائز والاحاسيس الانسانية
500 الوطنجيات
501 ما بيحضروا اعمال غيرهم
502 الغاء الاخر
504 التفتيش عن الذات
505 المسرح حاجة
506 حياتنا، تراثنا، قضايانا، جغرافية، فكر، تقاليد
508 الاسلام تحدثوا عن شوشو، شامل، مرعي
509 (المسيحيون ما جابوا سيرتو (شوشو مهرج
510 هناك عزل للمناطق
511 Hommage seperately celebrated in East and West
512
513
514 Interview
515
516 أنا لبناني بس مش لبناني بذات الوقت... غربي... أميركا، اللغة، طريقتهم بالحكي
517
518
519
520
521
522
523 عنا نمط حياة مختلف هون بالشرقية... غير عن الغربية...
524 نكت من المنطقة ع رئيس بيمون ع المنطقة تحت. كلمات من المنطقة.
525 نكت من المنطقة ع رئيس بيمون ع المنطقة تحت. كلمات من المنطقة.
526 نكت من المنطقة ع رئيس بيمون ع المنطقة تحت. كلمات من المنطقة.
527 نكت من المنطقة ع رئيس بيمون ع المنطقة تحت. كلمات من المنطقة.
528 أنا لبناني بس مش لبناني بذات الوقت... غربي... أميركا، اللغة، طريقتهم بالحكي
529 نكت من المنطقة ع رئيس بيمون ع المنطقة تحت. كلمات من المنطقة.
530 يا مش فاهمين شي من كل اللي عم نقولو... يا نحنا بايخين لدرجة فوق الطبيعة
531 نحنا منعرف من زقفة العالم بالآخر... سكيتش الملاك ... مع أنو هيدا أذكى سكيتش بالمسرحية ولا مرة بحس العالم
بيتجاوبوا معو...
532 بلد ديموقراطي وما فينا نحكي كلمة...
533 مجرد ما يسمعوا سبينا الحريري بيبطلوا يضحكوا ع شي...
534 موضوع السيكس: اذا من شباب، صهيل من الضحك، يوقفوا، وتحميس، اما اذا كان حكي من ولبس osé بنات
وكذا ما بيتقبلو... بيسكتوا... فيه شباب بيصوفرو... نحنا منجرب نخفف المشهد
535 موضوع السيكس: اذا من شباب، صهيل من الضحك، يوقفوا، وتحميس، اما اذا كان حكي من ولبس osé بنات
وكذا ما بيتقبلو... بيسكتوا... فيه شباب بيصوفرو... نحنا منجرب نخفف المشهد
536 ميشال عون صار آخر هم العالم. من 4 5 6 سنين كنت اذا سمعت اسمو يطلع زقيف وهيك... هلق صرلو 10 سنين
عايش بفرنسا راح من ذهن العالم
537 المعتقد بيأثر ع طريقة التفكير

538 باتمنى ما يكون فيه عنا افكار مسبقة ونقدر نعمل مسرح لكل لبنان... مش ننطر بكل منطقة نغير لانو نحنا منفكر انو هون مسرحنا متعلق بفئة معينة... بمرسي كتير كان فيه فكرة بتهم كل شخص... هوي كل واحد بيفسرها ع طريقتو بس بتهم كل العالم

539 باتمنى ما يكون فيه عنا افكار مسبقة ونقدر نعمل مسرح لكل لبنان... مش نضطر بكل منطقة نغير لانو نحنا منفكر انو هون مسرحنا متعلق بفئة معينة... بمرسي كتير كان فيه فكرة بتهم كل شخص... هوي كل واحد بيفسرها ع طريقتو بس بتهم كل العالم

540

541

542 مسرح مارك قديح بعد مرسي كتير معمول للمنطقة هون... لفئة معينة... ما عاد لكل لبنان

543 مع العهد الجديد خف حماس الناس لاشخاص واسامي، يعني صار فيه ناس بيضحكوا ع الحريري حتى لو كانوا من المنطقة الغربية وبيحبوا الحريري

544

545 يمكن عم يفهم الجمهور عم يضحك مع انو هيدا واقع عم نعيشو. يمكن comique الـ message مش الـ message الاساسي.

546

547.

548 لعب ع الكلام ومسبات بمشهد دوبلاج ماريو. الجمهور كتير بيحب هالمشهد

549 كل شيء ممنوع مرغوب... نحنا منقول اشيا ممنوعة منشان هيك بيحبوا العالم هالشي

550

551 مخصص لفئة من العالم TV كل سكيتش بالـ

552 بالنهاية الانسان اللبناني هوي لبناني... يعني عقليتو وحدي تفكيرو واحد عاداتو وحدي... بس في أوقات انو المجتمع... انو فيه شوية تقاليد بتتغير... يمكن... بس ما بعتقد انو فيه هالفرق الكبير... بتلاقي العالم وين ما كان تحت... وهون... يعني فيه

553 sex بس بيختلفو انو 3 فئات... ناس بتحب السياسة ناس بتحب الاجتماع ... ناس بتحب الـ المسبات... بيضحكوا عالمسبات... ناس بيحبوا الشكل... بس كلن مجتمع لبناني... تفكير لبناني ... ما بعتقد انو فيه شرقية وغربية..

554 sex بس بيختلفو انو 3 فئات... ناس بتحب السياسة ناس بتحب الاجتماع ... ناس بتحب الـ المسبات... بيضحكوا عالمسبات... ناس بيحبوا الشكل... بس كلن مجتمع لبناني... تفكير لبناني ... ما بعتقد انو فيه شرقية وغربية..

555 sex بس بيختلفو انو 3 فئات... ناس بتحب السياسة ناس بتحب الاجتماع ... ناس بتحب الـ المسبات... بيضحكوا عالمسبات... ناس بيحبوا الشكل... بس كلن مجتمع لبناني... تفكير لبناني ... ما بعتقد انو فيه شرقية وغربية..

556 برتاح هون أكتر... ليه برتاح هون أكتر ما بعرف... لانو تعودت... شغلي هون بيتي هون أصحابي هون... ما بنزل

كتير لتحت ... ما عندي شي أعملو [...] بهيديك المنطقة... بس برتاح هون... يمكن هلق لو منزل لتحت ومنشتغل تحت
...برتاح تحت..بس أنا هون برتاح اكتر ...هلق
557 برتاح هون أكتر... ليه برتاح هون أكتر ما بعرف... لانو تعودت... شغلي هون بيتي هون أصحابي هون... ما بنزل...
كتير لتحت ... ما عندي شي أعملو [...] بهيديك المنطقة... بس برتاح هون... يمكن هلق لو منزل لتحت ومنشتغل تحت
...برتاح تحت..بس أنا هون برتاح اكتر ...هلق
558 ...صار عمري 18 سنة ونص عم قلك... قبل ما كنت أنزل ع المسارح لوحدي أو أنا وأهلي
559 ...بلد ديموقراطي وما فينا نحكي كلمة
560 هلق فكر بحب... بخاف... لبعدين كتير فكر بحب ما...
561 بتمنى يكون فيه ضمانات من الدولة للفنانين... بتشوفن كلن قاعدين ببيتن وما معن ليرة... عيب عالدولة... بيروت عاصمة الثقافة...
562 فيه فن مظبوط هوي فن...
563 ...ا
564 ...
565 ما فيه شي غير انو عم تسب عالمسرح... بيزقفوا... وهو... بيصيروا يدبكوا ع الطاولات... عيب... مش كل شي
566 ...هيدا... لازم يكون فيه هيك تيضحك... مجبورين.
567 ما بتحس انو فيه عالم اجو كتير... شهر... مسرحية ثقافية بمسرح المدينة... ما فيها كتير مصاري... اذا ما فيها مصاري ما بشتغل فيها
568 الفن خلق ... واحساس
569 هيدا الاحساس شغلة بتجي من عند الله... ما بعرف... كل العالم عندها احساس
570 المسرح اللبناني يعني مفروض بالقليلة يكون الو هوية
571 ...هودي المثقفين والفهمانين والشاطرين والعميقين... هودي اكتر شي بيشتغلوا مسرح عالمي... بيبقى فيها غربة وبعيدة عن العالم...
572 ...هالكبار المخضرمين بالمسرح اللبناني... ما فيه تواصل بينهن وبين الشعب اللبناني
573 ...الانتاج خايف لانو فيه ازمة اقتصادية
574 "مسرح الشانسونيية عم ينضرب بالتلفزيون... مثلا نحنا "هون منع في لبنان
575
576
577 لو ...مشكلة نصوص... شكري فاخوري... نساء في العاصفة... محطوط عتلفزيون لبنان... كان LBC محطوط عال... نعملو بروباغاندا اكتر
578 بس أنا ما بلاقي غلط انو يصير عنا لغة لبنانية منبثقة من العربي ... نهضة ثقافية...
579 ...بيروت هي الميزان الحراري لكل هالبقعة من العالم
580 شئنا أم ابينا... عندنا حرية... لأنو فيه تعددية... كل واحد عندو حرية من منظر معين...
581
582 ...نهضة ثقافية... على نطاق 10 أشخاص أو على أكتر... قيام طائر الفينيق
583 المسيحي عندو الام الحنونة فرنسا صوب الفرنكوفونية... ولاء غربي... الاسلام عندهن انفتاح عربي... بس عم يتجهوا صوب الانغلوفونية
584 ...بالاسلام كدين المسرح محرم... ممنوع... حتى الرسم ممنوع... تجسيد الانسان محرم كفن
585 يلي أسسو المسرح بالبلدان العربية ... بعتذر اني قولها... لاني مني طائفي وطريقتي بالايمان خاصة... هني

المسيحيي... هني الرواد بالثقافة العربي... ما فيه يجي حدا يقلي بلكي بتعتبرو حالكم مش عرب... فيه ايه بعرف أنا

...مش عربي... بس أنا بالعربي احسن منك... مش بركي مش أنا كفرد
586 أكتر من ... من...المحيط المسيحي... الانسان ... الـ taboo بالعالم الاسلامي عندن sex كمان... فيه أفراد اسلام منفتحين... كمسيحين بيتقبلوا اكتر... الاسلام صار عندك مؤخرا نوع من الاصولية بينما المسيحية ما عندن

...أصولية... المسيحي عطول منفتح
587 اذا واحد بدو يعملك دعاية... بيفرجيك دغري فخذ... وحدي عم تلحس البوظة ومتلاية تما Gratuitement ...حليب
588 بأوروبا لما يكون فيه جسد عاري... ما بيطلعوا عليه من منظار جنسي... من منظار فني أو ثقافي...
589 على الجسد..المسيحيي بعد السينودس... taboo... المسيح مات بالزلط وخلق بالزلط بيرفضوا انو يكون فيه تعرية

...والاسلام تحصيل حاصل... والتشخيص ككل ...
590 مجدلون "فيه عندك رقابة اليوم..."
591 ...بعد ما فيه هوية لبنانية غير الطائفية... لبنان فيه عليه جيوش غريبة
592 بس بدي نزل النص على الامن العام... تيقللي واحد بركي ما بيكون عارف قرعة جدو من وين... انو هيدي الكلمة

...بدك تغيرها... أنا بركي هيدي الكلمة أخدت معي ليلة بكاملها
593 ليه بدهن يشخطوها لانو عم بحكي الحقيقة... يمكن مش الحقيقة بس رأيي... رأيي غلط... تعبير عن الرأي...
594 الهرمل... معقل حزب الله... وبدك تعدا انو متصلة بسوريا اكتر ما متصلة بلبنان.
595 تتفرجي شو لابس... x يعني جايي مدام show off جمهور بيروت جمهور صعب... وكمان أو جمهور جايي أو عالم جايين يشوفوا نوعية العمل أو سمعوا انو العمل حلو ... intellectuel يننتقدك لانو هوي جايين بعفوية

...كبيرة بالهرمل
596 ليك هيدا كيف عابط هالشقرا... بالهرمل... 300 شخص برموا كلن تيشوفوا مين هوي اللي عابط هالشقرا... وصار

...فيه جدال... مينو هالعكروت اللي عابط هالشقرا... براءة الجمهور... وعفوية
597 عندك الغشيم هونيك والغشيم هون... عندك المثقف هونيك والمثقف هون... وهودي بيتفقوا مع بعضن أكتر من

...صنفين بذات الملعب
598 فيه انو انا مسلم ما بحب المسيحيي وأنا مسيحي ما بحب الاسلام... هيدا مسيحي عامل مسرحية... مسرحيتو ما

...بتسوا... وهيدا مسلم ... يعني هوي بركي ما بيقولوا ظاهريا بيستحي... بس هوي داخليا بينحاز
599 ...معقول حسب المنطقة مش بس حسب الاشخاص
600 المسلم باتصور بيعرف حالو... بيعرف كتير منيح انو المنطقة المسيحية هيي منطقة الحرية الفكرية... يعني... منشان هيك تلات ارباعن... يعني المسيحيي والاسلام بيجوا بيسهروا بالمنطقة هون... ما حدا بيروح هونيك...
601 اذا صار فيه نكرزات بتكون على نطاق شخصي او تيار سياسي لمدير هالمسرح... عم جرب كذب عليك وقلك لا...

...بس هوي هالشي موجود... بس انا مش عم بتقبلو... لازم نشوف هالموقف الصعب ونطلع منو
602 فيه حزازيات... مش صحيح انو الحرب أهلية... داخليا فيه انتماء طائفي... فيه حوار حول الانتماء الطائفي... كل

...طائفة عندها تلفزيون

ARABIC TRANSCRIPTIONS

603 اعلام CNN ما ببلدي أنا بس... المطار طريق على الخميني صورة بيفرجوك ...هيك
معين طابع اعطي مفروض...
ايماني انا... شي والدين شي والطائفية شي الايمان... بيزعجني ديني شي كل انا... معينة لمنطقة
وبين بيني بعملو
ربي وبين وبين... حالي
604 بالمنطقة قصف ياكلوا عم كانوا لانو المسرح بقلب ينزربوا عالم فيه كان...
605 تسيس فيه... سياسي تيار فيه لانو يدعسوا حدا عاد ما المدينة مسرح... سكر بيروت مسرح
606
607
608
609
610 وعندو الاوركسترا مدير... المسرحي العمل عن والاخير الاول المسؤول هوي المخرج
للعمل تبعو التفسير... عمل
انطفاء... الحركة ووقفت الحرب اجت ...75 الـ لحد... الستينات أوائل قبل موجود كان ما المخرج
طلع... للحركة
اليومية النقدية والكوميديات بالشانسونييه واهتموا... التلفزيون من جايين جداد جماعة...
Interview ا مع 611
612 المسرحي العمل عن والاخير الاول المسؤول هوي المخرج...
613 للعمل تبعو التفسير وعندو الاوركسترا مدير هوي...
614 ووقفت الحرب اجت ...75 الـ لحد ...الستينات أوائل قبل موجود كان ما المخرج عمل
الحركة...
615 فيه صار
616 بالشانسونييه واهتموا ...التلفزيون من جايين جداد جماعة طلع ...للحركة انطفاء متل
النقدية والكوميديات
617 ما كمان نقدية مسرحيات يعملوا يعني... هيك يوصل بيقدر ما الشانسونييه... اليومية
lendemain الها
618 قبل بالحركة كانوا يلي مخرجين من قيمتها الها يلي المسرحيات بعض بالفترة مرق
الحرب.
619 فيه يكون لازم مسرح فيه ليكون أنا الى فبالنسبة... موجودة عادت ما هيدي mouvement
مسرح فيه عاد ما...
620 بلبنان...
621 فخاد... عالفخاد ويتفرجى ويسكي كاس يحط يروح بيفضل... موجود عاد ما الجمهور
والنسوان ...البنات...
622 كل يشوف يروح كان ملتقى انطوان يشوف يجي بس مش الجمهور كان... الستينات أوائل من... الجمهور ربينا
623 يروح بدو وين بيعرف ما اليوم الجمهور... جمهور هيدا... المسرحيات...
624 بالـ بيفعل... يفعل بدو اذا المسرح ...jeunesse الـ jeunesse ...بالبيوت تربية فيه ما أولا
تربية فيه ولا
625 موجودة منا... الشعب حضارة بتخلق يلي للعناصر صحيحة ورؤيا فنية تربية ...بالمدارس
626 الجمال حس بتربي ما لانها... الابتدائية المدرسة وخاصة المدرسة على المسؤولية بحط أنا
الولد عند...
627 الـ عندهن... واعيين اهلن ولاد عندك sens du beau
628 شي عالم دخلوا الحرب بوقت انو التلفزيون مشكلة... الدولة تلفزيون عندها... الدولة مسؤولية
تيعة شي تكتك
629 موظفين فوتوهن يلي... للمحاسيب يدفعوا عم المصريات كل هلق بقى... بالثقافة خصهن ما
الـ... عندهن dish مش
630 تجيبو قادرة العالم كل...
631 متل اجا المسرح... مسرحية تقاليد فيه ما عنا نحنا prise de conscience انو وعينا أنو
عنا فيه يكون لازم

632 ...مسرح لأنو المسرح مهم
633 كلمة مارون النقاش "ليس لهذا الفن مستقبل في البلدان العربية" بعدا دايما براسي...
634 ليش؟
entre nous يمكن هلق ليش... أنا بدي فوت لجوا عندو... أنو بما انو فيه بهالبلد... هلق هيدي يمكن انت ما
635 هلق هيدي... أنا بدي فوت لجوا عندو... أنو بما انو فيه بهالبلد... يمكن entre nous يمكن انت ما
تقدرش تقولها... انو بما انو فيه التعصب الديني... وخاصة وجود العنصر الاسلامي... هلق هوي تطور كتير لا
636 ضد التمثيل... مش هيك representation شك... بس العنصر الاسلامي يلي هوي ضد الـ عند العرب حتى
637 لانو هالفنانين arabesque بالفنون التشكيلية ما كان عندن شخص... منشان هيك طلعت الـ الموهوبين ما قدروش
638 يعملوا شخص... كانوا يعتبروهن مارقين... كانوا يعتبروهن كفار... لانو عم ياخد مطرح الله... قال هوي عم
639 يخلق... من هيك تحولت العبقرية تبعولتهن تحولت الى الخطوط ... الخطوط والرسوم يلي ما بتمثل حدن... يعني
640 رسوم مجردة... التجريد بلش عند العرب الاسلام قبل وين ما كان يعني... هيدا هوي الخطوط الـ arabesque ...
641 هلق هيدي أنا ما بقولا وين ما كان... أنا بقولا قدام ناس بيفهموا لانو اذا بقولها بالشارع... بيقولوا هيدا ضد الاسلام
642 الاسلام... علما انو عند المسيحية... كمان بالقرون الوسطى... مشي الدين المسيحي ضد التمثيل... لفترة معينة
643 ولكن بما انو عندن فكرة تحررية أكتر... ببلدان أوروبا... تخطوا هالشو أسمو... وعملوا اللي بدن ياه وما فارقة م
644 ...شو الدين وشو بيقول الدين... وشو اسمو
645 تسعين بالمية منهن عم ياخدوا آخر فقشات عم تصير بالغرب يلي هني كمان ضايعين بالغرب... بالمسرح بالغرب
646 كمان ضايعين... مضيعين هويتهن... عم بيروحوا بيتكلوا عالعبيد السود... الحركة السودا... جايين الشباب عنا عم
647 ياخدوا آخر فقشات انعملت هونيك ... ما الها علاقة فينا أصلا يعني... عم يبعد المسرح عن الانسان... الانسان ما
648 ...ما عاد الو حضور كإنسان robot عاد موجود ... صفى فيه حركات ... صار الممثل
649 انا ... psychanalyse دور المسرح... شغلتي اني اخلق لحظة من حقيقة... هي نوع من واياهن (الناس) منحس
650 بمشكلة... ولكن ما بتتوضحلن المشكلة... انا اذا كنت افهم منهن شوي وعيت المشكلة... باخد مسرحية بتبحث
651 بهالمشكلة... المشاهد بيشوف المشكلة وبيعرف انو فيه غيرو عم بيفكر فيها... المريض ليصح بدو يعرف مشكلتو
652 ...شو هيي
653 الشانسونييه تنفيس للثورة الداخلية...
654 كل مشكل يومي ... اذا ضل مشكل يومي بيأثر بس بالغريزة... هيدا ما الو مستقبل... وقت اللي هالمشكل هيدا الي
655 عم بيصير كل يوم... بيطرح عندو تساؤلات... فكرة ونفسية ووجودية ... ساعتها بيصير الو قيمة... وبيصير يؤثر
656 ...عالمجتمع... وممكن يعمل ثورة
657 المسرح مفروض يساهم بوصول الناس الى هالفكرة العامة اللي بدها تعمل تقدم بالمجتمع... بدون ما تقلهن روحوا
658 اعملوا...

659 هاللي نزلوا بمعترك الحرب... ان كان من جهتنا وان كان من جهة هوديك... كانوا عم بيقبضوا تنينات... هلق بدو
660 يتبين بعد فترة انو رفيق الحريري هو من اكبر مجرمي الحرب... هو اللي كان يدفع للقوات... وكان يدفع
661 فيه ناس بيقولولك... انو centre ville لهوديك... منشان تيتقاتلوا... منشان تيحرق دين الـ كان يدفع بملايين
662 ... centre ville الدولارات للقوات... وللي ضدن كذلك الامر... وكان مشدد اكتر شي عال وهلق نزلنا تحت دين
663 20 مليار دولار... الخواجا حريري مطلوب منو القضاء ع لبنان... وين حطهن؟ شو عمل
664 ...قبل الحرب كان فيه عندي اصحاب اسلام... ما كانت مطروحة... الوعي هو الاساس
665 هدف الحرب ... المنطلق تبعوا هو الصهيونية بواسطة أميركا... انو بدن يبرهنوا انو ما معقول طايفتين يقدروا
666 يتعايشوا... منشان هيك سموها حرب أهلية... مسيحي ضد مسلم
667 خلال الحرب فترة انعدام الوزن... لانو الناس اللي بيفهموا كانوا قاعدين بالزاوية... مين نزل عالساحة... نزلوا
668 الزعران عالساحة... يللي بدفعون المصريات منشان تيتقاتلوا... قبل الحرب كان فيه مفكرين كبار...
669 القبلية ما عادت موجودة... خفت... ما فيك تقول النظام اللبناني نظام قبلي... نظام طائفي ... ايه... مفروض ينحكم
670 ...لبنان من عدة طوائف... ويوصل للعقلانية
671 الشعب العادي بعدو عقليتو كتير طائفية... الحرب وعّت الطائفية بنفوس البشر... بس يكون بعيد عن المجتمع تبعوا
672 بينسى...
673 ...المسيحيي خلقوا الالحاد
674 ...بنظام القرآن... كل شي مرغوب محبوب
675 ...فيه ناس من عامة الشعب... انو هيدا واحد مسيحي ما بدي احضرلو مسرحيتو
676 ما عندنا هالعقلية... الفرقة تبعولنا كانت مخلوطة... يلي كانوا يطلعوا الاسلام من المعهد... كانوا يشتغلوا مع
677 ...الشعب معتر وبينساق... الكبار هني اللي عم بيسوقوا هالشعب
678 المسرح وسيلة تعبير... متعلقة بالجغرافيا... وبالتاريخ... وهيدا بيعطي الهوية... ولكن المضمون الانساني العام...
679 يكون عالمي... اللغة ما الها اهمية... اللغة اللبنانية... لغة غير لغتو الواحد مني موافق عليها...
680 ...لطيفة: نحنا هيك... مخلط عربي وفرنساوي وانكليزي
681 ثقافتي اجنبية... ولكن انا بحس حالي لبناني... التركيبة الها علاقة بالارض بالمناخ... اللغة ما بتغير الهوية...
682 ...منو تضييع هوية... عندك سطحيين
683 ...اللبنانيي شرقيين وبيشوفوا بكل جسمهن... العلاقة مع مكان الاحتفال
684 ...ما بعتقد فيه فرق بين الانسان المسيحي والمسلم
685 ...وسيلة التعبير هيي الهوية
686 الموضوع polarization: هو اللي بيعمل
687 الحدس (الغزالي)... والفكر الغربي (أنا أفكر، اذن أنا موجود)... طريقة تدريب الممثل تأتي انطلاقا من اليوغا...
688 مختلف عن الرياضة الغربية.
689 ...مع الكل interaction تعطي Scène centrale
690 ...الديكور يحد من حرية الممثل
691 ...تبويس ايدين... ويعمل زلمة فلان وفلان... تيوصل
692 ...الحكومة الحالية... شيل ميشال المر وفرنجية... جورج قرم
693 ...الطبقة السياسية العتيقة ضد الناس اللي بيفكروا

694

695 Interview

696 عملت مسرح للاقي جزء من حياتي...

697 بين وحدي بتحبها وبعدين بالواقع مختلف fluctuation مع emotional حاجة...

698 بحس انا انو الشغلة الحلوة بين الجمهور والخشبة لمن بحس انو الجمهور صار عالخشبة... هيدي هيي الـ

699 هيدي كتير he identifies لألي لمن بحس انو الجمهور صار emotional part لألي emotionally

700 بينك وبين live فيه اختبار كتير حلو وقت اللي بتكون عم تعمل satisfaction بتعطيني الممثلين وبينك وبين

701 الجمهور بيعطيك حيوية بحياتك... بيعطيك نشاط وتجدد... هالشي يلي الواحد بيبدلو عن المصاري...

702 تجاهو... المسرح التجاري واللبناني عندي رفض emotions المسرح الجامعي عندي هالـ وحساسية سلبية

703 تجاهو...

704 كل واحد عم يفهم الهوية اللبنانية بطريقتو... يمكن الخشبة اللبنانية اللي عم تموت... يمكن لانو ما فيه

705 عم تجرب تجسدها بهالمواضيع meaning of life...

706 بعدني عم بكتشف اذا انا هويتي عم شوفها كلبناني...؟

707 طانيوس شاهين ... مسرحية مارونية... حسيت فيها اجواء مارونية ... انا مني ماروني... حسيتها بتعالج يمكن

708 نوعا ما الهوية المارونية... بشكل ممسرح... والموارنة في لبنان عندهن قيمة وجودية في تكوين هوية البلد...

709 ...وهالمسرح هوي جزء من هالموضوع

710 طانوس شاهين لو كانت انعرضت بغير جورج الخامس... ما كانت نجحت... هيي انعملت لجمهور موراني

711 ...وكسرواني... بتحكي عن مواضيع بتهم عاطفيا الكسروانيين والموارنة they identify with it more

712 than other people ...

713 ...حسيت حالي كل ما مرق يوم the odd man out حسيت حالي اول شي I'm sharing with them

714 things... belong حالي حس كنت قبل ... alien اكتر.

715 الجمهور بيجي اوقات غروبات... الصالة بتصير تشكل حلقة عاطفية بمجموعة كراسي معينة... مرات بتسيطر

716 تبعولها... ايجابية أو غير ايجابية... فيه تأثير طائفي... بس reactions ع بقية الكراسي بـ طريقة حياة الناس

717 ...يللي عم تجي حسيت الها تأثير أكبر يمكن لانو ما كان فيه جمهور مسلم عم يجي

718 ...خزان عاطفي وفكري بيعطيك راحة مع نفسك

719 بيت الخازن... وقت اللي يكون خازني بالصالة كان يبين... أو مثلا من أهل ريفون. بتحس تجاوب غير

720 ...تبعن... صارت تعنيلي الجمل غير emotions بتحس فيه فهم أكتر... بتحس بالـ

721 موظفين الشركات والبنوكي ... بتحس عندن كبت... بيعملوا غروبات وبيجوا يحضروا لينفسوا من هالضغط...

722 فيه فرق كتير بين تلاميذ مدارس مختلفة... تلاميذ جامعات بيهتموا يحضروا مسرح متل ما تلاميذ المسرح

723 بالجامعات...

724 ...الجامعة بتأثر أكتر من الدين بعمر معين

725 بشوف الجمهور الاسلامي بيحب يحضر المسرح اكتر كعدد... الجمهور المسيحي مظنظر شوي... فيه شعبية

ARABIC TRANSCRIPTIONS

726 معينة... القاعدة الشعبية بتعتمد عشعنة المشاهد... الجمهور المسلم بيهتم بشو عم بيصير عالساحة الشعبية أكتر
727 ...من الجمهور المسيحي ببيروت... فيه عندو التزام أكتر بالقضايا اللي عم تصير عالارض
728 ...يمكن المسيحي عندو انتماء للبيئة الاوروبية أكتر من القضايا العربية اللي عم تصير هون
729 ...نتايج الحرب بتعريف هوية الانسان وشو خلفت عالارض
730 الجمهور المسلم بيحضر مروان نجار أكتر من المسيحي...
731 ...المسيحي متحرر أكتر من المسلم بانو يعمل مسرح
732 ...الشيوعية غطا... عند زياد الرحباني... هوي ما بيقدر يطلع من حالو
733 ...طربية... يعني reception صارت reception الـ
734 fusion de la conscience individuelle dans la conscience collective ... مع المتفرنجين... progrès de la
735 conscience individuelle avec l'extension coloniale ... هالتفاوت...
736 ...بيلقطوك الفلسطينيين وبيقولولك [...] انت مسيحي... يا عمي انا منكن وفيكن
737 ...سمة الحضارة الغربية هي فردية وسمة الحضارة التانية هي حضارة انتماء
738 amortisseur ... la civilisation الديموقراطية هي خلقت القلق يللي اجا المسرح يعملو
739 materielle tout est reduit à l'intelligence humaine... ... الانسان منفصل عن
740 ...الشمول... وبحالة تناحر
741 قول ايه لقول لا... هون ما في مسرح لانو ما فيه ...conflit بالعالم الاسلامي ما فيه
742 conflit ... ... appartenance à la totalité ... ... tout est en relation avec les
743 forces soujacentes qui sont dans le cosmos, c'est ca l'orient بينما انا بلعب
744 Antigone ساعة اللي بدي... قبل الظهر... مش ضروري من 8 عشية لـ 5 عبكره
745 انا مش قابضو جد المسرح العربي... لانو عندو الطرب يلي بيدخلو بحالة الرضى... بتحس
746 ...extase حالك ما بدك شي من الدني... متل انت وقاعد مع مرا
747 الانتماء بيحدد الهوية... الانتماء للأمة... للبوطقة للعشيرة للعيلة... أذا عندك ضابط كبير درزي ... وعندك واحد من
748 بيت جنبلاط هوي اللي بيملي عالكوماندان شو يعمل... وعندك واحد من بيت جنبلاط هوي اللي بيملي عالكوماندان شو يعمل
749 ...ما فيه ارتباط... تدمير منهجي لبيروت... الحريري والميليشيات
750 انا رائد المسرح السياسي في العالم العربي... برشت بالعو... وماركس بالعو... الـ
751 Volksbühne ...عشت فيها سنة
752 هني بيقولوا انهن منعوا التشخيص... ما صحيح... ما كانوا بحاجة الو... شو الهن فيه؟
753 ...الكوميديا سموها هجاء... والتراجيديا
754 فيه Sects كتير بالاسلام ... la trance qui est l'antithèse de la reflection
755 ...فاضل الجعايبي كان عم بيقول نحنا عم نروي قصص لعالم هني مش بحاجة لقصص
756 ...الجمهور العربي ما الو علاقة بالمسرح
757 هلق فيه الشيعة عم بيروحوا عالمسرح بس... لانو هني بحالة الـ promotion sociale, ils sont remis sur
la scène بيجوا من الضاحية الجنوبية وبيشوفوا منير كسرواني... واحد ماروني عم يعملهن هيدا
...اسماعيل
...والبنت اللي عم تعمل ام طعان وحدي أرمنية... ils se voient, c'est une promotion
pour eux هيدا شي جديد بالنسبة الهن... بس ما بيضاين... لمن طلع ... هيدا صاحبنا... رفيق علي أحمد... طيزوا عليه وسبوا... ولمن اجا لهون... انا جبتو لهون... ومشيتو... بالشرقية... حلي بعينهن... كنت مع وحدي بتقربو لكامل الاسعد... عم تقلي... شو هالكلب رفيق علي أحمد... نحنا أحلى ناس ... نحنا معلمين... عاملنا معازي؟... لمن مشت المسرحية بعد 6 أشهر... ما لقيتا الا ودركبت... عم يزقفولوا... هيدا واحد منا... هوي ليك الي ...بيصير عند المسيحي
...هوي سباق... بدو يصير عند الاسلام... بعد كذا سنة... يعني عون وجعجع بدو يصير بعد

275

758 بيجوا من الضاحية الجنوبية وبيشوفوا منير كسرواني... واحد sont remis sur la scène
759 ماروني عم يعملهن هيدا ... اسماعيل... والبنت اللي عم تعمل ام طعان وحدي أرمنية... بس
760 هيدا شي جديد ils se voient, c'est une promotion pour eux ... هني عم بيشو بالنسبة
761 ...الهن... بس ما بيضاين... لمن طلع ... هيدا صاحبنا... رفيق علي أحمد... سبوه
762 ولمن اجا لهون... انا جبتو لهون... ومشيتو... بالشرقية... حلي بعينهن... كنت مع وحدي بتقربو
763 ...لكامل الاسعد... عم تقلي... شو هالكلب رفيق علي أحمد... نحنا أحلى ناس ... نحنا معلمين
764 ...عاملنا معازي؟... لمن مشت المسرحية بعد 6 أشهر... ما لقيتا الا ودركبت... عم يزقفولوا
765 هيدا واحد منا... هوي ليك الي بيصير عند المسيحيي... هوي سباق... بدو يصير عند الاسلام... بعد كذا سنة... يعني
766 ...بعد كذا سنة... يعني عون وجعجع بدو يصير بعد عون وجعجع بدو يصير بعد
767 ...زغيَر حساس... لبنان ما الو دور laboratoire... لبنان ما الو قيمة... هوي متل ميزان
768 ...صيدا مدينة عربية... بيروت مش مدينة عربية
769 هيدا أنا قاعد هون... رح يجيني ولاد... رح سكنهن هون... نحنا عشيرة ما منبعد عن بعضنا...
770 منصير نركب فوق بعضنا... بتلاقي احياء فيه عصبيات بقلب المدينة... هيدي المدينة العربية...
771 ...مش معناتا انو مدينة فيها اسلام ما فيها مسيحية... المدينة الاوروبية c'est l'individu
772 ...ابني فل... يعني خلص... قطع الرحم مع الجماعة abstrait
773 بيروت est récente, et déjà elle a pris son extension avec l'acte colonial فيه
774 كركون الدروز وفيه الجميزة ... مارونية... اشرفية أورثوذكس... النهر أرمن... الطوائف بعدا
775 آخدي محلها... الحرب خلطتهم هودي... بتروح مثلا... حي التينة بلزق بكفيا روم... بكفيا
776 بيناتهن... هيدا نظام الملة... arbitre موارنة... ع أيام العثمانيين كان فيه الطوائف وكان فيه ما
777 نحنا رجال ... universel يكون نظام individuel ضروري النظام الديموقراطي الـ
778 ...المسرح هون دورنا
779 Interview.
780
781 غياب المساحة المشتركة... بعد فيه شرقية وغربية... أنا ابن الشرقية بس روح عالغربية... ما الي كلام بالغربية...
782 وكذلك ابن الغربية بس يروح ع جونية ما الو كلام... متل طلابي بس يروحو ع الشوف بيصيروا يحكوني عن الشوف كأنو عم يحكوا عن قبرص... أزمة مجتمع... غياب بؤرة التفاعل والتنوع الحريري غيبها... بعدها بيروت مشطورة الى شطرين...
783 بعد فيه شرقية وغربية... أنا ابن الشرقية بس روح عالغربية... ما الي كلام بالغربية... وكذلك
784 ابن الغربية بس يروح ع جونية ما الو كلام... متل طلابي بس يروحو ع الشوف بيصيروا
785 يحكوني عن الشوف كأنو عم يحكوا عن قبرص... أزمة مجتمع... غياب بؤرة التفاعل والتنوع
786 ...على غرار أثينا
787 ...الحرية والانفتاح في ظل خلق دولة اسرائيل
788 ...المسرح الغربي عم بيموت... ليش بدك نلحق المسرح طالما عم بيموت
789 ...المسرح ألغاه الطرب
790 مسرح مارون النقاش
791 مسرح أبو خليل القباني
792 سهرة مع أبو خليل القباني
793 ...حجازي والأخوين رحباني
794 ...الستينات... حلقة المسرح اللبناني... مع انطوان ملتقى ومنير بو دبس

795 الا ... كل المحاولات لمسخ النموذج الغربي... بقيت على هامش الادراك والوعي الجماعي
796 وارتياح ... حالة رضى... بما يناسب الطرب...
797 الحضور عن نيابة ويعيشه ... بيشحنك مسرح ... الغربي المسرح
798 le personnage sur la scène, qu'est ce qu'il fait? هو عم بيعيش المشكلة وانت عم
799 تعمل identification الضربة ياكل عم هوي بس ... عنو ... يعني...
800 Interview.
801 نبيه بو الحسن بيحسب كل نكتة قديش بتطلع... واللي معو هودي جلاميق ما بياخدوا شي...
   ...بدهن كل شي الهن
802 أنطوان كرباج صار عم يشتغل اش ما كان...
803 ...ما فيه فرقة... لازم يكون فيه هم مشترك شو ما كان يكون
804 ...كل سنتين تلاتة ليعمل الواحد مسرحية
805 ...معهد التمثيل ما انتج حدا... ما فيه برنامج
806 50 أحد المشاكل الاساسية يمكن الانتاج... اذا بدك تنتج مسرحية مظبوطة... البطاقة بتكلف
   دولار... ما عنا تاريخ
   مسرحي [...]
807 الكومبيوتر ...العولمة... ثقافية... عم بيفوت لجوا... نسفوا الثقافة وبدهن يخلوك تفكر متلهن...
   Microsoft... السعودية
   ...يمكن بتضامن... فيه دين
808 الشانسونييه...كاس ووحدي بتبين اجريها...
809 ...ما فيه شي بيحمي المسرح
810 كل الممثلين ملتهيين بالدوبلاج
811 ...كل الناس بتحكي متل بعضها
812 ...ما فيه تحضير للمسرح في المدرسة او بالبيت... ما حدا بيقرا بالبلد
813 ما كل ...؟للعرض اذا بس ... تابو السيكس نقول عم ما ... بالسيكس فالتين ... فايضة الدنيا
   ...بيعالج مشكلة كبو لشو
814 بيردو حدا وما ... بيسبك ... صاحبو كنت وما ... منيح عنك بيكتب ... صاحبو كنت ان...
815 21 تقسيم طائفي... مذهبي... ومناطقي... كل حي الو شغلة... صرنا على مشارف القرن الـ
   بعدنا لكن بعدنا عربان
   قبائل بدو...
816 الحرب قسمت ضهر الشغلة...
817 الفيلم بيطلع ... هيك هيك تعمل ... كلو بالكون تمشي بدها هوليوود تبع الراشته ... عولمة
   ...بدنا نبيع بهونغ كونغ
818 اذا ...بيروحوا العربان... عليه؟ تتفرج تروح العالم سكس فيه بأوروبا... الختيارية بيروحوا
   كانوا هونيك... عالم تالت
   بشكل المرا استبعاد ... المي متل محلولة ... بيروحوا ما الشباب ... افلام هيك ع بيتفرجوا بيروحوا
   غير لايق... انا ما
   وحدا تقعد نخلص بس ... تخدمنا وتصير أنا اقعد ... بيي يقعد ... عالسفرة معنا قعدت امي مرة بذكر
   الاشيا... تاكل
   هيدا ...المرا تنتاك تروح ... جنسي تحرر ... تفرخ بدها وين سوا كليتها feminism...
819 وتهيأ توقف عرفت ناس فيه ... عليها اللي عملوا ... انطفيت المنائر ...
820 اجا ... محيرة اسامي يسموا ضلوا ،... جورج يسموا قلب الهن كان ما المسيحي خصوصا
   مسرحية عمل جبارة ريمون
   ما ... بالبيكاديللي حطها ... هيك بينت ... لهونيك لهون مش لكن ... السماء الى يصعد قندلفت
   انا بيروح ...بيحضروهن
   واحد وكام وانت...
821 جمهور هيك بيفرز مجتمع هيك
822 عندن الرحباني ... formule ... هيك ... للدروز نقدمها نهار هونيك بدنا انو حساب بيضرب
   بدنا سميعا شعب نحنا
   اياه بيقبلك حدا ما الكلام عادي مسرح بتعمل ... الحلوة الكلمة منحب ... نسمع ...

823 ليه بيحط بوالعبد؟
824 هون :...
825 لا ... عندك هونيك... ليه بيحط بالشانسونييه بوالعبد... ليضحك عالاسلام... وهونيك بيضحكلها وبيعطيه مصاري...
826 التلفزيون بيفوت بالقوة ع كل بيت...
827 لمن اجا المرعشلي بالحرب عالبيكاديللي [...] مين كان مستلم هون الميليشيات... تيلعب بالبيكاديللي بدو يكون الميليشيات راضيين عنو... طيب هيدا ما معو مصاري يعطيهن... هيدا ميليشيا... جاب امو جاب اختو... يتفرجوا عالمرعشلي... جابوا معهن اللوبيات... جابوا معن الكوسى... جابوا معهن الطناجر... انو كيف بتقعد هيي عالتلفزيون بتصير اللوبية و... هيك صار بالمسرح... طبخوا... طبخوا كوسى... المرعشلي بيعرف يحكي معهن...
828 طس....: هل هوي متخطي الطائفية؟
829 لا... هوي بيحك عالجرب... ماشي الحال يعني... هوي ما بيفوت بهالشغلة... بيحكي بالجنس... بيضحك... بيرضي...
830 هون يمكن أكتر ما بيرضي هونيك... فيه شغلات مشتركة... التعب الجوع المرض الاكل الجنس الجنس تابو... ما فيك تمد ايدك عليه... بياخدولك الكتاب... بيسكرولك المسرحية... بعدين هيدا العالم المتخلف...
831 [...] الجنس شو بيفهمهن فيه؟... بيعرفوا النياكة النواب هيك والاكل هيك والشرب هيك والشانسونييه هيك... لحد ما... الدروز مش طالعلن شي [...] نبيه كان ذكي... كان يعرض عند المسيحي...
832 بالسعودية فيه طائفية؟... ما فيه مسرح...
833 طس....: يمكن الدين بيأثر عالمسرح...
834 طيب بليبيا... عد وغيرو... شمالي افريقيا... تونس ... صار فيه عندن مسرح... الدولة مهتمة... العراق ما فيه عندن مسرح مع انو عندن جيش من الفنانين... كان فيه مسرحية... ركعت وصارت تصلي قدام صورة صدام حسين... وتطلب يعفي عن ابنها... قلنالهن عيب... قالوا ع ايام المهيب... هيدا اللي قبل صدام كانوا يحطوا صورتو بهاملت... شو فيها
835 ديموقراطية كذب... نحنا لا مننتخب رئيس جمهورية ولا مننتخب نواب ولا شي... ما بعرف كيف بتصير...
836 ...مسرح بلا حرية... كيف ممكن يصير مسرح بلا حرية فيه هامش من الحرية... هون ستوب... اجمعهن كلهن عبعضهن... بعدين هيدا شعب 2 3
837 ملايين... عندو بيتهوفن... عندو برشت... انا مين فيه عندي... بتروح عالمدرسة كل اللي بيحفظوك بيتين تلاتة شعر من الجاهلية... وهيدا أحسن شعر بالعربي كان... ونتفة المتنبي والباقي كبو...
838 بدون نص ما فيك تعمل مسرحية...
839 إذا بدك تفوت دغري... ايه بدك تضرب راسك بالحيط... بيحطوك بالحبس... أو بيقاطعوك أو بيشيلوك من الوظيفة...
840 كان معي ماجستير مسرح ... ما كان يفوتني عالجامعة..يطلع تلميذ يلزقلي صورة... هون مسيحي نصراني... وهونيك شيوعي... رحنا جبنا دكتوراه... بدنا واسطة... هالدني كوتا... دخلتو عباسمك... كميل شمعون [...] من فرنجية من البطرك... من الحص... من جنبلاط... آخر شي جبتلو واسطة من البواب... كان بدن كلن يكونوا اسلام بالمنطقة هون...

الاحزاب... المرابطون... أمل... هالشي كان موجود... هيدي قابلة انك تحركها وقت اللي كان... هودي بتجي تحكي

معن بيقولك... ليك اخواننا المسيحيي ما تواخذني بهالكلمة... ونحنا عنا بالضيعة اذا شافونا دبانة بيقولوا هيدي أم محمد... هيدي اسفنجة... الطائفية موجودة وقادرين يحركوها بكل ساعة... تاريخيا الها تاريخ الطائفية...

بالنتيجة الناس بتقيمو طائفيا... لو بدك تحكي بالتلج تبع ألاسكا... بيضلوا يلاقولها... ليك بس 841 هلق خفت... هلق
...موجودة وبتقدر تشعلها ساعة اللي بدك... بس هلق خافة

842 Interview.

843

844 كاتب مسرحي غير متفرغ ... محامي... مواقف سياسية... المسرح اداة توصيل نظريات سياسية يسارية للجمهور...

اضراب الحرامية... 1970 اخراج روجيه عساف ونضال الاشقر في صالة أوتيل النورماندي ... الدولة والثورة

...لينين... الدولة هي اداة بيد السلطة المستغلة لتحقيق استغلالها

845 تأثير من برشت ودورنمات

846 ...بعدها توقفت عن العمل... لانو الناس ما حبوا انو يكون محاميهن عم يشتغل مسرح...

847 بنسيون الست نعيمة... اخراج جلال خوري...

848 بالاول كان فيه عندي حماس سياسي...مع الوقت تواضعنا... وصرت شوف اهمية العمل الفني بحد ذاته وصرت

شوف انو المسرح... يهدف الى... الى ... الى ... المتعة... وان يكون وسيلة لأستعادة تفكير... ان يكون باعث على

تحريك افكار وشعور المتفرج... وهو يختلف عن التلفزيون لانو مشاهد التلفزيون يتلقى بدون ان يشارك ويفكر...

بينما المسرح يجب ان يكون فيه متعة ... الواحد مش عم يدفع فلوس مش تيروح ياكل وعظ سياسي او اخلاقي

بطريقة فجة... بدو يفوت يلاقي شي يعطيه متعة... وهذه المتعة تختلف بين شخص مثقف مفكر وشخص موظف

عادي منو مشارك بنشاط بالحياة الفكرية بالبلد... قدرة الكاتب... الفنان... انو يقدر يؤدي عمل يعطي متعة مشتركة

لاكبر عدد ممكن من الاوساط والناس... يعني ما يكون عملي محصور بمثقفين او بشعبويين... متعة مجانية [...] هلق

...كيف بدو يعجبهن... اذا كان ما فيه قاسم مشترك ما بين انا ما افكر فيه وهني ما يفكرون فيه

849 أعمال قبل الحرب...كارت بلانش... روجيه عساف ونضال الاشقر... هي اقتباس لمسرحية 3 لجان جينيه... لكن

...معربة... ومعاد تأليفها

850 ...مسرحية جحا في القرى الامامية... جلال خوري

851 ...يعقوب الشدراوي عن مسرحية لمحمد الماغوط

852 ...نجاح باهر لانها بتتناسب مع ذوق الرأي العام

853 رفيق علي أحمد... الجرس... عملها عن الجنوب ... الحقيقة هالعمل لم ينجح في مراحلو الاولى قدام هذا الجمهور يللي

هوي الوسط الطبيعي لالو... رجع خطرت على بالو فكرة ... انو يقدمها بجونية... راح قدمها بجونية... هناك كان...

يعني... مع بداية مرحلة السلم... وبداية انفتاح اللبنانيين على بعض بعد انفصال... حبو الناس اللي هني ما بيعرفوا

اهل الجنوب ... ما بيعرفوا معاناتن... حبوا انو يشوفوا... ويتعرفوا على هالناس... فأجت... مجرد عم تقدم شغلة

لجمهور... ما بيعرفك... اجا ليتعرف عليك... على ما تمثلو انت على المسرح... فأعجبوا الناس بالعمل... وتدفقوا
حتى وصلت... انا حضرتا عدة مرات... انو فيه ناس يجوا من صور... لما راحت لعندن المسرحية ما شافوها... لما اجت ع جونية ولاقت هالنجاح... صاروا يجوا من صور ع جونية ليشوفوها... تصور الى أي حد يعني أعجبوا بقيمتها متأخرين... ولكن بعد ما طرح من الشعب اللبناني... حب يتعرف ع حياة ما بيعرفها هوي... هالمعرفة عملت هذا الوهج لهذا العمل

854 بدو قول انو بدون شك الحرب الاهلية... عملت نوع من التقسيم النفسي عند الناس بفكر هن... وغيرو ... لكنهن... مع بداية مرحلة السلم الاهلي صاروا بيحبوا يتعرفوا على بعض... يتعرفوا على آخر... مش انو واحد منهم... لحتى يصيروا بالاخير... كلهن واحد... ما يعودوا فريقين...

أنا ما بكتب لجمهور لبناني على الاطلاق... بفكر انا بالعمل... بقيمتو الانسانية... بيخطر 855 عبالي كيف بيتلاقها المتفرج العادي... بس مش انو اذا مسلم أو مسيحي...بصير انو هون عم بوقع ب... بالمسرح الفنوي ... يلي نبيه ابو الحسن اشتغل عليه اثناء الحرب اللبنانية...

856 منير ... يعني انا قرأت... ما شفت العمل... ولكن بعتبر انو... مسرح منير كسرواني يتوجه الى اهل [...] الجنوب بالذات... هذا المسرح انا...ما ... ما ... انا المسرح الذي يجمع

857 برأي لا يمكن تسمية مسرح الرحابنة مسرح... لولا موسيقاهم الجميلة... وغناء فيروز... ما كنت فيك تلاقي اقبال على مسرح الرحابنة... الرحابنة يللي عني مبدعين في مجال الموسيقى... وفيروز يللي هيي مبدعة وجمعوا ناس مبدعين متل نصري شمس الدين وغيرو... وعملوا اعمال لا يمكن ان تدخل في تاريخ المسرح... حتى ولا تاريخ ...المسرح الغنائي... لانو المسحر الغنائي يفترض تقنية مسرحية ورؤيا مسرحية هيي ما معن اياها

858 زياد الرحباني مختلف... عندو قلق...

859 فيه عقم سياسي بالبلد [...] وضعهم بالسلطة مرهون بقبول قوى غير لبنانية فهين... هذا الوضع السياسي بشكل... يعني الحياة السياسية بلبنان... منا حياة ديموقراطية صحيحة... وبما انو المسرح لا ينمو الا في نطاق جو ديموقراطي...

وبما انو التعبير عن الوضع بالمسرح صعب... وبالتالي فيه بدائل بدها تصير... ومن هيدي البدائل... مسرح ...الشانسونييه [...] يللي هيي تعبير عن بنية رجال السياسة الحاليين و هيدا تفكير هن يعني

860 أنا برأي انو رجال المسرح بلبنان. رجال متجاوزين... للتفكير الطائفي

861 بعض المثقفين في القطاع الغربي في بيروت... اذا جينا اختصرنا لبنان ببيروت... عم بيشاركوا بالحياة الثقافية اللي عم تصير في بيروت الشرقية... عكس... ما عم بيصير في المناطق الشرقية... الى حد كبير... ما يزالوا مقاطعين ...المسرحيات التي تقدم في المناطق الغربية

862 يعني فيه تغيرات... صارت بعد مؤتمر الطائف... صارت انو المسيحيين يفكرون انو سلبت منهم حقوقهم... واللي سلبوها هني المسلمين... ما بدنا نروح لعندهن... يعني منشتغل معهم... بس بدو يضل فيه حاجز بيننا وبينهم... هيدا تقديري...

863 ...الكاتب المسرحي... او المخرج... عم ياخد مادتو من هالناس... وعم يرجع يقدملهن اياه

864 ...الزواج المدني فصل بين الشباب والكبار بالعمر
865 رجال الدين ما الهن قوة انطلاقا من العقيدة اللي عم يدعوا فيها... بقدر ما القوى أو الدول يللي عم توقف وراهن...
يعني معركة الزواج المدني... المملكة العربية السعودية قامت ضد كل شي فيها... بدنا نقول المفتي ياخد موقف من مشروع قانون للبنان؟ ورئيس الحكومة ... كان رجل قريب للسعودية... وبالتالي خاض معركة كتيرة قوية ضد اقرار... ضد احالة المشروع الى مجلس النواب... دخلوا كدول وقوى سياسية مع الاديان ... ورجال الدين...
866 المسرح يجب ان يكون جزء من حركة سياسية وفكرية واسعة تهدف الى التغيير... باتجاه ارساء حياة ديموقراطية بالبلد... لحالو المسرح ما بيقدر يوصل للتغيير...
867 Interview.
868
869 ...نحنا عنا... عند العرب
870 ...عنا الحكواتي
871 ...المخايل في خيال الظل
872 لبنان... المونولوجيست... نحنا عنا مسرح الممثل... شوشو... شامل ومرعي...العالم تروح لتتفرج على شامل ومرعي...
873 ما عنا شي اسمو مسرح لبناني... عنا مسرح منتج... بيشوفوا الصندوق... وقف الصندوق... وقف العمل...
874 ...المشكل انو ما عنا تراث... أو تقليد مسرحي... مسرح يومي
875 عنا مسرح موسمي... اذا ما فيه منتج... ما فيه مسرح... لولا الجهود الجبارة للمخرجين المسرحيين... والممثلين... ما فيه عنا مسرح...
876 مسرحية ليعقوب الشدراوي... كانت المانية صارت مصرية صارت لبنانية.
877 هلق بصراحة... أولا وسائل النقل الها تأثير... نحنا ما عنا وسائل نقل منظمة متل أوروبا...اذا فيه مسرحية عم تنعمل بضيعة ... ايه ما ح يحمل حالو واحد يجي من البسطة... ويروح بسيارتو يحضر مسرحية ويجي...
878 ...فيه بيت العيتاني... اللي كانوا يقدموا بالبيكاديللي والاورلي... فيروز وعندك اختها
879 جمهور طلاب ومثقفين وفضوليين... يعني اذا حكيوا عن الجرس شغلة حلوة... هات تعا نروح نشوف الجرس... يعني ...ليك اذا بدهن يحكوا بالمجتمع يعرفوا هيدا كيف عملوا وكيف ساووا... أو بيلاقوها شغلة غريبة عليهم [...] المونودراما...
880 الممثل بيهموا يكون قريب للجمهور اكتر من الاتقان الحرفي... كل هم القرب للجمهور وشو بدو بالمخرج...
881 ما تصدق انو فيه عنا جمهور مثقف... لانو الثقافة ما داخلي بحياتنا... والتلفزيون يللي اجا لعنا ما وصلنا الثقافة...
والتلفزيون وصلنا برامج حزازير وفزازير... هيدي البرامج كلها اللي معباية التلفزيونات من المحيط للخليج...
وبيجيبوا اسئلة واجوبة متل كأنها للطلاب... منشان ليربح الواحد بالآخر تلفزيون أو براد... هيدي منا ثقافة... هيدا تدمير للثقافة...
882 التلفزيون بيشوفوا العالم كل يوم 5 ساعات... بيحضر مسرحية 1 أو 2 ساعة... شو بدو يبقى قدام هالبحر.؟
883 ...التلفزيون قتل الممثلين لانو اخدهن عالدوبلاج
884 المسلسلات التلفزيونية ما بتعبر عنا... عم تخلي الجمهور يكسل... وكمان ما عم تخلق حتى ستار... لانو المنتج كمان

...ما بيناسبو هالشي... حتى ما تطلع الاجارات

885 تصارع الهويات... ومن التسعين وجاي صار فيه محاولة تكوين مجتمع لبناني... وهيدا تأثير السياسة على الناس...

...وفيه كتير تغييرات ديموغرافية... فاختلف الجمهور

886 Interview.

887

888 أنا مواطن من الجنوب اللبناني... خلقت بمرحلة في بلد فيه مزرعة من المذاهب والتكسيبيين... وال... النظام الخاطئ

...اللي فيه ظلم وما فيه عدالة

889 وعيت على حالي عمالي صرخ... وعيت على شارلي شابلن... وعيت على نجيب الريحاني... بديع خيري... عمر الزعني... على الفن الملتزم [...] على كل فنان يصرخ... وابن البلد ما هوي الشخص اللبناني أو الجنوبي... ابن البلد هوي الضمير الشعبي... هوي الضمير العربي... هو المسحوق العربي... هو الرافض العربي... هوي الشخص اللي مجبول بالتراب... اللي لونو بيشبه لون التراب... ابن البلد لم يكن يوم له علاقة بالممثل... ابن البلد هو الانسان بيعبر عن حالة الطبقة الوسط اللي كادت ان تنخرط بالوطن العربي... نتيجة أوضاع اقتصادية...

وصراع انظمة... و.... ابن البلد بعدو لحد هلق لم يتغير... جلدو غير قابل للتلوث... رغم كل [...]... الزمن اللي ضدو

890 لانو هيدا النظام العالمي الجديد... نظام السكس. والدولار والمخدرات والهاء العالم بعلاقات كلينتون الجنسية وبشذوذ مايكل جانسون وبمادونا... وتمرير كل هذا المجزرة الثقافية... والهاء الناس عن [...] القيم الانسانية والقيم الدينية

...والروحية والقيم الالتزام والقيم القومية

891 أنا من هالناس اللي بيحبوا الحياة من هالناس المصدومين من هالناس للي رافضين الاستسلام و... بزمن ما بالستينات والسبعينات... كان فيه اللاآت التلاتة للزعيم الراحل جمال عبد الناصر... أنا اليوم حطيت صفرين فوق منهن... عندي 3 آلاف لا

892 لكل ما يحدث من استغلال المرأة كسلعة... من المواضيع التافهة مما يصدر لنا الغرب من ... ثقافات ما بتشبهنا وما بتشبه تقاليدنا... وللي غزت برامجنا المحلية وغزت شاشاتنا غزت بيوتنا... يعني. تصور من ضمن المهازل التي الى القداس والى المسجد والى الحسينية والى هالمقامات cellular يعاني منها الانسان ان يدخل الـ هيدي عداك بقى عن المسارح... ان يدخل هذا الجهاز اللعين الى أماكن... دون ان يعير قيمة لها المكان للي هوي فيه... تصور أنك بيرن بتاخدو وبتمشي قال بتحكي على جنب... cellular تكون قاعد عم تسمع قرآن وقدامك جهاز وهناك من يقرأ... قداس بالكنيسة ... بهذا الزمن... ما ممكن ابن البلد يستسلم ويتقوقع ويلبس كرافات ويحول مسرحو لكباريه [...] وشانسونييه [...] . وهيدا ابن البلد

893 المسرح هوي ابو الفنون... انا متواصل مع جمهوري... ما بتعاطى مع النجم... والاماكن المخمورة... المسرح هوي

...المنبر اللي بيعبر فيه عن موقفي الانساني والسياسي

894 اليوم بتلتفت على بعض المسارح بتلاقي فيه كيلوتات وفخاد والناس متخادة بكل غرائزها... ونكت تافهة وتنمير

... على زعماء سياسيين بشكل منحط ورخيص وتافه

895 المجزرة الثقافية... منبعها... الوضع الاقتصادي... ثم الوضع الاقتصادي... ثم الوضع الاقتصادي...

896 فيه اسر عم تفوت باشيا ودهاليز منها الها... انت لمن م تجوع ناس وتغرقها بالدين... منا مزحة... الشغلة منا مزحة...

897 أنا عندي قناعات... يمكن تشوفها غريبة بس هي قناعات... أي حرب بشعة بدها تخلف سلام ابشع... يعني ذات يوم مثلا... كان أي واحد من طائفة بدو يعمل خدمة... يروح للطايفة التانية ويطلب خدمة... ويخدموه... لانو بوق اعلامي بيحكي... لانو كان فيه نوع... رغم اخطاء الامتيازات... كان فيه... كان فيه مشروع بلد... مشروع قومي... مشروع حرية...

898 ...بيروت شغلة كبيرة... هلق انفرزت المذاهب

899 هلق بتحس فيه عرق اكتر مما كان بمرحلة الحرب او ما قبل الحرب... وهيدا شي سيء... انو تحددلي طموحاتي من خلال مذهبي... بهذا الزمن وبهذا القرن وبهذا العصر... شي مخزي... شي مخزي...

900 لا هيدا ما الو علاقة بالمسرح... هيدا البلد... نحنا... نحنا... ناس... عرب... عنا قناعات... عناوين... انا ما ناقل مذهبي على بيتي... انا ناقل بلدي على بيتي [...] وبقلن لولادي مين مثلي الاعلى [...] . من هالمنطلقات بحكي معهن

901 بس كمان نتيجة مواقفي... ايه طبعا... ما قدرت... ما قدرت... استغل شهرتي ونجوميتي... وتاجر بالناس... وصايرة القصة انو أي واحد صح ضمن مجموعة غلط عم بيصير هو الغلط...

902 بعتزل الفن وبشتغل مهنة تانية اشرف...

903 يدفع بالدولار... رايح يتعشى ويشرب... نحنا Drink جمهور الشانسونييه مرتاح... رايح ياخد جمهورنا جمهور الطبقة الوسط... للي ما بقى معو حق بطاقة... واللي هيدا المسرح عاملولنو اياه الو نحنا... لنحكي عن وجع لنحكي عن قهرو... لنحكي عن حبنا لهالبلد

904 أنا اصلا ما بسمحلو يشرب سيكارة بالصالة بدي اسمحلو يشرب... الفن ابن الوعي... كيف بدي قدملك فن انت وعم تشرب... شو هيدا أي نوع فن؟.. كيف بدي اسمحلك تطلع بفخذ مرا بدل ما تطلع بوجهي وبعيوني

905 الطائفية استعملت بشكل كبير... بذكاء خارق... الناس عظيمة... ما فيه اعظم من الناس... الناس عندها ثقافة اكتر من اللي بيمثلوها... الشعب اللبناني شعب عظيم ورائع...

906 البلد كلها وحوش

907 الشهيد ابن البلد... كان عم بيجيب ربطة خبز وعلقو ابناء الصف الواحد... هلق هي قبل ما يموت قتل مرتو... ليه قتلها؟ لانو اسمها مذاهب... مذاهب... هي ما بدو مرتو مذاهب... بدو بلد هي... قتلها... قتلها... بالأخرة طلعت متزوجة من كل طائفة واحد... 6 طوائف كبرى بالبلد بتخطفو بدها تحاكم... بالآخر بتنتهي المسرحية... بقلهن ما تخليها تتجاجر فيكن هيدي مذاهب... هيدي بدها تقصكن كلكن شققة شققة... اصرخوا لمذاهب... قولولها لا... لا... لا

... حرضت الناس على الـ لا... ما فيه دين مؤذي

908 ما بقى الا علاقة المنطقة بنجاح المسرحية... واكبر دليل انو الجرس نجحت هونيك ... قبل ما تنجح هون... المسرح

...جمهورو قد ما تحترمو بيحترمك

909 أنا بحب المسرح الشعبي... المباشر... كل تاريخي انا مرحلة مع شوشو ومرحلة ما بعد شوشو باشتغل الادب الشعبي... باشتغل الثقافة الشعبية... باشتغل المباشر... ما بحب الجمهور انا... تطفيلو ضو... وتعملو مشهد تعمل اسقاط فيه... بتضهر... ولك شو بيقصد؟... الناس ما بقى الها جلادة شو بيقصد... ضويلها ضو احمر... وتجي تحطلها خيال... وتلبس قماش اسود... وتعملها مشهد هيك سوداوي... رمزي... ما... اختباري... انا ما بحبهن

910 منير كسرواني...
911 بس نقعد لحالنا منحكي

912 فيه مسرحيات... فيه مسرحيات تدعي صفة الوطنية من برا... وهي تتكل على التهريج والسطحية والتجريح... الناس ما فيك تكذب عليها على طول... بمهرجان المحبة... الصالة تتسع لستة آلاف... هيدا النوع من المسرحيات السطحية اللي عم قلك اياها... اجا 200... بابتسم انت لبناني... اجا بين 12 و15 ألف بني آدم اجو على مسرحية انت لبناني... عرض واحد... بالشهيد ابن البلد... لمن مثلت لبنان فيها بمهرجان دمشق العاشر بدورتو المسرحية... 11 جريح راح بالشام كسروا البلور بالقوة بدن يحضروا. وعملت عرضين... والعالم على الارض بالبلاكين وبالشارع

...وما بقى فيه محل

913 ليه؟ بيعرفو انو فقير بيعرفو صادق وبيعرفو ابن البلد. بيعرفو انخطف مرتين... بيعرفو تقوس عليه بيعرفو تهدد بالقتل. تغير جلدي ما بقى حدا فيه يغيرلي جلدي. الناس ما بقى ما فيك تضحك عليها... انا بس اطلع كنت تلفزيونية... Interviewبخليك بالبيت... اذا ذاكرتك قوية. او بالليل المفتوح أو ببعد سهار. أو بأي الناس بتسمعني وكأنو عم بعمل اعظم مسلسل... بس لسلاطة لساني وجرأتي وعدم تمسيح الجوخ لكائن حي بهالبلد [...] هودي بيعرفوهن الناس

914 ...والدليل على ذلك خروج هالنص من الامن العام دون ان يشطب حرف منو... مع نقدي لكل الاشياء الجارحة بهالبلد...

915 نحنا عنا في لبنان بعدا حرية التعبير عنا افضل من أي مكان في الدنيا... في الدنيا...ما حدا بيقدر يقمعنا هون بالبلد... المهم ما قدرو يشترونا. ما قدرو يستعبدونا بلاقولنا سعر...

916 Interview.
917
918.
919 1847 مارون النقاش [...] 1960 منير ابو دبس.
920 عيلة ابو المجد 1966 نص اميركي ملبنن.
921 المسرح الوطني لعب دور كبير ومهم جدا في تكوين الجمهور المسرحي...
922 ليه شوشو عم ينجح عم بيقدم اعمال بتعني شي للناس [...] حولوا شوي الاجواء السامية تاعتن... نزلوا شوي على الارض...
923 جمهور الحرب اللي عايش بالخوف والذعر... وخايف. من الموت اللي يلاحقو باستمرار من زاروب لزاروب من شارع لشارع... هذا الجمهور صار يتطلب نوع من المسرح السهل... ما مستعد يشغل دماغو... ما مستعد يشغل

924 فكرو... لانو فكرو اساسا متعوب... رجال تعبان خيفان... فبدو شغلة سهلة... ولذلك نشأ مسرح خلال الحرب... مسرح لا يبغي سوى اضحاك الناس وتسليتهم والترفيه عنهم...
ما عم بشتغل مسرح لانو صرت بخاف... بخاف... كنت آخد النص اعرف اذا بينجح ولا لأ... بعرف بهذا النص
وين الجمهور بيضحك وين ما بيضحك... هلق ما بعرف شو بدو الجمهور...
925 أنا بعتقد انو اللبناني... لبناني... كلن بياكلو تبولة وبيشربو عرق...
926 في "حزب سعدلله" مع انطوان غندور في شاتوتريانو... تعابير اقليمية...تعابير كسروانية... سم سميمك ... سكوت
ولا كلمة... ابن كسروان بيفهما... أنا ما بتعنيلي شي...
927 الحرب عملت عجايب...
928 المرا استغربت انو فيه خوري عم يمشي ع كورنيش المزرعة... وانا جاري اللي تحت مني مسيحي... وعايش انا
وإياه متل الاخوة... انما هالجيل الجديد... زوجتو لهالشاب من الجيل الجديد... يمكن ما شايفة مسلم... انعزلت بمنطقة
جونية... ومحيطها كلو مسيحيين... استغربت جدا انو تشوف بمنطقة اسلامية خوري...
929 ضلوا في هون الناس مختلطة ببعضها اكتر... المنطقة الغربية ما تفرغت من المسيحيين... عكس المناطق الشرقية...
المسلمين خافوا واجوا عالغربية... خط الجامعة الاميركية كل عمرا هيدا خط... خط عروبي... الطلاب طبعا... مش
الجامعة... الجامعة اليسوعية فيها لبنانيين وبس... ما فيها عرب... من طايفة وحدة
930 بيقولولك تعايش وهي واحدة... ولمن انعقدت الشركة... كانت بنوايا غير صافية... بدك تغير كذا... بدك تكون
علماني... بصريح العبارة... وهيدي شغلة وراها مشاكل وقصص طويلة عريضة... ويمكن السياسيين اللي بيقولولك
نحنا مع العلمنة وكذا هني اول مين بيحاربها...
931 لا اشتغلوا عليها (الطائفية) ايه... اشتغلوا مش تيخلصوا منها... اشتغلوا عليها تتضل... وتتفاقم... ليش بيقولولك اشتغلوا
مزرعة... وبدهن اياها تبقى...
932 لا موجودة... ما فيي قول مش موجودة... ويجب العمل لأزالتها
933 الجماعة اللي اشتغلوا مسرح تجاري... اشتغلوا عليها
934 الله عاطيه موهبة حب العالم... الناس بتجي ومستعدة للضحك... فلو طلع زياد الرحباني عالمسرح وقلهن للناس الله
معكم... ح يموتوا من الضحك... شوشو كان يمد عصايتو من الكواليس... تقوم الناس تتنطنط عن الكراسي... استعداد
فظيع للضحك...
935 فيه اتفاق بين اللبنانيين جميعا انو الحرب حرقت دينن... البيئة الفاسدة هون اللي افسدها السياسة... والاعلام... يمكن
الاذاعة الوحيدة اللي ما اشتغلت على الطائفية هي صوت الوطن...
936 أنا خلال عملي ما صادفت أي مشاكل متعلقة بالحرية... بلبنان فيه مساحة من الحرية اكتر من أي بلد عربي
آخر...يمكن فيه بعض التابو...حتى فيه شغلات بالشانسونييه انا باستغرب كيف سمحوا فيها
937 شكيب... قلبو طيب... ما قدر انو خلال عز دين التشنج الديني... حزب الله من ميل وجماعة الاحباش من ميل وبدك
تجي تعمل مسرحية تهاجم فيها الله مثلا... ايه ما بتركب
938 هلق بالظروف هيدي ما بتمرق... حيد عنها وعن نقطتين سياسيتين تانيين... حر تقول اللي بدك اياه
939 بنتي عمرها 10 سنين وتكتب شعر بالفرنسي...مثلا

940 فيه خلاف قومي... لا خلاف ديني... لانو بخلال الحرب كلها ما سمعنا انو واحد مسلم حط الفرد براس واحد مسيحي
وقلو اسلم... ولا واحد مسيحي حط الفرد براس واحد مسلم وقلو عمول مسيحي...
941 الخلاف قومي المسلمين بيقولو نحنا جماعة عرب ويدعون الى القومية العربية والوحدة العربية... والمسيحيين بيقولو نحنا ما النا علاقة بالعرب... هودي العرب جرب جماعة متخلفين... نحن اقرب الى اوروبا... نحنا غربيين بتفكيرنا...
942 الخلاف قومي وليس خلاف ثقافي (...educational)
943 Interview¹
944
945 ما بقى فيه افكار مثلا... أفكار ما بقى فيه... لانو ما بقى ما فيه حركات فكرية بالعالم... كان فيه صراع بين فكرين
بالعالم... كان فيه الاتحاد السوفياتي... الاشتراكية... وكان فيه رأسمالية متوحشة... كان فيه الثورة بكوبا... كان فيه
الثورة الثقافية بالصين... حرب التحرير بفيتنام... المسرح كان جزء من هالحركات...
946 ما كان المسرح مفصول ابدا عن الحركة العامة لانو جزء من الحياة المسرح
947 مسرح الاطفال في لبنان كان جزء من حركة سياسية عامة...
948 خلال الحرب تم اختبار كل الافكار... من الماركسية... من اقصى اليمين الى أشد خيارات اليسار الراديكالية... تم
تدمير المساحات المشتركة في لبنان... في الاسواق التجارية...
949 عنا مرحلتين... الكسوف... يلي عم بيقولوا انو نهاية العالم... ومرحلة الالفية الثانية...
950 راحت التعددية وبقي صنف واحد. يلي هو الفودفيل... الذي يعبر عن خاصية اللبنانيين [...] بالظرف العام
951 الشانسونييه عبر عن الانهيار النهائي للطبقة الوسطى ... وقيام طبقة جديدة هي طبقة اثرياء الحرب...يلي الناس يلي
بيروحوا بيشربوا كاس وبيتفرجوا ع واحد بيسليهن... يا ريت بيشتغلوا متل ما هوي بالعالم... بس اللبنانيين
بشطارتهن يعني صاروا يشتروا المسرحية بشنطتها... يروحوا... يشوفوا مسرحي مشهور مثلا فولبوني... يشتروا
مسرحياتو بشنطة... يفتحوا الشنطة تطلع الماكيت كاملة... النص... الماكيت... الديكور... السينوغرافي الى آخره... بس
هني يعربوا النص ويوقفوا ممثلين... يجيبوا مخرج منشان يعمل عملية التنسيق الاخيرة...
952 بهيداك الوقت قدمت مسرحية قدمها حزب ديني... ورحت حضرتها المسرحية... لأول مرة بتاريخ المسرح بلبنان...
ويمكن بالعالم كمان... بيقسموا العالم شققتين... شقفة بيقعدوا فيها النسوان وشقفة بيقعدوا فيها الرجال... والمسرحية
كان اسمها "ثأر الله"... ايه... فالمسرح هوي جزء من حركة عامة...
953 بالحرب الاخيرة جرى اقلمة لبنان... صار بلد متلو متل... أي بلد تاني بالمنطقة... متلو متل... متلو متل... متلو متل
متلو متل...
954
955 متلو متل...العراق وسوريا... ما عاد يتمتع بأي خاصة من خصايصو العتيقة... وخاصة بعد التدمير المنهجي للطبقة
الوسطى يللي هي منتجة ثقافيا... بالعراق ما فيه طبقة وسطى... بسوريا ما فيه طبقة وسطى... بمصر ما فيه طبقة
وسطى... فيه يا اغنيا كتير يا فقرا...
956 الناس بشكل عام ما عم تضهر من بيوتها... الحالة الاقتصادية مع التلفزيون لعبوا دور اساسي في تفريغ المسرح من

957 كوادرو... الممثلين راحوا يشتغلوا بالتلفزيون فضعف الانتاج... والعالم مزروبة ببيوتها عم تشوف تلفزيون...
واحد متل انطوان غندور كان عم يشتغل (عهالصعيد الطائفي)... يوسف بك كرم... طانيوس شاهين...كل الناس
...بيعرفوا انو كان اشتغلهن لمناطق معينة... نبيه ابو الحسن... اشتغل بفترة من الفترات لمنطقة
958 ...منير ما قدم "بمناطقو" اذا بدك بين هلالين... بس منير عم يشتغل مسرح شعبي
959 المسيحي بيشوف شو رأي المسلم بالموضوع... والمسلم بيشوف رأي المسيحي بالموضوع...
960 الشانسونييه... هودي مش مسرحيين... هودي ناس لتاتين... حط بين هلالين اذا بدك هو الناس يعني...
...بيعتبروا حالهن مهضومين... الناس بيحبوهن لانن غلظا
961 لا لا لا لا الجمهور بشكل يعني لحد هلق ... حتى بالمحلات الخاصة... عم نكتشف ناس طائفيين كتير يعني... ما
بيكونوا بيعرفوا مين نحنا... فبيصيروا يحكوا عن الطوائف باعتبار انو نحنا من طايفتهن يعني... لازم المرء يعترف
بوجود الطائفية حتى يتخطاها يعني... منضل نقول ما فيه طائفية... نحنا لبنانيين ما عنا طوائف. لا في طائفية...
وطائفية موجودة بمحلات ما بيفكر الواحد انو موجودة فيها يعني... وفيه احقاد وفيه احاسيس متشنجة وفيه توتر...
...وفيه للي بدك اياه بالاخير
962 هيدا الجمهور ما بيهموا المسرح... بيهموا المواضيع اللي بتنطرح بالمسرح... بس لا اكتر ولا اقل... بيهموا الى حد ما
النجوم... يعني هالمسرحية فيها انطوان كرباج... بيروح بيتفرج ع انطوان كرباج... وبيهمو انطوان كرباج يقول
شغلات بتناسبو... وقت انطوان كرباج بيقول شغلات ما بتناسبو بيزعل منو لانطوان كرباج... لانو بيعتبر انو
هيدا ممثلو في هذا المكان. على هذا الصعيد... حتى روجيه عساف لمن كان يقدم الفرقة على اساس انها متعددة
...الطوائف. كنت اتخانق انا واياه... لانو نحنا مش مفكرين بالموضوع
963 يعني لبنان وين يعني... بانقلو للبنان بحطو بأوروبا يعني...؟... مهابيل هول مهابيل... واللي بيشددوا انو هوية لبنان
...هوية عربية مهابيل كمان بنفس الوقت... لانو لبنان... بشكل عام لبنان متخلف
964 ...بشكل عام لبنان متخلف
965 Interview.
966
967 أنا تركني الجمهور المثقف مع انو انا ما تغيرت... لانو الجمهور المثقف صار عمرو كبير... وبعدين اجت الحرب...
...وكان يعرف بيروت قبل الحرب... وبعدو عم بينبش ع بيروت قبل الحرب
968 يتناقض مع طبيعة اللبناني. هو كمان ساهم بإبعاد الناس عن discipline عنصر الـ المسرح... العالم
969 ...بتحب المسرح السهل... بدا تاكل بدا تشرب... ما بدا تجي عالوقت
970 ...مارسيل خليفة ... استقبلو كتير منيح بجونية
971 ...الحرية والاحتلالات ... كل الناس معو...منير كسرواني استغل قضية الجنوب
972 هلق مثلا سنة 1999 الجمهور اللي عمرو
973 علاقة الحرب مع العمر... ما فيه ثقافة... خلصت همن يلحقو الوقت اللي ضاع... هيدي عنا génération perdue
...بعد 5 سنين يمكن يطلع عنا جيل عندو شوية ثقافة
974 تبع الجمهور عليها... لانو اللبناني بطبعو بيحب reaction عندي مشاهد بالفرنساوي نفس الـ يتثقف ... بعدين حتى
...لو ما فهم ما بيحط ع نفسو انو هوي ما فهم

975 ...اللبناني فوضوجي وما عندو احترام لشي... بيبهر العالم بس يطلع لبرا
976 المسرح اللبناني هو اللي بيصور المجتمع اللبناني... مش اذا ترجمنا...مسرحية لارابال صار عنا مسرح
977 ...عوامل قتلت المسرح اللبناني
978 ...troque... التلفزيون اللبناني... ما حدا من الفنانين بيقدر ينجح الا ما يمرق بواسطتي
979 ...LBC شجعت مين ما كان يعمل مسرح... لحد 1992 كان كل شي عال
980 من 1993 اجو بقية التلفزيونيت عملو نفس الشي كل تلفزيون عندها فنانين او تنين او تلاتة عم بيروجولن
981 ...مات النقد الثقافي المكتوب... لانو التلفزيون كل يوم بيحططلك سبوت
982 ...الضمان... كسر حق المسرح... صفت الناس طلع دينها من المسرح... بطل فيه شباك تذاكر... بطل الشخص من تلقاء
983 ...نفسو يروح يشتري بطاقة لأنو بيجي بيقلك بكرا بيبلصوني ببطاقة الدعوات... بيجي واحد بياع...بيطلع من محلو بيقول... شو ما جبتنا بطاقات لمسرحيتك السنة... ولو فلان الفلاني
...فات جاب هونيك 20 بطاقة للموظفين كلهن
984 الضيقة الاقتصادية... 5 اشخاص مع الاولاد وكذا ندفع 100 دولار... بعدين صار فيه كتير تكسير اسعار من الفنانين
985 ...صارو يفوتو الناس بـ 5000 ل.ل أقل من السينما
986 Interview.
987
988 ...محاولة هرب عن طريق السرعة... البسط غير الـ... ما تنسى 15 سنة حرب
989 لجنة مهرجانات بعلبك الدولية... اللي عطت منير ابو دبس... واكبت هالقصة بعض المؤسسات الدينية الي كانت تنتج وخاصة بأوائل الحرب... وقبل الحرب كمان بشوي... وتدفع مصاري منشان تنتج... متل شربل مع ريمون ومحاكمة يسوع مع ريمون... وأعمال تانية... حتى جبران اللي أخرجها منير ابو دبس... بخص هون بالذات ...حركة انطلياس
...كان فيه ناس
990 فيه عنصر مهم هون هوي المنتج اللبناني... يللي كان موجود قبل الحرب... لان اللبناني عامة بيحط 10 ل.ل. أو تياخد 20 ما هيك؟ 15
991 الدعم المالي من المؤسسات الدينية توقف بالحرب... بقت الدولة...كانت الدولة قبل الحرب تساهم بالمهرجانات حتى
...ماليا... اليوم صار مطلوب أكتر... السينما لا تمول الا من المؤسسات الكبيرة
992 الازمة الاقتصادية... ما حدا بيقدر يدفع قرش الا بمحل محسوب... فيه ناس عم يوصلوا لحال الجوع بلبنان... هودي
...اذا بتقلو مسرح بيسبك وبيسب شكسبير... بدو يعيش
993 ...هيدا بلد مركب تركيبة عجيبة... حاربنا مع الطائفية وضد الطائفية... أنا مني طائفي
994 الفنون المشهدية... يمكن اكتر لوائها معقود للمسيحيي أكتر من الاسلام لاسباب بتتعلّق يمكن بتربيتن لاخواننا الاسلام الدينية...يمكن المشهديات بالاسلام منها مقبولة قد المشهديات اليوم بالدين المسيحي... بس اللي بدي قولو هلق بيعارض الفكرة اللي قلتلك اياها. بالبلدان العربية اللي فيها أقليات مسيحية... لواء المسرح معقود للاسلام... متل تونس
...وسوريا والعراق
995 أنا اورثوذكسي علمت سنتين بالكسليك... اكتشفوا الموارنة اني اورثوذكسي... عم بحكيك القصة عن مزح... قالولي
...عن مزح... ولك ضيعانك... ضيعانك... يعني منها طائفية القصة... مذهبية القصة

288

ARABIC TRANSCRIPTIONS

996 بعدين منير كسرواني فيه كتير ناس بيفكروه مسلم... الاسلام بيفكروه مسلم... وحبهم الو يمكن جايي من هالقصة...
وفيه كتير ناس بيعرفوا مسيحي وبيحبوه لأنو بيحكي وجعن...

997 انا بعتبر كرجل مسيحي... انا بحب المسيح كتير... بس انا بعتبر انو المسيح... هو أول واحد مسيحي ويمكن آخر
واحد..يمكن... أنا كمان مني شيوعي... بس كتير مع كلمة الدين أفيون الشعوب... كتير... جدا... الدين شغلة...

998 ليك الطائفية... الها رواسب بالحياة... وبس يرجع المسرح لاسبد ما ترجع تبين... نحنا ما شفينا من الطائفية... بعد
بلبنان... ما شفينا... هيدا كلو كذب ما شفينا...

999 طول عمري... من زمان تفكيري واضح... باخد عمل انا بحبو... وعامة بيكون او اجتماعي او انساني او سياسي...

1000 انا بستبعد انو انا شخصيا اعمل مسرحية ضد المسيحي او ضد الاسلام... لانو انا ما بتعاطى بالدين... بس الدين
بيحد ذاتو ما بيندقر...

1037 Interview.

1038

1039 أنا أؤمن انو اللي بدو يشتغل بالمسرح عليه أنو يكون مثقف فعلا مش قولا... وللأسف انو أغلبية من يدعو الثقافة
عنا هني اشباه مثقفين وليسوا مثقفين...

1040 تعرفت ع جوزف بو نصار... كان راجع من بولونيا... اشتغل مع واحد من اهم المسرحيين بالعالم... جرسي
غروتوفسكي... ايه كان يشتغل معو كان بفرقتو ع مدى كذا سنة وعاملين أعمال كبيرة

1041 العيلة توت" لستيفان اولكيمي ضمن اطار المهرجان الاول للمسرح والعروض المشهدية...اللي نظمو جان داود

1042 1984 لا باركا"... من المسرح الكلاسيكي الاسباني للكاردينال دو لا باركا"... "الحياة حلم

1043 1986 "الصابرون"... les patients تبع ماجركو ليبرتي

1044 و"البيت الحدود" لسلافومير مروجك [...] la maison frontière ...

1045 كان وقتها زمن الحرب وتحول المسرح الى الفودفيل والشانسونييه... والى تجارة سخيفة واعمال سخيفة... قليل تيلمع
فيها اعمال تضوي شوي او تلمع مسرحيا... كانت تجربة مريرة انك تجيب الناس ع هالنوع من المسرح عملية شبه
مستحيلة... فاتبعنا خطة بوقتها... انو نتصل نحنا مباشرة بالمدارس والاندية الثقافية واللي déjà
عندا حلول كان...

بلشنا بحوالي 500 600 شخص يحضرونا اول سنة الى حوالي 6000 7000 شخص بعد 3 4 سنين ce qui
fait انو عملنا جمهورنا...

1046 نعمل كل شي نحنا بالمسرح ...عشنا حياة انو ما عنا شي نعملو الا المسرح... بالمسرح
يالضياع بمعمعة الحرب...
بيلهينا عن اللي عم بيصير برا défoulement كان...

1047 قدرنا نكون جمهورنا... مش صحيح انو الجمهور بدك تكونو انك تجيب ضمانات... بتكونو بالصداقة أولا وبأنك
توعيه تانيا...

1048 أنك تقلو شو عندك... عزمنا واحد من المسؤولين بنادي الليونز...ايلي برتي... كان نائب الحاكم العام تبع الليونز
بلبنان... بالمنطقة 351 ما بعرف شو بيسموها... لبنان والاردن... وبما انو هوي مسؤول بالليونز صار يشجع اندية
الليونز يجوا يضمنو المسرحية ويشجعو العالم يجوا يحضروا هالمسرح الفقير... وهيك استمرينا...
عملنا جمهور

1049 الجمهور كان مدارس... طلاب... كتير... بتعرف طلاب بعمر معين وبزمن الحرب كان ما ...وهيدي خطوة كتير مهمة
عندن أي حس بالجدية... كان يجوا احيانا يتمصخروا علينا... نحنا وعم نمثل اعمال تراجيدية او درامية... يضحكوا علينا احيانا... بالجهد تيسكتوا ويسمعوا المسرحية للآخر... أول مرة هيك تاني مرة اخف... تالت مرة تغيرت القصة... الجمهور بدك تعودو على نوعية العمل... بيتعود بيصير يفوت معك.

1050 ...أنا رافقت الحركة المسرحية من وجهتي نظر... المسرحي والناقد
1051 ...كنت اسأل الناس ليه بيحضروا هالمسرحية مش هي
1052 ...أنا بدي اضحك... بحضر اخوت شانيه لأضحك
1053 ...أنا بحضر الرحابنة لانو عندن موسيقى حلوة... وتياب حلوة وعرض حلو
1054 ...ليه بتحضر شانسونييه... انا خيي ما الي جلادة بدو موّه عن حالي... وانسى الحرب

1055 صانع الاحلام"... 1987 طنطنت فيها العالم... رجع ريمون جبارة اعاد افتتاح المسرحية " مباشرة بعد مهرجاني
بغداد وقرطاج... بتذكر كان نهار أربعاء الافتتاح... الخميس انفتح غيشيه... رحت أنا بدي احضر تاني مرة
المسرحية... تشوفها... اكتب عنها... ما كان فيه حضور ... الجمعة كمان... ما كان فيه حضور... قام ريمون جبارة
وقف الممثلين... عالخشبة... وداروا وجهن صوب المقاعد الفاضية... وعطوا اشارة بعصة. صوب المقاعد الفاضية...
قمت خزقت اللي كنت بدي اكتبو وكتبت صانع الاحلام... جمهور فاشل حتى التفاهة... بعد اسبوع سكرت
المسرحية... ما عادت اشتغلت... بكازينو لبنان...

1056 ...مش صحيح انو الحرب يفرض مسرح التفاهة
1057 جلال خوري اللي هوي برشتي بامتياز وماركسي بامتياز... بيقول انو المسرح العالمي مر بتلات مراحل... المسرح
الاغريقي ومسرح شكسبير والمسرح البرشتي...
1058 بالمسرح البلدي...الضيف او العيلة توت اللي بتحكي عن تسلط العسكريتاريا بالمجتمعات... انعرضت المسرحية بأيام
الحرب... انعرضت هون وفهموها الناس انو هي ضد الكتائب والاحرار والناس اللي هون... وعرضناها بالغربية
وفيه ناس فهموها انو هي ضدهن وفيه ناس فهموها انو هي ضد اليهود... وفيه ناس فهموها انو ضد المحتل...
1059 ...الجمهور ما رح يطلع... ابدا ما رح يطلع من الطائفية... طالما الظروف هيك ما رح يطلع
1060 ([...]) حرمتها الكنيسة ([...]) يدافع عن الكنيسة لمنعها المسرح فهي منعته نتيجة مظاهر المجون... حرمتها الكنيسة.
العصور الوسطى...
1061 بالمقابل ... الاسلام كدين حرم المسرح... لانو اساسه وثني ممنوع المسرح... الشكل المسرحي... لها السبب اول شكل
ممنوع يعمل مسرح... l'ombre chinoise ...من اشكال المسرح عند العرب هوي خيال الظل لانو الانسان الذي
يتعاطى المسرح في الدين الاسلامي هوي انسان خارج... عن الدين
1062 وسيم طبارة ومحمد شبارو اتنين مسلمين سنيين من بيروت الغربية اشتغلوا ببيروت الشرقية... وممثل واحد درزي
الله يرحمو نبيه ابو الحسن يللي مسرحو اكترو كان بالمنطقة المسيحية... وما كانوا هودي يسترجو يروحو عالمنطقة
الاسلامية. بعكس زياد الرحباني... اللي كان مسرحو اهم مسرح اشتغل بالمنطقة الاسلامية... وما كان يسترجي يجي

1063 ...عالـ... الـ. فإذا مفهوم الطائفية ما تغلغل بلعبة المسرح الجمهور عندو هالوعي... ايه... المسرح الديني. ريمون جبارة عمل شربل... حزب الله عمل مسرح ديني... حركة امل

1064 ...عملت مسرح ديني... المسرح الديني يأخذ من الدين للدين ولا يأخذ من الدين لمعاداة الآخر

1065 ...ما فيه ما بحياتو كان فيه حرية بلبنان متل ما الناس بتفكر... وبالعالم ما فيه حرية المسلمين بيعترفوا انو المسيحيين والموارنة تحديدا كان الن فضل كبير على صون اللغة العربية ايام الاتراك...كان فيه خوف من التتريك...

1066 هامش الحرية عنا شوي محدود كتير... نسبة للماضي... محدود لاسباب سياسية أولا ودينية تانيا... ايه... لانو أنا تذكرت حادثة صارت... لمن قدم شكيب خوري مسرحيتو أمام الباب... توقفت المسرحية ... هجموا عليه جماعة حزب الله على المسرح... لمن قدمت لطيفة ملتقى مسرحية وصية كلب بالـ 66 لعبة سيدة الخلاص أو وصية كلب لكاتب برازيلي اسمو آريانا سوسونا... انو واحد غني كبير مات الكلب تبعو بدو يعملو جنازة بالكنيسة يعزم البطرك وكذا... وانعملت هالمسرحية تقدمت يومين تلاتة ومنعت بأمر من البطريكية المارونية...

1067 ...أنا بعتبر الزواج المدني بدعة صهيونية تهدف الى القضاء على مبدأ العيلة

1068 ...أنا ما بحب رجال الدين بس أنا بحب الدين

1069 Interview.

كل الناس اللي اجت حضرت مسرحية رفيق علي أحمد اجت غصمن عنا... لحالو وأكيد شي عن الجنوب... ومدري

شو... من بعد ما ضهرت من المسرحية كل الناس... بثبتها 100 بالـ 100 ووائق من كلامي لانو انا اخدت هالـ

هيدا من كذا شخص كانوا ضامنين... وفيه منن حكيو معي مباشرة... كل الناس اللي فلت من echo الصالة ندمت

كيف ما اجت حضرتها قبل [...] كليا... كليا...تغيرت الصورة عندهم كليا... يعني... نوعا ما الناس بالمنطقة... وقت اللي بتكون بتجهل شخص بالمنطقة التانية...

1070 الناس اللي اجت اكيد ناس منها طائفية... لانو لو ناس طائفية ما اجت.

1071 فيه ضمان من الضمانات... رئيس تجمع اجتماعي بمنطقة جونية... وتجمع مسيحي وملتزم كنسيا وملتزم مسيحيا... وقف فوق وقال... نحنا منشكر... رفيق علي احمد انو اجا عالمنطقة... وقدمنا هالعرض يللي نحنا كان مفترض فينا نروح محل ما هو نحضرو... يعني اعترف انو فيه تقصير من قبلن انو يروحو يحضرو مسرحية وين ما كان...

1072 ...أنا بثبت انو رفيق انسان غير طائفي

1073 Interview.

1074

1075 الحالة الاقتصادية... دعم الدولة... تعودوا الناس 20 سنة حرب يقعدوا ببيوتن... يتفرجوا عالتلفزيون...

1076 طـس: ليه هالاصرار انو يكون فيه مسرح؟

1077 بالستينات كان فيه حركة. نهضة فنية مهمة يعني... مشي الرسم التشكيلي... مشي المسرح. مشي الصحافة الادب...

الشعر... كلن هو دعموا بعضن...

1078 ...ما فيه عادة مسرحية بلبنان...(habitude) حضور المسرح عادة

1079 الحرب اثرت كتير...واحد ملتهي كيف بدو ياكل... وكيف يهرب من القذيفة ما بيحضر مسرح... الفنون فاكهة...

1080 بالحرب الجمهور انقسم عنا نصين...بدل ما كان عندك جمهور كامل... صار نص الجمهور عنا... اذا مثلت بالشرقية
...عندك نص جمهور... اذا مثلت بالغربية عندك نص جمهور
1081 جمهور المسرح قبل الحرب كانوا العقائديين الجامعيين... بالحرب ما عاد فيه عقائديين ...صاروا كلن طائفيين
1082 انعمل مسرح رخيص بالحرب... مثلا اذا انعملت مسرحية بالشرقية يشتموا الغربية... واذا نقلت هيي ذاتها عالغربية
...يشتموا بالشرقية... مسرح استهلاكي ... ما الو قيمة
1083 ط. س. : ممكن برأيك انو مثلا فكرة معينة ممكن يكون الها عدة مفاهيم حسب الطائفة؟
1084 لا أنا والله عملت مسرح بالحرب هون انتقدت فيه السلطويين بالمنطقة هون... بزرادشت (صار كلبًا)... طلبت مني بالغربية... ايه... قلتلن... أنا فيه رجل دين فيها المسرحية ... مسيحي. اذا بدي انقلها عالغربية... بدي حط رجل دين مسلم... ما وافقوا. قال ما فينا...ايه
1085 بيضل البيئة المسيحية فيها مجال للانتقاد اكتر من البيئة الاسلامية... يللي كتير متحجرة... يعني ما فيك تدق في... لا بالغربية منعولوا اياها... أمام BUC فيك تذكر... شكيب خوري بعد الحرب... عمل مسرحية بالـ الباب هددوه... كان بالغربية... اجاه تهديد من ... من BUC عم يعرضها... ما عاد عرضها هون كان عم يعرضها بالـ ايه ... جماعة متعصبة يعني...
1086 ...يمكن أنا ما بعرف
1087 ...
1088 ط. س. : شو سبب الانقسام هل هوي الدين... الحرب...؟
1089 فيه اديان...فيه اديان تركيبتها ضد الفنون... المسرح مثلا... يعني الدين الاسلامي... الدين المسيحي بيسمح... تعمل مسرحية عن المسيح او شي... الدين الاسلامي ما بيسمح تجيب سيرة الانبيا او النبي محمد... أو شي [...] حتى الانبيا المشتركة... مثلا ابراهيم... أنا عامل مسرحية "تحت رعاية زكور" ابراهيم بنزلو من السماء... الاسلام ما بيقبلوها...
1090 ط. س. : وقت اللي بتكتب مسرحية... بتراعي ذوق العالم...؟
1091 لا لا أنا لو براعي ذوق العالم... كان معي مصاري... أنا بعمل فن من متل ما أنا بدي... ان التقى معي واحد اهلا وسهلا
...وان ما اجا حدا كمان... اهلا وسهلا... معروفة عني... ما فيه
1092 ...حتى البولفار مش ماشي... ما فيه مسرح
1093 ...ط. س. : اذا بدنا نحكي عن الرحبانية وهيك
1094 ...أنا ما بحكي عنن ... ما بعتبرو مسرح... مسرح تنفيسي هيك وسلوغونات... وهيك
1095 ط. س. : زياد الرحباني...؟
1096 زياد [...] ما بين البولفار... والمسرح القوالين يعني... عرفت كيف... عندو حوار ذكي... بس بتصور كإخراج... شفتو
...ما ... بس شعبي... أنا بعتبرو مسرح شعبي... يعني بداية مسرح شعبي صحيح زياد
1097 ط. س. : شو العناصر اللي بتكون مسرح شعبي؟
1098 يعني فيه شغلات آنية للشعب... عرفت كيف... بعدين استقطب ناس... قدر استقطب ناس... هوي وشوشو هوي مسرح شعبي... وبو الحسن كان شوي هون
1099 ...ط. س. : اذا منحكي شوي عن منير كسرواني... واحمد الزين
1100 ما ما ... مسرح هيك... يعني هودي تجار... انا بالتجارة ما بحكي عرفت كيف...
1101 ط. س. : بالنسبة للجمهور... كيف بتقسم الجمهور.؟

1102 ...هلق بعد الحرب؟ [...]
1103 ط. س. : بعد الحرب... أو قبل الحرب
1104 قبل الحرب قلتلك... كان الجمهور المنيح هوي جمهور العقائديين... العقائديين... يعني [...] يللي هني بالاحزاب العقائدية مش الطائفيي... يعني الحزب الشيوعي الحزب القومي السوري... عرفت كيف... بالحرب صاروا طائفيين
...كلن... ويللي عارضوا قرضوهن... اذا مش اللبناني قرضوهن جهات اخرى
1105 الناس طالعلي صيت انو مسرحي صعب... انا بعمل مسرح متل ما لازم يكون المسرح... تعودو عالسهولة... بيشوفو مسرحي صعب...
1106 ...اللي بدو يكتب مسرح بدو يكون من المسرح والا بيطلع شعر قصيدة... ادب مش مسرح
1107 ما أنا بكتب متل ما بيكتب الشاعر قصيدتو... أنا بعتبر الفنون وجع بيختمر فيك بتعبر عنو... ما بفكر هيك... يعني أنا ما برتكب مسرح متل ما بيرتكبو جريمة عن سابق تصور وتصميم... انا بحس المسرح بكتب من عندي... ميلي...
...الطبيعي عبثي... الى الواقعي الى الرمزي
1108
1109
1110 ...
1111 ...
1112 رفيق علي احمد بيمشي بكسروان... بيجوا ليحضروه ليقولوا انو هني مش هيك... يمكن اذا راح البونا مونس
...عالغربية... بيحضروه ليقولوا انو هني مش ... طائفيين
1113 ...بعد الحرب الطائفية انقرضت شوي
1114 ...الشعب منو طائفي قد الحكام المسؤولين... يعني هني بيحركوا الشعب ليضلوا ...مستغلينو
1115 اللبنانين كلن قدريين... يعني عرفت كيف... الله بيعمل كل شي عنن... الله بيحارب عنن... والله بيموت عنن...
1116 ط. س. : مين الجمهور هلق؟
1117 ما تبقى من رواسب العقائديين والجامعيين... هو بيحبوا المسرح المنيح... الـ ... اللي بيطلعوا مصاري كتير الاطبا
وتجار البريما وتجار الصرامي وهو... لان اللي بيطلع بالنهار 20 ألف دولار بالنهار... هيدا بيحب يروح يموه عن فكرو... بيروح عالمسرح الرخيص يا شانسونييه... يا... التقريقات هودي... الطلاب الجامعيين عم بيروحوا عالمسرح ALBA الـ BUC الـ الجيد... وخاصة من الجامعات اللي فيها فنون... مثلا طلاب الاميركية الـ بيروحو عالمسرح الطلابي...
1118 المسرح فرجة... كل ضيعة... انا بلشت بضيعتي... الزجل مسرح... عند المسيحيي فيه كتير مسرح... سبت لعازر...
...كمان عند الشيعة... عاشورا... أنا كنت حابب اعمل عاشورا, تاخد الروح تبعا
1119 ع كل الاحوال بدي قلك شي... بيبقى المسرح بلبنان رائد المسرح بالدول العربية... كل ما ضهر واحد لبناني مسرحيتو بتاخد جايزة بالدول العربية... عرفت كيف... يبقى المسرح اللبناني رغم تعتيرو هو رائد المسرح العربي...
1120 ط. س. : فيه حرية بلبنان... ؟
1121 ...اكيد... انا عم بعمل مسرحية ما حدا بيشلي شي
1122 بين الناس ما فيه طائفيي... الرقي هوي اللي بيخليها تروح عطول... الزواج المدني... لو ما فيه طائفية...
1123

1124 Interview.
1125
1126 معهد الفنون المسرحية - موسكو. معهد بلوناتشيفسكي سابقاً... هلق صار اسمو "أكاديمية الفنون".
1127 ...هناك أزمة مواضيع... عملية انتقاء... خيار
1128 ما في أزمة جمهور... بلاقي انو الشباب بحاجة انو تطرحلو مشكلة عالمسرح بتهمو... ما عاد بدو هالمسرح السياسي
لانو فشلت كل الاشياء السياسية... ما عاد بدو هالاشياء الكوميك الفودفيل... لانو اظهر انو غريب وتافه... ولانو
تبعو ما بتـ مقربة لواقعنا... وقت اللي كلها بتحكي عن الخيانات... thematique هوي مقتبس... الـ وبيحطو الخيانة
كشيء مضحك... ولكن عندك بالمنطق الشرقي... الخيانة موجعة... موجعة... ولكن ممكن يضحك... ولكن يطلع بالنهاية
يحس حالو انو. ضحك عليه... في النهاية بلعو اياها... ولذلك أنا ما بلاقي انو الجمهور بعدو بينحي نحو الفودفيل...
بعتقد انو الناس بحاجة بالنهاية لمواضيع بتمس علاقاتن الانسانية الحميمية... مشاكل الشباب... مشاكل... وهيدا...
...ولكن المسرح يفتقد الى قضية سياسية ولكن المسرح مش بس بالضرورة مسرح سياسي .المنتحر لنيكولاي ايردمن
1129
1130 ...marketing ما عم ننزل بلعبة الدعاية ولعبة الـ
1131 يتماهى معو. مش بحاجة لعلاقة ذهنية... thematique الجمهور اللبناني بحاجة لموضوع بحاجة لموقف... تأثير
...انفعالي... يخليه بعدين يفكر... مش انت تجي تمارس معو الذهنية عالمسرح... والشعارات
1132 قدام اللحظة الجمالية كل الناس بتتساوى... بيبقى جايي وبيتخلى بالمسرح عن أي حكم مسبق ينتمي الى عرق الى طائفة...
1133 ...أكيد الوسط الفني متخطى المشكلة الطائفية بالبلد
1134 ...بيحط دعاية بماتش باسكت... مليونين شخص sponsor بتلاقي الـ
1135 المسرح اديه بيكون جمهورو بمسرح بيساع 250 كرسي... اذا فولت اذا فولت 7500 شخص... sponsor بيقلك الـ
...ما بحط دعاية لـ 7500 شخص
1136 ...عليها troque الشانسونييه بتروح النكتة بسهولة عالتلفزيون بينعمل
1137 تحديد علمي للمسرح الشعبي... المسرح الشعبي هوي اللي بطلو بيمثل بيجسد بيعبر عن افكار واعمال شعبية... هلق
ممكن انو منير كسرواني عم بيجسد انسان جنوبي... ومرا جنوبية... بس هوي عم يتوجه حصراً لمنطقة معينة...
بيجوز لاقي محيط عم بيدقلو ع وتر معين... مسرح مباشر دعائي بيزت شعارات... بيزت نكت بيزت هيدا... وهيدا
... ذوق الجمهور
1138 اذا عرض بالمتن بيكش دبان... هون الناس اوعى بتقدر تشوف وين اللي عم يستكرد... وين التجليط ووين... الـ
افترض زواريب... بتنعمل هون... بعد انساني... موقف انساني... الارتقاء بالجمهور للمستوى الثقافي...
1139 شو عملو ما عملو الا نسخوا... مسيرة التاريخ بتضلها ماشية... عندو احساس بالفشل عميق... هني ماتوا... نحنا
مهرجين اللبنانيين... انصاف مثقفين... اجوا من الثقافة عالمسرح بدون ما يكون عندو استعداد وادوات المسرح...
...صار فيه استنساخ للشكل المسرحي الغربي... جماليا بدون ما يكون يبحث عن ادوات تانية
1140 ...ما فيه بعد ما انخلق الكاتب المسرحي

1141 ...آخر ايام سقراط... حرام سقراط... آخر ايام مختار ضيعة
1142
1143
2182 Interview.
2183 كان حلمي اقرا غوته... كنا عم نقول انو لسوء الحظ يرتبط ببلادنا المستوى الثقافي بشي social status أي اسمو الارتقاء الاجتماعي... بتقل العفوية... بيصير فيه تطلعات تؤكد شخصيتهن الثقافية على حساب شخصيتهن الانسانية... تحقيق الذات الاجتماعية عن طريق المكتسب الثقافي... متل المكتسب المالي... بدي جخ وبدي اتفلسف كتير تفرجي اني مثقف... فبفقد كتير من عفويتي... ومن نفعي للناس تفرجي اني غني...
2184 الاهل بيعلموا ولادن تيشوفوا حالن فيهن... عنا بالضيعة بيعلموا ابنن بأميركا تيجي يعمر فيلا احلى من تبع الجيران...
2185 الانسان اللبناني احلى نفسية... بيعبونا حواجز طائفية shake the prejudice...
2186 انا عملت مسلسل برمضان اسلامي... اسمو مواسم الخير... غير المسلسل الاسلامي اللي عملتو من قبل اللي اسمو عرض بالسعودية (a تجارة عن تراض" يللي كلو مأخود من هالشهر الاسلامي... - بمواسم خير اسلامي... بس قلنالن اسلامي دغري... LBC وعرض عند حزب الله وعرض عل Label اسلامي... حطوه 12 بالليل... بيخبرني بيار الضاهر... قلي الاتصالات اللي اجت تطالب بتبكير عرضو 70% من المناطق المسيحية... وبرنامج اسلامي يشرح فكرة البنك الاسلامي...
2187 والاهل والبيئة ورجال الدين وكل الانظمة المطبقة والزواج media الـ...
2188 يتمنى نعمة الايمان لكل universel الدين المسيحي... شخص... والدين الاسلامي يتمنى نعمة الايمان لكل شخص
2189 وينن المسارح... انا حتى مني موجود... فيه مسرح اشبه بالمغلق عم بيكون صاحب المسرحية هو قضية نفسو. بدو يروح ومن وين بدو يجيب festival مش عن جد عندو قضية هي قضية نفسو... ع أي الجايزة تبعو... متل ما منقول اذا ما فيه فرمشية لشو فيه مختبر... اذا ما فيه فرمشية بيجي المواطن العادي بيستفيد من الدوا اللي عندا لشو فيه مختبر بيشتغل عالادوية...
2190 بقية المسارح متل الشانسونييه بس من دون كاس... اذا بتضحك ليش لأ... يعني هي نظريتهن هيدي بتضحك اذا بتضحك هيدي منيحة بدي ضحك الناس لطلع فلوس making people laugh by all means is a bad habit اللي position وعلى الـ attitude وعلى الـ taste عم بتأثر سلبا بالمجتمع... على الـ المواطن بياخدها...
2191 فيه عوائق... بوجه الحرية... مسرحية عن الزواج المدني...
2192
2193 Interview.
2194
2195 ما فيه مسرح لبناني لعدة اسباب... فيه أزمة نص بلبنان. فيه ازمة انتاج بلبنان
2196 العنصر الاهم يللي هوي الدعاية... ما فيه امكانيات... انا من وقت اللي جيت من اميركا لهلق ما عملت 1% من يللي ناوي اعملو...
2197 الدعاية التقنيات الصوت الاضاءة...
2198 نهاية الممثل اللبناني اللي حريص ع عملو... نهايتو معاناة كبيرة...

2199 مبارح تبلغنا هالشي وهلق اليوم... اليوم بدنا نطبقو... ايه تغييرات شكلية... ولكن مش بالمضمون اكيد... سياسية تركيبة النظام بالبلد...

2200 ...المسرحيين القدما... ثقافتن المسرحية عتقت
2201 ...الحريات محدودة... الثقافة محدودة... الحالة الاقتصادية معدومة
2202 ...[ ] كل واحد عندو ثقافة مختلفة جدا... كل طائفة عندها ثقافتها المختلفة جدا
2203 ...فيه ترمومتر عند الممثل... بتعرف انو الجمهور لقط الشغلة او لا... اذا ما لقطها you can skip it... and go to another thing...

2204 بكل منطقة بيضحكوا العالم من واقعن الاجتماعي... بالنبطية مثلا العالم يضحكوا على شغلات زغيرة لانن فاقدين شغلة كبيرة... يعني يعني... لانو ما عندن مسرح دويم هونيك... بيعتبروها شغلة كبيرة انو نراح لعندن وتقدملن عمل... [ ] فكان الجمهور كتير حلو وكتير فيه تعاطي بيني وبينو لدرجة انو صار فيه حوارات ...انفتحت بيني وبينو يعني بتضطر انو تكسر الحيط الرابع... بالنبطية كان غير نوع جمهور... وهون غير نوع جمهور...

2205
2206 Interview.
2207
2208
2209 ... المسرح مهنة... درستا وبأشتغلها... بتظن انها رسالة او شي
2210 المسرح بنا هندسة بشكل معين... وهوي كمان شكل من التعبير... استخدام ادوات ...استعراضية امام جمهور
2211 المسرح له مكان مميز في المجتمع المدني... المجتمع الريفي منو بحاجة لمسرح... المدينة لانها بحاجة للقاءات ...اجتماعية
2212 الانسان بيلتقي بالانسان... وبيعبر عن حياتو ومعاناتو بالقرن العشرين... مكان ترفيهي ذو ضرورة في حياة الانسان... التلفزيون بيلغي... حتى داخل عيلتك بتكون معزول... كل واحد لحالو... السينما كذلك ...المشاهد هوي الفرد ...وحتى فرديتو ملغاة
2213 ...اذا بتنحصر العملية المسرحية بالعرض المسرحي فهي ما شي... طريقة اعداد الممثل
2214 ما بتبقى اللحظة لحالها... فيها استمرارية... في علاقة بتستمر... بالخيال بالضمير ...بالوجدان... بالتصور
2215 الجمهور مش بس اللي قاعد بالقاعة... بس هني وعم يحضروا مسرحية بيمثلوا اكتر من حالن [ ] حجم او بعد العلاقة بين المسرح والجمهور بيتغير مع العمل المسرحي... ممكن مسرحية تنشاف من قبل عدد قليل من الناس وتبقى بمخيلة الناس سنين... بعطيك مثل... اليوم الناس اللي ما حضروا شوشو ولكن علاقتهن مع شوشو موجودة... اللي شافوا اللي عاشوا اللقاء مع الفنان على المسرح حولوها الى معطى ثقافي يبقى في ضمير ومخيلة الناس...
2216 ...الشخص يختلف انتماؤه من مكان الى آخر... هويتي الثقافية بتتأثر بالجمهور
2217 ...فيه مشكلة توثيق... فيه مشكلة تواصل
2218 خالدة السعيد ومهرجانات بعلبك... طلعوا كتاب... بس كتاب ما بيكفي لازم يكون فيه حركة لازم وزارة الثقافة لازم المؤسسات الجامعية...

2219 فيه نشاطات ثقافية تنتمي الى طائفة الى نخبة ملة معينة من المجتمع... وفيه انتاج مسرحي ...بيقصد الخليط المواجهة... تكون الفكرة مكونة من اعضاء مختلفة وتتوجه للجمهور ...بيهدف الانسجام مع الحالة الاجتماعية والتعبير عنها... التعدد مشكلة كبيرة مهمة... بيقولوا انو التعدد شي منيح شي ايجابي... لكن بيأدي لأزمات... لحروب... اذا فيه ناس عندن انتماءات ثقافية وطائفية مختلفة... لازم نستفيد من هالتعدد لعمل مشترك... لازم الثقافة تجمع...

2220 واحد يشتغل ضد هالمعطى صعب مش هين... وبيتطلب مش بس انك تعمل مسرحية موجهة للكل... لازم يكونوا اللي عم يشتغلوا بالمسرحية مختلفين... نحنا عم نحاول بشغلنا مش بس انو يكون العمل موجه لكل انواع الجمهور... لكن فريق العمل مكون من عناصر مختلفة... مختلفة بالانتماء الطائفي... مختلفة بالمدرسة الثقافية... مختلفة بالتجربة الاجتماعية... حتى مختلفة بالآراء... بدك تعالج موضوع العلاقات الثقافية... عداك عن العمل الفني البحت... الشغل

2221 double ضروري برأيي وأنا اغنى ولكن... ما فيه ملتقى حقيقي... يللي بيروحوا عهالمنطقة بيكونوا زوار... ما فيه ملتقى حقيقي... بيزوروا جونية. بيزوروا الحمرا... سواح...

2222 هي جزئيا نتيجة الحرب ونتيجة اكتر السياسة ما بعد الحرب... هيي التسعينات اللي اكدت عهالشي بتفريغ ما تبقى هلق القطاع الخاص صار يشتغل طائفيا اكتر من القطاع ...solidere من المساحة المشتركة العام... ما فيه شعور بالمصلحة الوطنية عند القطاع الخاص...

2223 بس العقيدة تتحول لمؤسسة... يعني تحول المضمون الى شكل والشكل يريد البقاء على نفسو على ذاتو...

2224 ما علاقة المسرح مع الدين علاقة مربكة... كل التجارب التاريخية... علاقة صعبة... انوجدلها حل جذري...

2225 كون المسرح فن جماعي واجتماعي... بيعاني من علاقة صعبة مع السلطة... الفنان او بيكون اداة للسلطة... والا مشكلة...

2226 ...البطل الرياضي... الزعيم السياسي... المرأة الجميلة... بيصير متل اله... معبود الجماهير

2227 ما فيه تواصل ما فيه تراكم ما فيه توثيق... حتى عند الفرد الواحد... ما فيه علاقة حية متواصلة مع الجمهور...

2228 ...اهم جمهور هوي الشباب... والمسرح بعدو بالطبقة الوسطى

2229 Interview.

2230

2231 ...يمكن قبل الحرب كان الها

2232 عم تضل بين بعضنا provocation ما عم تصير الـ competition

2233 ...ما بعرف... زياد بحبو مش حاضرتلو الا قبل الحرب... كنت بالمدرسة

2234 ...بالمسرح media فيه استخفاف بالـ

2235 مثلا بأوروبا فيه ثقافة معينة مشغول عليها ميات السنين نوعا ما بتوحد الاذواق... صار فيه تقريب... sensibilisation avec le théâtre

2236 ...نوعا ما صارت موحدة jeunesse فيه

2237 الو علاقة ثقافية... انو جامع انو سؤالك انت... انو هل الشيعي بيفهم اكتر أو الماروني بيفهم اكتر؟

... لانك مفتكر حالك ماروني... فهمت عليي؟ أنا ما رح اتواصل معك... مش انا

297

بكرهك... مش انا ما بحب المسيحيي... ما جوزي مسيحي... فهمت عليي... انو تلميذة راهبات... ومشربّة بـ ... بالمبدأ

تاعن... نصلي كل ما نطلع عالصف... بس ما ... فيه شي انو حاجز بالتواصل مع كل ... الـ ... المسرحية بيكون عندا حاجز انها تتواصل مع كل... مع حياله حدا... منرجع لقصة... السؤال بيكون لها المخرج لمين عم يتوجه... لمين بدو يسمعوا... والمخرج ما رح يعطيك جواب... لقتلك ليه... لأنو هوي ما بيعرف... فهمت عليي؟ هوي عم يعمل مسرحيتو... بس هوي عم يتوجه عمليا لحدا معين... مين هالحدا... بدك تشوف كذا مسرحية وتشوف مين حضرا...؟ شو ثقافتو شو مستوى ثقافتو شو دينو شو علاقتو بالمخرج... يعني الشغلة شائكة... أنا تجربتي مختصرة كتير كتير كتير انو اطلع عالمسرح ومثل... أنا ما بفكر مين رح يجي يحضرني بس رح آخر شي بشوف مين اجا...

2238 يعني بدك تتعرف هودي العالم هودي كمان...

ضحايا وجلادين للمسرح... فهمت عليي لمن بقول جلادين... يعني قرروا قرروا كيف يطبعوه كيف يوشموه...

2239 هودي متل يمكن اذا راح على صور على محيط شيعي شعبي بالمعنى الشعبي كنا قلناها هي مقولة انو كامل ما كامل عم يتعلم... فهمت عليي لمقولة كامل عم يتعلم... هولي بعدن تابعين لهالمقولة زقفولو انو هيدا عم يحكي وطنجي...

منرجع منقول الماروني عم بيروح يحضر الفودفيل انو يحضر شانسونييه من ارت الشانسونييييت بس حتى يشوف وحدي بالتنورة ووحدي بس عم تركب مقلة الحريري او مقلة فلان على شي ... فيه شي انا اسمو théâtre نسيت اسمها بالفرنسي بس انا شفتها بباريس شي رائع... يعني شغل مشغول فيه شي... ما بس انا عم هرج يعني... يعني... هيدا ماروني كمان... هالشيعي كمان للي بيزقف لكسرواني parodie اوطى درجات الـ الماروني اللي عم يحضر شانسونييه هوي ذاتو... بمستواه يعني فعلا بالاسفل...

ح.: الروم محسوبين عالتنين... روم بيروت بيحكوا غلاوي ... سنة بيروت عن جد 2240 مميزين... علمت بمدرسة كلها سنة بيارتي... مدينيين وانفتاحن عالغرب بيخليك تحس انو هني ما بينتموا ولا لطائفة... مع انن ملتزمين بدينن... عكس السنة بطرابلس... اذا بتحكي سوسيولوجيا...

2241 ح.: المسرح كتير بيعنيلي لاني بحسو تكثيف للحياة الانسانية كلها سوا...
2242 المسرح المعاصر بحبو... المسرح الكلاسيكي بحب اسمعو...
2243 ح.: انا كل اصحابي مش من طائفتي...
2244 ح.: مثلت بـ "اسكندرية بحرك عجايب" كتير حلوة... انت ما حبيتها
2245 انو عاملين بيروت incest ما الـ incest ح.: مجدرة... حلوة بس كتير زايدين قصة الـ القديمة كلها الـ ... مش غلط بس ... theme علاقات محرمة... انو ... مش هالقدي... بس فيها كتير تركيز على متل واحد مهووس... هوي مهووس... بيتجوز اختو... وهيديك اختو الزغيرة بلشت تعمل علاقة مع pédophilie ...واحد
يعني مش تارك نوع شي... وهيديك البنت اللي [...] . حبيت تنين موارنة وواحد شيعي...
2246 ح.: الماروني مدعي...
2247 ح.: السني... ما بعرفن منيح

ARABIC TRANSCRIPTIONS

2248 ...ح.: الشيعة ... متباينين
2249 ... complexe d'infériorité ح.: الروم... عقد الاقليات... يعني
2250 ...ح.: الارمن... ما فيني اوصفن كتير
2251
2252   Interview
2253
2254 ...المسرح والسمعي المرئي ...November 1988 فتحت الجامعة من 14 تشرين الثاني
2255 من الاول الطلب على المسرح ضئيل وخفيف... ومعدوم تقريبا عند الشباب... شب أو
...شبين
2256 ناس عايشين ما فيه 20 كيلومتر بعيد عنن مناطق اسلامية ... ما بيعرفوا شو يعني
رمضان... كيف بتريد؟ هيدا بيجي من المدارس بيجي من الثقافة من السياسة الثقافية بالدولة... انا ضد انو يكون فيه شو اسمو... تشيل الطوائف... لانو ... لبنان... ما تنسى انو هوي مركب من طوائف... وبدك بحرس كرامتو واحترام حياتو... لكل
...الطوائف
2257 ...مش لازم الطائفة هي تعطيك الهوية supra nationalité تبعك لازم يكون فيه
2258 أنا ولادي بيقولولو "We are American citizens and we are Lebanese too, my father and my
mother are from Lebanon" [...]
2259 ...عندنا دايما اختلاط théâtre Monnot نحنا بالـ
2260 الزواج المدني العولمة... الغاء الطائفية... عندي كتير افكار مضادة... بعدني ما وصلت لـ لـ
...مرحلة تفكيرية واضحة
2261 ...لازم نلاقي طريقة نجمع بين الهوية العامة والخصوصية لكل فئة
2262 وفيه التعددية الثقافية واللغوية... انا بطلع بلاقي انسان بيحكيني كلمة انكليزي كلمة عربي... ناس عنا بيحكوا كلمة
...فرنساوي كلمة عربي... انا هيدي ضدها
2263
2264   Interview
2265
2266 رولاند بارتس... بيني وبيني اختي... بيني وبينك يمكن تختلف الـ symbols, icons, signs... بين انسان وانسان
عايشين بنفس البيت في فرق بالـ signs.
2267 انك تعمل عنا ما انو لك culture... we are culturally imperialized... domination على بلد
بكل الغرب... لدرجة انو dominated culturally... بالـ american نحنا كتير culturally... عم نخسر الـ
شوف بالمسرح... بتعرف شو الحلو بمسرحية رئيف ...culture تاعيتنا. ما بقى عنا identity كرم... انو فيها
Lebanese identity... ان كان بالـ megatext... text او بالـ فيها هوية لبنانية...
2268 culturally imperialized لانو ... لانو مش فرنسا... وفرنسا... من أميركا... fran-cophone لبنان... انو منحكي french... ما بتقوي الجامعة اللبنانية... ما بتقوي اللبنانية... لانو الدولة ما بتساعد لتمحي هالشي... او العروبة
لالنا... بس credit هيدا كلو french w english تاعيتنا... انو بتجبر نتعلم... مش غلط انو نتعلم it's too
much... it's going too far too far كل شي بالـ كل شي ما مندرس عربي... english... كل شي بالـ
english... كل شي بالـ english ؟ [...] ليه

2269 لازم نقوي الـ culture ...تاعنا we wear French clothes we imitate the French eye glasses... we
make sure that our accent in English is so انو... ظابطة ....هيكي who cares... انو who cares...
انو who cares... شو عرفت؟
2270 ط. س : do we different cultures in your opinion, according to what?
2271 من الاشرفية ونازل French أكيد... ايه... مناطق... كومبلكس... من الاشرفية وطالع بيحكوا English... يحكوا
2272 انو شو يعني انسان لبناني. شو Lebanese identity اكيد المناطق طوايف مقسمة... ما فيه صفاتو؟ شو صفاتو
Steak او McDonald's... الانسان اللبناني؟ ما بعرف... شو بيحب ياكل اللبناني. بيروح ع Chips... ما
انا اللي عم بحكي ع الموضوع. ما عندي ...identity بعرف ... انا ما بعرف. حتى انا ما عندي identity...
2273 تاعتنا... انا اذا بدي سافر لبرا واعرف كيف mirror اكيد ببيين ... ما المسرح هوي الـ بألمانيا بيفكروا... بروح
بحضر مسرح بألمانيا... مسرحنا مرت كتير... ما عنا مسرح ... نحنا ناس معلمين بس مش مثقفين... منعرف math
ومنحكي 3 لغات بس نحنا ناس جهلة منا مثقفين... ما بيهمن المسرح بيهمن الـ algebra w business يعملوا
مصاري... يفتحوا مطعم... بس ما عنا مسرح... بعدنا متخلفين كتير كتير ما بقلك اديه... بعدو المسرح بيقوم على
مجهود خاص مش مجهود الدولة... انزل ع معهد الفنون ع يتمرنوا بأوضة بتنش بالشتوية... او روح على الفرع
التاني بفرن الشباك... محروقة قال البناية... ما عندن مسرح... بيروت قال عاصمة ثقافية... جابوا Pavaroti عطوا
شو عمل للبنان... OK... مليون دولار مدري اديه... ليغني ساعة وياكل كل انواع الفواكه وراح هيدا اجا ليلة... أكل
[...] كل انواع الفواكه وراح... طيب اوكيه هيدا شو عملنا للبنان
2274 قلت ...المسرح شيعت بمسرحيتي أنا no more theater...
2275 اربع سنين. ما بخبرك... اذا بعرف 20%... 18 % مجهود خاص مني... 2% عطتني اياهن الجامعة... مصخرة...
... for the money and the time and the energy [...] ...حسيت انو انضحك عليي
2276 ...اللغة العربية كتير دقيقة.. اذا بتغلط فيها نكزة بتبين جلق
2277 نحنا يعني اوروبيين... نحنا... ما لازم نكون بالشرق الاوسط... ما بعرف لازم نكون بغير... ما بعرف لازم ينقلوا
لبنان ويحطوه حد شي تاني... منا متل العرب يعني... نحنا مش عرب... بعرف نحنا ما شو بس ما بعرف نحنا شو...
...انو بعدني عم فتش نحنا شو بعدني ما وصلت. بس بعرف نحنا شو ما
2278 ...(نحنا فرنساويي وامركان وايطاليي وفينيقيي) (تضحك
2279 only the theater people are going to theater, the movement is not strong... for that
reason the producers fear to invest their money in theater production... because
nobody cares to come to theater they care to go to McDonald's or La Piazza... we
theater for the masses like Marwan Najjar, he corrupted the theater in Lebanon, he
pioneered for the corruption of the theater in Lebanon

ARABIC TRANSCRIPTIONS

2280 فيه ناس ما بتعرف بيضحكوا عليهن متل فلان مثلا... بس فيه ناس بتعرف ما بينضحك عليهم. انا بخاف
روح عالمسرح بيتخرب ذوقي...

2281 بـ $10000 ما فيك تعمل مسرحية... شي مسخرة... بس بيعطوا $800000 للرحباني يعمل "آخر أيام المسرح
اللبناني" play 2 شي... شي مسخرة... بتقرف... انا بـ كرست 10 دقايق من وقتي اتمصخر عليها... شي
قرف ما فيهن
ما هيك؟ ما قايلين Plato هيدا كتاب لـ "the Last Days of Socrates" يعملوا هيك... غير انو
هيك... انو
هني اللي مخترعينا... وسقراط عاملينو عبدو الهبيلة... وغسنتيت عاملينا بياعة البندورة...
اسقاطات... اسقاطات...
غير فيه بتخربط بالمعلومات... ليه لانو بتمرق عالناس... مثلا عملوا الامبراطور بالمسرحية...
وقت اللي انكتب آخر
ايام ما كان فيه امبراطور امبراطور شي روماني... من روما الامبراطور... رتبة رومانية... ...
يوناني... بتمرق
العالم ما بتعرف...

2282 ط. س. : حضروها العالم؟

2283 حضروها وزفقوا ووقفوا... أنا حضرتها صرت صرخ قد ما شي بشع...

2284 يات اوروبا... بس تعا بنت tv نحنا مناكل متل اوروبا ومنلبس متل اوروبا... ومنشتري
تعيش لحالها متل البنت
لا... فمناخد القشرة عطول... كتير ...cohabitation الاوروبية... والله بقوموا قياماتهن اللبنانيي
لبنان ...complex

2285 ط. س. : هودي التابو شو مصدرن؟

2286 الـ culture مصدرن؟ لانو العرب هيك... نحنا لبنان عربي كنا اساسا... هلق الـ
اجا بعدين... بس imperialism
نحنا كنا بيروت مدينة محافظة... بيروت والبيارتة... عيل محافظة... حتى الاشرفية... الاشرفية...
بيارتة... بيارتة مش
بمعنى سنة... بيارتة يعني من بيروت... عيل محافظة... يعني... لا الاسلام متزمتين اكتر... انو انا
مسلمة... لا ما
مسلمة ... انو بيي مسلم. انا ما شي... متزمتين اكتر... لانو دينن بيفرض عليهن هالشي...
المسيحيي انو غير... انو
وهيك... بس انو ضهروا لاوروبا قبل... راحوا fundamentalists غير شي... كمان متمسكين و
برا تعلموا اكتر من
الاسلام... الاسلام عن جديد يعني... كرمال هيك المسيحيي بيستخفوا بالاسلام لانو بيفكروهن
جهلة... بس هلق
الاشيا عم تتغير يعني...

2287 فيه طائفية بالمسرح كمان... بتعرف لو مسرحية مبارح حدا مسلم عاملها... كانت قامت
القيامة... بس لانو
من الاشرفية...ما حدا بيحكي شي... تمصخر كتير على سانت ريتا انو سانت ريتا عم ترفرف ...
وما بعرف شو... لو
عملها حدا مسلم كانت قامت القيامة كانوا الناس قاموا ضهروا... بس... لانو مسيحي اللي عملها...
غير انو
ما بعرف ليه... بس هيدي الحقيقة... ما بعرف priority التلفزيونات وهيك... المسيحيي الهن الـ
ليه... يمكن لانو
سياسي دبلوماسيي اكتر من غيرن... ما بعرف... والحرب... اصلا الحرب ما خلصت... انو
ايقاعاتنا كناس شوف
كيف منسوق... شوف كيف دغري منعصب... هيدا من الحرب كلو...

2288

2289   Interview.

2290 ... ممثل... كاتب ومخرج
2291
2292 أنا شخصيا ما قدرت شوفها كله...كان فيه انقطاع بين المناطق... ما كنا نعرف شو عم بيصير...
2293 بخلال فترة السبعينات بالحرب... ما فيه ما مرق سنة الا ما اشتغلت فيها ككاتب ممثل او مخرج...ما فيه شي وقف
بينما هلق. هلق. كثير انا متردد اني اعمل مسرح او اشتغل بمسرح
2294 من سنتين عملت مسرحية ... هيك مزاجية... هيك تسليت فيها... عملتها ببلاش... ببلاش 6 أيام... قدمتها بالـ centre c'est la vie... ايه اتكلت انو واحد culturel يخبر التاني...
بعدين عملتها شهرين مع دخولية بدون اعلان... جابت ناس متل ما بتجيب مسرحية مع اعلان... بشهرين جابت 3000 أو 3500 شخص بمسرح
مركز الثقافي الفرنسي... دفعوا وفاتوا لانو خبروا بعضن... ما بفتكر هلق اتخن مسرحية بتحط اعلانات... بتجيب
اكتر... يعني نسبيا ما بتجيب اكتر... بتجيب اكتر بس بتكون دفعت اعلانات... أكتر من ما... مش مهم...
أنا بسأل حالي... هل هي العمر يلي صرنا فيه افقدنا حماس المشاركة... هل هوي الوضع **2295** العائلي. انو ما بقى بدك
تقضيها رايح جايي عالطرقات بالليل لشي ما هوي شي؟ او انو صارت الشغلة ما بقى فيها شي يحمس... ما بعرف
هيدا مختصر هلق... بفوت بالتفاصيل اسأل...
شو عملوا؟ عم تحكي عن مسرح جامعي ومهرجانات؟ آه بسيطة... هو منن مسرح... انا **2296** برأيي منن مسرح... هودي
برأيي منن حركة مسرحية... حركة مسرحية بتشرك الشعب كلو... الناس كلها... بتصير الناس تروح عالمسرح... هون
الناس منا عم تروح عالمسرح... اذا بدك الجامعة اللبنانية عم تعمل اشيا من هالنوع... كل سنة عم تخرج 15
انسان...عم يعملوا كل واحد مسرحية احلى من التانية... ما عندن المطرح او الامكانات انو يسوقوها... في مسرح اذا
عم تحكي من هالنوع... اذا عم تحكي مسرح بالبلد... ناس تروح عالمسرح متل ما بتروح ع السينما او عالمطعم... ما بعتقد... فيه تراجع فظيع...
الاعلان مهم لتقلن للناس انو فيه مسرح... بس اللي صار شو [...] صار يعلن عن أي **2297** شخصين تلاتة بيطلعوا ع خشبة...
يعلن عنن مسرحية... ان كانوا شانسونييه او كانوا... أطفال... انخلطوا كل... شي. الشغلة التانية يللي هي الأهم...
كان المسرحيات يللي عم يعلن عنها... كان عم يعلن عنها مقابل تصويرا وعرضا... ما هيك؟... طيب... أنا عم روح
عالمسرح بجي عم تاني سنة بلاقي المسرحية اللي حضرتها انعرضت عالتلفزيون... فقسم مني يلي منو معود عالمسرح...
بقلك لشو بدي احضر مسرح وادفع مصاري... بشوفها عالتلفزيون... (شو بالنسبة للسينما؟)... هيدي نسبة مئوية من
الناس... يللي حضروا المسرحية... وعندك الناس يللي ما حضروا المسرحية بس شافوها عالتلفزيون مش بظروف
المسرح... بيقلك شو هالمسرحية كلها صريخ بصريخ منيح اللي ما حضرناها...فهيدا جزء آخر من الناس خسروا
المسرح... بيبقى الجزء التالت اللي بيقصد يروح عالمسرح... هالجزء يللي هوي اصلا قليل... قليل لانو كمان هيدا

مقسوم لقسمين... مقسوم لقسم يللي بيروح عالغيشه وبيقطع معود... وهيدا قليل جدا... والقسم يللي بيبيعوه بالبيت حفلة ضد لأني بعتبر already مضمونة... فأنا لما بدن بيبيعوني حفلة مضمونة بالبيت... بدي روح حالي انا مبلوص...

يعني رايح ضد... كمان جزء مني فات غصمن عنو... يعني سنة الجاي لمن بدي شوف ذات الشخص جايي لعندي عالبيت... بدي اسحب وقول... الله يعطيك تبرعنا يمكن لجمعية خيرية يمكن المسرحية اللي انت جايبها كتير منيحة...

ما بقى تفرق معي النوعية انا ما بدي انبلص... منيح؟ هيدا الضمانات... كمان هيدا جزء هرب... والحفلات المضمونة بتزيد عالكارت تتربح... وكل يوم بيجوا بيدقوا عليك عالبيت... واللي مسمح عالفن والثقافة بيقلك... شو عم تعملي عملولنا مسرح غير شكل... لمن بتعملو مسرح غير شكل بيقلك ايمتين بدك تعزمني؟ ما عزمتونا... وضع اقتصادي...اذا بيلاقي المسرحية عم تخسر بيقلك لشو؟ ما عم يتسلى آخر الليل...

المهرجانات اللي عم تنعمل هلق... كل الكلام عنها كل شي عن منظمينا... مش عن المعترين 2298 اللي عم بيبقوا الدم تيشتغلوا... عم يعطوا الواحد جمعة... جمعة تيعرض مسرحيتو... بس يصير الواحد مهم خلص ما عاد حدا ياخدو...

كنا نكيف انو يتلفنلك واحد من اصحابك بغير منطقة... انو جايين نحضرك اليوم... كنا 2299 نكيف... كنا هجنة... كانت هجنة... هلق مع انفتاح المناطق... باتمنى انو يصير فيه حركة... كل واحد منا غلطان...

عملنا مسرحية "بحسنة هالطفالي" بارودي عن مسرح الاطفال... ببلاش... ما كنت لاقي 2300 مسرح واحد يعطيني ليلة واحدة ببلاش... آخر شي المركز الثقافي الفرنسي... 6 ليالي... العالم خبروا بعضن واحد كتبوا... ما هو وظيفتن انو يكتبوا تيقبضوا معاش... بس بتقراهن بتلاقي انو هي 112 230 المقالة بتصلح لهي المسرحية... ولهاي المسرحية ولهاي المسرحية... هيي ذاتها... غيروا الاسامي لانو انت ما بتفهم شي من اللي بيكتبوه... انا نزلت كل الجرايد اللي مقصقصها من 71 لهلق عن الاعمال اللي انت مشارك فيها... خي بتقرا بتحس حالك انو عظيم جوا... بس ما بتعرف شو قايلين عنك... بتحس انو فظيعة هالشغلة... انا برأيي انو هودي النقاد الكبار ساهموا بابعاد الناس عن مسرح معين... ليش... المسرحية ما بتكون صعبة كتير... مقالتن عنا بتكون كتير صعبة... اذا عم تقرا بتقول ما فهمنا المقالة... كيف بدنا نفهم المسرحية... مسرح ريمون جبارة... منو صعب... بيكتبوا عنو مقالات انك ما تحضرو...

تحديد المسرح كما كان هوي مطرح بتترك بيتك وبتروح عليه... صار المسرح يروح عند 2302 الولد عالمدرسة يمثلوا عالطبقة وتحت الطبقة وبالملعب... ويجمعوا اكتر من 4000 ولد... وهدايا علكة وسوسيت... صار يبرطلوا...

اخترعوا قسم مسرح بكلية التربية... 2303
المسرح بيجمع فنون عديدة... هوي تهذيب للدين للعين... للسمع... من دون ما تعرف... ايه 2304 لا هوي بيحل مشاكل ولا بيعمل ثورات... ما تكبروها كتير... ليه بدو يكون فيه موسيقى.؟ حدا سأل ليه فيه غناني...؟ هيدا شغلة يومية

موجودة... ضروري... اكيد ضروري... اذا بتقدر تستوعب الشغلة... بتعرف بالحياة مين عم يضحك عليك مين عم يحكيك مظبوط... بتعرف من تطليعة الشخص اللي جايي يعمل مسرح... بتعرف اذا معك او جايي يلعب عليك... أكيد ضروري...

2305 أنا بقول انو مش الطائفة اللي بتميز... حاكي الجمهور المسلم والمسيحي...العبلن عالغرائز البسيطة بيتجاوبوا ذات الشي... العبلن عالاحاسيس الانسانية... بيتجاوبوا ذات الشي... ما فيه اسهل من انو تشغلوا ع غريزتو للجمهور بتاخد منو زقيف قد الدني...ليك... اذا هيك قصة مسلم ومسيحي... شو بتفسر انو خلال الحرب اغلب اللي برزت اسمائهن واشتغلوا بالمناطق المسيحية هني مسلمين...؟ بعدلك اياهن... كانت ناتجة عن عقدة نقص عند جماعتنا هون... كركلا... أبو الحسن... وسيم طبارة...ابراهيم مرعشلي... مني ضد... هو مسلمين ما هيكي... ؟ طيب كيف خاطبوا الجمهور المسيحي... كيف اجاهن الجمهور المسيحي واستوعبن؟ مش لعبولوا على غرايزو... ؟ هونيك مين اشتغل.؟ مش زياد الرحباني ومارسيل خليفة...؟ مسيحيي...وهلق منير كسرواني...بأحساسو وغرايزو... لعبو على اشيا... حكي اشيا بتعنيلو... بتلقطو... الرياضة سيسوها... بيقلك الرياضي اسلام والحكمة مسيحيي... ما بالحكمة فيه مصطفى فيه محمد قاشا وفيه الخطيب... 3 اسلام من 5 لعيبة... وهونيك مسيحي... البستاني مسيحي... عندك شربل وعندك خيو
لشربل. عندك 3 من 5 مسيحيي.

2306 بيت خالتي... بعد 4 سنين تلفزيون... مشيت المسرحية وجابت 70 ألف شخص... وكان اطارها الفني الداخلي بيتجاوب مع قناعاتي انو ما فيك تضحك عالعالم... بدك تعطيهن ديكور اضاءة موسيقى يعني المقومات الشكلية مسرحي rythme بدك تعطيهن ممثلين عم يشتغلوا... بدك تعطيهن situation وبدك تعطيهن الـ مرتب... واضح لما عملت مسرحية par contre... لانو هني جايين قاصدين الضحك... ما جايين قاصدين الوعظة بحسنة هالطفالي عملتا بقناعاتي انا للمسرحية من النوع اللي أنا بحبو... ايه. واجاها ناس من مختلف الاعمار من مختلف والفئات والثقافات ...من اللي بيعرف بالمسرح لاي شخص صاحب مهنة يدوية... وهوني خاطبت احساس وكنت تقريبا نفس الـ message للتنين... ردة الفعل بين التنين... يعني وصل الـ

2307 ...بكتب لحتى انا اعمل اخراج... بكتب الصورة اللبناني... دخل بالمسرح اللبناني نوع من المسرح public مروان نجار... عرف الـ 2308 المعروف عالميا... ومروان يتقن لعبة التسويق... وقلمو حلو... يشهد له انو قال للناس انو فيي ضحكن انا بدون ما يكون عندكن كاس وعم تلطشو عالسياسيين...

2309 زياد الرحباني... أنا من المعجبين فيه... انا حضرتللو عالمسرح مسرحية 2 3 ... وبعدين حالت الظروف انو... يللي هني سهرية نزل السرور وبالنسبة لبكرا شو؟... لا شي فاشل ما شفتها... بيكتب حلو... عمل طرح معين...

2310 شي فاشل مسرحية تقدمت بعد بسنة من انا ما عملت ضهر الشير... ضهر الشير هي مسرحية انعملت تقريبا

عالمسرح... بس انا بالنسبة لالي ... زياد اللي بحبو هوي الموسيقي...ما بعرف اذا نص زياد تقدم عالمسرح وخدمو

الاخراج... مني عارف... لو زياد كان فيه مخرج أو لو زياد بيحب يسلم لحدا... يمكن كانوا دوبلوا الناس... يمكن... ما بعرف...

2311 مشكلة معظم اللي بيشتغلوا بالمسرح... انو ما بيحضروا اعمال غيرن... ما فيك تقول مينو هي...؟ روح شوفو... في

شغلة... انو وقت اللي بيصرلو 10 15 سنة بالشغل... فيه شباب... بلشو هلق بالمهنة بلشوا عمرن قد ما كان عمرو

هوي وقت ما بلش يعد حالو مخرج... طيب ما هودي عم يشتغلو... روح شوف... وهيدا كمان بالجامعة... انت عارف

اني من وقت ما أنا فت ع معهد الفنون لهلق... بأي مسرحية شاغل فيها... مني شايف مخرج تلفزيوني جاي عم

يتفرج... قلال...يللي بيجوا يحضروا الديبلومات بالجامعة يجوا يشوفوا مين عم يطلع... كلن بيقعدوا بمكاتبن وبيكتبوا

وبيركضوا هالمعترين متل هالخواريف يتصوروا بالفيديو يعطيهن قياساتن...؟ casting بالجريدة ما بدا casting

الشغلة... اذا انت بتعرف وشايف... الدور بيصلحلو يا فلان يا فلان... جيبن... مش 33 واحد شي طويل شي قصير

طيب ما هيدولي مش كلن بيظبطوا لها الشي... معناة الحكي... الكل عاملين لحالن برج... مبسوطين فيه... كأنو ما فيه

...الا هالمطرح وهالكام واحد يللي بيزقفولن

2312 ...بالـ 3 ملايين واحد. بعتقد فيه 20 ألف واحد... بيحبوا المسرح
2313   Interview
2314
2315 **1982** ...بلشنا اول اجتماع منشان المسرح we know that there should be utility of theory, but in

order to have utility of theater there should be an established convention between

the work and those who come to see the work (play) ...

2316 ...نحنا ولاد كلمة مش ولاد مشهد... ما ربونا عالصورة ربونا عاللفظة
2317 ...ما بيأثر بذات الساعة cumulative المسرح
2318   survival was the most important thing
2319 celebration of life [...] dynamie de la forme [...] let's build a certain dynamism by

structuring the taste while celebrating while laughing [...] laughing is not a bad thing by

itself. No stars to climb on their shoulders. Don't create Shoushou, don't create Bou l-

Housn, the play should be the object by itself. 16 years... we were never dissapointed

by the audience [...]

2320   the people are in a mud hole... 3 attitudes to face that problem [...]
2321   either you say my hands are clean...
2322 either you jump into this mud to get the money of the people... then you become full

of mud...

2323 either you say »No... I want to shake them out" [...] then you dirty only your hands...

305

2324 j'ai les mains sales mais je suis pas sale [...]

2325 come enjoy laughter... because maybe later if the aim is not laughter... you will be able

to follow a story [...]

الى ان يصبح هذا النوع من المتابعة الذكية متعة عند المشاهد بدل المتعة التي يوفرها **2326** الضحك... سنبني هذه العلاقة

مع الجمهور...

2327 حالو entry ticket طبعا النقاد... سكان المقاهي. كان عم بيقولو مروان نجار عم يعطي تيعمل فلوس...

2328 I left advertising... I left the place where the money is...

2329 اكتشفت انو الجمهور كائن بشري له عقل... له قلب... وله اعضاء تناسلية... مثل أي كائن بشري... بللي بيقول انا ما

he is so sure that he is up... and I am not sure that the

احسده لأنو بنزل لعند الجمهور. audience is down [...] ... اذا فيه محبة بيحس فيها الجمهور... بس اذا بدك تلعبلو بغريزتو بينبسط ما بيقلك لا بس مش معناتا انو هيدي اللي بدو اياها...معناتا انت ما تعبت كفاية لقيت هي اهين... اذا بدك تطير فوق راسو بيقول

اسماله هيدا شو صعب وشو عبقري وما بيجي لعندك...

2330 do you have a cause, or are you the cause? [...] we are departing from the fact of the

existence of utility of theater... but we cannot take it for granted and impose it on

people as if everyting is done before...

رجعت بعد الحرب... لقيت مكتبي محروق... لقيت 100 مأساة... بس لقيت فيه شغلة **2331** تفرحني... صار فيي اطلع

that was a joy so how do you express it? عالرينغ... وبدقيقتين بصير بالحمرا... Theatrically [...]

something I was feeling and it's not personal it is national... so I want to share [...] ...

ماركس... مانيفستو... الشعوب تفضل ان تنسلخ عن واقع سيصبح ماضيا بشيء من الكوميديا... and how right

لقيت فكرة سواق التاكسي جوز الجوز [...] مجوز وحدة بالشرقية ووحدة بالغربية... he is مطمن انو ما رح يشوفوا

تبع هالزلمة... ما ضل لبناني الا ما بدو يشمت worries. بعضن...فتحوا الطرقات... وبلشوا الـ فيه... 16

ما scandalous ما عندي كلمة ... continuous months of full house performances عندي حدا عم

ما عندي ولا well known established star or stage يتعرى عالمسرح... ما عندي artificial device ...

and people came...

2332 ما بعرف ليه سكان المقاهي يللي هني ذاتن سكان الصفحات الثقافية... ليه ما شافوا هالـ phenomenon...

people came for a concept and not an exterior thing...

2333 مرا عملنا لعبة ...structured صرنا نفتش ع طريق... مرا عملنا كرمال المحروس كوميديا خفيفة بعمتي نجيبة...

تبع الاغنيا وحياتن... صرنا نفتش... بس حسينا انو الـ moral مرا عملنا فقرا بفقرا عن الـ audience عم تفتش

معنا... ولا مرة كان عنا اقل من 60 ألف مشاهد...

2334 ببعض الحالات رحنا فوق الـ 100 ألف مشاهد... وبحالة وحدة رحنا فوق الـ 200 ألف مشاهد يللي هيي عريسين
...فشو بدي اعتبرها بلبنان success تعتبر Westend مدري من وين... يللي هني بالـ
2335 reaction صارت لا صارتsexual freedom بأوروبا التعبير بالجسم تعبير... هون الـ
انو بنتي سلمت بالحرب ما صرلها شي خليها تمشي... هيدي خطرة لان هي البنت بعد كام سنة هيدي ام شو عم ينمى عندا style
الـ globalization فصرت ارتعب من التأثر بالـ substance... مش اكتر... ما عم ينمى of life artificial يللي
...عم يوصل لعنا

2336 even my identity with globalization is threatened...
2337 shake the prejudice... كبسة زر الهدف كان push button مسرحيتي اسمها
2338اذا خسرتلي 30 40 ألف دولار بخبرك انو ما ظبطت... بس اذا نجحت رح اربح رح اربح a new role for theater in my country this is my ambition [...] .
2339ما هي كيف صايرة القصة... ماركة مسجلة؟ I cannot say that Jawad el Assadi is not good
سماها جنون في الاسطبل... بكيت... بكيت ع Miss Julie بيفتكروني حمار... عمل جواد الاسدي ستريندبرغ... مش
عمل جنون في ...it was great ع ميس جولي... لا ما باخد ماركة انا... عمل الاغتصاب الاسطبل... it was
silly, shit... let's tell the truth... ولك اكبر عالم ما عندن a magic formula for success nobody has a magic formula for success [...] ...
2340 violence and sex are related...
2341they are violating values... سواء أكانت moral متعلقة بالـ sex أو وغيرو... بإحترام الناس... يعني تعى
خود الشانسونييه... هيدي احلى متل اليوم... يا بيزلطولك مرا وبيحكولك كلام زفر وبيحطولك صوفيرة عالشاشة...
...يا اما بيعهروا قيم اجتماعية انجازات احلام... بيعهروها لانو اذا عهرتها بتصير تضحك
2342the absence of harmony between cause and effect creates the ridicule... يعني لما بتجيب
...ridicule رفيق الحريري تيرقص مثلا... خلص... خلقت الـ
2343 parody... صار فيه comedy... اضحكوا..."... بطل فيه"
2344...حداي حداي فدائي خطاي صيبوا متل الترغلة
2345...حداي حداي كتابي خطاي صيبوا متل الترغلة
2346 ...مش بس فيك تقول فيه مسرحية هون بتقابلها مسرحية هون بيتشابهوا بس بيغيروا الاسامي نفس المسرحية الناس
يعني بتحضر مسرحية كذاب اللي انعملت بأول الثمانينات. بتحضرا [...] بالشرقية عم تنتقد الدور السوري... بعدين
نقلت هيي ذاتها بذات اشخاصا نقلت عراس بيروت صارت ضد الاسرائيلي... فيه استغلال فيه انتهازية عم تمارس
...ع مشاعر الناس حسب المنطقة اللي هني فيها
2347الـ لانو برأيي أنا ...clan على حساب الـ individual . عنا مشروع مسرحية بتكرس الدور السوري... بعدين only solution is to establish the individual... في عنا ...individuals نحنا مشكلتنا بالشرق انو ما فيه عنا clans... مشكلتنا
منو من بلادنا... عنا نحنا بيقولوا ربنا لأبراهيم بدك تقتل ابنك وتقدموا Oedipeus بالشرق انو ذبيحة... ابراهيم ما

بينما لو ... The individual doesn't exist. بيجرب يسأل ابنو شو رأيو بالموضوع Oedipeus ...من عنا
وكان اول ما قلو الاوراكل انت رح تقتل ابوك وتتجوز امك... كان قلها ماما انطريني بالتخت... انا رايح اقتل البابا
وجايي... he wouldn't have resisted...

2348   to establish the individual... هوي دور المسرح برايي انا
Joseph and Mary, a ...عم باحلم بمسرحية... ناقشتها مع بعض الزملا... مسميها انا2349 non religious play...
...اللي فيها

2350 الـ brand... الانسان he's branded... labeled... we want to label the Lebanese citizen as
an individual [...] ... ع بينزل العالم العربي او بلبنان فيه ما انو منعرف نحنا يعني الطريق منشان حق
من حقوقو المدنية... ابدا... بس بينزل عالطريق منشان بيار الجميل... بينزل عالطريق منشان ابراهيم قليلات...
بينزل عالطريق منشان نبيه بري... بس ما حدا بينزل عالطريق منشان رغيف الخبز منشان قرار مجحف منشان
حق مدني لالو... يعني انا بعرف بس دور الاعلام يللي هوي مشوه لحياتي اليومية... لو كانوا بغير بلد كانوا كسروا
وان TV نحنا اهم قضية لالنا ان كان عالـ fulfilled... منو individual كذا محطة تلفزيون... الـ كان عالـ
theater... هيي the fulfillment of the individual...

a system of va-القول المسلم... الزموهم بما الزموا انفسهم به... المهم انو يكون عندك2351 lues مش المهم انك تاخد
maturity, identity, اذا ما قدرنا نربي جيل هيك... ما منوصل لـ ...my system of values ما فيك... [...]
تعمل ندوة مع ملايين الناس... الندوة بتعملها مع اهل الاختصاص. وهون دور المسرح وهون دور وهون TV الـ
values... يعمل system انك تراكم عند الناس ردود فعل تتحول فيما بعد الى... media دور الـ
لما نقلت من جونية عالحمرا بقدر قلك... انو لعب الفار يللي نجحت نجاح على جورج 2352 الخامس ادونيس... نجحت
نجاح موازي تماما بعد كام اسبوع بالبيكاديللي بالحمرا... 100% نفس النجاح... ذات الشي عريسين مدري من وين
بالأتينيه... لقاءا كان في موسم رهيب بعد سنة بالبيكاديللي بالحمرا... موازي 100% ذات ردود الفعل... ذات الاشيا
اسمعا من الناس... الفرق بسيط قدرت المسو آنذاك... انو جمهور الغربية كان أكثر تسييسا من جمهور الشرقية..بشعر
انو... جمهور الشرقية كان مسيس على مستوى ردود الفعل فقط... قد ما مخوفينو بينما جمهور الغربية كان عندو
awareness للقضايا المحيطة فيه الى حد ما اكتر ... بغض النظر عن طايفتو... يعني المسيحي الساكن براس بيروت
يعني صار فيه مناخ منطقة اكتر ما ...reaction والمسلم الساكن براس بيروت يعطوني ذات الـ صار فيه تأثير
لعبت دورا الكبير... AUB طايفي مباشر... بالتعاطي مع امور رصينة... يعني انا... يمكن بيئة الـ يمكن بيئة الجامعة
الاميركية كان الها تأثير بنوع النقاش للي يصير... يعني هون النقاش صار... نقاش ع مستوى القهوة والمطعم
والمربع هونيك بقي النقاش مضمون بسبب بيئة جامعة اميركية وشوية حركة فكر ما ماتت...

308

ARABIC TRANSCRIPTIONS

2353 appealing لبياع الاطبا حبو مسرحي... المهندسين حبو مسرحي...يمكن مسرحي منو
خضرة او لاي واحد بعدا
يعني في طبقة اجتماعية لا يمكن تتمتع بكوميديا main issue حاجاتو اليومية بعدا هيي الـ
المواقف... تبدأ من
...حدود الطبقة الوسطى

2354 ...لازم نميز بين الذوق العام وذوق العامة
اللي جاب الناس عالمسرح بالاول ظاهرة اسمها صوت فيروز... وبعدين شوشو ظاهرة من
التلفزيون...
مجدلون ... منعت الدولة المسرحية... بيقدموا المسرحية على طاولات المقهى... النهار تغطى
الحدث على الصفحة
الاولى... اهتمام الـ masses بهيدي الفئة من الناس...
Scandalous انو للي بالنص هوي الموجود to make sure الدولة بتبعت ناس على المسرح عملوا ... effect
الضحك من هزيمة ...Curiosity based on scandal ...المسرحية التانية كارت بلانش
العرب بالـ 67...
Celebrating the same attitude, the poor egyptian soldier leaving his shoes behind on
the battle field... هزمنا الهزيمة...
ظهر الاخوت... اخوت شانيه... اخوت العرب... بعدين صار اخوت المنطقة الشرقية... الجمهور
عم يلحق ظاهرة... اهم
ظاهرة هي ظاهرة زياد الرحباني... Intuitive spontaneity ...
The audience is a wild genious... They simply behave... And we have to figure out what
 they want...
Wild collectivity to assume before we throw ouselves on the market...

2355   Interview
2356
2357   مهرجان بعلبك مع منير ابو دبس 1963...
2358   Le public libanais a recu un choque durant la guerre...
2359 نزعوا ذوق الجمهور اللبناني... وخصوصي الجيل الجديد... فكر انو هيدا الفن وتعود هيك...
وفيه الشبيبة اللي عم
تدرس بالجامعات... وفي عندا ذوق...
2360   ...ما عادوا هلق عم يلعبوا عالغريزة الطائفية بالمسرح متل ما كان خلال الحرب
2361   ...حضاريات... فيلم لبناني بانتاج فرنسي
2362 نبيه ابو الحسن... هوي درزي بس كان عم يلعب... وصار يحكي متل الناس بالشرقية عرفت
كيف؟... ضد السوريين
وضد فلان وضد فلان... مروان نجار...بس ما دخلوا بالسياسة... انطوان غندور... مسرح مروان
نجار ما بيعبر عن
انا بيقول هوي ما... je suis un amuseur... شي
2363 بتعرف انو انا ما بحب احكي بهالمواضيع...هلق بعد فيه كتير ناس طائفيين... بعدن ناس
متعصبين وما بيشتغلوا مع ناس
ومتشبصين بعقلن ...sorry من هي المنطقة... بس انا بالنسبة الي هودي ناس حمير... يعني...
2364   Interview
2365
2366 Qualité du texte. Une pièce qu'il faut écouter autant de voir. J'estime qu'au Liban nous
 avons passé de l'ignorance totale du théâtre à un théâtre avant gardiste en oubliant

toute la trajectoire que le théâtre a suivi, ce qui fait que nous avons une forme de
théâtre batarde que je deteste pronfondément parce que ça ne correspond à rien
finalement. Ca ne trouve ses racines dans rien... ni dans les traditions populaires... ni
dans les traditions sociales... ça ne trouve ses racines que dans les traditions commerciales et c'est très triste...

2367 Ensuite faire du théâtre pour une chapelle de pseudo... de pseudo-intellectuels qui
viennent et qui croient déchiffrer dans des rebus intellectuelles dans pensées on ne
peut plus ténébreuses [...] je n'aime pas cette forme de spectacle non plus...

2368C'est pour cela que je vais essayer de faire dans ma seconde tentative une forme de
théâtre très simple pour habituer les jeunes à venir voir au théâtre ... des choses
simples dites facilement mais toujours en prenant en considération que l'enfant est le
public le plus difficile qui existe... et qu'on ne peut pas le tromper et qu'on n'a pas le
droit de le tromper... et qu'on a une très grande responsabilité en tant que metteur en
scène vers le public d'enfants ... il ne faut pas déformer son goût... il ne faut pas
chercher à l'influencer... il faut lui présenter des choses simples dans lesquelles il se
trouvera et il comprendra de lui-même... on n'a pas besoin de lui ascéner des messages [...]

2369 Petit Prince... ils ont tout compris... Molière... j'ai monté »Le Bourgeois
Gentilhomme"...»Le Malade Imaginaire"... je vais monter »Les précieuses ridicules"...La
princesse Thurandaud...

2370 Le Bourgeois Gentilhomme"... tout le monde a retrouvé les côtés negatives d'une
société libanaise qui est tournée vers l'Occident... qui qui se pique de vouloir jouer au
bourgeois avant-gardiste... et qui n'a aucune culture et tout est superficiel ... c'est un
vernis de la société artificielle... c'est la seule pièce où j'ai ... parce que le texte le
permettais joué sur un côté oriental parce que il y a une turquerie dans le bourgeois
gentilhomme... dans la scène la plus spectaculaire... j'ai fait une Haflé à l'orientale avec
... du du ... Derbakké du Tablé avec danse orientale... ça a été un côté très libanisé dans

la pièce et d'ailleurs la pièce a commencé en arabe et s'est terminée en arabe
également... ce n'ai pas un mélange... j'essaie au contraire à travers de prototype de
personnages humains de faire passer cela auprès des jeunes et ils le comprennent
parfaitement... scolaires à partir de 7 ans...
2371 Ce qui nous manque c'est des auteurs dramatiques... ce sont toujours des adaptations...
2372 Qu'est ce que c'est que libanais? Traditions qui remontent si loin... ouvert à la mer ce
qui fait que le libanais ne ressemblent à aucun autre pays de la région ni du monde...
c'est un mélange de culture... sens de l'argent... sens du gain... c'est resté dans l'âme du
libanais...
2373 Ce sont des nuances d'après moi... le chrétien a pris du Musulman ... tout le monde a
pris de tout le monde...
2374 Rarement le public se mélange parce que les productions qui sont faites qui sont
faites au Liban sont faites en fonction d'un public... ils ne sont jamais faites dans
l'absolu ... on ne monte pas une pièce de théâtre parce qu'on aime cette pièce de
théâtre... il y a ceux qui font le théâtre de facilité ... dans lequel le spectateur entre et
sait d'avance qu'il ne va pas se casser la tête... qu'il entre ayant payé **15000** LL. Veut
s'amuser pour ces **15000** L.L [...] il y par contre un autre genre... le théâtre politique... et
se veut posant des questions mettant en cause le système dans lequel on vit et prenant
partie pour une cause determinée... il y a un public... pour ce genre... il ne pense pas
avoir des réponses à ses questions mais se retrouvera dans sa façon de penser et de
revoir la société libanaise sous cet oeil critique... ces deux sont des productions ciblées
vers le public... et automatiquement qui reçoivent en échange ce public pour lequel
ils sont destinées... il y finalement très peux de pièces qui ne correspondent ni à ça ni
à ça [...] ce genre de productions visent à attirer vers elle le spectateur qui veut s'amuser
en essayant de lui donner quelque chose de plus serieux sans tomber dans l'excès
contraire de lui donner des recettes politiques... de prises de positions... tranchées

nettes et catégoriques... ce genre de spectacle est malheureusement le grand sacrifié au
Liban... parce que jusqu'à présent il ne trouve pas un public... il cherche... mais ne
trouve pas encore...
2375 Quand vous faites payer **20$** pour voir une pièce... je trouve cela une barrière qui
empêchent beaucoup de monde qui aimeraient venir [...] et le théâtre est un plaisir que
l'on partage... il y a très peu de gens qui viennent seules au théâtre ... et cela revient
trop chèr... le théâtre n'est populaire que dans une forme que je deteste c'est le théâtre
de chansonnier... la les gens paient **21$** parce que on leur donne à boire on leur
donnent à manger... on leur donne un spectacle qui ne coutent rien parce que ça se
déroule sur un scène de **2** x **3** m. où l'on ne peut faire rien du tout... il n'y a pas de
costumes, d'éclairage, de mise en scène, rien du tout...(the extended version of
restaurant)... c'est de l'anti-théâtre... mis chemin entre le populaire et le politique...
c'est une forme batarde... un mélange...
2376 Censure dans le domaine de la liberté sexuelle... on est plus libre politiquement... cela
relève du fait que il ne faut au Liban ne heurter aucune susceptibilité [...] qui est une
forme de qualité... on réagit souvent par susceptibilité et pas par sensibilité [...] et c'est
dans les moeurs orientales...
2377 Le merchantilisme n'a pas réussi à imposer une liberté sexuelle dans le théâtre et dans
la vie de tous les jours au Liban... c'est une forme hypocrite de présenter le sexe...
2378 Le théâtre est entré dans les écoles... dans quelques années nous allons avoir un
public averti... chacun pourra retrouver dans ce monde du théâtre quelque chose qui
le touche... option dans le baccalauréat... on les envoie voir des pièces de théâtre ... il
n'y a qu'au Liban que ça se passe dans le monde arabe...
2379 Il y a eu des choses intéressantes qui n'ont pas été vues par tout le monde... elles ont
été vu par des spectateurs qui savaient qu'est ce qu'ils allaient voir et donc c'est
dommage parce que Il y a eu des pièces qui reflétaient une réalité que l'on ignorait dès

qu'on était de l'autre côté de Beyrouth... Beyrouth Est ignorait ce que vivait Beyrouth
Ouest et Beyrouth Ouest ignorait ce que vivait Beyrouth Est... Il aurait fallu au
contraire que les gens de Beyrouth Est sachent ce qui se passait et comment vivaient
les gens à Beyrouth Ouest et les gens de Beyrouth Ouest méritaient de voir ce que
pensaient et peut-être de cette rencontre de deux choses complètement différentes il
y auraient pu avoir des solutions à beaucoup de problèmes [...]
2380 Les médias ont été manipulées... il faut donner aux gens tout le temps de choses
sensationelles... la presse est devenue merchantile... il faut lui donner du sang et du
sexe... le public ne réagit plus qu'à ça [...] les médias désinforment... pour un but
lucratif... politiquement ... socialement ... moralement... religieusement... il n'y a plus de
conscience journalistique...
2381   Interview avec Berge Fazlian
2382
2383 Lebanese-Lebanese and Lebanese-Armenian are different... because the Lebanese-
Armenian have a tradition... they used to have a church... a school and always with the
school... theater place...
2384   1915 génocide arménien...
2385   1921 Armenia soviétique... tradition in theater...
2386 1960 Lebanon had no theater... but the Armenians didn't speak arabic...
2387 Lebanese audience is divided into two types... bourgeois high life speaks French for
which French troops used to come for 2. 3 days... that was enough... the other public
was attached to national values... it didn't have any theater only songs [...] variétés...
2388 Theater is not an isolated art it is related to other arts... vernissage... art... music... the
schools don't encourage the students to go...
2389 Christian was occidental educated the Moslem was educated Arabic way... form Egypt...
because they learned at the universities in Egypt... Arabic... because it was hard for
them to learn at the AUB or USJ...
2390 Shoushou... has become a symbol of Lebanon... like Rahbani... like Fairuz...
2391 At the beginning the Bourgeois didn't want to come to Lebanese theater... when it was

settled... with Mounir Abou Debs... Antoine Moultaka... Roger Assaf... they started
slowly to come...
2392 Shoushou was Sunni... but all the others were there.
2393 Tradition... we have no museum... nothing is kept from theater... no artifacts... not
even the place... at the universities there is education but not tradition...
2394 William Saroyan... American theater...
2395 1960 translations...
23961965 adaptations... La cruche cassée de Kleist... ضاعت الطاسة... Ben Johnson... لعبة الختيار...
2397 1970's writing theater... [...] الأزميل... الزنزلخت... جحا في القرى الأمامية [...].
2398عجايب بحرك إسكندرية... ... the imagination of the director is more than the imagination of
the author...
2399 Mounir... dans la première scène... avec la musique syrienne tout le monde a compris...
il n'y avait aucun mot sur la Syrie... aucun mot sur la politique... et le public a compris...
2400 Shoushou est un clown mais un clown inimaginablement fort [...] . le caractère qu'il a fait
est pris ni de l'Egypte ni des Arabes ni de rien... c'est un caractère typiquement qui se
trouve à Beyrouth... une sorte de charlatan... on voit le public au théâtre de Shehrazade... en descendant les retardataires entendent la voix de Shoushou et
commencent à rire... Shoushou est un génie... grand... comme Fairouz... on entend la
2401J'ai travaillé avec toutes les vedettes... Shoushou... Nabih Abou l-Hosn ... Mounir
maintenant... Fairuz... Sabah... tous sont faciles à travailler avec... ils se ressemblent
tous... ils viennent tôt... ils sont nerveux... ne veulent parler à personne...
2402 Il y a des tabous... وصية كلب [...] si je j'ai la liberté... je ne suis pas capable de ridiculiser
Mohammad... il y a une auto-censure... parce que pour ridiculiser Mohammad [...] ça veut
dire que je ne te respecte pas... le problème dans وصية كلب était ceux qui exploitent la
religion... parce que avec le Catholikos arméniens j'ai eu une discussion... ils m'ont
appelé... ils m'ont demandé qu'est-ce que c'est que cette pièce...?... J'ai dit... je n'attaque
pas la religion... mais est-ce-qu'il n'y a pas de gens qui exploitent la religion...? ils ont
dit oui... (de toute façon, la pièce a été arrêtée)...
2403D'abord... le théâtre c'est quoi... ? C'est un endroit où la société se ramasse [...] c'est un

spectacle... seul art qui peut être vivant devant une société pas devant un individu...
même le cinéma est individuel... quand on est seul dans une salle de cinéma on rit seul...
si c'est une comédie... mais quand c'est la même situation dans le théâtre on ne réagit
pas... mais quand tout le monde rit... on rit [...] donc le théâtre c'est un acte collectif... pas
individuel... comme dans une église ou bien un mosquée... il y a une communication...
aujourd'hui... l'homme est devenu individuel trop individuel s'assit devant la télévision...
et mange... voit dans l'Internet... la nécessité du théâtre... il faut à tout moyen
chercher a soutenir le théâtre parce que c'est un rassemblement collectif... l'église a
aujourd'hui perdu de valeur... qui a remplacé... côté sentiment... le football... oui c'est la
même chose... sentiment de collectivité... manifestation... collectivité... c'est cela qui
est important dans le théâtre [...] Rock ... Beatles... ils sont géniaux... les idéologies ont
toutes fait faillite…

2404   Interview [...]

2405

2406 بيروح يلي المتخصصين عندك ... الجماهيري الجمهور عندك ... النخبوي الجمهور عندك ... العالم بكل
بالفن معينة لناحية...
برأيي اشيا لعدة راجع هيدا...
1. التربوية المؤسسات... التعليم... التربية...
2. البيت...
3. الـ... عام بشكل... المجتمع... TV...
نخبوي... المقصود بها مجموعة زغيرة مش معناتا انو هيدي مثقفة احسن... انما اهتماماتا موجهة
لنوع معين من
الحاجات...الفن... هيدا بغير... مرجع للأساس يللي هوي الحاجات
بكل العالم ... عندك الجمهور النخبوي ... عندك الجماهيري... عندك المتخصصين يلي بيروح لناحية
معينة بالفن...
هيدا راجع لعدة اشيا برأيي...

2407   ليش الواحد بيروح عالمسرح؟
1. أول شي لانو اصحابو اخدوا عالمسرح... وهوي مش عارف شي من شي ...
2. لانو جمعية باعتو كارت... راح ليشجع الجمعية وهوي ما فارقة معو المسرحية ...
3. الاساس هوي حاجة تثقيفية وحاجة ترفيهية... كل شي معلومات جديدة ...بتفيدو... بتزيد من من
معلوماتو
ومعرفتو بتفتحلو آفاق جديدة... هيدي بعتبرا انا تثقيفية... كشف مواقف معينة... على العالم بشكل
عام... بيصير يلاقي
...المعرفة بتزيد مع الوقت مع كل عمل عم بيشوفوا
المحافظة على الذات... survival خلال الحرب كان فيه خطر عم بيهدد الناس... البقاء**2408**
... كل الفئات... كل الطوائف
...كان الفرز طائفي. حزبي. عقائدي... عشائري... عائلي... شو ما كان

315

2409 أديش... بعد الحرب رجع كيان الدولة... هلق الغاء الطائفية عم يعمل الغاء مصالح لناس... مستعدة هالناس تتخلى عن مصالحا... وتسلم الادارة للدولة. بس كمان الدولة ما بدها تهدد كيان فئة معينة... كل ما حست فئة معينة انو عم يتهدد كيانا... كل ما صارت تصرخ وتلجأ لحدا يحميها... الا اذا الدولة اخدت ثقة الناس فيها... وصار يحس الواحد حمايتو فيها...

2410 ...هلق الخطر صار اكتر من برا جايي علينا. ما ندوب بالعالمية
2411 ...المسرح ينبع من خلال انسان من مجتمع معين وفكر معين
2412 ...cinema كل الحركة المسرحية اليوم... الـ Dish والـ TV مضاربة من الـ
2413 انت بتعمل جمهور... مسرح ايماني... سمعتها طقت بدينتي الخبرية... أي ساعة بدو يحكي... انا اسست جمهور للمسرح الايمائي... ما فيك تقول انو بعرف يا غشيم... تاني عمل طرقتو موضوع عميق... بعدين عملنا نقاش مع الناس... من ورا مناقشتي صاروا يحضروا... بتعمل عمل منيح بيجوا الناس
2414 ...أنا برأيي المسرح يتعاطى بكل شي بس يضل مسرح... ما يصفي منبر سياسي
2415 منير كسرواني... ما كانوا قاصدين بالاول... وقعوا فيها... التنوا فيها... طلعتلن مصاري... مرق بمرحلة هالانسان المقهور المعتر... هيدي حالات مرق هوي فيها... أنا ما بلومو منير كسرواني... مرق بفترة بالحرب فنيت عيلتو كلها... وخلص هوي بعجيبة... لاقى انو هيدي شغلة هوي مرق فيها... عبر عنا هالشغلة معاناتو هوي... هيك تجاوب معو كمية كبيرة او مجموعة كبيرة من الناس كمان مرقوا فيها بنفس الوقت... هلق هالشي ما بدنا نوجدو عند جمهور هوي عم بيلبي حاجات ويدغدغ افكار واحاسيس فئة معينة من الشعب يلي مرقوا بهالظروف هيدي... وعم ترتحلا بيناتن... هوي عم يعطيهن شو بدن وهني عم combine الناس... يعني صار فيه نوع من الـ بيحسوا انو نوعا ما من تعاطف مع هالشي يللي قريب منن... فيه كتير اشتغلوا عهالنمط...
2416 ...مثل شي غيفارا... صار اسطورة يمثل تطلعات واهداف لرؤيا... من ورا صورة
2417 ...المسرح والمادة اساس الاقتصاد... فيه تكامل بين التنين
2418 ...المسرح لا يقوم على افراد... المسرح يقوم على مجموعة
2419 نحنا بلد زغير قائم على عائلات... فيه رابط القربى... ما لازم نخاف منها... لمن عم تفرط العيلة عم تفرط كتير
2420 ...اشيا... الحرية موجودة بشكل قوي جدا عملت عمل شاهنشاه... ملك الملوك... اللبناني... مملكتو الو هوي... امن كل شي ببيتو... بس حس انو بدو يعتدي على ممالك الآخرين... قلة وعي... جهل للاهداف الانسانية... احسن من هيك شي ما رح تاخد لا مني ولا من غيري...
2421 ...الجمهور... مقسم حسب المكان... والمعلومات الاضافية عن كل مشاهد موجودة هنا
2424 ..مقابلات أريسكو بالاس . الحمراء . مسرحية عربصات... خضر حسن علاء الدين
2425
2426 Christian, Maronite, male, early 40
2427 بصراحة نحنا كنا مستنظرين المسرحية ... متكاملة كاملة... يعني ... مش قضية سكتشات... ام يعني يتعرف... خضر منوش الا ممثل ما بينحكاش عنو الا بالمنيح المنيح... يعني... ع نسق بيو يعني... و... بفتكر انو هوي صار لاعب كذا مرة... يمكن ما كانتش عم تظبط معو... انشالله... هالمرة بتظبط معو
2428 ط. س. : موضوع المسرحية... كيف حسيتو...؟

2429	...ماتشات حلوين... مش عاطلين... ماتشات حلوين... مش عاطلين
2430	ط. س. merci : كتير
2431	...de rien
2432	
2433	
2434	Christian, Maronite, female, mid 30
2435	بس مهضومين كتير... كتير خفيفين... يعني ما حسينا.
2436	ط. س. : موضوع المسرحية...؟
2437	بس يكون سكتشات ما بيكون المسرح... موضوع متكامل... يعني... كل اسكتش الو ميزتو [...] المهضومة. الخفيفة... بس كتير خفاف... مرقت ما حسيتا...
2438	
2541	
2542	
2543	*********
2544	ممثل
2545	
2546	أنا دارس تمثيل وهوايتي كمان. المسرح عالم تاني وبحب كون فيه... مسرح منير بيعبر عن جرح الوطن...الجنوب...
2547	جمهور من كل الطوايف... مسرحنا. فيه من كل الطوايف حتى الممثلين من كل الطوايف... وعيلة وحدة... حتى
2548	...مؤخرا عرضنا بسوريا... مع انو اللهجة غريبة لالن بس لاقى نجاح كتير
2549	***********
2550	(ممثل)
2551	
2552	أنا من بيروت... مني دارس تمثيل... هيي كعرض للوضع بشكل عام. زلمة كتير طيب بيحاولو يستغلو بعض العالم...
2553	...على الآثار اللي التقت بقلب بيتو بعد القصف الاسرائيلي اللي صار بالبيت
2554	ممثلة
2555	
2556	...مغرومة بدكتور... استاذها بالجامعة... اهتم بالآثار وبطل يهتم فيها demoiselle دور
2557	
2558	*********
2559	مقابلات مع الجمهور خلال الاستراحة
2560	
2561	young man Shiaa. South Lebanon
2562	...الحلو يعني... الشي الحلو ما بتلاقيه هون بالمسرح
2563	ط. س. : بتعرف عن حالك... شو عامل شو دارس.؟
2564	...ما دارس شي
2565	ط. س. : بتحب المسرح؟
2566	...حسب المسرحية شو قيمتها... يعني بالوقت الحاضر بعدنا ما شفنا نتيجة هلق لعنا... يعني ط. س. : كيف شفت المسرحية؟
2567	مقبولة المسرحية... حضرنا مسرحية آخر ايام سقراط... مسرحية كتير حلوة والها معاني... كتير حلوة... لملحم بركات
2568	...الزوجة: ما بتتقارن بهيدي ابدا
2569	ملحم بركات مسرحية مهمة كانت كتير من سنة الماضية... مشيت بطريقي... يعني هو التنتين يللي بينو...

2570	ط. س.: يعني المسرحية الغنائية بتجذب أكتر؟
2571	...مش غنائية بمعنى غنائية... كانت موضوع حلو
2572	...نحنا مش قصدنا المطرب... المسرحية سمعناها... وحبيناها
2573	ط. س.: جايين من محل بعيد حضرتكم؟
2574	من الزرارية... من المنطقة من الجنوب.
2575	
2576	************
2577	Shiaa... South Lebanon. Late 40s.
2578	ط. س.: شو رأيك بالمسرحية؟
2579	...هي اجمالا كل مسرحيات منير كتير حلوة... فيها نقد... وبشكل عام مقبولة... منيحة
2580	ط. س.: عجبك أول مشهد؟
2581	كتير منيح
2582	ط. س.: بتحضر دايما مسرح...؟
2583	حسب الظروف... تقريبا... حسب الوقت... بشتغل تجارة حرة... حسب المسرحية ونوعيتها... حسب قربها بالدرجة الاولى... فيه مسرحيات كنا نقصدها لبيروت...
2584	ط. س.: شو بيعنيلك المسرح؟
2585	المسرح شي كتير مهم... و [...] يعني [...] احم... المسرح كتير مهم للبلاد اللي نحنا فيها... بالاخص المسرح للي فيه النقد
2586	...من المنطقة
2587	
2588	********
2589	2 young girls
2590	
2591	ط. س.: حبيتو المسرحية
2592	...نحنا منحب المسرحية واللي عم بيمثلو بالمسرحية
2593	تاني مرة منحضر منير كسرواني... دايما منشتريلو شرطان منحضرن بألمانيا... نحنا جايين من المانيا... صرلنا 10 سنين هونيك Dortmund...
2594	...المسرح بيعنيلنا كل شي... كل ما بيصحلنا فرصة... أم طعان وبس والحمارة
2595	
2596	********
2597	عايش في المانيا. في الخمسينات من عمره
2598	...المسرحية ما اشبا شي
2599	ط. س.: شو بيعنيلك المسرح؟
2600	...شوي بيفرج همومو الواحد... بيجي بينبسط بيضحك شوي وبينسى الهموم اللي هو فيها
2601	الزوجة: بيضحك ع حالو...
2602	ط. س.: بتحضر دايما مسرح؟
2603	والله انا بألمانيا عرفت كيف...؟ منحضر شرطان... مبارح جينا لقينا حفلة وجينا نحضرها اليوم... كسرواني... بيضل يضحك... ومبسوطين منو يعني... ومنتمنى انو دايما المسرحيات القادمة يكون نفس السيستام... يعني ... بتعرف المغتربين دايما بحاجة لضحكة لبسمة... ل... خاصة بيحكي عن الوطن عن الجنوب والحالة ...
2604	ط. س.: عجبك أول مشهد؟
2605	...كلن ملاح... كلن ملاح
2606	
2607	*********
2608	شابان في اواخر العشرينات

ARABIC TRANSCRIPTIONS

2609 الاول: thème... كنا منتمنى المسرحية اول شي يكون فيها لحد هلق ما حاسين انو في ...thème معين... منشان
هلق نحنا بعز هلق... ايام المقاومة والتحرير وغيرو... كنا منتمنى انو المسرحية.. تتطرأ لبعض المواضيع من هالنوع
هيدا... ما يكون كلها فيها... حاسس انو كلها بتدور حول مواضيع مسخفة... او اشيا ما بتمس لامان الانسان الجنوبي
بشكل عام...

2610 (هيدا اللي هلق خلص... كان بايخ كتير... يعني (استنكار بسبب مشهد السيكس
2611 ط. س. : اول مشهد؟
2612 الثاني: صح انو بعض الاشخاص بيتمنوا يسمعوا... بس مش الاكترية...مش رأي الناس كلها... فيه فلتان كتير
بالحكي... ممكن ينعمل مسرحية... بالجنوب... ينحذف بعض المشاهد منها... او بعض الكلام البذيء اللي عم ينقال...
2613 الثاني [...]: انو يتدارى الموقف شوي ... مش اكتر من هيك... لانو البعض منن بيتمنوا يشوفوا او يسمعوا... بس ولكن بصورة عامة مش الكل...
2614 الاول: نقد للدولة للادارة... لاصلاح البلد بشكل عام... المقاومة ... فيه مواضيع كتير الانسان بيتمناها ... مش انو الانسان يضحك وما ياخد عبرة من المسرحية...
2615
2616 ************
2617 مشاهد في الخمسينات...
2618 ط:س بدنا ناخد شوي رأيكن بالمسرحية بشكل عام
2619 المسرحية ع ...يعني بدي هنيهن
2620 بصراحة ما في مجال للنقد... كلها كاملة المسرحية مش ناقصة شي... يعني صراحة كلها عجبتني... عندي شغل بالليل وبالنهار...
2621
2622 **************
2623 مشاهد في الاربعينات
2624 مش رح فينا نوصف المسرحية اديش حلوة... من واقعنا... من مأساتنا... كتير مسرحية... بيتقبلها أي انسان... ما فيه عليها انتقاد... والله مش كل المسرح بينحضر... عفوا مع احترامنا للكل... طبعا الجمهور محل ما بيحب بيجي...
2625
2626 *********
2627 في الاربعينات
2628
2629 لو ما عجبتنا كنا جينا... انا كنت مسافر بـ 21 والاخ مسافر بكرة ع أبيدجان... بقينا لنحضر المسرحية... مفكرها قليلة...
2630 ما بتصور فيه نقد... الاداء كامل...
2631 ******
2632 مشاهد بالاربعينات
2633
2634 المسرحية حلوة كتير... انا مش عايش هون عايش بأميركا... بعتقد هيدي تاني مسرحية بحضرها. بس كتير حلوة
وبتعطي [...] انطباع كتير جيد... وانبسطت فيها كتير... الشخصيات لانو بعرفن معرفة شخصية الحقيقة... منير صديق

319

لالي... وتاني شي الموضوع... الموضوع كتير حلو وبيأثر بالناس... وبخاصة الانسان الجنوبي... انا بتأثر كتير

...بالجنوب وبالوضع اللي نحنا عايشينو هون... الحقيقة وبالناس اللي عايشة بهالبلد هي

2635   ...صرلي 15 سنة بأميركا... زيارة ورايح بعد اسبوعين

2636   ********

2637

شخص... جيدة كتير... حلوة كتير. شغلة كتير قوية ومنيحة... انا حاضر 3 مسرحيات 26383000
...لالو... وزارة للهوارة

وفلت الملق وهاي (فوق الدكة)... بتلاقي ما شاء الله انو فيه عطاء وفيه تجدد دائم يعني... بكل مسرحية... فيه اشيا

كتير جديدة بتخلق بوقتها يعني... او بظروف المنطقة اللي هوي بيقدم فيها... يعني مثلا بكل قرية... بتلاقي بيدخل

...شغلات كتير جديدة على المسرحية... وطبعا الفريق العامل بيبيض الوجه

الطابع اللي مشي فيه هوي... هيك... عن ابن قرية او ابن عيلة فقيرة او منطقة محرومة... 2639
...بيتهيألي انو هالاسلوب

او هالطريقة... كتير ناجحة... ليه... لانو 3 أرباع الناس... عايشة... نفس الاطباع ونفس المشاكل
...اللي عم تعاني منها

يعني يمكن هوي عم ينقل صورة عن مجموعة من الناس... هيدا كتير ناجح لانو ما بيخلص... بتطلع معو... مع كل
...بكل شي

يمكن بالنسبة للمواضيع الوطنية تطورت كتير بمسرحياتو... ووصلت لاقصى حد فيها... من 2640
...عمليات النضال

لعمليات القتال... والشغلات والدفاع عن الارض... يعني هيدا بتلاقي بكل مسرحياتو... نفس المواضيع... شغلة هيدي

ما بتصغر. وطريقة كتير منيحة... وجيدة... منير صديقنا وابن منطقتنا... حابين مسرحياتو بغض النظر عن علاقتنا
...الشخصية فيه

2641   **********

لاني   directement بحس... مثلا ... متل ريمون جبارة... ما رح يعيطلي لألي...مش لانو 2643 مسلمة...بس بحس... كأنو

...هيداك شعبو... هيدا بيرتاح معو

2644   Interview.

2645

قصة كاتبها... بحكي عربي...؟... ستانيسلاف ستراتييف... بلغاري [...] . اخدت هالقصة من 2646
...الكاتب البلغاري وعربتها

لبننتها... بقي فيها الفكرة الاساسية بس... أما الاحداث كلها تغيرت... ما بقى فيها الا الفكرة
...الانسانية... من المسرحية

انتو تبع الشعارات بتنادو بالانسانية وما بتهتمو بالانسان... كبيتونا برا... طيب وين الانسانية... ما اهتموا بأصحاب

البيت كمان... مش بس بالفسيفساء... انا عم بهتم بالآثار تأعمل محاضرات بلندن بباريس... بيقولها هوي... ما عم

...يهتم بالآثار كتار... بس تيوصل هوي عضهرن... هي الفكرة الانسانية

تاني فكرة... مهمة كتير انو الفقير ما الو حدا... مغلوب... هوي غريب ببيتو مثل ما اللبناني 2647 غريب بوطنو... هاي تاني

فكرة اساسية مهمة... انت هون غريب... بالحدود غريب... بالشمال غريب بالبقاع غريب ببيروت غريب. وين ما

كان غريب... بتعرف هالشي لما توصل عالحواجز كلها. وين ما كان... نحنا غرباء بوطننا... وهون اهمية

320

المسرحية... الفكرة اللي بتعالجها... مشكلتنا مش من اسرائيل بس... مشكلتنا من اللي عم بيتاجرو فينا بالبلد... زعماءنا اللي عم بيتاجرو فينا بالبلد وبيبيعونا... هون مشكلتو اسماعيل... كل واحد من اهل بلدو جاب الـ وفات ع OK
البيت وصار ينكش ... واحد جايب دفعة بـ 15000 بيعطيني 7000 وبياخد هوي 8000... او هيك او لا... عرفت كيف... الحل بالصراع... ما فيه حل... كيف بدا تنحل ما حدا بيعرف... انا ما بعرف كيف... كان فيه مقاومة منو هوي
...انا... كان فيه مقاومة مني

2648 ط. س. : ردات فعل الجمهور
2649 هالعمل مش عم بيمثّل الجنوب... هالمسرحية انعرضت بقصنون زغرتا... بكفرحلتا البترون... يعني بتنورين كمان ببعلبك... وين ما كان... كان التجاوب كتير كبير... ليش... لانو عم بيشوف فيها... انا هيك... انا متل اسماعيل
...مصيري متلو... حتى بسوريا كان التجاوب كبير
2650 انا عم بكتب للعالم [...] . اذا ما كتبتلن ما بعنيلن شي... ما بيحضروني... ما بعنيلن شي... ما بتقلن شي بعنيلن... الشغلة ... بدك تكتبلن شي بيخصن... لتحمسن... لتفعل فيهن... تت... تقيمن... تحس انو هيدا قضيتي...غير هيك لا بيصير فيه قطع... ما فيه تواصل يعني... بتروح عملية المسرح... Rupture بيصير فيه انفصام المسرح هوي تواصل بين الجمهور وبين الممثلين... اللعبة لعبة ممثل وجمهور. بس... شو انتي قادر تحكو... للجمهور... قادر
...تثيرو... بتكون لعبتك بالطريق الصحيح

2651 ط.س. : اول مشهد
2652 نحنا جايين لهون... بيصير بعد منو مشهد التلفزيون ... اشارة الى انو لبنان عم يتحول لسوق... يعني فيديو كليب ورقص وطقش وفقش... هاه... وفرح وحفلات وين ما كان... ويلا سهرة لمحمد اسكندر...
...سهرة لمادونا... كذا على مين... ع رقبتي ورقبة مرتي... عرقبة الانسان الفقير... بييتنا... بيتنا مخروب... العدو فوق راسنا... ومع ذلك بتروجلنا الدولة انو ما فيه شي. الجيش حامينا... وين حامينا الجيش... أي جيش... وين حامينا... كل يوم هون الطيران هون... كل يوم بالليل والنهار... هلق ما عم تسمعو يمكن... كل ليلة... الجيش حامينا... موسى الصدر... كلو نجاح... اكاليل غار ببيروت ... على الحواجز... حولو البيت لماخورة... ماخور [...] [...] على جمجمة هالناس المعترين... بيجوا بلاقوهن بالبيت... هيدا الاحتلال مش جايي من برا... منا فينا... مين عم ياكلنا... مين بيقطع خيط قطن بالجنوب... أي رجل بيقطع خيط قطن بالجنوب... بلا رندة بري... ونبيه بري... ما فيي شيلن انا خيي... هيدولي معن قرارات هون... الموضوع بيهمن للعالم ... الموضوع رمزي ... كل واحد بيفهموا قد ما بدو... منن بيفهموا انو والله اسماعيل حرام... فيه ناس بيقولوا انو شو هيدا بيزتو لبرا... فيه ناس بيفكروا بيعملولا بعد... كل
...واحد شكل
2653 الجمهور... كل واحد بيفهم ع ذوقو... الدكتور او المثقف بيفهم شي... والفلاح بيفهم عذوقو... الفلاح يمكن بيفهم انو

والله منير ركب عالحمار... الفقير... مبسوط فيها هي ...اووه ركب عالحمار... هوي كل يوم بيركب عالحمار... بس
... عالمسرح احلا... هيدا بيفهما هيك... ممكن
لا شك بقلك انو بـ جونية... يمكن ما بينعجقوا هالقد...يمكن ما بينعجقوا هالقد... ما بعرف **2654** بعد ما جربت بجونية...بس
عم بحكي عن المناطق بشكل عام... كلا تجاوبت... كان فيه تجاوب كتير حلو
عالسوري... كل العالم نفس الوضع... ليش هون بالجنوب ظامطين؟ [...] من الاولى لهون **2655** انو ظامطين من
المخابرات...؟... مش ظامطين... ضحكوا العالم انبسطوا... طيب ليه؟... هيدا وجعن... اكيد بغير محل يمكن ما بتعني
شي... انو نحنا ولاد جبل عامل... هيدا الارض اسمها جبل عامل... لحمنا مر... مش بسهولة فيها اسرائيل تاخد
راحتها... لحمنا مر... يعني شعب بيقاوم... بيعتو ولادو بموتن... بيقتل ابنو ع دبابة بس بيفجر الدبابة.. هيدا الخطر
بالموضوع... اكيد هيدي شغلة بدها تعني للجنوبي... اكتر ما بتعني غير انسان... بس حقيقة هوي... اليوم المقاومة منا
حكرا على الجنوب بس... فيه ناس من الشمال عم بيموتوا هون... من بعلبك... كل انسان عندو وطنية.. بتحركو
القضية هي...
من جونية... ؟... من جونية اذا كان حزبي... او شيوعي او قومي... بيجوز بيندفع ... غير **2656** هيك لا... انت عم تعرف
انو عم بيصير فيه ظاهرة... فيه موضوع اساسي هوي موضوع علاقة المسرح بالجمهور... اهم قصة.. مش عن
عبث بيجوا الناس... الناس بيجوا بدن يقولوا شو بدو يقول منير بهالعمل...؟... شو بدو يقول ... شو بيعالج ... شو
بيطرح؟. هيدي الظاهرة... بالمسرح اللبناني... اليوم... مسرح منير كسرواني ... مسرح اكتر شي بيستمر بالبلد... السر
قربى من العالم. مش ع تفاهة... على عمق... لانو الموضوع اللي عم بمسكو هالمرة هي... لتختار المسرحية وزارة
الثقافة السورية. هني عارفين شو عم يختارو... الموضوع فيه الو دلالة انسانية كبيرة للداخل...
انا اشتغلت مسرحية ببيروت 8 اشهر بالبيكاديللي... نسبة تدني الجمهور بالمسرح الثقافي... **2657** مسرح مثقف سقط
المسرح... منير كسرواني تخطانا بالجمهور... هيدا الجمهور ببيروت بدن شهرين ليجمعوا... بيضلوا يشتغلو شهرين
ببيروت ليجمعو... انا عم يحضروني بليلة... بعدين اذا اجو لهون عملو مسرح هني... ما بيحضرن حدا.. باتحداهن
منشان 4 5 بالبلد prestige ليه ما بيجيبوهن للعالم... ما الن حدا... وصنفوا حالن انو هني بيعملولن invitation
من ناحية... المسرح ما لازم يسمى حالو مسرح مثقفين... المسرح ... invitation ما بيجوا بالـ لازم يهتم بالجمهور
كتير... موضوع المسرح بحد ذاتو اساس... عند ما بتختار موضوع بيحك العالم... هيدي بداية النجاح... اولا... تاني
شي... لا شك انو الوضع الاجتماعي... الوضع المالي للعالم والمادي وضع مأساوي... قبل ما نروح عالمسرح... بدو
ياكل ويطعمي ولادو... فيه جوع... بلبنان فيه جوع... شئننا ام ابينا... اللي مش جايعين معروفين ... [...] يعني... 5 4
...العالم زهقت الطرب عالتلفزيون **2658**
كل سنة بجي لهون... كل سنة بتنتلي... حضرني 5 آلاف واحد بفرد ليلة بمدرج عقل **2659** شتورة... 5 آلاف... خمسة...

2660 ...انا ان فجرت بفلسطين كرشي اسرائيل بعملها خرابا
...بر الياس
.البقاع... الجنوب
...الزجل
...المواويل
...الوطنيات
...التحدي
...انا مقاوم جنوبي
...انا زلمة بلا صدر بلا ظهر
Direct from the area ...ببعتلك دورية من بيت حمية تقوسها
2661 ...نسيتي انو نحنا حد عنجر
2662
2663 مشاهد في الاربعين
2664 يعني كتير مزودينا من حيث... انو ليك فيه ولاد... ليك... ايه... بقصد انو كتير المجال... هلق المسرحية حلوة... ومنير
...كسرواني قد ما يكون... اهضم من غيرو
2665 ط.س.: بتحضر مسرح؟
2666 بس منير كسرواني... صرنا حاضرينو 3 مرات ... مرة بعقل بشتورا... مرة بعمر المختار وهلق هون... وببيروت مرة
...بالجان دارك
2667 شو بيعنيلك المسرح؟
2668 المسرح يعني [...] انو هيك بيمثل الواقع... عن قريب هيك بيختلط مع الجمهور... بحس قريب هيك... بيمثل عالمسرح
...ونحنا قدامو... الكلمة بتوصل اسرع
2669 ...ط.س.: بالنسبة لموضوع المسرحية
2670 الواقع اللبناني... مثلا انو العالم عم يهتم بالاثارات والبيوت عم تنقصف... مثلا يعني... هيك ...هذا بيحكي معاناة مثلا
...انو كل الاهتمام عالاثار وهوي البيت تهدم... ومش سائلين
2671 ط.س.: بتحب تحضر غير مسرح؟
2672 ...مش عم بيساقب وقت وقلال بالبقاع المسرحيات... يعني
2673 *******
2674 مشاهد في الاربعين
2675 ما عاش ماشي تخمين غير الاشيا... بتعرف انت... والا بشكل عام حلوين... مسرحيات حلوة ...بس فيها
2676 ...هاللي دارج ... عالدارج بدك تمشي
2677 *******
2678 مشاهد في الاربعين
2679 هيا ثاني بحضر مسرح... لا مرة ببيروت ومرة هون... هاو اياهن مرتين... تنتين ...لكسرواني
2680 ط.س.: شو بيعنيلك المسرح؟
2681 ...تسلية... وحلو... لحد هلق حلوة... انشالله يكفي هيك
2682 ط.س.: من أي ناحية؟
2683 كموضوع... هوي حلو... بيحكي عن واقع الحياة... بيحكي عن الشعب اللبناني كيف بيكون... الشعب بشكل عام
يعني... مش بس بلبنان... بشكل عام... انو كيف مستضعفينو لهالزلمة... مش معلم... فقير... عم ياكلولو ارضو... الصبية
...حلوة كمان
2684

2685 مقابلة - كفررمان - الجنوب - ومقابلات الجمهور.
2686
2687 .
2688
2689 الصوت كان كتير عاطل... اللي بدو يسمع ما قدر يسمع... جو المهرجان هون... داروها
2690 لعب... ما عم تقدر تركز...
2691 ممثل
2692
2693 يعني مش فرق بالجمهور... المسرح المسكر... اليوم فيه كتير ولاد... نحنا عملنا الموضوع ما فيه فزلكة... معمول للناس... بعد بيطلع معنا كتير... المسرح اللبناني... رغم هالفترة كان فيه اعمال مش مسرحية... هي مش مسرح هي تسلية... فيه ناس شغلتن المسرح... افضل شي... كل المهرجانات بياخدو الجايزة الاولى وبيجوا... ما بحمل المسؤولية للجمهور... حتى لو العمل هابط... بيكون اللي عاملو هابط... فيه اعمال محددة لجمهور معين... بيجي الجمهور العادي بيحضرا ما بيفهموا... مش لانو هني ما بيفهموا... بيصير مثل كأنو واحد حافظ نكتة قد ما هوي بيعرفا بس يتذكرها بتضحك... واحد بيشتغل مسرح لالو ولناس حدو... هيدي مسرحيات المهرجانات... بتنعرض مرة مرتين... بس
مسرح اذا بدو يستمر بدو يعمل شي للناس...
2694
2695
2696
2697 التأليف الشخصي... او اقتباس... عن موليير... لمؤلفين ومخرجين خاصين تانيين... تلفزيون... فيلم سينما بالانتاج والتمثيل... مش انا المنتج. بهيدا العمل. اسامة شعبان... ميرنا بشارة... طوني سعادة... وزينة سابا... الجمهور مش معود عالاعمال المسرحية... الوضع المأساوي اللي دائما المواطن الجنوبي عم بيعيشو صار يهمو الترفيه اكتر ما يهمو الطرح الجاد بالمسرح... انما الطرح بالقضية بيهتم فيه كتير الانسان الجنوبي... بس ممكن يكون فيه عملية shock... كان فيه نسبة زغار كتير... رغم انو هالعمل مش للزغار...
2698 من 10 أيام كان فيه منير كسرواني... من قبل بيومين كان فيه ابو سليم الطبل... عم بيصير فيه نشاطات بالبلد هون... الجمعيات والاندية عم بيهبوا سوا لاشيا معينة... مش بالضرورة بس المسرح...
2699 استطلاع مع مختلف الاعمار...
2700 *******
2701 الجمهور ...Audience
2702 شاب في اول العشرينات
2703 وقت اللي بيكون حامل القنبلة... كان من المفروض انو يكون في دخنة بالقاعة وتفجر القنبلة ع صوت صدى...
مظبوط...؟... هونيك بتضهر هيي ودخنة عازفة... منشان هيك نحنا مننزل بخار وما بيعود حدا يبين من ورا... يعني
اجمالا مفروض انو يكون هالشي صار... هيدا الشي الو رهبة كتير حلوة...
2704 بالنسبة لمنير اجمالا المسرحية كانت كتير حلوة مش اول مرة بحضرها... هاي تاني مرة بحضرا... الموضوع وعدة

ARABIC TRANSCRIPTIONS

تمثيليات يعني... اجمالا هوي انسان كتير محترم وشغلو كتير حلو... مش بس عجبني الي عجبنا كلنا نحنا بالشركة...
منير ... شغلو كتير حلو...

2705 التمثيل... الديكور... شوية تحسن اكتر... ما فيها شي اجمالا...
2706 Interview.
2707
2708 كان الافكار بالايديولوجيا رابطو كنت ما... مفتكر كنت ما بالاول... مسرح عملت
انعكاسو عليك بعمر 20 سنة انو تطلع عالتلفزيون... ويشوفوك الناس... وتشد البنات وتضهر بالطرقات ويقولو هيدا
اللي بيمثل... وكذا... جيت بظروف شوي صعبة انا... جيت مهجر من ضيعتي من الجنوب... فدخلت الى معهد الفنون
اللي منعملن بالمسرح... انو ما كنت exercice وصار انو وقت اللي اطلع على المسرح اعمل الـ جيب... من المسرح
العالمي المكتوب وقدم مشاهد... كنت دايما احكي عن حالي... اعمل كمان مونولوجات... التهجير... سكران... الوضع...
2709 اشتغلت مع يعقوب الشدراوي... اشتغلت مع الحكواتي... وكانوا عم ياخدوا موضوع الجنوب أكتر شي... ان بمسرحية
على اطروحتي basée من حكاية 1936" أو بمسرحية "أيام الخيام"... وايام الخيام هي اذا بدك" بالجامعة... one
كمان . اسما "حكواتي من جبل عامل" من الجنوب... وقت اللي عملنا ايام الخيام. man show اخدنا اكتر
المواضيع المعمولة بمسرحيتي ووسعناها. حواريا يعني... وبعدين اضطريت اطلع لبرا اشتغل مع نضال الاشقر
بجرش وبعمان وبطيب الصديقي... ورجعت عملت مسرحية مع نضال بقبرص... اسمها الحلبة... كتابة بول شاوول...
مع Bernard Giraudaux واشتغلت شوية سينما مع مارون بغدادي... عملت فيلم فرنساوي مع مجموعة افلام ...
اشتغلت مع برهان علوية... مع هاني سرور ... مع جان شمعون اذا بدك... وبعدين جيت عملت الـ one man
show طلعتو عالمسرح... كنت اعملن بالجامعة... رجعت كمان عملت مسرحية الجرس. فلاقت استحسانا شديدا
فضول انو كيف واحد لحالو ساعة ونص bouche à oreille عند الناس... وكمان كان فيه كتير عالمسرح... كانت
salle الناس عم تجي هيك... بلشت اعرض اعداد كتير قليلة... مرات يكون فيه عشرة بالـ اعرضلن... مرات 20
بعدين وصلت عملت عرض بعين زحلتا... بالمتن أو بالشوف بتصير... ايه [...] كان فيه خمس آلاف واحد جمهور...
احم احم [...] . عم يحضروا الجرس... ايه خمس آلاف... وكفيت... رجعت عملت مسرحية المفتاح وراها... رجعت عملت
هيدي. زواريب... هلق لاول مرة اذا بدك ... مسرح بيتجول... انو كنا عملنا تجوال بالمناطق اللبنانية قبل بالحكواتي
او باللي عملتن... بعدين انو عرضت تقريبا بكل العالم العربي... عرضت بفرنسا... وبلندن... رحت ع ديترويت...
شاركت بمهرجانات عربية ...تقريبا يعني كل المهرجانات العربية بشارك فيها... كنت عضو بلجنة التحكيم بمهرجان
مسرحية جديدة ... المسرح التجريبي... و [...] هلق عم حضر one man show... one man show يعني حسيت
انا بحبو... هيدي طبيعتي... بحب انو احكي لوحدي... ما انو تقصدت انو انا ممثل style انو هيدا قادر يوقف لوحدو

قدام الناس [...] مش هيدي الغاية ابدا ولا كانت بيوم من الايام... معروف هيدا الاسلوب بالعالم معروف... والو جذور تاريخية عنا بالمسرح... بالظواهر المسرحية العربية... لانو ما عنا تاريخ مسرحي... ما يسمى بال monodrame...

بينعرض جمعة... عشرة ايام 4 عروض... يعني منو شعبي... تجربة مسرحية بيعملوها... تحدي بينو وبين حالو الممثل... لما فيني قول انا انو قدرت اعمل هيدا الاسلوب المسرحي... مسرح شعبي... وقت مسرحية بتشتغل 7 6 اشهر... بوقفها بتكون مليانة الصالة مثلا... او الجرس اشتغلت شي 3 سنين وشي... بين سفرها وبين هون... مع تعطيل... فيقول انا انو الناس بتحب هيدا الاسلوب وانا انو هيدا اسلوبي يعني... برتاح كتير فيه... فكمان انا بكفي فيه...

سياسيا انا ما بشوف... مني معقدن او مسيس بالمفهوم الحزبي العربي... يعني منيش لا اتبع 2710 لقبيلة ولا اتبع لطائفة ولا اتبع لحزب... ما فيني شوف فنان أنا ملتزم حزبيا... في يكون عندك وجهة نظر سياسية يكون عندك توجه سياسي معين... تكون تنتمي الى اليسار او الى اليمين او او او... حر... هيدا طبيعي جدا انك تكون... والا كيف... بدك... ما فيه شي الا ما بدو يكون الو... ما فيه شي الا ما بدو يكون الو فكرة سياسية او اجتماعية ... والا بتكون خارج اطار المجتمع فنك... معزول... بس ولا مرة كان... فيني ... و الحزب بيفرض عليك تراتيبة معينة... فما بافهم انا انو الفنان ...يكون احادي الجانب... بس ما يكون مرتبط بفكرة وحدة

الحلبة كانت عن تنين ميليشيويي بيلتقوا بالشارع... بالحرب وبيحكوا عن حالن وعن علاقتن 2711 بالشارع وعن علاقتن بالناس وعن علاقتن بالقتل وعلاقتن بالافكار وعلاقتن وعلاقتن... هي صرخة كانت ضد ممارسات الميليشيات بالحرب... طبيعي جدا انو الاسلوب يختلف على مستوى النص وعلى مستوى الاداء... على مستوى الاخراج... انما ...الخط الاساسي هوي انساني... دائما منحكي عن الانسان

طرس : كيف عم ينطرح موضوع الجنوب بشكل عام بلبنان.؟ 2712 عم تسألني سياسة... يعني غير الحكواتي ما عم ينطرح موضوع الجنوب الا بشكل 2713 استعراضي تجاري...

طرس : منير كسرواني؟ 2714 احم احم... ما بديش سمي حدا... يعني ...بس حتى تحكي عن المأساة الحقيقية بالجنوب بدك 2715 تقول الاشيا شوي مباشرة... يعني... اذا بدك تقدم المواضيع بطريقة مواربة وغير مباشرة... بتكون عم تعمل أدب... بتكون عم تعمل مسرح... ما الوش علاقة مباشرة... بالناس... اذا بدك تاخد عامة... بدك تتوجه للناس... بدك تاخد لغتن... بدك تاخد مستوى الاستيعاب تبعن... طريقة تعبيرن كيف بيعبروا عن الاشيا... بدك تاخد لغتن بدك تاخد دينن... يعني مش انو بالصدفة... انو انا باخد يعني انو بحكي انو بيطلع شخصية لما بمسرحيات الحكواتي. وبستعمل بالتعبير المفردات الاسلام... لانو غالبية الناس بالجنوب اسلام... لو كانوا مسيحيين كنا انو طبيعي نحنا منستعمل نفس التعابير اللي بيستعملوها هني [...] بدنا نطلعن... بدنا نحكي عنن مباشرة... بتقلي وضع الجنوب ... وضع الجنوب ما بقاش هوي

هلك ... يعني ما كان ولا هلق هوي وضع جنوب لبنان... مسألة. يعني هي نقطة ساخنة بالنظام العالمي الجديد
بالصراع الاقليمي والدولي القائم... ساقبت اختاروا هالنقطة هي اللي هي الاضعف لحتى يعضوا على اصابع بعضن
فيها بانتظار ان يأتي شيء ما ... سلام... ما سلام ما بعرف شو... بس للأسف الشديد... بتقلّلي انو فيه احساس
بالمواطنية تجاه انو هيدا جنوب الوطن ومعزول ومعاني لأ... أكبر دليل على ذلك شفت كيف قدمت... حتى من الناس
السياسيين تبءول الجنوب يعني. او المسؤولين السياسيين. انا برأيي علاقتن الجنوب هيك... شعاراتية ... براقة
وبيرقصوا... وكذا... شوي night club تجارة مش اكتر. انو مسؤولين وهيك... وبيروحوا عالـ بيطلعوا بينخعوا
hard rock... تصريح... واذا انتخبنا ملكة جمال مثلاً... واذا عملنا حفلة كلا رقص... انشاله تكون وكل العالم ... أي
نوع اللي كان موسيقى والاحتفالات وكذا ... فيي مرق شي انو ديروا بالكن وتذكروا اهل الجنوب... منقوم نحنا وعم
نرقص ونحنا وعم نسكر وكذا منقوم منحيي الجنوب والمقاومة الصامدة بالجنوب وكذا...
ط.س. : هالطريقة بالتعاطي...مؤسفة شوي ... ولكن هل بتحسا موجودة بمناطق معينة او 2716 بكل المناطق؟
وين ما كان... ما شي انو بدك تقلي. خلينا نسمي الاشيا بـ... يعني انو بجونية مش موجودة 2717 بطرابلس موجودة يعني؟
قلب بعلبك مثلاً؟
حسب الطائفة... ما عم قلك ايه... كل واحد اليوم... لا شك انو مجتمعنا مجتمع طائفي... 2718 عرفت شو... لا شك انو كل
طائفة مرتبطة بالزعيم... وللأسف الشديد صار هيدا... متل قانون متل دستور عنا... ركبوا الدولة على هالاساس. انو
فيه الشخص... هوي هالمجموعة البشرية تتبع لألو... هوي قرارو هوي لالها... قرارا لالو...هوي هوي بيقرر...
بيوظفها... هوي بيطعميهم... هوي بيسقيها... مربوطة فيه... فاللي بيرضى عليه هيدا الزعيم... بيعيشوا منيح... واللي
بيزعل عليه. غضب الله بينزل على هيدي المجموعة... فصار كل شي يتجير على اساس الطائفة... والحصص
بالدولة انو كيف مناخدا يعني... فمن هون ما عاش فيه احساس بالمجموعة البشرية بالمعنى... انو ما عاش فيه
احساس بالوطن... لانو صار انتماء اللبناني لطايفتو... عرفت شو... اذا زعيم طايفتو استفاد من انو يكون تابع
للجنوب... آه... بيقلن الجنوب منيح ويلا نعمل... بس خلينا على مسيرة... الـ الاجتياح لهلق... انو مين عم بيقاتل ومين
عم بيقاوم ومين... خلصنا بقى... أهل الجنوب... يعني حتى ما نكون عم تتجنى على حدن... بس انو هيدا الشي. ايه
للأسف الشديد ... منتأسف انو يكون هيك... لأنو هيدا مش بس انعكاس على اهل الجنوب سلبي. انعكاس ع الوطن...
انو بقاش تتصور انو هيدا الجيل الجديد كيف بدو بالمستقبل يعيش مع بعضو يعني. اذا كل واحد بيعتبر انو وطنو
طايفتو... وانو الطائفة التانية بدا تاكلو اكلاتو... اكلاتو عرفت شو...؟ ومهددتو... انو بدن يقتلو لهيدا الآخر... كل
واحد بدو يقتل التاني. كلن مهددين من بعضن ... مين مهددن ما منعرف مين مهدد التاني... بس كلن فزعانين

وبيشكوا... والزعيم قاعد عالراس من فوق بيقلن انتبهوا هاه... اذا انا بروح اكلوكن... انا حاميكن... أنا هوي حامل السيف... ما جريس هوي والخضر... الخضر... هون... هوي ذاتو مار جريس والخضر... بس الخضر هون اسمو ...الخضر هون اسمو مار جريس

أنا ما عملت هيك... لانو انا ما اشتغلت عالعنصر الطائفي... ما ابتزيت الناس... لانو انا 2719 انتمي... متل ما قلتلك... ولا لقبيلة... ولا لطايفة ولا لحزب... منشان هيك انا بتشوف الناس اللي بيجوا لعندي هني من كل المواطنين اللبنانيين لانو... اولا ما سبيت حدا يعني مني واقف بزاوية حدا لسب الآخرين... دايما بحكي عن حالي... عن اللي بحسوا وما بجيب سيرة حدا... ولاني صادق... فأي حدن بيجي بيحضرني... وبقدم العمل بطريقة فنية صادقة فبيشوف حالو فيه... فاذا قلت انا خيفان هوي بيحس انا خيفان ... مظبوط انا متلو... اذا قلت انا مهدد... بيقول انا مهدد متلو...فبحكي عن موضوع المواطن الانسان بوجودو مش بالتفاصيل الحياة اليومية ما بحكي بالسياسة اليومية... سياسة الجرايد ما بحكي فيها... ولا بحكي على الوضع الداخلي ولا بحكي على الحكومة ولا بنكت ع السياسيين ... بفوت عالعمق ع وجدان الناس... بفوت عالحاضر اليومي... الحاضر اليومي بربطها بالتاريخ كمان. فمنشان هيك انو كل الناس اللي بيجوا بيحضروني... ما بيحسوا حالن انو مأذيين من كلامي... انو هيدا عم يحكي علينا... انا يمكن بحكي ع حالي... فلما بيجي الآخر بيشوفني... بيلاقيني عم سب حالي شو بدو يقول... فبيلاقي انو انا كمان لازم سب حالي...

مسرحياتي كلها بتنتهي بالموت... ايام الخيام ... الحلبة... الجرس [...] للمفتاح بتنتهي... بالأسر يعني تقريبا قد الموت .لزواريب بتنتهي بموت الصبي

طرس. : فيه حدا جايي يشوفك ع اساس انو هيدا شيعي شو بدي يحكي يحكي عن 2720 الجنوب؟

بعد 10 سنين بعتقد انو خفت كتير بالنسبة لالي... وكوني بطلع عالتلفزيون بمقابلات طويلة 2721 ببرامج وكذا... صار يعرفوا الناس انت شو بتفكر... وقت اللي بتربط الاسباب بالنتائج الآخر بيصير يسمع... اليوم .المواقف بالبلد طائفية وانت واقف ضد... هالمواقف الطائفية وبتسب النهج الطائفي تبع طايفتك... آه... اللي انا ما بانتمي ...اليها اصلا يعني وبتسب نفس الشي يعني بتحكي عن النهج الطائفي الغلط بدون ما تسمي الطائفي . فاللي عم يسمعك بيعرف انو عندك نهج توحيدي بمعنى انك بتؤمن بهذا الانسان كأنسان... وعم بتقول الاشيا اللي شايفا كأخطاء عندو... بيقبلك او ما بيقبلك... بس كنت طل بسقراط على مدة سنة... كانت توقف العالم... هيدا دليل انو هني بينتموا لها الفكر والنهج ...اللي انت بتقولو الجوهر الاساسي في حقيقة... الخير خير والشر ... فيه اختلافات سياسية فيه 20 سنة وفيه 2722 .قبل... ساهم فيها الغرب بس انو قصدي... هالدولة الكبيرة اللي كل دولة تبنت طايفة... بالقرن التاسع عشر... انو والله الانكليز بيتبنوا هالطايفة... والروس بيتبنوا الارثوذكس... والفرنساوي بيتبنوا الموارنة... وما بعرف شو... وبيركبوا التقسيمات

...الادارية بسايكس بيكو

2723 ما فيه خلاف جوهري بطبيعة البشر... ما عاداتنا هي ذاتها وتقاليدنا هي ذاتا... منغضب لنفس الشي... ومنفرح لنفس الشي...

2724 وقلنا بالاول انو مربوطة كل الطايفة بالزلمة هيدا... ما فيك تتوظف انت وجايي عامل دوكتوراه بكرا الا ما تروح قبلانو لهيدا... ميشال المر... انت مين OK انو référence عند زعيم الطايفة تبعك... بدو يعطيك ب...؟

2725 ...ط.س:

2726 هلق اذا بدك بما انو عم نحكي بالبحث ايه بشكل او بآخر كمان... المسرح كمان صار عم ينعمل مسرح طائفي...
وحتى المسرحيين كلن فاتوا بهيدي المسألة... انو صاروا... بديش سميلك هلق احس كمان ما انا ابن مهنة كمان... بس
صاروا يشوفوا هالطايفة تتبع لهيدا الزعيم السياسي... صاروا يفتشوا بالتاريخ على واحد بيشبهوا... آه... لعون مثلا...
ويعملوا مسرحية ويلمحوا انو هيدي مواقفو متل مواقف الجنرال هلق... وصارت تجي الضيع كلها بالسنجق
والنوبة والبوسطات وكذا... يحضروا المسرحية كأنو هيدا الزعيم اللي هلق هوي منو فلان الفلاني... بالتاريخ...
هوي هلق... يعني كمان الفنانين والمنتجين عم بيساهمو بطريقة غير مباشرة... لانن تجار... منشان انو يربحوا
مصاري بتغذية هيدي المسائل... شو دلالات والله انو ينزلوا اهل الجبال بكل هيدا التاريخ الفلكلوري التراثي...
ليفوتوا يحضروا مسرحية يعني... يعملوا العرس برا... وبعدين يفوتوا وبس كمان ينتصر البطل جوا يطلعوا يعملوا...
...وعلى جمل معينة يعلا الزقيف بالصالة ... آه... وما بيعود يهدا

كذب [...] كان احسن... كان معروف انو فيه طائفية... هلق الناس طائفيين اكتر من الاول **2727** ومش عم بيدبحوا عالهوية
بانتظار انو تفلت بيوم من الايام... خلي أي واحد من هو الزعما اللي بالدولة يقلها لطايفتو قومي نزل عالشارع
ولنشوف شو بدو يصير هلق... ما خلو ولا نقابة بالبلد الا ما عملوا عشرين نقابة... لحتى ما يخلوش فيه توجه
بمعنى وحدوي وطني يعني... انو يعني يتجمعوا هالعمال مع بعضن... بهدف انن عمال يطالبوا بحقوقن... عملوا
نقابة ونقابة ونقابة... وبشكل... من تحت الهوا عملوا هي النقابة تابعة لهي الطائفة وعملوا هالنقابة تابعة للاسلام
واللمسيحيي... ما خلوش حزب بالبلد... فرفطوا كل الاحزاب... طيب شو يعني... وين بدا تلتجي العالم... يعني شو
الغاية ما كنت ما اعرف انا من انو يعملوا نقابة جديدة يعني... مع انو فارطين تنين يعني... ما الن قيمة... بس هيك
لحتى انو هيدي نقابة وهيدي نقابة... هيدي بيتبناها هالمجموعة... وهيدي بيتبناها هالمجموعة... وبعدين انو مين
بياخد القانون أي نقابة ... بيقولولك انو ما منعطيه لحدا... بيقلولك انو اتفقوا... ولو خيي لشو عملتو تنين لتقولولنا
اتفقوا... ما كان فيه وحدي وخلص.

2728 il faut trouver dans chaque confession 2 Zaiim pour que la confession reste faible...

comme dans les syndicats [...] .

2729 الفنانين ما كتير طائفيين... لما بيصيروا طائفيين منشان التجارة لا اكتر ولا اقل... يعني بيعملوا رموز وبيصيروا يربطوها بالحاضر... للتجارة... فمن هون الجمهور بيصير طائفي بالاتجاه... بس بيكون الفنان غشو انو هوي متبني... ايه. حالتو النفسية والسياسية منشان بس يشلحوا مصاري ... يجي بس يدفع 10 آلاف عالباب...

2730 الجمهور اللبناني صار ...fast food... صار الجمهور يحب الاشيا السهلة ... الاشيا الخفيفة يسمع الاغاني باجريه... بدو نطبلو والمطرب قبل ما هوي يفوت عالمسرح بيبلش هوي يزقف... قبل ما يقول ولا كلمة فبيصيرو يزقفوا... هني بالصالة وبيقوموا وبيصيروا يرقصوا متل السعادين... احم احم

2731 الجمهور صار هيك عند الطايفتين... فيه ظاهرة اسمها منير كسرواني... منير ما زالنا عم نحكي بالعلم وهيك... مسيحي ماروني... اكتر واحد بيشتغل بالجنوب... وجمهوره كلو جمهور شيعي تحديدا... يعني 90 بالمية.. طيب انا شيعي وجمهوري كتير قليل جمهور شيعي... انا بحكي عن الجنوب ... انما بحكي بطريقة شوي عميقة سياسية اجتماعية الى حد ما... فنية ... ولا شك ... ومنير آخدها من فوق ... بالفلكلور تبعا... مش عم بحكي ضدو... عرفت...؟ وبيسب هالمسبات التقليدية وهاللبس العادي... وبيتجوز اربعة ... مع انو caractère بس بيعمل فيش حدا ...بالجنوب بيتجوز اربعة يا روحي... وحدة عم بيطلقوها... بقاش فيهن الاكل بدن ياكلو

2732 ابن البلد كان موقف سياسي بالبلد... اكل قتلة احمد الزين مثلا بالمنطقة التانية... اوائل السلم بالحرب وكذا... كان يعمل مواقف... لقطو الشباب باليمين ما بعرف شو اسمن... وتهدد كتير... يعني... وصل لمرحلة انو رح ياكل قتلة...

2733 زياد متميز... زياد بالتالي اذا بدك تحاسبو... فيك تقول انو والله اخد موقف هيدا الزلمة... وعاش كل الحرب ببيروت اخدوا مواقف ضدو وكان وقت اللي يطلع عالاذاعة اللبنانية تنزل القذايف متل OK ...الغربية الشتي... وقت اللي كان يطلع بهيدا بعدنا طيبين قول الله... بس... شي خلصت الحرب لاقوا انو اللي عم بيقولوا زياد الرحباني... منو caractère موقف غلط ... وزياد الرحباني مؤمن بهالبلد... وحكي عالطائفية هون وهونيك... ما عمل مسلم او tère ...مسيحي حكي عن التنين وسب التنين

2734 دايما الثقافة نتيجة... ما فيه هامش من الحرية بشكل انك تعبر عن حالك متل ما بدك... هيدا هوي الحرية شغلة اساسية للتعبير... طيب وقت اللي مجتمع مفروز هيك... وقت اللي بيجي وزير وبيحضر شانسونييه يلي هيي ما شي وما الها معنى... وبيتصور وبيحطوا عالتلفزيون... بيكونوا عم بيقولوا للناس انو هيدا المسرح اللي نحنا بدنا نحضرو... وقت اللي انت بتعمل مسرح جدي وهادف وفني وكل شي وبتاخد جوايز بمهرجانات... ما حدا بيطل عليك... ما حدا بيعطيك مصاري لتعمل مسرحية...

2735 بدها ثورة ثقافية ... بس هيدي بدها قرار... بس اذا كل طايفة مسكرة ع حالها... وبوابتها هيدا الريس تبعها... ما بدو يسمحلنا نفوت نحكي... ان كان رجل الدين... اذا بدك تحكي بالزواج المدني... مصلحتو ومصلحة هودي التنين رجل الدين والسياسي ع ضهر الناس...

330

2736 فيه مطربين كانوا يحطوا الكاسكيت العسكرية ع راسن ويغنوا... يوحوا للناس انو هني تابعين للتيار المعين... والناس تدب حالها عليهن عاطفيا لا شعوريا... وبعدين بس يتهددوا بطريقة انو انتو عم تعملوا هيك... يقولوا لا نحنا ما كنا قاصدين هالشي [...] .

2737
2738
2739 .مقابلات مع الجمهور
2740
2741 بعد المسرحية
2742 مخرج تلفزيون سينما... مسرحية كتير رائعة لرفيق علي احمد... عنيف مسرحياً... المشكلة بهالوقت من السنة يللي هوي الصيف والعالم لا بتحضر لا سينما ولا مسرح يعرضها بجونية... يللي هي منطقة اصطياف وبحر... مش مشكلة مناطقية... موضوع المسرحية لكل لبنان مش لمنطقة معينة...
2743 ********
2744 (مشاهدة في الثلاثينات من عمرها - (بعد المسرحية
2745 ط.س.: عجبتك المسرحية؟
2746 ...مسرحية كتير كتير حلوة... نص وطريقة اداء النص يعني الاخراج كان رائع
2747 ط.س.: شو بيعنيلك واللي انحكى بالمسرحية؟
2748 والله انا ما بعرف كتير بهالقصص... منشان هيك بنبسط وقت شوف مسرحيات وفلومة يحكوا عن الجنوب وعن الـ
ـوعن كيف البلاد متفرقة... بنبسط بصير اتعرف اكتر واكتر بصير حس بالقضية اكتر ...
2749 ********
2750 (مشاهدة شابة (بعد المسرحية
2751 ط.س.: شو اللي عجبك فيها؟
2752 ...بتحسها naturelle هيكي
2753 ط.س.: بيعنيلك الجنوب؟
2754 ...بيعنيلي كل شي ... كل لبنان
2755 ط.س.: peak المسرحية تبع... وين الـ
2756 (لا جواب)
2757 ********
2758 (مشاهد (بعد المسرحية
2759 ...ما فيه محل بتحس فيه انو بتنعس... بس يلا لنمشي نحنا
2760 ********
2761 (من جونية... (قبل المسرحية
2762 NDU بالـ Hotel Management سكان جونية ... عم بعمل
2763 ط.س.: شو متوقعة تشوفي بالمسرحية؟
2764 هي قصة حشرية اكتر... انو ... characteristic ...اول شي بدي اعرف ليه بيمثل لحالو فيه كتير عالم بيقولوا انو
...يبي ما منحبو لحالو بيمثل... ؟... فكرت انو ليه ما منحبو... بدي كون عكس انا بدي اعرف
2765 ط.س.: موضوع المسرحية بتعرفي شي عنو.؟
2766 different ما بعرف شي... جايي كرمالو هوي بس... شي
2767 ********
2768 (. قبل المسرحية)
2769 ...بالكسليك تاني سنة business اسمي ط. ض. عم بعمل
2770 ط.س.: شو متوقع تشوف بالمسرحية؟
2771 ...كل شي بعرفو انو متوقع شوف تمثيل رائع... واندوخ... حاسس رح اندوخ
2772 ط.س.: ليش متوقع تشوف تمثيل ؟

2773 هوي رفيق علي احمد بحد ذاتو رائع بالتمثيل... بعدين بحس صعب الواحد يمثل لوحدو message ويوصل لوحدو... ما بعرف اذا فيه كتير تعبير بالكلمات... بس بحركاتو بيقدر يوصل ميساجات كتير للعالم... بقى شي رائع...
2774 ط.س: وعن موضوع المسرحية بتعرف شي؟
2775 ...ما بعرف شي
2776 *********
2777 (قبل المسرحية .)
2778 ..باشتغل هندسة... وجايي من القطين
2779 ط.س: شو متوقعة تشوفي بالمسرحية... ليه قاطعة هالمسافة وجايي؟
2780 ...لانو بحبو لرفيق علي احمد... تمثيلو بيعقد
2781 ط.س: شفتي قبل؟
2782 ...حضرتا قبل... هي تاني مرة عم بحضرا
2783 ط.س: شو متوقعة تشوفي هون؟
2784 متوقعة شوف رفيق بقوة اكتر مما كان ... انو انا بحب كتير كيف بيمثل ... وهوي طريقتو عالمسرح بتعقد... لانو
...ايه... وهيكي... منشان التمثيل
موضوع بيزعل وبيضحك... بيزعل انو ابن ابنو بيموت بين ايديه ما بيلحق... لانو ابنو مشغول بالسهرات هوي
ومرتو... هيدا بيزعل انو كيف صارت لانو هو مقهور عليه كمان... وبيضحك انو كيف بيصير يحكي بالزبالة
وهيك قصص... انو شغلتو هوي كيف بيمثل لحالو عالمسرح... هي كتير فوق الطبيعة... كتير قوي... تيقدر يمثلها...
قضية الجنوب... كتير حلو انو ذكر الجنوب... انو ذكر مظبوط شو بيخص بالجنوب... مش هيك عالفاضي يعني...
وبس...
2785 *********
2786 (ط.س: شو متوقعين تشوفوا بالمسرحية هلق؟ (قبل المسرحية
2787 ...شي سياسي... ايه اكيد سياسي... وغير هيك... اذا ما لقينا حدا نقلع معو بقلع معو انا وهلا
2788 *********
2789 (قبل المسرحية
2790 عم بدرس Education بالـ NDU
2791 ...ط.س.: شو متوقعة تشوفي بالمسرحية
2792 ...متوقعة ازهق
2793 ط.س.: ليه؟
2794 انا بحب ... in the end ...انو اديه بدو يبدع ليبدع it's a one man show لانو المسرحية يكون فيه
different characters, music, danse (french) بيعطوا الـ genre بحس هولي اللي
عالمسرحية...
2795 ط.س.: فيه نوع مسرح لبناني بيعجبك اكتر؟
2796 سقراط... حضرتها للمسرحية... ؟... لا رحباني... ايه بحبو لانو فيها style ...بحب music يعني بحب action فيها
...مسرحيات رفيق علي احمد... بس ما بحس فيي فيهن يا كمل الوقت... بحب مشهد
2797 ط.س.: فيه اشيا معينة بتعجبك او ما بتعجبك...؟
2798 لتكون انت عم تدير مسرحية it takes a lot لا بحب... السلبية فيه انو جديتو... انو حلو انو وفيه... بمشهد انا
بمسرحية انا نسيت شو اسما بيكون هيك انو هوي محبوس... ايه حلوة هيك بيحسسك انو عن جد هوي محبوس...
...يكونوا arts كل الـ ... music, danse (french) حلوة... بس قلتلك بحب هيك الـ

2799	*********
2800	(مشاهد - (بعد المسرحية
2801	...من رقص لكتير جدي ... بالفعل بهنيه على هالفن
2802	********
2803	(. قبل المسرحية)
2804	...شيل هالمسجلة تتشوف اذا بدنا نقلع والله لا
2805	ط.س. : لا لا ما فيه شي اذا بتعرف عن اسمك ومنين جايي وهيك
2806	... جايي من الصفرا
2807	ط.س. : شو متوقع تشوف بالمسرحية؟
2808	والله لازم لاقي اول شي وجعنا... الوجع بالوضع اللي نحنا فيه هلق... بالبلد. من جميع النواحي مش وجع من مطرح معين... سياسي اجتماعي اقتصادي... حتى طائفي... انشالله نلاقي شي دوا عندو... لاي مرض من الامراض اللي نحنا فيها...
2809	ط.س. : بتلاقيا غريبة شوي انو رفيق علي احمد عم يعرض بجونية ولا كيف؟
2810	بالنسبة لالي شخصيا لا... يعني انا ما بعرفو شخصيا بس من خلال ملاحقتي لاخباري لاعمالو... بحسو انو بعيد شوي عن متل ما تقصد انت المناطقية ... او طائف... بديش قول طائفية... بالنسبة لالو ايه... بحسو بعيد هيك...
2811	...منشان هيك جايي احضرو اول مرة عم بحضرا... هاي النوعية من المسرحيات انا كتير بتستهويني... ايه... كتير... خاصة اذا فيها... نكزات ابديش قول نكزات هي موضة قديمة ... اذا فيها تعالج الموضوع بدون تنكيت بدون النمر اللي كانوا يمرقوها ببعض المسرحيات... مسرح الرحباني القديم... عم بحكيك بالستينات وبالسبعينات انا متابع كلن المسرحيات... كلن حاضرن... كنت حس اوقات اذا مضيع شي لاقيه بقلب المسرحية... مش بكلها... ببعض المشاهد او المقاطع... من خلال فيلمون وهبه الله يرحمو او الممثلين اللي كانوا معو... انشالله هون يكون يداويلو شي...
2812	ط.س. : من وقتا لهلق عدت لقيت شي عهالنمط... الرحابنة القدام حتى الرحابنة الجداد... منصور الرحباني... بمسرحية ... مع غسان صليبا... صيف 840 813 كان فيه شي ... بعرف... فيه هدف شخصي من وراها اللي عاملها هوي... ما بعرف شو هوي...
2814	ط.س. : هدف طائفي...؟
2815	...لا لا لا سياسي... سياسي... سياسي
2816	ط.س. : شو بيعنيلك المسرح؟ المسرح ... اذا بفوت عالمسرح انا... كانو خلقت من جديد... بدي تابع حياتي عالمسرح... عاللي عم يلعبوا عالمسرح. يمكن لاقي حالي انا وولد انا وشاب... انا وكبير بهاي المسرحية... قديش بتعلمني شي... اديش بتحفظني شي. اديش بترافقني بعد المسرحية... هون... هون هون دور المسرح انو يخليني احمل زوادة معي... انا جايي هلق تأخذ وروح... مش جايي تأعطي... بغض النظر عن المصاري... انشالله المسرحية تحملني شي اقدر فيد وطني فيد عيلتي فيد ولادي فيد ضيعتي... انشالله...
2818	*********
2819	(مشاهدة شابة (بعد المسرحية
2820	من بعد المسرحية؟ حبيتيها؟ impression ط. س. : اول

2821	ايه بتعقد ... حبيت فيها كلها... حكي عن مواضيع انو لازم ينحكى فيها... بعدين الحلو انو ما زهقت... زهقت انت؟
	صوتو بيعقد... يطلع وينزل بصوتو... يوصل لمحل هيك... يقب شعر بدني... كون عم بضحكك... بتضحك كتير
	musique... شوي بعدين بتوصل لمحل هيك بتدمع واو ... بتعقد... أي
2822	**********
2823	شاب
2824	ط. س. : عجبتك المسرحية؟
2825	كتير
2826	ط. س. : شو اللي عجبك اكتر شي فيها؟
2827	...شي بيغير
2828	ط. س. : شو الجديد؟
2829	...أول مرة بجي عالمسرح
2830	*********
2831	شابتان (بعد المسرحية)
2832	ط. س. : شو اللي عجبكن فيها؟
2833	...c'est un tout المسرحية كلها سوا يعني شي متكامل يعني. واكيد رفيق علي احمد هوي اللي عجب اكتر شي...
2834	ط. س. : الموضوع تبع المسرحية عجبكن كمان.؟
	...يعني... اللي بارز عالمسرح هوي رفيق علي احمد... فيه غيرو وما شفناه
2835	يعني الكلمات تبع المسرحية كتير حلوين كمان... يعني فيها [...] . ايه... ان اللبيب من الاشارة بفهم... يعني ... وفيها
	...تمعين كتير ... هيدي اللذة اللي فيها... بعدين البلد... مظبوط زبالة صاير... ها ها ها
2836	********
2837	(شاب (بعد المسرحية
2838	ط. س. : عجبتك المسرحية؟
2839	.منيحة منيحة... شاطر كتير قبضاي الزلمة
2840	..ط. س. : كتمثيل يعني
2841	...الزلمة قبضاي
2842	ط. س. : أكتر شي شو اللي عجبك فيها؟
2843	...يعني... تمثيلو الزلمة اكتر شي هوي اللي بيأثر الواحد... حكيو حكيو كتير حلو
2844	ط. س. : طيب موضوع المسرحية عجبك؟
2845	موضوع المسرحية كتير حلو ... سياسي اكتر شي... و.... بيقدر الواحد... كل الاعمار بتفهمو... this is it... و thank you...
2846	********
2847	(ح. (بعد المسرحية
2848	ط. س. : عجبتك المسرحية مدام؟
2849	...ايه حلوة كتير
2850	ط. س. : شوي اللي عجبك فيها اكتر شي؟
2851	...اول شي مسرحية بشخص واحد... يعني... معدد الشخصيات
2852	ط. س. : هي اول مرة بتشوفي مسرحية بشخص واحد؟
2853	...ايه
2854	ط. س. : وغير هيك شو اللي عجبك فيها... الموضوع؟
2855	الموضوع حلو حتير . موضوع حياتنا... موضوع حي... مش موضوع بالخيال يعني... موضوع عايشينو كلنا حسينا في لأنو عايشينو...
2856	**********
2857	(شابتان (بعد المسرحية

2858	...حاضرتا قبل بتعقد
2859	ط. س. : شو اللي عجبك فيها؟
2860	اول شي انو هوي تمثيلو كتير قوي... تاني شي انو المسرحية بتحكي عن المشاكل بلبنان... وهيك... يعني كتير حساسة...
2861	ط. س. : عن كل لبنان يعني؟
2862	(ما بعرف ما تسألني بقى... ما بعرف...(خوف من الاجابة وجهل
2863	***********
2864	(شاب (بعد المسرحية
2865	...انا اساسا رفيق بحبو كتير... بعرفو من قبل
2866	ط. س. : هي المسرحية حاضرها من قبل؟
2867	لا مش حاضرها... بس متل كأني حاضرها لاني معود عليه و ع طريقة حكيو... اوكيه... الحقيقة ما حضرتش كلها
	...لقلك وين احلى محل... بس حضرت النص الاخراني ... مهضوم مش عاطل
2868	***********
2869	ح. (بعد المسرحية)
2870	بتجنن
2871	ط. س. : اول مرة بتحضري هيك نوع مسرح؟
2872	...لا دايما بس عجبتني كتير
2873	ط. س. : اول مرة رفيق علي احمد
2874	...بيجنن موهوب... والمسرحية الها خلفيات كتير حلوة... الوضع اللي عايشينو
2875	*********
2876	معه في الاول قبل العرضInterviewشاب تمت ال
2877	ط. س. : خبرني عن الموضوع؟
2878	عجبني مشهد المرة الغنية. للي بتباهى قدام العالم بتلفت نظر العالم انو انا غنية. شوفو قصة العضام وما عضام...
	هيدا كتير night club هيدا المشهد كتير حلو... ومشهد لميس ... كيس الزبالة والبالونات... بالـ حلو... انو هني رقص
	وطقش وفقش وبعدين بيدخلك قضية الجنوب والبقاع الغربي... انو كتير... يعني هيدا يمكن هوي عم بيبرهن انو
	العالم بتفكر بس انا برأيي انو هيدا بيحزن اكتر ما بيبيسط... انو هيك اشيا ما بتتذكر بهيك وضع... بدها وضع
	...جدي... وضع مأساوي ما فيك تاخدو... مع وضع هالقد فقش وطقش
2879	*********
2880	ح. [...] بعد المسرحية
2881	...حبينا انو بيمثل لحالو
2882	ط. س. : الموضوع؟
2883	...ايه
2884	*********
2885	ح. ... بعد المسرحية
2886	...اللي عم بيصير فيها هيدا المظبوط... خاصة السريلانكية
2887	*********
2888	سيدتان... بعد المسرحية.
2889	الاولى: صرنا بوجع معاش عم نحكي بفرح... هيدا جيلي انا مين بدي احضر؟... يعني كنا نحضر مسرحيات
	فيروز... هلق حضرت انا كركلا... حضرت سقراط... بس انا مين بدي احضر... بدي احضر الـ théâtre de dix
	heures وهودي؟... هودي الشانسونييه... ما بيعنولي شي... بيحسسوك بالعيش وهيك... بس هوي بحسو غميق

2890 ...الثانية: جيت لهون حشريا جيت... لحالو ... كتير شاطر... لانو لحالو شاطر كتير... بس...
2891 ط. س. : موضوع المسرحية؟
2892 الـ musique الموضوع ايه. بس فيه شغلة ما كتير حبيتا انو لحالو لازم تكون اكتر... بدو شخص حدا بس كان فيه يستفيد منها اكتر... يقويها اكتر... هوي بيركز اصلا musique يساعدو... انو حط على الحكي...
2893 كل النهار... ولانو أي مطرح نحنا عم نروح musique الاولى : لانو نحنا تعودنا نسمع عليه كلو خبيط ولبيط
عم نسمع... خبيط ولبيط... ما بدنا بقى نسمع خبيط ولبيط... هوي مش مهم عندو لانو كل يوم عم نسمع الصريخ
والدبيك وغناني جديدة والخ الخ الخ... خلص قرفنا... يعني ... بدنا نسمع شي يفوت براسنا... خلص هاي هيي...
2894 ************
2895 ...شابة في العشرينات... بعد المسرحية
2896 ...الديكور هوي
2897 ط. س. : بالنسبة للموضوع... شو حبيتي بالموضوع.؟
2898 ...ما بعرف يعني ...critique كيف هيكي... عمل la façon ... ايه [...] . هيكي j'ai été très touchée بتعقد
يعني... هيدي تالت مرة بحضرها... الموضوع بعتقد شي شخصي نحنا منحبو لانو موت حدن زغير كتير بيأثر
فينا... والـ mise en scène للـ السيارة... من افكار... يعني روعة... boite de nuit عم يرقصوا... انو روجيه
بتعقد mise en scène... عساف كمان غير رفيق علي احمد هوي تمثيل رائع بس الـ
2899 ************
2900 .رجل مسلم بعد المسرحية
2901 ط. س. : حبيت المسرحية.؟
2902 ايه ايه حلوة ... بس انا جيت متأخر... يعني استاذ رفيق علي احمد كممثل وحيد عالمسرح... مسرحياتو جميلة... فيه
الها معاني... بتحس... صحيح عم تضحك... بس بتحس بنفسك بأسى وبزعل ... بتدخل بصميم القلب... بـ... بوضع
...المشكلة الشعب اللبناني وقضية كيف التعامل ان كان... معنا وان كان غريب مع الغريب
2903 ط. س. : جايين من محل بعيد؟
2904 ...جايي من الزيدانية الظريف
2905 ************
2906 ...رجل من عمشيت
2907 كان مهضوم... حلوة يعني ... كنت آخد فكرة غلط بالاول... كنت مفكر انو شي... ممل بس بالفعل حلوة...
2908 **********
2909 ...رجل من عين سعادة
2910 ...رفيق علي احمد بتصور اهم رجل مسرحي بلبنان... ومتفوق جدا... واقع المجتمع... مميز
2911 **********
2912 رجل: حكيت مع الزلمة هونيك... ابو عوينات؟
2913 **********
2914 شيوعي
2915 أنا معجب برفيق علي احمد... حاضرلو الجرس ... المفتاح... وآخر ايام سقراط... ومع الاسف... زواريب هي اول مرة
بشوفها... عندو نمط حلو كتير... اولا طريقة بالتعبير عن قضايا الناس اليومية... بلغتو بلهجتو بطريقة حكيو...

تمثيلو... بقدرتو على انو... يطلع بعدة شخصيات... هيدا نمط صار اسمو نمط رفيق علي احمد... يعني...

2916 ط. س. : رأيك بالمسرح اللبناني بشكل عام...
2917 اف... اف... عم تكتر كتير علينا... انت عند مين عم تشتغل...؟
2918 ط. س. : انا عم بعمل بحث خاص
2919 انا ما اختصاصي مسرح... بس انا بحضر كتير مسرح... بحضر من الخمسينات... يعني متابع الحركة المسرحية...
حركة مسرحية طبعا فيه الها رموز مهمة... منحكي عن الخمسينات والجاي... يعني... من منير ابو دبس... جلال خوري ...ملتقى... فازليان... يعقوب الشدراوي... الرحابنة... انا برأيي انو الستينات والسبعينات كانت متقدمة اكتر من هلق... من ناحية نوعية المسرح لانو المسرح هوي بيجيب جمهور... صار هلق الجمهور عندو مجالات مختلفة...
صار عندو تلفزيون الشاشة الزغيرة... بس مع ذلك بحاجة لنصوص مختلفة... لشارع مختلف... لفن جديد... انا برأيي انو ما تطور العمل المسرحي لحتى يواكب... الجمهور الجديد... منو نفس جمهور الخمسينات... ثقافتو كبرت ومطاليبو كترت اكتر... ولذلك كان لازم يكون الفن المسرحي اكبر قدرة على التكيف... اول شي نصوص مسرحية ما فيه... هيدي وحدي من العيوب الكبيرة... عنا نصوص مسرحية مش للتمسرح... بالمسرح اللي استمر من السبعينات وبالجاي هوي مسرح روجيه عساف... لا شك انو كان عندو طريقتو بالعمل المسرحي هلق عم يعمل شي جديد
بس ع كل حال مهم انو العمل المسرحي... متواصل... منتنى انو يكون اكتر ابداع من حيث النص ومن حيث الـ message...

2920 ط. س : merci... كتير
2921 (بعد لحظات يريد ان يكمل الحديث)
2922 مرة كنت... تقريبا حاضر كل المسرحيات اللي تقدمت... كلها... كان فيه جمهور حقيقي... اليوم ما فينا نقول انو فيه جمهور مسرح... هلق هيدا... مش بس الحق على الشاشة الزغيرة... دائما هل الميل انو الحق عالتلفزيون... طيب هاي السينما... رجعت وعاد رجعت طلعت ... ما ممكن الاستغناء عن الشاشة الكبيرة... التلفزيون ما بيحل محل الشاشة الكبيرة... بس لما السينما ما بتقدمش شي مهم بروح للشاشة الزغيرة... واوعى تفكر انو القعدة بالبيت هي احسن شي بالنسبة للجمهور... لا بيحب يطلع... بس لحتى يطلع... بدو شي يدفشو ليطلع... لمن بيلاقي شي برا بيطلع... وهيدا متعلق بكل انواع الفنون اللي فيها مشاهدة... ان كان مسرح او سينما... او مسرح غنائي ... او باليه او رقص... او أي شي... قدم للجمهور شي بيجي... الجمهور عندو دايما رغبة بالتنوع... والتجديد... هلق ما فيه منتجين... بس يلاقي فيه جمهور بيجي. بس يلاقي فيه مصاري بيروح... بيحطن... بدك تلاقي منتج الفن للفن... لا . المنتج بدو يدفع مصاري... تيرجع يرجع فلوسو... هاها
2923
2924 **************
2925 Interview

2926 المسرح هو دينامو الحياة... هوي دينامو التجديد هوي دينامو البحث عن الحقيقة... هوي التفتيش عن الذات ... هوي الهوية ... وهوي بنفس الوقت الابداع... المجال اللي بيهضم كل شيء... يعني هوي يتسع لكل الفنون... ليه بدو يكون حاجة لفرنسا والمانيا واميركا وما بدو يكون حاجة للبنان...

2927 ... فيه فرق بين ابن الجبل وابن الساحل يلي هوي اللبناني منفتح على كل التيارات
2928 المدارس الي اجت من برا... المدارس الاميركية... المدارس الفرنسية... والروسية سابقاً ... وال... ال... قلنا الروسية...

والانكليزية... والطليانية... والامركان هني اكتر دول اعتمدت شكل المسرح
2929 تلاميذ الامركان اكتر معرفة بالمسرح من طلاب المعارف... والفرنسية ايه بيعملوا مسرح للتراث تبع اللغة... بس مش هوي فاعل بالحياة اللبنانية...

المقصود بالهوية ... العمل المسرحي... عم نترجم حياتنا وتراثنا [...] . على المسرح... عم
2930 نجسد هالقضايا المحلية... هي

... محلية وبنفس الوقت كونية [...] انما بجغرافية بفكر بتقاليد بمنطق بفلسفة حياة لبنانية
2931 موانئ الحنين... واحد لبناني كتبها... قدر يشوف المستقبل...المبدع عندو خيال وعندو مسيرة...

2932 موانئ الحنين ... هي مسرحية من وجع لبناني قدر حس شو ممكن يصير... بعالم سابق مئات السنين من الحضارة التكنولوجية... مئات السنين تكنولوجيا سابق لبنان... بس قادر يشوف مخاوف الـ 2000 وما بعد ... قدر شاف مصيرو ... قدر شاف شو معاناتو وبدها تكون للانسان... في أي كابوس... او في أي فسحة من الحرية والحياة

والانسانية... القصة لما بتجي للفرد المبدع... ما عاد فينا نحد... متل الشاعر... هوي قريب للنبي
2933 Waiting For بس بدك تعمل مسرحية. بدك تعمل مسرحية للجمهور... لمن بيكيت كتب End Game و Godot

وغيرن... كتب لانو هيك شخصيتو... هيك بيعبر...
2934 المسرحية صحيح بتعالج زمانين ومكانين لا تنسى انو فيها الانسان... الانسان القديم يلي هوي بيمثلو الرقم... 739
يوسف يعني... الجمهور يلي عم بيشاهد المسرحية اليوم... هوي كتير جمهور متعاطف مع المسرحية. قبل المسرحية

فيه ناس قالولي يعني انت عم تحكي كل شيء نحنا ما قدرنا نعبر عنو يعني معنى المسرح هو... عنصر اجتماعي

بيعبر عن رغبات وطموحات وتساؤلات المجتمع...
2935 مشكلة اقتصادية... البلد جامد... انا عامل مسرحية بـ 10 آلاف ليرة لبنانية... يعني 10 آلاف ليرة بتاكل فيها صندويشة ونص بلبنان... يعني ارخص شيء بالممكن... وفيه مسارح بيبلش السعر بـ 15 و20 و30 و50 الف ليرة... واحيانا 165 ألف ليرة البطاقة لما بيجي واحد من برا... وبيروحوا الاغنيا الاغنيا الاغنيا ما بيروحوا الناس تلاميذ المدارس... يعني اذا بدها تجي عيلة عالمسرح... اذا بدها تجي عيلة عالمسرح... اذا بيجي واحد هوي ومرتو... 40 ألف... اذا هيدا 20... ارخص شي 15 20... انا عملتها بـ 10 آلاف يعني ارخص شيء ممكن بالعالم

لاني عارف انو ما حدا بيقدر يدفع مصاري... يعني بيوفر الضهرة من البيت... لأن ما فيه امكانيات... بلاش صرف البنزين... بعدين انا بضهر لاعمل متعة... بروح بحضر مسرحية بضهر برا بقعد بقهوة... المسرحية هي كمان بداية للمطعم... اليوم فيه ازمة مادية...

شكل المدينة الحضاري تبع بيروت... انكسر... يعني الحرب سلخت من بيروت... هالوهج 2936
اللي كان عم بيمد لبرا...
هلق لبنان بعد الحرب عم يزغر ويزغر ويزغر كأبسط دولة فقيرة بالعالم العربي... العالم الثالث...
المجتمع يللي هوي
من رواد المسرح والحركة التشكيلية والموسيقى والمهرجانات والندوات الفكرية... كل هذا
انحسر... سافر... انتقل من
العاصمة الى مكان ابعد... وهي صارت لابسة لباس غيرها... يعني بتمشي بعد الساعة سبعة
بتحس ان ما بقى فيه
حياة بمدينة متل بيروت... هيدا مأساة... كل هالمظاهر هي بتخلي الانسان يقلك لشو انا بدي اطلع
من بيتي... بضلني
قبال هالتلفزيون المرت بضلني اتفرج ع برامج صنع شعوب مرتة... متل اميركا والمانيا وفرنسا
وايطاليا... هو
شعوب مرتة... لانو مش عم يقدروا حتى ينتجوا لشعوبن شيء على مستوى موانئ الحنين... هني
شعوب تجار... عم
فجر Midi de France بالـ MacDonald's بيبيعوا ... يعني اذا بفرنسا اليوم... واحد فجر
المبنى حبسوه... صار
بطل لان قال انا ما بدي آكل همبرغر مرت شغل اميركا... كلو هرمونات كلو كذب... نحنا
الفرنساوي عنا اكل
طيب... وعنا لحمنا اطيب ونبيداتنا عظيمين... هلق صار بطل شعبي... بلجيكا كمان نسفوا 3 4
محلات من كام شهر
The لماكدونالز... نحنا داخلين بآلية الذهن الغربي التعبان... المجتمع اللبناني عم يتأثر متل [...]
Bald And The
يعني متل الهمبرغر... هالشي كان الو تأثير عالحركة المسرحية كمان مش بس الناحية Beautiful
الاقتصادية...
مجتمعنا عم بيصير كتير قريب لأن... وما بيروح عالمسرح...
العرب ما شي تلاميذ قدام التشاطر الغربي... والشراسة الغربية... والانانية الغربية... والغش 2937
الغربي... والاحتيال
الغربي. والخيانة الغربية... بييع الله الغربي... بس ما ح تكتبن هو انت... بييع الله الغربي...
تيربح... بيدبح امو تاياخد
دولارات... المجتمع اللبناني اذا منرجع للمسرح... مجتمع نخبوي... اذا منحكي بالمسرح بالمعنى 5
المطلق. يعني لما
منشيل الفولكلور عجنب والشانسونييه عجنب... ما فيه بحياتو المسرح بلبنان ما كان الو هالرهجة...
الو جمهور
واسع متل الفوتبول يعني... ما صار ابدا بحياتو...
قبل 1975 كنت اعمل مسرحية للكبار ومسرحية للاطفال... وانا اسست مسرح الاطفال 2938
بلبنان ع صعيد احترافي...
من بعدي كلن اجوا... كنت انا من خلال مسرح الاطفال عم بعمل جمهور لمسرح الكبار... "الكوخ
المسحور."
جمهوري كان من الشباب الجامعي... ما عملت جمهور فوق الـ 45 سنة من العمر... لان ما بحب
انا الشخص اللي
او غربي... العثيين... كان الجيل Experimental. تكسلن عقلو... لان كل مسرحي هوي تجاربي
الشباب قرف من
شكل المسرح التقليدي... علاقتي كلن طلاب... كان يجوا من مسافات يتحضروا مسرحياتي...
الحرب بلشت 1975
وانا عم بعرض الفخ او القداس الاسود...
هلق الجمهور ارتد لورا... من 84 85 خف الجمهور الا اذا جمعيات ضامنة العمل. جمعيات 2939
حزبية يعني نوادي
احزاب... مثلا اذا فلان قومي سوري كل فروع القومي السوري بدها تروح عالمدينة. اذا كان
حزب الله مثلا بدو

يشجع الشيعة... بدو يشجع ...البري بيضمن الكذا... يعني دخلت... دخلت ... بعد الحرب الطائفية في لعبة الجمهور... و...

و حتى الصحفي صار مهزوم... لأنو حس حالو انكسر بالحرب وخسر الحرب. لما خسر الحرب... صار هوي ماشي مع المنتصر... ومعروف مين المنتصر... فصار هوي يكره ماضيه... لانو هو انكسر وانهزم بالحرب... فصار يكره التجربة الاولى. ويناصر التجربة الجديدة لانو اذا ما ناصرا... القوى على الارض هي المنتصرة فما بيطلع مقال...

فهمت قصدي...

2940 يا مُسيّس الجمهور... بيلتزم... هلق اذا انا طرحت عالمسرح فكرة سياسية بتشمل الاحزاب الوطنية بالحرب [...] . وبتقول آراءها. انت بتعرف مين هني... بتعرف مين المخرج اللي عم يعمل هالاعمال والتزم القضايا الوطنية والسياسية وبعدو ملتزما... هلق هيدا... الاحزاب اكيد... فيه حركة باقسام الاحزاب... هيدا بهالحزب منطقة قريطم بتضمن... قسم قريطم بيضمن حفلة... وبتمشي... القصة الها وجهين... وجه عقائدي او سياسي... حزبي... او وجه طائفي...

2941 ...لما بتحكي على مستوى انساني... ما ضل على صعيد طائفي... صار ع مستوى وطن
2942 فيه مسارح كمان هي ملتزمة... يلي اخدو برشت ومشيوا عليه... و... وقلدو وقلدو غيرو واخدوا لوبيه دي فيغا...

قصص البطولة الشعبية... كلن هدف واحد... وغيرن... يلي بياخدوا شغلة وبياخدوا مانشيتات الجرايد وبينفخوها بقلب المسرحية. كأنك عم تقرا اشيا يومية ... احداث يومية... بتضحك على حدث ضخم... على [...] فضيحة كبيرة على سياسيين... هيدي بتنتهي... بس تخلص بتموت... حتى الجمهور... هوي وطالع بيصير يفكر شو بدو يعمل هلق...

أي مطعم بدو يروح عليه...

2943 أمام الباب" [...] هني اجتمعوا كل الاحزاب بهالقصة... الاحزاب اليسارية... بلبنان" والطائفية. يلي هني حزب الله والاحباش... والاشتراكية... وكل الاحزاب اشتركت فيها هي... وصار فيه تحقيق بالمخفر... واخدت سنة... وتدخلت السفارة الاميركية... انو هوني حرم جامعي... اجنبي... والجامعة... اجا الجيش... قالو لا انت بتكمل... مش الجيش الامن الداخلي مدري شو... قلتلن. لا انا مش ممكن جيب ممثل خاطر فيه وكذا... تروح اجرو او ايدو... لحقوهن للمثلين لبرا... يعني تصور جماعة طالعين من حرب... جايين من جونية. بدن يمثلو هون واول مرة... بنات صبايا راجعين بالليل عالبيت وتلحقن سيارات... وتوقف بنص الطريق... وينزلوا... ونازلين مزلطين...من صدورن ويقولون اسحى تجوا لهون [...] هيداك لحقوه عالبيت ويقولولوا اسحك تجي لهون منقتلك... يعني... أنا ساعتها وقفت المسرحية... لها الشي... يعني كلها ... الحجة كلها انو... انو انا كيف... انو انا بضرب الرب... انو انا بجسد الرب على المسرح هيك... ما بق اتذكر المشهد مظبوط... انو نحنا ... هي المسرحية اصلا ألماني... اسما هيي... اسما هيي... شو اسما بالالماني... ما بق اتذكر اسما بالالماني... هيدي مسرحية كتبها واحد ألماني كان بالحرب. مورشرت

المؤلف... هوي مات عمرو 22 23 سنة شاعر... راح عالحرب وكان ضد النازية... فالحرب بيلقطوا معو رسائل انو ليه الحرب... وكذا... فيحكموا عليه بالاعدام... ما بيعدم... هوي الوحيد. اللي ما اعدموا... بيجي من الحرب بسيبيريا... بيجي عبرلين بيلاقي مدينتو مدمرة... وبيعمل هالمسرحية... بيكتبها... كلها شعر... واشخاص وخيال ولا وعي... تمثلت بالمانيا... صارت المسرحية كلها شخص... وكلن... الاشخاص كلها واحد وما بقى فيه ديكور... وما بقى فيه شي... وبالحرب بيصير فيه تخوين للقيادات والشكل بالقيم والله ولو فيه الله ما كان صار شي. فهو هيك. بيقلوا وين كنت... وين كنت لما صار هيك... فأنا بجسد هالشي عالمسرح بعملو عنيف... هيدا زعجن... انو كيف الله... بمصر كمان اخدت الجائزة الاولى هيدي المسرحية. رجعت عمصر... المصريين قاطعوني... كل الصحف بعد هيدي المسرحية بدها تعمل معي احاديث... تاني نهار صرنا نحنا اعداء المجتمع المصري... وين ما نروح يهاجمونا... وين اي مسرح نفوت عليه يقول انتو كفار... بمصر فيه كتير اصولية ورجعية... بيخوفوا هني والتدين تبعن... يعني... انو انت كيف... وطلعت جريدة الاخبار ضدي بهالموضوع... ما عاد حدا يسترجي يحكي معي... بطل حدا يحكيني... وين ما فوت عالفرقة... قاعدين العالم عم يحكوا فيها المسرحية... وانتو لبنانيين انتو كذا... الجائزة الاولى... رهيبة هيي الذهنية اللبنانية اللي عملتها... مش لأنو الكاتب الماني... عرفت كيف. المخرج بيعطي هويتو عالعمل الآخر... من تراثو وتقاليدو ترجمها المسرحية... مجدي فهمي... من 30 سنة... ترجمها وبعتلي اياها عن الالماني... وانا 2944 ما بعرفو الشخص... قريتها حبيتها... بس بقت معي 25 سنة ما قدرت اخرجتها... الا لما نضج براسي تجارب الحرب... صرت افهمها وقدرت اعمل منها هالطقوسية ... هي منها طقوسية ... يعني قدرت ادخل عليها العنصر الطقوسي... واللي صارت هي كلها غناء ورقص ونواح... يعني طقوس ضلت بالمناخ الالماني... أنا بأرانب وقديسين عملولي مشكلة... فيه كاتدرائية... انا آلة تعذيب... بعدن لما بيرجعوا 2945 للوحشية تبعن هني بربر... انا فرحان انو الاسلام قادرين يشوفوا انو المنشد بيخصن... وهوي بيخصون لانو انا عاملوا شرقي عربي... والهندسة اللي حواليه شرقية... انما الاعلى هوي... كاتدرائية... يعني هون الخليط... في مسرحية جزيرة العصافير... لما بكون. قلت انا كانت هي طقوسها اسلامية عربية... اسلامية ... عالم فيه طقوس اسلامية ومسيحية سوا... لانو انا شرقي... انا ما بنكر انو انا عايش ع صوت المؤذن في طرابلس... صوتو بيغل بصدري انا وانيم... بحسو فات ع قلبي... لما بسمعو انا ونايم بالليل هيك او عند الفجر... الله اكبر ما في غير شي صوت بالفضا... ما فيه غير السكون ويطلع صوتو الحلو قبل ما يكون عالهوبارلورات ومكبرات الصوت المزعجة [...] كان حس انا بالطمأنينة... فأنا ابن هالتراث... فأنا ما فيني قول الا انا لبناني. متميز انو في عندي تنوع... الحضاري... فلذلك في مسرحياتي دائما فيه

الاسلام والمسيحيي سوا... يعني انا حتى روح الكون فيه موسيقى كنت رح حط الله اكبر على ناي عندي اياها تقريبا
او شي شرقي ناي هيك صحراوي... ناي لانو كنت دايما حس انو الحضارة رح تجي من الغرب... رح تجي من هون. فالناي لانو احن وكنت اطلب من الموسيقي دايما يعملي اياها... روح حط فيها البيزنطية لانو هني اساس الموسيقى... ومن هون حطينا الصوفية الدراويش... وكذا... يعني لانو... هيدا تأثير المجتمع لما فيه مسرحية وبتنجح كلن بيروحوا عليها... الجرس... لما لعبها بالجنوب... ببيروت... 2946 بالجونية... قضية لبنانية
موقف لبناني... بالنسبة للمقاومة بالنسبة للجنوب بالنسبة للبنان... نفس الشي ارانب وقديسين عملت نفس الشي...
تعاطف ابن كسروان مع قضية الجنوب... لما مسرحية بتقدر توصل بفكرة تخاطب الجمهور الواسع... صار خليط ما بقى مسيحي ومسلم... وحتى المسرحية بتخاطب النخبة بتخاطب التنين... مع انو انا مسرحيتي... ذهن مسيحي... فكر مسيحي. مبتكر مسيحي اغلب العاملين فيها مسيحيين... بالاول هي مسيحية... اذا بدي انطلق كمؤلف... هي نابعة من حضارتي... فما كان فيه عليها اختلاف عالجوهر...
فيه تنوع... شوف المسرح لازم ينشاف اجتماعيا خارج طبقات الحكام السياسيين... يلي هني 2947 مجبورين يشتغلوا سياسة طائفية لحتى يحافظوا على رعاياهن... يعني اذا الارثوذكسيي ما اهتم بالارثوذكسيين ما بيصير وزير للارثوذكس... والارمني. والشيعي... انو بدي مدير عام سني شيعي بدو ياخد محلو... لما كنا نروح نحضر نبيه ابو الحسن او شوشو... ما كان وارد هيدا شيعي وهيدا درزي... وشكيب ارثوذكسي... يعني هلق كشفت حالي رح تسبوني...
بيقول انو النص طويل... الكلام مش عم ينسمع... احيانا... انت لنعرف نجاوب العالم... هي 2948 معود ع عمل تلفزيوني... الجمهور عنا لبنان ما بيقدر يحضر مسرحية طويلة... اصلا ما حضروا بعد مسرح عندو قضية... كل المسارح على هامش الحياة... حتى اذا فيه مسرحية كبيرة مستهدبين عليها من نص اجنبي... بيدخلوا فيها قضايا ستي وعمتي وخالتي... وبيدخلك عيدي امين وقصص وبيقرق عالعالم وشو فيه اليوم مانشيتات بالجرايد...
بيدخلها بالمسرحية... بتكون مسرحية زغيرة ... اهميتها انها زغيرة... حدوتة... يا سكيتش... بينفخها بأشيا بلا طعمة...
بتضلها بمجال التسلية البسيطة... قلي حوارك انت اذا ما سمعنا كلمة ما منقدر نفهم المسرحية... يعني واحد ما عندو شخصية الا يسأل عم بيخدم الشخصية الاخرى... منو character...
هيدا... هون الحوار ما بتعرف من وين بينبع لان كل واحد عم بيقول شيء من عندو من خاصيتو من اوجاعو...
بتطور القصة وبتوصلها للموضوع... منشان هيك المسرحية بدها اصغاء... بيتعب المشاهد 2949 الشامل... نحنا عم نستعمل المسرح الكامل... le théâtre total ... هوي بتفوت فيه السينما... بيفوت فيه الرقص...
فيها كل شي... total عم هني ... الرسم ... السينوغرافيا... الكوريغرافيا... هي المسرحية مسرح بيصيروا مسرح الـ statement... بيلقي رأي ... شعارات... نوع من الشعارات الاخرى...

2950 فيه اشكال تستعير الشكل المسرحي... وتقدم عن المسرح... بس منها الشكل المسرحي يلي هوي قضيتو الانسان...
الطقس يكمل حيث يصمت الانسان...

2951 بالعولمة بيزتوا علينا فكرة لون حركة الخصوصية بدها تتعذب ولكن بدها تتمرد. لأن العولمة مش قادرة تمحي خصوصية الافراد والحضارات... ولذلك فيه ردة اسلامية ضد العولمة... المسلم اليوم في اميركا فيه حملات ضدو...

2952 Interview
2953

2954 ع. الجمهور تلات ارباعو من الفن... عدا عن انو جمهور اصحاب وهيك... كتير واعي تيستوعب
المسرحية... مثقف مسرحيا اللي عم يجي... الاشخاص الي جايين يحضروا مسرح لدكتور خوري déjà بيكونوا
يعني مش... elite حاطين براسن انو بدن يجوا يحضروا شي صعب مش شي كتير هين... للـ الشخص اللي بيحب
المسرح التسلاية. العالم اللي عندن هم ثقافي واجتماعي. مش بس حياتن الخاصة... بيطلعوا حواليهن... وبيشوفوا
عندن هموم. اكتر من اجتماعية... société لهالدني... كيف عم تتحول الـ evolution كيف فيه العالم مش عم
برا. وعم يسألوا سؤالات... اوقات بيقعدوا discussion تفل دغري بعد المسرحية... عم يعمل ساعة بعد المسرحية...
يسألوا انو مظبوط نحنا فهمنا الشغلة هيك... بيضهروا ومعن شي براسن...

2955
2956
2957

2958 من عكار. قضاء الشمال. نزلت ع بيروت كنت اخدت شهادة قسم تاني ونزلت ع بيروت لاتعلم [...]. رحنا عالبيولوجي... وبعدين فتنا عالفنون...

2959 انو عم قدم هالدور بموانئ الحنين ومع الاستاذ شكيب خوري... يعني ما الو spécial طعمة...

2960 مقابلات
2961
2962

2963 ر. م. آخر سنة مسرح
2964 ط. س. : قلتلي هالمسرحية لشكيب خوري بس [...] ليش؟
2965 لأنو هوي في قال انو ما حدا رح يفهما الا اذا حضرها عدة مرات...
2966 الثاني: سطل ما جرس... سطل حديد عتيق...
2967 بيناتن relation ر. م.: ما بيرمز للجرس... ما لازم تعمل.
2968 الثاني: هيداك سطل الحديد للتعذيب ... وهيداك شي خصو بالراوي يلي هوي...
2969 ر. م.: هوي الشي الاصلي الانسان البدائي يلي محاه التطور
2970 ط. س. : أي نوع جمهور بيحضر هالمسرحية.
2971 ر. م. : اليوم صار جايي تنين... ليك طلاب المسرح بيحبوا يشوفوا اشيا متل هي... بس الناس الناس...
يعني مش طلاب المسرح... ما رح يجوا انا اكيد...
2972 ط. س. : أي نوع مسرح بيجذب اكتر شي جمهور؟
2973 ر. م. : هيدا النوع... بس معمول بطريقة عن جد عم توصل ... الناس عم تقدر... شخص واحد عم بيمثلها...
2974 ط. س. : شو رأيك بمسرح منير كسرواني بالجنوب.؟
2975 ر. م. : ولا مرة حاضرو

343

2976 ط. س. : ولا مرة حاضرو... ليه؟

2977 ...بحسو عم يضحك عالعالم cheap... ر. م. : لانو هيك بحسو هيك

2978 ط. س. : هوي يعني منير عم بيجيب شوية عالم... عم بيجيب كتير عالم. مش متل هون بتعد واحد وتنين...

2979 ...تبع كسرواني style ر. م. : بركي لانو بالـ

2980 الثاني : بتوصل للناس اكتر.

2981 تبعو... يمكن نحنا style تبعو... عم بيوصل ... عم بيكون شاطر بالـ style ر. م. : لا ... الـ ما منحب الـ style اللي بيضحك تنقول عم بيضحك العالم... بس style تبعو... لانو هبل وسطلنة... بس بهيدا الـ style بهيدا الـ التجريبي هيدي انا بالنسبة لألي المسرحية منا مبكلة... انو منا معمولة احسن شي لنوع المسرح التجريبي...

2982 ا. ح. : انا صرلي 3 سنين بلبنان... معود عالمسرح بالبرازيل... يعني بحب المسرح لانو بحبو من البرازيل مش من هون... ايه... المشكلة بلبنان... المسرح مات بالحرب... العالم بطل فيها تروح وتجي... بعدين ما فيه هون ما بيعرفوا شو يعني مسرح. يعني فكرة المسرح غلط بالعالم... يعني بتقلو مسرح... يعني كلن بيفكروا chansonnier وكاس ويسكي وبزورات يعني... منها هيك... بعدين اليوم فيه كتير ناس اذكيا وفيه كتير ناس مدعيين بلبنان... يعني it's very... عم بقولها ... بس فيه كتير ناس ما الهن حق يحكوا sorry... بيفكروا حالن بيعرفوا good عم منجرب من كل الجهات انو نعمل شي مسرح... بس مين ما كان بيجي حدا يصورك كذا... بيطلع فيك من فوق لتحت انو مسرح... ما بيعمل مصاري... انو ما بعرف... فيه شغلة اساسية... انو السينما اللي جايي من برا ما بتعمل حضارة... يعني culture ولا جريدة ولا المسلسل المكسيكي بيعمل حضارة وبيعمل

2983 ط. س. : كيف بتلاقي جمهور المسرح

2984 ا. ح. : فيه مشكلة تعقيد يعني... مش من ورا المسرحيات للي عم نعرضها... كنت عم بسأل بنات عمي وهيك... يي ما الي جلادة... بفضل ادفع 5 آلاف احضر سينما مرتين ما احضر مسرح... ما بيعرفوا شو يعني مسرح... هلق بلش بالمدارس منهج المسرح بس كمان الشغلة مش كتير واضحة... يعني اليوم فيه مشكلة بلبنان ما بتعرف العالم شو المسرح المظبوط... ما بيعرفوا شو هوي اصلا مش انو ما بيعرفوا شو قيمتو... ما بيعرفوه... عنا مش بالسينما او بالمسلسل التخريفي بس تيبيعوا دعايات... بعدين ... culture ا. ح. : الـ

2985 المسلسل فيه خشبة magic روح... غير التلفزيون... مش عم يتعشى... المسرح بتكون ولع من جوا... فيها المسرح للي عم بيمثل systems مع انو انا بركب all that واللي عم يحضر... غير. كليا عن المكنات... والتكنولوجيا و انا ببيع computers it's all different...

2986 حتى بالثقافة... فيه snobish... ا. ح. : الغنية والفقيرة... المثقف يلي بينتنو وبيعطي قيمة جمهور مثقف بيقدر بيجي بيحضر... فيه جمهور بيجي بيحضر بيجي بيعرف... تيفرجي انو بيعرف تيشوف حالو... والقلال اللي اللي بيحب public بيجوا وبيجربوا يفهموا... تيجربوا يشوفوا شي اكتر من الي معودين عليه... الـ المسرح 10 آلاف

ما رح تأخروا... الشانسونييه مش مسرح ما فينا نسميه مسرح... فيه مشكلة مش طائفية... فيه مشكلة... كيف بدي قلك... فيه تصنف... يعني بيصنفوا العالم... يي هيدا هبيلة لاحقلي الاشيا اللي بلا طعمة... وبينهبل قدام العالم... انو بيصنف هيدا انو هيدا ما خصو... خلص ما بيفهم فيها الشغلة انو هودي انو بلا طعمة... هي المشكلة بلبنان... فيه بيشوفوا حالن على غير شي الي ما بيفهموه... بشوفها كتير هي... شو بدك بهالشغلة ما بتجيب خبز... انو شي يطعمي خبز... يوصل عالبيت بكير... ويهرب من العجقة...عم بحكيك من قرايبيني... شو بتروح تضيع وقتك بهالاشيا اللي بلا طعمة...

2987 ط. س. : شو الـ production

2988 ا. ح. : اللي عم يشتغل مسرح بلبنان... شو بدي قلك... شغيل عالبور؟. أهون من هيك ضلي عم نشتغل بالديكور للساعة 5 بعد نص ليل لحتى نعرض مسرحية... اذا رح نطلع شي هيدا منو مهم... اذا رح يكون فيه تقدير هيدا بيهمنا ما منعرف... اللي بدو يعمل مسرح بلبنان... عم يعمل... عم يفلح بأيدو... عم بيكسر حيطان...

2989 ط. س. : أي نوع مسرح بتروح عليه.

2990 ا. ح. : شانسونييه ما بروح... كوميديا... ا. ح [...] انا بالدكوانة... وبصيف بنبع الصفا... صرلي 3 سنين بلبنان...

بس هون ما فيهن culture ا. ح. : مشكلة انتاج... الدولة بتعطي منحة من الشركات للـ 2991 لانو بتكون كلها تفنيص بتفنيص... يعني. (وسايط)... مشكلة المسرحية... من الوزارة... الها حق يفوتوا بهيك مشاريع المسرحية... عم يعطوا عشرة بالمية...

2992 ر. م.: لا انتاج ولا شي ولا ناس. ولا دعاية. انو فيه مطارح خصوصي متل مسرح المدينة... بلا دعاية انو الناس دغري بتروح بتخبر بعضها... هي المشكلة بالابداع تبع الناس يللي عم يعملوا هيك نوع مسرح... هي السنة اجت مسرحية من هولندا... بتمثلها بنت لوحدا... الديكور كان ما شي شقعة بالة centre ville بالـ تياب... بالة تياب بيعقد... بتحس انو بتطلع راسك معبى من ممثلة وشقعة تياب... من spectacle وحبلة... انو كان ماشي يعمل شي... هيدا هوي اللي ناقص... بس العقل محدود صاير هون...

2993 ط. س. : يعني ما عم يوصل للعالم؟

2994 ر. م.: ما عم بيكونوا صادقين... عم بيكونوا فيه هيك تصنع. فيه تصنع... فيه... شي بيقرف... انو بيدعوا... وقد ما بيدعوا بيعملوا شي... هني مش مقتنعين فيه بس مش مفهوم... تيقولوا انو الناس ما فهمتنا... متل كمان... فيه واحد عمل مسرحية ما مشي فيها... ما خلى واحد ما جابوا... شي اربعين واحد عالمسرح... وفلسفة بلا طعمة... وغلط بشع يعني... مش مظبوط يعني لها النوع من المسرح... مش مقبول هالشي... مش انو الناس ما فهمت... هوي محدود...

2995 ا. ح.: عندك هالشغلة بلبنان... بيبطل الواحد يقدر يعيش متل ما بدو... بيبطل حر انو يفلت متل ما بدو...

3079 انني انظر الى هذه التجربة على انها خطوة في الطريق الصحيح للبحث عن فن عربي له «هويته وخصوصيته، وذلك

345

من خلال التعاون الجدي بين المثقفين والمبدعين العرب. كلي امل في ان تتلو هذه الخطوة خطوات اخرى من
«التعاون المثمر والبناء».

Appendix D: German Summary

Theater im Libanon
Produktion, Rezeption
und Konfessionalismus

Die Arbeit nimmt eine Typisierung des Phänomens: »Theater im Libanon« vor. Produktion, Rezeption und Performance werden anhand qualitativer Daten analysiert. Diese bestehen aus Interviews mit Produktions- und Rezeptionsakteuren sowie audiovisuellem Material und Beobachtungen verschiedener Theaterstücke. Nachdem erste Beobachtungen ergaben, dass Bedeutung und Konzept des Theaters sich von einem Gebiet zum anderen ändern, bot sich eine qualitative Feldforschung an, in der Daten aus Interviews mit den Akteuren des Phänomens Theater ausgewertet werden. Methodisch wird die Analyse der Daten mit Hilfe der »Grounded Theory« von Anselm Strauss, den Grundlagen der Verstehenden Soziologie, wie sie von Weber und Schütz erklärt wurden und dem Hermeneutischen Ansatz Soeffners durchgeführt. Nach diesem Ansatz kann die erlebte Erfahrung der Performance rekonstruiert werden, und die vorangehenden anderen Prozesse und Teilprozesse können erklärt werden. Die Funktion und Natur des Theaters zu erklären, bleibt so den verschiedenen Gruppierungen von Akteuren überlassen.

Das Theater im Libanon ist in seiner Umwelt verwurzelt. Die Sozialstruktur, die laufenden »Social Dramas« sowie die ästhetischen Elemente der Umwelt lassen sich auf verschiedene Arten im Theater darstellen bzw. widerspiegeln. Deshalb war es nötig, die relevanten Elemente der Umwelt, die gleichzeitig als Hintergrundinformation dienen, am Anfang zu gliedern. Libanesisches Theater ist damit eine soziale Aktion, die integraler Teil der gesamten gesellschaftlichen sozialen Aktion ist und nicht nur ein von der sozialen Umwelt isoliertes Phänomen mit begrenzter Außenwirkung. Um die Herstellung der Beziehungen zwischen Theater und seiner Umwelt deutlicher zu machen, wird im Laufe der Arbeit die Sozialstruktur und die gesamte soziale Umwelt als »R1« (Realität 1) bezeichnet, während die Performance, die konstruierte Realität in der theatralischen Performance, als (Realität 2) bezeichnet wird.

Die libanesische Sozialstruktur ist das Ergebnis einer Geschichte von Konfessionalismus, Regionalismus und Krieg zwischen den verschiedenen Gemeinschaften *(ṭawā'if)* der libanesischen Gesellschaft. Insbesondere im letzten Krieg (1975-1990) ließen sich diese Gruppen in zwei Hauptkategorien einteilen: Christen und Muslime, deren (politische) Hauptdifferenz die Vision der Nationalidentität ist. Während die Muslime darauf bestehen, die arabische Herkunft als determinierend im Bezug auf die Zugehörigkeit zur arabischen Welt zu betrachten, tendieren die Christen dazu, die arabische Identität höchstens an zweiter Stelle, nach einer eigenen Vision einer »libanesischen« Identität, gelten zu lassen.

Der Krieg spielte die Rolle eines geographischen und demographischen Katalysators: die Mehrheit der Christen sammelte sich in Ostbeirut, während Westbeirut zum Quartier der Muslime wurde. Entsprechend dieser Aufteilung kam es zur Nominierung »Östliche Zone« und »Westliche Zone«, jeweils für das christliche und muslimische Gebiet. Als Konsequenz dieser Aufteilung verstärkte der Regionalismus die Isolations- und Differenzierungsgefühle zwischen den beiden Gebieten. Daraus entstanden zwei »Soziale Welten«, die aber trotz scheinbarer Differenz abhängig von einander blieben. Diese Abhängigkeit zeigte sich auf der ökonomischen und politischen, sowie auf der kommunikativen und ästhetischen Ebene. Konkurrenz, Spannung, Isolation und immer geringere Kenntnis des *Anderen* sind charakteristisch für die Beziehung zwischen diesen Welten. Insbesondere seit Kriegsende streben Christen und Muslime eine zunehmende *ästhetische Differenzierung* an. Dementsprechend unterziehen sich die ästhetischen Elemente der Umwelt Prozessen, die dazu führen, dass sich die Umwelt in zwei *ästhetische Domänen* teilt. Sobald eine Seite ein Zeichen als Symbol adoptieren würde, würde die andere ein anderes paralleles, aber unterschiedliches suchen. Die Christen finden ihre Zeichen und Symbole in einer westlich-orientierten Ästhetik, während die Muslime sich auf die arabische Ästhetik konzentrieren. Dieses geschieht durch drei Hauptprozesse: *Polarisation* (Polarization), *Aufteilung* (Apportionment), und *Etikettierung* (Labeling). So werden neue ästhetische Elemente in der Umwelt des Theaters polarisiert, aufgeteilt, und zur einen oder anderen »Sozialen Welt« zugehörig etikettiert. Zwei Kriterien liegen diesen Prozessen zugrunde: Erstens die Identifikation mit der eigenen Ästhetik, Christ und/oder westlich, Muslim und/oder arabisch; zweitens, die Differenzierung von dem *Anderen*.

Auch Elemente der globalen Kultur werden so aufgeteilt. Ein Teil davon aber bleibt »neutral« und befindet sich in beiden Sozialen Welten. Dieser Teil wird hier als die »*ästhetische Domäne der Globalisierung*« bezeichnet. Institutionell gibt es trotz der ästhetischen Differenzierung eine Parallelität zwischen den Welten. Jede Welt kann als eine institutionelle Duplikation der anderen empfunden werden. Die Existenz von bestimmten Institutionen – darunter das Theater – kann als Ergebnis dieser Duplizität gesehen werden.

Im Rahmen der Sozialstruktur entwickelte sich das Theater zu einem Kommunikationskanal zwischen den beiden Welten, in dem die Konstruktion des *Anderen* und die Repräsentation des *Selbst* die Hauptrolle spielen. Nach der Goffman'schen Theorie erfüllt Theater eine Darstellungsfunktion für die konfessionellen Gemeinschaften. Die laufenden »Social Dramas« in der Umwelt reflektierten sich im Theater in »Differenzsphären« (Spheres of Discord). Diese manifestierten sich in vier Hauptdifferenzsphären. Die erste ist die für die Entstehung der zwei »Sozialen Welten« verantwortliche *konfessionelle Differenzsphäre*. Die zweite teilt die Gesellschaften zwischen *Herrschenden* und *beherrschten* Gruppen. Aus der Empirie können wir feststellen, dass diese Differenzsphäre sich als die Struktur *Za'īm (Leader)-Abhängige* manifestiert, in der die *Zu'amā'* (Leaders) auf der Basis ihres konfessionellen Rangs politische Autorität und Macht ausüben. Nur durch das Etablieren einer Verbindung – üblicherweise durch Familienbeziehungen – zwischen *Herrschern und Beherrschten,* die als *connections (wāsiṭa)* bezeichnet wird, können die *Beherrschten* ihre Alltagsangelegenheiten lösen. Ähnliche Strukturen sind in der Hierarchie der Theatergruppen reproduziert. Der *Theaterza'īm* – der große Name im Theaterstück – übt ähnliche Autorität über den Rest der Truppe aus. Das führt dazu, dass das Theaterstück ein dem *Theaterza'īm* entsprechendes konfessionelles Etikett (Label) erwirbt. Aus einem zusätzlichen Konflikt zwischen Kollektiv und Individuum entsteht eine dritte Differenzsphäre, die sich parallel in beiden »Sozialen Welten« befindet. Diese konnte sich entwickeln, da die Umwelt generell die kollektiven Werte auf Kosten der Entfaltung des Individuums fördert. In dieser Sphäre bietet das Theater einer solchen Entfaltung den nötigen Raum, und erlaubt eine Revolution gegen den kollektiven Typus. Die vierte Differenzsphäre ist die Kluft zwischen der Kriegs- und der Vorkriegsgeneration. Im Theater ist der Krieg ein Diskrepanzthema, das jedes Publikum polarisieren kann. Die *konfessionelle* Differenzsphäre steht jedoch über all den anderen, die höchstens eine Konsequenz daraus sind. Dies zeigte sich in der Empirie darin, dass jedes Thema, das auf eine Differenzsphäre hindeutet, zur *konfessionellen* Sphäre umgeleitet werden kann. So wird Theater zum Raum für diesen konfessionellen Zusammenstoß der es umgebenden »Social Dramas«. Begrenzt ist dieser Raum durch eine limitierte Freiheit sowohl in Bezug auf den Inhalt als auch die ästhetische Form eines Theaterstücks.

Im nächsten Schritt teilt die Arbeit die Ergebnisse entsprechend dem Kodierungsprozess in vier Levels: die Umwelt wird als Level I betrachtet, Theaterprozesse außerhalb der Performance werden als Level II bezeichnet. Level III ist die Performance selbst. Level IV, der Post-Performance Level, stimmt mit Level I überein, da eine Performance einen Zyklus im Theaterprozess und seiner Umwelt darstellt.

Entscheidender Faktor für die Rezeption und die Produktion außerhalb der Performance auf Level II sind die eigenen Einstellungen des Publikums. Neben der Sozialstruktur definiert die Interaktion zwischen den Produktionsakteuren und dem Publikum die Parameter des Produktionsprozesses. Diese reduzieren sich auf zwei Faktoren: Die Ökonomie der Theaterproduktion und die Freiheit der Produktion aufgrund der Sozialstruktur der libanesischen Gesellschaft. Um zu überleben, muss eine Produktion genügend Publikum haben, da das libanesische Theater über keine nennenswerten Subventionen vom Staat verfügt. Dies schafft eine starke Abhängigkeit der Produktion vom Publikum. Auf der anderen Seite ist die Freiheit der Produktion durch die Sozialstruktur begrenzt. Über Jahre von Spannungen sind viele ernsthafte politische und soziale Tabus entstanden, die Friktion in den Beziehungen zwischen den beiden »Sozialen Welten« verursachen. Dies betrifft insbesondere die Darstellung des *Anderen*. Im Theater hängt viel davon ab, *»wer wem was sagt und wo«*. Themen im Bereich der Differenzsphären verursachen Friktion und Konflikt, sofern sie inszeniert sind. Diese für das Publikum sehr attraktiven Eigenschaften sind jedoch für die Produktionsseite aufgrund der Freiheitsbegrenzung schwierig zu inszenieren, da eine harte Zensur mit weitgehender personenorientierter Diskriminierung nach den Vorstellungen der *herrschenden* Autorität von den Regierungsorganisationen durchgesetzt wird.

Gleichzeitig definieren die Einstellungen des Publikums gegenüber dem Theater die Funktion und die Rolle des Theaters. In diesen Einstellungen existieren deutliche Unterschiede zwischen den beiden »Sozialen Welten.« Die Christen tendieren dazu, das Theater als *l'art pour l'art* zu verstehen, wodurch die Ästhetik eine höhere Bedeutung als in der muslimischen Welt gewinnt. Die Bühne wird außerdem auch als Raum für die Entwicklung des Individuums betrachtet. Auf der anderen Seite muss das Theater in der muslimischen Welt eine konkrete »inhaltliche« Funktion haben, um seine Existenz überhaupt rechtfertigen zu können. Durch diese erzwungene Funktionalität werden Inhalt und Form stark beeinflusst. Muslimisches Theater benötigt einen stärkeren Bezug auf den Alltag, um überhaupt akzeptiert zu werden. Dadurch wird mehr *Realismus* in Form und Inhalt erwartet, und so nähert sich das Theater den Einstellungen des nicht-eingeweihten Publikums. Im christlichen Milieu tendiert das Theater zu einer stärkeren Ästhetik, die auch außerhalb des Alltagsrahmens gesucht werden kann. Das Thema wird als Brücke betrachtet, die die Ästhetik trägt.

Betrachtet man die Geschichte des libanesischen Theaters, ist dieses Ergebnis kein Zufall, da die Ursprünge des Theaters von den Christen aus dem Westen importiert wurden. Bis heute besteht das libanesische Theater aus »Kopieren«. Molière, Cheshow, Shakespeare, u. a. wurden unabhängig von den Interessen der Rezeption gespielt, weil das Theater an sich völlig unbekannt war. In einer späteren Phase kam die Adaptation *('al-'iqtibās)*, die in Bezug auf Namensänderungen, Ort- und Charakteradaptationen etwas elaborierter als die einfache Übersetzung war. Inzwischen haben die Muslime die arabischen Ansätze wie *ḫayāl z̧-z̧ill* (Schattenspieltheater) und *'al-ḥakawātiyy* (Geschichtenerzähler) nicht weiterentwickelt, sondern sind der Entwicklung des christlich-westlich beeinflussten Theaters gefolgt. Aufgrund dieses Duplikationseffekts entwickelten die Typen der Theaterproduktion in beiden Milieus später viele Ähnlichkeiten, während die Interessen des Publikums sich auseinanderentwickelten, und sich zwischen christlichem *Ästhetizismus* und muslimischem *Funktionalismus* aufgeteilt haben.

Aus der Empirie kristallisieren sich drei Typen des Theaters heraus: »*Seriöses Theater*«, »*Unterhaltungstheater*« und »*Populäres Theater*«. Seriöses Theater lässt sich weiter untergliedern in »Politisches Theater« und »Intellektuelles Theater«, »Chansonniertheater« und »Boulevardtheater« sind Unterkategorien des Unterhaltungstheaters. Diese Typen wurden »in-vivo« von den Akteuren selbst entwickelt. Gleichzeitig sind sie die Antwort auf zwei Bedürfnisse des Publikums: *soziopolitische Kritik* und *Unterhaltung*. Ein dominanter *Realismus* findet sich im populären und seriösen Theater; eine Tendenz, Abstand von der Realität zu nehmen, charakterisiert das *Unterhaltungstheater; Restbestände* westlicher Herkunft bestehen im auf dem akademischen Kreis begrenzten *intellektuellen* Theater. Um das Interesse des Publikums zu halten, agieren diese Typen als Funktion der Differenzsphären mit Berücksichtigung der Freiheitsgrenzen.

Ob die Form realistisch oder absurd ist, die Themen im seriösen Theater behandeln Alltagsbereiche, die nah an den Differenzsphären liegen. Dagegen bezweckt das Unterhaltungstheater eine wohlbedachte Ablenkung von diesen Sphären. Dazu werden zwei Strategien verwendet. Wie sich am Beispiel des Boulevardtheaters zeigen lässt, ignoriert die erste Strategie völlig den Alltag »R1« und bietet dem Zuschauer eine vom Alltag unabhängige alternative Realität »R2«. Dabei wird das Thema meist noch aus dem französischen Boulevardtheater importiert. Die zweite typische Strategie, die im Chansonniertheater häufig zu finden ist, besteht aus getrennten Sketchen, Bildern aus dem Alltag, die sich in der Regel um die Herrscher-Beherrschten-Differenzsphäre drehen, und in denen Karikaturen politischer Figuren dargestellt werden. In »R2« wird eine Version von »R1« konstruiert, in der der Beherrschte zum Herrschenden wird, damit er seine in »R1« entstandene Frustration abbauen kann. Im populären Theater vermischt sich »Unterhaltung« und »Seriosität«. Die Seriosität zeigt sich in der Deutung seiner Themen im Hinblick auf die Differenzsphären. Die Unterhaltung liefert ein oberflächliches Spotten über die politische Situation, das jedoch keine ernsthafte, fundierte Kritik darstellt. Dieses Theater kann aber nur *eine* Art von Publikum – entweder Christen oder Muslime – befriedigen, da die politischen Visionen in beiden Milieus unterschiedlich sind. Dafür tendiert die Produktion dieser Art von Theater in Richtung einer symbolisierten Ebene der *konfessionellen* Differenzsphäre, um mehr Publikum zu gewinnen. Typischerweise gehört sein Publikum dem einen Milieu an, während die als Karikatur dargestellten Politiker aus dem anderen Milieu stammen. Wie in der Arbeit gezeigt wird, existiert neben diesen Typen ein weiterer Typus, der aus der Problematik der zwei »sozialen Welten« entstanden ist, das »Crossing Play«. Dabei handelt es sich um Theaterstücke, die die Grenze zwischen verschiedenen Arten von Publikum überschreiten und von allen akzeptiert werden. Dieser Begriff summiert die gesamte Problematik der Theaterproduktion dadurch, dass die Produktion eines solchen Theaterstückes implizit alle Hindernisse des Theaters überwinden muss. Zwei Typen von »Crossing Play« lassen sich identifizieren: die »regionale Version«, in der die ästhetischen Elemente sich an die geographischen bzw. politischen Merkmale der »sozialen Welt« anpassen und das »Passe-partout Play«, das im voraus so geplant wird, dass keine Änderungen nötig werden. Beide Arten charakterisieren sich durch eine einflussreiche Neutralität, die alle anderen Elemente des Theaterstückes deutlich prägt, da auch in der »regionalen Version« die Anpassung der Elemente eher dazu neigt, positive Attribute der Region und ihrer Leader zu betonen, als die negativen der anderen Region zu zeigen. Letztendlich muss das Theaterstück in *beiden* »sozialen Welten« spielen können. Weiterhin ist die Erlaubnis des lokalen *Zaʿīm* nach Absprache mit dem *Theaterzaʿīm* eine Bedingung dafür, dass das Theaterstück überhaupt in der Zielregion gespielt werden darf.

Auf der Seite der Rezeption determiniert neben den konfessionellen Unterschieden die »Kultur des Theaters« die Rezeption des Publikums. Im Christlichen Milieu findet sich eine Tendenz zu aufsteigender Ästhetisierung, Exklusivität und zur Entwicklung eines Bilds des Individuums, während Funktionalismus, Popularismus und die Erhaltung des Kollektiven die Tendenzen im Muslimischen Milieu sind. Die Rezeption wird ebenfalls durch den Ort der Performance beeinflusst, sowohl im eigenen Sozialmilieu als auch beim *anderen*. Parallel zum Begriff des »Crossing Play« wird der Begriff des »Crossing Audience« für das Publikum eingeführt, das die Grenze zum anderen Gebiet überschreitet, um die originale, nicht konfessionell adaptierte Version eines Theaterstückes zu sehen. Typisiert man das Publikum, steht die Christlich/Muslimische Kategorisierung an erster Stelle. Danach tauchen die Ausbildung und die »theatralische Kultur« auf.

In der Performance, Level III, charakterisieren Interaktion und Identifikation die Beziehung zwischen »R1« und »R2.« Die Elemente Produktion, Struktur des Publikums und Ort der Performance beeinflussen die Situation der Performance. Die Anwesenheit des *Anderen* in einem gemischten Publikum führt gemäß des Themas zu Polarisierung oder zu Harmonisierung des Publikums, was Victor Turner »Spontaneous Communitas« nennt. Eine Verlagerung der Einstellung des Zuschauers zwischen dem Individuum und dem Kollektiven kommt hier zustande. Die Post-Performance-Phase kann auch als Pre-Performance betrachtet werden, da jede einzelne Performance ein theatralischer Zyklus in der sozialen Umwelt darstellt.

Insgesamt können wir folgende Schlussfolgerungen ziehen.

Erstens: Die Produktion des Theaters ist durch Konfessionalismus und die daraus resultierende soziale Struktur dominiert. Je mehr polarisierte Performances unter diesen Umständen zustande kommen, desto mehr wirkt das Theater in seiner gegenwärtigen Form einerseits als Verstärker der aktuellen Sozialstruktur und stellt andererseits gleichzeitig eine Folge des Konfessionalismus dar. Damit wird Theater Teil des konfessionellen Prozesses. Dies geschieht insbesondere, wenn »R2« »R1« kopiert, d. h. wenn wir mehr Realismus im Theater haben. So kommen wir durch exzessiven Realismus zu einer Verstärkung des Konfessionalismus. Da die Begrenzung der Freiheit in »R1« eine objektive offene Diskussion des Konfessionalismus im Theater, »R2,« verbietet, kommen statt dessen viele Vorurteile in Bezug auf die Konstruktion des *Anderen* zum Vorschein. Auf der anderen Seite wirkt die Verstärkung des Konfessionalismus wiederum als Ausdehnung der Kluft zwischen den bereits geteilten »sozialen Welten«. *Zweitens:* christliche und muslimische »Theaterkulturen« zeigen eine Divergenz: durch zunehmende Ästhetisierung und die daraus folgende Entwicklung des Symbolismus ist das »christliche Theater« besser geeignet, im Rahmen der derzeitigen Freiheitsgrenzen zu überleben, als das durch Realismus und Religion geprägte »muslimische Theater«. *Drittens:* Durch die »Scheidung« des Theaters von der Sozialstruktur d. h. der Trennung zwischen »R1« und »R2« und der daraus resultierenden höheren Autonomie für das Theater und eine zunehmende Freiheit, könnte das Theater umgekehrt positiv auf die Sozialstruktur einwirken und neue Perspektiven im Bereich des Sozialen aufzeigen. So kann das Theater Prosperität und Bedeutung in der Zukunft erwerben.

Bibliography

Adorno, Theodor W. *Aesthetic Experience and Literary Hermeneutics.* Trans. Michael Shaw. Minneapolis: University of Minnesota Press, 1982.
Adorno, Theodor W. *Aesthetic Theory.* London: Routledge & Kegan Paul, 1984.
Akutagawa, Ryunosuke, and Jürgen Berndt. *Rashomon: ausgew. Kurzprosa.* München: Beck, 1985.
Al-Hourani, Youssef. *Lubnān fī qiyami tārīḫihi: Baḥt fī falsafat tārīḫ Lubnān: Al-'ahd l-fīnīqiyy.* Beirut:'an-nahār, 1992.
Alter, Jean. *A Sociosemiotic Theory of Theater.* Pennsylvania: University of Pennsylvania Press, 1990.
Andersen, Martin. P. *The Speaker and his Audience: Dynamic Interpersonal Communication.* New York: Harper and Row, 1973.
Artaud, Antonin. *The Theater and its Double.* Trans. Victor Corti. London: John Calder, 1981.
Auwärter, Manfred, and Edit Kirsch. *Seminar: Kommunikation, Interaktion, Identität.* Frankfurt am Main: Suhrkamp Verlag, 1976.
Bab, Julius. *Das Theater im Lichte der Soziologie.* Stuttgart: Ferdinand Enke Verlag, 1974.
Bartsch, Shadi. *Actors in the Audience: Theatricality and Doublespeak from Nero to Hadrian.* Cambridge – Mass: Harvard University Press, 1994.
Basha, Abido. *Bayt n-nār: az-zaman ḍā'i' fī l-masraḥ l-lubnāniyy.* London: Riyad er-Rayes, 1995.
Basha, Abido. *Kitāb r-rāwiyy: siyar.* Beirut: Dār t-tanwīr, 1995.
Basha, Abido. *Mamālik min ḫašab: 'al-masrah l-lubāniyy 'inda mašārif l-'alf ṯ-ṯāliṯ.* London: Riyad er-Rayes, 1999.
Beck, Lewis White. *The Actor and the Spectator.* New Haven: Yale U. Press, 1975.
Beckermann, Bernard. *Dynamics of Drama.* New York: Alfred A. Knopf, 1970.
Benjamin, Walter. *Understanding Brecht.* London: New Left Books, 1973.

Bennett, Susan. *Theatre Audiences: A Theory of Production and Reception.* London: Routledge, 1990.
Bentley, Eric. *The Life of the Drama.* New York: Atheneum Press, 1964.
Bourdieu, Pierre. *Die feinen Unterschiede: Kritik der gesellschaftlichen Urteilskraft.* Frankfurt a. M.: Suhrkamp, 1982.
Brook, Peter. *The Empty Space.* Hamondsworth: Penguin, 1972.
Carlson, Marvin. *Performance: a Critical Introduction.* Repr. London: Routledge, 1998.
Chaikin, Joseph. *The Presence of The Actor.* New York: Theatre Communications Group, 1991.
Chekhov, Michael. *L'Imagination Créatrice de L'Acteur.* Paris: Pygmalion, 1995.
Clevenger, Theodore. *Audience Analysis.* Indianapolis: Bobbs-Merrill, 1966.
Dahir, Massoud. *'al-ğuḏūr t-tārīḫiyya li-l-mas'ala ṭ-ṭā'ifiyya l-lubnāniyya: 1697-1861.* Beirut, Ma'had l-'inmā' l-'arabiyy, 1986.
Dahrendorf, Ralf. *Homo Sociologicus.* Opladen: Westdeutscher Verlag, 1974.
Deeb, Marius. *The Lebanese Civil War.* New York: Praeger Publishers, 1980.
Dilthey, Wilhelm, and Manfred Riedel. *Der Aufbau der geschichtlichen Welt in den Geisteswissenschaften.* Frankfurt am Main: Suhrkamp, 1990.
Downes, D. M. *The Delinquent Solution.* London, 1966.
Duvignaud, Jean. *Sociologie du Théatre: Essai sur les Ombres Collectives.* Paris: Pr. Univ. de France, 1965.
Elam, Keir. *The Semiotics of Theater and Drama.* London: Methuen, 1980.
Erikson, E. H. *Childhood and Society.* New York, 1963.
Fischer-Lichte, Erika. *Die Entdeckung des Zuschauers: Paradigmenwechsel auf dem Theater des 20. Jahrhunderts.* Tübingen: Gunter Narr Verlag, 1997.
Fischer-Lichte, Erika. *Semiotik des Theaters: Das System der theatralischen Zeichen*, Band 1. Tübingen: Gunter Narr Verlag, 1983.
Fischer-Lichte, Erika. *The Theatrical Code: an Approach to the Problem.* Ernest W.B. Hess-Lüttich (ed.) Multimedial Communication 2: Theatre Semiotics. Tubingen: Gunter Narr Verlag, 64-62. 1982.
Fowler, Richard. »The Four Theaters of Jerzy Grotowski: An Introductory Assessment.« *New Theatre Quarterly* 1, 2 (1985): 173-8.
Fuegi, John. *Bertolt Brecht: Chaos, According to Plan.* Cambridge: Cambridge U. Press, 1987.
Gadamer, Hans-Georg. *Wahrheit und Methode.* Tübingen: Mohr, 1972.

Geertz, Clifford. *The Interpretation of Cultures: Selected Essays.* New York: Basic Books, 1999.

Gibson, James W. *Audience Analysis: A Programmed Approach to Receiver Behavior.* Englewood Cliffs: N.J: Prentice-Hall, 1976.

Gilsenan, Michael. *Lords of the Lebanese Marches: Violence and Narrative in an Arab Society.* London: I.B. Tauris, 1996.

Girard, G., Ouellet, R., and C. Rigault. *L'Univers du Théâtre.* Paris: Presses Universitaires de France, 1978.

Glinka, Hans-Jürgen. *Das Narrative Interview: eine Einführung für Sozialpädagogen.* München: Juventa Verlag, Edition Soziale Arbeit, 1998.

Gloversmith, Frank. *The Theory of Reading.* Brighton: Harvester Press, 1984.

Goffman, Erving. *Encounters, Two Studies in the Sociology of Interaction.* Indianapolis: Bobbs-Merrill, 1961.

Goffman, Erving. *Stigma.* Frankfurt am Main: Suhrkamp Taschenbuch Verlag, 1967.

Goffman, Erving. *The Presentation of Self in Everyday Life.* Garden City, New York: Doubleday Anchor Books, Doubleday and Company Inc., 1959.

Goodlad, John S... *A Sociology of Popular Drama.* London: Heinemann, 1971.

Gras, Henk. *Studies in Elizabethan Audience Response to the Theatre.* Frankfurt am Main: Peter Lang, 1993.

Grieder, Terence: *Artist and Audience.* Madison: WI, Brown & Benchmark, 1996.

Grotowski, Jerzy. *Towards a Poor Theatre.* London: Methuen, 1980.

Guy, Jean Michel. *Les Publics du Théâtre: Fréquentation et Image du Théâtre dans La Population Francaise Agée de 15 Ans et Plus: Résultats d'une Enquête Realisée par Sondage en 1987.* Paris: Documentation Francaise, 1988.

Habermas, Jürgen. *Theorie und Praxis.* Neuwied a. Rh.: Luchterhand, 1963.

Hamdan, Kamal. *Le Conflit Libanais: Communautés Religieuses, Classes Sociales et Identité Nationale.* Paris: Editions Garnet, 1997.

Hanf, Theodor. *Koexistenz im Krieg. Staatszerfall und Entstehen einer Nation im Libanon.* Reihe: Schriften des Forschungsinstituts der Deutschen Gesellschaft für Auswärtige Politik e.V., Baden-Baden: Nomos, 1990.

Hess-Lüttich, Ernest W.B. *Multimedial Communication* 2: Theater and Semiotics. Tubingen: Gunter Narr Verlag, 1982.

Hillmann, Karl-Heinz. *Wörterbuch der Soziologie*. Stuttgart: Alfred Kröner Verlag, 1994.

Hitti, Philip. *Lebanon in History: From the Earliest Times to the Present*. New York: Macmillan, St. Martin's Press, 1965.

Holub, Robert. *Reception Theory*. New York: Methuen, 1984.

Homan, Sidney. *The Audience as Actor and Character: The Modern Theater of Beckett, Brecht, Genet, Ionesco, Pinter, Stoppard, and Williams*. London: Associated University Presses, 1989.

Hudson, Michael C. *The Precarious Republic: Political Modernization in Lebanon*. New York: Random House, 1968.

Ibn Khaldun, Abd Ar-Rahman. *muqaddimat 'ibn ḫaldūn*. (1st ed. 1879). Librairie du Liban: Beirut, 1990.

Iser, Wolfgang. *The Implied Reader: Patterns of Communication in Prose Fiction from Bunyan to Beckett*. Baltimore: John Hopkins University Press, 1974.

Jauss, Hans R... »Theses on the Transition from the Aesthetics of Literary Works to a Theory of Aesthetic Experience.« *Interpretation of Narrative*. Eds. Mario J. Valdes and Owen J. Miller. Toronto: University of Toronto Press, 1979.

Jauss, Hans Robert. *Toward an Aesthetic of Reception*. Minneapolis: University of Minnesota Press, 1982.

Johnson, Michael. »Political Bosses and their Gangs: Zu'ama and Qabadayat in the Sunni Muslim Quarters of Beirut.« *Patrons and Clients in Mediterranean Societies*. Eds Gellner, Ernest and John Waterbury. London: Duckworth, 1977. 207–224.

Jones, David R. *Great Directors at Work: Stanislavsky, Brecht, Kazan, Brook*. Berkeley: University of California Press, 1986.

Khalaf, Samir. »Changing Forms of Political Patronage in Lebanon.« *Patrons and Clients in Mediterranean Societies*. Eds. Gellner, Ernest / John Waterbury. London: Duckworth, 1977.

Khashan, Hilal. *Inside the Lebanese Confessional Mind*. Lanham: University press of America, 1992.

Kirby, Michael. *Futurist Performance*. New York: E. P. Dutton, 1971.

Korm, Georges. *Ta'addud l-'adyān wa 'anẓimat l-ḥukm*. Beirut: 'annahār, 1998.

Kurayyim, Muhammad. *'al-masraḥ l-lubnāniyy fī niṣf qarn: 1900-1950*. Beirut: Al-Maqassed, 2000.

Lasswell, Harold D. »Who Says What, in What Way to Whom and in Which Effect? The Structure and Function in Communication in Society.« *The Communication of Ideas*. Ed. L. Bryson. New York, 1948.

Luckmann, Thomas, and Peter Berger. *Die gesellschaftliche Konstruktion der Wirklichkeit: Eine Theorie der Wissenssoziologie.* transl. Monika Plessner. Original title: The social construction of reality. Frankfurt a. M.: Fischer Taschenbuch Verlag, 1969.

Luhmann, Niklas. *Soziale Systeme: Grundriss einer allgemeinen Theorie.* Frankfurt am Main: Suhrkamp Taschenbuch Wissenschaft, 1984.

Mackintosh, Ian. *Architecture, Actor, and Audience.* London, Routledge. 1993

Mahfouz, Issam. *masraḥī wa-l-masraḥ.* Beirut: Dār 2002, 1995.

Makki, Muhammad Ali. *Lubnān: min l-fatḥ l-'arabiyy 'ilā l-fatḥ l-'uṯmāniyy, 635-1516.* Beirut: 'an-nahār, 1991.

Matthes, Joachim. *Zwischen den Kulturen?: Die Sozialwissenschaften vor dem Problem des Kulturvergleichs.* Goettingen: Schwartz, 1992.

Mead, G. Herbert. *Mind Self and Society.* Chicago: University of Chicago Press, 1934.

Meyerhold, Vsevolod Emilevich. *Meyerhold on Theater.* Ed. and trans. Edward Braun. New York: Hill and Wang, 1969.

Mitter, Shomit. *Systems of Rehearsal: Stanislavsky, Brecht, Grotowski, and Brook.* London: Routledge, 1992.

Moultaka, Antoine, and Nagi Maalouf. *'al-masrah.* Beirut: 'al-markaz t-tarbawiyy li-l-buḥūṯ wa-l-'inmā'.

Mourani, Antoine H. *Fī hawiyyat Lubnān ṭ-ṭā'ifiyya.* Beirut: 'an-nahār, 1994.

Mukarovsky, Jan. *Structure, Sign, and Function.* Eds. and trans. John Burbank and Peter Steiner. New Haven: Yale University Press, 1977.

Münch, Richard. *Sociological Theory: From the 1850s to the Present.* Chicago: Nelson Hall, 1994.

Nasr, Salim, and Claude Dubar. *Aṭ-ṭabaqāt l-'iğtimā'iyya fī Lubnān.* Beirut: Mu'assasat l-'abḥāṯ l-'arabiyya, 1982.

Naumann, Manfred. »Literary Production and Reception.« *New literary history* 8.1, 1976. 107-26.

Osgood, Charles E., George J. Suci, and Percy H. Tannenbaum. *The Measurement of Meaning.* Urbana: Univ. of Illinois Pr., 1967.

Parsons, Talcot. *The Social System.* London, 1951.

Passow, Wilfried. »The Analysis of Theatrical Performance: the State of the Art.« *Poetics Today* 2.3, 1981. 217-54.

Pavis, Patrice. *Problèmes de Sémiologie Théâtrale.* Quebec: Les Presses de l'Universite du Quebec, 1976.

Petran, Tabitha. *The Struggle over Lebanon.* New York: Monthly Review Press, 1987.

Pfister, Manfred. *Das Drama.* München: Wilhelm Fink Verlag, 1997.

Plato. *The Republic*. Ed. G.R.F. Ferrari. Transl. Tom Griffith. Cambridge: Cambridge University press, 2000.

Plessner, Helmut. »Die Antropologie des Schauspielers.« *Gesammelte Werke* vol. 10, 235.

Poyatos, Fernando. »Nonverbal Communication in the Theater: the Playwright, Actor, Spectator-Relationship.« *Multimedial Communication 2: Theatre Semiotics*, Tübingen. Ed. Ernest W.B. Hess-Lüttich. Gunter Narr Verlag, 1982. 75-94.

Raghib, Nabil. *Fann l-'arḍ l-masraḥiyy*. Beirut: Librairie du Liban – Publishers, 1996.

Rahi, Ali. » 'al-masraḥ fī l-waṭan l-'arabiyy «. *'ālam l-ma'rifa*. Kuweit: 'al-maǧlis l-waṭaniyy li-t-taqāfa wa-l-funūn wa-l-'ādāb, 1999.

Rapp, Uri. *Handeln und Zuschauen: Untersuchungen über den theatersoziologischen Aspekt in der menschlichen Interaktion*. Darmstadt: Luchterhand, 1973.

Rapp, Uri. *Rolle, Interaktion, Spiel: eine Einführung in die Theatersoziologie*. Wien: Böhlau, 1993.

Rieck, Andreas. *Die Schiiten und der Kampf um den Libanon. Politische Chronik 1958-1988*. Hamburg: Deutsches Orient-Institut, 1989.

Rieger, Brigitte. *Rentiers, Patrone und Gemeinschaft: soziale Sicherung im Libanon*. Frankfurt am Main: Peter Lang, Europäischer Verlag der Wissenschaften, 2003.

Roose-Evans, James. *Experimental Theater from Stanislavsky to Today*. New York: Universe Books, 1970.

Rossides, Daniel. *Comparative Societies: Social Types and their Interrelations*. New Jersey: Prentice Hall, 1990.

Saiid, Khalida. *'al-ḥaraka l-masraḥiyya fī Lubnān: 1960-1975, taǧārib wa 'ab'ād*. Arayya: Laǧnat l-masraḥ l-'arabiyy, 1998.

Salibi, Kamal. *A House of Many Mansions: The History of Lebanon Reconsidered*. London: I.B. Tauris & Co. Ltd Publishers, 1988.

Salibi, Kamal. *Crossroads to Civil War. Lebanon 1958-1976*. Delmar NY: Caravan Books, 1976.

Salibi, Kamal. *tārīḫ Lubnān l-ḥadīṯ*. Beirut: 'an-nahār, 1991.

Schechner, Richard, and Mady Schuman, eds. *Ritual, Play, and Performance, Readings in the Social Sciences/ Theatre*. New York: Seabury Press, 1976.

Schechner, Richard. *Performance Theory*. NewYork and London: Routledge, 1988.

Schechner, Richard. *Public Domain*. Indianapolis: Bobbs-Merrill, 1969.

Schechner, Richard. *Theater-Anthropologie: Spiel und Ritual im Kulturvergleich*. transl. Susanne Winnacker. Reinbeck by Hamburg: Rowohlts Enzyklopädie, 1990.

Schütz, Alfred, and Thomas Luckmann. *Strukturen der Lebenswelt*, Band 1. Frankfurt am Main: Suhrkamp Taschenbuch Wissenschaft, 1979.

Schütz, Alfred. *Der sinnhafte Aufbau der Lebenswelt: eine Einleitung in die Verstehende Soziologie*. Frankfurt am Main: Suhrkamp Taschenbuch Wissenschaft, 1974.

Shaoul, Melhem. *'al-'iftirāq wa-l-ğam': dirāsāt fī l-muğtama' l-lubnāniyy*. Beirut: 'an-nahār, 1996.

Shaoul, Paul. *'al-masraḥ l-'arabiyy l-ḥadīṯ (1976-1989)*. London: Riyad er-Rayes, 1989.

Silverman, D. *Interpreting Qualitative Data*. Newbury Park, CA: Sage, 1993.

Soeffner, Hans-Georg, ed... »Kultur und Alltag« *Soziale Welt: Zeitschr. für Wissensch. und Praxis d. sozialen Lebens*. [Soziale Welt / Sonderband]. Göttingen: Schwartz, 1988.

Soeffner, Hans-Georg. »Berger/Luckmann« *Hauptwerke der Soziologie*. Ed. Dirk Kaesler and Ludgera Vogt. Stuttgart: Kröner, 2000. 39-44.

Soeffner, Hans-Georg. »Schütz/Luckmann« *Hauptwerke der Soziologie*. Ed. Dirk Kaesler and Ludgera Vogt. Stuttgart: Kröner, 2000. 379-386.

Soeffner, Hans-Georg. *Auslegung des Alltags - der Alltag der Auslegung: zur wissenssoziologischen Konzeption sozialwissenschaftlichen Hermeneutik*. Frankfurt am Main: Suhrkamp, 1992a.

Soeffner, Hans-Georg. *Die Ordnung der Rituale: Die Auslegung des Alltags 2*. Frankfurt am Main: Suhrkamp Verlag, 1992b.

Soeffner, Hans-Georg. *Interpretative Verfahren in den Sozial- und Textwissenschaften*. Stuttgart: Metzler, 1979.

Soeffner, Hans-Georg. *Rezeption - Kommunikation - Situation: Vorschlag zu einem Begriffsrahmen für eine Theorie rezeptiven Verhaltens; Situation, Information, kommunikative Handlung*. Essen: Univ. Gesamthochsch. Essen, 1999.

Soueid, Mohammad. *yā fu'ādī: sīra sinamā'iyya 'an ṣālāt bayrūt r-rāhila*. Beirut: 'an-nahār, 1996.

Stanislavsky, Konstantin. *La Construction du Personnage*. Paris: Pygmalion, 1984.

Stanislavsky, Konstantin. *La Formation de L'Acteur*. Saint-Armand-Montrond: Editions Oliviers Perrin, 1994.

Strauss, Anselm and Juliet Corbin. *Basics of Qualitative Research: Techniques and Procedures for Developing Grounded Theory*. California: Sage Publications, 1998.

Strauss, Anselm. *Creating Sociological Awareness*. New Brunswick: Transaction Publishers, 1991.

Strauss, Anselm. *Qualitative Analysis for Social Scientists.* Cambridge: Cambridge Univeristy Press, 1987.
Strauss, Anselm. *Spiegel und Masken: die Suche nach der Identität.* Frankfurt am Main: Suhrkamp, 1974.
Suleiman, Susan R. and Crosman, Inge (eds). *The Reader in the Text: Essays on Audience and Interpretation.* Princeton: Princeton University Press, 1980.
Tan, Ed. »Cognitive Processes in Reception.« *Multimedial Communication 2: Theatre Semiotics.* Ed. Ernest W.B. Hess-Lüttich. Tübingen: Gunter Narr Verlag, 1982. 156-203.
Tan, Ed. *The Act of Reading: a Theory of Aesthetic Response.* Baltimore: John Hopkins University Press, 1978.
Tan, Ed. »The Art of Failure: the Stifled Laugh in Beckett's Theater«. *Theories of Reading, Looking and Listening.* Ed. Harry R. Garvin. Lewisburg: Bucknell University Press, 1981. 139-89.
Tan, Ed. *Toward an Aesthetic of Reception.* Trans. Timothy Bathi. Minneapolis: University of Minnesota Press, 1982.
Turner, Victor. *From Ritual to Theatre: The Human Seriousness of Play.* New York City: Performing Arts Journal Publications, 1982.
Turner, Victor. *On the Edge of the Bush: Anthropology as Experience.* Arizona: The University of Arizona Press, 1985.
Vorderer, Peter, and Sabine Trepte. »Medienpsychologie.« *Psychologie in der Praxis: Anwendungs- und Berufsfelder einer modernen Wissenschaft.* Ed. Jürgen Straub. München: Deutscher Taschenbuch Verlag, 2000.
Walcot, Peter. *Greek drama in its Theatrical and Social Sontext.* Cardiff: University of Whales Press, 1976.
Weber, Max (1922/72). *Wirtschaft und Gesellschaft. Grundriß der verstehenden Soziologie.* Tübingen: Mohr, 1972.
Webster, James G... *The Mass Audience: Rediscovering the Dominant Model.* Mahwah: N.J, L. Erlbaum Associates, 1997.
Wehr, Hans, ed. (1952/1977). *Arabisches Wörterbuch für die Schriftsprache der Gegenwart.* Wiesbaden: Harassowitz, 1977.
Wiles, Timothy J... *The Theater Event: Modern Theories of Performance.* Chicago: University of Chicago Press, 1980.
Willet, John. *Brecht on Theater.* New York, Hill and Wang, 1964.
Williams, Clifford John. *Theaters and Audience: a Background to Dramatic Texts.* London: Longman, 1970.
Wilson, Tony. *Watching Television: Hermeneutics, Reception and Popular Culture.* Cambridge, UK: Polity Press in association with Blackwell Publishers, 1993.

Printed by Printforce, United Kingdom